A FEAST
OF EGAN

A FEAST OF EGAN

- *The Borrowed Alibi*
- *Run to Evil*
- *Detective's Due*
- *The Nameless Ones*

by Lesley Egan

Nelson Doubleday, Inc.
Garden City, New York

CONTENTS

A FEAST
OF EGAN

THE
BORROWED
ALIBI

CHAPTER 1

When Vic Varallo resigned his captaincy on the Contera force, he'd figured the sensible thing to do was come down to the big town and join the force there. It was the job he knew. He'd have to start at the bottom again, which wasn't so good at thirty-three; but city forces paid higher, and Laura (against his private liking) didn't mind working awhile until they got some savings ahead.

He knew a couple of men in the L.A.P.D., and he knew that that crack force is perennially undermanned. But it was on the cards that promotion would come more quickly on a smaller force, that his rather unusual status as a cop of twelve years' experience, now again a rookie, would be understood and appreciated. In the end, he joined the Glendale force. Glendale was one of the larger towns-within-the-big-Town—most northeasterly city at that end of the San Fernando Valley, a hundred and twenty-three thousand.

It felt strange to be back in uniform again, a tan uniform instead of navy, and riding a patrol car. There were a few new things to learn since he'd last ridden a car, and a lot of different things to being a city cop; but people were people anywhere, he made some friends on the force—notably Sergeant Charles O'Connor—and most important of all, of course, he had Laura.

On the other hand, they made a few mistakes, trying to plan ahead. They decided it wasn't sensible to go on paying rent when they could be acquiring equity in a house; and, said Laura, it would be silly to start to buy a house they'd outgrow in a few years. Because when they could afford it they intended to have a family of two at least. The upshot was that they bought—or started to buy—the house on Hillcroft Road. Neither of them had ever owned a house before, and it turned out that they'd been a little naïve about this one.

It was a fine house, about twenty years old ("Because all these new ranch houses have such small rooms," Laura had said. "I like nice old-fashioned bedrooms with walk-in closets") and well-built, a stucco house of Mediterranean design. It had a separate dining room, three bedrooms and a den, and even—attached to the double garage—a room and bath meant for maid's quarters.

This section of town, the Rossmoyne section, had for long been one of the best residential areas; these days it was not as fashionable as some of the new subdivisions, but the taxes were still a little higher than in other places in town. That, they found out.

Laura didn't want to go back to the telephone company because it meant such irregular hours; she got a job in the Security Bank down-town, posting and filing. Of course that didn't pay so well. And there were Varallo's new uniforms to buy, and—because the .38 he had wasn't the regulation model—a new gun. He'd had a backlog of savings, and so had Laura, so they hadn't had to go into much further debt except for the necessary furniture. They'd finish furnishing the house properly as they could afford it, but meanwhile there had to be a refrigerator, a stove and a few other items. Both their cars—his seven-year-old Chevvy and Laura's eight-year-old Ford—were in decent condition, but you never knew.

They'd make it, though things were, naturally, a little tight. Prices were up, and the house payments a pretty big bite out of their joint in-come—the house really a bargain, as Laura said, at twenty-seven five, and much better value for the money than these jerry-built new places. But the payments were higher because of the higher taxes in this area; they'd just gone up, the voters having passed another raise to the school board.

"Which," said Laura, "is all to the good, isn't it? You have to look ahead. The Glendale schools are supposed to be good. As good as any of them are these days. And if we're staying here—*which* we are—"

Varallo said, "Yes, but it ups the payments, damn it."

There were summer uniforms to buy as well as the winter ones, and of course a certain amount of ammo because you had to keep up to standard on target shooting. And then the damn transmission went out on the Chevvy. . . . Sitting there helpless at (of course) the busy inter-section of Broadway and Glendale Avenue, Varallo had searched his memory for all the curses he knew in two languages, which affected the transmission not at all. And that was a hundred and seventy-nine bucks. . . .

"Darling," said Laura, "things come along. We'll—weather it. And we can't give up the house. We wouldn't break even. And what with your—your nursery of exotic females out there—"

Varallo said they weren't all exotic females. He called her attention to Fred Howard and Horace MacFarland, adding that he was, however, going to get rid of MacFarland. "Because I don't like pink ones. There's Dr. Huey too."

"There is also," said Laura, reaching to adjust his tie, "that duchess, who sounds to me like a high-class harlot. I'll bet she was."

Varallo told her she was a senseless female. "And I haven't spent much on them—not over twenty dollars, anyway."

"It's the principle of the thing," said Laura. "You will." She stood on tiptoe to kiss him. It was seven-thirty in the morning and he was on days this month. "Besides, think about *me*. Here I think I've married a big tough he-man cop, and what does he turn into? A damned rose fancier."

Varallo told her not to swear. "We'll make it somehow," he agreed. "But it's a little rough, sometimes. Because—" And he left it all unsaid. How time slipped away, and Laura was twenty-nine this year, and they wanted a family; and he didn't like her working, and did want to give her more than he could; and though he'd made friends, was getting along O.K. and liking this force, it was a little galling to be riding a squad car in uniform, to be plain "mister" off duty. She knew all that, and patted his chest, smiling up at him.

"It'll all turn out all right, Vic. Or do I sound like Pollyanna? It's all all right now so long as it's us together. Isn't it?"

And that of course didn't need answering in words. It was.

What Laura called his exotic females had been as much of a surprise to Varallo as to anybody.

They'd moved into the house on the first Saturday in December, a little over two months after they'd been married and a month after Varallo had joined this force.

Late that Sunday morning, a warm blue-and-gold morning, he had strolled idly out into the back yard because Laura said it made her nervous to be watched while she hung the curtains and, no, he couldn't help her, thank you—go away. The back yard of the house on Hillcroft Road was deep, and for the first time Varallo really noticed how many flower beds it contained, and all the lawn to be kept mowed, and felt qualms of doubt. He knew absolutely nothing about that kind of thing, and wasn't interested. The grass needed cutting now.

All the flowers seemed to be roses—one of the few flowers he could identify. The house was on a corner, and on that side, against a low cement wall, grew a tangled climbing growth sparked here and there with round yellow-pinkish roses. All over the yard were scattered small beds in various shapes with rose trees in orderly rows, or lower bushes. There was a pleasant brick-floored patio at the rear of the house, with a tall fan-shaped trellis partially sheltering it, and up that was growing another tangle of rosebush. The cement wall carried on across the back and down the other side of the yard; there were more small beds and about the middle of the wall another tangle of climbing bush sprouting roses of a different shade of yellow.

Varallo stood and looked at all the roses and thought the whole thing looked like the hell of a lot of work, for which he experienced—as someone had said—a deep feeling of no enthusiasm.

"Per Bacco," he said to himself, "I think we've been fools here." The real-estate woman, Mrs. Williams, had seemed a little stunned at the rapidity of their decision, but Laura had fallen in love with the house, and though the payments were high, they'd be just as high or higher on any house this size in this good a residential area. Which, of course, was the point. They should have found out more about the various sections of town before—

At that point he became aware that he was being regarded over the wall by a paunchy bald man of fifty-odd, with a pink face and horn-rimmed glasses. The man smiled and nodded at him. "You'll be our new neighbor," he stated, and came up to the wall to offer a somewhat grimy hand. "Name of Anderson—Marvin Anderson."

"Varallo," said Varallo, deciding to spare Mr. Anderson the Lodovico. "Vic Varallo."

"Varallo?" said Anderson involuntarily, glancing at Varallo's thick crest of tawny-gold hair, fair skin and blue eyes.

Varallo explained about North Italians. Anderson said, "Oh," cautiously. Varallo wondered if he'd now get a polite brush-off for possessing a funny foreign name, but Anderson only said, "I'm retired—had an automobile agency. What line you in, Mr. Varallo?"

The mister still sounded queer. Varallo told him, added (in sudden and unusual self-consciousness) that he'd ranked captain up to two months ago and was starting all over. Anderson said Oh again and

Tough luck, and seemed to warm up a little to so respectable a citizen as a man on the force. Of course this was that sort of neighborhood. "You a gardener?" he asked.

"I was just thinking it all looks like a lot of work. I don't know one damn thing about it."

"Now that's a damn shame," said Anderson glumly. In fact, he looked ready to cry. "All Fred's roses." He looked over the wall sadly. "That Duquesa de Peñaranda, way he'd nursed her along—and President Hoover too. It's a damn shame. . . . Fred Woolsey, that owned this place. Had his last heart attack six months back, and Mrs. Woolsey decided to sell and go live with her married daughter in San Luis Obispo, see. Built this place, Fred did, and planted everything here himself. A rose man, he was, like me. Matter of fact, it was Fred got me interested. Used to take prizes with his hybrid teas, he did. Two years running, with Charlotte Armstrong and Hector Deane."

It was Varallo's turn to say Oh. "I couldn't let 'em go," said Anderson apologetically. "Mrs. Woolsey arranged for a gardener, to keep the place in shape until it was sold, but—well—roses need more attention than once a week. I been coming over, mulching 'em here and there, like that. Fred was sure looking forward to seeing that Duquesa de Peñaranda. He just put her in last January and she hasn't produced yet. Something to see when she does." He pointed. "That's her there." It was just another rose tree to Varallo; it hadn't a bloom on it. "Shame he never got to see it."

Varallo agreed. "I never knew they had names. Names like that. What's that one?"

Anderson looked at the climbing bush on the wall and said, "Doubloons, that is. Pretty color, that deep yellow. Fred fussed around that Duquesa to beat all, it does seem a damn shame. . . ."

Varallo agreed it was a shame he'd never got to see it bloom. He really felt it was a shame. But then Vic Varallo was a very good cop, the one cop in about five hundred who had the flair for the job; and that meant, to start with, empathy for people. "What does it look like?" he asked casually.

"Oh, she's a beauty. A kind of long, tight bloom—neat and close, you know—and an awful clear light red, almost what they call a Chinese red. A little like Floradora, only even prettier. It's funny she *hasn't*," said Anderson. "She *ought* to have, by November. In this climate. Ought to be producing now."

"Is that so?" said Varallo. And presently said it had been nice to meet him and he hoped they'd find each other good neighbors, and gone in.

But that grass had to be cut; and of course they couldn't afford a gardener. So he bought a lawn mower—the old-fashioned kind—and inexpertly mowed the lawn. That was on Tuesday evening. There was a smaller front lawn to mow, too; and more rose trees and climbing bushes out there. As he worked back and forth, he found himself looking at the rose tree with the improbable name and wishing it would produce just one bloom. Maybe Fred Woolsey could see it from somewhere, and be pleased.

The day after that he saw Anderson in his yard in late afternoon, and asked him what to do to rose trees to make them bloom. Anderson talked for a long while, and it wasn't until Laura called him for the second time to dinner that Varallo realized it was dark.

The day after that he bought some rose food at a nursery.

"I've just *realized*," said Laura that night, sounding worried. "All this yard to keep up. We can't, not properly, Vic. Neither of us knowing anything—"

"Oh, well, mowing the lawn'll be good exercise for me," said Varallo vaguely.

"You haven't the time—"

And as time went on, he began to agree with that.

He started out just willing the Duquesa de Peñaranda to produce a rose. Just one. For poor dead Fred Woolsey, who had labored over her. He fed the duchess the best brand of rose food, and carefully gave her what Anderson said was the right amount of water. She continued to stand there greenly, putting out leaves and nothing else. Varallo got mad at her. Damn it, she'd be made to produce! Every day, the week after that, he'd come home off duty, kiss Laura and at once go out to look at the duchess. She didn't produce. Anderson said she should be producing now.

He also said, worriedly, that the Neige Parfum wasn't doing so well. Only one bud. He pointed it out. Varallo had never seen a rose that color. It was real silver—gray-white, luminous, a close-curled round blossom. There were holes in the green leaves around it. "That Goddamned aphis," said Anderson. "You ought to spray. And even that—Your best bet is Aerosect."

Varallo got some Aerosect.

On his next day off, he went to the library, got a card and brought home five books about rose growing.

"Darling!" said Laura.

"Go on and laugh," said Varallo. "By God, I'll get that damned Spanish duchess to bloom for me or know the reason why!"

Laura rocked with laughter. "What *would* the boys down at headquarters say?"

"I couldn't," said Varallo, "care less. *Silènzio, per favore.*" And he opened *The Rose-Grower's Guide.*

On the last day of January, the Duquesa de Peñaranda presented him with one perfect bud, which opened to one exquisite blossom—close-furled, long, of a peculiarly beautiful clear deep coral. He called Laura out to admire it, and that was the first time—looking resignedly and amusedly at Vic Varallo's six-one of hard compact muscle and very masculine good looks—that Laura brought out that remark about having thought she'd married a big tough cop. . . . But she duly admired the duchess, and (as an afterthought) added that she supposed a hobby was good for a man.

Especially—she had remarked several months later, after Varallo was really captured—for a good-looking married man.

"You have to look ahead, after all," she said, nodding her bright brown head at him, pseudo-serious. "I can just see myself, you know, looking perfectly awful, ready to go to the hospital for the first one— Well, but you *do* look awful at the last, you can't deny it—and you—bad policy to flatter husbands, but the uniform and all— But I wouldn't have, as they say, a moment's anxiety. Where other women were worrying about Harry or Jim taking up with some floozy, my husband, he'd only be out fooling around with his Spanish duchess."

"*Impertinènza,*" said Varallo. "You miscalling me—"

"I wouldn't dare. I only said—"

"So it's funny. Sure, so it is. It's—damn it, I think," said Varallo, "it's *because* I'm a cop. They defy you. Challenge you, do I want to say? In a kind of way. And then when they do come out, it's like a miracle—and all so different, you know. . . . And that Goddamned aphis— Remind me to get some more Aerosect."

In February he had planted his first tree—a Floradora, under Mr. Anderson's instructions. He had Neige Parfum blooming fairly well by then. A week later, the Duquesa put out three new buds; and Varallo had never looked back after that.

Then, in August, the transmission went out on Laura's Ford. Over two hundred bucks, that was. And the garbage disposal already installed in the kitchen when they bought the house needed repairs to the tune of twenty-three dollars more. Both of which came along just after the July income-tax installment.

And prices—

"We'll *manage*," said Laura. "Somehow. Next year—"

Yes. They were stretching a point for him, considering his background. They were letting him take the sergeants' exam next time it came up. And of course he'd already passed it—and the lieutenants' exam—once; he hadn't any doubt of doing so again. But passing it didn't mean automatic promotion—that would come, maybe, when there was a vacancy. Of course, Lieutenant of Detectives King was due for retirement next year, and very probably Sergeant Charles O'Connor would get his step to lieutenant then and leave a hole. A hole to be filled by one of, say, fifteen or twenty eligible men. If he made the highest score—

He thought he could. He had, before. And that would mean a fatter paycheck, and also on the way up again to superior rank. But that was at least eight months off. Now if he could qualify as a sharpshooter, that would mean another few bucks a month too—

"I've had an idea," Laura said tentatively that night over dinner. "Just an idea. Don't fly off the handle, Vic. But couldn't we rent the room and bath off the garage?"

CHAPTER 2

"And why should I fly off the handle?" asked Varallo.

"You do. Stiffnecked pride," said Laura.

"Don't be silly, it's an inspiration. A damned inspiration. What could we ask?"

"I haven't the faintest idea. Let's look at the ads."

They looked at the ads, in the *Independent* and the *News-Press*. It appeared, by the ads, that a furnished room rented for about forty a month on the average. "Furnished?" said Varallo. Laura said firmly, Good plain furniture—secondhand—leave it to her. "We can ask more. Fifty. A private bath, a private entrance. I'll even get a hot plate. Maybe even fifty-five. You won't *mind*, Vic?"

"There are things I mind," said Varallo, "and being over my head in debt is one of them. But we want someone—"

"Oh, of course, quiet and respectable. We will, I'll get busy on it," said Laura energetically. She did. When she showed it to him, a week later, Varallo thought it looked the hell of a lot homier and more comfortable than his Contera Hotel room where he'd lived the last five years or so. But Laura had a knack for making you comfortable.

There was a neat studio couch ($12 secondhand) with a neat brown corduroy cover. A bedside table (one of a pair from the house). A lamp ($2); a rug ($5); an armchair ($10). Curtains, beige cotton ("And *what* a job. You know how I loathe sewing"—$2.50 for materials) looking very nice; a writing table and straight chair ($5 and $2 respectively), and a small chrome table at the end of the room for a hot plate— "The cheapest was twelve something, and I thought we'd just say no objection to cooking and let it go at that, you know." There were a couple of pleasant pictures—inexpensive lithographs, a seascape and a copy of a Degas. It looked fine. Much better than his old hotel room—which wasn't saying much, of course.

"Ask sixty," he said. "We can always come down." He looked into the bathroom. Green plastic curtains to match the tile there, green terry towels and facecloths. Very nice.

"Well—" said Laura.

They spent a congenial hour composing the ad. "Not," said Varallo, "just anybody. Living twenty feet away. Better ask for references and so on."

And that was how they met Ross Duncan.

They had thought, perhaps, a young schoolteacher, someone like that. But Duncan was the first one who answered the ad. Varallo was on night tours then, and consequently just up, at three o'clock that Friday afternoon; he was sitting in the little covered patio at the rear of he house, with a tall cold Scotch-and-water in his hand, looking at his roses wilting in the hot September sun. It was around a hundred even in the sheltered patio. When the telephone rang he swore, heaved himself up reluctantly.

It was a man's pleasant voice. Was the room still available? Would it be convenient if he came to look at it now? Well, fine.

Twenty minutes later, Varallo found himself liking Ross Duncan. He was about Varallo's age, a couple of inches shorter, with a square pleasant face; if his dark eyes looked tired and blistered around the lids, well, it had been a bad week, temperatures over a hundred every day. He was conservatively dressed; he'd driven up in a dusty gray Anglia Ford about ten years old. He spoke well, answered questions openly.

"I'm in the insurance business," he said. And—"I can give you a couple of names of people who know me, sure," and had: an officer at the chamber of commerce, an officer at the Security Bank. Varallo, used to sizing people up and pretty good at it, decided they couldn't ask for a more satisfactory tenant. He put Duncan down as an insurance salesman, not the easiest way in the world to make a living. Neatly dressed, but the suit had seen better days, and the shirt collar was just slightly frayed at one side. Poor but honest . . . Eventually, thinking that, he came down to fifty-two-fifty for Duncan.

"There's no garage, of course," Duncan had pointed out reasonably.

He was certainly a quiet tenant. He moved in on Sunday, when Varallo was still asleep, and was pleasant to Laura. He asked if there was any objection to his bringing in a small apartment-size refrigerator, which he did. It was a very old one, its porcelain mostly chipped off.

He left a little later in the morning than either of them did: about eight-thirty, Varallo discovered—coming off night tours and getting home around then, to see Duncan leaving. He was always formally dressed in suit and white shirt. As, presumably, insurance salesmen were expected to be—like bank tellers and a few other unfortunates (in this weather). At least, one mercy, he didn't seem to own a radio or portable TV; they never heard a sound from the little room off the garage when he was there.

For no reason, Varallo took idle note of Duncan's comings and goings. He came home most nights about eight o'clock, sometimes earlier, and stayed in. One very hot night toward the end of the month Varallo, leaving for his night tour at eleven-thirty, had a glimpse of Duncan through one of the room's two wide-open windows—Duncan sitting, naked except for shorts, in the armchair, reading and holding a tall chilled glass in one hand. A quiet man relaxing after a trying day. He had a fine mat of black hair on his bare chest. He looked calm, serious and—as always—reserved.

Several times he came home, in daylight then at this time of year, when they were sitting in the patio over drinks or dinner. He smiled and lifted a hand, never offered to come closer, get better acquainted. Which of course was all to the good, the way they'd wanted it. An ideal tenant. But—

"But he looks nice," said Laura, after one of these occasions. "And lonely," she added after a moment. "Doesn't he? He never seems to go out in the evenings, as if he had a date. It's not natural, somehow."

Varallo gave her an amused glance over his glass. His darling Laura, looking deceptively cool in her mint-green sundress, her brandy-colored hair shining in the late sun. His sensible, practical Laura, still very female. "Women—you will find something to gossip about." But it was, certainly, a little odd that Duncan never went out in the evenings. A young, single man—even living modestly, you'd think once in a while—

And the next night, a Sunday night, he did. Or rather he didn't come in at the usual time.

"He's got a date," said Laura in satisfaction, as they washed the dishes together after dinner. "I hope a nice one. He looks nice. Solid, sort of."

"Next thing you'll be deducing the color of her eyes," said Varallo. But he felt—in some obscure way—oddly relieved. That was the word. The ridiculous word. It put Duncan back in the class of ordinary. Typical. His old-maidish routine had removed him from that, and as a cop Varallo disliked oddnesses in people.

Duncan came home just as Varallo was leaving that night. As he walked down to the garage, Varallo heard him coming up the drive, walking steadily, not too fast. He paused, waited to speak to him—for no reason.

"Oh—hello," said Duncan. He had a pleasant baritone voice.

"Still hot," said Varallo.

"You can say it twice. Even at this hour. I'd hoped it'd have cooled off a little by the time I got out of the theater. Been to see the new Disney," offered Duncan. "Very good." He smiled and nodded a goodnight before passing on to the narrow front door of his quarters.

So, not a date.

The rent fell due the Saturday after that, and Duncan stopped when he came home, to pay it—punctiliously, and in cash. He seldom went out on Sundays at all; if he did it was for a short while in the afternoon. Like themselves, not a churchgoer. But what, demanded Laura, did he *do* with himself, there alone? It wasn't natural. Varallo agreed, but certainly there was no reason to complain of him as a tenant. . . . Now, accepting the money from Duncan, he impulsively asked Duncan to join them; they'd been sitting in the patio over drinks. Duncan looked surprised and grateful, accepted a Scotch-and-water.

He was a quiet, withdrawn man; he talked easily, but not much, instead inviting Varallo to talk about his job. His eyes were as grave and tired as the first time Varallo had seen him. He had a habit of running one hand over his thick dark hair; there had been, Varallo suddenly remembered, a gold signet ring on his right hand that first time, but it was gone now. He didn't try to push a friendship, nor was he at all standoffish; he stayed a correct time over his drink, said, "I mustn't keep you from dinner," and stood up, smiling.

When he was inside his room, Laura said in a low tone that he *was* nice. But that it still wasn't—natural. "Just to a movie, once in eight weeks. And alone."

"So he's writing a novel in his spare time," said Varallo, and yawned, and added, "Thank God I can sleep tonight. And tomorrow." He was coming off night duty and would have the Sunday free before going back on days on Monday. And, heat or no heat, he ought to get those beds weeded—also thank God there was a sprinkling system installed—and those damned aphis were back again. . . .

He went back on days, riding a patrol car alone, on Monday. Like all city forces within the metropolis, this force was shorthanded, and there weren't any really bad slums around here: Glendale was a quiet middle-class town, mostly. On a couple of the routes they paired off, and mostly they rode in pairs at night, but days you were nearly always alone. It was a boring routine job, looking for the traffic violators, listening to the incessant radio, in your spare time studying the big page of hot plate numbers posted on the dashboard.

The route he was riding took in, among other areas, all of West Glenoaks Boulevard up to the Burbank line. When he was on it, Varallo usually stopped for his break at an inexpensive little coffee shop and restaurant at the corner of Brand, and today was no exception. The minute steak was as crisp as ever, and the coffee as fresh and strong, but it had started out being one of those days, and over them Varallo brooded gloomily.

In the first place, they'd given him that cranky 89 again. Most of the patrol cars were fairly new Chevrolets; 89 was only three years old, and supposedly kept in good condition, but in the opinion of anybody who had to drive it all day, it had been a lemon from the start. Its shift was sticky and hard; it ate gas faster than it should; it rode like a truck. . . . Four hours more on duty. Must be around a hundred now; looking at his watch he thought, five more minutes of air conditioning. . . . The extra money from Duncan helped a lot, but things were still tighter than he liked. If he could maintain top accuracy on the range for the required time, he'd get eight bucks extra a month as a qualified sharpshooter, which would come in very damn handy. . . . Well, damn it, he'd known what he was in for when he resigned; he'd been finished in Contera, there'd been nothing else for it. But Laura— It wasn't fair on Laura.

He paid the check and went out with a sigh to the black-and-white police car parked in the narrow lot. Righteously obeying traffic laws, he turned right on Glenoaks out of the lot, though his route lay left, to go round the block. Almost at once he was held up by one of those new block-long Lincolns maneuvering backward into a parking slot; and as he waited, he glanced idly at the sidewalk to his right.

There was half a block of modern, sleek business places along here, a joined row of French provincial architecture, smartly gray and white, with chaste, uniformly lettered signs: the whole, a high-class setup. An architect's office; two doctors; a real-estate office; a C.P.A.; and—

Varallo did a double take on that one. ROSS DUNCAN, INSURANCE OF ALL TYPES.

The Lincoln was parked; he stepped on the accelerator and manhandled 89's sticky shift into second. Now this was a thing, he thought. *Ross Duncan, Insurance*— He hadn't denied it: "I'm in insurance." Not very likely there'd be two Ross Duncans in insurance, even in a town this size.

But a setup like that spelled money. Substantial money, anyway. The lease of an office in that building wouldn't come cheap; and an insurance business that didn't pay its way wouldn't stay in a location like that long—couldn't. So what the hell was the presumed owner of the business doing living in a single cheap furnished room?

Or was he this Ross Duncan?

Varallo wondered about it off and on the rest of that tour. . . . When he turned in 89 at the headquarters garage, he said to Snead, "Look, Joe, all I ask is don't give me this bitch tomorrow. Pass it around—play no favorites."

"Shift sticking again?"

"And she died on me four times. It doesn't look just so efficient, you know, a squad car stalled at an intersection. Take her away and let the mechanics have a look."

"Rough day, Vic?" asked O'Connor, behind him. He turned, feeling a little better already to run into O'Connor, if only for a casual word.

"You've said it." O'Connor was a plainclothesman in the detective division. They'd met casually when Varallo was in the process of being sworn in, and O'Connor had gone out of his way to grease the wheels a little for him; they had taken to each other. Charles O'Connor was a dark, stocky man of thirty-one, in many ways a complete opposite to the quick, intuitive, impulsive Varallo; he was (Varallo thought) perhaps intrigued by the oddity of the situation—he a sergeant of seven years' experience, technically senior to a former captain with twelve years' service. On the relatively few occasions when they'd had time and privacy to talk, they'd got on first-name terms, and O'Connor had prodded him into reminiscence, listening flatteringly.

"This damn weather," said O'Connor, mopping his brow.

"You should talk. You can sit in a nice air-conditioned office all day."

"It is to laugh, friend. I've been out most of the afternoon—an assault over on San Fernando Road, one of those small-parts assembly plants. Though, speaking of air conditioning," added O'Connor thoughtfully, "I've got an idea if the place *had* had, there wouldn't have been an assault. Contributing circumstances, anyway. Isn't there some place in

Morocco where they don't count murders committed during the hottest season? You can see the logic in it." He turned in the car he'd requisitioned—"That damn thing of mine's in for another check-up—" and they went their respective ways.

Driving home, Varallo thought about Duncan some more. What it added up to was another oddity, and he didn't like it. He liked Duncan, the little he'd seen of him, but a few pro crooks he'd known had been likable. And this oddity was living twenty feet away from him—and Laura.

He thought he had a right to ask questions.

He got home at twenty to six, tired and hot after the little drive through traffic. To his surprise, Duncan's Anglia was sitting at the curb round on Loretta Drive where he parked it overnight. Varallo put his car away in the garage and knocked on the door to the little room, but got no answer. A glance through the window told him it was empty.

He told Laura about it when she got home. "But, Vic, it seems so—prying into his private business—"

"Prying hell. He's living on our property. I've got a right to know who and what he is."

"He left a lot earlier this morning. I heard him go out about seven. . . . Maybe the business *isn't* doing so well and he's saving money however he can."

"I'd just like to know," said Varallo obstinately. They sat there in the patio, waiting for the sun to go down and, maybe, a small breeze to come up. Presently he got himself a drink he didn't especially want. They couldn't afford much liquor, and brandy—which was his normal preference—was not a hot-weather drink, straight. He poured four ounces into a glass, shot some soda into it and added ice cubes. This damned Daylight Saving; you thought the sun never would go down. . . .

Duncan came home at eight-thirty. He came on foot; he must have taken the bus. The only bus through this section of town was the No. 2, and its nearest stop a good ten or twelve blocks away. His footsteps up the drive, in the dusk, sounded slow and tired.

Varallo got up. Laura said hastily, "I'll go and see about dinner. For goodness' sake don't lose your temper, Vic."

Varallo caught up with Duncan at the door. Duncan was fumbling with the key—as it turned and the door opened, Varallo said, "Oh, Duncan. Like a word with you."

"Hello. Sure," said Duncan. "C'mon in." He pressed the switch beside the door and the lamp across the room came on. "Welcome."

Duncan was a little tight, he saw with some surprise. Not very; just a little. "Siddown," said Duncan, smiling at him.

"That's a nice office you've got out on Glenoaks," said Varallo, standing. "I just noticed it today. It must run pretty high on lease."

"Brother," said Duncan simply. He opened the battered little refrigerator and took out the ice tray. Picked up a glass from the table, set it down again. Picked up the bottle of Scotch sitting beside it and squinted at it. "I won't offer you a drink," he said. "Not because I grudge it, my friend, but because I think there's just about enough left to tie a very nice one on me, and that is my full and deliberate intention this night. After what I've had. Already, that is. First time I'd been in a bar for over a year, imagine that. Just imagine. Cheaper to drink at home. Alone . . . The car went out on me. All I needed. From now on, the bus. And what a bus . . . Needn't worry, Varallo—I don't get noisy. At least never have, the couple times I've really loaded up. D'you know something very damn funny?"

"No, what?" said Varallo, watching him.

"For the first time in my life," said Duncan, carefully measuring six ounces of Scotch into a glass and adding water and ice, "I understand why a man could maybe turn into a deliberate drunkard. Old-fashioned word—excuse me—alcoholic. I could. A solution—in a sort of way, you know. But, damn it, I just can't afford it." He squinted at the bottle of Scotch, a cheap brand. "This is all until nex' month, see. Shouldn't buy any at all. Means cooking soup here instead of the fifty-five cents for a hamburger at the dime store. But a man's got to have something. One little nightcap, make him sleep." He drank.

"You've got that high-class office," said Varallo. "How's business, Duncan?"

"Business," said Duncan, "is just great." He looked at Varallo over the glass and smiled. He wasn't very high yet; just relaxed. "So you're wondering," he said. "And ordinarily I'd tell you to go to hell, Varallo. I'm not the kind to go spouting my personal business—looking for a shoulder to cry on. My business. My mistake. We all make mistakes, don't we?" He drank some more. "But maybe you've got a sort of right to ask questions. Maybe so. And—give me a minute till this hits me— don't like spouting off—sound like a martyr." He gulped more, quickly. "Sorry. A minute . . . Very funny, can't afford it. Know what I've got on me? After the bar and the bus? Just eleven cents. All the payments first, y' see, and it doesn't leave much for luxuries—like liquor. . . . But you needn't worry, Varallo. You'll get the rent on time. I won't rob your house or attack your wife. Seems like a nice girl. Nice domestic girl— Always been a very quiet conservative fellow, me. Only—it's O.K., set your mind at rest—*not* askin' for any pity, y' know—only—I'll tell you—only, I got married."

"I see," said Varallo. "And?"

"And," said Duncan. "And. Brother." He drank. "I'll tell you—"

Half an hour later Varallo came in by the kitchen door, found Laura sitting waiting over a large bowl of chicken salad, deviled eggs and iced coffee, and lifted her into his arms to kiss her very thoroughly.

"Well!" said Laura when she could speak. "What's that for?"

"For being you, *cara*. Just for being Laura . . . You know something? We're rich people, my darling. Very, very rich, and very, very lucky. We'll do no more worrying about anything from here on in."

CHAPTER 3

Ross William Duncan was thirty-two years old, and anybody looking at him from the outside might think he was one of the lucky ones. He was moderately good-looking, he was in excellent health, he had a flourishing business of his own and—most important of all—he had just met the One Girl, the real thing, and she felt the same way.

Her name was Susan Morgan and she had nice dark hair with a natural wave and very blue eyes and a slender rounded figure. She was a teller at the local Federal Savings branch. She was twenty-six and lived with her widowed mother. Her older married sister lived in Hollywood.

You'd think Ross Duncan had it made.

He'd gone to the local public schools, where he hadn't been notable for anything much, and then to U.S.C. He'd been an only child, and his father fairly prosperous, so— He'd gone into the business with his father, the nice little flourishing insurance business all built up over many years. They had a number of very rewarding accounts—a big chain of supermarkets, a few others like that, besides a lot of individual accounts. They took in a very nice gross indeed.

He fitted into the business because he liked dealing with people, if he wasn't the aggressively gregarious type. He understood and could deal with figures; he knew the business, and was conscientious—as his father was—with clients. As for hobbies in his spare time, he liked golf; and he read a good deal. He didn't much like the hearty club meetings, that kind of thing; you had to do a certain amount of it as a businessman, but it was always a chore for him. He was a quiet man. Maybe a rather ordinary man. Women, occasionally, yes; and that too, rather the ordinary thing.

It had been a shock to him, Dad dying so suddenly, so comparatively young. Ross had been only twenty-eight. His mother had died the year before, after a serious operation. He had loved his father, another quiet man, but somehow, well, nothing else to do, you carried on. He knew the business; and with efficient Mrs. Starr in the office he carried on, thinking that perhaps later he'd take on some bright young man, such as he'd been once.

He stayed on in the much-too-large house on Kenneth Road, telling himself he should sell it, move to an apartment. There was, with only himself in the business, plenty of money then to live very well, in a substantial way.

He hadn't done that, before he met and married Helene. And been divorced by Helene.

Helene—

Well, he was an *orderly* man, he thought. (To himself. He'd always been rather inarticulate, and anyway not at all given to spouting off about his private life, his private troubles.) He'd always taken it for granted that if you were honest, and moderately moral, and used common sense and so on, you couldn't get into much trouble. Certainly not from the law. Which was, in this place and time, very fair and just to the upright citizen . . . He still felt, above all else, an immense surprise that, by due process of the law of the land, he could be so—victimized.

For that was the word. The bored, careless judge—perhaps not even listening closely enough to distinguish "gross" from "net"? He would never know. . . . A flourishing business, yes. But not on that scale.

Up to a year ago (two years after she got the interlocutory decree) it had been—possible. Because of the money for the Kenneth Road house. But when that was gone (and some of it had had to go, inevitably, for due installments on income tax when he was caught short), very soon almost everything else had to start to go too. How else?

He did not dare move the office to a cheaper, smaller location. That would be a giveaway, that the business was faltering; which it wasn't, not by any means. On the contrary, he was grossing a little higher than they had when Dad was alive. But of course that shot up the income tax higher, so it came to nothing really—in fact, a little less net. But you had to keep up the front to keep clients. The Duncan insurance office had been in this building for twenty years. Besides, there was the lease. Five-fifty a month. On the dot. The middle-class apartment on Glenoaks had been a hundred and five; that had to go first. The two-year-old Oldsmobile had to go; it cost too much to run; he turned it in on the very much secondhand Anglia. They said, thirty-five to the gallon, but it didn't deliver that. He found another apartment for seventy, but even that—after a while—was too high.

A thousand a month. A thousand a month.

She was earning at least four hundred and fifty at that place. Damn her. Damn her. The damn judge—

Had to keep up the front. To keep business. There were certain bills to pay first—couldn't get behind, that would be fatal. Where did you cut down? Quite obviously, on yourself.

He had the suit repaired that, before, he'd have tossed into the salvage box. He looked for bargains in shirts, in underwear. He took his laundry to the laundromats, hunting for the cheapest ones—fifteen cents per load.

Eventually, he ran an ad in the *Independent* and sold the TV, the radio, the portable air conditioner, the typewriter.

Business was just fine, he thought bitterly. Only, the little difference between *gross* and *net*. Maybe the judge hadn't known about the difference?

The gross, of course, fluctuated. Some months more, some less. Any month, looking at the figures, it sounded like the hell of a lot of money. Sure, to the damn judge. But there was the five-fifty for the rent, four-twenty for Mrs. Starr, average of forty-odd for the phone bill, average ten for gas in winter, fifteen to twenty for the air conditioning in summer— He'd have done without that for himself, but there was Mrs. Starr, and you had to remember the clients dropping in.

A thousand a month. Before everything else.

Last month he'd had exactly one hundred and eleven dollars to call his own. His net profit from the flourishing business. And that was just twenty-two bucks more than the Old Age Pension.

Sure, very funny.

Four months ago he had sold his Longine watch to an old-gold shop and bought one of these cheap Swiss ones, six-ninety-five. Some while ago he'd sold his mother's engagement ring, his father's Masonic ring with the diamond. Odds and ends in the little box of family things his mother had kept: his grandfather's diamond stickpin ("Oh, well, these old-mine-cut diamonds, sir, not as valuable— I could offer you, er, thirty dollars?"), the garnet sunburst brooch, relic of some great-aunt ("Sorry, seven bucks is all I can offer").

What did a man do?

He saw an attorney, who was vague. "It's tough, very tough, I know. The bench always favors the female side, all I can say. . . . No, Mr.

Duncan, it's not fair, it's not justice, but that's how it is. You take it to court again, you come in for legal fees, and—I'm not a shyster, enough business I've got now—I tell you frankly, it's a hundred to one against you that you'd get it decreased. . . . You know how they figure—pure womanhood on the pedestal. Unless, of course, she's very obviously a cheap chippy out to dig gold."

Which, of course, she wasn't. Not obviously. To any damn near-sighted judge listening to her for fifteen minutes.

A thousand a month. For the privilege of, for the period of approximately one year—

What did you do, a man with a flourishing business drained, in vampire fashion, by this thing?

Duncan found out.

Eventually, you wore suits that needed cleaning because you couldn't afford the seventy-five cents. You put off the oil change, the grease job, on the car. You brought home cans of beans and stew.

You, belatedly, gave up the apartment and looked at the ads for single rooms. You tried to cut down on cigarettes, switched to the very cheapest brand and saved all the stubs over an inch long. In the single furnished room you had a little hot plate where you warmed up canned hash and made ice cubes for your coffee in the battered bar-refrigerator you'd picked up for ten bucks. You—

Because there were the necessary payments to come out, first and foremost. *A thousand a month.* The rent. Mrs. Starr. The utilities. The rent of a roof over your head. He'd have made some arrangements to live at the office, but it just wasn't possible: only that one small back room, and Mrs. Starr would spot— She'd worked at Duncan Insurance a long time, she was efficient, but she wasn't the sort of woman he could explain to frankly, ask for understanding, for— The necessary amount of food. The cost of running the car. Now, since the damn car had gone out on him, of the bus—thirty-eight cents a day—because who could afford a garage bill?

The month before this, he'd had exactly ninety-nine bucks and forty-three cents to call his own.

The month before that, a hundred and three and twenty-eight cents.

The month before that. When you met her. The real one. The forever one. No fooling. The one to live with for real, and have kids with, and make a family with. And she—

Only, of course, you couldn't. Ever. Quite out of the question.

Because a judge (bored, careless, half-listening) hadn't distinguished between *gross* and *net,* and had said, *A thousand a month.*

There was a little restaurant half a block from his office, where he'd usually gone to lunch. It wasn't an expensive place but there were other places cheaper; only he had to drive to find them. Once, quite seriously, he'd tried to work it out on paper—if he had to drive a mile, which used up how much gas, to find a place where lunch would cost him only sixty cents instead of eighty— But he still went there, mostly. You didn't have to have a regular lunch, with the salad and dessert. In the coffee shop he could get a sandwich for thirty-five cents, coffee for ten: cheapest items on the menu.

It was there he met her, having lunch with a woman he knew—not well; in fact it wasn't until she spoke to him that he placed her. A young woman, a Mrs. Carr—who was in the escrow department at Federal Savings. They'd met over that Goldman business, gone out for coffee together once, he remembered.

"—This is Sue Morgan, she works at Federal too. We're on our way to the beach. I just stopped to pick her up, and thought we'd have lunch first—" Mrs. Carr was garrulous.

Duncan said how do you do, and she smiled at him. She had very neat, shiny dark hair, which seemed to fit her like a sleek cap, and very white skin with a powdering of freckles across her nose. Her eyes were very blue and her mouth a little too wide, and her unplucked brows were oddly almost straight lines, which should have been unattractive but was just the opposite. Duncan thought absurdly, But she looks so *clean.*

A funny word for it, for the impression she made on him.

He sat down at the counter beside her and ordered. They were almost finished; it was barely five minutes he sat there talking with her—trivialities. And then they got up and she smiled and said, "Please don't bother" as he did too. "Nice to've met you, Mr. Duncan," and they went out together.

Only he kept seeing her. Looking so clean (which was, when he thought it out, the fumbling word his mind had dredged up as a synonym for *honest,* for *straightforward*). He'd liked her—

He'd liked Helene at first too.

How young and naïve he had been . . .

But she wasn't like that. You couldn't be childish about it: say, Because I was tricked by one of them, they're all false and devious. You grew up a little and were less naïve, was all. This girl—

It was, looked at logically, madness. Just madness. In his position. But he couldn't stop thinking about it. Daydreaming, could you say? For just one evening, to turn the clock back and enjoy things he'd never much noticed when he could have them any time. Such little things. The discreet quiet and outsize menu cards of a good restaurant. The deferential waiter giving good service. The pleasant sharp ice-cold tang of the leisurely preliminary drink. A carefully prepared meal, something fairly exotic like steak Marseilles. A pretty girl across the table, smiling at him . . . Not just any pretty girl: Susan Morgan. Who looked so *clean* . . . Just as if he was a real human being again, and a moderately successful one, instead of a machine for producing a thousand a month. Just as if the fifteen or twenty bucks it would cost him didn't matter, wouldn't mean skipping a few meals and—

(The attorney said, "I tell you. You could show it to be unfair, with a lot of figures—all your accounts. If you happened to get a judge who'd take the time to look at the figures. A lot of judges start out with the ingrained idea that any husband trying to wriggle out of alimony is a heel to begin with. A lot of judges haven't quite caught up with the times, don't take it into consideration that a young able-bodied woman without encumbrances can go out and earn a damn good living for herself. They don't—go into the pros and cons, some judges. And you've got to remember, one reason, the calendars are all damn crowded. They just can't spend too much time on—excuse me—minor plaints. It's just one of those things, Mr. Duncan.")

He was mad to think of it. Out of his mind. Besides, he didn't know where she lived. So that was that.

In the middle of filling out an accident form for a client the next morning, he suddenly remembered that Mrs. Carr had said, "I just picked her up." Didn't that argue that she lived somewhere around here?

He looked at the Morgans in the phone book. There were Morgans in the Verdugo Woodland area, and in the east part of town, and over toward Burbank—and one on Stocker Street, just four blocks up from Glenoaks. A Mrs. Catherine Morgan. Maybe her mother?

It didn't matter, because of course it was out of the question to—

He finally called the number two days later, at seven-thirty in the evening, from the office. He asked for Miss Morgan, and was asked to wait (in a woman's pleasant voice) and presently she said hello. It was the right one.

He felt as nervous and adolescent and terrified as the first time he'd ever asked a girl for a date, back in junior high seventeen years ago. His palms were wet and he had to clear his throat. "Miss Morgan—this is Ross Duncan, I—we met the other day, Mrs. Carr—"

"Oh," she said. "Yes, Mr. Duncan?" She sounded polite and cool.

"I—" He had to clear his throat again.

He hadn't taken a woman out—he hadn't gone anywhere, or done anything, with a woman for nearly three years.

"I wondered if you'd like to have dinner with me some night. . . . Friday night, maybe?"

"Well, that's—very nice of you." She said it playing for time, time to think, remember him. If she could. Barely five minutes there— "Friday? Let's see, I— Yes, Friday would be fine, Mr. Duncan, thank you."

He found he'd been holding his breath. He managed to sound normal, he thought, making arrangements about the time.

He took her, recklessly, to the Matador up on Foothill Boulevard. It was the first time he'd been in a decent restaurant in that three years too, except for a couple of times when he'd been the guest of a client. He forgot everything but right here and now, and they had a fine time together. They found they laughed at the same things, which was maybe the most important piece of any relationship; and they stayed until the orchestra came on, and found that their dance steps fitted too.

He drove her home after midnight, and just as he halted the car in front of the neat little California bungalow where she lived with her mother, he found he was thinking at the back of his mind, Eighteen dollars and seventy-two cents, for five hours of happiness. How many times in the next month to have just coffee for lunch, just chili for dinner? God—

She had turned to him, started to say something about enjoying the evening, when he brought one hand down smack on the steering wheel and said, "Oh, my God, I'm a fool! Why did I—why did I?" He looked down at her in the dark, the pale oval of her face, and he said abruptly, "It's just no good, Susan." She'd said people called her Sue, but she wasn't a Sue—a mindless, cuddly little kitten—she was straightforward, honest Susan. "I shouldn't have asked you out. Or anybody. I've got no business to. I—"

And without any exclamations she asked, "Why?"

He told her. It was a difficult thing to explain, without seeming to ask for sympathy. And of course, a divorce—well, there were still a lot of people (like himself) who felt vaguely that it left a little taint. Always faults on both sides . . . "It's just no *good,*" he said painfully. "I want to be honest with you—because—I felt you're an especially—honest—person yourself. You can see. It's not just the money. It's—like false pretenses. And just making it worse—for myself, too. I'm sorry, Susan, I'm sorry. I shouldn't have—"

Because now he'd be thinking about her, wanting her, all the more. All the time. And not just because she was the first girl he'd taken out in three years. Because she was Susan.

"We had a good evening together," he said. "Leave it at that. Thank you, Susan. For everything."

"I suppose," she said calmly, "that squandering money the way you did tonight means you'll be pretty short for a while? That wasn't bright. We could have gone somewhere cheaper."

"I—Susan—"

There was a little silence, and then she said, "You can't just—bury yourself, Ross. It's bad for you. You need to talk to somebody, have a little fun sometimes. Maybe just riding around a little, having a hamburger at a drive-in. And we'll go dutch on that, and you're not to go all silly and masculine about it."

"Susan—"

"Brooding's bad for anybody," she said. "Keeping it all inside. Much better for you to swear about it to a sympathetic ear. Thank you for telling me—I know it wasn't easy. Don't get out—it's all right. Next time we'll just have that hamburger. Thank you, Ross—goodnight."

CHAPTER 4

When he knew her better, he knew that she'd deliberately taken the chance, made the overtures, because she knew Ross Duncan for the kind of man he was almost on sight. And knew that he never would, that he'd just stand still for a long while and let life walk all over him. Awhile. Helene, of course, hadn't ever known Ross Duncan. Helene, being self-centered, never saw below surfaces. She had read Ross Duncan for a weakling because he was very slow to anger, a steady cautious quiet man. But in a lot of men like that, the iron was just buried deeper.

He thought, through the next weeks, that it was only Susan who kept him sane. Just by listening to him. It was a very long time since he'd had anyone to listen to him fully and sympathetically. He had friends—men he called friends, from school, from business association; all of them were married, had their own concerns, and he could not talk freely to them.

But all the time he knew they were sitting on a powder keg, he and Susan. His much-beloved Susan, who went at things direct and open, bringing daylight to life.

They drove down to the beach one Saturday, for that hamburger. They talked and talked. She got him to laugh. Other times, they just drove around town, talking. She was firm about paying for her own sandwich, malt. "You've got to be logical," she pointed out. But of course logic didn't quite cover that sort of thing. . . .

Once they went to a cheap movie, because it was a reshowing of a very good old comedy and she said he needed to do some laughing. He did, and he felt fine when they came out, and they went to a place swarming with high-school kids to have a soda.

But all the time, of course, sitting on a powder keg . . . And as an intelligent, imaginative woman, didn't she know that?

So, the night they drove over to Hollywood to the free art exhibit, and drove home—

"Not a moron," he said angrily, breathlessly, against her mouth. "You knew what we—what I was walking into—damn fool— Oh, God, I shouldn't have, shouldn't have—Susan, I love you so much, Susan—"

"I—thought—" But he stopped her mouth again. A long time later, faintly, she said, "I thought—I was so smart— Good for you, have somebody to talk to. I was sorry for you—I—"

"Sorry! Sorry! I don't want any damned pity from— Oh, my God, Susan, make me let go of you—I can't—"

"Don't want you to," she said, and with a violent effort he pushed her away, disentangled her arms from him and took hold of the wheel with both hands.

"Listen," he said. "Listen. Logic you talk about. My darling, my darling. Logic is money. I have to think twice about buying a new shirt. I can't afford the rent where I am, I've got to find something cheaper—a room. Can I say to you, my dearest darling, let's get married? I've got a vampire sitting on my shoulder. Am I such a heel to say to you, forget the ceremony, take our fun where we find it? It isn't that kind of thing I want with you—it's the home and kids and building something together— *You*. Just—just go away from me, Susan. That's all."

"No," she said. She reached for him again, blindly. "No, Ross— Ross, we *could* do it. We could manage, darling. With what I—"

"So I let you pay the rent and buy the groceries! What the hell kind of—"

"It's not your fault— I understand how—"

"No," he said. "No. It would come apart—it would come down to— little petty feelings. I can see it. Just stop it, Susan—cut it off. I'm a bad risk, I'm poison. You can find somebody the hell of a lot better for yourself, Susan. This is just—this— Let go of me, darling, for God's sake—"

And she knew, then and there, not being a fool, that with no effort at all she could have had him. Trapped, for keeps. A touch, a word, and he could not have helped himself, he'd have taken her there, savage. But she was his Susan, honest; she played fair. She leaned against the far door and she said steadily, "Ross darling, you know I love you. I never meant to—I never meant to—egg you on. I don't want anybody better. There isn't anybody better. But I know how you feel. We *could* manage, I know we could. Please, Ross, if you could try again—get it reduced—"

But the attorney had explained about that. "It's no good," he said dully. "Cut your losses, Susan. Forget about me."

"So easy to say. Will *you?* Ross, I'll always be here. That's all. There must be some way. There must. Ross, please—"

"Good-bye, my darling," he said. "That's the only way. Thanks, and good-bye, Susan. Find somebody—less shopsoiled. Please, Susan, go away from me now."

She obeyed him, got out of the car in the silent dark street. "But I'm always here, Ross—there must be a way for us, my darling—"

He revved the motor to a roar and left her there. He was blind, dumb with pain—with desire. He had four dollars and forty-three cents on him; he stopped at an anonymous liquor store and bought a fifth of cheap Scotch, which left him thirteen cents; he went home and drank almost half of it, too fast, and woke seven hours later with a blinding headache.

That was the day before he looked at the ads for single rooms, and found the one he was living in now.

She had written him a letter. A very—Susan-ish—letter. Susan didn't know how to be devious. Even her handwriting, rather large, even and precise, was—*clean.* "Ross, darling," she wrote him, "I love you very much. I understand how you feel about the money situation, but I still think we could manage it if you could get over feeling that way. I make four hundred and ten a month. You might be able to get it reduced, with a good lawyer, because you can show it isn't at all fair. But anyway, my dear, I love you and I'm always here for you. In any way, Ross. Please believe me. I couldn't bear it, never to see you again, please."

Couldn't bear it. Neither could he. Susan, the real one, the forever one. There were things you had to bear. After a while—a long while— could learn to bear. Surely?

He hadn't seen her since then. It didn't get any easier with time passing. He still wanted her, with such a savage pain.

Something in the Bible, wasn't it, about, it is not good for a man to live alone—

He found the cheaper room, and moved. The Varallos seemed like nice people—but he wasn't feeling much, these days, noticing much, except on the surface. The room was comfortable, except that he was alone in it. He had trouble sleeping. If he could have afforded it, three or four stiff drinks before bed would help that; but he couldn't afford it. From the cheap bottle of Scotch, he allowed himself one drink half an hour or so before bed; after the first week, that didn't help at all.

And it was so hot. So unbearably hot. Not cooling off much even at night. The cheapest electric fans at the Thrifty were four-ninety-eight. Maybe next month—

He lay flat on his back, naked, in the hot black night and thought— Her slim white neck between my hands. I could kill her. I could kill her. She has no right to spoil my life— She is strangling *me*. Helene of the soft sly voice. I could kill her. My life—what could be my life. A real life. Susan, my darling—a home, a real home—my children. She is murdering my children. Have *I* no rights? A gun in my hand—her throat in my hands—just one thrust of a sharp knife—a rope round her neck—

He thought, homicides. In this sprawling metropolis, every day, every week, people were run down by careless or drunken drivers—killed by muggers—dead in the ordinary household accidents, a leaking gas line, a fire, something poisonous in the wrong bottle—

But never Helene. Not Helene.

He could kill her. She had taken his life—his potential life. Hadn't she? She had stolen Susan from him, and his and Susan's children.

Soft, sly, vicious Helene . . .

He could not sleep. Now, these intolerably hot nights at the end of October (the worst month of heat in Southern California), he was taking four aspirins and the Scotch, in order to sleep five hours; he felt stupid and dull most of the day, and Mrs. Starr had had to remind him of renewals, forms to be sent in, several times.

It was no good, not seeing her physically; he was seeing her all the time in the eyes of the mind. And, in a queer way, perhaps even clearer, Helene.

Helene, so safe and evil, going her way untouched by the careless driver or the dark-street mugger. Lucky Helene.

Luck could change.

He lay flat in the humid dark and he thought, I could kill her. I could kill her. An eye for an eye. She has killed me—Ross Duncan, as a man. Not with her sly innuendoes, her cutting sarcasm, her blind desire for dominance. No. She had read Ross Duncan as a weakling, to be easily dominated. And—very belatedly a sudden sure spark of knowledge illumined his mind—that is why. Why she had to have—retribution. Because she found out he wasn't: that Ross Duncan was just a quiet man who didn't like rows, but, when it came to a row, had maybe a little more than the necessary amount of steel in him. It had irritated her. . . .

He lay still in the dark. He thought, I could kill her.

And he wondered (since, with one like Helene, he would not have been the only object of her machinations, ever) he wondered how many other people were, perhaps, thinking the same thing.

Heat or no heat, the bed soil had to be turned over once a week or so, to keep it from getting packed. This humid, still Sunday afternoon Varallo, stripped to the waist, was grimly making the rounds from bed to bed, with a long-handled cultivator, loosening the topsoil, checking each plant, clipping off dead blooms.

Aphis again all over Diamond Jubilee, damn it. But Condesa de Sástago, one of his special favorites, was producing very nicely. The Condesa had two new buds to show him, and four nice fully opened blooms; he looked appreciatively at their lovely clear coral so unexpectedly turning to gold on the outside folds. Damn devil grass all around President Hoover. The Duquesa had a new bud. Eclipse looked a little dry, better give it extra water. Well, he reflected, you couldn't have everything. In most places, roses didn't go on blooming most of the year as they did here, with only a couple of dormant periods. In this climate—so you couldn't really complain of the climate, which called for daily watering all summer. . . . Charlotte Armstrong looked fine. Jacotte, climbing up the trellis beside the patio, was looking healthy too. Mrs. Paul R. Bosley hadn't had a bud in several weeks; maybe a light feeding, even this late, would help. Neige Parfum had three new buds. Regretfully he clipped off two dying full-blown blossoms.

God, it was hot! Varallo straightened, dropping the cultivator and yawned, stretching. He lit a cigarette. He looked at Ulrich Brunner, which had six or seven new buds, almost resentfully. Why the hell had he had to get involved with these damn roses? It was a senseless kind of —well, call it hobby. *Roses.* Big tough cop Varallo. But there it was, they'd got hold of him. So he had to spend his days off (which this month happened to be Sundays) tiring himself out wet-nursing a lot of roses, instead of sensibly—like Laura—sitting inside, with an electric fan, reading a detective novel.

Must be over a hundred, he thought. Hope this is the last of it, end of October. He looked over at the door beside the garage, wondering how Duncan was spending his Sunday afternoon. Reading, in there, or just lying on the bed brooding? The poor devil . . . Very possibly, thought

Varallo, there was some girl he wanted to marry too, and obviously couldn't. Duncan hadn't said anything about that—he wouldn't, of course, a reserved man. Almost certainly, Duncan wouldn't have said anything at all if he hadn't been high.

The poor bastard. Laura said she'd seen him, yesterday afternoon, starting down toward Mountain Avenue with his laundry in a paper bag —taking it down to the nearest laundromat, over on Verdugo. Walking. Last Thursday, there'd been a garage truck sitting on Loretta when Varallo came home, and a mechanic looking at the Anglia. Later, when Duncan came up the drive past the patio, Varallo had called to him, "Can they fix it up for you?"

"For an estimated seventy-five bucks," said Duncan wryly. "Sure." He went on into his room. The Anglia continued to sit at the curb on the side street.

Again Varallo felt very damned lucky to be who and what he was.

He finished his cigarette and buried the stub carefully in the soil under Ulrich Brunner. Seven months since the last rain, and the fire hazard dangerously high. He picked up the cultivator again and went on to Floradora; and then straightened as Duncan came out to the yard.

"Where d'you get the energy?" asked Duncan.

"I haven't got it," said Varallo. "The damn things just have to be tended. How's it go with you?" He asked casually; a man like Duncan (who had never referred again to what he'd told Varallo that time) was —prickly to handle. Very reserved.

"About the same. I— Hell," said Duncan, angry at himself, trying to laugh, "I've been sitting in there trying to get up my nerve. Like a kid. I hate like hell to—ask favors, Varallo."

"Well, a lot of us do." It was borne in on Varallo that now—knowing Duncan's situation, feeling sympathetic toward him—if Duncan should get behind in the rent, ask for time, it would be quite impossible to act tough about it. The poor bastard.

"It's just—well, look. I've got the chance at a new account, and by the sound of it a pretty big one. It might make—quite a difference. But they made rather a point of my going to see the top man, there's an appointment set up—out in the valley to hell and gone past North Hollywood, and— What it comes to, I—could you possibly lend me your car to get there? I'll pay for the gas—"

"Oh," said Varallo. "Well, I don't see why not. When is it?"

"Tomorrow night—eight o'clock."

"Well, that's easy enough, no trouble. I'll be home by six, and we weren't going anywhere—if we were, there's Laura's car. Sure, that's O.K."

"I appreciate it," said Duncan. "Thanks very much."

"Quite all right."

They talked for a few minutes more, casually, and some of the strain went out of Duncan's voice. How this kind does hate to ask for anything, thought Varallo; Laura would say, stiffnecked pride. And maybe be right; he understood Duncan because he was like that himself.

He got home at a quarter of six on Monday; Laura was before him as usual. "Duncan in yet?" he asked, kissing her.

"I don't think so. It takes such a time, on the bus."

That he remembered from the two days he'd had to ride the bus, the Chevvy in the garage downtown. He took off his shirt and tie; Laura had changed to shorts and a halter. They sat in the patio over very mild, very cold highballs, and relaxed. He told her about the drunk he'd picked up two hours ago, who was so firmly convinced he was in Washington and kept asking the way to the White House.

Duncan came walking tiredly up the drive at six-twenty. Varallo told him to sit down, and made him a drink. "Here're the car keys. You'll be running into a lot of traffic at this hour—tough luck."

"I'm afraid so," agreed Duncan. He looked tired and hot. "I'll have to put this down and rush—want to shower and change my shirt, and I'd better figure on at least an hour for the drive." He finished the drink quickly, thanked Varallo again, and went on to his room. Twenty minutes later he came out again, in a fresh shirt and a different tie with his rather shabby gray suit, and turned to the garage.

"Good luck!" called Varallo.

Duncan lifted a hand in acknowledgment, got into the Chevvy and backed out carefully.

"Poor man," said Laura. "Some women! I don't think they should grant alimony when the woman's young and earning a living. If there are children, that's different, but . . . I suppose I'd better start thinking about dinner."

When they went to bed at eleven, Duncan hadn't come in. But the Chevvy was back in the garage at seven-thirty on Tuesday morning when Varallo came out. He hoped Duncan had clinched his deal all right.

He was riding a route southeast in town today, and along it there weren't any restaurants as good as the one on Glenoaks. He stopped for his break at a hole-in-the-wall hamburger joint which was a little better than the others, on San Fernando Road. When he came out to the car at a quarter to one, after the regulation break, the radio was blaring. He slid behind the wheel.

"Car 94—car 94—come in to headquarters at once. Code One. Car 94—car 94—"

He snapped down the switch. "O.K., I hear you, am coming in," he said, obeying the "Code One," which meant "acknowledge." What the hell? Come in? He touched the siren once to clear the road for a U-turn, and started back fast for Central Avenue. . . . *Laura!* he thought. The only reason he could think of, call a man in from his route— Something had happened to Laura, and they had to tell him right away—

They hadn't said use the siren, but he did, then. He hit seventy all the way up Central, slowed just enough to make the right turn on Wilson, heading down to the big new headquarters building at the corner of Howard.

He was out of the car almost as soon as he pulled the brake. Snead, a couple of mechanics—and O'Connor standing there waiting—

"Hi, Vic."

"For God's sake, what's happened? Laura—is it—"

"Here, take it easy," said O'Connor. "Never crossed my mind we'd scare you like that—you husbands. Nothing like that. It's just business. Prosser's taking over your tour." Prosser was just coming down the stairs. Still shaken, Varallo nodded at him.

"What the hell is this, anyway? Business—"

"I've got to question you, Officer Varallo," said O'Connor solemnly, "about a little matter of murder."

"*Per l'amore di Dio!*" said Varallo. "It's too hot for practical jokes, Charles."

"No joke. I recognized the guy's home address, and then I remembered you'd mentioned renting that room. It's your tenant—Ross Duncan. It looks as if he maybe committed a messy little murder last night."

Varallo stared at him. He leaned against the rough cement wall of the garage and got out a cigarette. "Who's dead?" he asked, suspecting the answer.

"Mrs. Helene Duncan, over on Chevy Chase. Two blocks east, she'd have belonged to L.A.P.D. His former wife. I've collected this and that on it, in just four hours, and several little things point the finger at Duncan. Maybe you can hand me some more."

"Maybe I can," said Varallo slowly. "The poor bastard."

CHAPTER 5

They sat in O'Connor's office over coffee in cardboard cups. "I'll fill you in on it and then see what you've got. The body was found this morning about eight-thirty by her sister, a Mrs. Mona Norman. Seems they'd arranged to go somewhere together today, and Mrs. Norman was to meet her at her apartment. So she got worried when she couldn't get an answer, insisted the manager open the door—and there she was. In the living room, stretched out under the windows. Our old friend the blunt instrument. To short-cut, four or five blows were struck, mostly on the back of the head. Cracked her skull in three places. No weapon around, but it might have been almost anything—might even be somebody just held her and smashed her down across the mantel or a table, and wiped it off afterward. The sister says nothing's been disturbed in the apartment—no hunt through her drawers or anything like that. The doctor says, between six and ten P.M. last night, but we've narrowed it down more. The sister talked to her on the phone from about six-forty to nearly seven o'clock, and she says Helene told her she was expecting 'company' very shortly."

"Not who the company was."

"All I've got there," said O'Connor, "is the implication that it wasn't unnatural she shouldn't. The sister admits she was a little secretive about her personal affairs, apparently even when there wasn't any reason."

"There are people like that. Like to sound important."

"Sure. So she was alive at seven. Then, she had a date to meet a fellow—a Brad Hunter, painting contractor, about forty, I didn't take to him, could be a nasty character—at the Casa Manuel, a cocktail joint up on Foothill, at eight-thirty. She didn't show. He—"

"Eight-thirty," said Varallo. "And expecting company at home at around seven. She didn't leave herself much time, did she?"

"So it looked to me as if maybe the home company was unexpected, last-minute. As if somebody called and asked to drop around—some urgent reason—and she said O.K., but I can only give you ten minutes. Something like that. Hunter was mad to be stood up. About nine o'clock he called her apartment, got no answer. So that sort of pins it down between seven and eight-thirty, it looks like."

"Loopholes," said Varallo. "But yes, on the face of it. Why do you want to pin it to Ross Duncan?"

"Maybe he's pinned it on himself. To start with, he dropped his pen in her apartment." O'Connor fished out an envelope and dumped its contents on the desk. A shiny black fountain pen. "It's been printed—had three prints on it, look like a man's. We're getting Duncan's from his army record to check."

Varallo picked it up. It was not a new pen, perhaps five or six years old, a Parker. It had Duncan's name in fine gold letters along its side. *R. W. Duncan.*

"It was lying on the floor just inside the hall door. Then there was the manager. Ess, I should say. Mrs. Burton. Also the owner. She lives in one of the front downstairs units, near the entrance to the building. She had her front door open for better air all last evening. She remembers being disturbed, at about a quarter past seven, by a woman talking 'too loud,' she says, out in the hall—man and a woman, or two women, just leaving the building. This woman was saying, 'Wasn't it funny, running into Ross in Helene's apartment?' Mrs. Burton timed it because she was watching *Outlaw Sheriff* on TV and it was at the middle commercial. She volunteered this, by the way. All excited and indignant about somebody murdering that nice Mrs. Duncan."

"Very convenient," said Varallo. "She didn't know who these people were?"

"No. I pressed the sister again, hadn't Helene given her some hint who she was expecting, but she went on saying no. I asked her what she knew about R. W. Duncan, and she got excited and said Helene had been married to him and divorced him because he was so mean and cruel to her and probably he's the one murdered her because he just hated her and was a very violent man and besides he grudged her her alimony even if he was awfully rich." O'Connor took a drag on his cigarette. "That type."

Varallo nodded, seeing a breathless, incoherent, agitated female.

"So I asked around a little about Duncan, but I didn't get much. Only he seems to be placed there, by inference, about the right time, and it could be he has some motive. I haven't turned up anybody else suggestive. Of course it's early to say. Haven't seen him yet, but—"

"Where," asked Varallo, "did you get his home address? He's only been there two and a half months."

"It was in her address book."

"*Per carità!* I wonder why—and how. That's very funny. I certainly got the impression he's had no contact with her for a long while. What did she look like?" asked Varallo suddenly.

For answer O'Connor opened the flap of a manila envelope and slid out a glossy 8 x 10″ studio portrait. "In a nice silver frame displayed on one corner of the mantel."

"I see. Kind of female kept pictures of herself standing around. That figures."

She'd had an excuse, maybe. Helene Duncan had been blonde—probably by request—and altogether a handsome piece of goods. Handsome was the word, not pretty. It was a coldly regular-featured face, with wide-spaced eyes, well-arched slim brows—a face, he thought, of strong character. He tried to remember exactly what Duncan had said of her; there hadn't been much, but— "Had to be boss," there was that; and, "If it wasn't her way, she wouldn't play." That fitted the face.

"She was a hostess," said O'Connor, "at the Thunderbird Inn. Big place on Angeles Crest Avenue in La Cañada. Monday was her night off. You know, one of the haughty females stands at the door to the dining room and says, Have you a reservation, sir?"

"And earning a nice salary for it," said Varallo. "Well, I'm damn sorry for Duncan, you know, but I can give you one dandy motive, Charles. He told me about it when he was a little high. He wouldn't have, otherwise. He's one of those very reserved, prickly customers—no sympathy, please. She was bleeding him but good. Some damn fool judge didn't look at the figures just so close, you see, to be sure how much he'd be good for. One thousand bucks a month alimony."

"Jesus H. Christ," said O'Connor. "Is there that much money?"

"It's a flourishing business but to pay all his other overhead he's had to live pretty damn close to the bone himself. He can't afford seventy-five bucks to get his car running. He's paying us fifty-two-fifty, and I'd guess it doesn't always come so easy. He told me that that month—last month—he came out with just a hundred and eleven bucks to live on.

Take-home pay, as it were. He'd tried once to get it reduced, but no dice."

"My God, the poor bastard. That's sure and certain a nice motive," agreed O'Connor. "And possibly had his eye on another girl? Not that Helene qualifies—she was thirty-five."

"Older than Duncan. Quite possibly. Or maybe he's feeling, once bit, twice shy. I couldn't say. About last night, he borrowed my car. His is out of commission, as I said. He said he had a chance to pick up a big new account, only he had this appointment in connection with it, 'to hell and gone out past North Hollywood.' He came in at about twenty past six, I gave him the car keys and he had a drink with us. Went to shower and change, came out again and left—oh, between ten and five to seven. Last I saw of him. He wasn't in when we went to bed at about eleven, a bit after."

"Mmh," said O'Connor. "Both of you go to sleep right away?"

"Prying into my private life. I'd say we were both asleep by twelve-fifteen, twelve-thirty. He hadn't come in."

"Well," said O'Connor thoughtfully. His square, ugly, dark face was serious over the coffee dregs. "Let's go see him, hear what he has to say. I think I'd like you sitting in on this with me, Vic. It shouldn't be more than a day or two, if it's what it looks like—and they usually are, aren't they? Little irregular, but your immediate boss owes me a couple of favors, and there's an excuse—you know the guy, you've got inside knowledge."

"Not much."

"Never mind. Make a nice change in routine for you."

"Don't think I don't appreciate it," said Varallo. "But I could wish it was for another reason, Charles. Damn it, I like the guy."

"Dead?" said Duncan. *"Dead?"* He stared at them with an expression of utter incredulity. Then he laughed, sudden and mirthless. "Dead," he said. "If I didn't know better, I'd think it was black magic. Ill-wishing. God knows I've wished her dead often enough. But what—"

Varallo shifted restlessly. So, unlock the door to the gas chamber yourself, he thought.

Duncan had looked merely surprised to see them when they came in, surprised when Varallo said, "Hello, Duncan. This is Sergeant O'Connor, who'd like to ask you some questions. Could you—?" and looked at the woman at the second desk. It was a small office, well-appointed, carpeted, saying discreetly, Success; saying, Reliability.

"Well, what on earth," Duncan had said, and then shrugged and said, "Mrs. Starr, d'you mind taking your coffee break now?"

"I just came back from lunch, Mr. Duncan—" She was eyeing big Varallo and his uniform and holster belt in half-repelled fascination. She was a thin, scraggly woman in her fifties, with pepper-and-salt hair and black harlequin glasses.

"I know, but these gentlemen evidently want privacy, though what the hell about—"

She fussed around straightening papers, finally took up her bag and left, darting curious glances at all three of them. Varallo latched the door against any inopportune clients, and Duncan's eyebrows shot up but he said nothing.

Now he was saying, "Helene, *dead*. It doesn't seem— But what—"

"Murdered, Mr. Duncan," said O'Connor gently. "And we'd like to know what you were doing, when and where, at certain relevant times."

Duncan sat motionless for one long moment, his eyes quite blank of expression. "Murdered," he said then. Expressionlessly. "That's—funny. Rather funny. Just the other night—I was wondering how many other people might have reasons for wanting her—out of the way. Because I doubt very much I was the only one, you know. Evidently I was right." He looked up at them. "Oh," he said. "Of course—I see. You don't know who, and of course—it might have been me. Naturally. Why don't you sit down?"

They both sat down, O'Connor in the client's chair beside the desk, Varallo in another a little farther off. He would have liked to say, "I'm sorry," to Duncan, but of course he couldn't. If Duncan had—

"It wasn't me," said Duncan. "God knows I can't pretend I'm sorry—it's a vampire off my back—but it wasn't me. I—one thing, you know, I didn't even know where she lived. She had a box at the post office, I always sent the check there."

"Is that so?" said O'Connor, still gently. And not mentioning, of course, that Helene had evidently been in close enough touch with him that she'd known the address he'd had for a rather short time. "Just a few questions, Mr. Duncan."

"Yes," said Duncan. "What d'you want to know? I suppose—you already know from Varallo that I borrowed his car last night. Or was it last night? You didn't say—"

"And you left Hillcroft Road at approximately five to seven, yes. Where did you go then, Mr. Duncan?"

"I still can't figure it," said Duncan, looking frustrated and annoyed.

"The damndest thing. Unless it was a practical joke of some kind, and I don't know who'd do a thing like that. That address— Well, the whole thing— I'd better give it to you from the start. If I'm too long-winded, stop me. I see you've got to ask. Last Saturday morning I got a phone call. It was a secretary—Miss Somebody, she said, but I didn't get the name. She said she was 'speaking on behalf of' Mr. Somebody Else who was with Allied Canning Products, and he very much wanted to contact me to discuss turning the company's insurance over to my firm. It sounded like a big deal. You see, the real money is in these big accounts, like supermart chains and retail-store chains. You can see that. Bread-and-butter. I—could use another big account like that. You know?"

O'Connor said he understood. "Wasn't it a little unusual that the client—prospective client—should ask you to come to him? I thought it was usually the other way round." If, of course, thought Varallo, there ever had been a prospective client.

"Not really, on a big company deal—a package deal," said Duncan. "A little, yes. But some of these high-powered executives— Well, we set the appointment up, and the secretary gave me the address. I wrote it down." He felt in his breast pocket, took out his billfold, took from it a square memo-pad page, handed it over. "Damn it, she even spelled it out for me. Mr. Richard Whipstead, 12905 Moorbank Avenue, out in Valley Village—other side of North Hollywood. I don't see how I could have made a mistake. I—you know about my borrowing Varallo's car. It was the hell of a drive, still quite a lot of homecoming traffic out there. And still so damn hot. I couldn't find the street. I wandered around hunting, but there just wasn't any Moorbank Avenue." He passed a hand over his hair, wearily. "I stopped at a gas station to ask, and they'd never heard of it—tried to tell me I meant Moorpark. But that's what I was given over the phone—Mr. Richard Whipstead, 12905 Moorbank. I—"

"A gas station," said O'Connor. "Could you say where and at what time?"

"I guess so," said Duncan. He thought. "It was about ten past eight. I was a fool not to've looked at a map before I started out, but the secretary'd said, just straight out Riverside to Fulton, and left there, and I'd hit it. I was late by then, you see, and I thought, better stop and ask. It was a Union station, the first one—on Coldwater Canyon Road, and I think the cross street was either Riverside or Addison. I stopped twice, I don't remember which was first."

"Ten minutes past eight the first time?" asked O'Connor, taking notes.

"That's right. It was just—I never did find it," said Duncan dully. "After the second gas station, I pulled up on the shoulder and looked in the glove compartment for a map. There were a lot of them." He looked at Varallo, who nodded. There were. This had all been strange territory to him when he landed here last year, and he carried maps. "I still couldn't locate it on any of them. I wandered around out there until ten-thirty, like a damn fool. Too late then, if I did find it, to walk in and say, Sorry to be late, but I had trouble locating your address. You know? They probably put me down as just unreliable, and somebody else'll get that account."

"If there ever was an account," said O'Connor without emphasis.

Duncan looked back at him quietly. "Alibi," he said. "I see. Maybe. Not just the hell of a good one, sergeant, or is it? If those station attendants remember me. That is—what time was she—?"

"I'm not giving information, I'm asking," said O'Connor. "Then what did you do? What time did you get home?"

"I'm not sure exactly. I was—annoyed. And mad. I felt—you know—nothing ever going right for me any more. I stopped at a bar. That was a little after ten-thirty. I could find it again, I think—place called Giuseppi's, on Riverside. I had two drinks, all I could afford. It was air-conditioned, and I was tired—I just sat, nursing that last drink along. I—yes, sure, I remember I did some talking to the bartender. It was quiet, not many customers. He was a little Italian fellow with a mustache, friendly. I asked him about Moorbank, and he'd never heard of it either. Finally I drove back. I'd make a guess I got in at about a quarter to one, one o'clock."

"I see. Now, do you recognize this, Mr. Duncan?" O'Connor produced the fountain pen.

"Why, yes, of course, it's—where'd you get that? It's my pen, I lost it about ten days ago—or misplaced it somehow. I've been hunting all over for it. It's the pen I always—it was a birthday present from my father seven years back, I—"

"We found it," said O'Connor, "in your former wife's apartment. Can you explain that, Mr. Duncan?"

Incredulity widened Duncan's dark eyes. "That's impossible," he said flatly. "I don't know where her apartment was. I can't prove that, but I don't. . . . For God's *sake*. You're not really thinking—" He looked from O'Connor to Varallo wildly. "My *God*. Talk about—out of the frying pan into the—"

"Take it easy," said Varallo. "If it wasn't you, we'll find out."

"Will you?" said Duncan. "This is— I don't know what more I can tell you. That's where I was. I don't know if it would clear me, if those attendants remember, and remember the time—I don't know when she—when it was done—but if they *do*, well, I couldn't have driven out there from Glendale in much under an hour, you know. If that says anything."

An alibi? An alibi thought out? O'Connor and Varallo exchanged glances. A very tricky little alibi, and how could he have been sure that they'd pin down the time of death so close? Unless, of course, he had known about the sister's phone call, the later date. Which he could have, from Helene. But the alibi he'd started to set up on Sunday, when he couldn't have known.

It was very much less than satisfactory. . . . O'Connor asked more questions. No, Duncan had had no contact with his former wife since about two years ago when he had written her asking that she agree to accept less alimony. She had called him on the phone to say no. He didn't know where she had been living. He had known where she worked, because it was the same place she had worked before they were married, and she'd spoken of going back there, at the time of the divorce. They had liked her, she was efficient, so he had assumed she was still there. He had lost or misplaced his pen about ten days ago. Yes, he had hunted for it, of course. He didn't remember whether he'd mentioned it to Mrs. Starr—probably not. Why not? Well, it was hard to explain—she was an efficient woman, yes, he liked her all right, she'd been here a long time, but—well, just not much social exchange between them. Besides, when he didn't find it in the office he thought—he always had it on him, you see—that he might have lost it in the bus, going home. He hadn't killed Helene Duncan, no.

"Do you know of anyone else who might have had a reason to want her—out of the way?"

Duncan shook his head slowly, blindly. "Not to *know*," he said. "But there probably were, sergeant. There probably were. Because she—interfered. She always had to interfere. Do you know what I mean? She always knew just what you ought to do, and the way you ought to do it. She wasn't backward about telling you. That kid sister of hers, Mona—she had her hypnotized. I don't think Mona ever bought a new lipstick without first consulting big sister. Now, darling, what you want to do is—" Duncan broke off suddenly, passed a hand across his mouth. "There's her husband," he said. "I don't know. It doesn't seem like—a reason for murder, but he didn't like it, you know. Helene—what it amounted to—running his wife's whole life. They'd only been married a year when Helene and I—I haven't seen either of them in three years, I wouldn't know how that situation is now. . . . Helene, dead. It takes believing. She had—so much force. If that's the word . . . Are you arresting me?" He looked steadily at O'Connor.

"I haven't applied for a warrant yet, Mr. Duncan," said O'Connor placidly. "We like to be sure." He stood up. "I'll want to talk to you again, of course. We'll see how all this checks out."

"Just what I need," said Duncan to nobody in particular. "Arrested for murder. So then the business goes to hell too, even if I'm acquitted. Which I wouldn't be. Naturally. *Whom the gods would destroy—*"

"Take it easy," said Varallo again. "We'll find out, if it wasn't you, Duncan. We're not exactly morons these days, you know."

Duncan met his eyes. Damn it, thought Varallo, I like the guy—and while there was never enough motive to excuse murder, well—

Duncan gave him a faint smile. "I've got to believe that, don't I?" he said. "Thanks, Varallo."

CHAPTER 6

"So?" said O'Connor in the car.

"I'll just say this," said Varallo. "Almost anybody might commit murder. But—differently. I can see Duncan killing, yes. He's a man like that one in the Bible, is it—the one slow to wrath? I'd say he gets mad about once in five years, and then, when he does lose his temper, he loses it one hell of a long way. I can see him going to beg her again, take less, and if she was sarcastic with him, losing his temper and bashing her with anything handy. What I can't see is Duncan planning it all out beforehand."

"Well, now, Vic—a canny businessman, dealing with figures, having to look ahead— I'd say just the opposite."

"No. That's got nothing to do with the natural man. . . . This reminds me of something, for some reason. I can't think what, but—"

"Try," said O'Connor, "the Wallace case." He shoved in the dashboard lighter. "England, the nineteen-thirties. Interesting case, it was—made quite a legal stir. Busman's holiday—I like reading up on the classic capers. "

"By God, yes, of course. Laura reads these things. I picked up one of her books— Of course. Husband and wife, only no motive ever suggested—"

"Except that one," said O'Connor the bachelor. "Funny, he was an insurance salesman too. And it was exactly the same kind of alibi. Mysterious new client—long hunt for a nonexistent address. Home again, my God, wife battered to death by unknown assailant."

"He was convicted, wasn't he?"

"It was," said O'Connor, "if I remember right, the only case where the court of appeal, whatever they call it over there, reversed a jury verdict in a homicide trial. They turned him loose, and he died a couple of years later, of cancer. . . . It just struck me, you know. Almost a carbon copy, the alibi. If that's what you can call it."

"It is, isn't it? The Wallace case was written up—where I saw it—in a book of British cases, Laura got it at the library—"

"Where anybody could get it. I liked him," said O'Connor obscurely, "before I met him just now. I liked him a lot—he looked like the best bet. Well, ninety-nine times out of a hundred, it's just what it looks like, isn't it?"

"Sure to God," said Varallo. "Most of them don't have many brains."

"And it is," said O'Connor, "a very artistic kind of alibi. A very natural-sounding alibi, and not so watertight that you automatically begin figuring how he juggled it. . . . But unless he's one damn good actor, he was surprised as hell. For real."

"I thought so too. But count me out, Charles— I'm prejudiced. I like him."

"I just don't feel," said O'Connor, looking earnestly at his cigarette, "that a man putting on a good act, at being surprised to hear about the murder and so on, would have come out with that little piece about black magic and wishing her dead. He wouldn't dare—he'd be too self-conscious. I don't know— I could be wrong—but I thought that came straight from the heart. But it could be he's a lot smarter than I think."

"Pay your money and take your choice," agreed Varallo. "Don't write it down on your 510 form, Charles, for the lieutenant—not yet—but, that pen. Nice tangible evidence. I seem to remember, in that Wallace case, it was pointed out that nearly every bit of evidence they had could point two ways—to his guilt or innocence. Confusing. We've got something of the same sort here. If Duncan really did lose it—or thought he lost it—as he says, well, that says something to us. Because there it was in her apartment. It says that maybe somebody is ringing Duncan in as a handy scapegoat. Doesn't it?"

O'Connor turned in his seat and looked at him. "Now that never struck me, I hadn't got that far. So it does. But it's the hell of a long chance. Things aren't generally so complicated."

"Once in a while—" said Varallo.

"I'm telling you," said Martin Norman, "that one was a real pain." He added where. "I'm doing no crying. I'm not surprised she got herself taken off. Mona thinks it was her ex did it. He could of. That's why he was her ex, I figure."

O'Connor asked him to elaborate on that one. The Normans lived in a small, new, bright pink ranch house in a new tract in Montrose, above Glendale. The living room bore much evidence of uncertain feminine taste—a good deal of pink, lampshades with tiers of maroon ruffles, a pair of china ballerinas on the mantel, a turquoise sectional and several early-American maple chairs covered in patterned chintz—chairs not big enough to afford comfort to masculine rumps. In the middle of this, Mr. Martin Norman (plasterer by trade, employed by a local contractor and making a good deal more money than either O'Connor or Varallo) looked very masculine and out of place. Mr. Norman was perhaps thirty-five, solid and stocky, with a barrel chest and many muscles. He was wearing an ancient pair of slacks and a damp undershirt, and drinking beer. He wasn't, he explained, on the job because he'd been called home to take care of his wife after she found the body and was questioned by the police—gone all to pieces, the poor kid.

"Take care of her!" he said. "My heart wasn't in it, I'm telling you. Sure you won't have some beer? Plenty on ice. What I wanted to say, Honey, you'll be a damn sight better off. She finally took some dope, she's asleep—you want to ask her some more?"

"No, we'd like to talk to you, Mr. Norman. Or rather have you talk to us. You didn't like Mrs. Duncan?"

"She," said Norman, "didn't like me. It was mutual." He scratched his chest, where a mat of black hair showed through the undershirt and continued on up to his throat. "Hell of a snob, that woman. I'm telling you, the only way I ever got Mona married to me was catch her and argue her into it while Helene was off on vacation. Twice she'd got Mona to break it off. She was so damn mad when she got back and found us married, she couldn't hardly see straight. Couldn't do anything about it then. See, I don't say anything against Mona, gentlemen, but no denying anybody could argue her into anything in ten minutes. Which was all Helene's doing too. She'd bossed her all their lives—five years older—and kind of got Mona in the habit of being bossed, if you take me. She didn't like me because I'm a common workingman, see. Never mind that I make damn good union wages, can give Mona most anything she wants. That cut no ice with Helene because times I don't talk good schoolbook American, and I sit round in my undershirt in hot weather." He finished his beer. "Quite the lady, Helene was."

"Did she try to interfere with your marriage, Mr. Norman?"

"Hah!" said Norman. "Did she try! I had Helene and Helene's ideas thrown in my puss morning, noon and night. For quite a while. Helene says it's awful old-fashioned to have a double bed. Helene says it's slack —whatever the hell that means—slack to eat in the kitchen, we ought to eat in the dining room with the good silver. Helene says I shouldn't let you sit down to the table without a shirt, Marty, it looks like peasants or something. Now I'm a patient man, and I love my wife even if she is a fool, times, but she couldn't seem to get it into her head all this I don't like one damn bit, all this Helene says. So finally I got good and fed up and I took my old man's advice and I belted her one. No good just using an open hand on a female—you give her a real good hefty one and it gets through. I never had no trouble with Mona, like that, again. She got the message. But acourse, Helene still went on talking to her. And once in a while she'd turn up here." He got up. "Excuse me, I'll get another can. Sure you won't join me? Well, O.K." He came back with a new can of beer, sat down and drank. "That bitch," he said. "Looking at the place like it's a dump, Tobacco Road or something, and at me like I'm a Skid Row bum. She got under my skin. Know something? She wouldn't of, near so bad, if she'd come right out and said things. But it was all round the back ways, with Helene." He gestured with the can. "She always talked nice and sweet as pie. And about an hour later, you all of a sudden got the point of what she'd really said —something nasty. Sarcastic, do I mean? No, it was—more than that. Like, she'd be here when I was maybe sitting around like now, and give me one of her looks and say to Mona, 'So informal, darling, but that's terribly *passé* now, isn't it?'—I dunno what that means, but anyway, without her saying it straight out, the message came through—me a slob from Slobville, sitting guzzling beer. And it upset Mona like hell, that kind of thing. She was always trying to make excuses, damn it—for me, to Helene, you know. Like, Oh, well, dear, Marty works so hard. And that made *me* mad—madder, that is. I'm telling you, I know she'd been at Mona a dozen times to leave me. But Mona won't do that, long as I'm still around to persuade her the other way." He laughed. "But maybe you place Helene's type. I'm not the hell of a lot surprised she got herself knocked off. She must've annoyed a lot of other people. Maybe at that place she worked. *And* I useta tell her she didn't have such a high-class job either, restaurant hostess, but it never registered. I guess she thought it was, because she had to be all dressed up swanky— better than some of the customers." And it was then he came out with his comments on Ross Duncan.

"What do you mean, 'That's why he was her ex'?"

Norman laughed and drank beer. "She couldn't boss that one. I only met him four-five times but I sized him up. *He* treated me O.K., like I was a human being—seemed a nice guy, and a halfway smart guy for an office man. Look, Helene was Mrs. God. She had to be better than everybody else around her, and they had to know it and knuckle under. All soft and sweet as hell, but that was it. The men she picked up—I mean, just to go round with, you know—they were always the kind she could boss. I figure she thought Duncan was too, and he had a nice business and all, and she grabbed him, figuring he was a good bet. But she found out different. That one she couldn't run. He wouldn't have any rows, he'd just go out and do as he pleased, and it must have made her mad as hell. I know when she divorced him, she let out to Mona she was going to get every cent of alimony she could out of him—she was real mad. And that figured too. She was mean as hell about money. I useta try get Mona to see it, but she never could. I mean, Helene, she'd give Mona some little thing cost maybe a couple bucks, for her birthday —and next day buy herself a fur coat. Nothing too good for Helene, but she didn't waste money on anybody else. And when she could, she liked a man along to pick up the tab. Don't get me wrong—I just mean, for drinks and restaurants and theaters and like that. Matter o' fact, far as *that* goes, I don't figure if you ever got her to lay down, you'd get much of a kick out of it." Norman drank. "Don't think I ever heard her say anything to anybody without scattering a lot of Darlings and Dearests, and that kind's usually strictly from Siberia."

"Isn't it the truth," said O'Connor amusedly. "Do you know the name of John Broderick?" Varallo looked at him; this was something new. "There was a letter from him in her desk."

"Sure," said Norman, "he's her other ex. Didn't you know she'd been married before? Come to think, I guess no reason you would—maybe even Duncan didn't know. She was married to him a couple years, Mona said. It was before I knew her or Mona, I just heard the name."

"Do you mind telling me, Mr. Norman, where you were last night?"

"Me? What the hell, you thinking I had anything to do with— What the *hell!*" Norman was belligerent. He set down the can.

"Just for the record, please."

Norman snorted. "I was nowhere. Just here. Got home about six, had a few beers, had dinner. Sure, Mona was here. Where else'd she be? She fixed dinner and we ate it. She washed the dishes. I looked at

TV awhile. Mona did some sewing. We went to bed about ten-thirty. That's it."

"O.K.," said O'Connor. "Thanks very much, Mr. Norman."

They went out to the car.

"Well," said Varallo. "Mona. Apparently a very easily persuadable female. And under her husband's thumb. As well as Helene's. Whichever was there at the time."

"And under his fist," said O'Connor. "I appreciated that. He may have something there."

"The Irish are an uncivilized race," said Varallo. "I was just thinking, you know. On the long chance that this is a frame, there was a woman in it."

"How come? Oh, the woman talking in the hall for Mrs. Burton to hear."

"Not only that, Charles. To frame a man successfully, you've got to know that he won't be able to turn up an alibi. That Wallace case—the same alibi—only, not a good one, pointing both ways. Suppose Helene was dead by seven-fifteen. Duncan could have been out there, an hour's drive away, asking directions, by eight-ten—after killing her. And on the other hand, if it's a frame, the real killer sent him out there, to insure that he'd be alone, hunting that address, at the crucial time. Instead of in sight and hearing of witnesses. O.K. That whole setup was arranged over the phone, by a woman calling herself a secretary."

"I'll buy that," said O'Connor, after thinking it over. "But it *is* the hell of a long chance."

"What about this Broderick?"

"She didn't keep much personal stuff. We only found a couple of letters in her desk—the rest was all receipts and stuff like that. There was a letter from an old aunt—great-aunt, the sister said—and this one from Broderick. Asking for a loan of fifty bucks. It's an address in Walnut Park, I want to see him. But probably not much in it."

"Funny. I don't think Duncan knew he was Number Two. . . . All that Norman gave us—nice lady. I've met a couple like that. And he's right about Duncan, too. She couldn't run him, and that must have made her mad. So she's taking him the only way she can, in revenge."

"And maybe signed her death warrant doing it," said O'Connor. "I feel fifty-fifty about it, Vic. You said, the kind that loses his temper once in five years. So he is. So he put up with this situation a long while, and then got mad. I'd also like to know if just maybe he's recently acquired a new girl friend and wants to get married. What they call impetus."

"He's obvious," agreed Varallo. "Don't listen to me too hard, Charles—I'm prejudiced. I'd like to think, Not Duncan. And I just got to thinking, you know—Mr. Norman in there. Also a fellow with a temper, and one much shorter than Duncan's. He resented Helene's influence over Mona, her attempts to interfere between him and Mona. Maybe he got to thinking the only sure cure was to put Helene out of the way permanently. . . . No, I don't say he could have persuaded Mona to act as an accomplice, not if she knew what she was doing. But if I guess right about Mona, she's not the brainiest female in existence. He could have made up some tale, got her to do the telephoning to Duncan—left her outside in the car while he went in and killed Helene, and told her another tale, get her to— Oh, all right, so I'm wool-gathering. It was just a thought."

"Let's go see where she worked," said O'Connor with a sigh.

"O.K. It's three-twenty. Afterward, come back home with me—we'll pick up some steaks on the way—and have dinner. When Duncan gets in, drive out there with him and ask those station attendants."

"Good idea," said O'Connor.

"Was she liked?" repeated Sandra Wyatt doubtfully. Varallo suspected that she had been born Luisa or Dorotea or Maria, and had also picked the Wyatt out of thin air. She was small, thin, dark, about twenty-five, friendly and intelligent. "I suppose so," she said. "We waitresses don't have much to do with the hostess." She'd just come on duty; they were lucky to catch her. The Thunderbird Inn opened at four, closing at two after the luncheon trade—all except the cocktail lounge, which was open all the time, 11 A.M. through to 1 A.M. Sandra was in the restaurant. It was a classy restaurant, undoubtedly expensive, with all the props: deep carpeting, lighting so discreet as to make menu reading all but impossible, waitresses in scarlet uniforms. "We called her the Duchess. She was—what we saw of her—well, I guess she thought she was something. I will say, we all kind of felt it was just as well she didn't have much authority over the girls—she'd have been a tartar, that one. . . . No, she never had any trouble with any of us, that I know of, and I'd have heard if there was. She didn't really have much to do with the waitresses, you know—she just kept track of reservations and like that, led people to tables or booths, and then the waitress'd take over. You mean she's really been *murdered?* Gee, it doesn't

seem—" She was eyeing Varallo interestedly. "Gee, that's something.
. . . I never knew much about her, personally, none of us did. She was
just the hostess. I do know, she had a run-in with Mr. Reilly last week.
Not that I guess Mr. Reilly'd be the one murdered her. Well, I mean—
he's not the type. I don't know what it was about. I'd just come on duty,
four o'clock, and I'd changed to my uniform in the waitresses' rest
room. You have to come past the manager's office—Mr. Reilly's the
manager, yes—and I heard them going at it in there. She was saying
something about a cut of the profits, and Mr. Reilly said she didn't have
one damn thing on him. That's all I heard, I went on past, but they
were both pretty mad. I—"

"You do anything about that?" asked Varallo, forestalling O'Connor.
She tilted her head to look up at him. "I don't get paid to think. Just
to carry trays. I just wondered if she'd get fired, talking up to Mr. Reilly
that way, but she didn't. No, I didn't think much about it. I work here
to earn enough money, pay my college fees—I'm going to be a teacher, I
go to L.A.C.C., daytimes."

"Mr. Reilly in his office now?"

"I'd guess so."

"So let's see him, Charles," said Varallo; and grinned at pseudo
Sandra Wyatt and added, *"Grazie, lèi è molto gentile, signorina."*

"Piacere—" and she reddened angrily. "How'd you know, anyway? I
don't—"

"Ashamed of it?"

"Of course not! I—it's just, up where I come from, it's kind of like a
brand, people acting—"

"This is the big city. People don't think twice, here. Forget it," said
Varallo, and turned after O'Connor.

He thought he'd seldom seen such a fishily cold pair of eyes as those
of Mr. Gerald Reilly. Mr. Reilly was impeccably clad, cordial and can-
did, in his chrome-and-leather office. He was perhaps fifty, round and
pink and groomed to the last inch. He said it had been a shock—a terrible shock.

"Such a nice quiet girl. So ladylike. She had been here for some time.
One of these sneak thieves—probably a dope addict—was it? A terrible
thing."

"We're not just sure yet," said O'Connor. "Just a few questions, Mr.
Reilly."

"Anything I can do to help you," said Reilly earnestly.

"Yes. We have information," said O'Connor, "that you had an argument with Mrs. Duncan one day last week. In this office. Would you care to tell us what about?"

Dark color surged into Reilly's face; he made a convulsive movement. "What damned sneak told— Ah—an argument? I don't— Really, I— Oh, ah, yes, I *do* recall now! I don't know who happened to overhear, sergeant, but what it was, well, quite childish, I'm afraid! In fact, nothing more nor less than an—ah—a little political discussion. Mrs. Duncan and I were on opposite sides of the fence, so to speak, and I'm afraid we both got a little excited. Probably our voices were raised. But I do assure you—" he laughed cozily—"it was all purely, ah, objective. In the end we both calmed down and, as I recall, had a cocktail together before Mrs. Duncan went on duty. It was—"

"Oh, yeah," said O'Connor, giving his impersonation of the rather stupid cop accomplishing routine. "I see. You know, we just got to ask. Thanks, Mr. Reilly. You can't tell us anything more about her, uh, private life?"

Reilly spread his hands in regret. "It is not good policy to be on too familiar terms with one's employees, you know. Mrs. Duncan was a pleasant, respectable young woman—she did her work here satisfactorily. We were all on good terms with her, but as for myself, it was a business acquaintanceship only, and I don't believe she knew any of the other employees well. . . . It's been a shock—she'll be hard to replace. . . . I do hope you find the criminal responsible, soon."

CHAPTER 7

"Would you have any guesses about Mr. Gerald Reilly?" asked O'Connor.

"Well, you know," said Varallo, "I've only been a city cop for eleven months, Charles. Out in the sticks we don't get much organized pro crime. On the other hand, I'm fairly bright at adding two to three. What our Sandra overheard—you take your choice, dope, illegal liquor, the numbers racket, a back-room roulette wheel. Stakes down, gentlemen. I'd pick one of the first two. Helene tumbled to it, and was trying to cut herself in. We seem to be getting into deeper waters."

"Not too deep," said O'Connor. "Thanks to the chief and commissioners of L.A., this metropolis is shut but tight to the syndicate boys, and long may it continue so. Small-timers, if too many of them, only. I'm with you all the way, and we'll take a long, hard look at Mr. Reilly. But do you see Mr. Reilly bashing a beautiful blonde over the head?"

"I don't think so. Maybe he has henchmen?"

"What pretty words you use," said O'Connor. "Let's go get those steaks. On me. If your wife won't mind unexpected company."

"You seem to visualize married life as one long battle," said Varallo. "Very unhealthy attitude, Charles. You ought to be psychoanalyzed. It's the Helenes are the exceptions, really. Most women quite nice people."

"Do I deny it?" said O'Connor. "For a while. A little while. Stop at the Country Squire on Verdugo, they've got a good butcher there."

The important thing, thought Duncan, was to keep Susan out of it. Not just on Susan's account, though that was important too: Susan mustn't be touched by this thing. This incredible thing. (God, yesterday he'd have said, if anyone came to tell him Helene was dead, he'd have felt like a million, he'd have—) But also, the police were not fools. They knew he had a motive. You don't have to pay alimony to a dead woman. If they found out about Susan, well, that more than doubled the motive.

There was no reason they should find out. Unless she got in touch with him. She'd see it in the papers—she might— Please God, Susan would have better sense than to—

The papers. The first reporters had landed on him just after Varallo and O'Connor left. The *News-Press*. The *Times*. The *Mirror-News*. It probably wouldn't make headlines, but it would be in the papers all right.

He didn't know where he stood with them. They hadn't given much away. He didn't know whether he was the only suspect. They might have a tail on him now. They might think they had enough, and be getting a warrant.

How the hell had his pen got into her apartment? How the hell?

He rode the hot, smelly, belching bus. He got off at Ethel Street and started the long walk, up Cortez to Rossmoyne, up Rossmoyne to Hillcroft Road.

That pen. He couldn't figure it. It was—

But hang on to the thought, it would be all right. It had to be. These days, the police weren't fools or bullies. They made detailed investigations; they didn't railroad people. When he wasn't guilty, he was in no danger of being charged. Naturally, they had to check him out, but an innocent man wouldn't be—

Is that so? said his mind back at him. The way you used to think, an innocent man was safe from the law? The courtroom law. By the law of the land, nine-tenths of his income had been drained from him for three years; the law hadn't troubled to use fair play there.

If that could happen—

No, he thought. No. It will be all right. They'll find out who. And Helene is dead, and then—and then—

He was very tired. The walk seemed longer than usual.

When he came up the drive, he heard voices; they were sitting in the patio. He didn't want to face them, talk to them; he felt, ridiculously, embarrassed.

But he couldn't avoid it. Varallo called him over, told him to sit down. Sergeant O'Connor was there; they'd been broiling steaks on the portable outdoor grill. O'Connor had taken off coat and tie, and looked less official; Varallo had changed out of uniform. Duncan thought again what a handsome fellow he was, in uniform or out. His eyes looked friendly. O'Connor didn't look any way at all. Just—waiting.

"After a while we're all going out there in my car, see if those attendants recognize you. Meanwhile, sit down and let's hash this over a little. O.K.?"

Duncan sat down; and Varallo's pretty brown-haired wife asked, "Have you had anything to eat, Mr. Duncan? You look awfully tired."

"That bus— Yes, thank you, I had a sandwich."

"Well, that's not very much. It's silly to make yourself ill, worrying. I'll get you something." He tried to refuse, but she got up and went into the house. Varallo said he'd have a drink anyway, went in after her and came back with a tall chilled glass. Duncan took it gratefully. He looked from Varallo to O'Connor. He wondered suddenly what Varallo was doing in this. He didn't know much about the police, but he did know that uniformed patrolmen didn't sit in on homicide investigations. But, he remembered then, Varallo had told him he'd been a high-ranking officer on another force, a little town upstate somewhere. Hadn't said why he'd quit: funny. Maybe O'Connor was a friend of his, and was letting him sit in because of the circumstances. Maybe—

"I don't see any reason," said Varallo, "why we shouldn't satisfy your curiosity a little, Duncan, and tell you that Mrs. Duncan was killed —by several blows on the head from a weapon we haven't found—between seven and eight-thirty last evening. Probably nearer seven to seven-thirty."

"I was on my way out into the valley then," said Duncan.

"But you'd have had time to drop by and kill her before you started," said O'Connor. "You can see that. It's not a great distance, is it?"

Duncan looked at him. "I don't know how far it is, sergeant. I don't know where she lived."

"You have any ideas how she happened to know where you live? She did. You've moved three times in the last year and she had all the addresses in her book."

"That's imp—" Duncan stared at him. "If you say so. But I can't imagine how or why. Why the hell should she be int— I hadn't seen her for three years! I— Wait a minute. I suppose—" He looked at them. He knew how it would sound to them, because they hadn't known Helene. "I can imagine a reason—of sorts. It'll sound crazy to you. But she was —a long planner. You wouldn't believe the trouble she'd take to make something come out just the way she wanted it to. And she—how can I explain it? You know the people save things, in case they'll need them some day—string, paper bags. In a sense, she did that with people. Calculated, about people—whether they could be of use to her. Now, or ten years from now. I know it sounds—implausible, but it could be she somehow kept track of me because some day she might find a use for me. She had a nice hold on me, you know." He felt his mouth tighten in a wry smile. "She could have come to me with some nasty little job she wanted done, and promise to take less, and I'd have— I know it sounds crazy. . . . And, sure, she knew the business address, but that'd be Helene—efficient—keep track all along the line."

"Well, you knew her," said Varallo. "We're learning about her. A lot of the spadework in looking at a murder is finding out about the victim. We'd like to hear your version of her."

The drink was picking Duncan up. "Prejudiced," he said. But he felt from Varallo, at least, a friendliness, a genuine interest; and the other man might look stolid, but he wasn't; his eyes were shrewd. Cooperate with them, try to impress them— As intelligent men, they'd take character into account. "She hooked me," he said slowly. "I can't explain it to myself even now. I was a fool, but— It was just after my father died. I was alone and—she was there. I met her at the Archers', people I know slightly. Three weeks later we drove over to Vegas and got married. In other words, I acted more like eighteen than twenty-eight. We were married ten months, and for about nine and a half of them I knew the kind of mistake I'd made. What was she like?— It's words, just words, but I'll—give you my version. She was a woman who had to dominate her whole environment, and everything in it. Not—the way some strong characters are—from, oh, a sense of responsibility, but for the sense of power. She had to be the boss. On the surface, she was very feminine, too feminine if you get me—the poor helpless little woman—but if you wouldn't knuckle under to her—!"

"Tantrums?" asked O'Connor.

"Oh, God, no. She had a tongue like a razor. The very cutting, subtle sarcasm. She had a way of—knowing what weaknesses to play on, too."

"What was her attitude toward money?" asked Varallo.

"Toward *money*? Well, like most of us she liked it. But yes, there's something there too. It was—well, I've said she was subtle. On the surface, she was. But actually, when I analyze some of the things I've known her to do, and say, she was crude. She was so busy thinking of herself, she didn't have any idea what other people were really like. She had no imagination at all, you know. She didn't know when she was being tactless. About money, she seemed to have the feeling that it all belonged to her, and in a funny way she resented any of it being spent not for Helene, if you take me. I mean, what income I brought home—it was perfectly O.K. for her to run up a five-hundred-dollar charge at some department store, but if I bought a new tie she resented it, said it was extravagant. She'd have liked to have had charge of the whole bundle, doled out cigarette money to me—like that. She was—miserly—with everybody but herself, if that makes sense."

Varallo said it did. He got up, went into the house, came back with a bottle of Scotch, soda and ice cubes, and renewed all their drinks. His wife followed him with a tray of fat sandwiches, a bowl of salad and sliced cake on a plate. Duncan said he really didn't—and absently started to eat a sandwich.

"Don't fuss," she said severely. "They'll find out who, Mr. Duncan. Of course, it's a pity that this—this fat Irish sergeant happens to be on it instead of Vic, but he must have a few brains."

"Hey," said O'Connor, "that's a lie— I'm just right, according to insurance statistics. Haven't you ever told her about official ethics, Vic? Shouldn't say such a thing in front of a suspect."

"Hah!" she said. "A mere technicality. You have to take character into account." She sat down again.

"You'll gather my wife is prejudiced," said Varallo, sounding amused. Duncan didn't know what to say; he smiled at her. "Go on. What about her family? We know she pretty well ran her sister's life—or tried to."

"Yes, she was always phoning her, meeting her, going shopping—but the Normans didn't come to the house often. Not more than two or three times. She—rather kept people in watertight compartments. Norman resented her ordering his wife around. Understandably, from what I knew of the situation. I never—I'll tell you how it was, not to sound—prejudiced—but she was a snob. She didn't like Norman because he's not a white-collar man. There was an old aunt—Aunt, Aunt Minnie or Mamie or something—Helene used to go to see her at least once a week, but she only took me once, to introduce me. About that I found out, inadvertently, from something her sister said, that the aunt has a lot of money in real estate. There's a son, who'll come in for most of it, but I suppose Helene was hoping for a share, so she kept the old lady sweet. The aunt's pretty old, in her seventies. The point is, Helene was ashamed of her family background, she tried to—cover it up." Duncan hunted for words. "Hell, it's not snobbishness to—classify people. They come all sorts. If I didn't want to make a bosom pal of Norman, for instance, it's not because he's a skilled laborer but because we didn't have much in common. The old aunt, her grammar slips once in a while and she—maybe she's the miser, if there really is money there—she lives in a mean little place cluttered with Victorian monstrosities, all very lower-middle-class. The sister also once let slip that their father was a brakeman on the S.P. Well, what the hell? My grandfather was a bookkeeper, and his father was a farmer. It doesn't say anything. But people like Helene are sensitive about those things. Come to think, maybe the only thing she was sensitive about. That time she took me to meet the aunt, all the way back she talked about what a 'quaint character' the aunt was, 'pretending to be so uneducated' and so on. You get the picture."

"Mmh," said O'Connor.

And Duncan added suddenly, "*Why* the hell? I've been asking myself ever since. Two weeks after we were married— I thought, for God's sake, I had a little more sense, a little more sophistication! It's not as if she was even very smooth—about covering up. I've wondered ever since how I was hooked so easy. Like a teen-ager."

"We all make mistakes," said Varallo. "Tell me something. This pen. You missed it about ten days ago? At the office, or at home?"

"At the office. I'm sure of that. I use it all the time. One afternoon when I reached for it, it just wasn't there. It was just after I'd come back from lunch, I think. But I couldn't tell you whether I had it in my pocket and lost it on the street, or had left it on my desk. I usually pick it up automatically."

"Do you recall any stranger being in the office around then? Someone who'd never been in before and didn't come again?"

Duncan looked at him. Were they believing him, looking beyond his obviousness for someone else? But why should— "I'd have to think back on that, a lot of people come in. But why should—" And his logical mind, trained to deal with figures, gave him the answer. He stared. "Deliberate?" he said. "Something deliberate? A frame on me?"

"It's an outside chance," said O'Connor.

"I'd take a bet on it myself," said Mrs. Varallo sweetly. "Ten to one, sergeant?"

"I'm not a gambling man," said O'Connor sleepily.

"Laura," said Varallo. She made a grimace at him.

"Oh, all right."

Duncan looked from her to Varallo to O'Connor. "You think—"

"I don't think anything until we know more. The hell of a lot more," said O'Connor. He looked at his watch. "Just seven. Those attendants should be on duty again by now, and also we'll take a look at traffic conditions on the way out. Suppose we get moving?" He got up and reached for his tie.

Varallo got up too. He looked very tall, very hard and masculine, standing there over Duncan. He had changed to gray slacks and an open-necked white shirt, and at the V of the shirt thick golden hairs glistened in the sun. He hadn't, thought Duncan, any business being an ordinary cop. He ought to be a movie actor. A make-believe sheriff on TV, and all the female audience swooning over him. Only, the blue eyes were too intelligent and friendly. "That phone call last Saturday," he said. "The woman who said she was a secretary. Somebody's secretary. Like anybody's voice you know?"

"Hell, I couldn't say," said Duncan blankly. "It was just a voice—a woman's voice. She sounded like a secretary." He thought about that. "You know, like someone used to doing business on the phone. She said—" he paused to remember— " 'Mr. R. W. Duncan? I am calling on behalf of—' and so on. And then later on, yes, I remember, I suppose there was an interruption, another phone call or someone coming in, and she said, 'One moment, please,' and toward the end, when I asked for the address, she said, 'One moment, please,' again. It was—oh, nearest I can come, a thin metallic voice. Very brisk and efficient."

"You didn't—" began Varallo, and was interrupted by his wife.

"She said that twice, Mr. Duncan? 'One moment, please'?"

"As I recall, yes. It—"

"Well, there you are, Vic," she said. "A lead, anyway. That wasn't a secretary. That was a woman who worked—or has worked—for the telephone company. I've sat on a switchboard long enough to say that, for sure. Who ever heard a secretary say that? A secretary'd say, 'Hold the line a moment, please,' or, 'Excuse me a moment, please.' That *One moment, please* is purely switchboard-ese."

Varallo looked down at her. "I see what you mean. But girls do quit jobs and get others."

"So they do," she said, looking deflated. "But it's something, Vic."

"It's something. . . . Expect me when you see me, *mia vita*." And he bent to kiss her, open and hard. Duncan looked away. Susan, Susan —if I ever get out of this mess—

*

They drove out there, through difficult traffic, and found the right gas stations, and what did it say? Nothing. The one where he'd stopped first, the attendant recognized him. Sure. But he couldn't swear to the exact time. "About a quarter past eight, I guess."

They still hadn't told him where Helene's apartment was, but evidently in Glendale somewhere, at a distance from Hillcroft Road where he could have stopped, murdered her and still driven out this far in the valley to be here at that time asking directions.

On the way out, Varallo had asked him casually whether Mrs. Starr had been in the office when that phone call came through. She had not been: it had come through in her lunch hour, twelve to one. Duncan took his break when she came back; he'd been alone in the office. Had he mentioned it to her? Yes, he had, but she hadn't heard it firsthand.

The second station attendant was also positive, and that said less. "About twenty to nine." It wasn't any kind of alibi, if Helene's apartment had been within ten minutes' drive of Hillcroft Road.

"But I didn't," he said, there in the dark. "You've got to believe me— I didn't. It wasn't me. God knows I've wished her dead, but—"

"Take it easy," said Varallo. "We'll find out. . . . Do you know anything about the Wallace case?"

"What? Wallace—I never heard of—what d'you mean?"

They were sitting three in the front seat, Duncan in the middle. He saw Varallo and O'Connor exchange a glance across him. Small panic filled him. He said, "I swear to God, I—what are you thinking? I—"

Susan, Susan. Oh, God, this is a nightmare—must be a nightmare. Nothing real. I, Ross Duncan, suspected of—

"Now, this bar—" said Varallo.

"Yes, it was about ten blocks from here—next turn left, I think I can spot it—"

They found the bar, and the Italian bartender. Who remembered him quite well. That he had asked about a Moorbank Avenue, which was— so far as the bartender knew—nonexistent. But that said nothing; it was too late in the evening.

They couldn't, these days, convict an innocent man. The honest, efficient police—

Susan, my darling. No. It would be all right—

If I had not been such a fool, he thought. In the first place. About Helene.

CHAPTER 8

O'Connor had succeeded in borrowing Varallo, off routine duty, for a day or so at least, though Jensen of Traffic had kicked. "I've just got a little idea," said O'Connor on Wednesday morning, sitting at his desk and looking at the autopsy report, "that this is going to be one of the complicated ones. They come along now and then."

"So you need my brighter brain and experience to deal with it," said Varallo, "obviously. I'll tell you the one thing says that to me. That very unnatural little business in the hall outside Mrs. Burton's door. The woman talking about seeing Ross in Helene's apartment—talking loud enough to be sure she was overheard. Almost by itself, that says to me, a frame."

"I don't see it's that important—"

"Think about it, Charles. That was at seven-fifteen. When Helene talked with her sister on the phone at about five to seven, she said she was expecting company, not that she had company. In fact, when she chatted over the phone for fifteen or twenty minutes like that, it argues she was alone. So if these people—the woman and whoever she was talking to—came later, they didn't stay long. We're asked to believe, by implication, that Ross Duncan arrived while they were still there, that they knew him well enough to call him by his first name. Are you with me so far? O.K. We are then supposed to believe that, with two witnesses knowing he was there, Duncan committed the murder after they left—"

"Blew his top," said O'Connor. "Forgot about them?"

"You can't have it both ways," Varallo told him disapprovingly. "Use your mind on it, Charles. Either he set up that tricky alibi himself and went there intending to kill her, or he just went to ask her again to

take less money, lost his temper and killed her. If he went there mean-
ing to kill her, he'd have put it off when he ran into the potential
witnesses. If he killed her on impulse, what becomes of this rigmarole
about Whipstead and Moorbank Avenue? Because there isn't a Moorbank Avenue anywhere in the county. I looked at the county street
guide. So that was deliberately set up by somebody."

"It could," said O'Connor mildly, "be both ways. He set it up, and
then meant to call it off on account of the witnesses. Then something
she said made him mad—"

"All right," said Varallo. "All right. Let's find the witnesses. I'll lay
you a hundred to one we don't. That that was another try to pin it
harder on Duncan—and it sounds to me like a spur-of-the-moment idea
when they saw the door open. Is there a sign saying that's the manageress's apartment? There is. So, it'd be a fair inference the manageress
would take more interest in tenants than other tenants, and remember
what she overheard."

"That's very fancy deducing," said O'Connor. "And all what's called
ephemeral. . . . There's nothing new in this," and he put down the autopsy report. He opened the door and said, "Leath—Waterman. I want
you to go up to the Thunderbird Inn, on Angeles Crest in La Cañada.
Not right now—the bar doesn't open until eleven. We think the manager
there, Reilly, and possibly some others, are mixed up with dope, illegal
liquor or gambling. Sniff around. Say it's just a routine check-up like we
run every so often." He came back and sat down, picked up another report. "The prints on the pen are Duncan's. On the other hand, there are
no other prints of his in the apartment. Which says nothing—he wiped
them off, dropped the pen by accident. There were several unidentified
prints here and there—in the living room, the bathroom. Betts thinks at
least three people, excluding the sister, whose prints we took yesterday.
I think I'd like to get Mr. Brad Hunter's prints to compare. Also Mr.
Norman's. And—yes—Mr. Reilly's. Like several other people, Hunter
could be X. On times. He didn't get to Manuel's until eight-fifteen, and
he lives alone. Who's to say where he was between leaving his office and
getting to Manuel's? Let's go call on Hunter."

Downstairs, however, they ran into the Normans first. Mona Norman,
Varallo thought, was a pale copy of Helene. Also blonde by request,
with regular thin features, she had no figure; her too-light blue eyes were
pink rimmed, and she had chewed off most of her lipstick. Her voice
was high and breathless.

"Please, it's about—we've come to ask—because there'll be all the *ar-*

rangements, and I want it at Forest Lawn and the man there said they'd have to know about something he called a release—"

"Oh, yes," said O'Connor. "I think the doctor's finished with the body now—"

She burst into tears, and Norman patted her shoulder. "Now, honey, she's gone, she don't feel anything." He looked at them curiously. "It said on the radio this morning that you'd questioned him. Duncan. Just a kind of announcement of her being dead, in the paper last night, but this morning— You figure he's the one?"

"Sorry, too early to say."

"Of c-course it was him!" sobbed Mona. "Who else'd want to hurt *Helene?* Everybody *loved* her! Why haven't you arrested him yet?"

"Well, now, we have to have evidence," said O'Connor. "Mr. Norman, would you mind letting us take your prints? For comparison. There were several unidentified prints in her apartment, and—"

Norman, inclined to belligerence at first, was calmed down and agreed. "And Sergeant Stein over there at that desk, he's the man to see about getting the body released. He'll give you a form to fill out. See Wilmot up in my office, and thanks very much."

The trouble was, as he and Varallo did not remind each other, they had evidence. Quite good evidence, as far as it went. There was the pen. There was the woman in the hall. (Two detectives upstairs were working their way through Helene's address book, calling all her female friends to ask whether they'd seen her at her apartment at about seven o'clock on Monday night, and met Ross Duncan there.) There was Duncan's unprovable, implausible tale about Whipstead and Moorbank Avenue. There was his motive; and no one else seemed to have so strong a motive, that they'd run across so far.

They started out again; and the uniformed man at the desk nearest the door, speaking into a phone, laid the phone down and came to intercept them. "Lieutenant King calling from your office, sergeant. He wants to see you before you leave."

"You were just too late to catch me, Jack," said O'Connor. The uniformed man grinned and nodded. "The lieutenant," said O'Connor as they went out into blinding heat, "thinks I should have applied for a warrant yesterday. He thinks there's plenty to charge Duncan on. He pointed out that even if he was recognized by those station attendants, he could have killed her before driving out there to bolster up what he calls a crazy amateur alibi. I told him about the alibi being out of a book, and he was annoyed. Books, he says. Books, yet! These amateurs.

Then he said, You just go out and find the guy's girl. Bound to be one. That's the rest of the motive, he wanted to get married again. Enough to charge him on now, but the D.A.'ll like it better if you can find the girl. . . . I'll have to see him sometime today. Let's hope we pick up something—" He let that trail off. Varallo had never had anything to do with Lieutenant Harold King, but he had heard a lot about him from O'Connor, and he knew exactly the kind of police officer King was.

They are found on all police forces, and they are good police officers —within limits. Almost always they have worked up to rank slowly and ploddingly, as King had. He had been on this force for a quarter of a century, and ranked lieutenant only eight years ago. He was an honest man, but a simple man; he possessed no imagination at all, and was incapable of seeing below surfaces. Generally, as Varallo and O'Connor had agreed, what it looked like was just what it was; crime is seldom subtle. But now and again it was; and the Kings were simply not equipped to deal with that.

"He says, open and shut?" said Varallo as they got into O'Connor's car.

"He does. He'll be calling for action by tonight, and he's the boss."

"So let's hope we pick up something," said Varallo.

Mr. Brad Hunter, seen in his Central Avenue office (Painting Contracts of All Kinds—Free Estimates—We Guarantee Our Work) was belligerent and voluble. Varallo didn't like him any better than O'Connor had. He was a big square man with an incipient paunch, all the false bluster of the weak man compensating for weakness, and, proclaiming masculinity, he seldom opened his mouth without scattering profanities liberally.

He had, he said, been damn mad, and who wouldn't be? That damn sly little— The way it was, he said, he had been going to see she paid off, if he had to keep at her for a year. Three months, trailing him along, letting him in for all the tabs at restaurants, bars, shows—and all the time playing the prim little miss— "As if she's a finishing-school debutante or something, for God's sake!" Excuses, he said, and the wide-eyed routine: What makes you think I'm that kind of girl?

Sure to God, he'd been fed up but good. Spotted her for what she was, by then: the one always reneged on you. But nobody got the best of Brad Hunter in the long run, and he'd sworn to himself he'd have her, if just once, to prove it—make the sly little bitch lay for him once anyway. "Not that she'd be worth it—that kind I know, icicles aren't in the running, my God." Only reason he'd gone on paying out money on her. And he'd figured she'd stood him up deliberately, so naturally he'd been mad. If they wanted to know, he was still mad, because somebody'd taken her off—probably not before she deserved it—and now he never could collect.

His *prints?* Why the hell? What damn qualified crap had they got in there— *Him?* Hell, he hadn't any reason to kill her—just the opposite! Damn dumb cops—

"Unidentified prints," said O'Connor, "in her apartment. We have to check, Mr. Hunter. Eliminate people. Had you been in the apartment?"

"Oh," said Hunter. "See what you mean. Sure I had, damn it. To pick her up and like that, you know. *Not* beyond the living room, you bet your sweet life!—except once when I bulled my way in for a last drink and used the john. Didn't do me any good," he added gloomily. "She'd had five Martinis too, and I figured—but she never turned a hair. Quite the hell of a dame, in her way. And now I never can get square with her. Hell and damnation." He agreed to drop in at O'Connor's office on his lunch hour and have his prints taken.

"You called her apartment at about nine or a little before? Yes. Then what?"

"What the hell d'you mean, then what? I was good and mad. I bought a new bottle and went home and watched TV, that's all."

Outside, O'Connor said, "Well?"

Varallo shrugged. "So look at it the other way around. We think she was killed a long while before eight-thirty, but maybe she wasn't. The doctor gave it leeway to ten o'clock. Maybe she really did stand up Hunter, and was in the shower or something when the phone rang. Maybe he went right around to the apartment, so mad at her coldshouldering that he killed her. Nothing to say yes or no. For that matter, nothing to say he didn't kill her at seven o'clock. Only that leaves out the frame on Duncan. I mean, that kind of motive—it'd be a murder committed on impulse, almost certainly."

O'Connor sighed and agreed.

They went on to the Bank of America, where they looked at Helene Duncan's financial record. It was, in a way, interesting. She made fourforty a month at the inn, take-home. Otherwise, her monthly income added to a nice round sum. She had evidently started out, three years ago, using Duncan's alimony as investment capital, and she had built it up. She was paying a substantial monthly installment on a sixteen-unit apartment out on Verdugo Road, and another on a twenty-unit place in

Pasadena. The gross monthly take on those two added to nearly three thousand. She had recently bought six lots in La Crescenta.

"She regarded that," said the vice-president who was letting them in on all this, "as an investment. Expansion, you know—lots of new building up there. She told me she expected to double her money on this. A very shrewd business head, Mrs. Duncan had." He looked regretful.

She lived well: the apartment rented for a hundred and twenty, and there were checks to Cash (probably representing grocery bills, cigarettes and so on) and checks to three department stores where she had accounts; but her personal expenses, though high, were not extravagantly so considering her income.

There was a savings account of seven thousand ninety-four dollars and fifty-two cents, and a checking account of six thousand eighty-six dollars and ninety-three cents. Both O'Connor and Varallo looked at the figures enviously.

"I wonder," said O'Connor, "who gets it." But the vice-president knew nothing about a will. If there had been one, probably the lawyer who drew it would call in. A holograph will was legal in California, but there hadn't been one among her effects at the apartment. They asked if she'd had a safety-deposit box. She had, a small one. After delay, authorization was obtained and in the vice-president's presence they opened it. It contained a legally drawn will leaving everything she possessed to her sister, but tied up in a trust to be administered by the bank; the deeds to the property she owned; her birth certificate; certificates of common stocks, fifty shares here, a hundred there, in eleven different corporations; a high-school graduation diploma; her two marriage certificates; the official death certificates of her parents, John M. and Marian L. Baumgartner; and a number of statements-of-account from a conservative brokerage in L.A.

"The string saver," said Varallo to himself. "Yes. How very efficient and businesslike. Of course, Baumgartner—you might know, German."

They made a list, thanked the vice-president. "I want," said O'Connor, "to see that aunt—only other relative. Also John Broderick. And—"

"I want," said Varallo, "to see Duncan again. Should have asked him last night, damn it. If he knew about Broderick. What she might have said about him. If he knew— Look, it's a quarter of twelve. See Duncan, have a quick lunch at that restaurant down the street, and go over to L.A. for the aunt and Broderick. O.K.?" Unconsciously he had assumed leadership here.

"O.K.," said O'Connor.

They parked in the restaurant's lot and walked down to Duncan's office. On the way they passed Mrs. Starr, heading for the restaurant on her lunch hour. She gave them a quick sidewise glance, recognizing Varallo though he wasn't in uniform.

They went into the office. Duncan was hunched at his desk over some papers, but his pen wasn't moving; he was just sitting there. He looked up slowly. "Oh—hello," he said.

"Just a couple of things," said Varallo. "Did you know she'd been married before? Who he was?"

Duncan looked surprised. "That," he said. "Yes, I did. She told me she'd been married less than a year—he turned out to be a bum, drank and beat her up. She was only eighteen then. No, I didn't know what his n— Wait a minute, sure I did, on account of the marriage license. She'd gone back to using her maiden name, Britton, but legally she still had his, she put it down on the license, it was Broderick, something like that."

"Wrong on several counts," said Varallo. "Her maiden name was Baumgartner. She married Broderick when she was twenty-two, according to her sister, and lived with him a couple of years. Apparently she got absentminded when she filled out the form for your marriage license. She put herself down as twenty-seven when she was actually thirty-one."

"*Thirty*— She told me— Oh, well, I'm not surprised," said Duncan wearily. "I didn't know all that, no. Why? D'you mean—"

The door opened behind them. And Duncan's expression changed to stark fear, to something like despair.

A woman's voice said eagerly, "Ross, my darling—" and then, seeing the others, "Oh, excuse me, I didn't—"

Varallo swung around. She stood there, hand on the open door, looking uncertain. A pretty girl, an unusual type. Dark hair, white skin, thick straight brows. A plain tailored blue sheath dress, nice figure. About twenty-five. She looked quickly from Duncan to Varallo to O'Connor.

"Ross—" she said again, and shut the door behind her. "I saw it in the paper last night, I came as soon as I could—my lunch hour—"

"I'm sorry, what is it you want, miss?" said Duncan. "The office is closed."

"You're a friend of Mr. Duncan's?" asked Varallo. "Miss—?"

She moistened her lips. "Morgan. Susan Morgan. Ross, what—"

Duncan stood up, violent on movement. "No," he said. "She must be a nut—or a reporter—claiming to be— I don't know her, never saw her bef—"

"Miss Morgan," said Varallo resignedly. So here—by Duncan's manner—was the reinforcement to motive, and Lieutenant King was going to like it very much indeed. "Have you known Miss Morgan long, Duncan?"

"I don't— I just *said*—"

The girl backed away suddenly. She looked at Duncan. "I don't underst— Yes, I'm a—friend—of Mr. Duncan's. Ross, what do you *mean?* I—it said in the paper last night—she was killed, by a burglar or something like— What *is* it? You look— Ross—"

"Maybe," said O'Connor, also sounding resigned, "you and Miss Morgan had planned—or hoped—to be married, Mr. Duncan?"

"Ross, who are these—I don't underst—"

"I never saw the girl in my life," said Duncan loudly. "Get out of here, you—you crazy female! She's just a nut—"

"Not that easy," said Varallo. "Sit down, Miss Morgan. We'd like you to answer some questions."

"No!" said Duncan. "No, I—"

"Take it easy, Duncan. The cat's out of the bag now. What I said still goes, you know—if you're innocent, we'll find it out."

The girl took two steps to a chair and sat down. Duncan said harshly, "She's got nothing to do with this. We've neither of us anything to do with it. For God's sake, believe me, she's— She couldn't—"

"Ross, darling, what *is* it?" she said. "What's the trouble, Ross?"

CHAPTER 9

"All right," said Duncan. "All right." He dropped heavily back into his chair and put his head in his hands for a long moment. "Would it expedite matters if I wrote out a nice neat confession now?" His tone was bitter.

"Did you kill her?"

"No!" said Duncan violently. "But it sure as hell looks just the opposite, doesn't it? I can hardly deny I had a motive. I'm so damn obvious. And now—now you'll bring her into it, and the damn newspapers— Oh, God, Susan, why did you come?"

She had turned very white, belatedly understanding—and understanding who they were. "They think *you*—did that? But you couldn't have—you wouldn't have, no matter what—"

"A few questions, Miss Morgan." O'Connor introduced himself and Varallo. He was noncommittal now. "And lies won't help Mr. Duncan, you know. Has there ever been any discussion of marriage between you and Mr. Duncan?"

"Do you have to bring her in?" asked Duncan in a low voice. "Let me take it. It's obvious that I'm—was—in no position to consider marriage. Susan knew that. I—"

"Yes. Are you hoping to marry Miss Morgan now?"

"No," said Duncan. "Probably not. You'll see to that, won't you?"

"Why do you think it was Ross, sergeant?" She had steadied quickly; she was an intelligent, level-headed girl, Varallo thought.

O'Connor said the whole question was still open; she understood they had to investigate. Mr. Duncan had a motive; others might have motives. They didn't intend to railroad anybody. If she'd answer a few questions—

"I made it worse," she said to Duncan. Blankly, starkly. "Coming. I'm so sorry, Ross. I never dreamed— I took it for granted, a sneak thief, something like that, from what the paper said. I'm sorry, Ross." Duncan was silent. "What do you want to know?"

O'Connor asked questions and she answered them, economically, succinctly. She and Duncan had known each other about four months. Yes, they had had dates together. Yes—since it wasn't much good denying it—they had discussed marriage. Yes, she supposed they both felt resentful toward Helene, but Duncan was not the kind of man to try to solve difficulties by murder. No, of course she had never heard him utter any threats to Helene. On Monday evening she had been home, from six o'clock on. Alone, because her mother was on a visit to some friends in La Jolla. She gave her address and occupation.

"So now," said Duncan, "come the reporters, and her name all over the front pages—girl friend of arrested man. And maybe she loses her job over it—maybe you'll say she was in it with me—"

"Ross," she said quietly. "They have to look. They're not stupid these days. You didn't—do that, so they'll find out. That neither of us had anything to do with it. Don't—"

"That's so, Miss Morgan," said O'Connor. But his eyes met Varallo's across her; both thought of Lieutenant King. "We may want a statement from you. I'll let you know. And we don't go handing out free information to the press, you know—there's no reason any reporters should get hold of Miss Morgan's name unless you give it to them."

Varallo said, "Duncan. I want you to write out a detailed account of all that business about the phone call. Every last little detail you remember. And will you also think back and try to remember any person who came into the office at about the time you misplaced your pen, any stranger to you, who didn't come back again. Maybe someone who came in ostensibly to discuss insurance, never came back. Like that. Write out a description, as near as you can. And ask Mrs. Starr if she remembers anyone like that coming in when she was alone."

Duncan looked up. "Don't tell me you still have an open mind?"

"Don't be a fool," said Varallo roughly. "Try to help us a little."

"All right. Sorry, Varallo. I'll do that."

They went out, and as the door closed saw her rise to go over to Duncan. O'Connor said heavily, "The lieutenant'll probably apply for that warrant himself. It makes a nice case."

"In spades," agreed Varallo. "And for ninety percent sure, somebody arranged it that way. But it's going to be damn hard to show."

"I don't go quite that far on it," said O'Connor. "Maybe seventy-five percent. Doesn't make sense to say he's a little too obvious, because, hell, usually the obvious answer is the right answer. But I don't like the feel of it. Which will make no sense at all to the lieutenant."

They went into the restaurant. "She looks like a nice girl," said Varallo. And, as they sat down on the two end stools of the counter, a little apart from other customers, "That's a nice piece of change the sister inherits. Probably—even if Helene was secretive—Mona *and* Marty could pretty well figure it would come to her."

"And nobody ever has too much money," said O'Connor. "So, find out if they're in urgent need of money, in spite of Marty's fat union wages. Doesn't say anything if they're not. They might still like the idea. . . . Make it a ham sandwich, on white, and coffee, please. No, hot coffee . . . But it looks to me as if maybe Mona's the only person who's really much cut up because Helene's dead. Of course, we haven't met many of her friends yet."

"I wasn't thinking so much of Mona," said Varallo, lighting a cigarette, "as of Marty. Mona may be a nice biddable wife, but he's a virile specimen—it could be he likes a change now and then. And roped some girl friend in on it. Not, of course, knowing about the trust. Because there was a woman in it, there had to be. That phone call and so on."

"Sure," said O'Connor. "I'll bet Marty spends a lot of time reading about famous British trials."

"That's the drawback," admitted Varallo. "Because whoever set it up was familiar with the Wallace case—had to be. The details are too close for coincidence. Another thing we have to keep in mind: whoever X is, he's got to be somebody who knows enough about Duncan to know he has a motive—not necessarily about the girl, the alimony is enough motive—and who took the little trouble to find out when Duncan would be alone in the office. And more little trouble to get hold of the pen. I don't think whoever it was was after the pen specifically, just anything easy to pick up that could be identified as Duncan's property. Stage prop to leave at the scene of the crime. Even if it turned out he'd mentioned some little loss like that to Mrs. Starr, it wouldn't carry too much weight—she's worked for him a long time, it could be she'd tell a little white lie for him. Or so somebody might figure. Nobody who knew Duncan could walk in there and give a false name and business, so I think X sent a henchman. Ess, as you'd say. The woman in the case."

"Why," asked O'Connor, picking up his sandwich, "not just a lone woman? Given a heavy enough weapon, a woman could have done it. Maybe Helene stole her boy friend. Maybe she told tales on her to a husband. And they tell me women gossip together about men. Maybe this woman had heard all about Duncan from Helene, without ever meeting him, and figured he'd make a handy fall guy."

"Implausible," said Varallo. "That kind of motive implies a sudden loss of temper—murder on impulse. Doesn't fit with the elaborate frame."

"So we sit here and tell ourselves fairy tales," said O'Connor. "I'll tell you, Vic, give us plenty of time on it, looking at everybody she knew—and that address book was full—and without much doubt we'd turn up a couple of other motives, several other very-much-possibles. What we know about her, I'd say she wasn't as universally beloved as Mona thinks. But I don't think we're going to have time on it. To the lieutenant, it looks open and shut."

And Varallo thought of what he'd said to Duncan—of what the girl had said. They don't railroad people now. Innocent people— But it could still happen. Even given a good, honest police force, and a legally fair trial. There had been his last case up in Contera, last year: the case he'd resigned over. An innocent woman convicted. It could still happen.

And what they had here, as well as Duncan's whole demeanor, told Varallo that Duncan wasn't guilty. Whoever had borrowed that very tricky little alibi from a book about modern British murder cases had a tortuous mind. Whoever had dreamed up the Wallace case alibi in the first place (whether it was Wallace or somebody else) had had that kind of mind: the chess player's mind. Of course, like every other piece of evidence here, that canceled out: it pointed two ways. To lift a plot idea from somebody else, you didn't necessarily have to have the same type of mind. But Varallo thought that that kind of idea wouldn't appeal to a person with a more direct, straightforward intellect. He couldn't see it appealing to Duncan. Duncan, supposing he'd made up his mind to kill Helene, would have evolved a much more elementary plan—probably something rather naïve, such as stealing out leaving a radio playing, or robbing her apartment to make it look like the casual hopped-up burglar.

"We'll cover as much territory as we can today," said O'Connor. "All we can do. And I wish to God I had more experienced men to send out." Before they went out to the car, he phoned his office and told the desk sergeant to dispatch Wright, Katz, Stepp, McMillan, Silvers and whoever else was available. They were to find out from Mona Norman who had been Helene's closest friends and call on them. Feel them out as to their actual attitudes toward her. Detailed reports, please.

In the car, Varallo said, "Broderick first." And then, belatedly, "Sorry, Charles. I'm acting as if I was still captain."

O'Connor grinned. "Getting back in practice. This time next year you'll have rank, anyway. I'll probably get King's desk, you know. O.K., Broderick first. Why?"

"Because I think he's one we can eliminate and forget about. She divorced him eleven years ago, but he could still write her and ask for a loan, sounding as if he expected to get it."

Broderick, run to earth in a very shabby apartment in Walnut Park, turned out to be an amiable, rather handsome fellow in the late thirties, who described himself vaguely as a salesman. Though he wasn't exactly working anywhere now, things had been tough, he was hoping to get taken on at Sears next week.

He hadn't seen the story in the papers about Helene, and when he heard, he started to cry. He had thinning blond hair and myopic china-blue eyes and a very large Adam's apple. He mopped at his eyes ineffectually with a dirty handkerchief, and said she'd been a wonderful person, it was a terrible shock, they must forgive him. He was afraid he wasn't a very strong or successful person himself, and Helene had grown impatient with him, left him—no wonder, really—but she'd always been so kind to him, ever since, and so generous. He had asthma and his heart wasn't too strong either, there were times he couldn't work, and employers didn't understand, he was always the first to get fired— But Helene understood, and many a time he wouldn't have had enough food in the house, if not for her. She came to see him sometimes too, tried to help him in all sorts of ways. She'd paid Dr. Walters' bill for him, last January after he lost the job at the Broadway—

They had to ask where he'd been on Monday night, futile as it looked. He didn't seem to make any deductions. He said (still sniffling) that he'd been right here, starting to come down with a summer cold. By the grace of God (colds always meant a long bout with his asthma) he'd warded it off, of course Mrs. Warren had been very good to him— she was the landlady here, such a nice woman—she'd brought him a hot-water bottle, and some hot lemonade laced with whiskey, and a special gargle, and some of her own cold tablets, and sat with him most of the evening—

"Nature," said Varallo in the car, "has a fine sense of order, you know. Odds and evens. I've noticed it before. For every Broderick, a Helene or a Mrs. Warren. With the Helenes, a love of power—with the Mrs. Warrens, I suppose, the maternal instinct. I had a hunch we could cross him off."

O'Connor said he supposed so. He added that he guessed Long Beach Boulevard was the quickest way to Bellflower from here, and turned onto it.

It was an old redwood California bungalow, on a shabby middle-class street. The lawn in front was brown; someone grudged the water to keep it green in summer. The front walk leading up to the porch was cracked.

At either side of the steps was planted a rosebush, and Varallo looked at them disapprovingly. The one on the left was a Mrs. Sam McGredy, and the one on the right a Rome Glory, and they hadn't had proper care in a long time. There were dead blooms on both of them. They hadn't been pruned in several years, there was devil grass in the tight-packed earth around them, and altogether it was a wonder that they were still producing buds at all.

He stopped, took out his knife, and carefully clipped off the dead roses. O'Connor laughed.

The ring at the doorbell—an old-fashioned one that really rang, instead of chiming softly—produced instant response. She popped up on the other side of the screen door like a jack-in-the-box.

"Are you police officers at last? I've been expecting you. It's about time you came. Come in. About poor sweet Helene."

"Mrs. Byrd?" asked O'Connor.

"Don't waste time, young man, of course I'm Mrs. Byrd. Mattie Byrd. Come in. Have you arrested that husband of hers yet? Of course he's the one. I don't approve of divorce—but they do say, exceptions prove the rule, and when she told me—weeping like a little *child* she was —about his beatin' up on her and all, well, the only thing to *do*. Get shut of him. Even if she was a lady and hadn't ought to go to law. Sit down."

They sat down, on a tapestry-upholstered love seat whose back and arms were carved profusely with flowers, spirals and irrelevant knobs. The long living-dining room was dim, shadowed by the deep porch, but most of the amenities could be seen as their eyes adjusted. Opposite them sat a large upright golden-oak piano. Displayed on its rack was an ancient piece of sheet music, *The Black Hawk Waltz.* Mrs. Byrd sat down beside it in the chair matching the love seat and stared at them avidly. The rug was a violently patterned American Oriental. There were marble-topped tables, one of them bearing a lamp with a domed glass shade. There were hard, small, low armless chairs upholstered in hot red velvet. The curtains were white mesh over plastic shades. Not a window was open. There were a great many small china figures standing about on all the tables, many empty vases. Over the flat brick mantel hung a large black-and-white picture, under glass, of several weeping veiled ladies in flowing robes supporting one another past what looked like a row of Greek statuary: *The Return from the Tomb,* said the script underneath. Many similarly cheerful pictures, large and small, hung at random on all the walls. On the mantel sat a pair of hurricane lamps and a marble clock, which consisted of a simulated log with a be-wildered-looking girl sitting on it, clad apparently in a bathrobe, and the clock dial let into one end. The room smelled strongly of dust, cats and recent cabbage. It was very hot.

"*Well?*" she said. "Cat got your tongue? Have you arrested him?"

"We're collecting evidence, Mrs. Byrd," said O'Connor. "That's all. When was—"

"Tosh!" she said impatiently. "Anybody with the sense God gave geese'd see right off it was him. Only met him the oncet, I did, but I didn't cotton to him then. He was too quiet. Men like that, they brood. Nor he didn't like her going to church, told me that herself—didn't hold with churches. You can see what kind he *is.* And beatin' up on her, whenever she asked him to stop his drinking. Brought up right, Helene was. I asked her faithful, ever' time she came, was she sure go to church on the Sabbath, and she allus did. 'Twasn't her fault she had to work amongst sinners and backsliders. Most folks are, nowadays. But she stayed a real good girl, Helene did, even if she had such awful bad luck with her husbands. I was assured o' that. *Well?* What d'ye want o' me?"

A large tabby cat came into the long room from a door leading to the hall, considered them with cold amber eyes, turned and stalked out, waving its tail insolently.

She was a little woman, plump as a robin, but with an oddly narrow, pinched face, a pair of piercingly sharp black eyes, thin white hair pulled back to a meager bun. She might have been seventy-five. She wore a very neat ankle length black-and-white cotton dress, thick stockings, old-lady oxfords and old-fashioned round pink-plastic glasses. Her pink pursed mouth was so small as to seem hardly a mouth at all, and her false teeth clicked as she spoke.

"You saw the newspaper accounts?" asked O'Connor.

"I never read about all this immorality and violence—all that's in the papers these days. My son read about it and told me. Poor sweet Helene, that awful man—*brooding*. I said right off, 'twas him. Couldn't blame Helene, she was so downright trusting herself, she was allus took in by men. *Men*," said Mrs. Byrd with loathing. It was borne in on them that *men*, automatically, were lewd, violent and unsatisfactory in general. "She explained it all to me, and I understood—knowing Helene. A lady, she was, and a real good girl. Just bad luck she had. 'Twasn't like that namby-pamby sister of hers, that Mona. I declare, runnin' off with a fellow like that no-good Norman—spend half his wages on liquor, and I wouldn't doubt on other women too. Helene said so. But that Mona never had no spine. Poor Helene—poor Helene." She dabbed at her eyes with a handkerchief produced from her sleeve. "I thought a deal of Helene, 'twas an awful shock. Closer maybe than my own flesh 'n' blood, being a girl and all. Well, what do you want of me, young man?"

"When did you see Mrs. Duncan last?"

"Week ago last Sund'y. She come faithful, but she says then as she prob'ly wouldn't come next Sund'y—that was this last Sund'y—on account there was a special meeting of the Sund'y school teachers she had to be at."

Varallo and O'Connor exchanged glances. That was a picture, blonde-by-request Helene as a Sunday school teacher. It was on the cards, as Duncan said he'd vaguely gathered, that the old aunt had some money and Helene had been keeping her sweet. Very artfully, it seemed.

"What church?" asked O'Connor, managing not to sound amused.

"Second Methodist. Acourse my father was a Lutheran minister, but the Methodists are good folk too, I guess. Strictly teetotal, and Helene—"

Five Martinis, Hunter had said ruefully, and never turned a hair. Varallo hastily looked away from O'Connor.

"That place she worked, she didn't like it much, selling liquor and all —but she was just in the restaurant part, acourse, she didn't have anything to do with that. And it didn't make no difference to her character, not Helene, nor going to law like that about those men, neither. She was going to quit work, soon as she could afford. Inherited her business sense from me, she did," said Mrs. Byrd with satisfaction. "A real smart girl she was. Buying up property—real estate, you know."

They thought of the deeds, the bankbooks, and agreed that Helene had been a real smart girl.

"Only all the bad luck— *Men!*" said Mrs. Byrd. And then her voice rose to a harsh shriek and she cried, "You, Henry! Fin'lly come home, have you? Come here and let me smell your breath! I know where you been—out after liquor!"

"Not guilty, Mother," said an amused pleasant voice. "I'm quite sober and of sound mind. Who're the visitors?"

They turned. He was standing in the doorway, looking at them inquiringly. A good-looking, middle-sized man of about forty, sandy, with a craggy, good-humored face, sharp-dressed in brown slacks and beige sport shirt. "You always will jump to conclusions," he said gently, and came into the long room, taking a cigarette case from his breast pocket.

"My curtains," she grumbled. "Indulgences o' the flesh," as he lit the cigarette with a silver lighter.

"Now, Mother. May I be introduced?"

CHAPTER 10

"This is my boy Henry. *I* remember when he used to be a good boy. He's a wicked man, he is, now. Consorting with sinners all the time. And he don't come to see his old mother near so often as he should."

"Now, Mother," said Byrd. He came to kiss her cheek lightly. "I was here just yesterday, wasn't I?" He looked at Varallo and O'Connor, and the rueful amusement went out of his eyes. "Let me guess," he said. "The arm of the law. About Helene." They introduced themselves; he offered a firm hand to both. "More familiarly known as Hank," he said absently. "Don't let Mother give you any wrong ideas. I'm an actors' agent. Mother doesn't approve."

"Actors!" she said, and unexpectedly gave a pleased cackle of laughter. "You skin 'em, Henry, that's one thing I'll say for you!"

"Well, if you call ten percent—" Varallo thought all this was wearily familiar exchange to Byrd; the old woman would certainly be what was called difficult. "What taradiddles have you been telling the officers?"

"You're a one, talk about taradiddles! I never said anything but the truth. Why would I? Just said it was most likely that husband of hers did it. Why, that was the reason she give when she went to law, cruelty. He was a broody sort of fellow, kind to turn violent—wasn't he, Henry? Why, the oncet they was here together, I—I saw with my own eyes, he hit her, he did—"

"Now, Mother. You never mentioned that to me before—isn't that just a little something you imagined?"

"'Tis not! I did so see him. She'd told me before, he did, and—and then I saw him do it. Just about something she said—I'll remember in a minute what that was, too. And I'll say so again to anybody. Henry, don't you *dast* put your nasty smelly tobacco ashes in my grandmother's cranberry glass—"

"Sorry, Mother. Look, why don't you go and make us some nice cold lemonade? Just the thing, afternoon like this. And I'll talk to the gentlemen out on the porch."

"Go telling 'em I'm a senile old lady? Well, I'm not, by a long ways, and well you know it!" She got up, grumbling.

"I know it!" he said, smiling, patting her shoulder, starting her toward the kitchen. "Come out here, we can—" On the porch, gesturing at the several dilapidated rattan chairs, he sobered. "Well, I needn't try to explain Mother," he said. "You can see for yourself. And still sharp as a tack, lots of ways. Great old lady, really . . . It *is* about Helene? Hell of a thing. I was with her just last Sunday. We—well, some ways Helene and I were almost like brother and sister." He tossed his cigarette stub over the porch railing, leaned back hands in pockets, rattling coins absently in his pocket. "The girls' parents died when Helene was only sixteen, and they came to live with us a few years, and of course Helene and I were closer in age. I never knew Mona as well. . . . Have you got any leads yet? Or can you tell me?"

"What do you think of your mother's idea, that it was Duncan?"

"Hell, I don't know. I suppose he could have. I only met him once, you know. If that sounds funny, well, I'm pretty busy with my own affairs and Helene never was one for cozy family get-togethers. Knowing Helene, I'd make a guess that she was taking him but good on alimony, and it could be— But I don't know him well enough to give an opinion. He seemed like a nice guy."

"You say, knowing Helene. You'd expect her to be—greedy and unfair about that kind of thing? And yet you—"

Byrd shrugged. "Greedy, yes. She had a pretty hard time growing up, she liked money. Don't we all? Helene had her head screwed on tight, as you've probably found out already. She wouldn't be above—pulling the fast one, if she saw any advantage in it. Oh, I don't mean anything illegal, but—"

"We've gathered," said Varallo, "from what your mother's said, that Mrs. Duncan had been telling her a few—um—taradiddles of her own, Mr. Byrd. At least, a couple of little things that don't square with what we've found out about her. Or do you know what I mean?"

Byrd laughed, shrugged, looking rueful. "You mean about her being such a faithful church attendant and teaching Sunday school and so forth. Well, look, you've met Mother—" he glanced over his shoulder as if to reassure himself she wasn't at the door, listening. "Shall we say she's old-fashioned? That kind of thing was just—smoothing things over, is all. Saved a lot of rows, and listening to a lot of lectures. Look, I'm fond of her, well, she's my mother after all, but I can't deny she's—difficult. And Helene was fond of her, Mother'd been good to her when she was a kid, reason she took the time and trouble to come and see her—but she knew she'd come in for some rows if Mother got the wrong answers to Do you go to church every Sabbath and so on and so forth. It was just—wasn't there a song about it?—little white lies." He shrugged again. "You know how it is."

"Sure," said Varallo, watching him.

"Keep our voices down, shall we?" Byrd fished for another cigarette. "Mother very seldom goes out, she wouldn't be checking up, you see. We used to laugh about it—just one of those things. Mother can be a tartar, if she thinks you're—" he grinned—"sinful. I do the same sort of thing myself. Makes things easier all round. You always come in for a kind of catechism, you see, details of what you've been doing lately and so on. The thing is, she's one of those mothers—among other things—who's never really realized that kids grow up and turn into men and women. She'd like me to've gone on living here. Well, I ask you." He lit the cigarette. "You see how it is. Helene was good about coming to see her, it's—lonely—for her, here alone, but she won't hear of moving anywhere better. But there was scarcely much point in coming to cheer her up, so to speak, and getting into a row because Helene told the truth and said she'd had two cocktails before dinner last night. I mean, silly little issues like that—" again he glanced over his shoulder—"you know. Maybe Helene wasn't the most admirable character in the world, but you know the one about casting the first stone."

"Mr. Byrd," said Varallo, "what your mother just said—about seeing Mr. Duncan strike Mrs. Duncan. Is that a lie she's convinced herself of, or could it be true?"

Byrd looked at his cigarette. "I thought," he said, "that she'd just made it up, but I don't know. I don't know Duncan well enough to say, and of course I wasn't here. She says—she's told me before—that Helene told her he had. I think when Helene divorced him it was on mental cruelty, couldn't swear to it. Maybe Mother dreamed it up from that. You're looking at Duncan? I suppose you would, first thing."

Varallo looked at O'Connor. And, having some experience of human nature, they were aware that, lie or no, the stubborn old woman would probably continue to swear to that. Nice evidence for the prosecuting attorney, showing the predisposition to violence. Almost certainly it was a lie. All of it. First Helene's, and then the old woman's. But how to prove that?

"Mind telling us where you were on Monday night, Mr. Byrd?"

"Me?" said Byrd, looking very much surprised. And then he laughed, without much mirth. "Hell of a thing to laugh about—Helene— Only, nobody ever suggested before I've got enough nerve to commit a murder. I was with a girl friend—Marilyn Marshall—from, let's see, about six-thirty on. . . . Want details? Well, sure, but—we had a couple of drinks at her apartment, the Garden Arms on Hobart Street, and went on to dinner at Frascati's, about eight o'clock. Got there, I'd guess, about eight-thirty. Had dinner. A leisurely dinner. And went back to her apartment." He gave a quick look over his shoulder. "She's not coming, is she? She doesn't like actresses, but me in an actress's apartment—!"

"How late did you stay?" Not that it mattered.

"About midnight. Matter of fact, it was all very innocent, we were discussing a new contract. But you're not really—"

It was all very unsatisfactory. About all they'd got was another small piece of pseudo-evidence that would tell against Ross Duncan. They stood up as the old woman came out to the porch with a pitcher of lemonade and glasses. They refused the lemonade politely. Byrd looked piteously at the tall glass she gave him.

"Before you go, can you tell me—"

"Sorry, we're not handing out any information, Mr. Byrd. Not yet," said O'Connor.

"I don't mean that. You'll think it's funny, but neither of us have Mona Norman's address. We lost touch with her some while ago—"

"Running off with that man! Half his wages on liquor, and ordering her round like she was dirt!"

"—and I expect she'll be—making the arrangements. I'd like to find out—"

"Oh, yes, sure," said O'Connor, and gave him the address.

Byrd thanked him, copying it down in his book. "Good luck on it, sergeant. Hell of a thing. Well, I mean—relatives, people you know, it just doesn't happen. It's been a shock. . . . Not at all, glad to oblige."

"It seems," said Varallo, "to have been a shock to everybody."

"So it does. I'm not liking this more and more. Of course we haven't taken a look at her female friends yet. But somehow I don't see a woman— Nothing, just a big bare nothing, except for Duncan the obvious. And I keep feeling it's the hell of a lot more complicated than that."

"A little psychological point," said Varallo. "We've agreed that that Whipstead-Moorbank business is definitely patterned on the Wallace case alibi—that whoever set it up, Duncan or X, was familiar with that case. Quite likely from casual reading—a lot of people read stuff like that. All right. In that case, the original case, Wallace the husband was found guilty by a jury. The jury didn't believe it was a frame. They thought he'd set it up himself. Do you think Duncan the husband would have picked that alibi to copy? Wallace didn't have such good luck with it. It's a very minor little thing, but it seems to me that if he was going to borrow a plot from real life at all, he'd borrow one that had once been successful. Like—" he cast around in his mind for some of them, gleaned from Laura's library books and modest private collection—"like Pritchard's, was it Pritchard, who combined the poisons—or Haigh, or that professor back in the '80's—"

"The one that burned another professor up in a furnace. No furnaces like that in California," said O'Connor. "It's a piddling little thing, Vic, but I see what you mean. Funny sort of thing for anybody to do, to start with, borrow a plot from real life. . . . I'll give you two more piddling little things in rebuttal. The British court of appeal evidently disagreed with the jury and let Wallace loose in the end. And he was an insurance salesman. It could be, say it *was* Duncan, that one little fact atracted him. Coincidence. Psychological."

"Hell," said Varallo. "Yes, I know. Everything we've got, pointing both ways."

It was half-past three. They didn't do much more talking, on the way back to Glendale. It was hotter in the valley, over another range of foothills from the ocean.

As they came into O'Connor's office, a man rose from the chair beside the desk, a very long, lean man in a wrinkled gray suit and crooked tie, a man with a long, lean face and sad eyes. "Sergeant O'Connor, by chance?"

"Yes, what can I do for you?"

The man produced an I.D. card. "Llewellyn. Narcotics, L.A. Will you kindly, sergeant, call off your amateur suburban bloodhounds from worrying Mr. Reilly at the Thunderbird Inn?"

"The hell I— What's the gimmick?"

They all sat down. "You've just," said Llewellyn sadly, "tumbled to the joint?"

"It showed on the edge of a homicide," said O'Connor shortly. "So what?"

"That's annoying," said Llewellyn. "Because we don't want anybody poking around, O'Connor. If you take me. Worrying poor Mr. Reilly and the owner. Especially anybody official like your eager young henchmen prying into store cupboards and annoying the chefs. It's a drop for the big H, and we're sitting on it waiting for a couple of the big boys to show."

"Oh," said O'Connor. "Awkward. I see."

"Cooperation," said Varallo. "Our corpse just maybe stumbled onto something about it. She was overheard asking for a cut, and Reilly saying she hadn't a damn thing on him. How likely is it that he took her off or had it done?"

Llewellyn looked at him speculatively. "Not very. Reilly—he has a short pedigree at Records—doesn't go in for violence. This is a small-time deal. A ring supplying maybe twenty pushers. Like that. He'd be a lot likelier to cut her in, under protest. They're not strong-arm boys. But we can do some looking for you, if you want. Corpse's name?" He was told. He wrote it down, with the relevant times, and stood up. "Please, call your boys in, sergeant. We don't like to overlap. The lieutenant was annoyed."

"Not half as annoyed as I am," said O'Connor when Llewellyn had gone. "'Amateur suburban bloodhounds,' hah!"

"Well," said Varallo, "the L.A. boys have been named by the F.B.I. as the top crack force anywhere, and they get consulted by Scotland Yard. They've got a right."

"So it goes to their heads," said O'Connor, "and they get snobbish about it." He looked at the papers on his desk. "Katz. Silvers. See what they've got to say." He read rapidly, passed the page over to Varallo.

Katz had seen two women named by Mona as close friends of Helene's—a Mrs. Louise Humboldt and a Miss Marian Blake. Mrs. Humboldt (husband a broker downtown L.A., expensive house in La Cañada, money) had gushed, about poor dear Helene and how close they'd been, such a sweet girl. "Female stuff," judged Katz. They had belonged to a little cards club together. Bridge. They usually met on Wednesdays when the club met. At alternating places. "Sometimes here, sometimes at Sylvia's—Sylvia Stevens'—or Norma Breck's." "A lot of talk," reported Katz, "about what a shock it was, how awful, etc., but I didn't get the feeling there was really much behind it. Subject good-looker, tall, blond, about thirty-two, nervous type, several good pieces jewelry, diamonds." "Katz," said O'Connor, "would know. His father's a jeweler." "Subject was nervous. Said had known H. D. about a year, since H. D. joined club."

Marian Blake. "Age about thirty-four, employed secretary at Glasscraft. Inc., Burbank. Said was old school friend, attended high school with H. D. (Hollywood High.) Did not see her often—maybe once in a couple of months. Had been invited to dinner and card parties in H. D.'s apartment. Subject reluctant to say much, finally said had turned down several invitations because she couldn't afford to play for such high stakes. Pressed, said stakes sometimes fifty cents a point. Says H. D. was very shrewd, lucky player. Says, liked her all right. Not enthusiastic."

"Well, well," said Varallo. "That could run into a little money, couldn't it? What you and I'd call money."

O'Connor, reading, said, "Try Silvers," and passed over another sheet.

Silvers had seen one Linda Walker. He noted a Kenneth Road address, very good residential section. "Husband, Dr. Arnold R. Walker, listed as consulting surgeon, office 633 Central. Mrs. W. member small cards club H. D. belonged to. Claims close friend, but talk slightly malicious (?). Says a couple of other members mildly resentful at H. D.'s good luck, winnings, in friendly games. Says Louise Humboldt may have quarreled with H. D. recently, as Humboldt 'made cracks' at H. D. when subject talked with her at recent dinner party. Says (pressed) Humboldt said something about H. D. being 'money grubbing.' Further said sympathized with Humboldt 'in a way' because of 'much older husband, so difficult,' and H. D. 'sometimes irritating, if she was a basically nice person.'" He was going on to see a Miss Catherine Goodman, and he added the time: 3:25 P.M.

"Card debts!" said Varallo. "I ask you."

"But what," said O'Connor, "did Mrs. Humboldt quarrel about with Helene? Just maybe something else? We're told she has a 'much older' husband. Just maybe had she acquired a younger, more interesting admirer—and Helene found out about it, maybe righteously threatened to inform the husband?"

"Talk about plots out of books," said Varallo exasperatedly.

"I know, I know—" And O'Connor broke off as the outside phone rang. He picked it up, said Hello, and Yes and Go on. He whisked out his pen and started to take notes. Finally he said, "Thanks very much for calling in," replaced the phone, looked at his notes and said, "So now we know. Helene was employing the Merritt Private Investigation Service to check on Duncan. As you might say, desultorily. That was Merritt. They have a clean record—small business, decamped creditors and so on. He says she just asked for a casual, occasional check on him —where he was living, whether he was dating a girl, like that."

"Keeping in touch," said Varallo thoughtfully. "Well, he knew her— he could be right when he says she might have been keeping him in reserve in case some little undercover job came along that wanted doing. If I had to guess, and of course it's way up in the stratosphere, I'd say some fast little piece of work in a business deal, where she might need him—known businessman of integrity—to back her up. Something like that. And I suppose we'll never know now. It's a very little evidence for Duncan, this. It backs him up that maybe he didn't know where she lived, when we know this is how she'd kept a check on him."

"You think so?" said O'Connor. "She'd lived in that Chevy Chase apartment for eighteen months—she was in the phone book. All he had to do was look."

"Hell," said Varallo.

And Sergeant Burr looked in and said, "Lieutenant King's on the phone, sergeant, asking for you to come to his office. I had to say you were in—"

O'Connor got up, heavily. "O.K., tell him I'm on my way." He looked at Varallo. "I'll try to sell him. Keep your fingers crossed."

CHAPTER 11

The lieutenant was querulous. The lieutenant—paunchy, bald, jowled, behind his scarred desk—asked O'Connor if he remembered one single thing out of the *Manual of Procedure.* He'd be obliged if O'Connor would hand him all the new stuff, if any. In his opinion, they had enough to make a case on Duncan now, and if O'Connor would get on the ball, they'd probably pick up more.

O'Connor had to hand him what little more they had, and the lieutenant pounced on the girl. There you are, he said. Motive, and the only motive they'd turned up. He pushed away the gentlemanly Mr. Reilly and his small-timer associates impatiently. Duncan was obvious, and it was about time O'Connor stopped talking, for God's sake, about feelings and borrowing plots out of books—books, yet—and remembered a few ordinary common facts about police work. The inquest was set for tomorrow morning and he'd like to avoid leaving it open—clean it all up at once with a definite finding against the guilty party, and make the pinch right then. He'd get on the phone to the prosecutor's office and talk it over with him, see what he said, but meanwhile O'Connor wasn't to hold out on him, had the search through Duncan's apartment and office turned up anything?

For Christ's *sake,* he hadn't searched yet? What the hell was the matter with him? One hot lead, since yesterday morning, and O'Connor hadn't— How the hell had he ever passed the sergeants' exam?

O'Connor admitted his fault. It was so; he should have got a search warrant after questioning Duncan the first time, or at least this afternoon after learning about the girl. But by then he'd come round to Varallo's feeling, almost to Varallo's certainty, that it was a frame. He said he'd get a warrant and look now.

And meanwhile, said the lieutenant, Duncan had had plenty of time to get rid of the weapon and anything else incriminating. Even if he hadn't on Monday night. Had O'Connor even looked for the weapon? Where he might have thrown it away, around that apartment somewhere? Of course O'Connor had—had men poke around the bushes and so on, and found nothing.

Another thing, said the lieutenant, what the hell was all this about O'Connor taking a regular patrolman off his tours to tag along? Jensen had a beef about it, and why, for God's sake—

O'Connor explained Varallo. A ranking officer of twelve years' experience, and—involved. The lieutenant said, in some one-horse town upstate, picking up chicken thieves. He said O'Connor was slipping, all right, blundering around like this with the guilty party staring him in the face.

Without much hope of getting across to him, O'Connor said again that both he and Varallo—also an experienced man, no matter where he'd had experience—had the definite feeling that this thing was a lot more complicated than it looked. That it could be a tricky frame on Duncan because he *was* the obvious suspect, and that a little more time for some careful looking into it—

The lieutenant reminded O'Connor that he, the lieutenant, had just eighteen years' more experience as a ranking cop than O'Connor, and he knew a good case when he saw one; but from even seven years' experience, O'Connor ought to know that lawbreakers of any kind are very seldom very smart, and consequently they didn't do "complicated" things. He advised O'Connor to get with it, or he'd take over the case personally and do so. And this what's-his-name, Varallo, was to go back on his regular duty tomorrow. Now, said the lieutenant, for God's sake go and get that warrant you should've got yesterday!

O'Connor went, thankfully but feeling helpless. If the prosecutor's office also thought it added to a case, it would be out of his hands; there'd be a warrant issued and Duncan would be charged and arrested —probably after the inquest tomorrow. Very likely the witnesses would be getting their subpoenas now, if the lieutenant planned to make it a full-dress business instead of just leaving it open. And the lieutenant would be passing on Susan Morgan's name so one could be addressed to her.

He went back to his own office and told Varallo. Who said, "Hell. And not one damn thing we can do about it."

"Of course he's right about the search warrant."

"Yes," said Varallo, "and I've got a little feeling, Charles, that you're going to turn up another helpful piece of incriminating evidence on that search. The pen made a very nice stage prop, and of course the motive's very obvious, and the tricky alibi—exactly the kind an insurance man would think up, which is maybe what the Wallace jury thought too—is useful, but to clinch the deal, I think X threw in something else. I could have a guess what, but I couldn't say where."

As a matter of fact, it turned out to be in Duncan's car.

It was after five. O'Connor resignedly set about getting the search warrant; Varallo collected his car and drove up to Duncan's office. He found Duncan in it alone; Mrs. Starr had just left.

"Funny woman," said Duncan aimlessly. "She's worked here for eighteen years, and the first time I found out anything about her but her name and address was when she wanted to switch her insurance to another company last year. She—as the British say—keeps herself to herself. I don't know even now what she thinks of me—I had to tell her about all this, well, of course she'd seen the papers—when I asked her about any strangers coming in. She just said, 'Yes, Mr. Duncan, I'll do my best to remember.' I—wrote it all out for you. Between us we figured out—"

"Fine. Look, let's go home and discuss it over drinks, O.K.?"

"Well," said Duncan, standing up, "I'd be much obliged for the ride, sure. That bus—"

Varallo didn't think there was any point in breaking the news about the lieutenant's impatience or the search warrant until they'd discussed whatever Duncan could tell him on this part of it. He drove home, Duncan silent beside him; Duncan looking very tired, making no mention at all of Susan Morgan. There, they automatically stripped off jackets and ties. Varallo made two fairly strong highballs and they sat in the patio. Duncan handed over a couple of typed pages.

"Here's what we came up with between us. Not very helpful, I'm afraid. In the ordinary way, not many strangers come in. That is, they do occasionally but they usually turn into clients, of course. Strangers coming in just once—it happens, but not often. And the time limit's pretty vague." He hesitated and then said stiffly, "I—haven't been sitting up taking much notice, lately. You know. Not sleeping awfully well, this damn weather. And—well, when my pen went missing, I hunted around, didn't find it, and just thought, hell, one more thing going wrong. If you take me. I have the impression that it was early afternoon, but I couldn't swear to the day. About ten days ago, say a week ago last Monday, a week ago last Saturday. I expect it looks funny that I didn't mention it to Mrs. Starr. But the way it was, I was feeling damned low, you know, and I just felt, Damnation, another thing, and—didn't do much about it."

And Varallo could see it happening just that way. And how would X know that Duncan wouldn't mention its loss right then? He couldn't; the chance he took. It really wouldn't have mattered much if Duncan had; the assumption would be that he'd found it again, had it on him to drop accidentally in Helene's apartment that night—because, there it had been.

"It's all damn vague," said Duncan gloomily.

Necessarily, it was. What Duncan could remember came first. He couldn't place the day, but thought it had been a week ago Friday or Saturday. A man had come in during Mrs. Starr's lunch hour, to ask about car insurance. He'd been about forty to forty-five, nondescript; Duncan had never seen him before. He'd given his name as Pepper. Just Pepper. He had been dissatisfied with his present insurance and wanted to know if he could get the same coverage cheaper elsewhere. "He couldn't. It all figures about the same, unless you let something go." Duncan didn't remember whether he'd left the man alone at his desk at any time; he might easily have done so, going over to the extra file case where he kept odds and ends, for a brochure or a statistical chart or something. Mr. Pepper had thanked him, gone away and never come back.

Either the preceding day or the next day, there had been a funny little thing that had never happened to him before. A man had come in, and introduced himself as an adjuster for a large insurance firm, and said he was after particulars on the Gorman claim. John Gorman was one of Duncan's clients: a high-school teacher, very nice fellow; and recently he'd been involved in an automobile accident, and was putting in a claim as the innocent party, to the other fellow's insurance firm. It was a rather tricky little thing, because what had happened— Gorman had been run into, at an intersection, estimated damage about seven hundred dollars—involved the interpretation of this new left-turn law, which some judges read one way, some another. If Varallo— Varallo nodded. Anyway, the man had given his name as Roberts, but had not offered a card or any identification. Duncan had trustfully talked to him for about five minutes, but became suspicious when Roberts showed ignorance of a few technical terms. Had asked him then for identification, at which Roberts had got mad, or pretended to, and walked out.

"I figured he was the party of the second part, or a friend of same, just trying to pump me," said Duncan dully. "You know. As it turned out, it was the second accident the fellow'd had in two weeks, so by the rules his license was in danger and they'd probably up the premiums on him. But I don't know— I didn't follow it up."

And those were the only two strangers he recalled coming in at about the right time, and not returning. Roberts had not been left alone at the desk, but he had, of course, sat very close beside the desk. "You've seen the office." Both strangers had come between twelve and one, when Duncan was alone.

Mrs. Starr had done better; she remembered three strangers. The first, definitely, had come in a week ago last Monday—Mrs. Starr remembered because it was her sister's birthday. This had been a large, genial, talkative man, middle-aged, speaking like a man without much education. He had come in, puzzled, saying that he'd been given this address for a certain James Brady, a realtor, and could she tell him anything about Brady? There was no Brady in this block of offices. Mrs. Starr had agreed, and suggested that possibly he wanted East Glenoaks instead of West Glenoaks. He had brightened, said maybe so; said it sure was hot, nice to step into air conditioning, he'd just got here from Iowa and hadn't thought California got all this humid kind of heat they got back there—in short, he had been garrulous, and only Mrs. Starr's prim monosyllables (it could be deduced) had chased him away at last. She thought she recalled that he had leaned against Mr. Duncan's desk as he talked.

A few days before that (she couldn't definitely say which) there had been the young woman. It had been, she thought, about one-thirty, when Mr. Duncan was out to lunch. A young woman had come in, looking very white and ill, and apologized, and said she'd suddenly felt very faint, could she sit down here a minute? Mrs. Starr had said of course, helped her to a chair—the chair beside Mr. Duncan's desk. This terrible heat—people did get heatstroke, and faint, from it. The girl had seemed very weak and sick. Mrs. Starr had hurried into the little back room, where a water cooler stood, and brought her water in a paper cup. The girl had taken an aspirin with it, thanking her; and after about ten minutes she had said she felt better now, and thanked Mrs. Starr again, and gone out. She had been perhaps twenty-five, slender, pretty. She'd had a scarf over her hair, so Mrs. Starr couldn't say whether she'd been fair or dark; she thought, medium. But she had the definite impression that she had seen the girl before somewhere, so possibly she lived, or worked, nearby.

And, sometime around then, there had been a woman—older, a dark, rather haggard-looking woman—who came in, during Mr. Duncan's lunch hour, to ask about the local buses. She wanted to know which bus to take to get to downtown L.A. Mrs. Starr had told her, and given her a bus schedule.

"It's not much, is it?" asked Duncan.

"You never know," said Varallo. He heard Laura in the kitchen, got up, went in and kissed her, and briefly brought her up to date.

She said, "Oh, Vic! But he's not the one—you don't think—"

"I don't know about the happy ending on this one, *cara,*" he said heavily. "We can try for it." Looking troubled, she went off to change. Varallo took more Scotch, soda and ice cubes out to the patio, renewed Duncan's drink and started abruptly to tell him the facts of life—and of police work. "—That's the way it is, Duncan. I don't think you're X, I'd stake my bank account on it, which is saying something—and neither does O'Connor. It's a frame. But the lieutenant's the boss, what he says goes. And there is a nice legal case against you, you know. It looks as if there's a good chance you'll be charged and arrested tomorrow, and after that it's technically out of bounds for the police. They've done their work."

"I see," said Duncan, who had gone a little pale. "I'd better think about what lawyer to call."

"Technically," repeated Varallo. "Damn it. Damn it to hell. There'll be other things coming along, you see, and O'Connor detailed to look at them. And me, I'm just a uniformed cop, the harness bull, riding a squad car. Neither of us has any business poking around more in a case already passed to the courts. Both of us could collect a black mark on our records for it, if the lieutenant felt like that."

"I see," said Duncan again. "Of course. Well, thanks for—believing me, anyway. I can see there's nothing more you can do."

"Who said that?" said Varallo softly. "I'm a cop, Duncan. I hope a good one. A good cop doesn't suddenly get that way the minute he takes the oath. Maybe he always was. Responsible—and curious. Charles O'Connor is another one. And he wants King's desk, and he might not get it if he collects a black mark over this thing, but if I know Charles he'll stay on it all the same. Only, I can't promise you that we'll get anywhere on it, working more or less alone the way we'll have to."

Duncan said after a moment, "That's—I don't know what to say. You can't be really sure—"

"I'm sure," said Varallo. "Not to flatter myself, it's just something I know about Vic Varallo, like the fact that my birthday's in January and I've got blue eyes—the feelings I get about people are so. About you, I know. You might have killed her, but you wouldn't have killed her that way."

And Duncan said in a low voice, "I'd thought about it, you know. I had."

And Laura came out, in a fresh sundress, and smiled at him; and Varallo heard a car pull up in front, and said, "Here's Charles and his minions."

O'Connor had two men from the night staff with him. With Varallo and Duncan looking on, they searched—thoroughly, quickly, deftly. The room and bath did not contain much besides what Laura had furnished them with. Duncan had brought in the small refrigerator, a cheap pine bookshelf filled mostly with paperbacks, an electric grill and hot plate, a couple of pans, a few cheap dishes, kitchen silverware. There were canned goods stacked neatly on the floor under the chrome table. The painted chest of drawers held only his clothing; the small closet only more.

"We'll want the key to your office," said O'Connor, and Duncan passed it over silently.

Varallo felt tension mounting in him. He thought there would be something: another thing to bolster the frame. But where hide it, in a single room, where Duncan wouldn't come across it? The back of the closet—but there was nothing there. The office? That back room? Much harder to get at—

There was nothing out of the ordinary at all, here.

And then he understood where it must be—would be. Of course.

"That's all, sergeant. All clean."

"Yes," said O'Connor. "The office— Oh, there's your car, Duncan. Just have a quick look over it, boys, before we go on to the office. The keys, Duncan?"

Slowly Duncan fumbled them out, handed them over. "I don't think it's locked." But O'Connor was already gone, after his men.

It was in the Anglia, sitting there dusty and immobile at the curb—on the floor of the back seat—that they found the weapon. A heavy wrench, outsize—with the kind of corrugated handle that wouldn't retain fingerprints—but with, on its business end, several long blond hairs stuck in a little mess of dried blood and brain tissue.

CHAPTER 12

It was, of course, a sad fact that in real life neither policemen, lawyers nor criminals behaved as they so often did in books. Duncan could say, But why should I do such a stupid thing as to leave it there in my car? Why in my car, anyway, when the car is not running? Doesn't that prove that someone is framing me, and not knowing that the car is not running, deliberately planted the wrench there? If I had used that wrench, why on earth should I bring it home with me? Surely you can see I'm a more intelligent man than that!

And within limits Varallo and O'Connor could agree; but of course a man who has just committed a murder is not always thinking logically. To Varallo, this was more evidence for a frame, because of one angle a bit too subtle to offer Lieutenant King or a jury. X would assume that Duncan would know of the murder, and of the police suspicion of him, very soon. He was not a fool. If he should come across that wrench, obviously planted on him, he'd scarcely be such a fool as to announce the fact and offer it to the police. He'd take good care to bury it, or throw it off a bridge into the Wash. But X wanted it there, waiting for a police search. X must be aware that the Anglia was not running, and that Duncan would have no reason to go near it. And Duncan said he remembered unlocking it for the garage mechanic, but had not locked it again. "Why? Nothing in it to steal." A very handy place for X to stash the weapon, where it would lie undisturbed until the police found it. X hadn't even had to pick the lock.

Lawyers and juries—even the bench—didn't go so deep into inherent psychological likelihoods, into the maze of pros and cons of character. The concrete facts were that Duncan had had reason to want the woman dead, and property of his (obviously dropped unwittingly) was found at the scene of the crime, and the weapon had been found in his possession. He could not prove he had lost the pen previously; he could not prove he had been elsewhere at the probable time of the murder. Instead, they had some indirect evidence (the woman Mrs. Burton had heard in the hall) that he had been at the scene of the crime quite near the time the murder must have been committed. Nobody knew better than police officers, lawyers and the bench, that the obvious answer was usually the right answer. It was (despite all the fiction) very seldom that you turned up a murdered body and found that a dozen people had had ample motive for making it so.

"Let's face it," said Varallo. "People in real life aren't half as smart as the people in books. It just doesn't work that way." They were sitting there still, in the growing dusk, in the patio—the four of them, because Susan Morgan had showed up as O'Connor and his men left.

She had said very directly to Varallo, "Ross told me how kind you've both been. You don't believe this, do you? Thank you." And they'd told her to sit down, which she did beside Duncan, and Laura had put on the expression she wore when she felt very low and was pretending hard otherwise, and said, "Get Miss Morgan a drink, Vic, and then I think there's enough odds and ends to go round—it's really too hot to eat much. . . ."

And they were still sitting there "listening to me lecture," said Varallo. "This about puts the lid on it, all right, and you'd better expect the worst, Duncan. And we're going to be hampered, Charles and I, in poking around any more. He'll have new business coming up, and I'm tied to a patrol car all day. True, I'll be going back on evening tour—four to eleven-thirty—next week. But still—"

"You're not going to stop—looking?" said Susan. "That's how I feel—we can't! There must be ways to find out— Tell me how I could help—"

Varallo shook his head at her. "Police investigation," he said, "is mostly just boring routine. The collaborative efforts of a lot of people all working on different aspects of a thing. And there aren't too many places to start work on, in this business. It may have been still light when somebody stopped for a minute, around there on Loretta, and tossed that wrench into the Anglia. If it was done right after the murder, it probably was still light. So, ask the neighbors if they noticed anything, a car stopping. The only ones really in a position to see it—if they'd been in their back yard, which practically everybody would be in early evening—are the Brownes across the street, because the Anglia's parked along our wall on this side. And if they didn't, it doesn't say that

X wasn't here then. Or he might have played it safer, come later, after dark. Yes, Laura and I were right here, but the house is between us and the car. And any time up to midnight, who takes any notice of a car door slamming, a car starting up and driving off? Not much there."

"But then what? I just don't see how—where to—"

"Those strangers coming into the office just once," said Varallo. "And no guarantee that those five are all there were—"

"No," said Duncan out of the shadows. "I think that's pretty accurate. It isn't—usual, and both Mrs. Starr and I would remember."

"O.K. That's a big help right there."

"How?" demanded Susan. "How on earth can we—"

"One of them gave his name. Pepper. Now if he was the genuine article, just what he said he was, very probably he lives here in town. Nobody would go into another town to find a new insurance agency to consult, there's plenty of choice right here. So we call all the Peppers in the phone book and ask if one of them really did come in to consult Duncan. And we find a Mr. Pepper who really did, then we've eliminated him—he's the real McCoy, and not the emissary who stole the pen. *Capito?*"

"But—you wouldn't have got anywhere proving that Ross didn't—"

"I said it's boring routine. Slow, too, a lot of times. So then we take a look at this fellow the teacher Gorman is having a claims suit with. I don't think that one's very likely, because how could X or his emissary have known about that suit, and the name and so on? But we'll look. Ask if he or a friend of his spun a tale to Duncan hoping to find out which way the cat would jump. He'll deny it, of course, but he might give himself away. And if he did, that's that one eliminated. Then the genial gentleman who was looking for James Brady, realtor. If we find there isn't such a Brady on East Glenoaks, well, then, he was the emissary. If there is a Brady, go and ask if one of his clients had trouble finding his address. And so on. The two women, not so easy. No line to take there, except to get a better description of them from Mrs. Starr and check all the business places in that area."

"What a job," said Duncan. "And even then—"

"Even then, yes." Varallo was silent and then said reflectively, "But with good luck—a lot of good luck—we should be able eventually to say pretty certainly which one of those five came to pick up something of Duncan's—as it turned out, his pen—to be evidence against him. Of course that's a long way from finding and identifying him, or X. But— And then there's the wrench."

"Not mine, I never saw it before," said Duncan.

"No, I don't think they'd have gone to the trouble of stealing a weapon which could be shown as yours. Why bother? And it could be that right there X made a fatal mistake. . . . I hope Charles will have enough sense— Of course he will, but I think I'll just try to catch him—" Varallo got up abruptly and went into the house. He was back in five minutes. "*Va bène.* I should have trusted him. He already has."

"Has what, for heaven's sake?" asked Laura. "Don't make mysteries just to sound superior, darling."

He smiled at her, over a new cigarette. "Has already tagged the wrench and dispatched it to the L.A.P.D.'s criminological lab with a polite request for the full treatment. Tomorrow morning Lieutenant King is going to be very annoyed about this and say, For God's sake why'd you do such a stupid thing, we don't need any full report like that! Whereupon Charles will give his celebrated imitation of a big dumb cop and say, Well, lieutenant, I figured you'd like to be thorough. And it'll be too late then, anyway."

"Why?" asked Duncan. "I mean, what could possibly show up? It looked like an ordinary wrench to me. Outsize, and not new. But that's all."

"Well, you never know," said Varallo, leaning back and shutting his eyes. "And whatever there is to be found out about it, let's find out." He grinned, thinking of Llewellyn and the amateur suburban bloodhounds, and O'Connor's annoyance. The fact was, the several separate police forces inside Los Angeles County were very damn lucky to have Big Brother, the L.A.P.D., so close. "You see, that crime lab down there—it's about the best there is anywhere. Scotland Yard comes asking its help. A lot of other forces. It could be it'll come up with something interesting on that wrench. There was the time, Charles told me, it proved out a case on a killer by just half a heel print—and another time, it caught a whole forgery ring by the chemical analysis of one finger of a glove. We'll be interested to hear what it has to say about that wrench. And then there's a lady by the name of Louise Humboldt. Remember the name, Duncan?"

"Doesn't ring a bell."

"So she'd met Helene since. She was a friend of hers. I say was. There's reason to believe that she'd quarreled with her recently. It seems that Helene and she both belonged to a little bridge club—I gather, of mostly youngish married women with money to spend—where the stakes were higher than usual for friendly games—"

"Helene was a fiend for cards," said Duncan. "She was always having people in for bridge. It was one of the— Well, if there's one thing that bores me, it's cards. Any kind of cards. And as you might expect, I'm the world's worst player. But Helene was good."

"So it seems," said Varallo. "From a couple of reported conversations, it might be that this Humboldt woman lost more than she could afford to Helene, and maybe was being dunned. Quite recently, Mrs. Humboldt—who, by the way, is married to a husband much older than herself—has been reported as calling Helene 'money grubbing' and so on. But, on the other hand, I see some reason to doubt that reading of it. It could have been that Helene was blackmailing her over something else."

"Too melodramatic," said Laura, shaking her head.

"Why?" asked Duncan.

"Rather elementary. You knew her, Duncan. If she gave someone credit, in a card game—carried her, so to speak—or lent money outright, would she have done it on trust, a verbal agreement?"

"Good God, no. She thought too much of money."

"Yes. She'd have got an I.O.U. And having it, and not getting paid, she'd have taken very good care of that I.O.U. But no such thing was found in her apartment or her safety-deposit box. That's why I say Louise Humboldt's bitter talk about her might be over a debt—less legal."

"What kind of woman is she?" asked Susan suddenly.

"Never laid eyes on her myself. The report said, tall, blonde, about thirty-two—nervous type, whatever that means—lives in an expensive house in La Cañada. Husband's a broker in L.A. I'd like to know more. There might be something—"

"Mr. Varallo. I want to help on this. I see how it's going to be hard for you, and the other—if he thinks Ross isn't guilty too, I mean that sergeant. I want to do something, and I think maybe a woman could—get at—this Humboldt woman quicker and easier. D'you see what I mean? Please—"

"Well—" said Varallo.

"*I* see what *you* mean, about police routine and so on. But sometimes—like the personal touch. You know? Let me have a try at her."

"If you tell me what you plan—" said Varallo.

And simultaneously Duncan said, "But your job, Susan—and I hate to think of you—"

She waved away the job impatiently. "Don't be silly, Ross, this is more important than any job! I've got a week's sick leave accumulated anyway, and if I do get in the papers along with you they'll probably be only too glad to let me take it. Don't fuss."

"I hate to think of you mixed up in this— Damn it, they'll make it sound as if—"

"He is," said Susan to Laura, "quite the puritan, isn't he?" Laura said men were, when it concerned women they thought of as lawful wives. As well as illogical.

"And I'm getting hungry," she added. "It's eight-thirty. I've got some potato salad left, and seven deviled eggs and two lamb chops, and there's ground round—we could have hamburgers—"

"Povera lèi. Finitelà!" said Varallo. He took out his billfold and riffled through its contents. "What do you say, Duncan, we pool our resources, forget all about tomorrow or next week, and take these two beautiful, charming females out to a really nice place for dinner? Last fling and so on."

"Toujours gai," said Duncan. "Let's do that. I've got—" he looked— "eleven dollars and forty-three cents."

"But I'll have to get *dressed,"* said Laura.

"But I'm not *dressed,"* protested Susan.

"Oh, well, I've got you beat—fourteen-eighty-four," said Varallo. "The Brass Ring, maybe—the Matador?"

"The Matador," said Duncan. (The first place he'd taken Susan, he thought. Might as well be the last place too.)

"Vic, you devil," said Laura. He pulled her to her feet, kissed her, turned her around and gave her a slap in the indicated spot.

"Ten minutes. You look fine now, but if you must, that green thing. I said *ten* minutes—make it snappy!"

"Men," said Laura, and went. Susan went with her.

Duncan asked, "What are the chances, Varallo?"

Varallo said, "Don't shove me. I don't know. It's like the case X borrowed from, friend—all up in the air. I'll promise you this, we'll have one damn good try at it. Because I'm curious. And, shall we say, don't want to see the world deprived of an honest insurance agent."

"Oh, well," said Duncan, *"toujours gai,* like I said before. Likewise *buona fortuna.* And what the hell? Take the long view—only another insurance salesman, lots of us around."

To Duncan, the inquest produced in him exactly the same feeling as had his divorce and consequent economic bleeding: an immense surprise. He had vaguely imagined an inquest to be conducted somewhat like a trial in miniature. But the inquest on the body of Helene Duncan, called at ten o'clock that Thursday morning, was held in a rather small, dusty room on one of the upper floors of the new county courthouse, presided over only by the coroner with the aid of a clerk.

Duncan had called a lawyer last night: a bare acquaintance, Boyd Garland, whom he had been introduced to, on the golf course, by a mutual friend. Quite some time ago: it had been nearly three years since he could afford golf. But Garland was the only lawyer he knew, and he remembered liking him, casually.

Garland was waiting for him on the steps when he and Varallo arrived. Garland was looking serious and upset; he looked more upset when he heard all the details. He kept saying unhappily, "But I haven't much experience in criminal practice—"

Everybody was there; evidently, said Varallo, this was to be a full-dress one, all evidence taken and a verdict delivered, instead of the police case being reserved and an adjournment given to allow more time for investigation. Evidently the prosecutor's office didn't think more time was needed.

The coroner sat at a long table, only slightly raised on a dais, at the far end of the room, with a shorthand clerk and another man who, O'Connor said, was from the prosecutor's office. All the police officers were called up first, one by one, to give evidence: the squad-car man who had been first at the scene of the crime, Varallo, O'Connor, the two searchers. The pen was examined. Though the room wasn't large, the acoustics must have been bad, for their voices were hardly audible to the other witnesses in the row of folding chairs near the door, where a fat bailiff sat presumably to prevent any of them escaping.

The coroner asked inaudible questions, the witnesses gave inaudible answers, and the clerk took it all down on his shorthand machine. After the police, the police surgeon was called, and then Mrs. Starr. Neat and noncommittal in her smart black cotton, she trotted up to the table. She was not kept long. Then Duncan's name was called, and he got up, feeling absurdly nervous, the way he used to feel in school when he was called on to recite, and walked up to the long table and sat down in the folding chair beside the coroner.

The coroner was a long thin man, looking gray and rather bored. He led Duncan through the whole thing again: the divorce, the setting of alimony (Duncan could not remember the name of the judge, which made him feel like a fool; the coroner said impatiently, "Oh, we'll find it, we'll find it"), the effort to get the alimony reduced, the failure. The measures to which he had been driven in consequence. The loss of his pen (Duncan almost expected him to say, alleged loss), and failure to mention it to anyone because— "What? I didn't quite get—" Duncan told him what he'd told Varallo last night: how he'd felt it was just one more thing, and said Damn and let it go. It sounded very lame. But surely, he thought, they can see that a supposedly intelligent man wouldn't have acted so stupidly— And remembered that Varallo had said the facts were the main thing, all they'd look at. He was asked about Susan, and said just as little as possible, feeling the sweat in the palms of his hands. He was led through all the business about the phone call, and borrowing Varallo's car, and driving out there to hunt for the nonexistent address. He made the mistake (apparently it was a mistake) of trying to tell the coroner what he'd just learned himself last night, that that whole business had been borrowed from a British murder case of twenty-five years ago. The coroner interrupted him testily, saying that had no bearing on this present case. He was asked formally if the murder weapon found in his car was his own property, and denied it. "All right, that's all," said the coroner, and Duncan walked back to his seat beside Susan.

She was called next, but was kept only a few minutes. Then the name of John Dolan was called, and Duncan wondered who he was, belatedly remembered: the attendant at that first gas station. He looked nervous; but he was not kept long either.

During Duncan's questioning, a newcomer had arrived: a stocky, paunchy, bald man. Varallo said *sotto voce,* "King." He looked, thought Duncan, exactly the way O'Connor had described him. After Dolan, there was a pause, and King walked up to the table and held a low-voiced conference with the coroner and the prosecutor's representative, and they all looked at a folded piece of paper from his pocket. The coroner, who had been taking occasional scribbled notes of his own throughout, glanced over them, asked King a few questions, and nodded. He said quite audibly, "I agree with you," and picked up a small gavel and banged it on the table. "Virtue-of-authority-vested," he gabbled—Duncan didn't catch all of it—"after-due-consideration-evidence—hereby-find-said-Ross-William-Duncan-responsible-death, and-so-order—" Bang, went the gavel, and he stood up at once, shuffling his notes together.

And Lieutenant King turned and marched down to Duncan, said he had a warrant for his arrest on a charge of first-degree homicide, told him his rights and privileges, and formally charged and arrested him.

Susan looked very white. His darling Susan—poor darling, dragged into all this—not fair—

Defiantly, she kissed him, and held his hand tight. "It's got to come out all right, Ross. We'll all just never let ourselves think it won't, that's all. Don't go to brooding, darling, please. I d-don't know if you'll be allowed visitors—"

"Neither do I," he said.

"But I really haven't much experience in criminal practice," said Garland distractedly.

Most oddly, they all just stood around awhile, King going back to confer again with the prosecutor's man. There wasn't much to say except what they all said—take care of yourself, don't give up yet, we're all pulling for you.

And presently King came up and took his arm, quite impersonally, and said, "O.K., let's go, Duncan." The bailiff came with them, out to the elevator, and down to the police car waiting. They drove the four blocks to the police building in silence. On that short journey, Duncan grew a bitter resentment for King. King, who did not look at him or speak to him; King, to whom he was, apparently, a species apart—the lawbreaker, who did not deserve any of the smallest courtesies.

There, he was asked to empty his pockets, and they took his pocket-knife away, giving him a receipt, but let him keep everything else. He was fingerprinted, and taken upstairs to a not unpleasant small cell. It had a window, barred, through which he had a view of the foothills above Glendale. Its walls and ceiling were painted light blue. There was a neat cot with immaculate bedding, and behind a screen a lidless toilet and basin; there was a straight chair. There was a very small table with a chipped glass ashtray on it. Duncan lit a cigarette.

Garland had said he would bring him pajamas and clean shirts.

Duncan stood staring out the window for some time after he was left alone, staring aimlessly up at the tallest peak of the range of foothills which marked the northern boundary of the San Fernando Valley. There was a big white H painted on the side of the mountain. Periodically it was renewed by a volunteer crew of freshmen from Herbert Hoover High School; but as a matter of fact, he remembered, the H hadn't originally stood for Hoover High but for the name of the mountain, which was Mount Henry.

He wondered who Henry had been.

After a while the ragged fading H began to annoy him, so he turned back into the cell and sat down on the cot.

CHAPTER 13

"It'd be silly to say, cheer up and don't worry," said Varallo to Susan. "But we're going to go on working this thing, and sooner or later we'll get a break—a lead. For one thing, we've got time in our favor, wouldn't you say so, Charles?"

They had taken Susan (very pale and fighting tears) to that nice quiet little place near Duncan's office, for lunch. She wouldn't eat anything, but had had two cups of coffee, and was looking better.

"I'd say so," agreed O'Connor. "The court calendars are pretty full. You see, Miss Morgan, it's only since last year when the new county courthouse was built here, that there's been a facility in Glendale to try criminal cases. They all used to have to go downtown to L.A. But even so, the calendar's full enough here. And there'll be the grand jury finding first. I don't think his trial will be scheduled for, say, eight to ten weeks. Maybe longer."

"He has to stay there *all that time?*"

"Now, Miss Morgan. It's a nice, comfortable, clean new jail, and it serves good food. There's no bail on a homicide charge, you know. Don't worry about Duncan—he'll be O.K. The thing is, as Vic says, to go on looking and find a lead. Somewhere. Somehow."

Susan's small firm jaw came forward. "And I'm going to help you. We *will*. We've got to. I—I haven't thanked both of you for—"

"Not necessary," said Varallo. "Just the job. If you happen to be—as we flatter ourselves we are, don't we, Charles?—fair to middling good cops. And you might say there's some selfish interest involved, too. Cops are a lot smarter these days than they used to be, but they still make occasional mistakes. And the mistakes get known, and the public says, Yah, dumb cops. Which isn't the opinion we like to—foster, from the public we're trying to protect." He smiled at her. "As a man in uniform, I'm safer, I find the job easier, and so does Charles as a plainclothes sergeant, if the public believes we're reasonably intelligent, honest, efficient professionals. If you see what I mean."

She nodded. "I want to go after that Humboldt woman. Will you give me her address?"

"If you'll promise not to do anything foolish," said O'Connor. "One thing, Miss Morgan. Don't say to anybody that Vic and I are still poking around."

"I wouldn't, I've got some sense—please let me try to help."

"Wait just a minute there, Charles," said Varallo. "Why must we be so modest? Me, I think it might be very useful to us to let everybody know that. Stir them up. Right now, X thinks he's a pretty smart boy, the police have taken his bait and arrested Duncan. I say, let's spread it around that the police aren't satisfied. No need to let it out that it's just you and me, that the lieutenant isn't behind us, that we're not exactly official. If you see what I mean."

O'Connor massaged his jaw and said he saw. "Might be something in that." He gave Susan the Humboldts' address. And looked at his watch, and said he ought to be back in his office.

Varallo said ruefully, "And I'm due in to ride half my tour anyway." On the way back to where Susan had left her car, he added, "You can help on the telephoning too, Miss Morgan. Checking up on those men."

"Yes, I will," said Susan. She was still looking stubborn and determined, and obviously thinking about Louise Humboldt. It was to be hoped she wouldn't do anything silly . . . but of course she was an intelligent female.

At ten minutes after twelve, a woman had called in to headquarters and said she thought there might be something wrong next door, would the police come and look? She gave her name as Mrs. Ruth Simpson, and an address on Colonia Drive in Verdugo Woodlands. What was the trouble? Well, she didn't *know* that there was any trouble, which was why she'd hesitated so long before calling; but it was unusual for her not to see Mr. Ingman, or Mrs. Ingman, or Roberta Ingman, sometime each day—just to notice, or wave to, you know—going and coming. She almost always saw Roberta leave every morning. She, Roberta, that is, was a teacher and left early. And she hadn't seen any of them since last Sunday, except for Julian Ingman, who in her opinion was *odd* and always had been. In fact, she was a little frightened of him, and didn't like to go to the house and ask— But there hadn't been anything said about going away, and anyway old Mr. Ingman would never let his beautiful lawn go unwatered for *five* whole days, if he could help it—

Resignedly, Communications issued instructions to the nearest car: to Prosser, profanely riding car 89. Prosser went up to Colonia Drive, to the expensive and well-groomed Mediterranean stucco belonging to Mr. August Ingman, and rang the front doorbell with Mrs. Simpson watching him anxiously from her front porch next door.

The door was opened by a very large, round, pink young man of about thirty, who smiled vaguely at him and said, "Oh, you're a policeman. I thought maybe I'd go to a policeman and say I'd done it, but then I thought maybe I wouldn't. But if you know already—"

In the house were three bodies, all five days dead. The old father, the old mother, the once-pretty young schoolteacher sister. They had all been killed with something like an ax, and very messily too, with unnecessary violence. Shaken, Prosser called in for assistance, and got it promptly.

O'Connor was to be very fully occupied for quite a while with young Mr. Ingman, the vexing question of his sanity, and all the red tape in connection. But, as Varallo pointed out, there was a saying about an ill wind. The press fell with delight on the strange and macabre saga of the Ingman family, and consequently relegated Ross Duncan—after all, that was just another of these rather ordinary triangle love nest things—to a brief article on the fourth page.

"You must be able to remember something more," said Varallo, glancing at his watch hurriedly. Now he was just as happy he was riding a tour alone, for if he hadn't been he couldn't have taken this chance, stopping in at Duncan's office where Mrs. Starr was holding the fort. But he couldn't stop long, be off the radio more than ten minutes. "She had a scarf over her hair, yes, but what color were her eyebrows? Did she wear glasses?"

"Oh, no. No. I do see it's important—" Mrs. Starr shut her eyes—"let me try to visualize, now. Yes, her eyebrows were dark. Dark brown. Though she had quite a fair complexion. Of course she was pale because she felt faint. Wouldn't she be? I think her eyes were light—blue or gray. She was a pretty girl, nice regular features, you know, a straight nose and rather a high forehead. And she had a nice voice too—a warm voice, you'd call it. Even when she was feeling sick. And I had seen her somewhere before, I know—only I can't place where. If I do remember—" She was silent, and then said, "I have the impression—this sounds silly, but I have the definite impression that it was at a dance. I think she was in evening dress."

"Oh. What dances have you been to recently?"

"Well, I don't, of course, as a rule. The only time I can think of—my sister's husband belongs to the Elks, and they held a big party about two months ago—my sister asked me to go, and I did. That's the only time I—"

He mustn't stay longer, must get back on tour, where he was supposed to be. He looked at his scribbled notes. Not much. The other woman, about forty, very dark, "haggard," not very well dressed. The girl who felt faint, a blue sundress, dark glasses which she'd taken off, blue scarf over her hair, pretty. And seen before, possibly at an Elks dance two months ago. "You'd recognize her?"

"Oh, yes, Mr. Varallo. Of course. I couldn't be too sure about the other one, but that one I'd know. I see it's important," said Mrs. Starr. "I thought it might make a difference, my telling the coroner that Mr. Duncan *had* mentioned losing his pen to me, but it didn't seem to. Maybe it will at the trial. Or, let's all hope, you and that nice-looking sergeant will find the real murderer before then."

"What?" said Varallo. "He *had* mentioned it?"

"Oh, no," said Mrs. Starr. "I just said he had, and that he'd probably forgotten doing so. He hasn't been himself at all, well, no wonder—I quite saw why he hadn't. But it would have been the natural thing for him to do, so I said he had."

Varallo stared at her. "Mrs. Starr, you were testifying on oath this morning. You'll be doing the same at the trial—if this comes to trial."

"Oh, yes," she said. She smoothed her neat pepper-and-salt hair, adjusted the smart black harlequin glasses.

"If you swear to a lie, you could be charged with perjury. You know that."

"Oh, yes," she said. "But he's not guilty. Of course he's not guilty, he couldn't be. And anything to help him—it's only sensible."

Sensible. Varallo looked at her. The woman who—Duncan said—kept herself to herself. The woman who had worked here for eighteen years, and he still didn't know much about. Or how she felt about him.

He said, "No, I don't think he's guilty either. But—"

"He's a great deal like his father," she said thoughtfully. "A quiet man. A—conservative man." And she smiled at Varallo. "I've been in this office since I was thirty-six, since my husband was killed and I had to go back to work. At one time I thought I was foolish to stay, because of course Allan Duncan—well, it was quite foolish, because he was devoted to his wife, and she was a nice woman too. But—I stayed. Ross is so like him. The same quiet kind, that goes on—withstanding. He never did this, and we've got to get him off somehow."

"I know," said Varallo. "Yes." He wondered if Duncan would be grateful to know about this, or—merely embarrassed.

"Would it be helpful, do you think," she asked, "if I said I'd come back from lunch early that day—that he remembered wrong—and *did* overhear that phone call?"

"I—no, not when it's in the record he says not."

"He could say he'd forgotten. I must talk it over with his lawyer," she said thoughtfully. "We might fix up something. Even if he is so tiresome—so *much* like his father—about telling the truth. We'll get him off."

"I hope so," said Varallo. And he mustn't delay longer. "Thanks very much, Mrs. Starr."

"Not at all," she said, smiling mechanically.

That evening Varallo and Garland got busy, on the two phones in Duncan's office, trying to check out those three men. They had a little luck. There were eighteen Peppers in the Northwest section phone book, and Varallo hit the right one on the thirteenth call. It was a Mr. Jason R. Pepper, and he said—sounding puzzled and curious—that yes, he had stopped at the Duncan Insurance Agency, about ten days ago, to ask about a possible change in his car insurance. But really, what—who— He stopped, and said, "Oh. There was something in the paper—about a murder, and—"

"Yes," said Varallo. "We're just checking. Thanks very much, Mr. Pepper." So that was one mysterious stranger eliminated.

When he'd come off duty at five-thirty, he had driven up to the corresponding address on East Glenoaks, and discovered that sure enough, there was a James Brady, Realtor. The office, however, had been closed. Realtors sometimes keep odd hours, and now Varallo tried to get him on the phone; but evidently the office was still closed.

He did not want to talk to the third man, whose name was Ferguson and who had been involved in the accident with Gorman, on the phone. That one, he wanted to see in person, because it would be easier to judge lie from truth.

"This—this peculiar thing about that old murder case," said Garland. "I can't make it out. And I don't know whether it's anything to bring up to a jury. Sort of complicated little thing that confuses juries. And anyway—"

"Yes, of course," said Varallo, "if Duncan's guilty he could just as easily have done the borrowing of the alibi. You don't think he's guilty, do you?"

"I don't know," said Garland frankly. "You certainly don't seem to think so. But legally speaking, it's a hard case to answer."

Varallo said he knew that. Said that police officers had to know some law, of course. And there wasn't anything more they could usefully do that night. Varallo went home, and wondered how Duncan was sleeping on his jail cot.

On Friday morning, O'Connor snatched ten minutes from his new chore to call Llewellyn, at L.A. headquarters, to ask whether they had anything, from or about Mr. Reilly, *et al.*, pertinent to his corpse. He was asked whether he supposed the several Narcotics men working that case were really much concerned with a Glendale corpse. "Patience, sergeant," said Llewellyn. "There are—signs—that that one might break any day, so then we move in and Mr. Reilly and some of his pals will be available for questioning."

"Won't that be nice," said O'Connor. "You know his pedigree. You say it isn't very likely he'd use strong-arm tactics himself—but a few of the boys he's dealing with might?"

"Very possibly," agreed Llewellyn.

"Well," said O'Connor, "let me know what goes on, will you? Thanks." He couldn't really see Mr. Reilly as X, or one of the strong-arm boys in a pro ring of pushers. Because hoods like that wouldn't bother to fix a frame—or if they did it would be on some rival hood and a very crude frame. How would they have known about Duncan, anyway? No.

X knew quite a lot about Duncan. His lunch hour, and that his car wasn't running, and—probably—about Susan Morgan, the added motive. Of course, X had probably spent some time studying Duncan.

Helene had known about Duncan, from the Merritt Agency. Oh, Merritt had said, a casual check—she just wanted to keep in touch. Whether he had a girl, where he was living and how. Most obviously, Helene hadn't set up the frame. But it was possible that she had, casually, passed on her casual information. In gossip with female friends?—"That ex-husband of mine isn't loving me these days, he's got another girl friend and can't marry her because my alimony keeps him broke—and I couldn't care less!" That sort of thing. So a woman such as

Louise Humboldt might know, and see Duncan as the perfect sitting duck. Or, come to think (thought O'Connor suddenly) she might have said something like that to Reilly. They didn't know what sort of terms those two had been on: possibly quite friendly, before Helene tried to put the bite on him. (How had she tumbled to it?)

The trouble was, of course, would Louise Humboldt, or any such socializing, card-playing females—or the gentlemanly Mr. Reilly—amuse themselves reading about famous trials? Who could say? A lot of people did, all kinds of people.

O'Connor sighed and called the L.A.P.D. crime lab. The lab told him severely that they weren't finished with the wrench as yet. They'd let him know.

And that was about all the time O'Connor had to spare for Duncan that day.

Varallo, signing off for his half-hour lunch break at twelve-thirty, looked in at the hole-in-the-wall joint on San Fernando, said, "A tuna sandwich on wheat and coffee—I'll be back for it," and went into the public phone booth on the street. He fished out a dime and dialed James Brady's office; got a female secretary and asked to speak to Brady.

"Well, he's pretty busy," said the female voice doubtfully.

"This is a police officer speaking," said Varallo sternly. "Official business, miss. Very urgent that I speak with him."

"Ooooh!" she said. "Oooh, yessir, right away!" And almost at once a heavy male voice, sharpened by anxiety, came on.

"Police? What—is it an accident, or—"

"Nothing like that, Mr. Brady. We're checking up on various people in a case," said Varallo vaguely, "and we'd like to know if you happen to know a certain fellow, who may be one of your clients. That is, whether he *is* one of your clients. He's a big middle-aged man, talkative, not well educated, and may have landed here recently from Iowa. The first time he went to see you—if he did—he had trouble finding your office, went to West Glenoaks instead."

"Wait a minute," said Brady. "Give me that again, will you? I'm no electronic brain, captain."

The innocent, casual *captain* sounded good. . . . Never mind, some day he would again be captain. . . . He gave it to Brady again, slower, and Brady said, "Well, let me think. I dunno, I get a lot of people coming in. I dunno, but—"

Of course, it was a chance that if the man was genuine, even so he might not have mentioned his difficulty over the address. But if he was genuine, then his talkativeness was natural, and he probably would have. And if he was genuine, then what he'd said was true and should serve to identify him in Brady's mind.

"Iowa," said Brady. "Well—and middle-aged? What the hell's he done, anyway? I don't get this—"

"Do you know the man? Recognize the description?"

"It might," said Brady cautiously, "be Mr. Jenkins. I couldn't say. But now I think, I do recall he said something about having a little trouble locating the office, and he told me he'd just come here from Cedar Rapids. Him and his wife—retiring. Wants to buy a house and settle down."

"Fine," said Varallo. "Can you give me his address?"

"Sure. They've been looking over a lot of different places, decided on Glendale. They're living in a little court over in Eagle Rock, on La Roda Street," and he named the number. "What the hell's he done? Seemed like a nice old guy, kind of simple and honest. I don't get—"

"He hasn't done anything that I know of. Just an innocent by-stander," said Varallo. "Thanks very much, Mr. Brady." He went back to the joint for his sandwich and coffee. It looked as if Mr. Jenkins could be eliminated too, but of course he had to be seen. Drive over there tonight, thought Varallo.

CHAPTER 14

Susan Morgan sat in her six-year-old Ford coupé, across the street from the Humboldt house, and debated various approaches to Louise Humboldt. She had decided on the basic approach, but she thought it would go much better if she could make the casual contact in public instead of marching up and ringing the doorbell. Yesterday afternoon she had come up here, *and* rung the bell, with a story—of sorts—ready; but there'd been no answer. Now she was glad. She had, overnight, perfected a better story; but what excuse could she give for coming to see Louise?

It was an expensive house, all right. On about three lots, used-brick and flagstone, a long low L-shaped house, with—probably—an outsize swimming pool in back. Money, very definitely.

She sat and cudgeled her brains. For Ross. For darling, stupid, puritanical Ross in jail . . . Mother, she reflected, would probably come haring up from La Jolla the minute she saw a paper. But she'd back Susan up; probably, if Susan knew her, want to get in on the amateur sleuthing herself. She liked Ross. . . . *How* to get at this woman? What excuse—?

She might not need one, if that was Louise Humboldt coming out. Susan craned her neck. At nine-thirty in the morning, it wouldn't, would it, be a visitor?

The woman was tall, slender, blonde. She was smart in a short-sleeved apricot sheath, white costume jewelry, white sandals and big white bag. She crossed from the front door to the curving drive, went down it and into the just-visible open triple garage. In a moment she backed out down the drive in a brand-new violet Cadillac coupé.

Susan's heart rejoiced. Now if she could just keep her in sight— She started the motor. The Caddy turned the other way from her and started down Lynnhaven. She gave it a little headway, made a U-turn and went after it.

It was easy to follow, on these quiet streets; also more likely that Louise would notice that she was followed. But later on it got a little more difficult. The Caddy went down to Angeles Crest, turned there, went on to Foothill and on Foothill to Verdugo Road. These were busy, main streets, and Susan began to feel a little tense, keeping the Caddy in sight but not daring to follow too close. Louise Humboldt was an erratic driver, making too-wide turns, speeding up, slowing down.

They went down the winding length of Verdugo into Montrose, to La Crescenta Avenue, and down that into Glendale. Verdugo turned into Glendale Avenue; they went all the way down that, into L.A., to the Golden State freeway, and down toward the big feed-in and exchange where all the freeways came together.

By that time Susan was clutching the wheel tensely, eyes straining ahead for the Caddy, and the small part of her mind not fixed on the job was thinking how easy this kind of thing sounded in books. Tailing, they called it. Well, maybe to the experienced sleuth— But there had been the rattly old panel truck cutting in ahead of her, the awful moment when the Caddy had changed lanes for a left turn and she *couldn't,* traffic thick to her left, and had only managed it by signaling frantically and making a blue Plymouth stamp on its brakes (probably profanely), and that horrible bus, about a block long, looming up beside her just as the Caddy changed lanes again—

Oh, Ross, she thought. Please, we've got to have a little luck!

At the exchange, the Caddy turned off onto Figueroa, and went down to Sixth Street. The traffic, as usual, was very thick, but mercifully slow, off the freeway. They crept along. By now Susan thought she had an idea where they were going immediately, and felt a little more confident, still keeping a nervous eye on the violet gleam ahead—two cars ahead. They went down Sixth Street toward Hill, the Caddy changing into the right lane. Susan threw a frantic glance behind, signaled and started to switch lanes; four cars slammed on their brakes and doubtless some harsh things were said about crazy women drivers, but she made it. As she'd thought, the Caddy was turning down one of the entrance ramps to the big three-story underground garage under Pershing Square. She did too.

They went (obedient to signs) all the way down. Susan kept well back, but had to pull up just behind the Caddy. She rummaged aimlessly in her purse, head down, while Louise Humboldt got out, accepted a parking-ticket stub, and started for the escalators. Then she got out, took her own stub and went after her.

She rode up on the escalator, into the little square building which existed only to house the escalators, in the middle of the park. Five steps ahead of her was the apricot sheath. Susan felt easier, much more confident. There were always crowds in downtown L.A., easy to hide in —and the apricot sheath shouldn't be hard to keep in sight.

In the park, her quarry hurried. Hurried awkwardly, on stilt heels, out of the park to the corner of Sixth and Hill. Turned down Sixth to Broadway, a block down, and turned left on Broadway.

Susan, who had on walking shoes, had no trouble keeping up, keeping her in sight, but she was puzzled and curious at that left turn, which led the apricot sheath down toward Fifth and Fourth and Third, whereas all the kind of places where the apricot sheath (considering that house and the Caddy) would naturally shop lay the other way.

Two blocks. Three blocks. Second Street. Now, many of the passing crowd were talking in Spanish; there was a fair sprinkling of Negroes. Suddenly the apricot sheath veered off the sidewalk and entered a building. An old, frowsty office building.

Susan darted in after her and then hung back as she saw Louise Humboldt standing before a double elevator cage, waiting. Slowly, interminably, an elevator descended. Peering around the door, Susan saw her get in; heard the door slam shut. She went into the little lobby, stood before the doors and watched the floor-indicator hand earnestly. It stopped at five.

She found the office directory under flyblown glass at the end of the lobby. On the fifth floor there was a dentist, a chiropractor, two doctors, an optometrist, a private detective (Complete Confidential Service), an employment agency and Allred's Quick Loans (No Security Asked, Your Signature Only, Any Amount up to $5,000). Well, thought Susan. She copied down all the names in her address book.

She waited in the lobby for nearly three-quarters of an hour. Whenever either of the elevators came down, she bolted to the back of the lobby nervously. At long last the apricot sheath stepped out, and Susan followed it.

She was beginning to develop great respect for the detectives who did this sort of thing as a regular job, the underlings who tailed people and reported to the lieutenant so he could look so smart at the end of a case.

The apricot sheath went, hurriedly, up to Broadway. Hurriedly up to Fifth—Sixth—Seventh. Back in possible regions now, although the central downtown L.A. shops had what they called "run down" in the last few years; it was the big suburban department stores that were more fashionable now. Still— She was going into Bullocks'. Susan went into Bullocks' after her.

And stopped. Louise Humboldt had stopped, almost at once, at the real-jewelry counter just inside this door. She browsed among diamonds. Smiled and shook her head at a hopeful salesman. Wandered on into costume jewelry. And wandered back, circuitously around several counters, to the diamonds.

There were three oval counters of real jewelry, and as usual very few customers congregating there. At the moment, Louise and Susan had the department to themselves, except for the hopeful clerk and other clerks farther off. Susan stood about fifteen feet away from Louise Humboldt and, pretending to look at diamond watches, had her first close look at the other woman's face.

It was not a bad-looking face—pretty, in an insipid way. Regular features, rather thin and the nose rather long, but not at all bad-looking. It was also a—harried?—face. Her expression was pinched, worried, even a little wild. She turned, and pale china-blue eyes roamed unseeingly over Fine China in the far corner, over Silverware a little nearer. Susan bent her head over the watches.

"May I help you, madam?" Another suave salesman.

"Oh!" said Louise Humboldt. "I—no, thank you, I was just—looking. Just—admiring." Her voice was thin and metallic.

"We're having a sale—"

But she had gone. She went rapidly to the escalators, and rode up to the fourth floor, Susan three riders behind. She walked around at once to the down escalators and went back to the ground floor, and strolled back toward the real-jewelry counters.

Susan wondered—

But, she thought, that house. The husband a broker.

She didn't think Louise Humboldt was remotely aware that she was being followed. Well, she wouldn't expect it, of course.

This counter displayed a number of diamond rings and bracelets—all inside the glass case. It was the middle counter of the three, and had a single attendant: a youngish man, round-faced, beautifully dressed. Louise Humboldt hung over the display, deeply interested. And Susan, lurking around the oval end of the counter, looked at diamond-and-pearl pendants, watching Louise from the corner of her eye.

It really couldn't be that—

The clerk was heading purposefully for Louise when from the next counter a woman called, "Oh, Mr. Adams?" A worried female face looked round the edge of a cash register. "If you'd just certify a check, Mr. Adams—"

The beautifully dressed youngish man passed to the next counter, with a backward glance at Louise. There was no one else at the counter, and Susan thought she was out of Louise's sight, had not been noticed. Very casually Louise Humboldt slipped halfway behind the counter, through the gap in its middle, and tried the inside door of the display case. Through carelessness, or because the store was so recently opened to customers, the case was unlocked. She took out one of the ring cases. She admired it, turning it this way and that—and darting nervous side glances in all directions. (Susan took care to be studying the pendants deeply, head well down.) Then she slipped the case into her capacious bag and turned, walked away not too rapidly toward costume jewelry and handbags.

Feeling immensely surprised and confused, Susan followed. Louise Humboldt, a shoplifter? Or, probably, considering her social position, they'd call it a kleptomaniac. That house in La Cañada—the taxes alone must run nearly a thousand a year. What on earth was this? And she should point her out to a clerk, of course—

A little delay wouldn't matter, she'd be telling Varallo and O'Connor and they could—

This time the apricot sheath rode an elevator. The one of the many elevators which went to the twelfth floor. To the tearoom.

It was early, only eleven-thirty-five, and there was no waiting line. The hostess admitted her at once, and Susan after her. The hostess, in fact, gave Susan exactly the opportunity she had been waiting for; for, beaming falsely at them, she asked, "A table for two?"

"No, I'm—" Louise started to say, but Susan cut in.

"I'm quite— Why, it's Mrs. Humboldt, isn't it? What an odd coincidence! Maybe you don't remember me? We were introduced at Helene's, oh, last month sometime. My name's Robinson, Sarah Robinson. How nice to run into you like this! Are you alone too? Do let's have lunch together."

"Oh," said Louise Humboldt. "I—did we? Robinson— I'm afraid I—"

"People never remember me, it's awful." Susan smiled. "It was a little card party at Helene Duncan's. My *dear,* have you seen—about Helene? Isn't it awful?"

"Yes," said Louise. "Awful." By this time they were being led toward the banquette; the hostess settled them, side by side, and carefully pushed the little table closer, and left menus.

"I mean, people one knows—it just doesn't seem possible, a sensational thing like that. Her ex-husband—it said in this morning's paper he's been arrested, did you see? Of course, as I said to myself when I heard, in a *sort* of way one can see why. I mean, Helene *was* greedy about money, wasn't she? I was a little offended with her, I'm afraid—poor thing—the last time I saw her, she was actually dunning me for a tiny little debt I owed her from our last card party—I mean, as if she was a—a loan shark or something—" But I never talk like this, she thought; I'm a pretty good actress, putting this over. If I am. "Wasn't she?"

"Helene—" said Louise Humboldt, and stopped. There was something definitely wrong with her, thought Susan interestedly; she was nervous as a witch. (Why as a witch?) Her hands fumbled ceaselessly at her bag, her eyes were fixed, her voice oddly flat. "Helene," she repeated, and then looked at the big menu on the table before her and said, "What am I doing here? Why did I come here? I don't—" She looked at Susan. "Did I meet you—at Helene's? I don't remember— But I—" And quite suddenly she got up and walked out of the tearoom, rapidly.

No waitress had as yet come up to serve them. Susan went after her. A dilemma now presented itself to her: only one elevator came up this far, the floor below being given over to administrative offices. But if she followed Louise into the elevator, Louise would know she was, well, following her. Would that matter? Varallo had said, stir them up. She waited at the turn of the corridor until she saw the light come on above the elevator door, where Louise was tapping one foot, restlessly fumbling with her bag, biting her lip. When the elevator door opened Susan hurried the few feet and entered behind Louise.

She said sympathetically, "You don't look well, Mrs. Humboldt. I don't think you should be alone, really—"

"Oh, don't bother me, go away," said Louise. But she said it without anger, abstractedly. The pretty Negro girl running the elevator turned and looked at them. But she must, in the course of a day's work, hear a lot funnier things than that, thought Susan.

"Main floor," was all she said, expressionlessly. This was an express elevator; it hadn't taken long on the way. Louise pushed ahead of Susan rudely and all but ran out into the crowds of shoppers, turning sharp left down a corridor leading to Books. She didn't go that far, but disappeared into one of the public phone booths. Susan could see her groping for change.

The booths, six of them, were built in a row; all the inside ones shared walls. Louise had darted into one of the middle ones. Susan slid into the one next to it and, careless of any curious passer-by, laid her ear to the lefthand wall.

She heard Louise dialing, the click and whirr of the dial, but very faintly. When Louise spoke, she found to her disappointment that she couldn't distinguish words unless her voice was raised. Some seconds after Louise had first spoken, Susan heard her say sharply, "But it must be worth at least two *thousand*—" And then silence. And a murmuring, and finally Louise said angrily, desperately, "Oh, all *right!* But I don't know where—" And then, audibly, she hung up.

Susan waited until she heard the door open, opened hers and took up the pursuit. She was feeling, now, rather excited and self-confident. Tailing Louise in the car had been nerve-racking, but on foot it had proved quite easy and certainly productive. It began to look as if there were something very odd indeed about Louise Humboldt. Shoplifting a diamond ring. Behaving so erratically. Going into that frowsty old office building—Susan's mind (as she followed the apricot sheath rapidly through Notions, Handbags and Millinery) made a dazzling leap. Allreds' Quick Loans, and the theft of a diamond ring. Louise needed money. Maybe she already owed money to Allreds' and had failed to get the loan extended, hence the shoplifting. Had the phone call been to Allred, to offer the ring as payment? And he had refused to accept anything but cash. So now Louise would have to sell the ring.

It made sense, of a sort. But why did she need money? Her husband— Someone blackmailing her?

Varallo had said that X could be a woman. Louise was a tall, athletically built woman. And until recently she and Helene had been friends; Helene could have told her about Ross, enough so that she'd realize he would make an obvious scapegoat. Never mind why they'd quarreled—Helene dunning her for a debt or something—but they had, and she'd committed the murder. And it could be that someone else had somehow found out and was—

Where was she?

In one half second, it seemed, the apricot sheath rapidly weaving through the crowds ahead had disappeared. Susan broke into a trot, murmuring, "Excuse me—I'm sorry—excuse me—" as she veered around a mountainous Negress, tripped over a silver poodle on a lead, and inadvertently ran into a small boy, who wailed. Damn it, she'd simply vanished— No! There, just going out the Hill Street entrance—

By the time Susan got to the street, there was no apricot sheath in sight. She halted, debating with herself quickly. There was, she thought, a good chance that Louise had gone back to the garage for her car. It was very likely that Louise might (if all that nice story Susan had dreamed up was so) think she could make a better deal for the diamond in some local place where she was known and her possession of it would not be questioned.

Susan turned and started down toward Sixth Street and Pershing Square, only a block away. She hurried; Louise had a head start. Of course both traffic lights were against her: the Hill Street one saying *Wait* even if it was green, the Sixth Street one red. When that sign flashed to green and *Walk,* she ran across to the other corner and then had to wait long seconds there. At the corner opposite, where the great wide brick wall cut diagonally into the park, she ran again, past the benches of derelict old men, the pigeon feeders and lounging young louts with an eye out for girls, down toward the little building housing the escalators. It sat midway of the block between Sixth and Fifth, on the Hill Street side of the square. She reached it, and had her hand out to the door, when up there at the corner she saw a flash of violet.

Louise. It was the violet Caddy, coming too fast up the exit ramp, catching the green light at the corner, and disappearing down Fifth Street.

"Oh, *damn!*" said Susan.

CHAPTER 15

Varallo, on his way home at nine-thirty, was thinking about needles in haystacks. Of the five mysterious strangers the two women were the most elusive—that he'd seen at once. And it now appeared that X's emissary had been one of them.

Mr. Walter Jenkins, retired grocer from Cedar Rapids, remembered going to the wrong address, looking for Brady's office. He just hadn't realized there was an East and West, was all. But why was it so important to the police, for goodness' sake? And wouldn't—er—Sergeant Varallo join them in some nice cold lemonade? Mrs. Jenkins sure made good lemonade, always had. Mr. Jenkins really didn't see why the *police—*

As he'd been told, Mr. Jenkins was voluble—a simple, very respectable man who carried snapshots of four grandchildren in his billfold and belonged to the Moose Lodge and bemoaned the difficulty of getting vests with suits any more. Varallo managed to escape the lemonade, but it was three-quarters of an hour before he got away from the Jenkinses'.

Mr. Dan Ferguson was a horse of another color. Varallo had got the address from Duncan's files, an address on Pioneer Street. It was a block of middle-aged, middle-class frame bungalows (Varallo reflected, the kind of neighborhood where he and Laura should have bought a house, but that was past praying for now), neat enough, but too near the twenty-four-hour roar of San Fernando Road. Ferguson was home alone. Friday night, the stores all open, he said, the missus and kids downtown. He was a sandy-red bull of a fellow, about forty, with sharp little too-light hazel eyes. About five-eleven, broad and chesty, a lot of jaw, and his left eyetooth had a gold filling.

The minute Varallo laid eyes on him he was sure. Duncan, asked for a detailed description of the supposed adjuster, Roberts, had said, "He was a hefty fellow, about my height but twice as broad. Medium coloring—reddish sort of hair, and—oh, yes, he had a gold filling or inlay or something, it caught the light when he talked."

It was almost unnecessary to ask the question. To see Ferguson's eyes flicker, hear him say flatly, No, he'd never done such a thing, nor no friend of his either. Sure, he'd been interested in how the company was going to decide, and the damn D.M.V. too, but he hadn't— And why the hell the police were snooping around—

"Has the case been decided yet, Mr. Ferguson?"

"Yeah," said Ferguson without inflection. "The bastards took my license away for six months and I got to pay double premiums a whole year."

"Too bad," said Varallo. "Thanks very much." He hadn't much doubt that, confronted with Ferguson, Duncan would identify him with Roberts. But that wasn't necessary now. All he wanted was the private certainty of who he was looking for.

One of the two women. And his bet was on the pretty girl who'd felt faint, thus sending Mrs. Starr scurrying into the back room for a glass of water. The pretty girl possibly seen at an Elks dance two months ago. The other woman even more elusive, nowhere to start looking for her. He sighed. Find out which Brother Elk had organized that affair, get hold of a guest list. How many women? Very probably more than a hundred.

In this weather.

And his roses needing attention.

Hell.

He rolled quietly up the drive and saw that the yellow patio light was on. But when he came down from the garage, Laura was not sitting there alone. Susan Morgan was with her.

"Vic, the most extraordinary thing—and what it means I can't—tell him, Susan!"

Susan obliged with her story. "And so then," she concluded, "I came back to Glendale, but of course I hadn't a clue as to where she might go, there was no place to count on picking her up. But I thought about what it might mean, and—"

"It looks very suspicious to me," said Laura. "We've been talking it over, and, Vic, it could have been a woman. Susan says she's a tall, strong woman. If they'd quarreled over a debt or something—and

Helene might easily have told her about Ross—and now somebody's blackmailing her—"

"Hold it," said Varallo. "I think I need a drink to assimilate this." He went in and got one, brought it back to the patio and sat down again. "She had one hell of a lot of luck over that ring, you know. Department stores have professional spotters all over the place, on the watch for shoplifters, and I should think there'd be one on permanent duty in real jewelry. I'd make a guess that that was her first attempt at it, and she had beginners' luck, all right. I'll be damned. She must be desperate for money—"

"*And,*" pointed out Laura triumphantly, "for something she can't tell her husband about. Or she'd ask him and he'd give it to her."

"You go so fast," said Varallo. "All sorts of possibilities. Maybe he's a miser, begrudges her every dime however much he's got. Maybe he's very tired of her extravagances and won't listen to her pleas any more."

"Oh, *Vic,* can't you see—"

"There's nothing to say that Louise's problem has any remote connection with ours," said Varallo. "You've got to admit that. Maybe she's collected a lot of card debts and the husband disapproves of gambling, so she can't tell him. Maybe she's being blackmailed over a youthful indiscretion—or a present lover. Maybe she's fallen for a charming gigolo and needs money to support him in the style to which—*pace, calma!*" He dodged the cushion Laura threw at him. "I know, I agree she's got to be looked at closer. It could be this ties in. And what a damned funny thing . . . I'm going to try to get Charles, see if by any chance he can spare a couple of tails for her." He went in to the phone, but O'Connor was absent from both office and apartment. Still busy with red tape on those Ingmans, probably. Try later.

"I want to have another try at her," said Susan stubbornly when he came back. "She was so upset—in an odd sort of way—terribly nervous, you know, that I don't think she paid much attention to me, even when I approached her like that. If I can try again—my idea was that if I got it across to her that I hadn't liked Helene much, maybe Louise would—"

"Feel a kindred spirit and open up and say Yes, she was dunning me for money too, and explain why," said Varallo absently. "Yes. Not too bad an idea, Miss Morgan . . . This is a damn slipshod, chancy way to work a case. Damn all stupid lieutenants." Slipshod, you could say; my God, one inexperienced girl instead of three trained detectives! And the few leads they had so very damn nebulous . . .

Of course, the woman who had mentioned "seeing Ross," loud enough for the manageress Mrs. Burton to overhear, had never turned up. Varallo still had the feeling that that had been makeweight, a little thing tossed in at the last minute; it could never have been used legally. O'Connor said that the lieutenant said robustly, Oh, well, it was some friend of hers who didn't want to get mixed up in the case and wasn't admitting it, that was all. Maybe some woman who'd been with a man she shouldn't be with, something like that. Sure, sure. Only—

And there was Brad Hunter. He hadn't liked the feel of Hunter. Absolutely no alibi. But a woman mixed up in it too . . . Had Hunter, contrary to what he'd said, been very ready to part with Helene, having a more complaisant girl friend elsewhere, and Helene proving difficult about letting him off the leash? Possibly holding something over him?

And how the hell to get legal proof on any of it?

Martin Norman, too. A distinct possibility. Despite Helene's secretiveness, he thought she had had sufficient human vanity to have done a little boasting; her sister Mona had probably known that she had a respectable capital. And Helene had been just the type to tell Mona how her will read, to keep the whip hand over little sister. You be good and do what I say, or— And Mona, not secretive. What Mona knew Marty would know, and it could be he had liked the idea of getting rid of big sister and laying hands on her money at the same time. Not knowing about the trust. Yes.

And how to prove it? They'd need a lot of nice watertight legal proof on X before Ross Duncan would be released and X put in his place.

Laura and Susan were talking excitedly, going on building up a fine fairy tale about Louise Humboldt. Varallo interrupted without apology.

"Look," he said to Susan. "I take it you're going to have another try at her tomorrow."

"I am indeed—"

"Yes, well, look. Don't try to keep it a secret. Let her see she's being followed. When she's so nervous and intent on her own affairs, she may not notice anything—extraneous, of course. But no harm if she does. Try to make a chance to approach her again. Get her attention, make her listen to you, see?"

"Yes."

"You can make it sound natural enough—supposedly you knew Helene too, and as friends of hers you'd naturally be interested in the murder. Tell Louise, all girlish and excited, you know the kind of thing—"

"Yes."

"—that you actually know the wife of one of the police officers on the case, and that she let it slip to you that the police aren't satisfied with the case against Duncan, are still investigating, looking for someone who might have framed Duncan. Can you—"

"Yes," said Susan. "I will. Her reactions should be—interesting."

"I wonder," said Varallo. He was interested in Louise Humboldt, now, but he still felt that this was a man's crime. That a man's mind had plotted it. But there was a woman in it. Louise? No, Mrs. Starr's description of those two women—neither of them had been Louise, tall and blonde and insipidly pretty.

But of course—hell and damnation—X had not necessarily got hold of that pen through an emissary. It could be—it just could be—that Duncan had left the pen at the office (he'd said he hadn't been operating on all cylinders) and that X had got in, some quiet midnight, for a leisurely look around. It was a Yale lock front and— He didn't know, about the back door onto that little alley backing up to the Wash. Have a look. It would be a convenient place, certainly, to do a little quiet burglary. With a skeleton key or a key made from a wax impression . . . The ugly, utilitarian Wash slashed through Glendale and out through the valley—the ancient bed of the Los Angeles River. Tourists stared and laughed at its forty-feet-high cement walls—for nine months of the year its concrete bed was dry as a bone; but the tourists didn't know that before the Wash was built, the winter flash floods had come, a torrent down from the mountains, bringing devastation. In January, he had seen thirty feet of water come roaring down those cement walls, carrying three-ton boulders at thirty miles an hour. . . . Those office buildings, backing up to the Wash, with only a fifteen-foot chain-link fence guarding the drop, and two hundred feet or more away across the Wash, the backs of dreary apartment houses. Who to see?

Hell and damnation. A woman in it, because of the secretary on the telephone (Laura said, somebody who'd worked a switchboard), but not necessarily the fainting girl or the haggard woman, stealing the pen.

All up in the air.

Louise Humboldt—

But it was a mind, Varallo thought suddenly, of a certain sort: the kind of mind which would think of borrowing that alibi from a famous British trial. He didn't like that; it felt to him as if someone was amusing himself—mischievously. Also, poking some subtle fun at the police, assuming those stupid clods would never realize it.

The Wallace case. A teaser of a case, as he remembered the account. It had been a masculine intelligence that had plotted that plausible alibi in the original case, an intelligence that liked to dwell on details. The same kind of mind had borrowed it here.

A teaser of a case. As you could say this one was. Especially the way they were having to work it.

He finished his drink, went in and called O'Connor again. This time he got him, at the office, and told him the latest developments.

"I'll be damned," said O'Connor. "Now *what* the hell? So I call up Bullocks' and tell them I can put the finger on a shoplifter?"

"I think we lie back and watch her some more. Am I an optimist to ask if you've got some men to spare?"

"Ha-ha," said O'Connor gloomily. "Three men on eight-hour shifts? Don't be funny. . . . I will be damned. I wonder—"

"So do I," said Varallo. "Well, I'll have Sunday off, anyway—more than you will, probably. If you have any bright ideas, let me know."

On Saturday morning Susan parked her Ford across the street from the Humboldt house at eight o'clock. She was feeling very pessimistic. She had lost Louise yesterday at about noon; Louise had had plenty of time to dispose of that ring and do whatever she wanted to do with the money. She might not be planning to leave the house at all today, for all Susan knew.

She sat there for half an hour, smoking too much, feeling more and more pessimistic, and then things began to happen. The front door opened and a man came out. Susan could see Louise in the doorway behind him. He looked about fifty-five; she was too far away to see his face clearly, but he had his hat in one hand, and he was quite bald. He was just Louise's height, only average height for a man, but he was very fat; seen in profile, his paunch was almost gross, and he waddled rather than walked. He said a few words to Louise, kissed her, and turned toward the garage. Louise shut the door rather abruptly.

Goodness, thought Susan, the husband. He must have a *lot* of money. And while she'd agreed with Laura's eager theories last night, about the secret lover or the gigolo, it hadn't seemed quite real, she couldn't connect that kind of thing with Louise—average-pretty, mysteriously agitated Louise. Now she could. Almost any woman with such a husband might very plausibly have sought diversion—or forgetfulness—elsewhere. Or, being sought, have succumbed.

Susan wondered thoughtfully how long they'd been married.

The man—Arthur Humboldt—having opened the garage door by pressing a button set into the doorpost—backed out of the drive in a new black Cadillac two-door sedan, and drove off sedately. Susan went on waiting, and twenty-five minutes later Louise emerged. Today she was smart (only not really smart, thought Susan, because she doesn't know how to wear clothes—the clothes are smart, not Louise) in a plain black cotton shirtmaker, stilt-heeled black patent sandals, and white costume jewelry, the same big white bag into which a diamond ring, property of Bullocks' Department Store, had yesterday disappeared.

Louise went into the garage and a moment later backed out in the violet Cadillac. She went down to Angeles Crest, and turned on Foothill, Susan close behind her, and down to Verdugo Road. Susan wondered whether yesterday's expedition was to be repeated; but, Verdugo Road becoming Glendale Avenue, Louise followed it only as far as Wilson Street, and turned right there. And a block later, the Caddy slowed.

Susan's heart jumped. Police headquarters was on this—

The Caddy speeded up. Louise had slowed for a dog trotting diagonally across the street.

When the Caddy was between Louise Street and Maryland it started signaling a left turn; it turned on Maryland and almost at once turned again, into the big public parking lot just down from the corner. It took the first entrance; Susan took the second. This early, the lot was almost empty and both found spaces at once.

And now, damn it, thought Susan, I lose her right away because I haven't got a single nickel and will have to use the coin changer— But she had three, and slid them all into the meter, just in case Louise planned to leave her car the maximum time.

You could go out through the back of this lot, across a delivery alley, and onto Brand Boulevard, emerging in the little gap between Paddocks' Books and Stationery and a jewelry shop. Louise did so, and turned right. The light was against her at Wilson; she waited. Again, today, she was nervous; she moved restlessly, tapping one foot, as she waited. Susan hung back, pretending to read the headlines on the papers locked in the glass-fronted case on the corner. When the light changed, Louise hurried across and started up toward California, past the big men's store on the corner, the teen-age shop, the cafeteria, the wide tiled entrance of the Alex Theater. But there she turned and started across Brand by way of the pedestrian safety crossing in the middle of the block. One thing you could say about Glendale, that was a law the police enforced; you got a ticket for ignoring safety zones twice as easily as for anything else. Traffic came to a halt, while two women crossed the wide street, one after the other.

Immediately facing the safety zone was the glittering red and gold front of Kress's. Louise walked past it, turning right, and went up to the Brand Jewelers two shops up the street and went in.

Good heavens, wondered Susan, more shoplifting? She stayed outside, looking into the window. The display cases curved around, leading up to the entrance, and she stared earnestly at the display nearest the door, three tiers of men's watches, while trying to see Louise inside. It was a big square store. Louise turned to her right inside—Susan saw her through two thicknesses of glass—and then, apparently finding no clerk, turned back the other way. Susan transferred her interest to Ladies' Birthstone Rings in the lefthand display case.

Louise was talking to a clerk. She set her handbag down on the counter, half-turned, reaching into it, and brought out something.

Susan couldn't see the clerk. Then Louise moved and she could; the clerk was smiling, but shaking his head.

The ring? But why hadn't she sold it yesterday? She'd seemed in such a hurry, or had she, in that bit of the phone call Susan had overheard. Or, for all Susan knew, she had sold the ring somewhere yesterday, and had an orgy of successful shoplifting afterward and had more loot to dispose of today.

However, the clerk was still shaking his head. Come to think, thought Susan, probably retail jewelry stores wouldn't buy anything, at the most take in old-fashioned things as part payment for a purchase, or resetting, something like that. Their business was selling.

Louise came out past Susan's back; the click of her stilt heels on the pavement sounded angry. In a moment Susan turned; Louise had turned left and was heading up toward California Street again. She crossed California, went on to the middle of that block, to the Schaeffer Jewelers, and turned in there.

In a lucky moment of belated caution, Susan didn't follow at once, but stopped and looked into the window of a smart dress shop next door. Almost immediately Louise came back, stood irresolute, looking angry and somehow wild, and then started back the way she'd come. Risking a glance into the store entrance before following, Susan understood: the Schaeffer Jewelers didn't open until ten o'clock. It was only a quarter to ten now. Louise, apparently, was in a hurry again.

CHAPTER 16

This early, as a rule, the streets would be thin of pedestrians; but this was Saturday, and Glendale was a Saturday-shopping town. Already few parking slots were empty along this main street, and the sidewalks were fairly crowded.

Louise threaded her way among the crowds quickly, heading back toward Wilson. Trying to guess her new destination, Susan decided it was the real-jewelry counter at Webbs' Department Store on that corner, or any of the three small jewelry shops in that block.

She was wrong. Louise crossed Wilson, but there turned down Wilson and passed the rear entrance to Webbs'. The sidewalk was narrower here, and twice she nearly ran into people walking the other way, did not apologize, but only hurried on—past the hat shop, the photography shop, the little imported-giftware shop, the shoe-repair place and the shop where they sold very elementary practical-joke gadgets. And went into the old-gold shop on the corner.

Susan looked thoughtfully at the dusty collection in the window. A pile of silverware, little boxes of old-fashioned stickpins, napkin rings, trays of old rings, watches, brooches. A little handful of things in one tray with a sign: WE PAID $30 FOR THIS. Another sign: LOOKING FOR DISCONTINUED PATTERNS?—on the pile of silver. She edged nearer to the door, looking at a big velvet case of rings, and as the door was open could see that Louise was alone in the shop, except for the proprietor, a tall red-haired man. Oddly enough Susan knew a little about him, because old jewelry interested her and she had several times bought inexpensive things here, and once come looking for a couple of sterling forks to replace those lost from her mother's set. He had an unexpected British accent and was something of an authority on antique cameos.

She wondered how much he'd offer Louise for what she was trying to sell. And, if this was the diamond ring or some other piece of shoplifted loot, what excuse Louise would offer for wanting to sell brand-new jewelry—for jewelry it undoubtedly was.

Anyway, he was evidently buying, because Louise didn't come out. Also evidently, they had quite a haggling session, because it was forty minutes before she did come out.

Which was awkward for Susan, who felt after ten minutes or so that she must be horribly conspicuous, staring into this one window so long. Probably she wasn't; probably no one was taking any notice; but she couldn't be sure. There was a small open market across the street, and the clerks might— She strolled over there, looking at fresh fruits and vegetables— "Lotsa nice bargains today, miss!"—keeping an eye on the old-gold shop. She crossed back to the right side and looked into the window of the dress shop next to the old-gold shop. She looked at the practical-joke gadgets in the next window. She looked, often, at her watch. . . .

After what seemed an endless time, she heard the unmistakable click of Louise's high heels. She turned out of the entrance to the import shop and came face to face with her. Louise was looking angry, frustrated and oddly excited all at once, her eyes fixed as if she focused on something far ahead.

"Why, it's Mrs. Humboldt!" said Susan. "What a coincidence! Running into you yesterday, and now again today! You do remember me, don't you? Sarah Robinson—we met at Helene's." And she remembered, suddenly and irrelevantly, that Sarah Robinson had been (in one of those collections of famous murder cases) a peculiarly cold-blooded person who had poisoned numerous relatives, including several of her own children, for their life insurance. So that was what had put the name in her head. . . .

Louise stopped short, nearly running into her. "You—" she said. "I don't—" Her nostrils flared; she was breathing quickly, heavily. "What—what do you want?"

"Want? Why, nothing. I just said it's a funny coincidence. But, my *dear,* I do have something terribly exciting to tell you! I mean, you knew Helene too, didn't you, and 'll be terribly interested! It isn't *really* violating a confidence, because Laura didn't *say* don't tell about it— Don't you want to hear the latest news about poor Helene?" Louise had tried to pass by, push her aside; Susan took hold of her arm.

"Helene—" said Louise. "Helene—"

"You *must* hear—it's quite electrifying, my dear! You know they arrested her ex-husband? Well, but I just happen to know the wife of one of the officers—a *police* officer, Mrs. Humboldt—on the case—and she told me in confidence—"

She babbled on, but was not certain that Louise understood, took it in. Louise's eyes were strangely blank; she breathed heavily, she looked at Susan with an unfocused stare.

"—Quite thrilling, like a book or something, isn't it? If he didn't *really* do it, and someone *framed* him—anyway, the police seem to think—"

Suddenly Louise pulled away. "Let me go," she said harshly. "Let me go. Helene—of course he did it. She told me—she boasted to me—how she was taking nearly everything he had. Bitch, bitch—never thought of anything but money—oh, my God, *money*—" Her voice rose, and a few people passing slowed and stared. "Money—money—money—never enough! You— You've been following me! I don't remember meeting— *What do you want?*"

"Nothing, Mrs. Humboldt," said Susan. "I haven't followed you—but I expect the police are, you know. Because you didn't like Helene at all, did you? You hated her, didn't you? And if—"

"Oh, my God," said Louise, and plunged past her and almost ran, awkward in her high heels, up toward Brand. She did not look back; her big white bag jolted ungracefully on her arm. Susan went after her.

She never looked back, but went rapidly across the boulevard, and past the shoe shop, the dress shop, Paddocks', to turn left and cross the alley into the parking lot. Susan hurried too, then, almost running down to her own car in the lot now nearly filled with cars.

Where now?

Maryland was a one-way street, so the Caddy had to turn right. But it circled the block and headed up the next north-south street, Louise, to Glenoaks. Turned there and went all the way up to Glendale Avenue. Out Glendale until it turned into Verdugo.

Going home?

She was driving very erratically, much too fast, straddling the white lines, wandering from lane to lane. Susan hoped neither of them would be stopped by a squad car. She hoped if either of them was, it would be Louise.

Going home. The Caddy turned off Foothill to Angeles Crest. But it shot up past the turn for Lynnhaven, a mile, two miles, and swerved too

fast into a big parking lot at the side of a restaurant, a big restaurant—
In fact, the Thunderbird Inn.

Where Helene had been the hostess. The inevitable hostess in such
places, looking elegant and haughty, asking about reservations, saying,
sorry, it'd be half an hour.

Susan turned in after Louise, openly. But Louise was doing no looking back. She ran from the car to the restaurant entrance.

There was only one other car here besides hers and Susan's. Most
restaurants opened at eleven, if they didn't serve breakfast, and this
wasn't the kind of restaurant that would. It was just five past eleven
now.

Susan trotted after her. She felt that a large portion of her life had
been spent in trailing Louise Humboldt. At least, she thought, if nothing
else comes of it I can say I've had experience and hire out at a detective
agency. Susan Morgan, Girl Sleuth. If they fire me at Federal because of
being in the papers— If the trial— *Oh, Ross, my darling.* It *wouldn't*
happen. They'd find out the truth, and—

Louise darted through the wide double doors, and Susan was in time
to see her turn left, past a doorway marked COCKTAIL LOUNGE in red
neon. She turned after her.

It was even darker than most cocktail lounges, which was saying
something. For a moment, coming in from the blinding hot sun outside,
she could see nothing, and was aware only (gratefully) of refrigerated
air conditioning. Gradually outlines came clear. A long, narrow room;
bar down the right side, booths to the left. Voices up ahead.

Louise, sharp and breathless, "I want to see Mr. Reilly *right now!*
I've got to—"

A male voice, muffled, only partly audible, "—tell you! Cash . . .
You got to unnerstand—" She moved toward the voices in the gloom.

A quiet voice at her elbow, "What'll it be, miss?"

Susan jumped—she had the feeling, a foot in the air—so startling was
the voice; no idea there was anyone near her. There was: a white-
jacketed bartender, peering at her over the bar.

She went on moving toward Louise's voice. She didn't want a drink
at this hour. She said, "A glass of sherry, please," and sat on a stool.

"—*got* it, I tell you! Look, you can see for yourself—"

Louise somewhere near, a dim outline at the upper end of the bar—
The man spoke again. And then Louise, "Please, please, oh, please go
and tell him—ask him—"

"O.K., O.K., keep your shirt on."

A man came swiftly past her, another white-jacketed bartender. He went out of the lounge. Susan was served with sherry she did not want, and listened to Louise moving restlessly about on her stool, tapping fingers on the bar, sighing heavily.

The man appeared again at the doorway. Louise made a sound, something between a sob and a laugh, and came hurrying down the long room past Susan. Susan turned her head and saw her vanish down the corridor between the lounge and the restaurant.

She took a sip of sherry. Mr. Reilly. Hadn't Varallo said something about a Mr. Reilly?—of course, he was the manager here.

Susan took another sip of sherry, feeling puzzled.

Mrs. Adalia Burton invariably went to bed at eleven o'clock. Ordinarily, she slept soundly through the night. But as it happened, on Friday night she went to bed in a worried state of mind, and did not sleep. That Gray Boy, Mrs. Burton's big gray-and-white tomcat, hadn't come in at his usual time—hadn't, in fact, come home at all. Of course, cats—but Gray Boy was a neutered tom, a very non-aggressive quiet cat in spite of his impressive jowls, his nineteen solid pounds and his long masculine whiskers; and he liked his nightcap of warm milk.

Mrs. Burton lay awake worrying about Gray Boy. He never wandered far, and he was six years old, not an inexperienced kitten, and afraid of traffic so he never crossed the street. But—

At midnight she got up, put on a robe, looked out the kitchen door and called him, softly. She waited, but he did not come. She went back to bed and lay wake, worrying. Gray Boy was about all she had, of her own.

She was still awake at ten minutes past one when she heard noises overhead. In Helene Duncan's apartment. Or what had been Helene Duncan's apartment up to last Monday night. It was directly over her own, and these postwar buildings, no denying, weren't as solid as they might be.

Mrs. Burton was a healthy woman of fifty-two, with normal blood pressure, an excellent digestion and few nerves; the thought of ghosts did not enter her mind. The thought of burglars did. She got up and called the police.

A patrol car arrived four minutes later. Officers McCarthy and Keller came out of it and, directed by a decently robed Mrs. Burton, crept upstairs and found the apartment door ajar. They prudently drew their police specials, crept in, switched on the overhead light and found a big dark fellow pawing through the desk.

The fellow said, "Oh, hell," and several other things. He offered no resistance. He did offer Officers McCarthy and Keller fifty bucks apiece to forget about this, at which McCarthy and Keller said several things also. They took him, not too gently, down to the jail, where he was booked on suspicion of burglary. He gave his name, sullenly, as Joe Smith. Maybe it was.

Mrs. Burton, clutching her robe around her and looking after the patrol car, there in the front hall, was aware of warm fur pressing against her bare ankles. "You wretch!" she said delightedly, stooping. "Where have you been, *bad* cat? You deserve to go to bed hungry!" But she warmed his milk for him, all the same. . . .

The night-duty sergeant on the desk recognized the address, and said to McCarthy and Keller, "That's a funny one. That's the apartment where that dame got knocked off last Monday night. Maybe somebody on that ought to hear about this."

So when O'Connor came in on Saturday morning, he found a note on his desk about it, and said, "I'll be damned," and although he had plenty to occupy him went right over to the jail to have a look at Joe Smith. Who turned out to be Mr. Bradley Hunter.

"All right, what were you after?"

"Something that belonged to me," said Hunter sullenly.

"What?" Hunter was silent. "What was it? I'll go on asking until I get some answer, you know," said O'Connor mildly.

"Look, it hasn't got one damn thing to do with the murder. My God, you know I didn't murder her—"

"Do I?"

Hunter stared up at him. "It was Duncan. You've arrested Duncan."

"Well, a few interesting little things have showed up that say maybe it wasn't. That maybe somebody framed Duncan."

Hunter turned an ugly muddy color. "Well, hell, *I* didn't have anything to— What the hell would *I* want to kill her for? I didn't— I told you how it was, damn it, I was going to see she paid off if—"

"So you told us. Before. What were you after in her apartment?"

"Something—something I'd loaned her and wanted back. Nothing to do with any of this damn—"

"What?"

Hunter thought. You could see him thinking. He said, "A—a gadget, it was. A cigarette lighter made to look like an automatic, see. She had to drive home alone nights, late, and she said—she told me—she was a little nervous, you know, and this thing looked just like a damn gun, see, and she asked—"

"Where'd you get it?"

"Uh—that special tobacco shop on Wilson."

"How much did it cost?"

"Hell, I don't—why should I—somewhere around three bucks, I guess it was—"

"Wouldn't it have been easier for her to go and buy one for herself?"

"I don't know, damn it, how should I—"

"Did she ask where you got it?"

"No, she—"

"Or how much it cost?"

"No, damn it—it was just—you can see it didn't have one damn thing to do—"

"I can't spare the time right now for a long ride on the merry-go-round, Mr. Hunter," said O'Connor gently. "What did you really want in that apartment?" But what puzzled him here was that the apartment had been thoroughly searched by his own men, and nothing incriminating to Brad Hunter had come to light. Was it something she'd had and, unknown to Hunter, disposed of? Had his farfetched idea about Helene blackmailing Hunter been so? But any evidence for blackmail, Helen would have hung on to tight, and they'd have found it.

"I *told* you what I—"

"No," said O'Connor. "Let's forget about the lighter that looks like a gun. What did you really—" They went on like that for quite a while, and O'Connor began to feel exasperated at this stupid bull of a fellow. He had an appointment with the lieutenant, over this Ingman thing, in half an hour; it couldn't be helped. This obviously had to be looked into too, let King rant and rave as he would. O'Connor, presently, turned and called the jailer. "Would you call my office, please, Sam, and tell Sergeant Dick to tell the lieutenant I'll be late—something's come up I've got to stay with. Now, Mr. Hunter. We've got all the time in the world, you see. I'm staying right here until you come clean with me."

"I *told* you, Goddammit!" Hunter was, however, getting flustered. He would have understood, and stood up to, physical force; this mere calm repetition of patient questions was infuriating and confusing him. "I *said*— Not one damn thing to do with—and none o' your Goddamn business either, anyway! When you didn't mention it, I knew you hadn't—" He shut up with a little gasp; but he'd said enough.

"Oh?" said O'Connor. He thought a minute, a little puzzled. Everybody was fallible, of course. It could be that whatever it was hadn't been there at all. On the other hand, anything very important to Hunter —important enough for burglary—Helene would probably have kept. And—there was always the chance of human fallibility. He said to Hunter, "Stay here and be a good boy. I'll be back."

He went back to his office and called in the three men who had officially gone through the apartment. Forbes, Wayne and Poor. Forbes and Wayne he was pretty confident of: efficient men. Poor had only recently passed the exam and graduated to the detective division; he was a good boy, but lacked experience. O'Connor asked them to cast their minds back to Monday and that apartment. Which of them had looked where? "Let's go over it in detail." Obediently, they did.

Living room. Desk? Wayne. Under the chair cushions, under the rug, in table drawers? Yes, Wayne and Poor together. Kitchen. All the drawers looked into? Yes, Wayne and Forbes had done the kitchen while Poor started in the bedroom. They'd looked in all the cupboards, and Forbes had poked a spoon down in the sugar and coffee cannisters—"Favorite hiding place of my mother's," he explained. Then they'd gone on to the bedroom. All the bureau drawers? Yes. And the dressing-table drawers. Through the pockets of clothes in the closet? Yes. Under the rug, under the mattress. Bathroom. No drawers. But they'd gone through the medicine cabinet, and in the little hall outside, the linen shelves.

"I see," said O'Connor. He thought, and asked, "Which of you went through her extra handbags?"

"Extra—oh," said Wayne, "there were half a dozen of them, hanging on a kind of chain in the closet. Jim did. He was just finishing when we came in."

"Well," said Poor, "I—as a matter of fact I didn't, sergeant. I was looking at a handbag when—when George and Howard came in, but it'd been on the bed, I guess it was the one she'd been carrying. I—never thought of the—"

"You never thought," said O'Connor. "I see. You'll think next time, won't you?"

"I'm sorry as hell, sergeant—"

"Yes. Just get over there now, fast, and look through those bags. On second thought, I'll go with you," and O'Connor got up.

It was in the third bag he examined— Probably, thought O'Connor, the bag she'd intended to carry the next day—that they found a manila envelope, marked FOR SAFE-DEPOSIT. In it were a recently dated insurance contract increasing her life insurance, and two I.O.U.'s. The first was for the sum of a hundred and fifty dollars, and was signed by Louise Humboldt. The second was for five thousand dollars and was signed by Brad Hunter.

CHAPTER 17

"So," said O'Connor, back at the jail, "even cops make mistakes. We've got it now." He let Hunter see it.

Hunter said, "Hell and damnation."

"I see it's dated about three months back. Now we know this much, you might as well tell us the whole story."

"Oh, hell, all *right*. There's nothing *in* it, damn it. I'd dropped a bundle, see, down in Gardena—"

"Poker palace? Which?"

Hunter said yes and named it. "The boss was dunning me—it's a sort of tough place, he uses the strong-arm boys sometimes, see? I was scared, I don't mind saying. And, hell, Helene was the only one I knew could fork out that much cash—if she wanted to—and—" Momentarily his piggish face wore a very ugly expression. "And did she make me go on my knees for it, the bitch! Listen—so all right, I owed her. Listen, it was only natural—I don't say it was leveling, but it was *natural*—you don't say one word about it, so I tumble that you don't know, hadn't found it, and I think if I can get it back—"

"Oh, yes, I see," said O'Connor. "Didn't it occur to you that she might have put it in her safety-deposit box?"

After a moment Hunter said sullenly, "It was a chance, that was all."

And O'Connor decided that Helene, having probably kept the I.O.U. along with Louise's (which was only a month old) in her desk, had belatedly meant to stash them away at the bank. It didn't matter much. "Had she been dunning you?"

"All *right*, so she had! I wouldn't—hell—*kill* anybody, over— Listen, it was a little bind, but I could've paid her back by next month, I told her that, it was all O.K. with her, she knew she'd get it. But, for God's sake, when this happens, see, and you come around asking questions and don't say one damn word about— Well, damn it, I know you haven't found it, and if I can get in— It was only *natural,* Goddamn—"

O'Connor agreed that it had been a human impulse. "Why not until last night?"

"Oh, for *God's* sake," said Hunter. "You had a damn watchdog on the place up to Thursday night. You know that. I went and saw the landlady, kind of a nice old biddy, Helene liked her, and she said that. I asked—I figured you would. Then I saw in Thursday night's paper you'd picked up her ex, Duncan I mean—"

O'Connor nodded. The Prosecutor hadn't figured that Hunter's contributing evidence was necessary to put in at the inquest; he'd be wanted for the trial, of course.

"—So I thought the watchdog 'd be gone. He was. But the Goddamn people across the hall were throwing a party, they had the door open for air—it was a crowd, see?—and I didn't dare— Damn it, they went on until three A.M., and I just finally— But I kept thinking about it, damn it, if I *could* get hold of— It was only natural, hell, she was loaded, and— It wasn't anything to do with—"

"Well, so you say," said O'Connor. "Get you out? You got yourself in, Hunter. Breaking and entering. You'll get bail, I suppose. Depends what judge you get, how stiff the sentence is. But this does give you a nice motive. We're still looking, you know."

"Oh, God*damn* it to hell," said Hunter despondently.

O'Connor, belatedly, went on to his interview with King (who uneasily brushed off the Hunter business as irrelevant) and to other interviews. Was called in on a new accidental death—a four-year-old and some ant poison—and later to a particularly messy accident in which three people had died (negligence or malice? It wouldn't be the first time an automobile had been used as a deadly weapon); and by six o'clock he was feeling very tired and generally sorry for himself.

He was just about to leave off writing reports and go out for a drink and dinner, when his outside phone rang. It was Varallo.

"Charles? If you can spare the evening, or part of it—things are breaking. Here and there. We've got a lot to talk over. You ought to hear this, it calls for official action. We've also got steaks, after a couple of drinks—if you'll bring a fresh pint with you?"

"I'll be there in twenty minutes," said O'Connor. "I've got something to tell you, too. Four Roses O.K.?"

*

Despite the still-blinding glare of the merciless sun, it was comfortable in the sheltered patio, sitting on cushioned redwood chairs, holding very cold frosted glasses. O'Connor had stripped off his tie, opened his collar. Laura looked deceptively cool in a strapless yellow sundress, and Susan Morgan was looking not so cool, and very astonished, in a strapless blue sundress.

"Heroin?" she said. "But that's awful— I never dreamed—"

"No, of course you didn't know," said Varallo. "Inside information. But it explains Louise, doesn't it, Charles?"

"It looks like it," agreed O'Connor.

"She's been hooked. Probably quite recently, or her husband would have noticed something, obviously. She's run through her current bank balance, doesn't dare ask him for more for fear he'll suspect something —he probably makes her a generous allowance and would ask questions. Yes, it adds up. What's the current asking price, Charles?"

"What the traffic will bear. Among clientele like Louise, who are good for the really long green, pretty damn high," said O'Connor sleepily. "Maybe a hundred, hundred and fifty, two hundred a cap—or even more."

"È vero? That high? So she must be really strapped. Hooked but good, needing two or three caps a day maybe—that kind, they don't generally get down to stealing until they've run through everything. I'll bet if and when she's looked at hard, it'll turn out that she's hocked everything of value she has—that her husband wouldn't miss right away. Fur coat and so on—"

"Yes, and I'll tell you something else," said O'Connor. "I think this gives us an idea how Helene got onto Reilly and his pals."

"So it does," said Varallo. "That I.O.U. Louise—not a strong character—well, people who get hooked on to heroin very seldom are strong characters—Helene probably got the whole story out of her in ten minutes. . . . That restaurant, big fashionable place, and not far from where the Humboldts live. Maybe they went there a lot. Maybe Louise was in the habit of dropping in there for lunch. And I think, possibly, a personable good-looking young waiter or bartender—?"

"The husband," said Susan suddenly. "He's bald and terribly fat. I told you—I mean, she probably married him for the money—"

"I," said Laura, "can make some guesses about that. I've been sleuthing too. I sacrificed my lunch hour and went to Vital Statistics and looked. They were married nineteen months ago. So—after all, I gather that Humboldt is a fairly prominent citizen, there'd have been something in the papers—I went to the *Valley News* office and looked up the back numbers." She sipped her drink.

Varallo said, "So you're a very bright young lady, *cara*—the point is made and we're hanging on your words. What showed?"

"I was late getting back, I'll probably get docked," said Laura irrelevantly. "Well, he'd been a widower for two years. No children. He was fifty-six then. She was described as a 'clerk in a local branch bank.'"

"Oh," said Susan. "She'd have been about thirty. And not really terribly attractive. Just young—to him. And probably, to herself, rather desperate?"

"It reads like that," said Laura, sipping. "And just lately, maybe, she's found she couldn't take it—even with all the money—*or* met somebody who charmed and flattered her into—?"

"Even from a distance," said Susan, "he's—gross." She gestured. "A big stomach. The kind that wobbles. You know."

"Mmh," said Laura. Her eyes slid to Varallo, appreciating his big hard masculine fitness.

"Whichever way," he said, "that's the story." He smiled at her.

"But—aren't you going to do anything about it?" asked Susan. "Tell somebody? The—the narcotics bureau, or— I mean, it's awful, she should be—"

"Well," said O'Connor, looking at his cigarette, "it's out of our hands in a way. L.A. is sitting on this one, waiting to get the goods on a couple of big boys. Llewellyn said, maybe within two or three days. I'll pass this one on, of course, but they may not want to pick her up until they've pulled their raid and shut the place down, picked up who they're after. Then, of course, they will want her."

"Yes, I see. . . . *Could* she have?"

Varallo swirled ice in his glass. "She could," he said meditatively. "Did she? What we always come back to," and he drank, "is Dorothy Sayers."

"*Dorothy Sayers?*" said Susan. "Lord Peter Wimsey?" She said it a little wildly.

Varallo laughed and said no. "That book. Containing an account of the Wallace case. Laura says—and she ought to know—the only account of it ever published, so far as she knows. Each case was written up by a different detective novelist—British mystery writers' association. The Wallace case was done by Dorothy Sayers. Very lucidly, as I remember. The point is, would anybody in Louise Humboldt's mental state be thinking clearly enough to set up this elaborate frame on Duncan, a frame borrowed from that murder case? Even granting that she is—like Laura—a long-time fan for such reading, and familiar with the details of dozens of famous cases. Which we don't know at all."

"But—well, yes, but—"

"Heroin," said Varallo, "does things to the mind. As well as the body. If she's been a mainliner for even a couple of weeks, she's really not capable of conceiving or carrying out a plot of any kind. You've talked to her—seen her. She's—unfocused. Not thinking straight."

"Yes," said Susan unwillingly. "Maybe. But drugs—they destroy all the inhibitions, don't they? All the moral— If Helene did know, and—"

"Oh, it's an idea," said Varallo, "sure. Louise borrowed money from Helene, when she began to run short. And Helene, prying, got the story out of her. And disapproved—threatened to tell the husband? Also, of course, tried to cut herself in on the racket with Reilly. So, shall we say, not so much disapproved as blackmailed. Helene seems to have liked money wherever it came from. I still ask you," and he looked at O'Connor, "do you see Louise—muddleheaded, desperate for money to buy more heroin, not at the best of times a very intelligent woman—building that tricky little frame on Duncan?" O'Connor was silent. "Louise had a motive, all right. But if she killed Helene, it would have been in sudden anger, on impulse. No build-up. And ditto for your Brad Hunter, Charles. I don't like Hunter for it either."

"Why not? It could be. Considering. He's— I don't say he's *bright*," said O'Connor, "but he runs a fairly successful business, you know. He had a reason. I got the idea it wouldn't be just so easy for him to pay off that I.O.U. He—"

Varallo was leaning back with his eyes shut. "Two questions, *amico*. Has he got a library card?"

"What?" said O'Connor. "I don't—" But he had looked over Hunter's possessions at the jail, as a matter of routine; he thought back. Membership card in the American Legion; Social Security card; driver's license; Kiwanis membership card; a couple of snapshots— "No, why?"

"The book's out of print," said Varallo. "He could own a copy, but he doesn't strike me as a man likely to have much of a private library. Probably the only place anybody could have got that book was the public library. What's the title, Laura?"

"The Anatomy of Crime. I think about 1935."

"Yes. And tell me why," said Varallo, "if Hunter committed the murder, he didn't immediately hunt for the I.O.U. and find it? He had time—a reasonable amount of time. He didn't show up at that Casa

Manuel until just before eight-thirty. The I.O.U. was his motive for the murder. He'd have found it and taken it."

"All right," said O'Connor. "Though I'll add that he might have been excited and upset, and missed finding it."

"Whoever killed Helene," said Varallo, "didn't get excited and upset very easy. Not that kind of mind, Charles. The chess player's mind . . . There's still Mr. Martin Norman. I rather like Mr. Norman for it."

"But, Vic, there's the same objection—a man like that, he looks at sports on TV, he doesn't read about famous trials."

"For God's sake," said O'Connor exasperatedly, "let's make up a list of all the people who read about famous trials! And *I* don't see—" He fell silent, massaging his jaw.

Varallo got up and freshened their drinks. Laura said, "That cousin of hers—with the funny religious-fanatic mother—"

"Well, with what motive?" asked O'Connor.

"Duncan thought there was money—reason Helene took the trouble to keep her sweet," said Varallo. "But most of it would go to the son, of course. . . . Me, I'm still thinking about Martin Norman. A nice direct motive, money."

"Famous trials," Laura reminded him.

"That be damned," said O'Connor. "You say the alibi was borrowed. It could be just coincidence. It's the obvious kind of—of lure, for an insurance agent—promise of a big new account. X needn't have known one damn thing about the Wallace case, or even that there was such a case."

"Well, it's possible," said Varallo, "but I don't think it was coincidence. There are too many points of similarity. Also some differences, but the setup was the same. For one thing, two rather subtle little points are exactly similar. As I recall, the nonexistent address Wallace claimed he was given was Something Gardens East—and there really was a Something Gardens West in that area. Duncan was told, Moorbank Avenue—and there really is a Moorpark Avenue out there. And Wallace's mysterious new client had an unusual name—I forget what it was—"

"Qualtrough," said Laura.

"Yes. And somehow Whipstead—bears the same trademark," said Varallo. "You can't get away from the borrowed alibi. The details were changed a little, to allow for differences in British and American usage, but— The borrowed alibi, or the borrowed frame. Which was it in the

Wallace case? Anybody's guess. We know which it was here— So who built it?" He set down his empty glass with a little impatient smack.

"Vic. Is there a chance at all to find the right one, and get Ross off?"

"I don't know," said Varallo. "We've found out a few things, but we're still a long way from even guessing about X. Most of the time, even in a major crime, you've got a pretty good idea who you want—you just go hunting for legal evidence to prove it. Sometimes it gets complicated, like this one." He stuffed his shirt into the hamper and stood there absently at the window, looking out on the side garden where Alida Lovett climbed up the wall showing her many blooms to bright moonlight, with Brandywine, Eclipse, and Lady Margaret Stewart in their individual beds flanking her.

"What are you thinking about?"

"All those jolly party-giving Elks," said Varallo. "They'll probably be quite cooperative, and dig up a guest list for me. With about a hundred women's names on it. And Mrs. Starr and I will go joyriding all around to look at every one of them—only way to do it, you know. And when we find the girl—if we do—she'll turn out to be absolutely innocent, no connection with the case at all. Because X himself could have got in the back door of the office some night."

"Oh, lord, I suppose *so*," said Laura. "I'm so sorry for Susan. . . . Well, it was bad—for *us*—the way it was, a senseless fight and—wasting all that time—but, so much worse for her, with him— It's not fair, Vic. Innocent people don't get convicted, do they? In this day and age?"

He turned from the window. "Not very often," he said. "It can happen. It has. There was that case last year—up in Contera."

"But she got off in the end. You and Jesse Falkenstein got her off."

"With a lot of hard work and luck. The trouble is here, damn it, not a single real lead. Just—odds and ends. We don't even know that X is somebody we've remotely connected to the case so far. . . . But I'm going to spend tomorrow getting around amongst them and—being indiscreet and sinister. Pass on the news that we're still sniffing around hard, and drop hints that we're not quite so dumb as somebody thinks. Who knows, that kind of thing sometimes gets people to worrying, and then they try to clean up after themselves a bit more, and that sometimes hands us a lead. We'll hope, anyway." He switched off the light and got into bed beside her.

Out of the darkness Laura asked, "Haven't you any—favorite for X?"

"No hunches, not on this one, *cara*. Anybody from Martin Norman to Reilly."

"Susan—" she said. "You've *got* to find the right one, Vic. . . ."

Susan went home to find her mother, hat still on, calling everyone they knew in search of her. Mrs. Morgan, as Susan had anticipated, was fiercely partisan for Ross (whom she'd met twice), indignant at the stupid police, worried about Susan and generally upset, angry and curious. Susan sat down to tell her all about it, with many interruptions and digressions; in the middle of the story the phone rang and it was her sister, to whom someone had just pointed out Susan's name in the *Citizen-News*. The press had only got hold of her name today.

They sat up until midnight talking about it.

"I talked to his lawyer, Mr. Garland, yesterday. He said Ross can have visitors but I mustn't come—it would just make it look worse. I suppose at the—the trial he's going to try to make it seem as if we barely knew each other. . . . I keep thinking of him—in *jail*—oh, I know it isn't the way it used to be, but—and you know how he'll get to brooding. But—I told you how nice the Varallos and this sergeant have been, they're— We've got to find the right one, just got to. . . ."

Talking wasn't doing, of course.

At eleven o'clock O'Connor, sitting somnolently in his office finishing his last report, was startled by the outside phone. He picked it up and said his name.

"Policeman's lot," said Llewellyn. "You too, I see. We're pulling that raid tonight—in an hour. Birds in the net. So tomorrow you can come and ask Mr. Reilly questions at the county jail."

"Don't think I won't," said O'Connor. "We think we've identified one of his customers for you. We let her lay because of your operations, but you'll want to pick her up—probably find some in her possession." He gave Llewellyn Louise Humboldt's name and address. "Llewellyn— little favor. Can I sit in on that pick-up?"

"Don't see why not. She ties up to your corpse too?"

"Pretty close. Just let me know when, O.K.?"

"O.K.," said Llewellyn. "We're just getting under way now. See you."

At midnight Ross Duncan still lay awake on the quite comfortable cot, with bright moonlight streaming in the barred window. It didn't matter so much if he didn't sleep; he hadn't anything to do tomorrow.

It wasn't the confinement he minded, the boredom. But he didn't know what was going on outside, what they were doing, what they'd found out— If only he knew what they were doing to help him—they had said they would help him—

Garland, so damn vague. Ask Garland tomorrow, find out— If only he knew what was going on—

CHAPTER 18

Varallo was up early, not of personal choice but because he had a lot to do today. Thank God, at least this next month he'd have most of his days free. He put in an hour's hard work, while it was still reasonably cool, on his roses, and found that Chevy Chase had three new buds. As he'd transplanted it only last week, he was surprised and gratified; and, he thought, maybe it was a token of good luck. (Helene's apartment was on Chevy Chase.)

Laura asked if there wasn't something she could do. "I kept seeing Susan's face all night," she said miserably. "And remembering. About us. I mean, it was bad—being separated—but at least I knew you were *there,* all right and not in any danger. You know."

"I know, *amante.* I don't think— Yes, there is," said Varallo. "You can go through the preliminaries with the Brother Elks. On the phone. Or would they be more cooperative with a real police officer? Oh, hell, just let them think the police are using female secretaries these days. Most civilians don't know damn all about how a police force operates. What I'm after is a guest list of that dance. Better call Mrs. Starr first and find out the date."

"I will. I'll—"

"Hang on a minute, I want the phone first. Some of this I can do on the phone. Byrd, because he's a very long chance, not very important, I think—and some of her other friends." He found Henry Byrd's apartment and office numbers in the book, and tried both, but got no answer. "Well, well. Somehow I had the idea that actors' agents would be late risers. Especially on Sunday mornings."

"Maybe Mama's hauled him off to church with her."

"What, at nine o'clock? She goes to the Lutheran church."

"But a lot of them have two morning services now, one quite early. You must have noticed, on the signboards—"

"I notice as little about churches as possible," said Varallo; having suffered much from paternal priestly admonitions in childhood, he had early turned his back on religion.

"Well, they do. Even Methodist and Baptist churches. Because a lot of them have such big congregations."

"Yes, there are a lot of fools in the world," agreed Varallo. He looked in the appropriate directory for Mattie Byrd's number, and discovered that she didn't, apparently, have a phone. Typical. "Oh, hell, I'll have to drive out there. I don't want to see her again, no reason, but he might be there, of course. Dutiful son—all the same like Helene— keeping the old lady sweet so she won't leave everything to the church. . . . All right, love, I'm off—you can start your job." He kissed her and went out. As he shut the back door he heard her dialing.

It wasn't quite so hot today; was it starting to taper off? The thermometer hanging beside the garage door read 89; this time yesterday it had been 93. Well, on the second of November— But with Southern California you never knew. At least, today, he was out of uniform, in light slacks and an open-necked shirt. He was, however, wearing a thin sports jacket, because he had unearthed his shoulder holster. He scarcely thought any of the people he'd be seeing would be physically dangerous; but he wanted to show very obviously as a cop. All of these people had met him before with O'Connor, in plain clothes; they would assume he was attached to the detective division. As he'd said, few civilians knew much about the police. They wouldn't know, for example, that a detective very seldom went around alone asking questions of important witnesses; they traveled in pairs, to have a witness to the answers. And he wanted—or hoped—to alarm somebody. No knowing who. In the mirror, the shoulder holster with his police special in it made a rather obvious bulge under the light jacket; it might help with the alarming.

He backed out the Chevvy and started for Bellflower. Today he was going to be getting out and around.

He got to Mrs. Byrd's house at three minutes to ten. If what Laura said was so, she might not be here, damn it. The rosebushes at the top of the front walk needed water badly, and both had dead roses drooping from them. He got out his knife and cut them off.

"You leave my flowers alone!" she said sharply from the front porch.

"Good morning, Mrs. Byrd. Well, roses," he said, "you ought to cut off the dead blossoms, you know. It stimulates new growth." She was obviously dressed for church, in a black rayon dress, newer old-lady black oxfords, and a black straw hat with a very wide brim. The hat made her look rather like a squat mushroom.

"What you want now?"

"I'm looking for your son," said Varallo. He came up to the porch.

"Oh, for the land's sake, sit down!" she said. "Get a crick in my neck lookin' up at you. Never did hear your name right."

"Varallo."

"Hah!" she said. "Eye-talian."

"Yes," said Varallo. "Are you expecting your son to come and see you today?"

"Him!" she said. "Don't s'pose so. I'm just setting here waiting for Mis' Schwarz. Allus picks me up and drives me to church, see. 'Twas a nice morning, and I got everything redded up early."

"We have a few more questions to ask," said Varallo. "This and that's turned up, and we're—I tell you frankly—we're thinking of letting Duncan go. It looks as if somebody framed him, that he's quite innocent."

"Him! Innocent? You're a fool, young man. Nobody but him 'd want to harm poor Helene. Such a good girl. I did think a mite of Helene."

"Yes, I know you did. So you want to see her murderer caught, don't you? It wasn't Duncan, you know. But we'll get—the right one. Do you have any idea where I might find your son?"

"Consorting with sinners," she said emphatically, and added unexpectedly, "Or in bed. He came to see me yesterday. Don't come as often as he should. Coming down with a summer cold he was—*I* told him that, and what to do for it. Henry always did get colds easy. I told him, honey and lemon to gargle with, and don't eat no meat, and a poultice—but catch Henry listening to a word I say!"

"Well—" said Varallo, and got up. "I'll see if I can contact him."

"I don't hold with all these newfangled diseases," she said. "Just another way, get more money out of you for specialist doctors. That Dr. Gray, try to call my rheumatism bursitis or some such fancy name. Never heard of such a thing before. Here's Mis' Schwarz." She stood up. "Don't you be a fool, young man—'twas Helene's husband killed her, plain as—"

"But you never did see him hit her, did you? That was—"

Her too-small mouth primmed itself, worked contortedly. "I did *so!*

Just like I said— I can't stay talking to you no longer—" And she trotted away down the front walk, to where a dusty old black sedan waited.

Henry Byrd's apartment was on Edgemont Avenue in Hollywood. He wasn't there. His offices were on Santa Monica Boulevard, which rather surprised Varallo, who had vaguely assumed that all actors' agents had offices on the Strip. He wasn't there either. It was a middle-aged office building, not in a very fancy area of the boulevard.

Well, find him somewhere later on.

"What the hell you mean?" asked Martin Norman. "New evidence? You saying he didn't do it?"

"It begins to look as if he was framed," said Varallo. "I can't say any more right now, but we're pretty sure who—" He caught himself, obviously. "Do you still stick to your statement that you were both here from six o'clock on, Monday night?" He bent a stern stare on them.

"What the *hell?*" said Norman. "I don't get— You trying to say—"

Mona Norman just stared, mouth wetly open; belatedly grasped it and turned an ugly mottled pink. "My own *sister,*" she said shrilly. "You couldn't think—"

Norman said belligerently, "We was here. Together. All the time. I guess you dumb cops figure on account Mona gets all Helene's money— But it's crazy, you can't prove— Because we was *here.* Together. See?"

"Of course we were! It's— I don't see how you could *think—*"

"Have either of you," asked Varallo conversationally, "ever heard of the Wallace murder case?"

They stared at him. "What's that, you goin' to try pin another murder on us?" asked Norman. "What the *hell—*"

"All right," said Varallo. "Just asking. Just asking, Mr. Norman."

"—Because," said Varallo, "I think you'll be meeting some other policemen quite soon, Mrs. Humboldt. On, shall we say, a connected matter."

She just stared at him. Looking her over, he felt repulsion and pity. The blistered skin around her too-pale eyes, the trembling hands, the vague stare, the furtive scratching, told the tale on her. The deadly thing about the big H was that it took almost no time to get you hooked. Once, twice, and you had the habit to support. It took most people down but fast. And if she was paying out what Charles said she might be, it wouldn't have taken her six weeks, two months, to run through everything. . . . Probably she'd borrowed from that shady loan company downtown as well as from Helene. And pawned a lot of things her husband wouldn't miss immediately. This was a rich man's house, he thought, looking around the long L-shaped living room, but curiously impersonal. As if a decorator had planned it, brought in the furniture, the little touches of decoration—the Venetian glass fish on the coffee table, the reproduction of the Degas over the mantel—and nobody had touched it since: no magazines laying around, no ashtrays filled, no impress on the fat chair cushions. He found it a depressing room. . . .

"Do you understand what I'm saying?" he asked her sharply.

"Yes," she said dully. "I guess so. I thought he killed her. Helene. God knows he had reason."

"*You* had a reason too, didn't you, Mrs. Humboldt? You owed her money—she'd been dunning you for it—and you couldn't ask your husband, could you, Mrs. Humboldt? Did it occur to you that if she was dead—"

"Me?" she said. She sounded a little, mildly, surprised. She was down now, he saw: some while since she'd had any. Presently she would begin to feel the awful itchy craving; right now she was just dull and vague. He wondered if she had any in the house. Almost undoubtedly, because if she hadn't she'd be out acquiring some against the dire need. "Me?" she said. "I was glad she was dead. I didn't kill her, though. She was a Goddamned bitch but I didn't kill her." In this state, her original accent showed through, the original background; for a moment she sounded incongruously like Martin Norman.

But it was starting, and it would come on fast—the nervous twitching, the rising hoarseness in the voice, the hair-trigger nerves—

"It must've been him," she said. "Nobody else—you arrested him for it. The papers said— Such a bitch she was, maybe other people had reason, I guess—but I—but I— What do you *want?* I don't know anything—"

"But you had a better reason than the money, didn't you?" he asked quietly. "She knew something about you. Something bad. She was getting more money from you, for not telling—wasn't she?"

"I—I— Damn you, Goddamn you, I don't know what you m——"

"Louise, my dear," he said from the doorway. Varallo turned. A gross man, as Susan had said: a fat, petulant, jowled face, glasses, bald head, protuberant paunch. He had a section of the morning *Times* in one hand. Dark slacks (probably custom tailored, they'd almost have to be, those short legs and that stomach), a white shirt. "I couldn't help overhearing some—my dear, what is it? Who is this gentleman?"

Varallo introduced himself, showed his badge without mentioning rank. "Oh, I see," said Humboldt. He had a flat, high voice. "But you have no right to upset my wife with your—your crude questions. Now, my dear, try to control yourself. I understand you must ask questions, but Louise was a close friend to this poor woman, and—"

"Make him leave me *alone!*" sobbed Louise. "He said—he said— Don't *let* him, Artie!"

"Now, my dear. I'm sure the officer didn't mean to frighten you— You must understand, my wife's very delicate, officer, very sensitive—"

"Yes," said Varallo, eyeing her. She was trembling convulsively now, her mouth working. In a moment she'd be dashing off to privacy, to wherever she kept it, shaking hands manipulating the teaspoon, the hypo— He stood up, consciously impressive beside Humboldt. "I don't think your wife is at all well, Mr. Humboldt. You should call your doctor and have him—"

"*No!*" screamed Louise. "I don't *want* a doctor— I won't—" And she ran; she ran from both of them, and they heard a door slam.

"Dear me," said Humboldt. "She's upset, poor girl. She was such a close friend—"

He finally got hold of Byrd at one o'clock, at his office, by phone. Varallo said his piece again, sinister and emphatic. Duncan probably framed, and they were looking—"Well, I'll be damned," said Byrd after a moment. "Just like a script. What do you know? What put you on to it?"

"I can't say anything about that," said Varallo sternly, "sorry. You understand. What I want to ask you, Mr. Byrd—"

"Hell, *I* wouldn't know anything to help you. Hadn't seen her for a week before."

"Yes, I know. Do you know anything about the Wallace murder case?"

"The— Excuse me a second," said Byrd. In a moment he was back. "Looking for an extra handkerchief. The Wallace—? Never heard of it. Local case?"

"Not exactly," said Varallo. "O.K., that's all, Mr. Byrd. Oh, one more thing. The address of that girl you were with on Monday night— Marilyn something. If you please."

"Marshall," said Byrd. "Sure. Just a minute." He gave an address on Hobart Street. He said, "For God's sake, are you sure about this—a frame? Like a damn script, victimized hee-roh. This other case you mentioned, what's that got to do—"

"Sorry," said Varallo. "Confidential. You understand. Thanks very much, Mr. Byrd."

He hung up and, leaning against the scrawled-over wall of the stuffy little booth, thought of what he had. Not so damn much. They had all seemed innocently surprised. But X would be a quick thinker, able to cover up right away.

He wondered what Laura had.

O'Connor had tried the alarming act on Brad Hunter. Now Varallo had several more people to see—these intimate girl friends of hers, and one thing he wanted from them was the possible names of ex-boy friends of Helene's. You never knew. And then, sit on it awhile and wait for X—just maybe—being alarmed, to do something silly.

He wondered if X was among these people they had connected to the case. There was something in that idea about ex-boy friends. . . .

And then, the Brother Elks.

He got back into the broiling-hot Chevvy and started for his next scheduled stop, over in Burbank, to see Marian Blake.

The morning papers had had a front-page story about a raid on the Thunderbird Inn. Reilly, two bartenders, a busboy and two other men—the wholesale suppliers L.A. Narcotics had been waiting for, presumably—were in custody downtown. Sometime today they'd be picking up Louise Humboldt and Charles would be questioning her. He wondered what Charles would get. If anything.

O'Connor was getting nothing. He hadn't been let in to see Reilly until two o'clock, until the L.A. boys had finished with him. He didn't know whether Reilly had been voluble with them; he turned very talkative with O'Connor, after O'Connor asked him about Helene.

That one, in Reilly's opinion, had been a first-class bitch, but, for God's sake, *he* hadn't anything to do with taking her off! (Mr. Reilly's precise, polite accent had disappeared; it was as if it wasn't worth the trouble anymore.) He knew cops got some crazy ideas, but that was really a dilly. Him, doing a murder . . . Yes, she'd tried to cut herself in. Had cut herself in, a little. Which he hadn't liked one damn bit, but— No, he didn't know one damn thing about her ex-husband. Hadn't known where he lived, who he was, until he saw in the papers he'd been arrested. For, he pointed out, Helene's murder. Why the hell was O'Connor looking for anybody else?

And of course there was no evidence at all. O'Connor didn't really consider Reilly as a likely suspect, for Helene. Nor any of the strong arms he might employ.

After that, he went out with Llewellyn and another man named Knapp to sit in on Louise's arrest. That turned out to be quite a little business, as he could have foreseen, because they got to Louise not long after she'd taken herself on another little sleigh ride. In fact, they walked in on the husband trying to get a doctor; he didn't have any idea what was wrong with her, thought she was hysterical. Between his horrified exclamations that there must be some mistake—after they finally got it across to him—and Louise's screams and struggles, things got a little out of hand.

By the time the police ambulance got there, and took her away, Llewellyn had one sleeve torn out of his jacket, four bloody scratches down one cheek and a bitten left hand; Knapp had had the wind knocked out of him with a modernistic bronze statue and was still sitting on the couch making crowing sounds, and O'Connor had a nasty bruise on his temple from a chair leg. Two dining-room chairs were smashed, and a good many small items of glass and china, and one leg of the coffee table was snapped off.

Llewellyn said sadly, "Any day I'd rather have to pick up the toughest hood with us, than a female." He thought, and added, "Any female."

The husband just sat there, bewildered and horrified.

They looked—they didn't have to look far—and found three decks of heroin and the rest of the paraphernalia, in a drawer in her bedroom. By then, the husband was asking them questions. They told him what they knew: told him where she'd be, and when she'd be arraigned; that he could, probably, get her out on bail but he must realize that she needed medical treatment and supervision. As usual, O'Connor thought, the judge would commit her to one of the hospitals for a cure; and as usual, probably, she'd go back on the stuff as soon as she got out.

In any case, there was no chance of his questioning her right now.

He thanked the L.A. boys for an interesting afternoon and started back for his own headquarters. It was time he tried again to show the lieutenant that there were a couple of other people around with motives to want Helene out of the way. Maybe, with Louise, he'd make a little headway this time.

He wondered what Varallo had got—if anything.

CHAPTER 19

Varallo was reflecting gloomily that he had more than he wanted. With Laura's warm, practiced voice in their ears, the Brother Elks had come through very nicely. It had been Mr. Reinfeldt who had organized that party—that is, with several others assisting him, but if a list of those attending still existed, Mr. Reinfeldt would have it. Of course, he might have counted the names already and destroyed the list. Counted the names, obviously, so that in their yearly report of activities they could say how many had attended. Members had been asked to bring as many guests as they liked—it had been a very successful party.

It seemed that Mr. Reinfeldt, contacted at home, was behind with his counting; he still had the list. (Laura didn't ask why they had not just counted the ticket stubs.) Members' names he had from the tickets sold; and guests had signed a book, entering. He was very curious as to why the *police* should be interested—oh, hunting for a witness, but—at an *Elks'* party? Really, he was quite sure no such person— He was calmed, and reluctantly promised to deliver up the list. Laura had energetically driven right over to get it; and Varallo looked at it when he got home.

It contained the names of one hundred and eighteen women. No addresses. Laura was now sitting at the desk with all four phone books, looking up addresses. Some, inevitably, they would miss—the ones down as Mary Brown or Mrs. Jane Smith, no husband's name, no way of guessing the husband's name. On those, they'd go back to the Brother Elks for more help.

One hundred and eighteen. Mrs. Starr, Laura had said, had been quite pleased and eager to help. She'd expect him at nine o'clock tomorrow morning.

And Laura had had an idea which would help. Why, she said,

couldn't Susan take part of the list and go looking at women, to check off impossibles? They had a pretty definite description—age, coloring, figure and so on. Quite a good many of the women on the list would be impossible at first glance. That way, with Susan weeding them out, as it were, there'd be a number Mrs. Starr needn't go to look at, at all. It would be a help. Called, Susan had been as eager and pleased as Mrs. Starr.

Varallo, who was spending the remaining daylight weeding his rose beds, was not feeling eager. He had the growing conviction that that list did not contain the name of the fainting girl.

And what a way to have to work. This was the kind of job that, in ordinary police routine, perhaps twenty men would be doing. The quick, economical way to work it.

He'd called O'Connor and had the story of his day. Nothing there. The lieutenant, said O'Connor, hadn't liked hearing about Louise; he'd been a little uneasy, because—as he rightly said—you never knew what a junky might do; but he still thought Duncan was guilty.

Varallo straightened; was that a vagrant breeze? The sun was almost down. He went over and looked at the thermometer. It said 82. Last night at dusk it had said 86.

The heat was breaking, thank God. Each day would be a couple of degrees better, now.

"I keep feeling that it's so stupid of me not to remember more," said Mrs. Starr.

It was ten o'clock on Monday morning, and they'd just got back in the car after looking at the fourth woman on the list. It was slow work. Varallo had foreseen that even a brief rehearsal of the true story—looking for an important witness—would take up too much time. There would, inevitably, be many they'd find out and have to come back to. Ostensibly he and Mrs. Starr were poll takers, asking about favorite TV programs. Even then, it took time.

One piece of luck, of course, was that all but a handful of the women lived around this area—mostly Glendale, Burbank, Montrose; some in La Crescenta, La Cañada. There were a few in Eagle Rock, one in Tujunga, a couple in Sun Valley. And Susan, with a copy of half the list, was energetically driving around looking at women too.

"You remembered about the dance," said Varallo. "We wouldn't have had any lead at all, if you hadn't."

"Well, I suppose," she said. "It's only—I can't say honestly that I remember her at that dance, you see. I just have the definite impression that when I saw her before, she was in evening dress and dancing."

"And that's the only party you'd been to in some while where there was dancing, you said. So—" Varallo checked the next address, Grandview Avenue, and turned the ignition key.

"Yes, of course . . . I can *see* it," said Mrs. Starr. "It's quite distinct in my mind, in the oddest way, like a photograph. She was dancing with a tall man in a tuxedo, smiling up at him. I— But that's very peculiar. I just thought—"

"What?"

"The men weren't," she said. "I've always thought it looks odd, but you see it so much in California, don't you? The women in evening clothes and the men in just dark suits—or at the most white jackets. I'm sure at that affair none of the men were in evening dress. But I distinctly remember seeing her dancing with this man in a tuxedo."

"Well, so there must have been one," said Varallo.

"Yes, I suppose so. Of course it was quite a big affair, there must have been over two hundred people there, and I wouldn't have noticed them all." And she was silent until they parked in front of the next address.

A neat stucco house, with a well-kept lawn, opposite the wall of the Grandview Cemetery. Varallo rang the bell. In a moment a woman opened the door.

"Good morning, madam. Mrs. Richard Harkness? We are taking a poll for a local TV station. Do you mind telling us—"

The woman was about fifty, plump and brown-haired and still pretty, with graying ash-blonde hair and brown eyes.

Three minutes later they got back into the car. "How queer," said Mrs. Starr. "She didn't *look* like a person who'd enjoy *Outlaw Sheriff*, did she?"

At approximately the same time O'Connor was rereading the lab report on that wrench, and feeling frustrated. It had arrived, with the wrench in a separate neat parcel, ten minutes ago, by special messenger.

Thorough, you could say. That crime lab always was. And if and when they ever got X, this might be very useful evidence. But he couldn't see that it suggested an immediate lead, which was what they'd been hoping for.

The wrench, said the report, had been manufactured by Hope Brothers, a factory in Inglewood which turned out a great variety of hand tools. It was not the stock size usually purchased by individuals, but the size purchased in mass quantity by most big-car agencies, to be included in made-up tool kits, and also by a number of garages. This particular model of a Hope Brothers wrench would be found in a few hardware stores—and could, of course, be ordered from same—in many repair shops, agency garages and like places. This particular wrench was about four years old, and had not been much used for its intended purpose. The lab was of the opinion that it had not been used in a repair shop, but had probably been owned by a private individual (as part of a tool kit) who had not had occasion to use it more than half a dozen times.

Being thorough, and having been informed which corpse the wrench was relevant to, the lab had made other tests. The wrench was undoubtedly the weapon which had ended Helene Duncan's life. Both the hair and the blood type checked.

The only other interesting thing about the wrench was that at some time in the very recent past, somehow quite a quantity of ephedrine had been spilled on the handle. Certain tests (O'Connor skipped the technical terms) had positively identified the minute residue. Ephedrine.

"What the hell," O'Connor asked himself aloud, "is ephedrine?"

He had a dictionary somewhere— He found it, but of course all it told him was how to pronounce it. And even that was a little surprise.

He shook his head at the report, put it away and started downtown to question Louise.

She was in the hospital ward of the jail, in bed. They told him that the husband had wisely decided she was better here than under his sole supervision at home, and had waived bail.

Louise was way down now, just lying there vague-eyed. He wondered whether he could get through to her, get her to answer, but she was oddly docile. She answered his questions sluggishly, with long pauses between phrases. She didn't seem surprised when he asked her about lifting the diamond ring at Bullocks'.

Yes, she had done that. She had taken it to a jewelry shop in La Cañada, where Artie had bought her things and they knew her. But they had refused to buy it, and Mr. Gregor had looked "funny" and asked questions, and she got frightened and went away. Home. She'd called Mr. Reilly before, but he wouldn't take the ring, he wanted cash. And that loan place wouldn't give her any more money, she owed them so much now. And by next day she just had to have some stuff—"Like I will," said dreamy-eyed Louise, "in a little while again now—" and she'd tried another jewelry shop in Glendale—

"Yes, we know all that," said O'Connor, and reminded himself that somebody would have to see the proprietor of the old-gold shop and break the news to him. But then, Bullocks' would be insured. "You did finally sell it at the old-gold shop?"

Yes, she said. The man had argued. He didn't want to buy it; he said he didn't keep a pawnshop, and he couldn't offer her much. In the end he had given her two hundred dollars for it. And probably, thought O'Connor, congratulated himself on a profitable deal. She'd been disappointed, but had to take it. And she—

The rest of that he knew. He asked her where she'd been on Monday night. A week ago tonight.

After a long silence she said, "Home. That's all."

"Your husband says you weren't, Mrs. Humboldt. He says that you weren't there when he came home at six-thirty, and didn't come in for about an hour. Where were you?"

"I don't—remember," she said. Her eyes slid over him, briefly sly. "Just—out. It was so hot—I thought maybe if I drove around in the car, there'd be a breeze. That's—where I was. Just—in the car."

Or up at the inn getting another deck? Or off somewhere with a hypothetical boy friend, possibly the one who got her hooked to start with? Or, just possibly, murdering Helene?

Because while Varallo was right about what heroin did to you eventually, well, just at first it could act like a few drinks, stimulate the brain waves for a while. She could have plotted the thing, carried it out. It wasn't impossible. . . .

Varallo and Mrs. Starr called it a day at three-thirty. He had to report in in an hour, and wanted a little while to relax before that. She politely refused the offer of a drink, and he dropped her at the office and drove home.

They had looked at twenty-one women, none of whom at all resembled the fainting girl.

He went home, took a shower, and in nothing but shorts wandered down to the kitchen and made himself a long cold drink. He sat in the kitchen with it, not thinking, his mind just ticking over lazily. The house felt very empty without Laura in it. He thought, Next year— Let him make sergeant, and Laura could stay home, they could start a family. A regular home, Laura in it all day. Maybe a dog. All dogs didn't dig up plants—wasn't it just terriers? There was a dog he'd seen once, a man driving through Contera, heading, he said, for a field trial down in Kern County, where the dog was entered. A medium-sized, medium-long-coated dog, a rich amber color; the man had said, a golden retriever. Varallo had liked the dog; the dog had such warm, kind, dark eyes. And the man had said wonderful with kids.

Next year . . . And where would Ross Duncan be then? Up in San Quentin, or just maybe occupying an unmarked prison grave? And if he was, how could Vic Varallo—

They'd never find the girl this way. If they did find her, or the other woman, would it be any use? It was very far from sure that either of them had one damned thing to do with it. . . . Damn it, if they only had a lead of *some* kind—

The phone rang. He took his drink with him to answer it, and it was O'Connor. He'd seen Louise; and that lab report on the wrench had come through. . . .

"Do you know what it is?"

"No idea," said Varallo. "How's it spelled? Oh. That's funny, I'd have thought—"

O'Connor said he would too, but that was what the dictionary said: *ephedrine* was accented on the second syllable, not the last. And that was all the dictionary said.

And that was all O'Connor had. Except Louise being out somewhere alone at more or less the crucial time, and a voluble Mr. Reilly denying any knowledge of Helene's murder. Otherwise, O'Connor said, he had odds and ends to clear up on that Ingman business, and an unidentified corpse found along the railroad tracks, and he'd better be getting busy on that. . . .

It was five past four; Varallo should be leaving to report in. He looked at the phone, finishing his drink. Ephedrine. It sounded more like something vaguely medical than chemical. Or did it?

They'd had occasion to go to a doctor only once since they'd been here; Laura had had a virus infection last February. On the Andersons' recommendation they'd gone to Dr. Libby on Central Avenue, and liked him.

Varallo dialed. Yes, the doctor was in. Who was calling? Hold the line a moment, please. . . . "Hello, doctor. I'm just after a little infor-mation, if you've got a minute. Do you know what ephedrine is? Is it a medicine of some kind?"

"Well, I suppose a layman would call it that. It's a proprietary solution used to relieve congestion."

"Lay terms, doctor, please? What's it used for?"

"Sinus infection," said Dr. Libby, "chiefly. Postnasal drip. About the only thing to do for congested sinuses, short of surgery. Why?"

"Just a little something came up on a case. How's it used? As a spray. I see. Thanks, doctor." Varallo put the phone down. There was something—what was it?—a very little something, trying to get through to him. . . . Ephedrine. Sinus congestion. On the *wrench,* for God's sake, a medicine for sinus trouble . . . Something— No good, it was gone.

Whatever it was.

Four-fifteen. Varallo swore, and made a quick change into uniform.

At nine-fifteen the three women were sitting in the patio talking desultorily. Susan, with her mother, had dropped by to report progress on their way to dinner, to leave the part of the list she'd covered, and Laura had suggested that they stay to keep her company, Vic being on duty. They'd sat here talking about Ross, about the case, talking round and round the whole thing—largely, thought Laura, just being futile and partisan.

Vic didn't seem very hopeful. . . . But innocent people couldn't be— They'd find something, some lead, and eventually find X. They had to.

Susan— Laura's heart contracted. Vic would get there somehow. . . . It had been bad, that two years of alienation from Vic, a senseless quarrel, her fault—but he had still been *there*. Alive, walking around. But for Susan—

They had sat here talking, round and round. For a little while now there had been silence, and all three of them jumped when the phone shrilled, loud and imperative.

Laura got up, went in and caught the third ring.

"Mr. Varallo—"

"This is Mrs. Varallo, may I—"

"Oh, Mrs. *Varallo!* This is Mrs. Starr—she's on right *now,* on the television—that girl! I recognized her right away—in a play, I know it's her—"

"What channel? Did you see her n—" No, credits came after a play on TV.

"I don't—let me—it's channel two—a thing called *Mystery Theater*— she's—"

"All right," said Laura, sounding very calm to herself as her heart thudded, "that's enough to identify her."

"Her voice—I recognized—"

"Yes, we'd better all check the credits at the end, see what her name—"

"Oh, my, *yes!* I will—" The phone banged down.

Laura called to Susan and Mrs. Morgan, and plunged for the living room and the seldom-used TV. It had been her mother's; she and Vic hardly ever—

"An awful thing," gabbled Laura excitedly, "supposed to be a suspense story, but you could spot the villain in thirty seconds, and the acting was terribly third-rate. And *then,* of course, we realized that *we* couldn't identify which girl it was, because we'd never seen her and there were three of them in the play—at least, two girls and another youngish woman who might have been. Because of course we couldn't tell about coloring, naturally, and light brown hair photographs quite dark sometimes—you see, of course, Mrs. Starr must have remembered her from seeing her in TV before, in some play where she was dancing, in evening dress—"

Varallo shook her gently. "Take a deep breath and calm down. Now. So what did you do?"

"Why, we wrote down the names of all the women in the play. Five, because there were two older ones too. And they run the credits so fast, and on this one they just ran the actors' names without saying what part they'd—"

"*Allora tutto va bène,* that's fine, and anyway the station would know. What were the names?"

Laura pressed the slip of paper on him eagerly. They were still standing in the service porch, where she'd been waiting to pounce on him the second he got home.

Varallo looked at the hastily scrawled names, reflecting absently that if he hadn't known it was a list of actresses, the names would have told him. Sonia Cheney. Virginia Lee. Amalia Hart. Elaine Parr. Marilyn—

"*Per l'amor di Dio— Possible?* Well, I will be damned!" he said. And then he said blankly, "But what the hell was the motive?"

"Does it tell you *who?* Right away? Oh, Vic, do you really—"

Varallo headed for the telephone, muttering to himself. Damn the hour—he dialed O'Connor's apartment. "Charles, we've got him. About evidence we'll see, but now we know, for sure." He told O'Connor about the girl on TV, told him her name.

There was a short silence, and then O'Connor said, "Well, I will be damned!" And after another short silence, he said blankly, "But what the hell was the motive?"

CHAPTER 20

As the polite and very curious young clerk at the Information Desk of C.B.S. hurried away to fetch a higher authority, Varallo suddenly swore and snapped his fingers. "*That* was it! Another little piece of the puzzle."

"It's still a little puzzle," agreed O'Connor. "What?"

"The mother. She said he had a summer cold, was all. And later on, that she didn't hold with newfangled diseases . . . Oh, the ephedrine—you don't know about it. It's for sinus trouble."

"I'll be damned," said O'Connor. "I see. But *why,* in God's name? I don't see any reason—"

Higher authority appeared, was given explanation and shown credentials, and eventually parted with information, some of which was interesting, and the address, which they already had. It was a good address, on Hobart Street between Hollywood and Franklin.

In the car, Varallo said, "The money. It's got to be the money. What kind of things did she say?—about Helene, and about him? Just suppose—"

"But how do we show it?"

"She'd be—difficult, in court. Sure. If it's a holograph will— But if it isn't, the lawyer."

"Well. See how it works out. Hope this damn female's at home and we don't have to—"

"An actress, at nine in the morning? She'll be home."

She was home. She was a pretty girl with dark-brown hair, blue eyes and a very nice figure—they had an opportunity to notice that because she was wearing very short white shorts and a halter, nothing else. But she seemed to be a nice girl too, and didn't ask them in until they'd told her who they were and shown identification. Then she looked very frightened and backed away from them, into a violently modern small living room.

"I haven't done anything—what do you *want?* I haven't—"

O'Connor told her what they wanted. She kept shaking her head dumbly. "No," she said. "No, that's not true. I never did—I don't know anything about it—no—" She was very frightened, and she was a very bad actress.

"Maybe," said O'Connor, "you're in love with him, and thought—"

"No. No, that's not true. I never— I don't know anything about—" She stopped abruptly and sat down.

Varallo laid a hand on O'Connor's shoulder, looking at the girl. "That's not quite the way it was, was it?" he asked quietly, smiling at her, consciously using the weapon he knew (without vanity) he possessed, his masculine good looks, his warm deep voice. "He used you, telling some story about—maybe—a practical joke? And for the obvious reason you went along. And when you found out what it really was, why, then you were tied into it as deep as he was, weren't you? Which he pointed out. Of course he never expected us to drop on him. He never thought we'd look beyond the handy scapegoat, naturally. He wasn't much worried about you."

"No. I don't know what you're talking about. No." Her voice was shaking badly.

Varallo went over to her, squatted beside her chair. "Now just think about it," he said gently. He smiled at her. "You were used, that was all. You didn't know, did you? I doubt it very much. And now you're scared. But policemen and judges and juries have some sense, you know. If you tell us the whole story, and it's what I think it is, you're in no danger at all—you'll just be a witness. A very important witness. You see? You're an honest citizen, aren't you?—want to see the right thing done? Sure. There's no reason to be frightened if you tell us the truth."

"I—" she said with a little gasp. "No. No!—I—it's no good, you couldn't ever prove anything and so he wouldn't be in jail and he could —he said about k-killing *me* if— No—"

And Marilyn Marshall began to cry.

They were patient with her. Cops learn to be patient. . . .

On their way to the next indicated place to go, O'Connor said, "Pity if the prosecutor's office thinks she's lying about that practical joke business. Seems like a nice girl, if not too bright."

Varallo agreed. All that was for later on—all the legal red tape.

It took them a while, collecting the odds and ends of evidence, now they knew where to look. The lieutenant had not been pleased; he would be less pleased, when he saw all the nice evidence they were getting. Nobody liked to show as the sucker who had fallen for a trick. . . . They saw the old woman. They saw a lawyer, who opened up reluctantly. They got a search warrant and searched an apartment. When you knew where to look, it was surprising how many little things turned up.

At two-thirty that afternoon they went to Henry Byrd's office on Santa Monica Boulevard.

"Well," said Byrd genially. "Surprise, surprise. Come in. What can I do for you?"

It was not a very prosperous-looking office. It tried hard to look prosperous, with a big mahogany-veneer desk, modernistic plastic-covered chairs, a reproduction Picasso; but everything was faintly shabby. "Sit down," invited Byrd. "You've arrested Duncan, I see. Poor devil, I suppose he—"

"I don't think," said O'Connor, "that Duncan will stay in jail much longer, Mr. Byrd. Do you, Vic?"

Varallo shook his head at Byrd. "You clever fellows will go on doing it. Underestimating our intelligence, that is. Always a mistake, Mr. Byrd. How's your sinus trouble, by the way? It was awkward, forgetting that bottle of ephedrine in your pocket when you dropped the wrench in on top of it—"

"What the *hell*—" said Byrd loudly. He had been lighting a cigarette; he dropped the lighter and it bounced to the floor. He sat motionless, making no move to pick it up. "I don't get—"

"Would you like us to tell you every move you made, and why?" asked Varallo. "We can, you know. I don't suppose you either liked or disliked Helene Duncan, much. But she was in your way, because your mother liked her and approved of her a lot more than she did you, and she'd made a will leaving three-quarters of what she has to Helene. Helene was very convincing, to your mother. And so were you, unfortunately for yourself—you'd convinced her that your business was so flourishing, she didn't worry about cutting you out almost altogether. She'd told Helene, and it's on the cards Helene told you, in her little sarcastic way. And your mother's an old woman and might die at any time. You—"

Byrd said, "What the hell is this—a frame? You can't prove—" But he had gone white; his eyes were curiously blank.

"Little shock, Mr. Byrd?" asked O'Connor. "Didn't think the stupid cops would ever get within a mile of you, when you'd so cleverly handed us Duncan on a silver platter?"

"Didn't think," said Varallo, "that the stupid cops would recognize that borrowed frame—alibi—from the Wallace case. Not that it mattered much, that it *was* borrowed—except that it showed us somebody was being—mischievous. Laughing up his sleeve at the dumb cops. It never crossed your mind we'd catch up, did it? Keeping that book right out in plain sight on your bookshelf at home—*The Anatomy of Crime*. Quite a crime fan, aren't you?"

"Go on and talk—you can't—"

"We know every move you made, Mr. Byrd. You saw that Duncan was an obvious scapegoat, and you watched him unobtrusively for a little while, got to know his schedule. I don't think your business is actually very flourishing, you had time on your hands. And it amused you to steal that frame from an old murder case. You told Marilyn Marshall—"

"That lying little bitch! She—"

"—that it was a gag, a joke on this guy—big laugh. You're her agent, she's dependent on you for jobs—she had to play along. She pulled the fainting act, got hold of Duncan's pen for you, sliding it into a nice clean envelope as per instructions for any little personal item she could pick up, to preserve the fingerprints. And she made the phone call for you—the famous Whipstead-Moorbank phone call. She used to work at the telephone company, did you know? We'd already guessed that. Just another little piece of the puzzle. You took her along when you did the killing, because you'd be on your way to alibi yourself afterward. Left her outside while you went up to see Helene. About this I'm guessing, but maybe you'll be nice and cooperative and tell us? I think you'd set up that appointment with Helene the day before. Said you wouldn't keep her long, but had something important to tell her? Some favor to ask? Anyway, up you went and killed her. Nice timing. About ten minutes after Duncan would have left on his long hunt for the nonexistent Mr. Whipstead. Only, when you left home, you'd had a little accident, dropping that wrench into your pocket and breaking the bottle of ephedrine. We've got the jacket, you know, and the lab can say what that stain—"

"You bastards, sneaking into—"

"With a search warrant, Mr. Byrd. All very legal. You didn't waste much time killing her. And down again—but you noticed the landlady's open apartment door, so you added a little something—brought Marilyn in to say that little piece about seeing Ross in Helene's apartment. Not a bright idea," said Varallo. "Of course, none of it was very bright. Especially roping in an accomplice."

They looked at him. He sat there frozen, unlit cigarette still poised, his face gray. He said, "What the *hell*—you can't prove any of this God-damned crazy—"

"An innocent accomplice," said O'Connor, "who has come apart and bared her soul to us, and is at the moment making a long statement to my lieutenant."

Byrd swore, obscene and expressionless, and then he tried to run. He plunged between them for the door, shoving O'Connor off balance. Varallo caught his arm and swung him around, dodged a wild haymaker and got him on the jaw with a short left. Byrd staggered back against the bookcases, slid down sideways and took another nasty crack, on the temple, from the corner of the desk, and sprawled still.

"Well," said O'Connor, annoyed, "now we'll have to wake him up to make the charge and arrest."

"But it's been hours *now*," said Susan, fidgeting. "You said— Why doesn't he—"

"Well, there's a lot of red tape," said Varallo soothingly. "Don't worry, it'll be O.K."

"I can't *help*—"

"*I* want to hear all the rest of the details," said Laura. "Then what? After the murder, I mean? I suppose he wrapped the wrench in a piece of newspaper or something, and—"

"That's a guess. The girl told us all she knew, finally. She's not very brainy, or she'd never have fallen for his crude little lies, you know. She says when he came out of the apartment—he'd told her it was just a business call—he went around and opened the trunk of the car. Stashing the wrench away, obviously. We've got the lab working on his car. It's a big Lincoln, and the agency says the regulation tool kit includes that model of wrench. Very nice legal evidence. We've collected a lot of evidence on him, more than we ever had on Duncan. Once we knew where to look, it turned up all over the place. They may, we hope, find some blood in the trunk. Probably no hope of finding what he used to wrap the wrench—there's a big basement incinerator at his apartment. After the impromptu business about 'seeing Ross,' Byrd drove the girl back to

Hollywood and they really did have dinner at Frascati's, because of course that we could check. Which is all she knows. I don't think he came back here to plant the wrench in the Anglia until a lot later—two, three in the morning maybe."

"Why *don't* they come?" asked Susan. "Sergeant O'Connor said—"

"All because of that will," said Laura. "I can see why he resented it, you know. After all, he was her own son. And Helene was a scheming little—"

"Don't swear."

"—miser," said Laura, "who was just a little better at fooling that tiresome old woman. You know what I—"

"It never entered his head that we'd drop on him. After all, Duncan was very obvious. And with the planted evidence on him— He was just a little too clever," said Varallo, "stealing that plot. That, I should think, amused him. He's that kind. . . . And when the Marshall girl started to add two and two, with what she saw in the papers—"

"Yes, of course, he pointed out that legally she was accessory to the crime, and if she told—"

"He also threatened her physically. But he made a bad mistake in picking her for the part, too. She's an honest, fluffy-headed girl who— yes, a little like Mona Norman—can be re-persuaded quite easily by any personable male. Of course—"

"Hey," said Laura severely, "don't go all egotistic on me."

"Oh, I meant Charles," said Varallo blandly. "Charles the gay bachelor. Of course Byrd never thought she'd be put to the test—"

"It's *hours*," said Susan despairingly.

"Red tape," said Varallo. "Don't worry—even Lieutenant King had to listen to this evidence."

"You know what I'm wondering?" said Laura. "If he had got away with it, as he fully expected to—how long would it have been before he got impatient with his mother for not dying sooner?"

"There is that," agreed Varallo. "He might have, very easily. I— Here's Charles now."

But Susan had already seen them. Susan ran. Walking up the drive beside O'Connor, Duncan looked tired, looked older; but he lifted his head when he saw her, and began to hurry. They were both reserved, rather shy people; they just held each other's hands very tightly and smiled.

It was seven-thirty and ten degrees cooler than it had been at this hour last night. The heat wave was broken. Varallo had got off this tour of duty because of all the red tape, his necessary statements for head-quarters.

Looking at Susan and Duncan, he smiled, fishing in his pocket, and went over to them. Duncan looked away from Susan to him. "You know—" he began. "I mean—there's no way to—"

"Don't bother," said Varallo. He brought out the little bunch of keys. "Maybe you'd like to borrow the Chevvy again. Take your best girl out to a nice place for dinner."

Duncan grinned at him a little shakily. "I'll just do that. I'll just damn well do that, and— Thanks. I guess you'll be advertising for a new tenant."

"A nice maiden-lady schoolteacher," said Laura. "Stop crying, Susan —everything's all right now, and men hate it."

"I *am*," said Susan. "I mean, I will. In a minute . . ."

They watched the Chevvy back out. "I think," said O'Connor, "we might go out and celebrate too. What about it? Split the check with you."

"I shouldn't," said Varallo absently. He walked over and inspected Alida Lovett critically. "Any free time I get I ought to— That God-damned aphis is back again. And I want to dig that compost hole deeper. I—"

"Vic!" said Laura firmly, and turned him around and gave him a lit-tle push. "Go in and put on a tie. We're going out to dinner. And if I hear one more word about your damned roses all evening—"

"Don't swear. I'm going, I'm going. . . . But remind me to get some more Aerosect tomorrow," said Varallo.

Their feet run to evil, and they make
haste to shed innocent blood . . . Isaiah 59:7

RUN
TO
EVIL

CHAPTER 1

"Thank goodness," said Mrs. Anderson, "school starts tomorrow." She heaved a sigh over the low cement wall separating the Andersons' yard from the Varallos'. "Seems the kids get noisier every year. And that Brandon boy—! I see he's been bothering you lately, too."

Laura said fervently that he had. "We never saw much of him until I quit work, you know— I suppose that was it, we were only home in the evening and I will say they seem to keep him in at night."

"Oh, they're nice people, the Brandons, sure, try to bring him up right. But that boy— And you may not have seen much of him, but he was telling everybody about you before you'd been moved in a month, if you'll believe me. How your husband has two eggs for breakfast and likes his bacon real crisp, and you only have coffee and toast. But you ought to be having more *now*, dear, you know. About four months along, are you?"

"But how on earth could he— Do you mean to say he'd been snooping around looking in windows and listening? I never—"

"He doesn't mean any *harm*," said Mrs. Anderson. "But what I say, he'll grow up to be a private detective." And added, "Oh, lordy, those potatoes!" and ran for her back door.

Really, thought Laura, starting back to the house, having added the coffee grounds to Vic's compost heap as he'd asked. Really, that boy . . .

They'd lived here almost six months without hearing much about Paul Brandon or meeting him. It wasn't until that first summer he'd bothered them much; and, both of them being away all day most days, it hadn't been too much. But then last April Vic had got his promotion, to Detective, and after all they weren't getting any younger and with the raise in pay they could manage, even with the size of the house payments—so the baby got started and Laura quit her job and stayed home. And the Brandon boy began to be more of a nuisance. . . .

She remembered the first time she'd seen him, when they'd been living here about six months. She'd been standing at the stove, peacefully watching potatoes boil and stirring the warming asparagus, about six-fifteen. Expecting Vic any minute, she turned when the service-porch door opened, not startled, though she hadn't heard the car. And in had walked this perfectly strange boy, a boy about nine, a sandy-haired, freckled boy with a wide friendly grin. Nonchalantly coming into the kitchen, saying, "Hi, Mrs. Varallo. I'm Paul Brandon, everybody around here knows me, I figured it's time you folks did too. You want me to cut the grass or maybe run any errands for you? Got a new stove, haven't you? A Westinghouse, I guess they're pretty good, the Bradleys down the street got one too."

Taken aback, Laura had stared at him. Obviously a boy from a good home. His slacks were newish, clean, and he had on a clean shirt. He spoke up well, grammatical, and his grin was utterly confident. But just walking in— She said something about that; his grin never faltered. "Oh, you don't want to mind me, Mrs. Varallo, everybody knows *me*. I just like to get to know people, see. People, they're kind of interesting." And his bright blue eyes under their sandy lashes were darting around, absorbing every detail of the kitchen: the new stove, the round maple table and chairs in the breakfast alcove (because Laura detested those cold chrome things), the cheerful yellow curtains matching the linoleum and the yellow-enameled cupboards, and the portable mixer left out on the tiled drainboard.

"Oh, you got a Kenmore mixer," he said interestedly. "Mrs. Anderson and Mrs. Keith both got Sunbeams." And then the car did come up the drive and Vic came in, in uniform. Ridiculously handsome, tawny-blond Vic, and her heart still turning over at the sight of him. He looked at the boy in surprise. "Gee," the boy said admiringly, staring back at him. "I never saw you in your uniform before, sir. What do you do in the cops, drive a car or stay at headquarters doing something?"

They'd got rid of him finally, and Vic asked, "Where did that come from?"

"It simply walked in," said Laura. "A funny one, isn't he? I mean, you can't say he isn't polite, but—"

After that they heard a little about him from the Andersons. The Varallo house was on the corner and they hadn't got acquainted with anyone in the neighborhood except the Andersons next door—Mr. Anderson retired, nice people in the sixties. By then Vic had got captured by his roses and Marvin Anderson being a rose man too, they foregathered over the wall quite a lot. Everybody, said the Andersons, certainly did know Paul Brandon. For several blocks around. And he knew everybody. No harm in the kid, you couldn't even say he was brash; just an awful friendly kid, and friendly the way one adult would be to another—people on equal standing. And one awful damn curious kid, said Marvin Anderson. He liked to know everything about people. Just to know.

The second time Laura had encountered him was on a hot October Sunday; Vic on duty, she was sitting in the living room under the electric fan reading the latest Doris Miles Disney when the Brandon boy rang the doorbell. Ostensibly he wanted to ask if he could do any errands for her, he was going down to the market for his mother; but he came into the entry hall as he asked, and inventoried what he could see of the living room as she answered. Three minutes later when she shut the door on him, Laura was amusedly aware that he could tell anyone who wanted to know all about the Varallos' plain beige rug, rather shabby old couch and chair in tan tweed, one new plastic-covered armchair and ottoman, middle-aged twenty-one-inch TV, mahogany coffee table and the reproduction of Vermeer's "A Woman Weighing Gold" hanging over the mantel. Not that he'd know what that was; he'd probably say, a funny old picture of a lady in old-fashioned clothes with a big stomach. (Why, she wondered irrelevantly, were so many of Vermeer's women so obviously pregnant?)

And then she thought of Aunt Lorinda, and sat down and laughed and laughed.

Aunt Lorinda hadn't been a mean gossip, or really a gossip at all; but she had been, well, nosy. She liked to know about people, the smallest things about them—whether they used handkerchiefs or Kleenex, slept in nightgowns or pajamas, and where they kept things in the kitchen, and what time they had dinner. It wasn't as if she went around (having found out) saying, "You know, that Allister woman *does* dye her hair," or, "Mr. Clarke lost forty dollars at the race track last Saturday." She just liked to *know*.

And the look in ten-year-old Paul Brandon's blue eyes had been the exact look that came into Aunt Lorinda's when, having stormed the citadel of new neighbors, she made amiable small talk while cataloguing the furniture and her hostess's clothes, and accurately estimated incomes.

Aunt Lorinda and the Brandon boy . . . It was a queer quality to find in a ten-year-old boy, but then, as Vic said, people came all sorts. And the Brandons, as Mrs. Anderson said, were quite nice people. They lived a block up on Hillcroft Road. Paul's father was a salesman of some kind, a big, hearty, sandy man. Laura had met Mrs. Brandon a few times at the nearest supermart—a little, dark, untidy woman with the same wide friendly smile as her son. He was an only child.

Very fortunately, when they'd had their murder last year (as Laura always thought of that Ross Duncan affair) the Brandon boy had been (probably to his frenzied frustration) in bed with the measles. . . . (So innocently they'd fixed up the maids'-quarters garage apartment to rent, and then discovering that it was illegal in this single-residence zone! A pity, too, the money had been useful. Oh, well.)

Since Laura had quit her job, she'd seen a good deal more of Paul Brandon, it being summer vacation. He'd turned up that first day she stayed home—neat and clean at that early hour, smiling and polite at the front door.

"Hi, Mrs. Varallo. You've quit your job, haven't you? Because you're going to have a baby—that's nice. What you want, boy or girl? Well, I just came by, tell you, any time you want any little errands done, anything like that, I'd be obliged, see. Being it's vacation now."

Once or twice she'd taken him up on that, too lazy to get her car out, and let him bicycle down to the market, the drugstore, for her; and he was quick and reliable, cheerfully refusing any little tip. "That's O.K., I get a good allowance, just like to oblige, Mrs. Varallo." But then, very obviously he admired Vic—big, handsome, tough-cop Detective Varallo.

No, you couldn't say he was exactly brash. Just friendly—and curious. That you could say. Talk about the Elephant's Child, thought Laura. . . . At this end of another summer vacation, she could agree with Mrs. Anderson, thank goodness school was starting. The Brandon boy safely confined elsewhere six hours a day anyway. She wondered what his teachers made of him. Probably a highly intelligent boy . . .

Smiling a little (for nobody could really dislike the Brandon boy, even with his 'satiable curiosity), she came back to the kitchen and finished getting dinner on the table. Coffee keeping warm on *simmer,* she drained the peas, turned over the hamburgers a last time, stirred a large dollop of butter into the mashed potatoes. Got the salad out of the refrigerator. And called Vic, who'd come in ten minutes ago looking tired.

"Tough day?" she asked sympathetically.

Varallo, feeling better for dinner, sipped coffee gratefully, groped for cigarettes, and said, "Maybe it's the hot weather. Everything coming along at once. I remember seeing some statistics a while back—the murder rate always goes up in summer. Not, of course, that all the current cases are murders. But all the red tape— We picked up those vandals, by the way."

"Oh? The ones who started the fire at the school?"

"Two fourteen and one twelve. And already talking up smart to the cops. . . . My God, what's the answer on them? I don't know. . . . And then there was a holdup—broad daylight—at a liquor store out on Glendale Avenue. Squad-car boys got him, but of course we had all the red tape and paper work on it. Maybe I was a fool to want to make rank again." He smiled at her across the table. With twelve years' service on another force upstate, ranking captain when he resigned, he'd joined the Glendale force thinking that he might get more rapid promotion; but that didn't come very fast on any police force. "The squad-car boys just turn him over and get back on their tour—we get the real work. . . . And then Charles got a hot lead on the Kreiss burglary and we went out on that. And when we got back, here's an urgent message from the Feds, to every single law-enforcement office in California, that just maybe the Armagast kidnapers are heading west and'll end up in our territory, kindly keep an eye out. And then—"

"Oh," said Laura. "That awful thing."

"Yes." For a moment Varallo looked grim. "Not a nice bunch." The kidnaping of small Robert Armagast, back in New Jersey two months ago, had been a rather brutal affair, ending in the clean escape of the kidnapers with a couple of hundred thousand dollars, after the child's body had been found: the two-year-old child dead of starvation and exposure, tied up in a deserted mountain cabin in deep woods. The FBI was chary of giving out information, but let it be known economically that they thought two men and a woman were involved, and that they had a couple of leads. "What the hell," said Varallo, finishing his coffee, "do they expect us to look for? They can't give us anything but a couple of vague descriptions. One man about thirty-five, medium-sized and dark, calling himself John Newhall—which he obviously won't be now. A fattish woman about forty, dyed blond hair, known as Marion

Stepp. Neither of them ever picked up, so no prints or nice profile shots. Just that. The other man they think is one Joseph Adam Kallman, and him they have a pedigree on—but it's not certain any of them are here, and there's a lot of California outside L.A. County."

"Yes. I never can understand a woman being mixed up in such a thing."

"*È vero.* As Charles said, it'd be very gratifying to catch up to those jokers, quite aside from the nice publicity we'd get, but pretty farfetched that they're anywhere here. . . . And then, just as we were finishing up the paper work on the burglar, the lead on the vandal case came in—reason I was late. I was a hell of a lot better off riding a squad car. Regular hours."

"Don't show off," said Laura severely. "You know you love it, being back in a little authority again. And *I'm* just as relieved—regular hours or not—to have you out of uniform. You catch enough feminine eyes as it is, without— And I'm a fool to say so, turn you into an egotist." She smiled at him, knowing Vic Varallo for what (regardless of looks) he was: a man quite without vanity, despite his handsomeness *or* brains: a quiet man who liked to grow roses.

"And," said Varallo, "the Keene trial starts tomorrow and I'll have to give evidence. Probably waste the whole day. And there'll be something new overnight—armed robbery or another burglary. And by the way, they've got Mountain shut off now—from Jackson down to Cedar. Damned nuisance." The residents of Glendale, far from being grateful to the progressive city fathers, were cursing them these days for the major project under way of reconstructing the main sewage lines and water mains. All over town, men and large machines were busily ripping up whole sections of streets, setting up signs reading DETOUR and CAREFUL! and closing off blocks to maddened residents, shutting off through intersections on main roads. Peacefully traveling some familiar route, drivers found intersections unexpectedly blocked, or had to nurse their tires over wooden planking. "But," said Varallo, "I haven't asked what sort of day you had, *cara.* Feeling all right?"

"Never better. Babies seem to agree with me. Except that I'm getting to *look* so awful. . . . Don't be so damned polite, you know I do—"

"Don't swear."

"Old-fashioned! I wonder if it could possibly be twins, the way I'm—Well! Nothing very exciting, I went to the market and came home and washed my hair, and finished the new Ursula Curtiss—very good."

Laura was a mystery fan. *"And,"* she added, "had a phone call from Thalia." Her tone was significant; Varallo looked at her.

"Thalia? Oh. The one—"

"Thalia Winters. A very nice girl"—a girl who'd worked with her at the bank—"whom I mistakenly introduced to your fat woman-chasing Irish lieutenant, Charles O'Connor."

"Now, look," said Varallo defensively.

"I thought," said Laura, "that the police were expected to have high moral standards these days. After all, Thalia's a very nice girl. And this rake O'Connor—"

"Oh, well, not exactly a— So she is, no harm done, she turned him down and that's that. *Sta bene.* Charles—"

"That O'Connor!" said Laura.

Varallo grinned at her. "And I should be damned relieved the famous Celtic charm doesn't reach you." She was just being female; she liked Charles well enough.

"Charm!" said Laura. "That gorilla? Oh, well, Thalia just doesn't like autocratic men. . . . And then, just before you came home, I had the Brandon boy."

"That kid," said Varallo, extending his cup for more coffee.

"Saying he noticed we'd got some new furniture—he'd seen the truck delivering the crib and so on—and he'd be glad to help me move things around if I was going to, and he hoped I was feeling O.K."

"That one," said Varallo. "Damn funny kid, like a nosy old gossip in ten-year-old jeans."

"Elephant's child," agreed Laura. "But a nice enough boy, in a way, Vic. I suppose he can't help it. He had another boy in tow today. That's funny, too, when you see him with another boy, the other one never says a word. I suppose he teams up with the silent ones so he can do all the talking."

Varallo laughed. "Probably grow up to be a gossip columnist."

"I have," said Laura, "either homemade lime sherbet or store-bought ice cream. Which?"

"Neither right now, *amante.* Maybe later." He stretched. "Ought to go out and do some weeding—check for aphis."

CHAPTER 2

During the next couple of weeks, various people were thinking various thoughts about the Brandon boy.

Mr. James Keith, who owned the almost-new Spanish stucco around the corner from Hillcroft on Carmen Drive, thought about Paul Brandon in something like panic, not unmixed with hatred. That Goddamned nosy kid! Hadn't thought there was a soul in hearing, and then the doorbell, just as he put the phone down, and that damned kid— Damn it to *hell*. And he wasn't sure what he could or should do about him. Make a big deal of it, approach him direct and offer him five or ten bucks to forget it—that would tell the kid there was something fishy for sure. Bring it up casual-like, explain it as a joke, or— What the *hell!*

Listen, he said to himself, did the kid even understand? He sort of looked as if he had. But he hadn't said anything, not really— Not to *him*, thought Keith. But, he went on thinking, sweating profusely at the mere idea, for all he knew the kid might be spouting off all over the neighborhood, to his mother, Mrs. Riegler when he cut her lawn, Ella Knox, other kids who'd tell their mothers—oh, God!

If Alice ever found out—

Next time he saw the kid— Got to do *something*, thought Keith.

Steve Morehouse was also thinking vengeful—and scared—thoughts about Paul Brandon. He'd threatened to give him the beating of his young life if he told anybody, but he wasn't sure he'd really scared him, damn it. A damn funny kid, that Paul. And, well, brought up right, so maybe he'd get to thinking—

Oh, God, thought Steve. He went hot and cold at once when he imagined how it'd be, Mother and Dad ever finding out. It just *couldn't* happen—mustn't happen! And that damned kid knowing—

Steve, who had also been brought up right, felt as if he'd got into one of those mazes the psychologists put rats in. Why the hell he'd ever, in the first place— But, my God, he was eighteen, not a baby, it was his own business— Only if they ever got to hear about it—!

I could kill that damn snoopy kid, he thought in panic.

Wilma Starke was also feeling jittery about the Brandon boy. Damn little nosy-parker, she thought, with panic fluttering its whirring wild wings all around her. If Ken ever found out— And a *kid*. Only ten years old. You couldn't count on a kid, they didn't have good sense. Sure, sure, so he looks up all friendly and sympathetic and says, "Why, no, Mrs. Starke, I won't tell anybody if you wouldn't like it. Honest I won't, you don't need to be scared." A *kid*. Forget all about that by next day, come out with it to somebody like Ella Knox or Mabel Anderson, anybody—he got around, that one did—and everybody knowing, so Ken knowing. . . .

God. If he found out *again* . . . Just thinking about it unnerved her, and she had to go out to the kitchen, get down his bottle of whiskey and swallow some. She nearly gagged, choking it down; she hated the taste of the stuff, she didn't like any of it, gin or vodka or whiskey, *that* wasn't her trouble. But in a minute, when it hit her, she began to feel a little better, more optimistic.

Maybe he'd forgotten all about it.

But she knew he hadn't. That snoopy kid. So damn interested in everybody, in finding out things about everybody. Bad as a gossipy old maid.

Ken— Last time, last year he'd said he'd stop letting her have even housekeeping money. Or maybe leave her altogether, if it happened again.

They weren't the only ones who were thinking about Paul Brandon. . . .

The subject of many long thoughts didn't know or care who was thinking about him. He was methodically kicking the low wire edging around a flower bed near the high fence of the Verdugo Woodlands Elementary School. That Miss Mason was nice, real nice, he thought, a good teacher too. But she needn't have kept Gordon in after, just because he got those fractions wrong. He wondered why she wasn't married; she was real pretty. She wasn't engaged either, she didn't wear a ring on that finger. Just a little one with a dark stone on her little finger, and on the other hand one like a college ring of some kind with a seal on it. He wondered why Gordon was so dumb about the fractions. He wasn't, lots of other ways. Kind of a funny kid, though.

He wondered— Well, here was Gordon. "She pretty mean?"

Gordon Bicknell shook his head. He was a thin, dark boy with a sallow skin and dark eyes habitually fixed on the ground. A little undersized for ten years old, he slid his hands down the sides of his new-looking blue sports shirt, as if nervously. "She just ast a lot o' stuff about what things I had in school last year, and like that. Well, gee, I tole her, I was sick a lot." That was quite a mouthful for Gordon, who wasn't much of a talker.

"Fractions are easy really," said Paul. "I'll show you, you want."

"Don't matter," said Gordon indifferently, shrugging. They went out the gate and round front to Verdugo Road. They'd have to wait for the three-forty bus now. Damn, thought Paul. Oh, well, there'd still be time, stop by the Kaufmans' on Moncado and see those puppies again. Dad said maybe, even if they did want forty bucks apiece because they were thoroughbreds.

"Anyway, I kinda like her," he said.

Gordon looked at him in blank surprise. "Teacher? Nuts."

Paul told him about the pups. "It'd sure be swell, have a dog again. They're Springer spaniels, see, and awful cute—my dad said maybe when they're weaned— Our old dog died last year, he was half collie and half German shepherd, old King. I'd sure like— You want to come 'n' see 'em?"

"Don't care," said Gordon. "What's the big deal about a dog, anyways? O.K., if you want."

"They're awful cute," said Paul. He glanced sideways at Gordon. A funny kid, he thought. He'd just taken up with him this last two-three weeks, since Gordon's folks had moved to their house on Rosemount from over the other side of town. Well, people were interesting, and all kind of funny when you knew them. A thing his dad was always saying. When you came to find out about them, well, gee, you never knew what *would* show up. Most people, he thought, were kind of nice, but all so different—and sometimes funny. Like Mr. Keith that time, and Mrs. Starke—she'd sure been scared he'd tell somebody about that. Funny . . .

"Verdugo much different 'n where you went last year?" he asked.

"Glenoaks School," said Gordon. "I went there last year. I guess not much. School's school."

"What were you sick with?"

"Oh, measles and different things."

"Oh. Well, you say you got a football?"

"Sure," said Gordon.

"Well, we get to your house before ours, s'pose we stop by and get it and we can—there's that empty lot on the corner—"

"O.K.," said Gordon, and added uncertainly, "but, see, you better not come in with me. My mother, she gets these awful headaches and lays down a lot, she don't like to be bothered—"

"Oh," said Paul, filing that information.

He didn't really know why he liked finding out things about people. He'd never actually thought about it. He just did; it was interesting. He mostly liked people, and he guessed they mostly liked him; so he liked knowing about them, that was all.

Katharine Mason was not thinking about Paul Brandon at the moment, but about Gordon. She sighed, sliding open the bottom drawer of her desk and taking out her bag. Gordon had a long way to go, she thought. He seemed normal, if a good deal too withdrawn and un-cooperative (this educational-method jargon!) but he'd certainly had a very poor foundation from his previous teachers.

Better ask Mr. Harwell for his records on the psychological tests.

Oh, well, Friday-thank-God. She walked sedately down the hall to the teachers' lounge, went in to repair facial ravages before starting home; she had to stop at the market.

Combing her hair, using lipstick, she thought about tomorrow night and made a grimace at herself in the mirror. Why on earth she'd said she'd go out with Lester Carey again—a deadly dull bore, and so damned polite, and insisting on talking shop. Lester Carey taught sixth-grade science, and moreover he had long ago taken Dewey as his only god and prophet. Which Katharine, having some common sense, had not.

Besides, he was going bald.

She just hadn't, she told herself, stopped to *think*. You thought naturally, work a few years and get married. And she liked children, liked working with them, so— If her common sense had been operating, she reflected, it would have told her that you just didn't have an opportunity to get married unless you were in a position to meet a few men. And for a fact, Lester Carey was the only man on this whole faculty (not many of them, of course) who wasn't married; and where else did she stand a chance of meeting any men?

Oh, in the three years she'd taught here, since graduating from U.C.L.A., she'd met a few people outside those at the school. The nice young couple across the hall from her, a few friends of theirs; Mr. Thompson's sister Marge (he was the registrar) and some of her friends; and she'd had friends of her own, before, of course. But most of her old friends from school were married and busy with young families; the couple of men she'd dated in college had either married somebody else or drifted off into distant jobs. She didn't, at the present moment, know one eligible and attractive male. And shut up five days a week here with all the kids and other female teachers—

She looked earnestly at the mirror. Katharine Mason wasn't really so bad, was she, even aging rapidly at twenty-seven? Very white skin, very black hair in a short smooth cut, and gray eyes *were* unusual—even if her nose was too short and her mouth too wide, and she was too tall and thin, nearly five-eight and fifteen pounds under what the insurance statistics called for, with not much figure.

She thought about that police officer, and sighed. The interesting ones were always married. Quite something, he was. An awful fuss there'd been, those vandals setting that fire three days before the beginning of term—*what* a mess Miss Barr's room had been, between the fire and the firemen. Several of the staff had been here that day, and Katharine had been one of those the police officer talked to. Ought to be on TV, she thought. Detective Varallo—north Italian, he'd be, with that crest of blond hair, and handsome— But she remembered him saying something casual about his wife. Of course, of course.

Well, one thing, after tomorrow night she wouldn't go out with Lester Carey again. She wouldn't settle for one like that, just to have a husband.

And she thought, The vanity of the woman. He hadn't shown any signs of asking her yet.

Oh, well. She snapped her bag shut and went out briskly into the mid-afternoon heat, to the parking lot and her five-year-old Dodge. An early dinner and then get those papers corrected. Several interesting, promising kids in this new class. That Brandon boy, bright as they came— Miss Barr had mentioned him, she'd had him last year. I.Q. in the 120's, she said—a very bright boy indeed. And the Kelly girl, definite artistic talent there: and Mary Wells. A couple like poor Gordon too, of course . . .

*

Gordon got home at ten to six. Albert Bicknell was in the front room, drinking beer and watching TV. He said sharply, "Pretty late to get in, kid. Have to stay after school?"

"Yes," said Gordon because it was the easiest thing to say.

"Yes what?"

"Yes, Dad, sir— I'm sorry," muttered Gordon.

"O.K.," said Bicknell. "You just remember—no playing hookey or anything. Who'd you play with today? That kid was here the other day?"

"We just came home together, that's all. Paul's O.K."

Bicknell drank. The boy waited, stolid, for whatever he'd say. But all the man said was, "Dinner's about ready, you better get washed up."

Paul Brandon got home at six, but they never had dinner until six-thirty or seven because his dad didn't get home until then. His mother was fussing around the kitchen. He told her about those pups all over again. "It'd sure be swell to have one—"

Margaret Brandon smiled at him. "We're going to."

"*Honest*? Oh, boy— I know *which* one I want, Mother—only I guess he's about the best of the litter and maybe they'll want more than forty bucks for him—he's a real he-dog, you can tell, and smart— For *sure*?"

"For sure, Paul."

"Oh, boy . . . Mother. It's not like—being sort of disloyal, like, to— to old King, is it?" For a second he looked troubled.

She bent and kissed him. "No, darling. They just don't live as long as we do, that's all. They—sort of just go on ahead, you see—and I don't think they mind when we get new ones to love. I really don't."

His face cleared and he kissed her back. He went to his room, excited and happy, thinking about the new pup. A real swell pup, mottled, kind of, black and white, the biggest one in the litter. What'd be a good name? You wanted a *real* good name for one like that. He sat down at his desk and wrote out some names to look at. Chief. Caesar—that was a sort of Roman word for king, wasn't it? Colonel. Prince? Kind of ordinary . . . Well, they'd talk about it at dinner, Dad always had some good ideas about things like that.

He opened the top drawer, the one that had a lock, and took out his Book. It had a lock too. He opened it—it was half filled with his careful printing, rather smaller, neater printing than most ten-year-olds might produce.

It was almost two years since he'd invented the Code, and he hardly had to think about the letters now, which meant which. He started to print carefully: T. Y. NLGSVI SZH SVZWZXSVH—

At six-twenty on Saturday night Charles O'Connor said, "So that's that," and leaned back in his chair, dropping the last page of the latest report. "Why the hell did I ever join the force, Vic? Always something unexpected coming up—now I won't have time to shave again, I said seven o'clock and she lives to hell and gone out in West Hollywood."

"Well, if you didn't have this outside hobby—" said Varallo. "The only solution is to get married, Charles, instead of playing the field." He surveyed O'Connor amusedly, from perennially blue bulldog jaw to shoes in need of polishing. O'Connor was never a dressy man; and even his wide bull shoulders, in the ready-made jacket, couldn't quite conceal the bulge made by his favorite revolver, that S. and W. .357 Magnum with the 8⅜-inch barrel. Better than anything female (though they ranked a close second) O'Connor loved his collection of old and new handguns; he was a top marksman, had won the state peace officers' medal for target shooting last year, and was reputed to sleep with that particular favorite S. and W. with its custom rosewood grip.

"What, walk into the trap deliberately?" said O'Connor. "Not such a fool, my friend. There's that Feinberg thing, damn it—let it go until morning— I'm off," and he stood up, a broad solid hefty man who'd just scraped by on minimum-height requirements at five-nine, but made up for it in breadth. He reached up to adjust the shoulder holster absently, and picked up his battered hat.

"Have a nice time," said Varallo. "Tell me, just out of curiosity, don't any of them ever object to the gun digging into them? In the—er—preliminary stages, that is?"

"I never asked," said O'Connor seriously. "See you at eight," and he went out. Varallo laughed to himself, left a note for the night-duty man, got his own hat, and started home.

Remembering the clutter of men and machines along Mountain, and the five-block detour, he went out Glenoaks Boulevard, to turn on Cordova. At the corner of Everett he found himself facing a cordon of yellow sawhorses with lanterns and large DETOUR signs, and three Martian-looking machines parked overnight.

"*Per l'amor di Dio!*" he said, irritated. He turned up Everett to Mountain, had to detour again there, and finally reached Hillcroft Road by way of Rossmoyne Avenue. At the junction of Rossmoyne and

Hillcroft, there was a deep hole dug in the middle of the intersection, shored up with planks and surrounded by protective sawhorses studded with reflective lights spelling out CAREFUL and DETOUR. Three or four boys were playing in the hole, taking turns sliding down the heaped earth. Varallo circled the hole carefully and drove on home.

It hadn't cooled off much yet—September and October the worst months for heat—but he ought to finish weeding those beds, and do some spraying too: that Goddamned aphis—

CHAPTER 3

Over the weekend, two more schools were hit by vandals—an elementary school northwest in town, and a junior high a couple of miles away. Nothing was taken, and not too much damage done: the vandals had just created a mess, throwing ink around and breaking windows. No typewriters hammered to bits or furniture broken. That made it look like fairly young kids; it was the teenagers that could be so savagely destructive.

No lead showing up to say which fairly young kids.

Varallo finished his weeding and worried about Neige Parfum, which was covered with aphis. Laura said, "I think you worry more about those roses than me. Traditionally, you're supposed to be hovering over me asking how I feel every ten minutes."

"I read somewhere once," said Varallo, "that that's actually a subconscious pose and indicates masculine insecurity. Besides, you're obviously blooming—it does seem to agree with you, you haven't even had any morning sickness."

"I'm beginning to think," said Laura with a sigh, "I should fake some symptoms to get attention."

"Damn," said Varallo. "I'm out of Aerosect. . . ."

On Monday Gordon Bicknell was absent from school. When he showed up on Tuesday without a note of excuse, Katharine sent him up to Mr. Harwell; and Mr. Harwell, who was a rather old-fashioned disciplinarian, called Gordon's mother on the phone. Mrs. Bicknell was agitated and apologetic; she'd meant to write the note but had put it off; it was all right, she'd had to keep Gordon out to take him to the dentist. Mr. Harwell thanked her and sent Gordon back to Katharine.

Paul Brandon left the schoolyard alone after the last period and rode the bus up to Mountain. On his circuitous way home—he had different routes he took, dropping in to see different people he knew—he stopped off to see Ella Knox first. He liked Mrs. Knox. She was as interested in people as he was, even if she was pretty old. She lived alone with her three cats, and usually she asked him in and gave him some cookies or something. He stopped off at her place pretty often because she really needed errands done for her, poor old lady, she'd broken her hip a couple of years ago and was awful lame. And she really liked to talk to him, because of being interested in people too. In fact, old Mrs. Knox was about the only one Paul could talk to about, well, people.

Some way, his mother didn't understand his being interested; she even said once, when he was telling her about the Andersons' new living-room rug, that it wasn't *normal*. "You shouldn't go right into other people's houses, dear, it isn't polite. And why on earth you should be interested—" And she'd looked at him sort of funny. Another time he'd heard her and his dad talking about it, and she'd said, "Honestly, Harry, he's as bad as some nosy old-maid gossip! It's *queer*—a boy his age—" But his dad had just laughed and said, "Paul's O.K., Maggie—he just takes after me, the gregarious type that likes people. He's really just interested in them, in what makes them tick, that's all. Ask me, it shows how bright he is."

Paul didn't think much about that or worry about it. He knew he wasn't "queer," so it didn't matter. But he didn't try to tell his mother little interesting things he found out after that; so it was mostly Mrs. Knox he talked to about people.

One of her cats had some kittens, and she said today she was trying to find homes for them and would he ask around? "Sure," said Paul enthusiastically. He looked the kittens over carefully—there were two black and white ones, one all black, one gray and black striped with a white front, and one mostly gray—so as to be able to do a good job of selling. He thought about what people might be persuaded to take one. Mrs. Anderson, maybe. Mrs. Keith didn't like cats. He didn't know, but he suspected that probably Mrs. Starke didn't either. But Mrs. Varallo might. They didn't have a dog, and Detective Varallo liking to work in the yard, he wouldn't want a dog; they could be persuaded that a cat didn't dig up things. And maybe Mrs. Riegler and Mrs. Williamson—

He went straight off to the Varallos' from there and tried to sell Mrs. Varallo on the idea. He liked Mrs. Varallo a lot, now she knew him she was nice, and he thought she looked awful pretty in her green dress, with the sun making her brown hair kind of reddish, even if she was getting fat with the baby.

"You'd like the striped one," he said confidently. "See, a cat wouldn't be digging up your husband's flowers all the time."

"But we're going to get a dog," said Laura. "Vic wants a golden retriever. Really, Paul—"

"Big dog like that'd be digging the whole *yard* up," said Paul. "You'd be real sorry. And this is an awful cute kitten, Mrs. Varallo. Honest— Look, just s'pose I bring it up and you can see it. You'd like that one!"

"No, really we wouldn't—" said Laura helplessly.

"You think about it, anyway!"

It was almost five-thirty then. He walked down a block to Rosemount, to where Gordon lived, and rang the doorbell. He hadn't been inside Gordon's house yet, and he was curious.

It was Gordon's mother came to the door. She was sort of fat, and had dark hair she hadn't combed very smooth, and a high voice. "Hi, Mrs. Bicknell," said Paul. "Is Gordon home?"

"Oh—" she said, as if she wasn't sure. She had on an apron, so she was probably cooking dinner. Maybe they ate early. She stepped back a little, so Paul went just inside the door, looking around interestedly.

It wasn't as big as their front room. A lot of the furniture looked new, just a couple of old chairs, and there was a big what they called sectional, dark green, and a color TV, and the curtains were a gold color like the rug.

Mr. Bicknell was watching TV. He was a thin dark man and he looked tired. Paul wondered what kind of work he did. He looked around sort of sharp and said, "Gordon can't come out, kid, it's nearly dinnertime."

"Oh, well, O.K., then," said Paul. He guessed maybe Mrs. Knox was right; she thought, from all he said, the Bicknells had just started to make more money than they'd had before, maybe Mr. Bicknell had got a promotion or a better job, so they'd moved into a better house.

Anyway, it was interesting. Paul started home. Tomorrow he'd show Mrs. Varallo that kitten. He bet she'd like it, all right. Take it around late when Detective Varallo was home. Boy, he was sure big and good-looking, thought Paul. And a real nice guy when you got to know him, too—he'd said some Saturday he'd show Paul all through headquarters, how they worked and all. . . .

*

"But we really don't want a cat," said Laura. The kitten was, of course, charming as all kittens were. Paul said confidently that it was the biggest and best of the litter. It was still quite a tiny kitten, wearing an elegant gray coat evenly striped with black, and a spotless white shirt front. It had a smudged black nose and chartreuse eyes, and it waved its ruler-straight tail at her. "Vic," said Laura, "doesn't like cats."

The kitten crouched and pounced on Varallo's left shoe, and pretended to demolish it, rolling over on its back with all claws extended. Varallo laughed and bent to pick it up; the kitten dug claws into his shirt and uttered a loud baby squeak.

"It *is* a darling, of course, but—" Laura stroked the elegant stripes and the kitten started to purr. "But we were going to get— I *thought* you didn't like—"

"Well, I've never known many," said Varallo. "Pretty markings, hasn't it?"

"See, a cat wouldn't go digging things up the way dogs do," said Paul earnestly.

"Something in that, I suppose," said Varallo. He put the kitten down and it began to wash its face, prim and graceful. "Er—which is it, do you know?"

"Oh, it's a boy," said Paul quickly. "So that's O.K. too, it doesn't cost nearly as much to have them done, you know. A lot better than a dog." Personally, give him a dog any day, but he was helping out Mrs. Knox.

The Keiths' middle-aged black cocker came up the drive just then, spotting Paul, who was an old friend. He trotted into the patio amiably; the kitten immediately swelled to twice its natural size, uttered an astonishingly loud hiss, and dabbed at the cocker's nose with a short right jab. The cocker, who had had sad experiences with cats before, didn't stop to notice this one's diminutive size; he yelped and fled, and Varallo doubled over with mirth, along with Laura.

"*Il bellicoso! Che gatto!* Undoubtedly twice as good a guard as any dog! All right, you sell us—he's our cat, and his name is obviously Gideon, which means 'great warrior.' "

"It is not," said Laura, stooping to stroke the kitten. "I've been studying that dictionary of names too, and his name is Algernon—that means 'having long whiskers.' "

"A lionhearted creature like this, Algernon? Ridiculous," said Varallo, picking up the kitten. "Attila the Hun's more like it—"

The kitten was finally christened Gideon Algernon Cadwallader, the latter apparently signifying "battle arranger."

On Wednesday morning Gordon Bicknell showed up at school with a black bruise on one cheekbone. He told Katharine, when she asked about it, that he'd fallen down.

On Thursday, Lester Carey asked her at lunch to go out to dinner with him again on Saturday, and Katharine politely declined, making up a plausible excuse.

Overnight on Friday, more vandals broke into Hoover High, smashed a few desks, splashed ink all over the principal's office, broke most of the ground-floor windows of the administration building, and stole two new electric typewriters. There weren't any immediate leads to the kids responsible—but, for pretty sure, it had been kids. Probably teenagers.

O'Connor swore. "And with everything else we've got on hand right now! I can't understand it—why the hell doesn't the Board of Education hire night watchmen?"

Laura had just finished giving herself a manicure, and Varallo was playing with the kitten, trailing a piece of string, about eight o'clock on Saturday night, when the phone rang. Gideon Algernon Cadwallader bristled and fled under the handiest chair, and Laura, who was nearest, picked up the phone.

"Oh, Mrs. Varallo—please, is Paul there?" An agitated voice she didn't recognize at first.

"Why, no, he's not. Who—oh, Mrs. Brandon. No, I haven't seen him today."

"Oh, dear, what shall I— I've been calling everybody I can think of— my husband's not here, he had to meet a customer— I'm just worried sick! He's always home for dinner, usually by six— I just can't imagine—" Incoherent, breathless spate of words running together. "I know he likes you people, I thought— Oh, Mrs. Varallo, do you think I should call the *police?*" Margaret Brandon's voice began to shake badly. "If—if there was an accident—but there's identification on him, in his— I just don't know—"

"I think maybe you should," said Laura slowly. "Yes. My husband's right—" but she was interrupted.

"Oh, no, it couldn't be— I don't know what else to do—always such a good boy about coming home on time, he's *responsible,* you know— Oh, but I *haven't* called those new people—thank you—" a gasp, and the connection broke.

"I do hope nothing's happened— It's Paul Brandon, Vic, he hasn't come home, and that poor woman's there alone. She's wondering if she should call the police, she expected him home at the usual time, about six, she said. But she said he carries identification, if there'd been an accident surely they'd have let her know by now? I do hope—a nice boy really—"

"Did she know where he was going?"

"She didn't say, I don't think so."

"Have his bicycle?"

"I don't know."

"Well—" Varallo looked at his watch. "He's over two hours late. Not so good. I'd think he'd be a pretty responsible boy about time—"

"She said that. What could have happened? D'you think—"

"I don't know enough to think anything, but—" he picked up the phone book, flipped pages, found the Brandons' number, and dialed. "Hell, busy signal. She'll be on the line, of course. I think I'd better drop around and find out more about the circumstances."

"I'm coming too," said Laura. "I do *hope* nothing has— Well, he can be a pest but he's a good boy, isn't he?" She was looking worried.

On the doorstep of the pleasant Mediterranean stucco a block up Hillcroft Road, they waited some time before Margaret Brandon opened the door to them. "Oh— I was on the phone— *Paul?*"

"I thought I'd better ask some questions, Mrs. Brandon," said Varallo gently. "If you know where he was going, and—"

She stepped back, tacitly inviting them in. She'd been sitting or wandering the house, worrying—more desperately as time went on—for nearly two hours now; dinner left to grow cold on the table. Her hair and her eyes were wild. "I don't know where—always *responsible* about being home on time— I th-thought he'd naturally be at the Kaufmans' playing with the puppies, or—but he hadn't been there at all— *Where is he?* Oh, my God, and I don't know where Harry is to call him—"

"Mrs. Brandon!" said Varallo. "Is there any liquor in the house?"

She stared at him dazedly. "I—we don't—much— Harry has a highball sometimes—kitchen cupboard—"

Varallo found the half-full bottle of bourbon, poured a stiff slug, and stood over her until she swallowed it. Laura made her sit down on the couch. "Now," said Varallo, when he saw that the alcohol was reaching her. "Was he riding his bicycle?" She shook her head dumbly. "When did you last see him?"

"After—after lunch. About one o'clock."

"Did he say where he was going?"

"He said—he said he was going to t-take one of Mrs. Knox's kittens up to show Mrs. Williamson on Harrington Road. I don't know the Williamsons, but Paul—knows everybody. He— Oh, my God, I never thought about it—letting him go all over alone—my fault, whatever's happened—he's *responsible,* not a baby, and such a nice quiet neighborhood, nice people— I never thought—"

"That was all he said? You called Mrs. Williamson?"

"He'd—been there. About three-forty-five. But he went—somewhere else—from there, after she said she'd keep the kitten— No, she didn't know where— Oh, God, *something* must have happened to him or he'd have come—"

"All right," said Varallo. "Take it easy." He went to the phone and called headquarters. Poor and Forbes were on night tour this month; he outlined the situation quickly to Forbes. "Send up three cars, will you? And one of you come up—there'll be a good many people to see and ask questions of, quite a little area to cover. The boy—well, got around. And this isn't exactly the best-lighted section of Glendale, you know." With Daylight Saving still on, it was just dusk now, but the light was fading rapidly.

Laura was asking Margaret Brandon whether she had any sedative in the house. "There's no sense tearing yourself to pieces this way until we know something definite. Please, Mrs. Brandon—"

"He's our only one," said the other woman starkly. "Oh, please God, not Paul—"

The cars were all there ten minutes later. Varallo sent them off to fan out in different directions, gave the boys some names and addresses to visit, where the boy might have been. (Mrs. Brandon wasn't making much sense by then, or they could have eliminated some by what she'd got from her phone calls.) The hell of it was, thought Varallo, what *could* have happened to the boy? An accident, to prevent him coming home by six, must have happened more than two hours ago; and if the boy had identification on him, the police or emergency hospital would have called long ago. But just on the chance— He called headquarters again and asked for a check on all the accidents since about four o'clock; any unidentified ten-year-old boy?

There weren't many empty lots in this area; it wasn't the kind of neighborhood where the elderly homos, anybody like that, would be wandering around—though God knew you got those anywhere—

"What I've been thinking about," said Forbes, "is all these damn excavations. Kids always playing in them, and sometimes—" Forbes was a fairly new ranker, but a very bright boy. "You see what I mean. That thing just the other day, kid playing alone in a place like that, and a cave-in—"

Varallo stared at him, hand still on the telephone. "Yes, I remember. It's a thought. Somewhere else to look, anyway—come on."

It was Forbes, nearly two hours later, who found the Brandon boy. Found him mostly covered with caved-in earth, at the bottom of the deep hole in the middle of the intersection of Rossmoyne and Hillcroft Road.

He had, the ambulance interne said, been dead for about three and a half hours.

CHAPTER 4

"I tell you nothing could've caved in, so help me!" said Warren Golder passionately. "Aren't we warned about it alla time, I ask you—don't I keep telling the men alla time! I got kids of my own, mister—most o' the men got kids. We're not damn fools, we see the kids playin' around excavations alla time. We fix things so they're left safe—we got to!"

"But a couple of kids fooling around together—pulling away boards or—" Varallo didn't doubt him; he was the foreman on the job; but you never knew what kids would do.

"I tell you—! All right. All right. Let me take a look down there and I'll tell you—"

They hadn't taken more than a cursory look last night. At Forbes's alarm, they'd converged on the excavation, and a couple of the boys had helped him get the boy up, get the earth and planks off him. Varallo remembered standing here, feeling a little sick, hoping against hope the boy wasn't dead and knowing he was, and wondering how in God's name they were going to tell that poor woman. And the boy's father, who was home by then.

What it looked like, Forbes had said, scrambling out of the hole dustily, was that the boy—or boys—had accidentally pulled away a couple of the boards shoring up the side. Or deliberately, not realizing it would be dangerous. The boy's body had been partly under the boards, heaped earth on top of the boards where it had slid and shifted. He had probably died of suffocation, caught under the piled earth. There would, of course, have to be an autopsy.

Damn, damn these senseless things, thought Varallo. The Brandon boy, ten years old. A good boy, a bright boy. And the only child, doubly precious. A silly, unnecessary accident. While kids like those smart-aleck louts who'd set the school fire stayed alive. Sometimes it made you wonder if whatever was running things didn't slip up occasionally.

Because they would want to find out exactly what had happened, they'd routed Harrison out to take some flash shots of the site. The rest could wait until morning. And somebody had to tell the parents. He had plodded back to the Brandon house with Forbes. . . .

His most vivid memory of the night—not Margaret Brandon's hysterics or Laura's quiet tears, the neighbors milling around—the father, dazed and colorless, under control but hardly aware of what he was saying, saying over and over, "But he never played that way, in those excavations, he wouldn't have been playing there—he thought that was for babies, little kids. He never played that way—" As if trying to deny it had happened at all.

And he'd taken Laura home, leaving Forbes to set up a case file on it. Tomorrow, try to find out more.

He stood above the excavation again now, listening to the foreman on the job passionately deny that any accident could have happened. Beside him, Forbes yawned; on night tour up to midnight or not, Forbes had had to get out this morning, being on the case.

Varallo didn't think there had been any other boys down there with Paul. Ten-year-olds weren't babies; a boy his age, who he'd probably have been with, would have had the sense and responsibility to run for help. And as for Paul not playing in such places, there was always a first time—a nice deep hole like that quite a temptation to any kid, he'd think. Or it was possible, of course, that the boy had accidentally dropped something down there. . . .

"All *right!*" said the foreman, climbing halfway up again. "You come down here, mister. Show you something. You just come down."

Varallo backed down the wooden ladder and stepped into powdery dry earth to his shoe tops. Golder took his arm. "Now you look here." The hole, at its bottom, was about ten by fifteen; at one narrow end a section of pipe three feet in diameter gaped, ready for its new connection. The hole was about fifteen feet deep. "Look," said Golder. "Right here, wasn't it?—poor damn kid— I got eyes. We got to be careful, my God, of our own skins too! Damn dirt anywhere around this part o' the country, all sand, nothin' but sand—you go down a foot, she starts to move on you. We dug down here *careful,* mister. Look at the way she's shored up tight and strong! You try to shift one o' these planks, go on 'n' try—tell me if you think a ten-year-old kid could do it. Look—" he was almost incoherent in self-defense—"it took two men to get most o' these planks in place to start with! I ask you—"

Varallo tried to shift the plank and failed, even when he put out his full strength. It was not only three-inch oak planking, but it was—necessarily, he could see—wedged very tightly between its neighbors.

"Look," said Golder. "Dirt, it weighs heavy. It's like deep-sea diving—pressure and all that jazz. We got to figure these things, my God. No use to stick a few boards up against its shifting—they got to go in tight together and they got to be heavy, or just naturally that dirt's going to shift and slide where we don't want her. You tell *me* that any ten-year-old kid could move them two planks alone? You're just nuts, mister."

Varallo looked at the two planks out of place. Like the others, they were twenty to twenty-five feet long, three inches thick, about three feet wide. He remembered that last night it had taken three men to lift the planks and earth off the body. The two planks lay half across each other now, perhaps a quarter-ton of earth released by their removal heaped on the lower half of their length. As Golder said, sandy soil, practically no rock. He took hold of the nearest upright plank and shoved at it; he felt it move, but this one he could get a grip on, as there was a gap where a plank was missing.

He was six-one, a hundred and eighty-five, and in prime condition.

"One man," said Golder, "could move one o' these out, if he was strong and had a tool—crowbar or something like that. But if he hadn't no crowbar, no go. You don't tell me a ten-year-old kid did it with his hands."

"*Per carità!*" said Varallo softly to himself. So, all right, there had been a couple of other boys. All fooling around down here. And for some reason—

Reason be damned. His own reason rejected that. He couldn't believe that any boys of Paul's age (or even a couple of years younger) from around here, would have simply run away from such an accident, not gone for help. He couldn't believe that Paul, an intelligent youngster, even if the others hadn't realized, would have failed to realize how dangerous it was to meddle with those shoring-up planks. And he couldn't believe that even half a dozen boys that age and size would have been able to move those planks without a tool.

"There weren't any tools of any kind left here overnight?" he asked Golder.

"Mister, you think we're nuts too? We got orders. These days, you leave a twenny-nine-cent screwdriver out, somebody swipes it."

"Yes," said Varallo. He felt a little cold trickle up his spine. It was impossible, but— "Jeff!"

Forbes peered down over the edge of the hole. "What's up?"

"You didn't see any kind of tool down here last night, did you?"

"No, but I wasn't looking— I was concentrating on the boy, in case there was any chance of bringing him to."

"I know." A good man, Forbes; he'd pulled the boy out, kept up artificial respiration until the ambulance got there. Just in case.

These damned holes, all over town. . . . Necessary things that had to be done, but— That other kid, only a few days ago, a six-year-old that one, the same sort of— Playing around close to home, after dinner, after the men were off the job, because with Daylight Saving—

Quite suddenly he went cold all over.

No, he thought. Impossible.

But—

"All right, thanks," he said to Golder, and started to climb out of the hole.

"Wait a minute, mister—look, you finished here? We got a job to do. Is it O.K., we get back on it tomorrow?"

"No," said Varallo. "No, I'm afraid not." His voice sounded a little strange even to his own hearing. "I'll let you know. I don't want any of you down here again until we've had a much closer look. Sorry, but there it is."

"Oh, for God's sake," said Golder. "For God's sake."

Varallo climbed out of the hole. "Jeff. It was about ten o'clock when you spotted him here."

"About that, why? You know how it went—the cars out, and when we got the lead that that Mrs. Starke had seen him about four-fifteen, and she seemed to be the last one had, we were looking down on Mountain where she lives. I covered all those excavations down there before—"

"Yes. When you finally got round to this one, did you spot him right away? Did you have to get down in the hole to see him?"

"I did not. I'd gone down most of them, or one of the other boys had, with a flashlight, to be sure. And he might've been covered completely, of course, I'd even dug around a little in some of them. But when I shot my flash down here, I saw him right off—saw his legs sticking out from the pile of dirt. Why?" And then— Forbes wasn't lacking in brains—he said, *"Oh, my God,* Vic! No—not a *kid!* Not a ten-year-old *kid!"*

Varallo said, "We heard the interne. Internes not always right—we'll hear what Dr. Goulding says. But something—" He dropped his cigarette, stepped on it. "Daylight Saving, you know. . . . Go and call up some boys, Jeff, use my phone, and have a damn good look down that hole. For anything. I'll be at the office, probably. For a while, anyway."

"A *kid!"* said Forbes. He looked shaken. "But—why the hell, Vic?"

"I don't know," said Varallo. "We'll look."

He went back downtown, up to the one big room of the Detective Bureau, to his wide desk alongside O'Connor's. O'Connor was on the phone. Varallo dialed the morgue, got Dr. Goulding.

"The boy—that accident last night. I suppose you haven't done the autopsy yet?" A routine thing—until, all of a sudden just now, he'd put a few facts together.

"Just about to, why?"

"You examined the body when it came in last night?" The body. Confident, eager, bright, young Paul Brandon, ten years old.

"I did. Why?" Goulding was a little impatient.

"Tell me, doctor—the interne in the ambulance said the boy had been dead about three and a half hours when he saw him. That was at a little after ten o'clock. Do you think that's more or less correct?"

Goulding reflected. "About that, yes. I'd have put it a little less myself. I saw the body—these damn senseless tragedies!—about ten-thirty, and I'd say he'd been dead about three and a half hours then. Of course, he wouldn't have died instantly, an accident like that—may have taken fifteen or twenty minutes to suffocate."

"Yes," said Varallo. "This kind of accident—it usually is suffocation, the actual cause of death?"

"Bound to be. The cave-in—"

"Doctor," said Varallo, "take a thorough look at this one, will you? Because the way it's looking now, it wasn't an accident." He hung up on Goulding's startled expletive and looked across at O'Connor. "We've got a real something here, Charles. This boy—the Brandon boy. I think it was murder."

O'Connor put down his pen and asked what head doctor he was going to for his trouble. "Not funny," said Varallo. "I didn't see it myself until I went down that hole." He described the setup. "He was a bright kid, Charles. Brighter than average. I don't see him finding it any fun to fool around with those planks—he'd know the danger. He'd point out the danger to other kids if they were doing it. Without some tool, I don't think a few kids could have shifted those planks. And they were shifted, deliberately—they didn't just fall out from where they'd been wedged. But apart from that, there's the times. My God—it doesn't seem possible, but that's what all the facts say, when you think about it—"

"What about the times?"

"Two doctors say the boy died, well, call it between six-thirty and seven. We'll know more after the autopsy, know whether he died quick or slow, but even so—Paul knew he was expected home by six, and he was a responsible boy. He'd have been home by six, or before, if he wasn't prevented. So there's a time gap. Say he took fifteen minutes or so to die, after the cave-in down there—the accident wouldn't have happened the minute he was down in that hole, you know. Those planks—nobody could shift them in thirty seconds. So, where was he at six—just before? Hurrying home, maybe? So why should he stop to go down that hole—voluntarily? To play around, when he knew he was expected home?"

"Kids—" said O'Connor.

"There are kids and kids. You haven't heard the pay-off. With Daylight Saving on, it was still broad daylight at six-thirty. It was just starting to get dark at eight, when we began hunting. Full dark about eight-twenty, eight-thirty. And, the way these damn sewage people are going at the job, anybody who lives in that area, for about six blocks around, right now—listen to this, Charles—has to take Rossmoyne up to that particular intersection, and pass that particular excavation. I can testify that as you pass it, even in a car, you can see the bottom. Sure, not everybody looks down a hole in the street, especially as we're passing so many these days. But— And Jeff, who found the boy, says he spotted him right off, just flashing a light down there—from street level—in the full dark. He wasn't covered up—just the upper part of his body."

O'Connor jerked upright in his chair. He said, "Who looks down holes? What time were the workmen off the job?"

"Five o'clock."

"All right. Nothing in that."

"The hole's fifteen feet wide. You don't tell me that of an estimated—how many?—forty, fifty cars passing that intersection—it's not a wide street, you have to pass close to the hole—between five and six-thirty, not one driver looked down, to stop him if he was there. *Fandonie!*"

"You're telling me something too, boy—a ten-year-old kid, from a nice respectable home, nice quiet neighborhood—deliberately—"

"I'm telling you that's how it was. He was put there, Charles. It was a staged accident. And, by God, he was put there after dark. He had to be. No matter how he died, he couldn't have been at the bottom of that hole, to be seen right off by anybody who casually glanced down, at six-thirty. My God, if I'd only looked myself!—but I didn't happen to. We'll ask, and I'll bet you we'll find a few people who did look. He'd have been found long before. He wasn't there until after dark. And, by God," said Varallo furiously, "*che barbaro coraggio!*—the nerve of him—the boy was put there, the accident was faked, while we were hunting! Because it couldn't have been done until after dark. I hope to God Goulding can give us something—"

"For the love of God!" said O'Connor very quietly. "I see what you mean—but there are loopholes, Vic, it isn't certain. It could be that just nobody did happen to look and see him. Because what possible reason, damn it—"

"Yes, I know. I've been doing a little thinking on that," said Varallo. "I tell you, Charles, he wasn't the ordinary ten-year-old kid. Not by any means. He—"

The inside phone rang on O'Connor's desk; he picked it up. "O'Connor . . . Yes? Name? O.K., thanks, Dick. . . . Some woman just called in, all excited, just heard about the Brandon boy. Said she saw him at five o'clock yesterday afternoon. A Mrs. Knox, on Sinaloa Drive."

"Oh, really. Let's go and see her." Varallo got up abruptly.

"I don't know that you sell me on this—a damn far-fetched—"

"We'll see what turns up. I know, I know. But, knowing the kind he was, I'm just wondering—my God. My God, what a— Up there, in that nice respectable section of town. All those upright honest citizens . . . But at that, when you come to think—" Varallo broke off and laughed, sharp and mirthless. "Standards," he said. "Standards. Higher at that end of the scale, sure."

"What are you talking about now?" They came down the steps to the parking lot and got into O'Connor's new Ford.

Varallo laughed again. "People," he said. "That pro burglar we just picked up, for instance—quite philosophic about it. Just one of those things, and the food in jail is pretty good. And he didn't mind at all—never entered his head to worry about it—that we knew he'd been shacking up with that blond. Perfectly natural thing."

"And so what?"

"Different people," said Varallo, "have different standards. The people who live up on Hillcroft Road, Mountain— I can see any of them getting very worried at the idea of secrets a lot less venal coming out. And Paul Brandon—"

"I still don't see this. You've been reading too many of your wife's complicated crime novels."

"I'll tell you about Paul Brandon," said Varallo.

"The kitten," said Ella Knox. "He had the kitten—" She had almost stopped crying, still dabbed at her eyes with a wadded-up handkerchief. She might be seventy, she might be older, a thin scraggly woman with neat gray braids round her head, still bright blue eyes, most of her wrinkles laughter wrinkles: a nice old lady, neat in her blue printed house dress. "Oh, dear, I can't get over it— Paul—such a nice boy! Such a good boy, so polite and obliging about running errands— His poor mother and father! She's just prostrated, no wonder, but I talked to Mr. Brandon— I suppose we've got to think, just God's will, but—"

"The kitten, Mrs. Knox?" said Varallo.

She sobbed again, raised the handkerchief. "He was such a nice boy— such a bright, intelligent boy. It doesn't seem *right*. Please excuse me, I thought an awful lot of Paul—I can't help— But I know you want to figure out just how it happened, and anything I can—"

"Take your time, Mrs. Knox. I know. I knew him too, it's a bad thing to have happened."

"D-did you? Yes, it just doesn't seem— The kitten," she said. "He had the other black-and-white kitten. He was going to take it to show Mrs. Riegler over on Carmen—he thought she'd take it— That was about five o'clock, and he didn't come back with it, so of course I thought she *had*— I don't know the Rieglers, but Paul thought— And the kitten, I've worried, silly I suppose when Paul—but—I called her to ask, and she didn't, and—"

"Mrs. Riegler didn't keep the kitten?"

She shook her head blindly. "She said he took it away with him. And he never brought it back, so, you see, it must have been right then— And it *is* silly, I suppose, worrying over a kitten—but, only three months old and I can't help it. It wasn't—*there,* was it, with him? I didn't—"

"No," said Varallo. "No. Thank you very much, Mrs. Knox. I know how you feel—a tragedy, yes. But maybe you've helped."

Outside her neat, old-fashioned living room, he said to O'Connor,

"So let's find the kitten. If it isn't dead down there in the hole, which I doubt very much it is. Call up the boys and ask house to house—the people he knew on Carmen Drive, Sinaloa, all around."

"What the hell?" said O'Connor. "I like cats, sure, let's find the kitten and be sure it's taken care of—but what importance—"

"If he didn't find a home for the kitten," said Varallo, "he'd have brought it back to Mrs. Knox. He wouldn't have left it in the street somewhere. We don't know what happened to Paul, when or where, but the odds are he got separated from the black-and-white kitten when he met whoever it was killed him. When he ran into whatever trouble it was. However. For whatever reason. So let's find out, if we can, approximately where the kitten was abandoned, and narrow it down."

"For God's sake," said O'Connor. "Talk about the wild blue yonder! You're seeing ghosts. Murder. A ten-year-old kid. Even if he was a nosy parker who found out things about people."

"We'll take a hard look at it, anyway," said Varallo. "It's a bad one, an offbeat one, sure—but I think I'm right, Charles." And he thought of how Laura would feel too—she'd liked Paul; well, most people had. He had himself. And the Brandons—that poor damned woman . . . He felt a kind of righteous cold anger rise in him for this incredible and evil thing. "We'll look at this one very damned hard," he said to O'Connor.

CHAPTER 5

They started to look for the kitten; it was a funny angle, but made sense of a sort. They sent Wayne, Forbes, and Poor out, to start from the Riegler house on Carmen Drive and try to find out what had happened to the kitten.

There were other, less ephemeral cases on hand; until they got something definite, this was still up in the air. O'Connor went back downtown; Varallo, disliking the job, went to see the Brandons.

He hardly recognized the ravaged face of the man who opened the door to him. Overnight Harry Brandon seemed to have shrunk. He stepped back, identifying Varallo, and said dully, "I suppose—official red tape on it. All right, come in."

"I'm sorry," said Varallo. "I know how it is."

"You don't know how it is," said Brandon. "You haven't lost your only boy."

What could you say to him? And Varallo didn't tell him about this new, incredible thing—time enough if it proved out. Time enough for more shock and, with that, the bitter anger and the need for revenge. He said as gently as possible, "I just want to ask you a couple of questions, Mr. Brandon, and then I'd like to look at Paul's room. I haven't a search warrant, but I don't suppose you—"

"All right," said Brandon. "Why? No, that's all right. I—my wife—our doctor's put her in the hospital for a day or two, she was— What do you want to know?"

"Can you tell me the names of the boys he played with mostly?"

Brandon was silent for a moment. "I guess so. Don't see why you— D'you mean you think he wasn't—down there—alone? That some other kids ran off and let him—let him—"

"We don't know, Mr. Brandon. We have to figure out what happened exactly, if we can."

Brandon shook his head. "I can't see any of Paul's friends—any youngster that age, not babies, just running away like that. I can't figure it myself—any way." He was clenching and unclenching his hands. "Paul never played in those excavations—he was—mature for his age, he thought that was baby stuff, you know— I just can't figure it—"

"If you could give me some names, please?"

"Nicky Morehouse," said Brandon. "Over on Sinaloa. The Morehouses moved here about the same time we did, Paul and Nicky started school together. And Pat Emmett, I don't know where he lives. Johnny Parr, and a boy called Kevin, don't know his last name, and—oh, sure, Randy Latour. We know the Latours pretty well, nice people." His tone was dull, unemphatic. "He knew other kids, sure—another one he'd just got to know, a Gordon something— Paul had just teamed up with him lately. Margaret would remember, I'm sorry but I— But those were the boys he knew best, I guess."

And Varallo thought, Better see his teacher too. She might give them just a little something—you never knew. "Thanks very much, Mr. Brandon." Nothing else really to ask him right now; it would be the mother to ask for details of that last day. . . . "If I could see his room?"

Brandon got up heavily and led him down the hall from the living room. "You'll—excuse me—if I don't come in," he said, indicating the door. He turned away blindly, incurious in grief.

Varallo was as pleased to be left alone. These people—and Paul. An eye for an eye, said the old law. Was it enough? If the boy had been murdered, and if they were smart and lucky enough to catch up with X, the law would deal with him: he'd be shut up, or given the gas chamber. And like most cops Varallo was not among those who disapproved of the death penalty *per se*—for one thing, so much more economical; but, not exactly a fair exchange, for the Brandons or for Paul. If the sentimentalists were right in saying that the death penalty was nothing more than crude revenge, well, my God, he thought, could it ever be enough revenge—for a bright ten-year-old boy?

He looked around the room. The boy had been loved, and cherished, and happy. It was a nice room. The bedspread was printed in color with all the breeds of dogs; the curtains matched it. There was a cork pegboard on one wall, where the boy had pinned up pictures, newspaper clippings, anything of current interest to him. A new-looking carpet, a desk and chair, another larger chair; sliding doors to a wardrobe, and the wardrobe neatly in order.

Varallo looked at the pegboard. Some animal photographs, and human-interest stories about animals from the papers: an article from the *Times,* he remembered it, about statistics—queer interest for a kid. Pictures of cars, of boats. And—he looked closer—that little story from the *Independent* last year, the time when, still riding a squad car, he'd picked up that mugger: "Officer Varallo apprehended Clawson as he—"

He smiled, and suddenly found his eyes wet. Damn it, damn it—things happened, and you couldn't change them.

The boys out hunting a black-and-white kitten three months old . . . A kitten, and a ten-year-old boy— He thought, Anything alive in the world is taking chances every hour against staying alive. A long time ago he'd quit believing in some benevolent Arranger rewarding the righteous, punishing the evil-doer—wishful thinking. But it was a tenacious idea, old in the human mind; so that when you saw the innocent hurt, the first reaction was, Not fair. . . .

He turned to the desk: not a large desk, and oddly neat for a boy's desk. A bookshelf above it with two shelves of well-worn books; some obvious juvenile things, *Science for Boys and Girls, The Age of Dinosaurs, Our Earth, Space Travel*—books about animals, *Our Friend the Collie, Introducing Dogs,* some juvenile fiction.

Seven drawers in the desk. The top one yielded a couple of packets of notebook paper, a couple of ballpoint pens, a bottle of ink, a cheap fountain pen. Other drawers, a miscellany of rubber bands, library paste, a bag of marbles, a box of dominoes, a half-empty roll of Life Savers, bitten pencils, an advertisement for portable typewriters and a touch-typing keyboard chart, drawing paper and colored pencils, a sheaf of drawings of dogs and horses, showing not inconsiderable talent, and finally a navy-blue plastic-bound book with a diminutive lock, labeled in gold *My Diary.*

Paul not the manual type: not too much interested in sports, and no attempts at building model airplanes, anything like that.

You could say, Paul's main interest had been people.

Varallo looked down at the diary is his hand with speculative interest. It was locked. Paul had probably kept the key on his person—ask at the morgue. But a flimsy lock like this— He opened his pocket knife, inserted the smallest blade, exerted a little pressure, and presently heard a sharp crack.

With silent apologies to Paul, he opened the little book.

The first page—and, he discovered, riffling through, more than half the pages in the book—was filled with neat, careful printing. He stared at it.

WZM TZEV NZIB Z EZOVMGRMV—

A code of some kind. What was this? A boy's crude, simple code, for writing down—what? A mere diary of his ordinary routine?

Varallo took a last look around the room—the boy's nice comfortable, largely anonymous room. Carrying the diary, he went down the hall to the living room.

Brandon was sitting on the couch, head bent between his hands.

What did you say to these people, who had lost so much of what made up their lives? An insult to offer the bromides, the hurt will lessen with time, or, just destiny, or, you can adopt a child. There was nothing to say to Harry Brandon.

Varallo went up to him and said, "Mr. Brandon. I'd like to take Paul's diary away with me for examination. Is that all right?" Because you had to go by the rules.

Brandon raised his head slowly. A big, hearty, happy man: overnight he had shrunk; his round face was drawn, his mouth pinched, and his eyes were sunken and blistered. He said uncomprehendingly, "Diary? No, it doesn't matter—all right. I don't see why, but— Red tape. That's all right." He blundered to his feet. "I'm sorry, not operating on all cylinders—you're Varallo, live up the street, don't you? Sorry—your wife was very good—to Margaret—last night. Thank her— Oh, God, why'd this have to happen to *us*? I don't—"

The inevitable, age-old question. Varallo hadn't any answer for it—yet. He said meaninglessly, "I know, Mr. Brandon— I know. Thanks very much."

And instead of driving right back downtown to headquarters, he stopped by home to see Laura. . . . "Oh, no, Vic! Not a *deliberate*—who could be wicked enough to— Oh, no!"

"We don't know for certain, *cara*. Just, I think so."

"If it was, you've got to find out—and—"

"Yes. I'm wasting time. Just, all of a sudden, for this reason and that, I wanted to see you. See you're O.K. and behaving yourself." He contrived a smile for her. "And minding the baby . . . He said to me, You don't know how it is—when I'd said that meaningless little thing. What can you say to them?"

Laura leaned against him. "I don't know, Vic. There's nothing *to* say, no. . . . If someone deliberately—" And she gave him a little push, stood away from him. "You've got to find out, that's all."

"*Siete voi che l'avete detto*—we'll do that thing," said Varallo grimly.

O'Connor looked at the diary interestedly. "It's just possible," said Varallo, "that he wrote down some little secrets in this. Secrets which might offer us a lead or two to whoever thought it necessary to kill him."

"If he was killed. I'm waiting for the autopsy report to make up my mind."

"Let's hope Goulding can give us something definite, yes."

O'Connor was riffling through the little book. "A code. Sort of typical, would you say—that age? Maybe. Can't be a very complicated one if he made it up himself, though I'm damned if I can see any obvious— Tell you what, let Forbes look at it. He's pretty hot on this kind of thing, hobby of his."

"O.K. I wonder what luck they're having."

"A kitten!" said O'Connor. "Three trained detectives, out wasting the afternoon chasing a kitten. And all the paper work still waiting on that Feinberg thing—"

"I also think," said Varallo, "it might be a good idea to talk to his teacher. She just might know a little something to suggest a lead."

O'Connor agreed dourly. "You can do that. Why don't I ever get involved in one of those cases out of books, with beautiful girls and millionaires? All I get are dumb pro crooks and old-maid schoolteachers."

Varallo grinned at him. "Times have changed, *amico*. Some of them well worth looking at these days. That school fire—at least one I saw was quite a looker. Only, come to think, you go for blondes, and like them well-covered. This one—"

He was interrupted by Jensen of Traffic: the Feinberg business was tied up to Traffic and Jensen wanted to know if the red tape was finished on it. "Give us an hour," apologized O'Connor hastily.

"Sit around up here playing cards, I always suspected," grumbled Jensen. "God, what a weekend! Is it the hot weather? Twice the usual number of accidents, and now this hit-and-run." He sat down and mopped his face. "Now it'll be manslaughter, when we catch him—the woman just died."

"I hadn't heard about that—tough one?"

"About as tough as it can get. Happened late yesterday morning, up on Kenneth Road, about eleven o'clock. This Mrs. Waring was waiting for a bus at the corner of Ardmore—middle-aged woman, worked as a maid for some people up there. By all we've got, this car came down Kenneth going a lot too fast, hit a dip in the street and was thrown out of control—came up over the curb and hit her. Next minute, evidently, the driver's in control again and goes tearing off. That hour of the morning, up there, nobody around outside to see it happen. What we got came from a Japanese gardener half a block up the street, who did see it—but from that distance—and a Mrs. Meyer who lives in the corner house and happened to be looking out the window. She doesn't drive, doesn't know one car from another—elderly woman—and she can't give us any idea whether it was the size of a Fiat or a Rolls-Royce. All she tells us is, it was light green. This we knew, because it also hit the street sign there and left some green paint on it. The Jap doesn't get around too well in English, but he helped a little more—he says it was a medium-sized car, like a Dodge or a Buick, and he's pretty sure a sedan, but whether two-door or four-door he couldn't see. Can't offer any guesses as to the actual make—but he also says it wasn't a new car. Not new, not old, he says—maybe four, five years old. And he thinks the driver was alone."

"Not much there," agreed O'Connor. "Not a thing, I suppose, on the plate number." He sounded resigned; this one was heading his way when the victim was dead. A little more red tape, and Jensen would hand it to the Detective Bureau with his compliments.

"I ask you, do we ever have it that easy?"

"Sometimes," sighed O'Connor. "Not very often, no."

Jensen went away, and Varallo started to clear up the paper work on the Feinberg case. He had just got it tied up when Forbes wandered in.

"Well, I found your kitten for you, I think," he announced.

"We haven't actually got it, but we know about it—if it's the same kitten, which it sounds like. We started ringing doorbells, you know, and about an hour ago I got to this Mrs. Dyer on Cordova Drive. I asked if she'd seen it, and she said right off she had, all the time giving me a pretty cold eye, and she started to tell me off but good. I haven't any right to own an animal, she says, when I don't take better care— Well, I managed to get it across that it isn't my personal kitten, and she calmed down and told me the story." Forbes leaned his lank length on a corner of Varallo's desk and lit a cigarette.

"Which is?"

"Seems she likes cats, and last night about seven-thirty she was out gardening in the front yard when she spotted this kitten hiding under a bush. I got her to describe it—a long-haired black and white kitten, a female, about three months old. One of its hind legs was hurt—broken. She asked the neighbors, thinking one of them had just got it and she hadn't heard, but they didn't know anything about it. Well, she hasn't got a cat now, so she decided to keep it, and anyway, as she said, something had to be done about it—that leg. So like the nice kind woman she is, she put the kitten in the car and drove to a vet's, and that's where the kitten is now, at the Small Animal Hospital on Los Feliz, recuperating. I went back and checked with Mrs. Knox, and the description tallies. She was relieved to know the kitten was safe, by the way."

"So. On Cordova Drive," said Varallo. "With a broken leg . . . Used up one of its nine lives yesterday, all right. I wonder, now—any other injuries?"

Forbes shook his head. "One reason she lit into me when she thought it was mine. She'd thought it had probably been hit by a car, but the vet said it had more likely been kicked hard by somebody, because there wasn't another mark on it and any small animal hit by a car usually has a number of injuries."

Varallo sat up. "Well, well. At about seven-thirty, over on Cordova Drive. And a kitten with a broken leg wouldn't get far from where it happened—or would it? Or would it? Three good legs to use, and it was probably very frightened, made tracks out of there fast. . . ." He rummaged in a drawer, found a map. "Which block on Cordova?"

"Fourteen hundreds."

"Oh." Cordova ran at right angles to Hillcroft Road; that was the block just below Rosemount, which was the next street down from Hillcroft. It was a short block away from Carmen, running the same way as Cordova, two blocks from Sinaloa. "We could draw a provisional circle—ask the vet for an opinion on how far the kitten might have got after being hurt. But, still some way up in the air."

"Say it twice," said O'Connor. "Here's another little job for you, Jeff. Not that I'm going along all the way that it's murder, until we get the autopsy report. But you might as well take a look at this, anyway." He showed Forbes the diary, explained.

"Well, a code," said Forbes, interested. "That's something I know a little about—"

"Why else am I handing it to you? I don't expect it's anything very complex, a ten-year-old."

"Let's have a look." Forbes studied the first page. After a long moment he said, "Oh," disappointedly. "About as simple as you can get, yes. All he's done is use the alphabet backwards. Z for A and so on."

"I'll be damned," said O'Connor. "We *are* getting bright boys these days. One look and you spot it. How?"

"Anybody who knew anything about codes would spot it," said Forbes disparagingly. "All those W's and Z's and V's—letters from the end of the alphabet. Obviously used for vowels. And most of the vowels occur in the first half of the alphabet. So— All the same, a tedious little job to decode it. I suppose that's my job too?"

"All your own."

"A ten-year-old's diary. But if he was deliberately killed— God, what a thing—yes, sure, maybe a lead or two. I'll get on it."

"Four-thirty," said O'Connor. "Hell, isn't Goulding ever going to call?"

Twenty minutes later Goulding called. O'Connor listened to what he had to say, scribbled some notes; his expression tautened to grimness. "O.K., thanks, doctor—send the full report up, will you?" He put the phone down and turned to Varallo. "So now we know. It was murder— for pretty damn sure. He didn't suffocate, he died of a blow on the head. He probably lived about an hour, an hour and a half, after getting it, but in deep unconsciousness."

CHAPTER 6

"And doesn't that give us a few interesting ideas," said Varallo slowly. "He was struck on the head some time between five-fifteen—that's when Mrs. Riegler saw him—and, say, five-forty-five. Yes. Mrs. Riegler on Carmen Drive . . . Damn it, what a hell of a thing—and I'll make a tentative prophecy right now and say that the motive was a fairly slight one. . . . I think we can say he was on his way to take the kitten back to Mrs. Knox. He wouldn't have had time to show it to anyone else before having to be home at six."

"Logical," agreed O'Connor.

"So he'd probably start down Mountain toward Sinaloa. Only he never got to Mrs. Knox's." Varallo pushed the map away and thought. "Well, leave that until we get a few suspects. This one we'll get, by God —of all the cold-blooded—! Up to a point, it wasn't a bad plan, to cover up murder. He underestimated our intelligence a little, but they will go on doing that. He set it up to look as if that blow was struck by a falling plank. Where he really slipped up was in not realizing we'd spot how hard those planks were to move—he probably used a crowbar himself. Which tells us one thing, it was probably a man. And what nerve—he must have realized that by dark the boy would have been missed, and ten to one we'd be alerted and looking. The safest way, the only way, would be to use his car. Park as close to that hole as possible—it's damn dark up there, street lights a good way apart, and the one at that corner is—"

"Out," said O'Connor smugly. "It's in Forbes's report. Well, street lights do go out—you all took it for granted it'd just died of old age. But —we'll have a look at it, and I'll bet we find it smashed. . . . I'm seeing something else, Vic. I think it could be he got stuck, so to speak, with that head wound. That maybe he got mad and lashed out at the boy, some reason, and knocked him against something or hit so hard that it was a killing blow. So whatever fake accident he set up, it had to account for that wound. In nontechnical terms, the blow was on the left temple and Goulding says he thinks the boy was knocked down against something—table, raised hearth, something like that—because the wound was made by something ruler-straight and fairly sharp."

"Possible. Anyway, there he is with the unconscious boy. Can we say he realized right away that the boy was dying? Has he, maybe, had experience before with that kind of injury? Or did he just intend, having started the job, to finish it later with another blow? However, there he is. He's got to stash the boy somewhere temporarily out of sight, while he works out the accident plan, or if he's already worked it out, until after dark. And you might think," said Varallo, looking earnestly at his cigarette, "that that tells us he's living alone, but it doesn't really. Because, say he's a family man just by chance alone in the house when he hit the boy, he could have put him at the back of a closet, under a bed—or, the best way, under a rug in the car, right away. Yes, and that gives me another idea too. The chances are he wouldn't have realized the boy was dying, so he'd probably—"

"He did," said O'Connor, blowing smoke at the ceiling. "Goulding found that too. The boy had been tied up and gagged."

"*Diavolo!*" said Varallo.

"Nice fellow," said O'Connor, agreeing. He sat back and absently patted the bulge which represented that favorite .357 Magnum. "Could be, too, it actually happened in a garage—you said the boy wandered in everywhere. So the car was handy. If he is a family man, a lot easier than smuggling the body out of the house later. . . . He plans the fake accident. After dark, and not so long after, I think he went up to that intersection first and took care of the light. God, he took some chances, didn't he? With you hunting around the area already. Just luck he wasn't spotted—"

"He may have been," said Varallo. "Ask the people who live in those corner houses. Who'd have thought much about seeing a vague figure going down that hole, or noticing a flashlight at the bottom? We're so used these days to seeing these damned sewage people anywhere and everywhere. They'd just think, the foreman checking on something. But we'll ask, sure. . . . The actual cave-in wouldn't have made much noise, you know. Just those planks falling and then no noise to speak of as the earth shifted."

"True," said O'Connor. "Then, when he'd put out the light, he went back and drove down there with the boy. Possibly—this is another thought—he had an unpleasant surprise when he got down the hole with the boy—who was dead by then—and found those planks so hard to move. Had to go back to the car after a tool of some kind. But it was too late and too dangerous to change the plan. He just hoped we wouldn't think about it. Or that we'd think there'd been several kids down there when it happened, and the rest had run off scared and are lying about not being there. . . . He pried away the planks, after putting the boy in position, jumped back from the cave-in, and got out of there—"

"Sure, sure, so we can guess what he did!" said Varallo savagely. "All that's obvious. How does it help us find him, Charles? This cold-blooded devil who kills a bright ten-year old without any more compunction—"

"Not a nice customer, no. The hell with Jensen's hit-and-run and anything else that comes up, this one we work hard, every man we've got. . . ."

"But," said Varallo suddenly, "that's his character, isn't it? Because he kicked the kitten. Yes. We don't know much about this yet, but I think I see that detail. Paul dropped the kitten when he was struck, and X kicked it away."

"Could be," said O'Connor. "Could be." He got up and stretched. "Wait for what comes in. For what Jeff deciphers out of the diary. For what we get out of the kids he knew. We'll get some lead, somewhere."

"So, forget it until tomorrow," said Varallo, still sounding savage. "Pick up your latest blond and go out on the town, until office hours start—"

O'Connor looked at his hat, massaging his heavy blue-black jaw. "Well, now," he said softly, "twelve years on the force hasn't turned me just so tough as all that, boy. No. But sounding off about it isn't going to get us there any quicker. And as a matter of fact, I'm taking a night off from the blonds to get in a little target practice. If I'm going to get that medal again this year—and, damn, I only shot ninety-six last time."

"You're slipping. Sorry, Charles, but—well, damn it, there just aren't so many Paul Brandons around that we can afford to lose them. . . . I keep thinking about the rest of them we see—those vandals, that gang of high-school kids last month, riding around breaking car windows be-cause they were bored—all very much alive and making new trouble for us every day, that kind. And this bright, honest, nice kid—who knows what he'd have grown into? Somebody important to the world, maybe."

"There's never an easy answer," said O'Connor, still looking at his hat.

"I don't know how you feel," said Varallo abruptly, "but me, I don't think any cop can honestly believe in God—any of the earnest reassurances from the churchmen. Life doesn't bear it out. Crime does pay, God knows, and the ones hurt worst—in every way—are usually the innocent honest citizens."

"Well," said O'Connor, "I don't go to church either—they've all got a few ideas I don't go along with—but, you push me hard, Vic, I've got to confess to a vague sort of feeling that, comes the time all the chips are down, it's been arranged somehow that the do-good people always take the jackpot. In the end. In the long run."

"I wish I could agree with you," said Varallo, and laughed. "God sitting up there like a pro sharp, dealing off the bottom against the devil?"

O'Connor grinned and slapped on his hat, slanting it debonairly. "Damn sight better idea than the way most people think," he said. "God sitting up there disapproving of every little thing that's any fun for human people."

"Including blonds."

"Including blonds. Hell, we're only young once. . . . See what turns up tomorrow. I'll see you."

"Good luck on the range," said Varallo.

Forbes had taken the diary home with him. In the few pages he had decoded, nothing of interest had shown up—comments on kids at school, on teachers, on small happenings around the neighborhood.

"Just the kind of things a smart kid that age who was interested would put down."

"Are the pages dated?" asked Varallo.

"Just 'Monday' or 'Tuesday,' and that's not consistent."

"Well, to save time, why not start at the other end? The last pages? Go back, as near as you can judge, two or three weeks. If there's any lead for us there, I don't think it'd be too far back."

"I see what you mean, I'll do that."

It was too late today to do much more on it. Tomorrow, visit the school, thought Varallo. See some of the kids Paul had known best. The teacher . . .

At the last minute O'Connor came with him, on that. "We'll get on this one, all right. I'd like to hear what these kids have to say—if he talked any little secrets at all, it'd be to other kids, not grownups— I remember that much."

"What'd you shoot?"

"Ninety-eight," said O'Connor, sounding happier and patting the shoulder bulge.

It was a fairly new school, with a large playground. They went into the main building and immediately felt awkward. Everything, in keeping with modern theory, was graded in size to the size of the majority of the inhabitants. Feeling about nine feet high in comparison to the desks in an empty classroom they passed, to the height of drinking fountains and glass display cases, Varallo led the way down to where a sign said PRINCIPAL'S OFFICE.

"Shades of my past," said O'Connor *sotto voce.* "I used to spend a lot of time in places like this. You'd never've thought I'd grow up to be a respectable cop." He told the sallow, thin girl in the anteroom they'd like to see the principal, introduced themselves.

"Oh, dear," she said. "Oh, yes, about that poor little boy—such a tragedy— I'll tell Mr. Harwell."

The press had reported it as just another tragic accident. Let it go that way for the time being. If it got out that the police were asking questions pointing at murder, there'd be headlines. Eventually the parents would have to be told. . . .

"A dreadful tragedy," said the principal. "Dreadful." He was a portly bald man with a benign expression; he looked from O'Connor to Varallo with a hint of bewilderment. "But I confess I can't imagine why you want to see his teacher, or— It was on Saturday that it—"

"We haven't quite figured out just how it happened," said O'Connor noncommittally. "We'd like to, if we can. And it could be that some of the boy's friends can tell us something. Sorry to disrupt your routine here, but—"

"Oh, of course, any cooperation we can give—but I don't—"

"Well, you see," said Varallo, "sometimes kids this age get a little nervous and shy with police officers, lie to cover up little things. And probably the teacher would spot that where we might not." He didn't add that they also wanted to talk to her. He hoped she wasn't the garrulous, fluttery kind; in that case, tell her nothing. But if she was the sensible type, take her into their confidence?—because just maybe, seeing the kids every day, talking with them, she'd hear—or be able to extract—something of importance.

"Oh, well, of course we want to cooperate—" Mr. Harwell still looked a little puzzled. He opened the office door. "Miss Edwards, look up Paul Brandon's record, will you—whose class was he in?"

"It was Miss Mason's, Mr. Harwell— Katharine Mason. I know, because I saw her when she came in today, she was talking about it, how terrible—"

"Well, send her a— No, I had better go myself, yes, that will be best. If you'll just wait here a moment, gentlemen—" Mr. Harwell trotted out of the office.

"Use an empty classroom," said Varallo. "More informal atmosphere. Kids can be tricky to handle." O'Connor agreed. And presently Mr. Harwell came back with Katharine Mason—who was also looking a trifle surprised—and introduced her.

"Well, of course, anything I can do," she said. "We were all so shocked about Paul—an awful thing! But I don't quite understand what—"

Varallo waited for O'Connor to explain; O'Connor said nothing. Varallo looked at him. O'Connor was staring at Katharine Mason absorbedly, looking pleased and delightedly startled at finding this in these dusty, plebeian surroundings. Well, well, thought Varallo, amused; and not Charles's type, either. But there was that saying about variety. He explained all over again, and Katharine said, "Oh, I see. Of course I'll be glad to help, but—" she looked at the principal—"it'll mean interrupting the English period, I—"

"We must cooperate with the authorities," said Mr. Harwell sadly. "You will—um—leave a monitor in charge, or perhaps Miss Edwards could—"

"Yes, please," said Katharine. "With just a monitor, either the Emmett boy or Kevin Crandall would have the room in an uproar inside five minutes. Of course, if you want to see Paul's friends you'll want both of them. I think one-oh-three's vacant this period—"

In 103, Varallo looked at the miniature desks and resigned himself to standing. Katharine smiled. "Just a minute, we'll find some human-sized chairs, if one of you—" There were a couple in the next room; Varallo carried them in. O'Connor just stood watching Katharine fatuously, very obviously approving of everything about her.

"Charles!" said Varallo loudly. "Were there some questions we wanted to ask Miss Mason?"

O'Connor woke up and gave Katharine his best smile. He took her arm and steered her unnecessarily to a chair. "I think so. You look like a sensible girl, Miss Mason, as well as— So I'm going to ask you to keep to yourself everything about this little interview. O.K.?"

"Why—all right. But why—" She drew back from him a little, from the very masculine aura that surrounded him. Varallo watched, interested—it was the first time he'd seen O'Connor in action.

"Fine." O'Connor beamed at her. "Now, let's see—" He drew up his own chair close. "School just started a couple of weeks back, didn't it?"

"Three weeks, yes."

"Mmh. This is the first year you had Paul Brandon in your class?"

"Yes, it was. I liked him, a nice boy, and—"

"Yes. Did he talk much to you? I mean, about things other than schoolwork and so on?"

"I don't know what you— Why?"

O'Connor's dark eyes met hers seriously. "Did he? He was a queer sort of boy, you know, in a way. He liked to—find out things—about people. About the neighbors—everybody he knew."

"Oh," said Katharine. "I didn't— It's so near the beginning of the semester. I hadn't really got to know him very well yet—any of them. But I don't remember that he'd ever said much of anything to me—except about his schoolwork. I don't understand—what do you mean?"

"You just remember your promise now and don't repeat this," said O'Connor, "but then I know you won't, you're a good level-headed girl and want to help us—" and he started telling her about Paul.

CHAPTER 7

"I dunno," said Gordon Bicknell. "He never wanted go down those places any time with me." He kept his gaze on the floor.

"Did you see Paul any time on Saturday, Gordon?" asked Varallo. The boy shook his head without speaking.

O'Connor leaned forward. "Did Paul ever say anything to you about anybody living around his neighborhood? You live near where he did, don't you?"

The boy looked up and shot him one involuntary glance before dropping his eyes again: a glance compounded of startlement and fear. He shook his head.

"You'd been playing with him some, though, the last month or so? What kind of things did he talk about to you?"

Gordon made a vague gesture. "Gee, I—just things— I dunno. School, and that."

They exchanged impatient glances. Kids—how did you get to them? Katharine said, "Gordon." Her tone was level, though she was still white—her pale skin even paler than usual. "You know about this awful thing that happened to Paul. The officers have to find out how and why. They aren't going to punish anyone for anything. They just want to know the truth. Did you see Paul on Saturday?"

"No," said Gordon stolidly.

"Are you sure? They'll find out if you're lying, you know."

Gordon smiled nervously. "I dint see him, honest." And he raised his head and gave O'Connor a clear direct limpid look from his dark eyes.

"All right—you can go back to class." Katharine looked at them and shrugged as he went out in a hurry. "We don't seem to be getting much, do we?"

O'Connor smiled fondly at her for the "we." "You're good with them, lady—know how to get at them, which is more than we do."

"I still can't believe—such an incredible thing—how anyone could be so—"

"Very nasty. But we're working on it. Something's bound to turn up somewhere. We flatter ourselves we're pretty smart these days." In another minute, thought Varallo, he'd be patting her hand. Little change for Charles, who liked the well-stacked blonds—this slim elegant dark girl nearly as tall as he was.

They had seen six boys who, by what the father and Katharine said, had been Paul's closest pals. Two of them, Pat Emmett and Kevin Crandall, had seen him on Saturday morning—they'd all been down at the civic swimming pool—but not after lunch. They sounded as if they were telling the truth. Who could say about the other four? They were self-conscious, questioned by big-as-life policemen like on TV. They wriggled and stammered. Well, gee, Paul just talked about ordinary things. No, sir, I never heard him say— No, sir, I never saw him all day Saturday— No, sir, I dunno know what you mean.

Varallo frowned. Something about that Gordon kid puzzled him. That direct honest glance at the last: it reminded him of something. . . . It would come to him. But they sure as hell hadn't got anything here. Of course, by what emerged, Paul hadn't been the kind to acquire many very close pals. Hadn't been interested much in the things most boys this age were interested in: Little League baseball, any sports, that sort of thing. Something of a lone wolf. So maybe even the boys he knew best wouldn't know anything useful to them. "Well," he said, "thanks very much, Miss Mason. We don't need to ask you to keep your ears open for anything about this."

"Of course. I can't *believe*—it's incredible, a little boy. But anything I can do—and I must go to see the Brandons—" She got up, still looking shaken; O'Connor took her arm.

"You go on back to the car, Vic," he said casually. "I'll just see Miss Mason back to her classroom. Now you don't want to fuss over it, we'll find out all about it—" He steered her out and down the hall, murmuring confidentially.

Va via, a maraviglia! thought Varallo. The Celtic charm in action. She looked like a nice girl too, but somewhat bemused already. How the hell did he do it? You couldn't say he had any pretensions to good looks. And a smile like a friendly alligator.

Well. Varallo went out to the car and smoked a cigarette before

O'Connor joined him. "Enjoy yourself?" he asked. "Making up to a new quarry instead of sticking to business?"

"Brother," said O'Connor. "Isn't she something? *I* never had a schoolteacher like that. Really something. My God, and I nearly left this bit all up to you." He looked shaken for a minute. "My God . . . I'm taking her to dinner Wednesday night."

"*Davvero?* Talk about fast work. The famous Celtic charm."

"Celtic charm be damned," said O'Connor. "I just don't see any sense in wasting time." But he was wearing a peculiar expression. He looked rather like a man who had just been sandbagged and hadn't realized it yet. He sat there and stared at the steering wheel, no move to get out his keys. "Life's too short," he said.

"And quite a departure for you," said Varallo. "A good-looker, yes, but not your type—dark, and too thin. What was the elegant expression I heard you use once, you like to hug a girl without getting bruised by her hipbones?"

"You just shut up!" said O'Connor coldly. And looked, oddly, a little puzzled. "Well, I know, but she's— Well, I mean— You go to hell."

"I don't think you'll make any time there," said Varallo. "Quite a nice respectable female."

"You go to *hell!*" said O'Connor, sounding outraged. "Sure she's a nice girl! You and your damned dirty mind—" He got out his keys and jabbed at the ignition. "You think a girl like that— Well, you just lay off, that's all!" He got the key in finally, started the engine with a roar.

Varallo stared at him and began to laugh. "*Capperi—che tipo, bravo!* Our gay rake Charles— I recognize the symptoms—captured at last, don't tell me!"

"Don't be a damned fool," said O'Connor stiffly, and maintained a cold silence all the way back to headquarters, while Varallo went on grinning to himself. But as he pulled the brake, switched off the engine in the parking lot, O'Connor added absently aloud, "Isn't she damned good at handling those kids, though?"

Nothing from the kids, at least not yet; but now they had something, from Forbes and the diary. They had, in fact, a hell of a lot—and some provisional suspects.

Forbes said the diary, decoded from its simple secretiveness, was mostly what you might expect. The boy's comments on the people he knew, was interested in: things they had done and said. And also a brief record of his own routine: things that had happened to him. A good deal of it was about kids he knew at school, teachers, and neighbors. Allowing for the boy's offbeat interest in people, normal . . . The Andersons had a new living-room rug. He liked Miss Mason, she was a good teacher. Mrs. Riegler was sure a good housekeeper, way she was always dusting and cleaning. Mrs. Varallo was awful pretty, and nice too. (So she was, thought Varallo, smiling.) The Kaufmans' Springer spaniel was going to have puppies, real thoroughbred ones. He felt sorry for Mrs. Knox, so old and lame; he'd bicycled down to Verdugo to get groceries for her today. . . .

But there were, sandwiched in amongst all this, a few suggestive entries. On a Saturday three weeks ago, Paul had written:

I guess Mr. Keith has a girl friend, he was talking to somebody named Sharon on the phone. Looked awful mad when he saw me, like he knew I heard. Like those salesmen Dad talks about only he doesn't know I heard him. Mrs. K. is kind of plain, Dad says she has the money whatever that means. He looked funny at me all right.

And another item, the day before:

Funny how Mrs. Starke acted about the card party she's going to. Like it was something wrong. Mother has card parties, nothing bad about that but Mrs. S. was scared, asked me not to tell I heard her and that man talk about it. He was almost whispering when he said the address and she wrote it down, I just heard San Fernando Road, and when he said about roulette. I think thats a card game. He only had one eye and he limped like Mrs. Knox, I never saw him around here before. Mrs. S. was sure scared, said her husband didn't like her doing that. Funny but I said I won't tell. Nothing bad about playing cards, Mother does and Dad sometimes.

And then, the Tuesday after that (nineteen days before he died) Paul had written:

N.'s big brother Steve was awful mad about a thing I heard him and Jerry Emmett talking about. It was a thing about some girls I guess he said about a motel and Greta and Rose and getting some whiskey. People under 21 cant buy whiskey, I heard Dad say, state law that is so Jerry Emmett couldn't because he's only 18. I asked Steve and he was mad. He scared me a minute. I wonder if I ought to tell Dad but I guess its nothing because if its a state law Jerry couldn't get any whiskey, all the cops are honest now like Mr. Varallo says and they wouldn't let people break the law.

And five days ago, another little item:

I stopped ask Mrs. Bradley should I cut their grass this week. She said while she was talking to me about Mr. B. working late last night at his place. But he wasn't either because I saw him when Nick and Pat and I came out of the movie. Right where Dad was waiting to pick us up in front of a Cocktail place, he was coming out with that maid Mrs. B. has. I never said but its funny. She's awful pretty but dumb.

Varallo looked at those passages in Forbes's neat writing. The casual little secrets stumbled on by the boy, only halfway understood as secrets; the social importance, to the secret keepers, not comprehended at all. *Like Mr. Varallo says* . . . Leads. Very probably the boy had died without knowing why—without ever realizing how important his little knowledge was to his killer.

"Leads," he said thoughtfully. "Leads? These people, nice upright honest citizens—higher social standards. Sure. Didn't I say it? Little things, the extracurricular blonde and so on, but— Does one little thing there ring a bell with you, Charles, the way it set bells ringing in my head?"

"And me the lieutenant?" said O'Connor dreamily. "I'm conscientious, I am, I remember details and pedigrees. 'He only had one eye and he limped.' Just imagine that. Faro Joe Schultz, after all this time. We all thought he'd gone back East."

"It appears that we've got at least one undercover gambling joint in our territory. Roulette, no less. That's a fool's game."

"This terrifying innocent," said O'Connor. "He didn't even know what he knew, did he? Writing it down alongside the name of the movie he saw last and stuff about schoolwork and the Andersons' new rug. My God. 'Said her husband didn't like her doing that.' Understandable. And what's this about somebody's big brother? Illegal liquor—girls. And this Keith—what the hell, Vic? Motive for murder?"

Varallo laid down Forbes's transcript. "What constitutes a motive, Charles, depends on who has it. You know as well as I do. Murder done for a nickel in change—or a million bucks. For a second's loss of temper. What the hell indeed. But I can see it, in a way. People like these, keeping up appearances. At least it gives us places to look and questions to ask. . . . And if we can locate him, you know, we really should pick up Faro Joe, shouldn't we? Battening on the citizenry with his crooked roulette wheels—if it *is* Faro Joe."

"Oh, I think so," said O'Connor contentedly. "Fellow with a limp and one eye— I think so. I think you'd better go and see this Mrs. Starke."

"I don't," said Varallo gravely. "I think you'd better go and see her, Charles. I look too much—*scusi*—like a gent. I think you'd scare her a lot more, you look more like a cop. One of these tough brutal cops."

O'Connor stood up and reached for his hat. "You could be right at that," he said amiably. "A pleasure. Not that I really enjoy bullying females. And you can't outlaw human nature, and gambling's a very natural impulse—on occasion, I've been known to play a few hands of draw myself—but we really can't have gentry like Faro Joe operating in our territory. I'll see what I can get out of her. You might start following up the other leads."

But before Varallo left the office, the formal autopsy report arrived. He looked it over: nothing they hadn't known. Along with it, however, came the contents of the boy's clothes, and he looked at those with hopeful interest. The clothes themselves were now, as per request, at the L.A.P.D. crime lab being thoroughly examined. The Glendale force maintained a small lab of its own, but on this one the full treatment was indicated, and they didn't come any better than L.A. for that.

Contents of the pockets: A ballpoint pen. A worn leather wallet containing a dollar bill and twenty-four cents in change, and in the little plastic slots an I.D. card, a few snapshots—Paul and a big dog, his parents, himself and a couple of other kids on the beach—a library card, and a card testifying that all charges having been paid, Paul Brandon would be admitted to the junior swimming class at the civic pool. The key to the diary. There was the inevitable pocketknife. An unopened package of chewing gum. A little booklet of bus passes; he'd taken the bus to school, of course. A long piece of string, carefully saved for some unknown project. A shopping list in a woman's hasty writing.

Nothing there at all, damn it.

Varallo left the report and the other items on O'Connor's desk and went to see Mrs. Riegler. It was just possible that the boy had said something to her as he left—whether he intended to take the kitten elsewhere or back to Mrs. Knox.

The Riegler house was near the dead end of Carmen Drive, where it ran into Rosemount. It was a neatly maintained Spanish stucco. The front-door chimes produced only silence, but he could hear noise of some sort at the back; he walked up the drive. The double garage doors were shut, but somebody was pounding metal inside the garage.

"Mrs. Riegler?" he called, and knocked on the small side door of the garage. The pounding stopped; at once the door opened and a man came out, pulling the door to behind him.

"Mrs. Riegler's at the market. What d'you want?"

"Mr. Riegler?"

"That's right."

Varallo introduced himself. "We're still getting this business cleared up, you see, I've a couple of questions to ask your wife." Riegler was a thin dark man in the forties, going gray; deep worry lines creased his cheeks, and his eyes were bitter.

"Oh, yes," he said. "Bad business. Well, I expect her back any time, she just—in fact, here she is now." A car was turning in the drive, a blue Chrysler a couple of years old. The woman who emerged from it was as fat, jolly, and talkative as her husband was the opposite.

"Oh, that awful thing—he was such a dear boy, he took care of our lawn, you know, did a real good job too and only three dollars a week. I just *cried* when I heard, his poor father and mother— Mrs. Brandon just prostrated, and no wonder. Beg pardon? . . . Oh, you mean when he was here that day? Oh, I just can't bear to think about it, standing on this very spot he was, because I'd been at the market then too and he heard Mr. Riegler back here and came back just the way you did, Mr. Varallo. Sometimes it makes you wonder— But no, he never said where he was going next, home or somewhere else. I like cats well enough, and it was a cute kitten, but there's Mr. Riegler's allergy. So—"

Varallo thanked her, extricated himself, and debated who to see next. "N.'s big brother" probably referred to Nicky Morehouse, one of Paul's pals. Steve Morehouse. About high-school age, probably, and he and this Jerry Emmett experimenting with girls and whiskey. Well, there had to be a first time. And boys from homes up here, respectable and conventional families, would be keeping such activities very dark indeed, and the possibility of parents getting to know—

Motive for murder? You never knew. Depended on the boys. On what kind of parents, what punishment the boys might expect. See them both, get the story out of them, deliver a lecture—and incidentally find out what foolhardy retailer was selling the liquor to them and take away his license. Size them up.

But right now they'd be in school.

The philanderers, Mr. Keith and Mr. Bradley. He'd looked them up. Keith was personnel manager at a local department store; Bradley had a Buick agency in town.

Keith had known about Paul's knowledge; there was no indication that Bradley had, but he could have.

Varallo sighed and drove downtown to see Keith. He had to wait in the anteroom of Keith's office; when he was finally admitted, it turned out to be a handsome one, carpeted and expensively furnished.

The same could be said of James Keith. He was in his forties, looked younger, and obviously thought a good deal of himself. Neat dark mustache, automatic friendly smile, consciously pleasant baritone voice. His suit hadn't come off a ready-made rack, and an aura of woodsy masculine cologne surrounded him.

"Ah, yes—Varallo?—and what can I do for you, sir?"

Varallo told him. Keith's smile tightened a little, but he came out with all the obvious comments at once, plausibly.

"A dreadful accident—we all feel so sorry for the Brandons! I tell you, I've given my own two boys strict lectures about those excavations. It's disgraceful that they should be left uncovered at night. But I'm afraid I can't help you, I hardly knew the boy, our boys are younger, and—"

"Well," said Varallo, "it's just a little thing. I understand that a while ago Paul Brandon had inadvertently found out about your—shall we say extracurricular activities? By the name of Sharon."

"For God's sake!" said Keith wildly. His precise manner fell from him all at once; his eyes rolled whitely, startled; he dropped his cigarette on the desk blotter. "Oh, my dear God, he did tell somebody—he—how'd you— Listen, that's not so. That's—"

"You'd better rescue that cigarette or you'll have the blotter on fire. He wrote about it in his diary. Now just calm down, Mr. Keith, and answer me, please. Had you asked him not to talk about it?"

"Look," said Keith. "Look." He yanked at his collar as if he was strangling. But he looked a little calmer since Varallo had mentioned the diary. "I don't know what he wrote down but he got it all wrong, there's nothing to it, see? He happened to hear me talking on the phone with, er, one of our employees here—very nice young woman, Sharon Harker—a mere matter of business, I only know Miss Harker *as* an employee—you can ask her, it wasn't anything! But that boy, damn it, nosy as a gossipy woman, not normal if you ask me! I could see what he thought, and you can understand that I was afraid of his coming out with it to someone—an irresponsible ten-year-old, he wouldn't understand that— You know how gossip— And I've got a reputation to maintain, damn it! There was nothing *to* it, but you can see—"

Varallo said he saw. "Mr. Keith. What time did you get home on Saturday night?"

"On S-Sat— Why? I don't underst—" Keith stopped and looked at him with horror. "You don't mean you think somebody—that *I*— *Oh, my God!*"

"You'll be tearing your shirt if you yank any harder on that collar. What time, please?"

"Oh, my God. About five-thirty, it'd be—usual time."

"Your wife home? You spent the evening together?"

Keith shut his eyes. After a long moment he said, "You're not telling me you think somebody deliberately— Nobody could do that. A kid . . . No. No, she'd—there was this movie the kids wanted to see, over in Hollywood—and she had some damn P.T.A. thing until three o'clock. She took them then, and they had dinner out—afterward. I—"

"What time did they get home?"

Keith licked his lips. "About—eight o'clock, it was. But look—"

CHAPTER 8

So there was one possibility, all right. Keith could have done it. It emerged that Mrs. Keith, tired out, had put the two boys to bed and gone to bed herself about nine o'clock. So Keith could have faked the accident.

Would he? To prevent the boy's possible gossiping? The boy had known about the girl friend for three weeks; any gossiping he was going to do would probably have been done—three weeks was a long time in a ten-year-old's life. And a ten-year-old hadn't yet much interest in girl friends and boy friends, no real comprehension of sexual relationships. (Yes, and that also said that whatever he'd heard on the phone must have been pretty definite, or he wouldn't have got the point at all.) Would he have talked about it? Found it interesting enough to talk about?

So maybe he had, and the gossip had already reached Keith's wife. Revenge on the boy? For putting Keith in bad with Mrs. Keith—who "had the money"?

Varallo shook his head in dissatisfaction. It was *possible,* but he didn't like that idea much. Keith was all front, no real guts; Varallo couldn't see him taking such positive action. And it needed a rather special type of man to kill a child in cold blood like that. . . .

He had an early and mediocre lunch, at the nearest place, and afterward found a phone booth and dialed the house on Hillcroft Road. "It's me, *cara.* Do me a little favor? Call Mrs. Bradley up the street—Mrs. Brian Bradley—and say you've heard she has such a nice reliable maid and could you have her name because you need some part-time help yourself—"

"As if we could afford it," said Laura. "And if we could, much more useful after the baby's here. I won't ask questions now, but I'll want to hear details when you get home. All right."

"Wait a minute, I'm in a booth," and he gave her the number. It was only three minutes before she called back.

"Mrs. Bradley isn't home, the maid's there alone. She sounds terribly young, Vic."

"I'm in luck— O.K., see you, darling." He drove up to the Rossmoyne area fast, to the Bradley house a couple of blocks down from their own.

The maid was young, no more than nineteen. She didn't ask why a detective officer was interested in her; she was too awed. Her name was Sally Hopper, and she was the most luscious thing Varallo had laid eyes on in quite a while, if you liked the obvious type. A natural blonde, with a creamy complexion and very blue eyes, a figure designed for a calendar, and—he decided five minutes later—a mental age of about six. A nice, well-brought-up six.

Oh, sure, the Bradleys were nice people. She worked here three mornings a week, and then at the Williamsons' and some people named Harding on Kenneth Road. Oh, well, about that, Mr. Bradley was just being nice was all, there wasn't anything wrong about it. Sort of fatherly he was, you know. He didn't mean anything bad, and it was only twice yet he'd invited her out with him, she kind of figured he wanted to let her see, just because she was only a maid he didn't look down on her or anything. He was a real nice man if he was sort of old, maybe about fifty. He'd given her a present on her birthday, ten whole dollars. There wasn't anything wrong about that, was there? Only she hadn't much liked the places he'd taken her, he'd ordered a thing called a gimlet for her and it tasted funny, she didn't like it, but he laughed and said—

Varallo sighed, feeling oddly protective himself, and started a little lecture, as tactfully as possible, about middle-aged gentlemen who acted fatherly and ordered gimlets for nineteen-year-old blondes. He could see Bradley's point in a way, but after all—

He went back downtown to see Bradley at his Buick agency. Bradley's much-enlarged photograph smiled down from above the neon sign on the building: round grinning face, horn-rims, curly gray hair, honest direct glance— What did that remind him of?

Bradley was out with a customer, but Varallo was seized by a garrulous young salesman who, in his zeal to sell Varallo a new car, saw nothing odd about the questions he asked and answered them in between extravagant praises of this new model, you'd never regret buying this one, no, sir, and they were practically giving them away at this end of the year—

Bradley wasn't alibied either, if his salesman had the facts straight. On Saturday afternoon he'd left about four-thirty, remarking jokingly that he was a temporary bachelor, his wife was going out to some hen party for dinner and an evening of cards, and he'd have to get his own dinner.

Well, well. Of course inquiry might tell them that he'd gone out to a restaurant, called on a friend afterward, that he was out of it. But— And had Bradley known that Paul had seen him with Sally? . . . Girls like that shouldn't be allowed out alone. . . . Paul had just liked to know about people, he hadn't talked about it much, by all appearances. And this too was something he wouldn't have had much interest in, as per Keith and his girl friend. Bradley could have known—could have also recognized Paul there, and known his reputation.

On the other hand, Sally hadn't realized there was anything clandestine about the fatherly Bradley's behavior. She might have come out with it, artlessly, to anyone at any time. Even to Mrs. Bradley. And with Bradley's sort, probably Mrs. Bradley knew him for what he was by now. Why should he worry about Paul knowing, when Sally—

Steve Morehouse. When was school out? About three. God knew when a teenager would actually be home, though. And also, would home be the best place to tackle him? No. Better catch him alone, somewhere. A little tricky to handle, persuade the story out of him . . . The school. He'd go to Glendale High, almost certainly. A motel, girls and liquor—almost certainly, a high-school kid. Even these days, the junior-high kids didn't get started quite that early. . . . Get there just before three, see the principal. O.K.

It was one-thirty. Varallo went back to headquarters and found O'Connor sitting at his desk reviving himself with black coffee.

"Females," said O'Connor. "How I hate hysterical women."

"Did you get anything out of her?"

"More than I wanted. When I said my little piece and started to ask questions, she came apart at the seams. . . . One of those little, dark, intense women, lipstick on crooked, safety pins holding her dress together. *Oh, my God, you know—oh, officer, please don't make me—if my husband finds out—* Practically down on her knees to me. *And,*" said O'Connor thoughtfully, "she also came out with some nasty words about Paul—*that damned prying horrid little boy, I knew he'd tell, I knew he'd forget promising not to—*and so on. Like that. A few scattered facts emerged from the hysterics, and I managed to get her calmed down enough to answer a few questions. After a while. And then she put on a nice act, trying to make it sound perfectly normal and natural—her husband just puritanical and suspicious, nothing *immoral* about a little friendly gambling on a card game, after all!—but she was so unlucky, and well, he was rather miserly, he disapproved of it because of that too, she did lose most of the time. He'd just been brought up strictly—" O'Connor gestured, his voice rising to nervous falsetto, and Varallo grinned, seeing the restless, chattering little woman—"and he actually *spied* on her. But when Gwen Evans told her about this nice little private club, really a very respectable place, where you could—" O'Connor sat back and drank. "You get the picture."

"In full color. How much is true?"

"Well, it's a little something," said O'Connor. "I went and saw Starke, because of course we have to know, and I had an idea about our Wilma. He's a purchasing agent for an assembly plant in L.A., by the way—seems like a very nice fellow. He went straight up in a sheet of flame, and I don't think Wilma's going to be very happy the next few weeks. You can hardly blame him. She's one of these compulsive gamblers, can't leave it alone. Until he found out, she'd cleaned their joint account a couple of times. They've only been married four years. Naturally he's tried every way he knows to keep a check on her, but you know that kind. It's an addiction like any other addiction, they'll lie and steal, get money any way they can to satisfy it. He was so mad he didn't keep anything back— I heard the whole story. She's pawned all her jewelry, she's pawned furniture, she's sold everything of value she can lay hands on. He doles out housekeeping money and she loses that, so he comes home to no groceries in the house. He stops giving her an allowance, does all the marketing himself, and she rifles his billfold, sells the TV—well, you know the pattern. That kind, it's no use at all to tell them the truth about gents like Faro Joe. They just don't believe it—or don't care. So long as they have the chance to watch the little ball spin round, or pull the lever on the one-armed bandit, or shuffle a deck of cards."

"He's got a problem," agreed Varallo. "I can just understand why anybody can get addicted to the other things, drink or drugs—there's some inducement, in a sense—at first anyway they give you a lift, you feel fine. But gambling—maybe it's growing up in a household where fifteen cents for a day-old loaf of bread came the hard way, but I can't bring myself to bet a nickel on anything. Damned funny sort of obsession."

"I agree with you," said O'Connor, whose mother had been born in Edinburgh, "but there are people like that. Starke has a problem all right. He said the last time she went off the rails, he threatened to leave her. . . . She's never worked, lived at home with Mama on Papa's pension until she married Starke. Motive for murder, Vic? She's not trained for anything, might find a living hard to earn. And she might be very crazy about him—he's good-looking, there aren't any kids. I wonder. She did a lot of talking about Paul, name-calling—vindictive. She's not a big woman, but for sufficient reason and with a good strong crowbar she could have shifted those planks."

"Yes. Alibi?"

"Wide open," said O'Connor, and finished his coffee. "I asked. Starke was so upset he never asked why. He had to work late on Saturday, some business fouled up that morning he had to straighten up, and he didn't get home until nine-thirty. He waited in his office after dinner for a long-distance call."

"You don't say. I've got some more of the same." Varallo told him about Keith and Bradley. "I thought I'd catch the Morehouse boy at school."

"Good idea."

"Did you get a line on Faro Joe, I hope?"

"Oh, sure. No trouble. Our Wilma parted with the address right off. I don't figure she realizes it's an illegal business, actually—she's not very smart, of course these people never are. As soon as I got back I sent Forbes to pick him up, and anybody who's in it with him. All legal, with a warrant."

"That much accomplished," said Varallo, "at least."

Footsteps in the corridor, and Detective Fred Wayne came in, looking tired. "We found a funny little something for you in the hole, lieutenant. Give you three guesses what it is."

"Smart as I am, I'm not omniscient," said O'Connor. "Let's see."

Wayne said admiringly, "Three-syllable words yet! It's a very funny little something—and for pretty certain, dropped by X, because we asked all the men on the job and they all say they never saw it before."

Since noon yesterday Wayne, Poor and Katz had been getting some unusual physical exercise, shoveling and sifting all that earth from the cave-in in that hole. Looking over every shovelful for anything extraneous it might contain. Because you never did know: and murderers were sometimes careless like other people.

In the end, in a very real sense of the word, they'd hit pay dirt.

"We got down to the planks finally," said Wayne, flexing weary muscles, "and when we moved them, there it was, right out in plain sight. I figure it fell out of his pocket when he bent over to lay the kid out in the right position so the planks would hit him. And if you can say what it is, you're smarter than the rest of us." He laid an envelope on the desk and watched rather maliciously while O'Connor upended it. "It hasn't been printed yet."

It rolled out on the desk smartly, bounced off the file tray, and came to rest. A coin. A large silver coin, stamped with strange letters and figures. A foreign coin.

"What the hell," said O'Connor.

"Just," said Wayne, "what we said, lieutenant."

O'Connor examined it. On the side uppermost was a human figure carrying a lute; the figure seemed to be standing on a sea shell, and in the background were the buildings of a city. There were also a rayed sun and some Hebrew letters. Round the edge ran an inscription: TU TANDEM ABIECTAM REDDES DEUS ALME SONORA.

"What the *hell*," said O'Connor. He flipped the coin over with the tip of the letter opener. On the other side was an elaborate coat of arms. Round the edge was another inscription: D G RUDOLPH. AUGUSTUS DUX BRUNS. ET LUN.

It looked like a very old coin.

"I will be damned," said O'Connor blankly. "And it looks as if it might be worth something, too."

Varallo studied it. "You know, Charles," he said meditatively, "what it says to me, this is the sort of thing somebody might carry as a kind of lucky piece. A talisman . . . If so, let's hope his luck is running out, since he's lost it."

They now had Jensen's hit-and-run to work on, as well as several other things. A couple of nights ago the vandals had hit a junior-high school. It looked as if the first couple of cases weren't hooked up to these last three; in those cases, only random damage had been done, nothing stolen, whereas at the two junior highs and one senior high hit, there had been thefts.

They went to work on that as they could: getting the serial numbers of the stolen typewriters and office machines, to send to all pawnbrokers. The hell of it was, high-school kids these days were so mobile, as O'Connor put it; most of them drove, a good many of the boys owned cars—they could drive fifty miles off to dispose of the loot.

There wasn't much of anything to do about the hit-and-run: a question of time. They knew that the car had a smashed head lamp and without much doubt a good-sized dent in one fender and/or the front grille. Its owner wasn't going to drive it around like that: the story had been fully reported in both Glendale papers and picked up for a briefer article by the *Times*. Probably the owner had made up some tale to account for the damage, but he was in a spot. Even if he was living alone, he'd have friends and neighbors familiar with his car. He wouldn't dare take the car in for repair at any garage in Glendale; they'd all been alerted to watch for it. Of course, he might not be a Glendale resident; but regulation fliers had gone out, as a matter of routine, to garages in all the surrounding area. Unless he drove outside L.A. County for the repair job, the car should be spotted. And it would look very odd indeed for him to do that, to people who knew him.

Of course, if he didn't come from around here (maybe the damned car had worn New York plates, they didn't know, nobody could tell them), was just passing through, he could have been up in Santa Barbara by dark, the blood wiped off the car, leaving it at a garage there. Or Bakersfield. Or anywhere. In that case, they'd never catch him. They were just waiting to see what might turn up.

They had Paul's whole diary decoded now, and nothing else of any importance had showed up. It was, viewed one way, a pathetic document, terrifyingly innocent indeed and yet the product of a good, if immature, mind. Comments on other kids, on teachers, on schoolwork, on people . . .

They had had, of course, to tell the parents, who reacted with the expectable incredulity. They had let the parents take their time in accepting it, believing it; and had asked patient questions.

"No, oh, no," Margaret Brandon had sobbed. "I just can't believe *anyone* could be so cruel as that, kill a *child!* It's not human—" And later, in better control, "S-something he'd found out—oh, God, I should have stopped it long ago, all that—he was too interested in people, I shouldn't have let him— I should have—"

And of course the father, when he understood it was certain, incoherent with anger, find the bastard and kill him! "I'll help you—tell me what I can do to help you—hell with the job—by God, if I ever get my hands on the—"

"That's our job, Mr. Brandon. We'll find him."

And, pressed, neither Margaret nor Harry Brandon could remember

Paul saying anything at all remotely suggestive. Asked, just on the chance, they had denied that the coin had belonged to Paul.

They had sent the coin to an L.A. numismatist, to be identified. Not that it would do them much good to know what it was. They wanted it back very soon, to spring on the principals in the case, asking if they recognized it: somebody might reveal something.

And they had a print from the coin. Or about three-quarters of a print. It wasn't in anybody's files, even in Washington. However, sometime in the future it might be useful.

CHAPTER 9

"Gordon," said Katharine, "you must know perfectly well that 'street' isn't spelled S-t-i-t."

"I can't help not knowing," he said sullenly.

"I'm sorry to ask you to stay after class, but you're not going to pass A-five if you don't do better, you know. Maybe if your mother or father tried to coach you, you'd—"

He gave her a glance of silent, surly contempt. Katharine pressed her lips together. She said, "I don't understand how you ever got out of B-five. Who was your teacher last year?"

For a moment she thought he wasn't going to answer. Giving her the old silent treatment. Then he said, "Miss— Miss— I guess I don't remember."

Which was ridiculous. Katharine refrained from saying so; it was a score for these kids if you lost your temper. She'd seen his entry test by now. Kids entering a new school were given a couple of elementary psychological tests to determine their level. Gordon wasn't retarded; he tested on the normal level, but either he was doing incompetent work deliberately, making silly mistakes to get attention, or he had had very poor teaching in the past.

It puzzled her considerably. The Glendale city schools were good on the whole, not overly progressive. If a child failed to accomplish satisfactory work in a grade, he wasn't automatically passed on to the next. And Gordon, at ten, could barely read. It was painful to hear him, and even more painful—because she could imagine his embarrassment— when the other kids laughed at him openly. Or was it embarrassment? Was it? Was he, for some reason, putting all this on, and getting a great kick out of being the center of attention? You never knew what kids would do, *or* for what reasons either.

And though she didn't go along with the notion that, psychologically speaking, kids were tender, delicate little plants, of course children could be disturbed by bad home conditions, and show it in queer ways. There'd been Rita Gaynor, last year: quite a bright little girl, suddenly turning sullen and seeming to forget half she knew, getting F's on every paper. All because, it emerged later, Mama and Daddy were planning a divorce. Things like that.

"Now, Gordon," she said. "You know you haven't forgotten the teacher's name."

He gave her a direct honest look. "I did too."

If necessary she could find out from the other school, contact the woman. "Oh, well," she said, "I'll get it when they send on your records." She felt very tired of Gordon suddenly. He was, after all, only one of thirty-nine kids she was supposed to teach fifth-grade English, and social subjects, and arithmetic. You tried to reach them, tried to help them, but sometimes— "Gordon," she asked, "is everything all right at home? Do you like your new house, living there?"

He shot her a quick glance, unfathomable because he dropped his eyes too quickly for her to read the expression in them. "Sure," he said indifferently.

All right, the hell with you, my little lad, thought Katharine. For now. Sooner or later, something would have to be done about Gordon. . . . Gordon, who had been a new friend of Paul Brandon's. She felt her heart jump. "Gordon!" she said sharply. "Please tell me the truth, do you know something about—how that dreadful thing happened to Paul? Are you worried about it, did you—"

"I don't know nothing about Paul. Why'd I be worried about anything?" He didn't look up.

The conviction seized her that he was lying. He did know something. And by itself, that wouldn't account for his poor work, because *that* had been constant from the start of term, but it did seem to be getting worse just lately. . . . But he baffled her. Usually, she could get to the kids; sooner or later, get them to open up with her. She couldn't reach this one.

She looked at him a moment more, a thin dark nondescript boy standing head down beside her desk, mutely awaiting release. "All right," she said at last, "all right, you may go. But please try to do better, Gordon."

He didn't answer, just turned and went out.

"Brat," thought Katharine. Wasting time on him. Go home and get those papers corrected fast, because this was Wednesday night.

And she must have been out of her mind, saying she'd go out with the man. That O'Connor. Out of her *mind*. Life was ridiculous—only the other day, thinking that she didn't know one single eligible and attractive man; and then, like a bad joke, fate offering her Lieutenant O'Connor.

Why on earth— She must have been hypnotized. She'd never liked short men; anyone as tall as she was wanted the six-footers. She was nearly as tall as he was; of course he made up for it in breadth. An Irish cop, and his suit looking like a hand-down, and that awful tie. One of those men who always looked as if he needed a shave. Curly black hair all over the backs of his hands. Like a gorilla. The only remotely attractive thing about him was his nice deep voice, and Katharine decided it must have been that that had hypnotized her. The first time she'd met him, saying—

And, come to that, the nerve of him. About an hour after he'd met her, presuming to— And quite confident and cool, as if taking it for granted she'd fallen for his manly charms. Well, that was probably a very appropriate adjective: she should be smart enough at twenty-seven to have spotted a wolf quicker than that. Probably spend the evening fending him off . . .

Paul Brandon. That incredible thing. What kind of man could be—*wicked* enough to murder a ten-year-old boy? She tried to forget how the Brandons had looked when she'd seen them on Monday night.

Keep her eyes and ears open, O'Connor had said, for anything from the kids. It was just possible that Paul had said something, that a couple of the kids did know something useful, not clearly realizing it, shy or wary of telling a grown-up for some reason.

Well. Go home, get these papers done, have a bath and change—the green chiffon, with the jade earrings, the new white sandals.

Gordon Bicknell . . . She got up and folded the papers together briskly. It was a quarter to four.

Gordon got off the bus at Mountain and started home slowly. He wasn't feeling good. Not sick, just not feeling right in himself like. For one thing, he was scared.

Paul—

It hadn't been so bad at first, but now, after that, he was scared of the Man. Cold scared inside; because he knew if the Man took it into his head, he'd kill Gordon just as easy and quick as he'd killed Paul, and never think twice about it.

Sweet Jesus, thought Gordon, if his dad just knew, if he could tell Dad! But he couldn't, that was all, he was all alone in the middle of this thing. . . . Dad spoke up sharp sometimes, and sometimes when he was a little tight or worried about something he might give you a cuff, but he never meant it; you always knew he was right there backing you up, because you were his boy. Dad was O.K., very much O.K., and you both knew things were O.K. between you.

He never thought much about his mother; she wasn't important to him, very. He liked his Aunt May better. But he couldn't talk to *her* either, she couldn't do anything about this. About anything.

The cops. Asking. Dumb cops. He thought he'd acted O.K. with them, but— Teacher, asking. Why had she? He hadn't said nothing, showed nothing. He was afraid; he tried to push away his fear.

If Dad could only—if he could tell Dad—

Well, he couldn't, that was all. Stop thinking about Dad.

It had been all right, at first. But now— The Man scared him. You thought about it straight, anybody who could do a thing like that, killing a little kid, might do *anything*. Just anything.

And Gordon knew all about him, and he knew Gordon knew.

It was all right—all right, he told himself. The Man knew Gordon wouldn't tell—didn't dare tell anybody. Nothing bad was going to happen. . . .

He tried to stop thinking about the Man. He thought about Teacher, asking all those questions. He didn't like school and he didn't like teachers. All the time asking questions. Gordon, why can't you? Gordon, why did you? Gordon, why won't you? Nuts. All that stuff never be any use to a guy, reading books, those fraction things, history. So he didn't know how to spell street right, so what? Dad always said book learning wasn't everything.

But the Man—

Gordon put a hand to his face, where the Man had hit him. Calling him names.

All *right*. It'd be all right, the Man knew he wouldn't tell. Only it was all so different now, here—

School and all. He didn't get it, it was another funny thing, other kids laughing because he got things wrong at school. Making fun of him. It wasn't *natural*. Not for the first time, he felt homesick for the old gang back home, Bill and Joe and Rudy—all his old pals, they knew he wasn't somebody to laugh at. . . . And Teacher asking funny questions about did he like the new house and all. Other teachers had just asked the why questions and sometimes got awful mad at him, and so he hadn't gone, and the truant officer like they called him had—

He turned onto Rosemount Avenue. *Oh, Dad!* he thought in silent panic.

Paul, down in that hole—

I needn't, thought Katharine, have got dressed up at all. He'll probably take me to a hole-in-the-wall hamburger joint. She surveyed O'Connor beside her exasperatedly.

His gray suit needed pressing, his tie was garish and crooked, his shoes needed polishing, and a heavy stubble of black beard shadowed his heavy jaw. He wasn't looking at her because he was driving, but he was talking in his—yes, definitely—charming deep voice. And apparently not realizing that he was talking to a lady, or a reasonable facsimile thereof.

"We usually get them in the end, as I told you. We get the tough ones like this— Listen, you bastard, get over in your own lane!—but things turn up eventually. We've got a couple of leads on this already—a very offbeat sort of thing, sure, and they're offbeat leads. Motives for murder, you run into the Goddamnedest things sometimes—just sometimes. Usually very routine— Son of a bitch, didn't even signal—but once in a while the plots out of books. Like this thing. My good Christ, look at that guy changing lanes—hell of a good way to commit suicide." He flicked on the directional signal and turned into the parking lot. Not a joint. The Chef's Inn up on Foothill. "Traffic statistics," he said, "are never any surprise to me. The idiots they give licenses to." He actually came around to open the door for her.

Inside, settled at a table, he asked a little doubtfully if she'd like a drink. Katharine said yes, please, a Martini. "Oh," said O'Connor. "Well, Scotch and soda for me . . . I thought teachers had to be pretty careful about—"

"We're allowed a little more leeway these days," said Katharine.

"Thank God," said O'Connor. "I've been having visions of spies from the Board of Education accusing me of corrupting your morals. Damn it, why the hell did you have to be a teacher?" He scowled at her.

"Why shouldn't I be a teacher?" she bristled. "I like teaching. What's it to you, anyway?"

"A *schoolteacher*," said O'Connor. "Of all things. Damn it, I should have let Vic go alone. What the hell got into me—" Their drinks arrived and he took a quick gulp, still looking black.

"If," said Katharine haughtily, sipping her Martini, "you are trying to convey to me that you're regretting asking me out, I may say that *I'm* regretting—"

"Now, now, Katy," said O'Connor, and grinned at her. "Don't be hasty. I grow on people. Especially females. I just—"

"Some females, possibly. And when did I invite you to call me— *nobody* ever called me—"

"Life's too short to waste time waiting for invitations. I like Katy— suits you some way. Only I think I've all of a sudden gone crazy—you're not my type at all. I like the little bouncy blondes."

"*Really,*" said Katharine, outraged at this bald pronouncement. "And *I* might say, Lieutenant O'Connor, that I think *I* was crazy, agreeing to—"

"And a temper," said O'Connor sadly. "I don't like the temperamental strong-minded kind. Never have, damn it. I like them to hang on my arm adoringly and tell me how big and strong and smart I am, no question. What the *hell* got into me—"

"Lieutenant O'Connor," began Katharine coldly, "I—"

"You'd better learn to say Charles," he said gloomily. "Whatever the hell got into me, you'll be seeing quite a lot of me, Katy."

"I will *not*—" And suddenly, at the sight of his depressed expression, Katharine burst out laughing. "Well, you needn't sound so sad about it!"

"Now that's better. Sense of humor anyway. I wonder if there's one single little thing we have in common. I did go to college two years, but I didn't graduate. And I suppose you go to some church every Sunday all righteous—"

"As a matter of fact I—"

"And approve of all this progressive education, way you've been taught. And like classical music. And modern poetry and art. And going to lectures on serious subjects."

"I *detest*—"

"And concerts. And—"

"In fact, I don't at all like—"

"And," said O'Connor mournfully, "you won't know anything about guns."

"Well, no, I—"

"There you are. Why the hell I ever—"

"You're interested in guns," said Katharine. "I suppose natural for a police officer."

O'Connor suddenly beamed at her. "I've got quite a collection, sure. I've got a couple of the first Colt-Patersons, and an eighteen-sixty model Cone, and an Adams Percussion— Of course, it's a kind of expensive hobby, you could say. And of course, you can't *use* those old babies. Nothing to touch the modern ones for accuracy and range. We arm the boys with thirty-eights these days—little less weight to carry than the old forty-fives, and not much difference when it comes to the kind of target shooting we get on the job—but I don't like the short barrel, see. A hell of an argument I had with the Chief—it's not regulation— but I pack that S. and W. three-fifty-seven Magnum, with that you've got everything—control, range, impact." He patted the bulge at his left shoulder complacently. "Of course, I had to have the holster custom-made, on account of the long barrel—"

"Another drink, sir?" asked the waitress, pencil poised.

"What? Oh— I don't think so." He looked at Katharine.

She found she wanted to laugh. She shook her head speechlessly, and looked down at the menu, ordered almost at random.

"Damn it, I'm sorry, you're not interested in all that," he said when the waitress had gone.

"Why shouldn't I be?" She smiled at him. She knew suddenly, in some odd way, fatal in the ordinary way to encourage Charles O'Connor, but for her quite safe. She finished her drink. She said, "You asked me to—watch the kids. For anything. There's a boy named Gordon Bicknell—I've got a funny hunch he knows something. I can't imagine how, or what, or why he's lying about it, but—you know how you get these feelings." She looked up at him.

O'Connor leaned across the table. His mouth straightened to a grim line; his dark eyes looked grim and absorbed. "Gordon Bicknell. Have you worked on him? What'd he say?"

She started to tell him about Gordon. And she discovered that—well, she wasn't quite sure how she felt about Charles O'Connor, personally, whether she liked him at all or disliked him intensely—this bull-shouldered Irish cop—but just by the look in his eye, she was suddenly and oddly sure that he'd get there in the end, he'd find out who had murdered Paul Brandon.

CHAPTER 10

"Well, of course it was a mess," said Varallo. "Quite a mess. These things always are. I— What's the matter?"

"Nothing really," said Laura, looking uneasy. "It just kicked me again. I read somewhere that you're supposed to feel all sweetly maternal and sentimental when it starts kicking, but as far as I'm concerned it's just terribly startling. And disconcerting. As if I weren't in control of myself any more, somehow. Heavens, there it goes again."

"You certainly don't sound very maternal," said Varallo. "Calling my first-born It."

"Well, we don't know," said Laura reasonably. "It's a very odd feeling, all I can say. I wish it'd keep quiet. It can take all the exercise it wants afterward. . . . Go on, I want to hear about this."

He stopped smiling at her and put out his cigarette. "Quite a scene," he said wryly. "Several scenes." Having missed Steve Morehouse and Jerry Emmett at school yesterday, he'd held off until today. "I explained to the principal—the old boy was horribly shocked, bless his proper little heart—and asked to use his office, see them alone. He wanted to stay, but I thought they'd open up sooner to a stranger, without anybody there who knew them. They wouldn't open up very easy at that, I knew." He started to open a new pack of cigarettes, and Gideon Algernon Cadwallader appeared, a small striped streak, at the rattle of cellophane. He crouched at Varallo's feet, chartreuse eyes round and intent, tail twitching. Varallo laughed at him, rolled the cellophane into a ball and threw it. Gideon fielded it neatly and began to bat it around the floor.

"For goodness' *sake*," said Laura suddenly, "why can't you be quiet?

It's got hiccups or something, Vic—a very funny feeling. I'm not so sure I should have started this project at all."

"Are you going to turn out one of those unnatural mothers? And I'd remind you that it wasn't you who started it."

"How right you are," said Laura, still looking uneasy and sitting bolt upright. "Well, go on and tell me—it'll help to take my mind off . . ."

A mess you could say, in several ways. The teachers had sent the boys up about ten to three. The principal had introduced Varallo and gone out, as agreed. The boys were nervous then; they got a lot more nervous as Varallo sized them up in silence for thirty seconds.

Both big boys, physically mature; they were both eighteen. Steve Morehouse was a big All-American type, a good six-three, sandy blond; his round snub-nosed face looked out of place, oddly immature on that big body. He was, on looks, a good deal less emotionally mature than the other one. The Emmett boy was more slightly built but also tall; another one like O'Connor, dark, who grew a heavy beard—he'd probably been shaving for a year or more. He had a thin face, regular chiseled features, a would-be cynical look in dark eyes. Both of them were scared, but Steve more so than Jerry.

Varallo told them to sit down. Then, without any comments, he told them quietly that they'd found out something about them from Paul Brandon's diary. An ugly little scene, the one that followed. Blustered attempts at denial, panic growing in Steve Morehouse's voice, weak cynicisms from the Emmett boy, an attempt to talk man-to-man to Varallo. It was, of course, Steve who broke first, turning on Jerry, "You got me into this, damn it, you said—"

"All right," said Varallo, "take it easy, both of you. Suppose you tell me some names and places."

It wasn't, of course, as easy as that. It never was. Teenagers were as tricky to handle as younger kids, or more so. It took a lot of patience to get all the details, but he finally extracted most of what was important, he thought.

And, looking at it in his abbreviated notes, he felt impatient and angry. . . . It was Jerry Emmett who had first picked up this one girl, Greta Hansen, at a movie over in Hollywood. The other one, Rose Garcia, was a friend of hers. It emerged pretty clearly that both girls were teen-age tramps; the boys hadn't corrupted any morals, that had already been done. By what the boys said, the shoe was on the other foot, and even though that was a natural claim for them to make, Varallo was inclined to believe it. For one thing, boys like these, living in that section of a town like Glendale, were very unlikely to have had any idea where to find a lenient motel, a lenient liquor dealer. They said the girls had known; both were in Hollywood.

Have a look at the girls, sure; that would tell them rather definitely where most of the guilt lay. But technically—

"Hell," thought Varallo to himself wearily. He looked at the two boys, now completely demoralized and even more scared than before. In a very real sense, the thing was ridiculous. These two were physically mature adults, with adult urges and emotions. In a good many other cultures—in another period—boys their age were married and fathering families. They hadn't done any harm to these girls, who had asked for it; if the girls hadn't been visiting motels with Steve and Jerry, it'd have been with others—lonely servicemen, anybody—who'd offer free drinks and a little fun. The whiskey had been the girls' idea, too. Not that he thought Steve and Jerry had needed any persuasion. But, what the hell? There had to be a first time.

So in this particular social culture, boys from homes like theirs were expected to go on to college, wanted to go to college, make something of themselves, get started in a career before they married at twenty-six, twenty-seven. Nature didn't give a damn for social cultures. And also, he thought, an operative phrase was "homes like theirs"; over in east L.A., a lot of other places, who'd make a big deal out of a couple of eighteen-year-olds shacking up? They were old enough.

On the other hand, of course, most of them simply weren't mature enough in other ways to shoulder the responsibility of marriage. They still had education to finish. It created a little problem, which frequently resulted in such situations as this one.

Only in this case, with boys from this end of town— Because you couldn't just let it go with a stiff lecture, which would be his private inclination. Not by the letter of the law, you couldn't. There'd be the ridiculous technical charge, contributing to delinquency, and a hearing before a juvenile-court judge, and—probably—probation, after the stern lecture. And the odds were pretty damn high, thought Varallo sardonically, against the solemn judge's having gone to his marriage bed a virgin. Society promoted some funny rules and regulations.

There was also the fact that the scenes these boys would be getting into, with their parents and so on, could result in some unfortunate emotional tangles. Not that Varallo went along with the head doctors all the way, but a little of what they said was just common sense.

He sighed over his notes and looked up at the boys. "You've been

very cooperative, thanks. Now look—this is just my job. After all, I'm
human too. Having a little sense, I don't think you two have been committing any major crime with these girls. Maybe your parents will, I
don't know—I hope they'll be understanding. If we handled these things
the way I'd like to, I'd deliver a little lecture to you and that'd be that.
And come to that, would I have any right to lecture you at all? But—"
He went on and told them what he'd been thinking, frank and friendly,
and their expressions relaxed a little.

Nevertheless, they'd have a little ordeal to go through. He couldn't
help that. It wouldn't get into the papers, they protected kids these days
(in some cases he disapproved of that, but in this one it was just as
well), but there'd be a little gossip. He couldn't help that either. And
there was also another aspect. "Now," he said quietly, "I've got a few
more questions for you. About Paul Brandon . . ."

"But, Vic, do you think—*could* they have? Just because of that?"

"That's the hell of it," said Varallo. "They could have, very well. On
several counts. Teenagers—damn it, they're not on an even keel in life
yet. You know what I mean. Still in between, in most ways. Things that
aren't really very important look very important to them, and vice
versa. I don't know the families, but by the exhibition the Morehouses
especially put on, typical upper-middle-class conventional people." He
smiled. "Bob Emmett took a little more realistic view— Jerry won't
have as bad a time as Steve." Of course the parents, informed, had gone
up in sheets of flame. The Morehouses and Ellen Emmett, anyway.
Their boys couldn't have done anything bad like that, the police
were quite wrong, nice boys from good neighborhoods didn't get into
trouble—

Convinced, the Morehouses had eyed the miserable Steve grimly.
They were orthodox church people, originally from a small middle-west-
ern town. Ellen Emmett had burst into sobs and how-could-yous and
the usual "After the respectable bringing up you've had—" until interrupted by her husband, who was the grown-up edition of Jerry: a successful lawyer, a handsome lean man with an amused and cynical eye.

"Don't be a damn fool, Ellen," he'd said. "Social laws or any other
kind can't outlaw human nature. Don't want the boy to stay a baby all
his life, do you? What the hell, no harm done—you might say, a chip off
the old block," and he grinned. "I'm only sorry there has to be a little
legal fuss, but there it is. . . ."

"The point is," said Varallo, dangling string for Gideon to stalk,
"they weren't sure what awful punishment might result if their parents

knew. It's a funny age. A lot of their fear might have been fear of all the embarrassment—kids that age, physically mature, sure, but they haven't quite got used to the idea of sex yet, you know. I should say, kids from homes like this. Because that enters in too. The ones from the slum sections, the tough kids, they're adults at eighteen, they're cynical and experienced. But parents like the Morehouses, they keep them kids longer—sheltered. For whatever reason. They don't think of them as even physical adults at eighteen. So for one thing the parents would be a lot more upset about it—which the boys would know—and for another, boys like these would be more apt to be a little unstable—the immature reaction. Can you say? The first instinct, somebody knowing their secret, might have been—Steve, at least," he added to himself, "is the type to have an immediate physical reaction. Any threat to his security, hit it."

"A mess all right," said Laura, "if they did. What a dreadful thing, if it was one of them. Incredible. Do you— *Oh!*" She jerked upright. "It's a pro-baseball player or something, Vic, jumping around like this! I can't tell you how peculiar— I wish it'd stop. . . . Do you think Steve could have? That he did?"

"I don't know," said Varallo soberly. "I'm going to take a long hard look at him, *amante*. I hope not, but—"

"But," said O'Connor the next afternoon, "there's the same objection. Paul had known about it for the better part of three weeks. If he was going to talk, he'd have talked before."

"You haven't read Steve's statement," said Varallo. He'd been out all morning, seeing the other boys and getting through some of the red tape on this; this was the first chance they'd had to talk it over. "He told me all about it finally. Sounding nice and honest. Paul came home with Steve's kid brother Nicky that day, and while Nicky was in the bathroom Paul wandered into Steve's room and happened to overhear Steve and Jerry talking. You remember what the diary said—a ten-year-old not very sex-conscious, Paul was more concerned about the possibility of the whiskey-buying being something bad. Steve and Jerry were scared to death when he showed up and asked a couple of questions. They frankly admit they did all they could to scare the daylights out of him, make him keep quiet. Threatened to beat him up. Actually roughed him up a little. They thought he'd be too scared to tell. All right.

"But the effect of threats wears off. I asked Steve if he'd seen Paul recently, if he thought Paul was still scared of him, if he and Jerry were still afraid Paul might tell someone. He said he'd seen Paul that Friday, and he didn't know if Paul was still scared. He and Jerry looked at each other and shut up on the question of whether they were still afraid Paul might tell. So I think maybe they'd discussed it, and they were."

"Teenagers and a ten-year-old," said O'Connor. "I don't like this case." He grimaced. "Where were they on Saturday?"

"I only know where they say they were," said Varallo. "And I don't like it much either, Charles. They say they were down at the beach—Santa Monica—with two other boys, Rodney Hart and Bruce Lyon, and didn't get back to Glendale until seven o'clock. Very reluctantly, when I pressed them, they admitted that these other boys knew about the girls and in fact they'd got Greta and Rose to fix up a date for them with a couple of other girls, only it hadn't come off yet. So—*è chiara!*—you see how it could have been. One of them or both of them could have got very worried about Paul, decided to get rid of him for safety's sake, and asked the other boys to back up him—or them—saying they were meeting the girls."

"But what a motive—"

"I'll tell you why, though I hate to think so, Steve is our top suspect. Just possibly Steve and Jerry together. Kids that age aren't thinking quite straight about emotions, Charles. Aren't feeling quite straight. As I said to Laura, little things look very important, and vice versa. They're apt to go off half-cocked, for what looks like very small reason to an adult mind—and at the same time, they're smart enough to make quite good plans. In a funny kind of way, if I read them right and remember myself at eighteen, they haven't quite jelled. And because of that, they can be frighteningly cold-blooded."

"Yeah," said O'Connor absently. "That's all very true. If so, my God, what a thing . . . Just for *that*. It's a damn funny thing, you hear a lot of talk these days about moral standards getting lowered, but, my God, when *I* was eighteen nobody thought anything about a thing like that—young fellow that age picking up an easy lay. Live and let live. Of course I will say I didn't live in an upper-class part of town."

Varallo laughed. "I know. Neither did I. Maybe the lower classes take a more realistic view of these things? But anyway, there it is. . . . I saw Rodney and Bruce, sure. They swear Steve and Jerry were with them all day. I don't know whether they'd go on swearing if they knew we were suspecting Steve and/or Jerry of murder. If I came out with that, it'd be letting the whole story out. What's called an impasse—I thought I'd check with you. Of course, what we've said to a couple of people has told them what we suspect, but they have good reasons not to talk. The boys would spread it, and we'd have the press on our necks. Do we want that?"

"The publicity might help," said O'Connor, trickling smoke through closed lips. "We'll have to, sooner or later, Vic. I want to question Wilma Starke again, too. . . . Nobody will feel very sympathetic to Paul's killer. I think you'd better ask the boys. Do you think they're good enough friends that they'd alibi the other kids for murder?"

"I'd say no," said Varallo, "except for the fact that who knows what kids that age will do? Their emotional reactions aren't established. Reason they *can* be cold-blooded on occasion. And, without going all Freudian on you, I'd remind you that the motive goes straight back to a rather primal instinct, sexual gratification."

"Um," said O'Connor. "Also a point." He looked resentful suddenly. "This damn case. Getting me involved with a schoolteacher, of all things. Damn it, she's not my type at all, why I—"

Varallo laughed and said sooner or later every man met Nemesis. "You go to hell," said O'Connor darkly. "Well, there's a little work to do on this. Fortunately, some of it the Hollywood boys are doing for us." Varallo had passed on the girls' names to the Hollywood boys yesterday afternoon; they'd pick up the girls and suitably chastise the motel manager and the liquor dealer.

And Varallo would go to question Rodney and Bruce again, let out the news of the murder, and see whether they changed their stories.

"But you know, Charles," he said, getting up, "there's something else in my mind now. Because these little secrets that Paul knew—they didn't really interest him very much, he hadn't talked about them. They were adult secrets, to do with matters Paul didn't find very interesting—as we said when we came across them in the diary, he didn't have any emotional understanding of why Keith was upset at his knowing about the outside girl friend—or Bradley, if Bradley knew—or Steve and Jerry. We know he didn't talk about them in the two or three weeks he'd known. He was a lot more interested, by the diary, in the new house being built over on Cordova, and the Kaufmans' puppies, and the Bicknells' new furniture."

"Bicknell," said O'Connor. "Yes. I wonder if that boy— But they couldn't be sure he wouldn't tell, casually."

"No. But considering what we know now," said Varallo, for several men had been out gathering in routine details, "I do wonder—"

Bradley had an alibi. His wife at her hen party, he had taken himself

out to dinner at an expensive restaurant up on Foothill. Had had several drinks, a very lavish dinner, and returned home about eight-thirty.
He'd been alone then until eleven, but that didn't matter; at the crucial
time of Paul's murder he was alibied.

Keith was not; but Varallo really didn't see Keith, all front, doing
that singularly cold-blooded murder.

He too wanted to confront Wilma Starke again, who'd been so vindictive about Paul; show her that coin, get her reactions. She wasn't
alibied either; and a woman—but for sufficient reason (and these compulsive gamblers, like other addicts, were fanatics; and with a tool of
some kind—

They knew now what the coin was, which was interesting but not immediately suggestive. The L.A. numismatist said it was indeed worth a
little something. It was a coin minted by the German province of Brunswick about 1685, a silver quadruple "Mining" *taler*. It was in fair condition and would be an interesting addition to any collection.

Somebody's lucky talisman? Somebody who had ancestors coming
from Brunswick?

If those other boys persisted in alibiing Steve and Jerry— And quite
true, Alice Keith had inherited a nice little piece of change; the Keiths
probably could not live quite so well on just what Keith earned; but
would she have broken finally with Keith just over one girl friend? Unless the girl friend was the latest of a long procession, and Alice Keith
had got fed up? Also true, Keith was weak; and that was often an ear-
mark of murderers. All the same—

Varallo thought (much as he disliked the idea) that Steve was the
hottest suspect they'd turned up. But there was also this other idea.

"I wonder," he said, "if what we've got from the diary are dead
leads, Charles. If he never got a chance to write down in the diary a
lead to what the real motive was. Whether it was something Paul had
seen or heard just that Saturday afternoon—something dangerous to
somebody, a lot more so than the girl friends—that constituted the motive. So he had to be—shut up."

"That could be too," said O'Connor. "And how the hell can we find
out what it was, if so? Then there's the boy named Gordon— Katy
thinks he knows something—"

"Katy? Talk about fast workers."

"Mind your own business. Yes. See what turns up. Try to work back
over his route that afternoon, where he'd been?"

"I think so," said Varallo. "And I haven't seen that vet, ask him how far the kitten might have got. Picayune little thing, but—" He shook his head. "I'd like to turn up another hot suspect besides Steve. It's a nasty enough case as it is, but adding in a basically nice honest teenager— *Diavolo!*"

CHAPTER 11

"Mrs. Starke, have you ever seen this before?" Varallo extended his palm, the Brunswick coin on it.

"No, why, what is it?" A little thin intense woman, O'Connor had described her graphically. She was nervous and frightened; beside her, her husband looked grim. But so far as Varallo could judge, she didn't react to the sight of the coin. He put it away.

O'Connor asked her conversationally, "When you saw Paul Brandon on Saturday, Mrs. Starke, did he mention this little, um, secret between you?"

She pushed back wisps of dark hair, her mouth working; it was an extraordinarily mobile face, not unpretty, but her neuroticism had spoiled any attraction she'd once had. Nervously she contorted her mouth as she talked, and her hair was uncared-for, her dress not clean, with buttons missing from it. "That boy—that damned boy! I knew he'd let it out—always nosing around, he was, not *normal*— Why should he care what I do? Why should anybody care? You'd think I'd done something *immoral*— Everybody likes to—"

"Control yourself, Wilma," said her husband sharply. He looked at O'Connor and Varallo with weary resignation. "Since you know so much about us as it is— I've arranged to take my vacation now, until we can settle this some way. I'm trying to persuade her to see a psychiatrist."

"As if I was *crazy!* You're the one who's—"

"I thought," said Starke, "that you boys were pretty good at keeping these joints down, in a county as clean as this. But she usually manages to find one—or, of course, if she can't, there're always the private parties. But we've been over all that." He sounded detached; Varallo thought he wouldn't stay by Wilma much longer. Who could blame him? This kind impossible to cure; and she'd probably lost all her attraction for him.

"Don't talk about me like that! Don't— Ken, oh, please, darling, don't be so unkind, don't sound so— Please, give me another chance, darling, I swear I'll never do it again, I'll promise on anything you want me to, only don't leave me, please, Ken—another chance—" She was sobbing, clutching at him wildly.

"Control yourself!" he snapped, flushing at this public display. "We'll discuss that in private. The officers have some questions to ask you, they said— Pull yourself together, for God's sake, and try to answer them sensibly. When you saw the Brandon boy on Saturday, did he—" And then he looked at O'Connor and asked curiously, "Why?"

O'Connor said unemphatically, "Because it wasn't an accident, Mr. Starke—the boy was murdered."

"Oh, my God!" said Starke blankly. "My God—a *kid*—who could—?"

"*Murdered!*" said Wilma Starke in a high, wild voice. She went greenish-white, staring, licking her pale lips. "Murdered—you think *I*—" And she began to scream, "I didn't, I didn't! I never did such a— I couldn't— Stupid damn cops, get out of here, leave me alone, I didn't—" She trailed off into incoherent obscenities, and Starke slapped her across the face. She stopped screaming and sank down on the couch sobbing uncontrollably.

"Sorry," said Starke. He looked white himself, and was breathing hard; he passed a hand across his face. "I can't take many more of these scenes," he said as if to himself. "Damn it. . . . My God, that poor boy, what was he, only ten? Who'd want to murder a—? But if you are thinking about Wilma in connection with it, lieutenant, I think you can write that idea off. She's neurotic, yes, but I really don't think she's capable of murder, you know. Of murdering a child, for God's sake. I suppose you're thinking she had a motive—well, yes, of sorts. But not a big enough—"

"You never know what'll be enough," said O'Connor, looking at the disheveled sobbing woman with distaste. "Well, we won't get anything out of her in that state, obviously." He looked at Starke. "When she calms down a little, will you try to find out what exchange there was between her and the boy? Or what she says it was."

"Yes, of course." He accompanied them to the door. "What a hell of a thing. How did you find out it was murder? Everybody took it for granted, a thing like that—"

"Oh, various little things showed up," said O'Connor vaguely.

"I suppose you can't answer questions. . . . Excuse me, but could you—" He looked at Varallo. "You men run across—the ones like Wilma, don't you?"

"Only now and then. You've got a little situation there."

"You tell me nothing," said Starke. He looked tired. "She makes these promises, never again, but of course it doesn't mean a damn thing. Do they ever get over it? Would psychiatric treatment help? Hell, it doesn't sound like much of anything, not anywhere near so bad as alcoholism or drug addiction, but it can be twice as—demoralizing."

"So it can," said Varallo. "In my experience, Mr. Starke, it's just part of the personality, for some reason, and it can't be amputated any more than a tendency to freckles."

"I see," said Starke. "Well. This boy. Have you thought about that fellow who—was here that day? I gather the proprietor of the joint, collecting a back debt—"

"And passing on his new address," said O'Connor. "Yes."

"Because, if he knew—she may have told him the boy knew—"

"It's pretty farfetched, for this reason and that," said O'Connor. "Thanks very much, Mr. Starke."

"Well, I suppose you know your own business," said Starke, and shut the door.

Faro Joe, snugly lodged in the new jail, was pretty farfetched when it came to Paul's murder because the killer almost certainly had been someone who knew Paul, someone up in that area. Wilma could have passed on information, yes, but the boy wasn't that much threat to Faro Joe; the boy didn't know there was an illegal aspect to her secret, didn't know the address of the joint. And like all pro gamblers, Faro Joe was utterly nonviolent and harmless personally.

"What about our Wilma?" Varallo asked O'Connor.

"What about her?" O'Connor shrugged. "I don't know. In a way, I can see her doing it, Vic. We talk about motive and what's enough motive. Well, the little things the boy knew—if he did come out with them, easy to say a ten-year-old's lying or imagining things. I think what happened here is that somebody lost his temper for a minute, struck out in sudden rage—and got stuck with a murder. And I can see Wilma doing that. For some reason lashing out at the boy, knocking him down against a table or something. And then seeing he was badly hurt, and thinking, a chance to be rid of him for good. She knew she had the time— Starke had called to say he'd be late."

"Two things," said Varallo. "Would she have had the strength?"

"For sufficient reason, she could have. People find they can do all sorts of things in an emergency. I remember," said O'Connor, "when the Fairlane Hotel caught fire in fifty-six, one old man carried a steamer trunk down three flights of stairs. Full, too—the trunk, I mean. Ordinarily he couldn't have lifted it. It's the extra adrenalin."

"I've studied biology too. Second, has she got the brains and control to have carried out that plan? A fool of a woman, going off half-cocked at a word."

"That's so. Well, we just can't say, can we? And how do we prove it yes or no?"

"That's the snag," agreed Varallo. They got into the car.

Rodney Hart and Bruce Lyon stuck to their story, as did Steve and Jerry: they had all been at the beach together Saturday afternoon. . . . "*Murder?* That little *kid?* Who'd do a thing like that?" Identical reactions. The double-take, and, "You think *Steve* or *Jerry*— They wouldn't do a thing like that! Honest— Well, sure, none of us wanted our folks to know, but— Hell, our own business, but— They never did!"

And by four that Thursday afternoon, three hours after Varallo and O'Connor had seen the Starkes, an excited reporter from the *News-Press* was at headquarters: "Listen, boys, what's this about a murder? Murder of a kid? It's an exclusive, friend of mine knows somebody knows somebody who has this high-school kid, and he said one of the kid's pals called—"

"Publicity," said O'Connor thoughtfully, after he'd given the *News-Press* man a story; and he called the L.A. *Times,* the *Herald,* and the Hollywood *Citizen.* A good many of the people in Paul's neighborhood wouldn't take the local paper but one of the L.A. sheets. Let it out—it might jog a few memories.

From what they had already, and the little more Wayne and Forbes had gleaned yesterday and today, they had pieced together Paul's itinerary that Saturday afternoon fairly well. He'd left home after lunch, at about one-twenty—all morning he'd been down at the civic swimming pool, with his junior swimming class. He'd gone first to see Mrs. Knox, to see if she wanted him to go to the grocery for her as she sometimes did on Saturdays. She had given him a small shopping list and the money, and he must have gone home for his bicycle, for Randy Latour had seen him at about a quarter of two, riding down Mountain. (Mrs. Brandon had gone out in her own car, immediately after he'd left, for an appointment at a beauty salon; she didn't get home until three-fifteen.)

One of the checkers at the Country Squire Market on Verdugo re-membered Paul passing through his stand at about two-twenty— "Or it might've been five minutes later, I was watching the time on account my break's at two-thirty, see." By a quarter of three Paul had delivered the groceries to Mrs. Knox, and leaving his bicycle at home had set off for the Bradleys', a couple of blocks beyond his own home on Hillcroft. He mowed the Bradleys' lawn on Saturday afternoons, the Rieglers' on Wednesdays after school. He used the Bradleys' lawn mower; it took him only about half an hour, because they just had a strip in front, not much more in back. Mrs. Bradley paid him a dollar and offered him a glass of lemonade, but he said he had to get back to Mrs. Knox's, he'd promised to find homes for her kittens and he wanted to get busy on that.

He didn't press a kitten on Mrs. Bradley; the Bradleys had a poodle.

He went back to Mrs. Knox's house and took the male black-and-white kitten, and went up to the Williamsons' on Harrington Road. Mrs. Williamson liked Paul, and liked cats, and she fell in love with the kitten and said she'd keep it. Paul left there about four o'clock, and got to the Starkes' house over on Mountain two blocks down about five or ten minutes later. Wilma Starke had told them (before she was further involved in the case by Paul's diary) that he'd asked her if she'd like a kitten.

"I told him I loathe cats," she'd said rapidly. "I'd as soon keep a snake, and he said he didn't think I would, he'd just stopped to ask just in case—and he went off, and that's the last I saw of him—little nosy parker, not a nice boy at all, he—"

About four-thirty he was back at Mrs. Knox's, to pick up the female black-and-white kitten. He'd stayed ten or fifteen minutes, she said, tell-ing her what a nice home the other one would have, the Williamsons were nice kind people and crazy about cats. He'd said he was going to show this kitten to Mrs. Riegler, and of course that was where he had ended up, about five o'clock. As they knew from Mrs. Riegler, he'd tried to persuade her to take the kitten, but there were Mr. Riegler's al-lergies, and she'd refused. "I didn't see which way he went," she'd said on being asked. "I had to get dinner started, I went into the house just as he was leaving."

And that was the last glimpse they had of him. About five-fifteen, there in front of the Riegler garage, the kitten in his arms. Nobody admitted to seeing him after that. And not very long after that—within the next half hour—he got the killing blow.

On his way to take the kitten back to Mrs. Knox? His quickest route would have been straight down Rosemount to Sinaloa, and down two blocks to her house. Or down to Mountain, down that to Sinaloa.

The kitten—frightened and hurt—found some two hours later over on Cordova, a block down from Carmen, two from Rosemount, two from Sinaloa in the other direction.

They had thought they had leads—suggested motives—but did the motives amount to anything? Would those boys go on backing up a fake alibi for Steve Morehouse when they knew it was murder? Varallo didn't think so. Wilma? It was possible, damn it, and that was all you could say.

Or—X? In the very short space of time between five-fifteen and five-forty-five, had Paul inadvertently stumbled across some new, more dangerous secret, and so had to be silenced?

He would have had time, Varallo reflected—he would just have had time, to show the kitten to someone else before going home: if the someone else lived close to where he was, or on his way back to Mrs. Knox's. . . . And Paul had been such a nice obliging boy, anxious to help out Mrs. Knox by finding good homes for her kittens.

Well.

Varallo sighed over the detailed reports. It was still all up in the air. See Steve Morehouse again, try to get a better impression of him, lean on him a little and see if anything emerged. . . . Would he get anything out of the vet except personal opinion?

They had other cases on hand, and just so many men to work them. He glanced over reports that had come in just today; he hadn't been in the office since checking in. All negative on the hit-and-run. The school vandals, who had obligingly left a few prints on the Hoover High job, had left a couple of the same prints last night when they visited Burbank High, and the Burbank boys, on discovering it, were understandably annoyed. Wayne had left a note: "Sgt. Fremm says tell us their own troublemakers can raise enough hell, why don't we keep ours at home?" Varallo grinned. Nothing had showed from any pawnbroker on the stolen office equipment. Well, something eventually should: kids from a town like this wouldn't know where to locate a crooked pawnbroker.

They might be out-of-towners, of course. But it wasn't likely; for some reason, school vandals raided their hometown schools mostly.

There was another flier from the FBI. Attention all peace officers. One of the Armagast kidnapers was now definitely known to be in California. John Newhall. They evidently hadn't got much on him yet, for there were no vital statistics—just a vague description. A medium-sized dark man in the late thirties. How many men in California would that fit? Hell, thought Varallo, it fitted several men he knew on this force. That was a tough one all right, when even the Feds didn't know more after three months' work on it. . . .

The inside phone rang and he picked it up. "Varallo."

"Say, Vic," said Sergeant Dick downstairs. "I've got a guy on the phone who just might have a little something for you on that hit-and-run. You want to talk to him or shall I just take it down?"

"I'll hear him. We can use something on that one!"

CHAPTER 12

Varallo lit a cigarette one-handed, waiting. In a moment he heard a man's voice, full of suppressed excitement but outwardly cool, say, "This is John Howerton, sir, excuse me, what name did the other officer say, Var—"

"Detective Varallo, Mr. Howerton. I understand you think you've got a lead for us on this hit-and-run?"

"I don't *know,* see," said Howerton. "It just looked funny, and just in case I thought we'd better tell you. I've got Bill Bergman right here beside me, to tell you— Excuse me, I'd better tell you from the start— See, I've got the Dodge agency in Pasadena. Two-twenty-four Orange Grove, Howerton Dodge. And when Bill told me—well, we both read the papers, you know. And that flier you sent— It just looked funny, because not many people these days try to do their own major repairs. You know? Except maybe the hot-rod kids always tinkering around. And Bill says he looked like an office-type. Hell, I'm getting this all backwards, sorry—tell it straight—"

"Please, Mr. Howerton," said Varallo, reaching for a pencil.

"Well, a couple of days ago this fellow came into our garage, and Bill Bergman waited on him. He said he wanted a headlight replacement—whole installation—for a fifty-seven custom sedan. Said he'd do the installing himself. Which struck Bill as a little funny, because it's not very usual for a customer to do that kind of work himself. Little things, like—oh, new rubber on the windshield wipers, or like that, sure, but a fairly big repair job like a whole new headlight— But anyway, Bill told him he'd have to order it, and said it wasn't just such an easy job for somebody not a mechanic, and wouldn't he prefer—you know the song and dance."

"Yes. And?"

"Well, not a hope. Fellow just said, order it for him. So Bill did, and said it'd probably come through today, which it did, and the fellow came in to pick it up about half an hour ago. But meanwhile, Bill had done some thinking on it, and told me, and of course we'd both seen this flier you sent out—that hit-and-run car had a smashed headlight among other things, medium-sized car—and, well, it just occurred to both of us, it *could* be, you know. Could be the fellow's figuring on fixing up the car himself, in private, to—"

"It could very well be," said Varallo. "Hell, and I suppose all you can give us is a description."

"Little more than that," said Howerton. "I think we've nailed him as your boy, all right. Which doesn't help you catch him, but I think you'll be interested. We talked it over, see, Bill and I. And when this fellow came in to collect the order, about half an hour ago the way I say, Bill asked him to sign for it. We don't usually, of course, but he made out it was regulations or something."

"Very nice," said Varallo. "So if we can ever pin down a suspect, we'll have a handwriting sample. What'd he put down?"

"Well, that's the clincher," said Howerton. "He called himself J. Reising, but he also put down a nonexistent address— Bill asked for that too. He put down two-eleven Bracey Street, L.A. We looked it up— no Bracey Street in the county."

"I'll be damned, very nice indeed," said Varallo. A little something. "It looks like our boy."

"Well, that's what we thought. Now, I never laid eyes on him myself, I was out with a customer when he came in both times, but Bill can give you a good description—"

"So let me talk to Bill, please," said Varallo.

"Sure." And a moment later another voice came on the wire. "Bergman here, sir. I took a real good look at him the second time, because by then Mr. Howerton and I had started wondering, you get me. He's about my height, five-nine, a little bit more. Kind of dark. I'd say about forty-five. Dark hair going gray on the sides. Dark eyes. He looks—oh, like one of these worrybird types, got a lot of deep lines in his face, sort of bitter and, well, worried. And both times he was in he was wearing a dark gray suit, white shirt and tie—like an office man of some kind, and—"

Suddenly Varallo's mind made a lightning leap from one place to another. Call it inspiration, intuition, anything you pleased—just, suddenly in one piece he saw it, clear and plain. He dropped his cigarette and said, *"Che dice? Diavolo!* Wait a minute—wait a minute, now—"

J. Reising.

"What?" Bergman was saying.

"Listen, Mr. Bergman—" Varallo rescued his cigarette—"would you recognize him? You can identify him?"

"Oh, sure, easy. Know him again anywhere."

"Benissimo! Come to Papa, friend, right away, *all'istante, immediatamente,* and I'll take you to look at somebody. O.K.?"

"You got a line on him just from what he looks like?" asked Bergman, excited. "Sure! Sure, I'll be right over, sir—"

Varallo put the phone down. What the *hell,* he thought. A line. Could it be? Was he counting too much on just a wild hunch?

A line, maybe, on two problems, not just one.

J. Reising.

John Riegler.

The description certainly matched damn close. That didn't really say anything, but—

Riegler hammering metal behind a closed garage door.

Mrs. Riegler artlessly saying something about the very spot you're standing on now, heard Mr. Riegler back here and—

Paul Brandon, stumbling on the guilty party in a manslaughter case? That hit-and-run—if it had been Riegler, he could be put away on a heavy charge, maybe a seven-to-ten if he got a tough judge. Talk about motive. A very nice motive.

If this wasn't just a brainstorm—

"You might as well answer me, Gordon. We're going to stay right here until the one o'clock bell, and I can be just as stubborn as you can."

Gordon sat there, head down, staring at the dusty ground. He felt resentful and worried. Why'd she keep *at* him like this? Why'd she suspect him? She couldn't have any real reason, he'd been careful all the time, just like the Man said he should act. Never give nothing away.

Kind of exciting— But since that awful thing had happened, Paul, he'd been feeling worse and worse. Mixed up, like. He felt right now like he hated this school and this teacher ten times as bad as he'd ever hated any school or teacher, and that was really saying something. She was all the time picking on him, and he couldn't get away from her. Because he couldn't do like before, like he mostly always had about school, just not go. Because they were keeping a check on him now, *making* him go every single day— He sat there seething with sullen hate and fear.

And the other kids—it wasn't *natural*, it was funny. He hadn't made any friends here, it was like the other kids here thought *he* was funny and didn't want to take up with him. The whole day just plain hell— *school*—because she kept picking on him, he didn't know this, he couldn't do that—as if it *mattered,* this dumb history and reading and the fractions! He had to do *something* besides sit there, so he was all the time in trouble—just for sticking out a foot to trip Bob or something like that—these damn stuck-up kids, the way they acted to him—

He'd never felt so alone and miserable and scared in all his life.

"Gordon—"

She'd cornered him here sitting at one of the outside tables, just finished with his lunch. He had fifty cents a day, buy lunch at the school cafeteria. A couple of times he'd sat down at a table with Randy Latour and Kevin Crandall and other guys in his grade, but they'd either pretended he wasn't there or called him silly names and said to go away. So now he just sat by himself.

Paul had been different. He guessed Paul had liked him O.K. Gordon had just tagged onto Paul because Paul let him, the only one who did; but now he missed him something terrible, like they'd been best pals since they were babies.

Paul, down in that hole—

And afterward, the Man so mad and even a little scared because he'd lost that thing— "Damn it, my lucky piece! God, I never been without it —got to get it back, wherever the hell I—damn it to hell—"

But later, when nothing bad had happened, he'd stopped being so worried.

"Gordon, look at me. Answer me, please." She put a hand on his shoulder. "I'm sure you know something about Paul. I don't know why you're lying about it, maybe you're frightened that whoever did that to Paul would know you had told and—hurt you? But, you know, Gordon, policemen these days are honest, brave men and they have all sorts of— of scientific things to help them— They wouldn't let anything bad happen to you. And it's the duty of anyone honest and—and on the right side, to help the police. You know that, Gordon."

"I don't know nothing about Paul," he repeated dully.

She sighed. "I want you to tell me what you did last Saturday, please."

"Nothing much. Just fooled around." Why couldn't she let him *alone?*

"What did you do after breakfast?"

If he told her, maybe she'd shut up and go away. Dumb old teacher. Dumb old school. "I just went out. Went and watched the men working on that new house. And the men in the street."

"How long?"

"I guess till noon and they stopped. I went home and had lunch. And the men working in the street came back but the carpenters didn't, and I—and I—then I saw Randy and Kevin and Bob and they were going to practice football in that empty lot and I went too."

"And you played football?"

"For a while and then Kevin said it was too hot and they were going to his house and I thought I'd go too but they said—they didn't want me to— I didn't care! Damn silly stuck-up kids—"

"You mustn't swear, Gordon. So what did you do then?"

"I—just watched the men in the street awhile, and then—and then I just went home. To study like you said I should," said Gordon, with the sudden vague hope of pleasing her enough that she'd leave him alone.

"Oh, you did? Well, I hope that's true. And when did you go out again?"

"I never," he said breathlessly. "I stayed— I stayed home. Honest I did. Studying. And then—and then my—dad came home—" (*Oh, Dad!* he thought fiercely, if I could only tell Dad!)—"and we had supper and I went to bed— I don't know nothing else to tell you, you leave me alone!"

"Well," she said. "All right, thank you, Gordon. But— Oh, well," and she got up at last and went away.

Gordon just sat there, waiting for the bell to ring. When it did, he got up and trudged slowly back into the building, to Room 112, and sat down at his desk.

School all day. *Every* day. Because they made him, now. Before, ever since he'd been supposed to be in school, he'd got out of going most of the time, four days out of five. So he didn't know much about it, really. Just sit there, and all this dumb stuff he didn't know, couldn't make head or tail of. He felt so mixed up and terrible inside, and all the while more and more scared of the Man—

Teacher came in, and the tardy bell rang. She said they were going to do about history now, and which book to get out. Gordon fumbled listlessly under his desk and got out the blue one, and then he saw all the other kids had the red one out. The names looked kind of alike, one about the same sized name as the other. He got the other one out, but Nicky Morehouse across the aisle had noticed and grinned at him.

"Old dumb Gordon, can't even read the name of a book!" he said in a whisper.

It just wasn't natural. . . . The thought crossed Gordon's mind again, vaguely, that he might not feel quite so bad about having to go to school, shut up here all day, if he knew a little something about all this stuff. But the couple of times he'd really tried to follow what Teacher was saying, just for something to *do,* well, he couldn't very well. She'd say something like, "You remember from last year, when you learned about the Pilgrims," and gee, he didn't remember and what were Pilgrims anyway? And sooner or later she'd say, "Open your books to page—" And say they had ten minutes to read so much. And the other kids, most of them, would get all through while he was still trying to make out what the first line said. Sure, he knew how to *read* all right—only some letters he got mixed up, ones that looked a lot alike—and all these books had awful hard words in them, words he'd never heard of before. Well, so it was because he hadn't gone to school much, before—just when that truant officer had caught up to him— But he wasn't *dumb!* Resentfully he thought, Damn it, was every kid in this school a genius or something? It wasn't *fair.*

Mostly he'd stopped trying. But he couldn't help hearing Teacher. "Now who can tell us about how Virginia was settled? . . . Very well, Mary."

Some prissy girl across the room got up and started to talk. She knew all about it, whatever it was. He sat head down, looking blindly at the open book on his desk.

All of a sudden Teacher was saying his name. "Gordon! You're not paying attention."

"I am too," he said sullenly. All the time picking on him.

"Then suppose you tell us—it's right there on the page you're looking at—who was the leader of the Jamestown colony?"

He stared at the black lines of print without recognizing any word he could spell out. "I dunno," he said. All the other kids giggled.

"Gordon, just look at the book, please. The second paragraph."

He didn't know what a paragraph was. He didn't care—what the hell was all this dumb stuff, anyway? He tried to remember some names he'd heard lately when they were doing this history stuff, and clutched at the only one he could think of. He stammered, "A—a lady named Frances Drake, it was—"

And they all laughed. Laughed like he'd said the funniest thing they'd ever *heard*—all the other kids, laughing their heads off at him, and even Teacher smiling—

Damn them, damn them, damn them! If his dad was here, he'd sure tell them off—he'd—

Gordon had never hated anybody so much as he hated these Goddamn snobby kids and this nosy-parker teacher. He felt the hate filling him up inside so he was nothing but hate, nothing but— He screamed out at them, almost sobbing, "Goddamn all you bastards!" and he ran out of Room 112—had to get away from them, had to—

Had to get away . . .

The Man. Just as easy, kill Gordon too—if he did anything, said anything—

He was all alone with it. He'd never felt so alone in his life. He stood there at the end of the hall, shaking all over; and he put both hands over his mouth in involuntary gesture. Just keep quiet, keep quiet. The Man knew he wouldn't talk. It would be all right. Keep quiet, and act natural, that was all.

But the Man just didn't know how hard it was—everything here so *different*, and school all day—and the other kids—

Katharine watched Randy Latour and Kevin Crandall leave the room and wondered if she'd found out anything definite. She felt very troubled over Gordon. She wondered what the parents were like, if she should go and see them. If they were sympathetic, if he trusted them—if it was a good home environment—quite possibly the parents could persuade him to tell. If he knew anything; and maybe it was only a wild hunch, but she was convinced he did.

A puzzling boy. She didn't like being puzzled by her kids. She ought to be smarter than they were, after all.

She had an idea, knowing that the Bicknells had recently moved into this school district, that the father had just got promoted, something like that—that up to now they'd lived in a lower-income neighborhood. Not to be snobbish about it, but— Gordon's grammar slipped quite a lot; of course, boys this age, even with educated parents, came out with some atrocious grammar, but Gordon's was consistent. And boys from the kind of homes this district took in didn't often swear, at least out loud and in front of grownups. How the kids talked, what they said, reflected what they heard at home to a great extent.

She thought too that these days most boys this age hero-worshiped the cops. From what they saw on TV and so on. Maybe if a personable police officer sweet-talked him—

Personable. Well, at least you couldn't overlook him, thought Katharine to herself, and laughed.

She gathered up her bag and papers, went out to the parking lot for her car, and drove home to her apartment on Lorain Street. She shut the door behind her, put down her burdens, kicked off her shoes, and realized how hot she was. This climate! She went out to the kitchen and found enough coffee left from breakfast, broke out ice cubes, and came back to the living room with a tall glass of iced coffee. Stacked today's papers for correcting on the desk, and got to work. Have it off her mind.

But every now and then she found her glance straying to the telephone. . . . When she finished, with a groan of relief, and put all the papers back into the big manila envelope, she looked meditatively at the lone ice cube left dwindling in the glass, and took up the phone book, looked up the number, and dialed police headquarters. . . . "I'd like to speak to Lieutenant O'Connor, please."

About thirty seconds later his deep voice said impersonally, "O'Connor speaking," and Katharine wondered belatedly how to address him: this wolf in gorilla's clothing who so casually bestowed a silly nickname on her the first time—

"This is Katharine Mason, lieutenant, and I—"

"Now, Katy," he said. "Why so formal?"

"Well," she went on, bypassing that one temporarily, "I've been working on that boy. The one I told you about. I don't know that I've got anything very definite, but a little something. Not from him, but from a couple of other boys—about Paul too. And I thought I'd better ask you how you think we should handle it. I thought of going to see Gordon's parents—they might help a lot, if it's a good home atmosphere. But I don't know them at all. And then I thought, you know how most kids that age admire policemen—"

"Yes. Just a minute, we've just had something break here too—" He said, off the phone, "What's the time? Five-forty-five—oh, well, I'm not selfish, it was your little brainstorm, you can handle all the red tape on it."

Varallo said in the background, "Damn you, Charles, I won't get home until ten o'clock! And I haven't done any weeding in a good ten days, and that Goddamned aphis—"

"You and your roses," said O'Connor, and came back on the phone. "Katy? I'll pick you up in an hour for dinner. Hear what you have to tell me. O.K., see you," and he was off the phone before she could say yes or no.

Of all the nerve, thought Katharine crossly, banging the phone down. The most *impossible* man— If there was a type she detested, it was these autocratic males, ordering women around by natural right. This Irish *cop*. Just like that, no polite inquiry, If you aren't engaged this evening, or Would you like, et cetera.

Really. The bouncy little blondes, he said outrageously. And probably that kind went around saying, Yes, Charles, and No, Charles, and looking up worshipfully at the big strong he-man. Little idiots. He was welcome to them. The lot of them—and there probably had been a lot of them.

Damn the man, she thought. She went into the bedroom, undressed, and had a bath. Dressed except for the smoke-gray silk sheath that matched her eyes, she sat down to make up. Eying herself in the mirror with dissatisfaction, she reflected that she ought to drink malted milks or something: she hadn't any figure at all. They always said tall women showed off clothes better, but that was small consolation for feeling like a giantess, having to look down on half the men you knew.

She splashed on cologne generously, stepped into the dress and zipped it up, put on earrings and a bracelet. Reaching into the shoe bag for the gray lizard sandals, she stopped and said, "Damn." Three-inch heels, they'd make her top O'Connor by two inches. She put on the old black sandals with one-inch heels instead.

CHAPTER 13

The brainstorm had been a real fourteen-karat one.

John Riegler owned an independent drugstore down on Colorado; he was a licensed pharmacist. Varallo had taken Bergman, when he showed up, straight down to have a look at Riegler.

And Bergman had taken one look at the thin, dark, bitter-faced man behind the counter, counting out change to a fat female customer, and said, "That's the boy all right. Know him anywhere."

Varallo said contentedly, "Isn't that nice. All right, come on back to headquarters—"

"Aren't you going to arrest him?"

"Well," said Varallo, "the law is very testy about citizens' rights, you know. Red tape. There are a few formalities. You've got to make a statement, and I've got to get a warrant on him, and confront him with the evidence and ask him questions and so on—"

And, owing to O'Connor's unselfishness—prompted by a phone call from his schoolteacher, thought Varallo irritably—Varallo got all the red tape. Though at that, it was always gratifying to see a thing come unstuck like this. He called Laura to tell her he'd be late, and managed to snatch a hasty meal.

By eight he was ready to confront Riegler. He took Forbes and they went up to the Riegler house. . . .

"No," said Riegler. "No. It's a lie, the man's mistaken, that's all, I wouldn't do a thing like that, you're all wrong—" But it was automatic defiance. He had, hearing the charge and the questions, seeing the warrant, gone a curious gray color, and he was shaking like a man stricken with palsy. "No," he said. "No."

His wife just sat there staring, a pleasant-faced plump matron, seeing her pleasant humdrum life dissolve around her, un-understanding, re-fusing to accept what was happening. "Why, that just can't be, John would never— John, tell them—"

"We'd like to see your car, Mr. Riegler. It's a nineteen fifty-seven Custom Dodge, isn't it? Please take us out to your garage."

"No," he said in a high frightened voice. "No—"

"John, tell them, dear! They've got it all wrong. Just because you're trying to save a little money!" She was indignant, but under that lay un-comprehending fear. "People just don't *understand* how hard it is these days for small businessmen—all the taxes, and having to pay union wages—it isn't *fair!* Surely—you explain how it was, dear—he was run into at an intersection by one of these careless drivers—not *much* dam-age, but some, and a headlight—he was just trying to save a little money, do the repairs himself, weren't you, John? He's always been pretty handy about— *Tell* the officers how it was, dear—"

"A little accident nobody reported to the police," said Varallo. "Which by law— The garage, please, Mr. Riegler."

"Oh, my God!" said Riegler. "Oh, my God. I knew I wouldn't get away with it. My God, what a fool! But I didn't know she was hurt—that bad. I swear to God I didn't. It was only a second I lost control—over in a flash, and I—I swear to God, I didn't know what I was doing, everything went black, I was so scared—all I could see, oh, God, more money, more money— You don't *realize*—and the damn lease running out and they're upping the rent seventy bucks—I— *Oh, my God!*"

Varallo went out and looked at the car. The green '57 Custom Dodge sedan. Riegler would have cleaned it of any bloodstains, or thought he had—the lab boys were pretty smart at finding that kind of thing, in hid-den crevices; they'd have a look. Riegler had done some hammering, trying to straighten out a dent in the right fender. The new headlight in-stallation was lying on the work bench, still wrapped.

He went back to the living room. The nicely furnished, conventional living room of a nice respectable couple living in a good neighborhood. Riegler sat on the couch, head buried in his hands, and Forbes watched him. Mrs. Riegler sat opposite, staring at her husband.

"John wouldn't do a thing like that— John, you're not saying you did a thing like that—"

Varallo called up reinforcements. (O'Connor out on the town with his newest quarry, damn him.) They towed the car in for thorough ex-amination. They took Riegler in, booked him, printed him, took away his belt and pocketknife, locked him in a cell.

Varallo and Forbes sat in the big, bare, nearly deserted room of the Detective Bureau and drank coffee out of cardboard mugs. "What d'you think?" asked Forbes. "Did he?" He didn't mean the hit-and-run; that they had tied up, with Riegler's confession.

"I like it," said Varallo. "I like it a lot, Jeff. Because it's the best motive we've turned up."

"Is it, Vic? The thing just happened that morning—the kid didn't know there'd been a hit-and-run. Why should he think there was anything funny about Riegler working on his car?"

"We'll find out details. But I can see it. That might have been— Riegler had to put in regular hours at the store—his first chance to start cleaning up the car at all. There might still have been blood showing somewhere. And Paul wandered in everywhere. I can see him, hearing noises at the back, going down the drive, pushing open that side door to the garage all innocent, and maybe seeing blood on the car, blood-stained cloths Riegler had been using— You're going to say, so he didn't mention anything about it after Mrs. Riegler turned up. So all right, his mind was on the kitten, it wasn't until after she'd gone in the house that he said, What happened to your car, Mr. Riegler, or some other remark that showed Riegler—"

"Well, all right," said Forbes. "People do have accidents. Riegler could have told him the easy story he told his wife, and let it go at that —no reason to suppose the kid would ever hear about the hit-and-run, or link it up to him."

"It'd be in the papers, he could expect somebody to mention it in front of Paul. But also, don't forget, Jeff, he'd still be very nervous and scared about it himself. What's that line from the Bible?—*The wicked flee when no man pursueth.* I can see him, with Paul asking bright questions, lashing out more in fear than anger—and then—"

"I see what you mean," said Forbes. "That could be."

"Well." Varallo finished his coffee. "Nine-forty, damn it. But I think I'll go see him—ask him some questions about it. Soften him up, if possible . . . I get the feeling, he could be a nasty customer with his baser emotions aroused. This could be the answer—we'll do some work on it, anyway."

"Mr. Riegler, about last Saturday. When Paul Brandon came down the drive about five o'clock, were you in the garage working on your car?"

Riegler had been sitting on his cell cot, his head in his hands. Now he glanced up in dull surprise. "The boy? What's he— Yes, that's right."

"But I don't think you'd have heard him coming, if you were hammering on the fender. Did he come into the garage?"

"Why?" asked Riegler. "I don't— That was a tragedy, wasn't it? Only child. Seemed like a nice boy, and the Brandons— We were sorry." His tone was dull, emotionless.

"Did he come into the garage, hearing you in there?"

Riegler nodded. "I seem to remember— I looked up when I heard him say my name, and— Please tell me something. Do you think it'll be very bad? What am I likely to get? I— I really think I blacked out for a second, you know, wasn't really *responsible*—"

"It depends," said Varallo, "on what the charge is, Mr. Riegler. What were you doing when Paul came in?"

Riegler hesitated and then said unwillingly, "I—was going over that fender with a rag. Why, what's all this about—"

"What did you do when you saw the boy?"

"Well, naturally I—didn't want anybody looking at the car too close. I took his arm and sort of led him out with me—just naturally, you know, so he wouldn't see— I don't think he noticed anything, probably thought I was just washing the—"

"But it must have looked a little odd, if he'd thought about it, a man working on his car in a closed garage on a hot day. Did he say anything to you about it?"

"No," said Riegler, head down.

"All right. Now, when your wife went into the house Paul was still there, wasn't he?"

"There was a man asking about that the other day. I seem to remember the boy was just going off down the drive—"

"Was he, Mr. Riegler? Or did you go back to the garage and did he follow you? Did he notice the car and ask about the accident? You'd told your wife not to mention it because neither you nor the fellow who'd run into you had reported it to the police—too much trouble—so it was just as well to keep quiet about it. But you couldn't tell Paul Brandon that. And Paul got around, didn't he? He'd very likely mention it to a few people, just casually, because he wouldn't see any reason not to—poor Mr. Riegler had an accident with his car. And the news about that hit-and-run would be in the evening papers and the Sunday papers. If Paul didn't think there was anything odd in your working on the car in a closed garage, other people might."

"What—what are you talking about?" asked Riegler. He was looking bewildered and frightened. "I don't— I never saw the boy again, he—"

"Or maybe nobody would have thought much about it even if they knew—little accidents happen all the time—but in your first alarm you magnified the danger he represented and struck at him in panic. Is that how it was?"

"You're not making sense," said Riegler. "I hit the— That's not so— that's just crazy. Everybody knows what happened to Paul, he was fooling around down in that hole and there was a cave-in—"

"No," said Varallo. "You missed the newspapers today? It was a faked accident, Mr. Riegler. As maybe you very well know. The boy was murdered."

Riegler stared at him. "Murdered— My God, I don't believe— It's impossible, I— My God, you're trying to pin it on *me*? I couldn't— I never—"

"Your house is the last place we know he was. And he got a killing blow between then and half an hour later."

"Oh, Christ," whispered Riegler. "And I've been worrying over a manslaughter charge— Listen, all I can tell you is, no. I couldn't do a thing like that, any reason—a little boy! I never— It doesn't seem possible, the boy—"

"If he had seen and asked questions, you had quite a motive, Mr. Riegler. The manslaughter charge. A jail term. Maybe a damage suit. The probable loss of your pharmacist's license."

Blindly, silently, Riegler nodded agreement to all that. "But I didn't— How can I convince you? He didn't seem to notice anything—he didn't ask any questions. He was thinking about that kitten. He went off down the drive— I swear to God that's so. Oh, God, this can't be happening to me—"

Varallo went on asking questions, but all he got out of him after that were head shakes and a dully repeated, "He went off down the drive with the kitten and that was the last I saw of him."

He gave up and went home. They had put a seal on the garage doors; tomorrow a team of men would give that garage a very thorough going-over. If they found anything connected with Paul in it—with luck, something blood-stained and the blood his type—

Question Mrs. Riegler again. Had she actually seen the boy leave?

Varallo thought the chances were good that Riegler was the man they wanted. But the hell of it was, without more definite evidence they wouldn't have enough to charge him with Paul's murder. Moral certainty was one thing, evidence another.

But he couldn't forget Steve Morehouse either. He wanted to question Steve again too.

He was tired; it had been a long day. And another day when he hadn't had time to work around his roses. All the beds needed weeding, there was aphis all over Ulrich Brunner and the Condesa de Sástago, and it was time the lawn was cut. . . . Laura was waiting for him in the kitchen, having heard the car; she kissed him and said, "I suppose you had a sandwich at some hole in the wall. . . . I thought so. Like something now? There's some cold ham, and bless this packaged stuff, I can do some mashed potatoes to go with it in no time, and the leftover peas— And a nice long drink before? You look as if you could do with it."

"Probably give me indigestion at this hour, but I would indeed, *cara*."

"You take your drink into the living room and relax. I'll have it ready in ten minutes. . . . Yes, yes, I've been feeling fine."

O'Connor had taken Katharine to a restaurant in town; when they were settled over drinks he told her about Riegler. "Vic thinks he could be X for the boy too. It's the last place we know definitely the boy was, and if Riegler was afraid he suspected about the car—if the boy asked questions—he might have hit him in impulsive panic, and—"

"Well, I'm very sorry to upset any theories," said Katharine, "but maybe I've been doing Mr. Riegler a great favor. If that boy is anywhere near right about the time. You see—"

"What? What've you found out now, and how?" He scowled at her across the table.

"Well, in the first place I tried to get something out of this boy Gordon. I can't tell you why, but I think he does know something. He's a queer boy—different from any ten-year-old I've ever known. I don't know what to do about him, either— I mean just as his teacher. For one thing, I simply can't understand how he ever got into the fifth grade. In some school systems, where radically progressive methods are used, the kids are passed to higher grades automatically, whether they're really doing work on that level or not. On the theory, you know, that you'll do them some psychological harm by humiliating them, keeping them in an age group below their real one—"

"I have read a couple of books," said O'Connor.

"But we don't operate that way. In this school system, a child doesn't get promoted unless he's doing satisfactory work. In theory, we do try to—to sort them out, as it were. Separate the sheep from the goats, you know—the bright students from the mediocre. But at Verdugo at least, the last couple of years we haven't had enough teachers to do that. Mr. Harwell's very worried about it—you know how the population's been increasing, but they voted down the last school bonds. If we tried to run two classes for every grade—one for the bright children and one for the slower ones—it wouldn't be fair on the teachers, some of us would end up with classes of about fifty kids, and others with only about twenty. Which explains why I have both Kevin Crandall and Gordon in my class—and at that, I've got a class of thirty-nine, really too many. You can't possibly give them all individual attention. What happens is, you naturally have to give more attention to the backward ones, which isn't fair to the bright ones. Take that Crandall boy—he tests out nearly four years above his age level. But I have to gear the teaching to the pace of Johnny Keller and Linda Bays. And Gordon can't even do *that* kind of work."

"Shop talk," said O'Connor. "Get to the point, Katy."

"I *am*. So you can see how hard it is to get at that maddening boy, I've got to give you some background. He can hardly spell c-a-t cat. The first day of school, he couldn't even fill out his transferal form. He transferred to Verdugo from Glenoaks Elementary, so he had to fill out a form for our records—his past history, you might say, parents' names and so on. He just sat and stared at it, and when I came to look all he'd put down was his own name—and he'd misspelled his last name at that— and in the end I had to fill it out for him. He answered all the questions, he's bright enough in a way—knew his new address and where his father worked and so on—but what it comes down to, he just hasn't learned to read and write. Not beyond a very poor first-grade level. And of course, all the other schoolwork depends on that. It's no wonder he's bored and restless and gets into mischief—he probably can't make head or tail of what's going on half the time." Katharine broke off as the waitress came up to take their orders.

When she had gone, O'Connor said, "You're aiming for a point, you said?"

"You let me tell it my way, you big Irish ape," said Katharine with dignity. "You may be missing some of the subtler points, but I can't help that."

"Oh, we're real smart these days," said O'Connor with a grin.

"Heard of psychology and all these other newfangled things. All right, go on, go on."

"If you'll quit interrupting. But, while he was bad before the murder, he's deteriorated horribly just this past week. Last week, for instance, he *did* remember, on an arithmetic review, that ten and ten add up to twenty, and then this morning he made a mistake adding one to nine. I'm waiting to get his records from his old school—funny they haven't been sent by now. They usually are by the first month of a semester. And he's been a lot more subdued this week, hasn't got into nearly as much mischief. Of course, it could be just natural deterioration as the term goes on—he can't be feeling very happy. He hasn't made any friends here yet, the other kids think he's a queer one too and of course they laugh at him." She told him about Gordon's "lady named Frances Drake," and laughed herself, but sobered at once. "It could be that all this is just getting him down more. He's such a sullen, funny kid— Well, for instance, he was absent one day and showed up without a note, so I sent him to Mr. Harwell. And Mr. Harwell called Gordon's mother, and it turned out she'd taken him to the dentist. Now why couldn't he have told me that, or Mr. Harwell? But he just turned dumb—in the literal sense—and even more sullen than usual. Well! I tried to get something out of him, but he told me just as little as he could." Salad arrived and she began to eat automatically. "By what he said, he went home about four o'clock on Saturday and says he didn't go out again. And then I had another idea.

"It occurred to me that while we'd asked the boys who knew Paul about seeing him that day, we hadn't asked the ones he didn't go around with. The ones who'd know him, from class. But first I tried to check on Gordon. He said earlier he'd played with Randy Latour and Kevin Crandall. I asked them, and they said, sure, he'd tagged onto them, they hadn't asked him—don't like him. Later on they got rid of him by—boys that age, they can be little sadists!—just telling him they didn't want dumb old Gordon around, go home, kid. But when I asked whether they'd seen him later, Randy spoke up and said sure, when he was on his way home about five-thirty he saw Gordon walking up Mountain— probably going home too. You see?"

"Complicated though it is, I follow you," said O'Connor. "The question is, where? And if you eat all that rabbit food you won't have room for the steak."

"Oh, yes, I will. And before that, I took the last half hour of the day and delivered a little lecture. Reminded them of the awful thing that had happened to Paul—of course they've been talking about it all week, everybody liked Paul. . . . It still seems so incredible. . . . And I told them the police were still trying to find out exactly what had happened, and of course we all wanted to be good citizens and help our gallant police, and if any of them had seen Paul late that afternoon, would they please tell me? And, just like that, Johnny Keller raised his hand and said sure, he'd seen him. This," said Katharine, laying her fork tidily on her empty salad plate, "is the point I've been aiming for. Johnny Keller saw Paul at about five-thirty on Saturday afternoon, walking up Rosemount Avenue."

"Now I will be damned," said O'Connor. "Is he absolutely sure of the time? A kid that age?"

"I pressed him about that, of course. After all, a ten-year-old can tell time, and he's got a cheap wristwatch. So maybe it was fast or slow, and naturally he didn't look at it then. But he says when he got home it was a quarter of six and his mother scolded him for being late. And—I looked—he lives up on Imperial Drive, which by the map looks about fifteen minutes away, by bicycle, from where he saw Paul."

"Which was?"

"He thinks somewhere around the corner of Carmen."

"Oh. Did he notice whether Paul had the kitten?" The steaks arrived.

"No—apparently he just glanced at him across the street, saw who he was. He didn't know Paul too well, just from being in the same class. So by that, Paul *did* leave the Rieglers'—"

"Did he? This boy remember which way he was walking?"

"There I'm afraid I fail you," said Katharine, attacking her steak with gusto. "Johnny isn't one of my brighter pupils. I did think to ask him that, and he got confused, said first Paul was going the opposite way to him—which would be, I take it, toward Carmen or Cordova—and then said no, the same way, and finally said he didn't remember. Which is natural enough—he just noticed him casually. This is a very good steak."

"Isn't it," said O'Connor. "If I remember back right to the days when I was ten, I didn't have much time sense. Boy going any place, home or elsewhere, there's a certain amount of fooling around. Detours through empty lots and half-built houses. Aimless delays kicking a can along the gutter. So he had a wristwatch. He wasn't looking at it every minute. He could have seen Paul on his way from Mrs. Knox's toward the Rieglers', half an hour before, and lost track of time, and got home forty or forty-five minutes later instead of fifteen minutes."

"I don't know," said Katharine doubtfully. "It seems a long time to—to be wrong about, doesn't it? . . . They never give you enough butter. Just two little pats—"

O'Connor beckoned the waitress and ordered more butter. "For a ten-year-old to be wrong about? Well, I don't know. I don't know, Katy. I think we want to see this boy, sure. Try to pin him down . . . Hell and damnation, Riegler looks like such a hot suspect—but if this is so, it clears him provisionally. But is it so? And this other boy, this Gordon—"

"Yes," said Katharine. "I'm going to set up a meeting with his parents. I'd have to soon anyway, to discuss his school problems. I haven't met his mother yet, she didn't come to the first P.T.A. meeting. But I'll tell them privately that I have this hunch he knows something about Paul's death, and maybe they can persuade it out of him—if I'm right. At least he seems to have a very good relationship with his father. I remember one day—somehow, in connection with our basic productive economy—there'd been a little discussion of the kind of work the kids' fathers do, each one telling about it. Of course, the neighborhoods our district takes in, a lot of them are professional men, white-collar men, you know. . . . Do you want that last roll? Well, in that case . . . And when Gordon said his father was a mechanic at Lockheed, a couple of the other little monsters made a few snobbish remarks—funny how they pick up these attitudes that young. And Gordon was furious. He yelled out at them, how his dad was the best dad anybody ever had, no matter what anybody said, and so on. So I thought maybe Mr. Bicknell can work on him, get whatever's there to be got."

"Yes," said O'Connor. She looked up and found his dark gaze fastened on her. "Aren't you quite the little detective? This is all very interesting, but something else interests me a lot more, Katy. I noticed it Wednesday night, sure, but I just thought maybe you'd missed lunch. How the hell can you eat so much and stay so damned thin?"

Katharine sat back and laughed. "I know, it's awful. What they call the basic metabolism. I never gain a pound, and I know I'm underweight, but there it is. I can't help it, I'm sorry. Do they charge for extra butter?"

"If they do, it's almost worth it," said O'Connor. "I don't know what the *hell* got into me. I don't believe in wives working, and you'd be twice as expensive to feed as most females."

"Well, really—" said Katharine, trying to sound offended and feeling herself blushing. "About these boys," she added hurriedly, "I think—"

"Dessert, madam? The caramel cream pie is very nice today—"

"Oh, yes, that sounds good."

"Three times as expensive," said O'Connor sadly. "Just more coffee, please."

CHAPTER 14

News of the murder had broken in yesterday's and today's papers. Also the news of Riegler's arrest. The *Times* story pointed out significantly that the dead boy had last been seen at the Rieglers' house.

And they had had Harry Brandon calling in every day, of course—had they found any leads, did they have any suspects; but on Friday morning they got him in person. Incoherent with rage, shock, surprise. "By God, was it him, was it Riegler?—do you think it was him? Because he was scared Paul would— My God, John Riegler's in the same Masonic lodge with me— Oh, my God, if I thought— Beat it out of him if it was the last— Please tell me, for God's sake, was it? Just because he did that, didn't have the guts to—"

They tried to calm him down; when at last he collapsed, sobbing, they called an ambulance and then Mrs. Brandon.

And Varallo said to O'Connor, "I predicted at the start, the motive was a slight one. I'm not so sure now. It never looks slight to the murderer, of course. But—a bright ten-year-old—even if it was a real, bigger-than-life motive—could it ever be really enough? For Paul Brandon? Those poor damned people."

A crew was examining the Riegler garage inch by inch. More men were examining Riegler's car.

These school kids. O'Connor was going to see Johnny Keller some time today. Try to get some impression whether he was right about that time.

"I know," said O'Connor. "Riegler didn't react to that coin at all?"

"Not that I could tell—said he'd never seen it before." Varallo stood up. "I am going out on a wild-goose chase. Kill two birds with one stone."

"Oh? In which direction?"

"Laura, who knows about cats, tells me there's a thing called feline enteritis—very fatal, contagious disease. You think anything of cats, you get them inoculated against it. Three injections, two-week intervals, at four bucks apiece. So I'm going to take our intrepid Gideon for his first injection, to the Small Animal Hospital on Los Feliz, and ask the vet there about Gideon's sister. About how far she might have got on three legs after she was kicked."

"Oh," said O'Connor. "Only opinion. Piddling little thing."

"Sure. But it all adds up."

"Nice little cat," said the veterinary surgeon, patting Gideon's head. Gideon hissed at him indignantly. "Just hold him firmly on the table, please."

Varallo did his best to obey, discovering just how difficult it is to hold even a three-month-old kitten somewhere the kitten has no desire to stay. The doctor took a hypodermic needle out of the sterilizer and rummaged in the refrigerator in the corner of the surgery. Gideon squirmed and wriggled, and Varallo hung on to him desperately. The doctor came back to the table, grasped Gideon by the rump, pinching up a fold of skin, and jabbed in the needle. Gideon yelled and spat.

"Nice little cat," said the doctor. "Bring him back in a couple of weeks for the first booster shot."

Varallo tucked Gideon back into the stout cardboard box with the air holes bored in it and retied the rope around it. Gideon muttered vengefully inside the box and one striped paw was waved out an air hole, all claws extended. "By the way, doctor, while I'm here I wanted to ask you—" He explained the problem; the vet was interested.

"That kitten. A nice little girl—she's coming along nicely, be good as new in a few weeks. I see. You're asking me how far away she might have got. Well, it's very hard to say, you know."

"I realize that. Just an opinion—"

"Yes. We had a cat in recently who'd broken his shoulder falling out of a tree—people saw it, so the owner knew where it happened. He managed to get three blocks, to reach home. But that was a grown cat, who knew where home was. This was the first time the kitten had been away from its mother? Well, knowing something about cats, I don't think she'd have gone far. I think someone kicked her, as I said. She'd have been scared and confused, she'd probably have bolted blindly and run as far as she could, and then gone to ground in the nearest hiding place.

I don't think a kitten that young would have tried to get back to home and mother—wouldn't have known how to. But cats are funny, they do unexpected things."

"Well, thanks, anyway." Varallo paid the receptionist and carried Gideon back to the car. Gideon thrashed around in his box and continued to talk, probably telling Varallo what he thought of him for bringing an innocent helpless kitten to this strange place where perfect strangers with odd-smelling hands jabbed needles into him. "Never mind," said Varallo, "it's all over now and we'll soon be home." Gideon snarled, disbelieving him.

Well. The kitten found over on Cordova. The Rieglers' house was a good four blocks from there. Rather a long way for a kitten to bolt, on three legs?

And damn it, if that Keller boy was right about the time he'd seen Paul, it looked as if Paul had left the Rieglers'. And how to prove whether the boy was right or wrong?

Of course, the Morehouses lived on Sinaloa, a block down from where it crossed Rosemount: about a block and a half from where the kitten was found.

Steve Morehouse . . . "You be quiet," he said to Gideon. "We'll be home in ten minutes and you can tell Laura all about it. . . ."

Grant that Steve had the guts to do it, he could have. Varallo had worked it out, and asked questions.

Wherever he'd been that Saturday, he came in about seven, Mrs. Morehouse had confirmed. She was a large buxom woman with a plain face: no fads or frills about the Morehouse ménage. Morehouse senior was the treasurer of a big manufacturing outfit in L.A. and a pillar of the church. They were ultraconventional people, of very orthodox moral principles. "Mixed up with *police!*" Mrs. Morehouse had said indignantly. For a fat woman she had an oddly thin, cold voice. "We've certainly tried to raise him to be a decent honest boy, and then to find out *this*— Well, it's been a shock, I don't deny. But you can rest assured he'll be punished for it. *Well* punished . . . What? Well, why should you be asking— Oh, well, of course, you people can just barge in anywhere and ask whatever you like, and ordinary citizens can't complain. *What* did you say your name was? . . . Oh. Italian."

Varallo had maintained a polite smile with some difficulty. "Did you see Steve get out of Rodney Hart's car when he came home?"

"No, I can't say I did. It was a hot night, we was all out in the patio at the back. . . . What did he *do?* Well, really. I must say I can't see the point, but I suppose you've got some reason for asking besides annoying me just when we've had this terrible shock about Steve. I never did approve of high-school kids going out on dates, just children they are—it just puts ideas in their heads—and all these immoral movies they make nowadays—"

Varallo thought somebody ought to tell Mrs. Morehouse a few facts of life; but that wasn't his job.

"What was the question again? . . . Oh, well, I asked him if he wanted any dinner, but he said they'd stopped on the way home and had something. He just went into his room, to read or study or something. I guess to do some homework, because he had his door mostly shut—he says the TV and Nicky's phonograph bother him when he's studying."

"Mrs. Morehouse, will you think back and tell me when was the next time you saw Steve, after he'd gone to his room?"

"What *is* all this about, anyway? At least we know he wasn't doing anything bad *that* night. I must say. . . . Well, I guess it'd've been about ten o'clock when he went to the kitchen for a glass of milk. But why on earth—"

He had, he remembered, thanked her and in reply to her own questions tried to explain the legal procedure to come—this was down at headquarters when the parents had first been told. And Morehouse had come up from a sullen, scared Steve. He was a big florid man run to paunch; Varallo reflected that if he had abstained from the more obviously deadly sins he seemed to condone gluttony. But, by his authoritative voice and manner, a virile specimen; Varallo eyed him thoughtfully. "Come away from this place," he'd said, taking her by the arm and looking around the spanking-new modern premises of the police building distastefully. "We've a good deal to discuss. I most certainly never expected to be called to a place like this to be told that *my* son—*my son*—was a juvenile delinquent!"

"Scarcely that, Mr. Morehouse. After all, it's a natural—"

"It is no matter to me, officer, what *your* moral standards happen to be. I trust I know right from wrong."

"That's sometimes rather a hard line to draw, sir," said Varallo quietly.

Morehouse stared at him contemptuously. "I know there's a great deal of moral laxity these days. But I should expect to find the police somewhat more upright. At least we have you to thank for exposing this precious pair of—" He had had a row with Bob Emmett, half an hour before, about Emmett's cynical and good-humored acceptance of Jerry's enterprise, and wasn't in the best of moods. But his arrogant righteousness made Varallo mad.

He stood up, to top Morehouse by a couple of inches. He said, "Not to quarrel with your moral precepts, Mr. Morehouse, cops see a lot of human nature. Which is pretty similar from generation to generation. You might think back into your own past and remember a few incidents —and decide not to be so hard on Steve."

Morehouse had turned purple and gobbled at him. He shouldn't have said it. But he'd take a bet that old turkey-cock had tumbled a few girls before he walked up the aisle with his singularly plain bride. Another case of do as I say, not as I do; letter of the law. He felt sorry for Steve. . . .

But, so Steve *could* have done it. He could have planned it out. Getting very nervous about Paul's knowing, thought (kids that age sometimes peculiarly cold-blooded) he'd be better out of the way. He could have asked the other boys to back him up with an alibi, giving any handy excuse. The Morehouses being what they were, there were probably a number of things Steve was forbidden to do. He had gone off with those boys about noon; but they could have dropped him somewhere. And it needn't have been planned at all; in fact, that sounded more plausible, that it hadn't been. Because Varallo was inclined to go along with O'Connor on that, the blow had been struck in impulsive anger. Say that Steve had wanted to see a movie his parents disapproved of, something like that, and had been coming home from his little clandestine venture, maybe to meet the other boys at an arranged time and place, so it would seem he'd been with them all day. And he ran into Paul—Paul on his way back to Mrs. Knox's with the kitten. And—

But, on the street? Broad daylight? And where?

And then suddenly Varallo had thought, *Cordova Avenue.* That new house going up. Union rules, the workmen off on Saturday afternoons.

It could be as simple as that. And if it had been, would there be anything left to find—any little clue—when the men had been back at work for four, five days? Hell. But they'd take a look.

Steve, meeting Paul—Paul going somewhere, then, if it had been there, to show someone else the kitten. Steve, saying he wanted to talk to him privately, taking him into the deserted half-built house. And getting mad enough, or frightened enough, at something Paul said—

Afterward, having the further idea of making it look like an accident. He could have got out of his bedroom window—

Well. Something to think about. See Steve again . . .

Varallo delivered Gideon back home. Released, Gideon sat down and began to wash thoroughly, after giving Varallo a cold look.

During her lunch hour on Friday, Katharine looked up the Bicknells' number and dialed. She waited through four rings before the phone was answered. "Hello?"

"Mrs. Bicknell?"

"Why, yes."

"Mrs. Bicknell, this is Miss Mason, I'm Gordon's teacher. I'd like very much to discuss Gordon with you, his schoolwork and so on. He isn't going to pass this grade, you see, unless he starts doing a lot better. I'd like to talk it over with you and his father— I thought if I could come to see you, this evening if you're free—or tomorrow?"

"Oh—" said Mrs. Bicknell. She sounded alarmed and puzzled; she seemed to be breathing rather heavily. "What d'you mean exactly, Miss —Miss—"

"Mason."

"I don't get what you— Just because he isn't doing so good at school? I mean, it's nice of you, take so much interest—"

"Well, there are a couple of other aspects I'll explain when I see you. We try to give the children as much individual attention as we can, you know, and Gordon—well, he rather puzzles me. And I don't suppose this is the first time you've had one of his teachers talking to you, is it?"

"Well—" said Mrs. Bicknell. Katharine thought she didn't sound very intelligent. "Well, his father— I mean, he'll be kind of mad— You want to come by the house, see us?"

"If it wouldn't inconvenience you, please." The woman didn't seem to realize that that was a little unusual, a busy teacher taking the time to do that. Usually, the parents would be asked to come to the school.

"Oh. Well, I'm sorry, we got—we got people coming for dinner tonight. Maybe tomorrow night?"

"That's fine. About seven-thirty? Thank you, Mrs. Bicknell, I'll be there then."

Nothing showed up in Riegler's garage. There were several lengths of old clothesline in a corner which could have been used for tying up Paul, nothing outwardly to say they had been. But they'd be sent into the lab, for analysis of dust and so forth, to see whether some link emerged. There were a couple of bloodstained cloths, probably the ones

Riegler had used to clean up the car, nothing to do with Paul. And unfortunately Mrs. Waring, the hit-and-run victim, and Paul had had the same blood type.

Mrs. Riegler, gray-faced, blank-eyed—her nice conventional life in ruins—had yet retained some of her wits. The news out that Paul had been deliberately murdered, she saw the way their minds were working and was steadfastly maintaining that she'd seen Paul walk off down the drive. And who could say, lie or truth?

"John could never do a terrible thing like that—please, you've got to believe me— He loves children, he liked Paul, such a nice boy— John could *never*—"

"Mrs. Riegler," said O'Connor unemphatically, "last night you were saying that he could never do such a thing as run away from that accident. But he did."

She turned away blindly, crying, groping for a handkerchief.

It was an unproductive day.

Varallo went home at six, and after dinner spent an hour and a half over his roses. He sprayed generously, got almost half the back-yard beds weeded, and clipped off all the dead blossoms. Doubloons was drooping a little—no wonder, in the full sun all day, and the thermometer read 91 at seven-thirty. God, this climate. He gave Doubloons extra water and a little rose food. Chrysler Imperial was doing very well and had a few new buds to show him; Brandywine had aphis, damn it, but Chevy Chase was blooming cheerfully, in excellent health. His special favorite, the Duquesa de Peñeranda, had seven new buds. . . . He straightened from yanking out the last weeds at her feet, and grimaced. Why the hell he'd had to get involved with all these damned roses—

When it was too dark to work, he went in. He'd meant to see Steve Morehouse tonight, but he was too tired to concentrate on what might be a tricky questioning. What with the heat— He felt drained of mental energy as well as physical. He took a long cool shower, and simply clad in shorts made himself a stiffish brandy-and-soda, sat opposite Laura in the living room. Laura was browsing through the dictionary of names.

"It's difficult," she complained. "I suppose my own fault for marrying anybody named Varallo. It seems to call for a Latin name, but *I'm* not Latin—my mother's maiden name was O'Brien, after all—and I don't want a boy named Luigi or a girl named Maria."

"There's no law about it," Varallo pointed out. "Neither do I, actually. You can name him Aloysius or her Bridget if you want to. Not that I'd allow—"

"What revolting ideas you have," said Laura. "I suppose you're right, but it's not every ordinary name that seems to go with Varallo. Do you like Matthew?"

"Not much."

"Oh. What about Michael?"

"Well—"

"Yes, I know. Mike Varallo. Sounds like a gangster. We could fall back on John, but it's rather too ordinary. . . . Nicholas? I'm thinking seriously of just plain Mary for a girl."

"Very nice," said Varallo somnolently, and yawned. Gideon clawed up the chair, jumped into his lap, and sniffed interestedly at his drink. "You're starting young," said Varallo, laughing at him.

CHAPTER 15

Katharine pressed the doorbell of the Bicknell house, feeling very curious about Gordon's parents. It was exactly seven-thirty on Saturday evening.

Almost at once the door swung open, to reveal a plumpish dark woman of about thirty-five. "M-Miss Mason? Come right in, I'm Gordon's mother. It's real nice of you to take the trouble—"

"Not at all," said Katharine meaninglessly. Mrs. Bicknell was a little nervous. Typical ordinary housewife, not used to having many visitors, maybe even a little awed by an educated teacher? She wasn't bad-looking, if a trifle overweight; and she'd taken trouble with her makeup, her clothes. She wore a plain black crepe dress, a discreet costume brooch at one shoulder, matching earrings.

"Come right in—this is Gordon's father— Miss Mason, Bert—"

"Nice to meet you, Miss Mason." He wasn't bad-looking either, neat in clean sports shirt and slacks; his handshake was firm, and his smile made him almost handsome, showing even white teeth. "Sit down, won't you?" Gordon wasn't in evidence, which was just as well. "Now, we're a little puzzled at what this is all about, see, Miss Mason? You say the boy isn't doing so hot in school?"

"He's doing very poorly," said Katharine. "I'd like to talk to you a little before we have him in, please—he's home, I suppose—"

"Oh, sure. In his room. That's O.K., sure." Bicknell was relaxed and friendly; his wife sat pleating her skirt nervously, silent.

"He's had a very poor grounding in reading, and of course that's such a basic thing— Naturally he finds it very hard to follow the classwork, and doesn't try. I thought, if you could possibly arrange for outside tutoring? It'd help him enormously, I'm sure, if he'd *try,* because he's really a bright little boy." At least normal, she added to herself; but you had to flatter parents.

Bicknell looked at his wife, and got out cigarettes. "Well, I'll tell you, Miss Mason, and I suppose it'll be no surprise to you—I can see you know kids—we have had a little problem with Gordon playing hookey. Last year, the year before. I've tried to talk to him about it, but, well— you know kids. It's been a little problem."

"But that was only to be expected," said Katharine. "Naturally he's bored and restless at school, because he *can't* join in the work. I haven't received his records from his old school yet, but I should be getting them any day. I want to see what other teachers have had to report about him. But if he can manage to catch up to his age level—sometimes a good remedial reading course can do wonders—and once he gets interested, I'm sure he'd get to like school." She was still puzzled that Gordon had been allowed to get as far as the fifth grade, but she didn't say so.

"You really think so? Maybe you can recommend some teacher like that who could—?" He sounded interested and receptive.

"Of course. I do wish you'd think about it, Mr. Bicknell, and enter him for a remedial course. As it is, he's— And there's another aspect too. You see, he doesn't seem to have made any friends at Verdugo at all. The other children think he's, well, backward because he can't read well and so on. It's very bad for him, you can see, feeling left out of everything."

"Yeah," he said thoughtfully. "Excuse me, offer you a cigarette?"

She took one and he lit it for her. She thought, a skilled workman: it was the union men made the salaries these days. He was probably earning twice as much as she was, but maybe hadn't graduated from high school. But an intelligent man, even a shrewd and imaginative man, by his eyes. More so than his wife, who might be rather stupid. This living room was conventionally furnished, a good deal of unimaginative new furniture, few ornaments. The woman still said nothing.

Katharine leaned forward. "Mr. Bicknell—that's just one reason I wanted to see you. There's another. You know about this awful murder —a little boy Gordon knew, Paul Brandon."

His expression tautened suddenly. Any parent thinking about that, she thought. "Yeah, I know. The very hell of a thing, that was. The papers said— Just a kid. Tough on the parents."

"And in such a nice respectable neighborhood!" broke in Mrs. Bicknell in a high nervous voice. "It doesn't seem possible—"

"Well, it's just a wild hunch, Mr. Bicknell, but I think Gordon knows something about it and is afraid to tell. I've asked him, tried to talk to him, but he won't say anything. I thought if you tried, maybe—he seems to be very fond of you—"

"Something about *that?*" Bicknell sounded astonished and upset. "Why, I don't see how he could—and if he did, I think he'd've come out with it to one of us, don't you think, hon?"

"Of course he would have! He's really a good boy—we've raised him right, tried to—"

"I think you're way off the track there, Miss Mason, but, sure, I'll ask him. If you really think— *Gordon!* Come in here!"

A long moment later the boy appeared. Katharine thought he looked even thinner, that he'd lost weight; he was certainly very white. He stopped on the threshold, and seeing Katharine suddenly looked abjectly frightened. "What's she said about me?" he cried in terror. "She's alla time *picking* on me—it's not so, whatever she said—"

"Hey," said Bicknell good-humoredly, "you stop saying bad things about Miss Mason. Come here—come here, son."

Slowly, unwillingly, the boy crossed the room to stand before him. His father put his hands on Gordon's shoulders. "Now, Miss Mason's just trying to help you, kid. That's all. She's a good teacher, likes to help the kids in her class. And she's got a couple ideas about you, boy, that's all she's been talking about. Now you answer me straight, see? You know I'm your dad, I'm on your side, right here to back you up and not let anything happen to you. Hmm?"

"Yeah," muttered Gordon. "Sure." He stared at the carpet.

"O.K. Now, Miss Mason's got a funny little idea you maybe know a little something about this pal of yours who got killed. That was a pretty damn awful thing, wasn't it?"

"Yeah."

"You look at me, Gordon. *Do* you know something about that? I don't see how you could—seem to remember you came home kind of early that day—but if you do, well, you know, kid, we all got to help the cops—"

"I *tole* the damn fuzzes all I knew!" the boy burst out desperately, frantically. Katharine saw the man's hands tighten on the thin shoulders. "I *tole* her—she's just nuts, that's all! I don't know nothing, I can't tell nobody nothing more 'n I did— If people'd just leave me *alone*— I don't— She's just *nuts*—" He broke away and ran out of the room.

"Of course he couldn't know anything about that," said Mrs. Bicknell. "How could he? He'd have *said*— You know he'd have told us, Bert—"

"Sure," said Bicknell. "I think so too." He looked at Katharine. "I tell you, Miss Mason, something occurs to me about this, see? It could be he's kind of upset right now because this kid, this Paul, was about the only new pal he'd made here. And so he's, you know, missing him. Because I just don't see how he could—"

"Well, I suppose that could be," agreed Katharine slowly.

"Maybe it was wrong to pick up and move," he went on ruefully. "I never thought of the effect on the kid. I don't know—take him away from his old friends and so on. But, well, after all, I was making more money, better job, we wanted a nicer home and all, better neighborhood. There were a couple of kids he used to go around with we didn't think much of, see—we thought, get into a classier district. I used to be with Bob Wegge, Pontiac agency over on San Fernando, but of course the money's better at Lockheed, and you got to think of the future—pension plan and all like that. Only I guess, now I stop to think, it's been rough on the kid, changing neighborhoods—"

"He'll get over it, Bert. It'll be O.K., he'll make new friends and all—"

"Well, if you ask me, Miss Mason, that's all it is—he just hasn't settled down like, yet. But I'll sure keep it in mind—he was upset just now, but I'll have a serious talk with him and try to find out if he *does* know a little something. I guess at bottom he thinks enough of his dad to trust him when the chips are down." He smiled at her.

"I thought you'd have a better chance of getting it," said Katharine. "I hope you will, if there's anything there to be got." She stood up. "And I hope you'll think about the remedial reading course for him. Not really very expensive, and if he'll cooperate, he could go a long way toward catching up to his age level. I'll ask Mr. Harwell, our principal, and give you some names and addresses."

"We'd sure appreciate it," said Bicknell. "It's nice of you, take all this trouble over the boy."

"No trouble," said Katharine, smiling at him. "We try to do our best for them, you know. And you *will* keep—the other thing—in mind?"

"I sure will. Thing like that—hell of a thing to happen . . . Been very nice meeting you, Miss Mason."

"Yes, it's real nice, your taking an interest in Gordon," said Mrs. Bicknell, sounding a little more forthcoming.

"Not at all," said Katharine again.

*

Technically speaking, Varallo wasn't having Sunday duty this month, but of course police officers didn't take regular days off when they were working a case. Not the ranking officers, anyway. He got downtown about ten to nine and had a look at what had come in overnight.

"Here's one you can go out on," said Poor, shoving a work sheet over to him. "I'm on desk duty, Wayne is out with an attack of neuritis —he says it was all that digging in your hole started it up—and Katz is on this new burglary."

"We do earn our money," said Varallo, and looked at the report.

Last night the vandals had visited two schools, an elementary school and the junior high across the street from Hoover High. Since the wave of vandalism had started, Saturday night being an obvious one for kids raising hell, one of the maintenance men at all public schools was detailed to make a routine check on Sunday mornings. These two had called in with the usual incoherent rage and astonishment, you never saw such a mess, send somebody quick.

"Hell," said Varallo. He went down the hall to Prints and borrowed a man. He meant to see Steve Morehouse sometime today, but this was more urgent.

They drove to the elementary school first. The janitor was waiting for them on the steps of the main building, a bald, spare, elderly man. "You sure took your time getting here," he said resentfully.

"Sorry, we've got other business as well—Toll Junior High got it too."

"You don't say. Be damned. These damn kids—people just don't try teach them any morals any more, I swear, and then too they don't get enough work, at school or at home—and like we all know Satan finds work for idle hands. My name's Fisher, by the way. You never saw such a *mess*." He was leading the way into the building. It was an older school than Verdugo, but laid out in much the same way. "Acourse I called Mrs. James, the principal, right off—she oughta be here pretty soon. In here. I figure they busted a window to get in." He threw open a door.

They looked, and Burt, the man from Prints, said, "Sweet Jumping Judas!"

It was the main office of the school, a room about thirty by forty, a long counter running wall to wall down the length of the room, making a corridor about ten feet wide at the front. At one end, this side of the

counter, was a door marked PRINCIPAL; at the other end a door marked
REGISTRAR.

In the larger space behind the counter had stood a number of steel
file cases, typewriter desks for clerks, all the office paraphernalia, with
almost continuous tall windows above. All the file cases had been
thrown down on their sides or backs; all of the drawers had been pulled
out. Their contents had been hauled out, torn up very thoroughly, and
heaped in a confused pile in the middle of the floor, and what must
have been several quarts of ink poured over the lot. All but one of the
windows were broken. Typewriters had been tossed on the floor, tables
overturned. One of the swinging gates in the counter had been torn off
its hinges. A gallon can of white paint had been overturned on the
counter top, to discharge its contents, both sides, on the expensive vinyl
flooring.

"They got *that* outta the basement," said Fisher; the man was liter-
ally shaking with rage. "That ain't all. Look in Mrs. James's office.
Damn little bastards—way I figure, when you catch up to 'em, you
oughta make *them* do the cleaning up!"

"Not at all a bad idea," said Varallo. They looked in Mrs. James's
office, and Burt said "Sweet Jumping Judas" again. The pile carpet had
been slashed in several places, and more ink thrown around. A couple
of file cases against the back wall were overturned, and the same trick
had been played with their contents. Two windows were broken. The
wooden desk chair had been broken apart by something like an ax, to
kindling wood.

"Didja ever *see* anything like— Morning, Mrs. James."

"Oh!" said the woman in the doorway. *"Oh, my heavens!"* She was a
stout motherly-looking woman, and right now looked ready to burst
into tears. Varallo couldn't blame her. "What—an—awful—mess! I never
imagined— These horrible vandals!" She looked at Varallo and Burt. "I
suppose you're police officers? Why can't you *catch* these delinquents,
anyway? Just children, really—"

There wasn't time to explain to her the various reasons why the vandals were hard to catch up with. Since the series of vandalisms had
started, of course there'd been increasing publicity about it, and a couple of local editorials asking the same querulous question. The public
didn't stop to think; it just wanted results.

"We do our best, Mrs. James," said Varallo with a sigh. "What we
can't understand, if I may say so, is why the Board of Education doesn't
protect its schools better. This kind of vandalism isn't just local—there's

an outbreak of it the year round, one place and another, especially in big-city areas. The total cost of everything destroyed and stolen must be a great deal more than it would cost to install reliable burglar-alarm systems."

"I *know*," she said angrily. "We all know that! But it's a state matter —all the red tape— Of course it's ridiculous, but they won't take action. Heavens, what a dreadful *mess*—Fisher, you'll have to call the rest of the men. We can't work in here tomorrow with the place—"

"I'll do my best, ma'am, but there's more than a day's cleaning up to be done here," said the janitor sourly.

"Have you touched anything in here?" asked Varallo.

"Not me. We all got instructions from you fellers, since this been going on. Not to say you won't prob'ly find some of my fingerprints around, naturally. I opens the door and reaches in to switch on the light, and I saw all this, and I said—well, never no mind what I said," said the janitor, looking at Mrs. James, "and then I went and called you."

"O.K.," said Varallo. "You can probably get to work in here in an hour or so. We want an inventory too, Mrs. James, to find out if anything's been stolen."

He and Burt got to work themselves, dusting everything for prints. This sort of thing was a nightmare of a job, one reason it was slow work. The vandals usually made a beeline for the administrative offices, as here; and in the natural course of events offices like that were already coated with hundreds of prints. After collecting all there were, you had to eliminate the innocent ones, those belonging to the staff, to visitors, and so on. To collect the two unidentified prints they had which pretty certainly belonged to the vandals, they had taken over eight hundred prints from innocent people, including numerous school kids.

A hell of a job. And from there they went on to Eleanor J. Toll Junior High, where much the same sort of damage had been done. Here, the vandals hadn't bothered to empty the file cases, but had hammered several of them so savagely that the clerks would probably have to use a blow torch to get at any of the files. Windows had been broken, chairs smashed, and two typewriters and an adding machine stolen.

By the time they finished there, it was past lunchtime. They stopped at Pike's on the corner of Glenoaks and Brand for lunch. "*I* think," said Burt, "Fisher reads it right. Kids haven't got enough to do any more, and partly that's natural. Life a hell of a lot easier now, all the gadgets, no chores for kids to do at home the way there used to be. And they treat them a hell of a lot easier at school, too. Not near so much home-work. My God, you should see the papers my boy Dan brings home—if I remember right, kind of stuff *I* had in second or third grade, and he's in B-five! And in high school, all these fool classes in baton twirling and ballroom dancing instead of solid subjects. Anyway, it's natural that they get restless, and it's just a step from there to raising some kind of hell."

"What gets me," said Varallo, "is the way they're let to wander around, nobody keeping a check. The ones we picked up who set that fire—twelve and fourteen, my God—out alone at midnight. Sure, I know it's only a minority, most parents are responsible and conscientious, it's the kids who do get into trouble we see. But some of them—" He con-templated his sandwich wryly. "One of those kids—as per the usual pat-tern, mother a divorcée out at a bar with some pickup. Jimmy? she said, oh, Jimmy was O.K. alone, he was a big boy now. And then it's the kids we punish." He looked at his watch. "Speaking of kids, I want to go and see Steve Morehouse again—this Brandon thing." Burt knew all about that, of course, having done some of the technical work.

"How's it coming?"

"Not so hot," said Varallo. "Where's any proof, either way? I still like Riegler for it, but if this new kid who just turned up *is* right about seeing Paul at five-thirty—and he seems damn positive— And I can't overlook the Morehouse boy. The unstable teenager—it's possible. I should think his family's being damn rough on him—very strait-laced people, you know—and he'd know how that would be. I've built up a way he could very well have done it."

Burt said cynically, "Seems to me we operate a damn funny way sometimes. Technically speaking, it's against the law however old you are, but the only cases we ever do anything about are the juveniles. In the next twenty-four hours, Vic, just right here in L.A. County, you want to guess how many people are going to be hopping into bed with somebody they're not married to?"

"I wouldn't dare guess."

"—But it's only if they happen to be under twenty-one that we make the big fuss and haul them in to lecture them. When we catch them . . . My grandfather," said Burt, fishing an ice cube from his iced coffee to suck, "he came west in a covered wagon in eighteen eighty-four, and by the time he was twenty-one he had his own ranch and'd been married three years and had two kids."

"It was," said Varallo, "a simpler age, yes." He wondered what had happened to O'Connor today; Katz had said he hadn't been in. Taking the day off? Very unlike Charles when he had his teeth into something . . .

CHAPTER 16

O'Connor was off on what he thought was a very wild wild-goose chase. It was just a little something he'd like to know about. . . .

Last night, by prearrangement, he'd called Katharine at nine o'clock. "Get anything interesting?"

"I don't think anything at all. They're nice enough people, they seemed ready to cooperate, enter Gordon in a remedial course—which could help him a lot, if *he'd* cooperate. I'm thinking now maybe Mr. Bicknell was right. He was very surprised at the idea of Gordon's knowing something about Paul's murder, he was positive the boy trusted and loved them enough to tell them right away. He suggested that Gordon's acting upset because he's missing Paul, and the shock of the murder, too— Paul was about the only new friend Gordon had made here."

"Could be, I suppose."

"I will say, he seems very good with the boy—as I told you, Gordon's very fond of him apparently. I think if there was anything to be got, he'd have got it. Or will. I'd say he wears the pants, definitely—"

"Tut-tut, Katy, slang."

"It's out of working hours," she'd said, and laughed. "Mrs. Bicknell seems rather timid, she didn't have much to say—let him do all the talking and deciding. I wonder if I've just been woolgathering. The boy's in a funny nervy state, but come to think, there's enough reason for that— his situation at school, and the other kids making fun of him, and then the only friend he *had* managed to make— At least I picked up one of the new slang words," and she laughed again. "And I wonder what on earth the connection—"

"What d'you mean?"

"Oh, these kids. Not quite as bad as the teenagers, with their own version of English, but they're on the way. Like a private code. But this was a new one to me. When his father was pressing him about knowing anything, he came out with it—said, 'I told the fuzzes all I knew.' I took it to mean the police. But—"

"Now I will be Goddamned," said O'Connor. "Sure about that, Katy? He said *fuzzes?*"

"Yes, why? You—"

"That's slang, lady, but it's pro-crook slang, current usage. I'll be damned. I wonder where the hell a ten-year-old kid—"

"What? Really? How funny. They're quite respectable people, you could see that— He's a skilled workman, probably neither of them has much education, but they're honest citizens. In fact, he said it was partly on Gordon's account they moved to a better neighborhood."

"Yes? From?"

"I don't know exactly, somewhere the other side of town. Gordon went to Glenoaks Elementary last year."

"Oh. You any idea what the father does and where?"

"He works at Lockheed now. Wait a minute—what was it he said?— yes, he used to work for a Bill Wegge at a Pontiac agency garage on San Fernando Road. Why? They're quite ordinary people— I rather liked her, she's shy, I think, because she realizes her lack of education— quite nice people."

"Um," said O'Connor. "And their backward boy Gordon coming out with the pro slang. A funny little something. O.K., thanks, Katy—"

"I wish you wouldn't call me—"

"It suits you. Can I afford to take you to dinner, say, Tuesday night? I guess so. Seven o'clock."

"You just wait a minute! You ask me politely instead of taking it for granted I'll be falling all over myself to say yes, and maybe I'll think about it! Didn't anybody ever teach you any manners?"

"Oh, I'm just a dumb Irish cop," said O'Connor. "You know that— what d'you expect? I'd say tomorrow but I've got to get in some more target practice. See you, Katy," and he put the phone down.

A very funny little something indeed. O'Connor hadn't been much interested in Katy's boy Gordon up to now; it was just a female's hunch. But now he found himself interested in the whole family, despite what she said.

On Sunday morning he found a Pontiac agency on San Fernando Road, and asked if there was a Bill Wegge around.

"Sure," said the salesman who had buttonholed him, looking disappointed. "He's our garage manager, head mechanic. Not here today, naturally."

O'Connor got Wegge's address, Garfield Avenue, and drove down there. Wegge was home, a little leathery fellow about forty-five, with the strong, well-shaped hands of a mechanic. He looked nervous when he heard O'Connor's name and job.

"What the hell d'you want with me? What've I done?"

"Nothing that I know of," said O'Connor. This was a neatly maintained old frame bungalow on a quiet side street. In the comfortable, if slightly shabby, living room were evidences of family life: a few women's magazines scattered around, a pair of boys' sneakers abandoned under a chair, a high-school notebook on the table beside the door, its cloth cover neatly stenciled MARION A. WEGGE. Rest of the family out? There was a little clatter from the kitchen and a woman's voice called, "Bill, you'll have to fix that darned stove drawer, it's stuck again."

"In a minute," Wegge called back. "What *do* you want?"

"Just to ask if you know an Albert Bicknell."

"Oh," said Wegge. He groped in his shirt pocket for cigarettes. "Why, sure. Sure I know Bert. Used to work at our garage. Why? What's he been—"

"Nothing wrong, far as I know. When did he quit at the garage?"

"Lessee," said Wegge, inhaling deeply. "Some time around last March, it was. Why the hell? . . . Well, no secret about it, I guess— I didn't blame him, he's a hell of a good mechanic and could earn more at Lockheed, and then there's the pension plan and all."

"Sure. They've moved just lately—where were they living then, you know?"

"What the hell this is about— Bert's an O.K. guy, he wouldn't be up to anything wrong! Well, I'd have to think—seems to me it was somewheres over toward Burbank—wait a second, I'll have it, I got a good memory for addresses and I drove him home a couple of times his car was on the fritz—thirty-four something Longa Way, it was. Listen, why the hell are the cops asking about Bert? I don't get—"

"Just a very routine check," said O'Connor. "Thanks very much, Mr. Wegge."

As he came back down the front walk to his car, an ancient battered Chevy drew up at the curb and a pretty blonde teenager jumped out of it, yelled, " 'Bye!" and came skipping up the walk. Her eyes were curious on him as they passed.

He drove out to Longa Way, having to look it up on a map. It was a narrow old street almost up to the Burbank line; this was a poor area of town, shabby and run down. The drab street here was lined mostly with duplexes and old-fashioned four-family apartments. The thirty-four-hundred block wasn't, fortunately, very long. O'Connor parked the Ford at one end of the block, got out, and began to ring doorbells.

On a hot September Sunday, a full-fledged lieutenant out tramping the streets . . . But it was such a nebulous little something that he'd rather waste his own time than another man's.

In a district like this, the tenants came and went. Rather frequently. The houses all needed painting, few lawns were kept green and smooth, there were a good many kids playing in the street. Not to be snobbish about it, it wasn't a very classy district. It was only a step below the street O'Connor had grown up in, over in Hollywood.

He rang doorbells and asked questions. He thought he'd hit pay dirt at one apartment building, where an immensely fat landlady said, "Bicknell? Seems like I remember that name—was they the ones had two-oh-two awhile? Oh, no, sure enough, their name was Bickfelt. I can't call to mind—"

He got there finally (without much doubt) at 3427. The youngish fellow in shorts, polishing the five-year-old black T-bird in the drive, said, "Bicknell? I seem to recall—yeah, Bicknell, Bickell, Bicker, some name like that, I remember, sure. Guy and his wife and I don't remember how many kids, two I think—"

"Just one boy."

"Was it? I s'pose the kid showed up with pals so often— Why you asking about them? Skip tracer?" His eyes turned shrewd.

"No, just checking," said O'Connor vaguely. "What'd he do?"

"Hell, I don't remember if I ever knew. We hadn't been here long ourselves then. One thing I can tell you, maybe, why they moved—on account a couple of other families round here, they moved same time, see. All of a sudden it turns out this Russ Galetti downa street, he's a real pro heist man. Brother, there was some excitement, I tell you!—the cops come down on him sudden, see, and we had shooting yet, time they took him. And the Moores in the flat next door, they said they didn't figure raise their kids in a slum, see, and a couple other people with kids felt the same way. So maybe these folks you're asking about thought so too."

"You don't tell me," said O'Connor. He vaguely remembered Galetti's name—small-timer, and it hadn't been his pinch. "You're behind on the pro slang, by the way, they call themselves elevator men now."

"No kidding? Well, anyways it was some excitement. And like I say some people— Doris and me haven't got any kids yet, *which* is O.K. by me, see, and—"

"This Galetti live alone? Any family?"

"Jesus, that was half the excitement, way they carried on. You know these Italians. You shoulda seen— He lived with his folks, see, old man Galetti and Mama and half a dozen kids younger—and when the cops come hunting him—well, it was something! And like I told you—"

"Yes, thanks, I see," said O'Connor. He started back to the car. Waste all morning on this very nebulous small something and then, of course, have it peter out on him.

So Katy's puzzling little boy Gordon had come out with some pro-crook slang. Funny, when the parents looked respectable. And what did it come to? Nothing. Gordon had lived, until recently, in an area where a pro elevator man also lived; and the pro had younger brothers. Without much doubt Gordon had played with them, and picked up a few words of pro-talk that way.

It was nearly noon. O'Connor, feeling disgruntled and irritated, unprecedentedly took himself out to lunch at Pike's Verdugo Oaks, and had two drinks beforehand.

Varallo got to the Morehouses' about two o'clock. He was feeling as disgruntled as O'Connor; they were getting nowhere fast on this one. The lab report on the boy's clothes had come in, and it said absolutely nothing. They had even collected dust samples from Riegler's garage for the lab, in the hope of establishing some link; that lab had given them solid evidence from as ephemeral things before now. But nothing.

At the end of eight days' work on it, what did they have? They knew Paul Brandon had been murdered, and how. They had a few suspects who could have done it, if they had felt that way, or lost their tempers. Keith. Wilma Starke. Steve Morehouse. John Riegler.

Wilma Starke the least likely. A woman, and not as strong. And the boy had been at her house at four-fifteen, he'd have no reason to go back so soon. Keith unlikely too.

They had an antique coin which was almost surely the murderer's, dropped by accident when he put the body in position before staging the cave-in. A lucky talisman? If he habitually carried it on his person, probably. So, mark off, say, eight or ten square blocks up there, start ringing doorbells: "Do you recognize this coin? Does anyone you know carry it as a lucky piece?"

It might come to that. Detective work could get that simple—and that tiresome.

Meanwhile—Steve Morehouse.

The teenagers of Steve's type usually could be broken down. In the end, they usually confessed, if handled right. Varallo thought this was the right time to work again on Steve, and he thought he knew the right way to do it.

He parked in front of the house. Steve was mowing the lawn with an old-fashioned hand lawn mower; he was in shorts and T-shirt. He looked grim, and hot, and unhappy. Varallo waited until he looked up at the end of a row, and beckoned to him. Steve dropped the lawn mower and came to the curb; Varallo opened the front door of the car and said, "Get in a minute, Steve. I want to talk to you."

"O.K., sir." But he'd hardly sat down before the front door of the house opened and Mrs. Morehouse came out. She waddled down to the curb, talking as she came.

"You get right back to work, Steven, hear me? No gadding around with your delinquent friends—"

"Mom, it's *not*— I—"

"I'm sorry to interrupt Steve, Mrs. Morehouse. I want to talk to him again."

"Oh." She peered in. "It's you. I declare. Just keeping it all in his mind, ask me. As if it wasn't bad enough, the neighbors knowing and all. Well, don't you keep him too long—he's got work to do!" She went back to the house.

And just how, Varallo wondered, had the neighbors found out, if the Morehouses hadn't told them? He looked at Steve. The boy was looking down morosely at his clasped hands. "I'm sorry," said Varallo sympathetically. "It's being pretty rough?"

"Damn it," the boy burst out resentfully, "you'd think I'd committed a murder or something! I mean, well, all right, it was a wrong thing to do, but—well, gee, look at how Jerry's father said—and I mean, Mr. Emmett knows how things *are*, how most people think about things. And—they don't have to be so damn *righteous* about—"

Varallo could see Morehouse senior being very righteous—and self-righteous.

"It's not fair," said Steve sullenly. "The Emmetts aren't doing anything to Jerry— I sort of figure his father was even kind of *pleased* with him." Naïve astonishment on that. "And me—it's like I was in jail. I can't have any more dates ever while I'm living with them, they said. I can't use the car, even once a week, and I don't get any allowance, just money for lunch, and I have to come straight home after school, and—it's not *fair*. I'm captain of the football team this year, I got to be there —they don't understand! They just said, well, you can't be, that's all. How can I tell the coach that? And—and why? All the kids knowing, and me looking like a five-year-old, have to do whatever Mama says!" His voice shook with rage.

And of course it wasn't fair. The humiliation worst of all. These people. "Well, I don't think it's fair either, Steve," said Varallo. "Especially when nothing's happening to Jerry. But, you know, your parents look at these things differently from the Emmetts—and some other people. . . . Cigarette?"

The boy glanced at the house. "No, sir, I better not, thanks. I don't much anyway, on account of keeping in training. . . . Damn it!" He pounded a fist on his knee. "Like I'm just a little kid! Sure I know they're strait-laced and all, but— I'll tell you one thing," and he sat up straighter, his mouth a grim line; he looked suddenly more mature. "After I graduate next June, I'm getting out. So they want me to go on to college, the hell with that. Or if I go, I'll pay my own way somehow. I'm done being ordered around like I was ten years old, and dragged off to that church every— Do you know they say I've got to go to *every* single service, every Sunday? From now on? That fat preacher— And I know for a fact he tries to flirt with the girls in the Youth Group, Nora King told me. I won't—"

"That might not be such a hot idea, Steve. Not so easy to work your way through college. What were you going in for?"

"Engineering, sir. I don't care. I'm done being treated like a kid."

"Well, think it over. . . . *Did* you commit a murder, Steve?"

The boy's head jerked up; he stared at Varallo. "What—what d'you mean?"

"Did you kill Paul Brandon?" Sometimes, if you showed them how smart you were, to build it up and guess how it had all happened, they would break down; it would all come out. Varallo lighted his cigarette, his eyes holding Steve's. "I can build it up, the way it could have gone, Steve. I don't think you planned it out—you didn't mean to kill him. I think you wanted to go somewhere that Saturday—a forbidden movie, maybe?—and got Jerry and Rodney and Bruce to say you'd been with them. I think you were coming home when you met Paul—over on Cor-

dova. Weren't you? You'd been worried about Paul knowing your little
secret, you'd talked it over with Jerry, hadn't you? Yes. Wondered
whether the effect of your threats had maybe worn off. And you thought
this might be a good chance to remind Paul again, threaten him some
more. You got him to go into that half-built house there with you.
You—"

"No!" said Steve, finding his voice at last. "No, please, I wouldn't do
a thing like—"

"I don't think you meant to," said Varallo, still holding Steve's eyes
with his own. "No. I think possibly you were only cuffing him a little to
back up the threats—but you're a big strong fellow—and you knocked
him down and found you'd hurt him badly. Is that how it was, Steve?
And then you thought, might as well be hanged for a sheep as a lamb,
and you figured out how you could fake an accident—"

"No! I never— I couldn't do a thing like that!" exclaimed the boy;
there was horror and panic in his eyes. "A little *kid*—I couldn't— Sure, I
was afraid he might tell, but just on *that* account I wouldn't! You can't
think I did a thing like *that*—"

Varallo went on looking at him for a long minute; and then he said
flatly, "Well, I guess I don't, no, Steve." The ones like Steve were not
very accomplished liars or actors. That had been genuine reaction. He
didn't see Steve planning it out beforehand; and if it had happened the
way he had outlined it, he didn't see Steve planning so carefully as to
look around for rope, tie the boy up, think that far ahead.

The half-built house was the only possible place Steve Morehouse
could have concealed Paul prior to staging the accident: the only place
he could have struck the blow. And if Steve—or anyone else—had struck
the blow there, how much easier to stage the accident there too. To
make it look as if Paul, prowling around among lengths of timber and
sacks of concrete, had stumbled and fallen against some sharp surface.
Very natural and nobody's fault.

Another very little thing: he couldn't see Steve kicking the kitten.

He had always liked Riegler better for the part. Now he relinquished
Steve Morehouse with a sigh.

"Please, sir, you got to believe— I never did a terrible thing like that!
I couldn't—"

"All right, I said I believe you. It was just an idea. This is a tough
case, Steve, we have to look at everybody remotely concerned."

"Haven't you any idea who—?" The boy sank back against the seat.
"An awful thing, just a kid, just as old as Nicky. I thought—the paper
kind of made it sound as if Mr. Riegler—"

"Well, we haven't any real evidence." That was another thing: the papers were making a Roman holiday of it, an offbeat murder.

"And that was another thing," said Steve dully. He wasn't really thinking about anything but his own situation at home. "A man everybody always thought was honest and so on, doing a thing like that, running away from that accident. The way *they* act—" you could guess that that *they* referred to his parents, bitterly— "you'd think nobody grown up ever did anything wrong! Like being an outcast or something . . . D'you know I can't eat with the family any more, like I'm supposed to be a bad influence on the younger kids—they said— Well, I'll have to stick it until June, but then I'm getting out."

More than a little revolted, Varallo hardly knew what to say to him. He wondered if people like the Morehouses would ever learn. If there was, at one end of the scale, the half-tight divorcée leaving Jimmy home alone, there were at the other end the overly protective, possessive, puritanical parents like the Morehouses. Keeping as sharp and suspicious an eye on a basically honest, responsible eighteen-year-old as on an irresponsible kindergartner. In this instance, as in many others, it had just resulted in the opposite effect to what it aimed at. They were driving Steve away from home, from any brand of religion, and probably depriving him of a college education; as Varallo knew from fifteen years back, it wasn't so easy to work your way through—maybe harder now. Just to get the personal liberty his grown-up body and nearly grown-up mind demanded, Steve would get out as soon as he could. And who could blame him?

If the Morehouses would acknowledge a few elementary biological facts, and think a little less about the letter of the moral law than about Steve— But it was too late for that, and it wasn't his business anyway.

"Just think it over, Steve," he said. "You might regret it a lot later. And you'd be away from home at college, you know."

"Oh, no, I wouldn't. They've got it all fixed. I'm to go to Glendale College the first two years and then L.A.C.C. so I can live at home. Cheaper. I wanted to go to Berkeley, but—" He shrugged and opened the car door. "Well, that's off anyway. I'll get out where I can live like a human being."

Varallo sighed after him, watching him trudge up the walk to the lawn mower. And from his own university years he dredged up a quotation he had always liked—Wilde, wasn't it?— *There is no sin except stupidity.*

È vero, isn't it the truth, he thought wryly, and turned the ignition key.

CHAPTER 17

Gordon wasn't really thinking any more, he was just feeling. Mostly feeling plain scared of the Man. After what he'd said.

And Teacher coming, and all. And they said he'd have to go and take that other thing, rem-something, because— Another dumb school! Nobody'd bothered him much about school before, except the truant guy— He just didn't *get* it.

If he could just get *away*—away from all of it. Clear away. Back before it all started—

He lay in the dark, scared, his heart beating with loud thuds. If he *could*—he wouldn't care what happened after that. Only they'd come after him, of course, and then—and then—

But he went on thinking about it. Hard.

Dad always said, Keep your head, keep cool, don't panic. Think what's the best thing to do, and then go and do it.

Anybody who could do a thing like that to a little kid—to Paul (Paul, who hadn't minded him tagging along, talked to him friendly)—he'd do just *anything*.

Had to get away from it, all of it. To anywhere.

Could he?

He knew where she kept all her money, and there'd be about fifty, sixty dollars now because they hadn't done the main week's shopping yet—that was tomorrow. If he could get it, get a ticket on a bus, a train somewhere—

The boy named Gordon might be barely literate, but he had a good, active mind. He thought of a number of difficulties and pitfalls ahead of him, and thought of ways to get round them. He lay there in the dark, with terror in his heart, and made cool plans to get away safe.

He thought, Get to a railroad station first. Go a long ways off—this was an awful big town, a lot of towns all running into each other—and ask the way. Then, wait around careful until he saw a lady with a kid, or maybe two or three kids, going to get on a train. And follow up behind, like he was one of the kids belonged to her. Nobody'd ask questions, he could get right on the train after her, and then—and then hide in a toilet until the train started. Easy.

A train to any place. Any place away from here.

Awhile ago, his Auntie May had taken him on a train to see his grandfather. Before Grandpa died, that was. He'd been a real little kid, only seven, but he remembered. There was a thing called a diner where you ordered stuff to eat. He'd have money to do that. If the nigger waiter thought it was funny he was alone, he'd say—sure, he'd say his aunt was train-sick and sent him alone to get dinner.

He could get right away. . . . And he didn't care what happened after that. It didn't matter what his mother had said, about minding and being good and all. . . .

He didn't sleep all night. He was too busy thinking. Or maybe he slept just a little while, before it started to get light.

He got up just like always, and dressed, in his new dark-blue pants and a light-blue shirt and brown shoes. He had breakfast with them, not saying much, and pocketed his fifty cents' lunch money.

"You got everything now, honey?"

"Yeah," he said. "I guess I'll go to the bathroom again." He went quick down the hall and into their room, and straight to her old black purse on the dresser. He opened it, opened the billfold inside, and took out most of the paper money—not all, or if she looked at it very soon, they'd *know* too soon. He stuffed it in his pants pocket without counting it, went into the bathroom, and flushed the toilet and came out again.

"You be good now, and try to pay attention to the teacher like I said."

"Yes, sir," said Gordon. " 'Bye." Just act natural.

He left the house. He walked down Rosemount to Sinaloa, down that to Mountain, and down Mountain to Verdugo. But he didn't stop there, to wait for the bus. The eight o'clock bus would have a lot of school kids on it, some who knew him, in his class, and they'd think it was funny, and talk about it, when he didn't get off where Verdugo turned into Glendale Avenue, for school.

He saw Kevin and Bob sitting on the bench waiting already. So he went back to Ethel Street before they saw him, and down that. He

walked all the way down to the corner of Ethel and Glenoaks Boulevard; by the time the bus got to there, all the kids would have got off.

When it came, he didn't give the driver a torn-out slip from the little
book of passes, but the half dollar. Maybe the driver wouldn't look up
to see him, just give him change. But the driver, a fat man with a jolly
smile, did look.

"Well, hey now, what're you doin' out of school?" he asked in a
friendly kind of voice. "Oughta be on your way up to Verdugo right
now, hadn't you, if you live around here?"

"Sure, but I got to go to the dentist, I got excused," said Gordon.

"Goin' all alone? You're sure a brave boy," said the driver, handing
him change. Gordon dropped seventeen cents into the box, went to the
rear of the bus, and sat down. This driver would remember him. Damn,
he thought.

He didn't know where this bus went from here, and he didn't like to
ask the driver. He thought the only railroad station would be down in
Los Angeles, and he did know there was a bus went there. It went down
Brand Boulevard: a big green bus.

He got off at the corner of Broadway, by the rear door. He walked
all the way down Broadway to Brand. By the time he got there he was
tired and sweating; it was awful hot already. He was thirsty, too.

There was a policeman standing by the Drug King there; he couldn't
ask him, but he asked a funny-looking old lady on the corner by the
bank, and she said, "You ought to be in school, young man, not traips-
ing around on buses."

"I got to go see the dentist," Gordon told her, giving her his honest,
limpid look. "It's not all the way *to* Los Angeles but I got to take that
bus, see. Please—"

"And whatever your mother is thinking of, to let you go alone! Well!
It's *that* corner, where the bench is, but you've just missed one. The
next one'll be along in about half an hour."

Gordon went into the drugstore, feeling nervous as he passed the
big policeman in his tan uniform, and had a Coca-Cola. He felt better
after that. He came out, and there were public rest rooms there on the
corner, down steep cement steps. He went down where it said MEN;
there wasn't anybody else there, so he took the money out of his pocket
and counted it. There were two twenties and a ten and a five and three
ones. A lot of money. Enough. He put it in his plastic wallet. He
climbed the stairs and waited on the corner until the light turned green

and crossed the street to sit on the bench and wait for the bus into Los Angeles.

Gordon was absent. Katharine wondered, Playing hookey again or what? She hadn't yet given the Bicknells the information about available remedial courses—she must see Mr. Harwell some time today, she wasn't sure which schools were offering those this year.

She finished taking the roll call and started the day's work. . . .

Before the last bell rang at three o'clock—thank God the last bell—she had interrupted three fist fights, confiscated ten mouthfuls of illicit chewing gum, managed to check one bout of nervous giggling before it got out of hand, suffered the retailing of three very old and elementary jokes, and rather guiltily overheard the confidences between Mary Wells and Linda Bartlett, which revealed the interesting fact that the Bartletts had had an awful fight—"because Mama said she was going to have her hair done this new beehive way and Daddy said over his dead body because you know the President's wife has one and we're good Republicans, Daddy's what they call a Goldwater Republican and he was just awful mad."

If the parents knew what kids came out with—

It was one of those days when she thought she ought to have had her head examined for having decided to be a schoolteacher. Of all things.

And during her lunch hour Lester Carey had approached her and asked her, in his Victorian-polite way, to go out with him on Friday night. To a very interesting lecture on the uses of psychology in teaching, over at U.S.C. Katharine said, "I'm so sorry, I have a date Friday night." And found herself—astonishingly—thinking about Lieutenant Charles O'Connor with something approaching approval. Even warmth. The wolf in gorilla's clothing. At least he was a hundred percent masculine, that you could say twice. He didn't say, "Er-hmm," before every sentence, like a sheep bleating, or call her dear lady, or talk about the essential principles of the Dewey method. . . . *How* he would shock Lester, she thought suddenly, and leaned back in her hard wooden chair and laughed aloud in the empty classroom. Lester, who never said *damn* or *hell* before a lady—and maybe never at all.

That O'Connor.

She collected her papers, went out to the car. Stopped at the market for a few items. Drove home, put groceries away tidily, changed into a housecoat after a shower, and with a glass of iced coffee at her elbow started to correct papers.

She had just finished washing her dinner dishes and was about to set-tle down with a library book, at seven-fifteen, when the phone rang.

"Oh, Miss Mason—" a high breathless voice. "Please, was Gordon to school today? Oh, I forgot—this is Mrs. Bicknell—was he? He hasn't—"

"Why, no," said Katharine, startled and surprised. "Didn't you— Well, I did wonder if he was—"

"He hasn't come *home,* see, and he always comes straight home, he's got orders about that, strict— His d-dad's just about *wild*— An' if he wasn't to school, then it—it looks like he's—just run off—"

"Oh, dear," said Katharine inadequately. "But— Did he leave at the regular time, as if he was going to school?"

"Just like always— When he didn't come home, we didn't know *what* to think, and then his d-dad— He's just *wild*— And we thought, find out if he was to school— An' if he wasn't, oh, my God, we—"

"Good heavens," said Katharine. "Mrs. Bicknell, you'd better call the police. They'll surely find him, a ten-year-old couldn't just disap-pear—"

"Been just *wild,*" said the other woman, panicky and confused. *"Po-lice?* Well—but I don't guess— Well—"

"You'd better call them right away," said Katharine distinctly. Surely the man would realize that. "Listen, Mrs. Bicknell, hang up now and then call the police. He can't be far away, they'll find him." She hung up herself.

But Gordon—in his funny nervy state . . . A boy from an ordinary, fairly good home—respectable quiet people—what had shaken his little world enough to make him run away from home?

Katharine thought, It could be natural—nothing to do with Paul Brandon's murder. Difficulties at school, and with the other kids—the upset of moving to a new neighborhood—and losing the only new friend he had managed to make. But—

And then she went suddenly cold, and she thought, If he did know something— And if Paul's murderer knew he knew—

Was Gordon down a hole somewhere, dead like Paul?

O'Connor. At headquarters this late?

She looked in the telephone book. Charles V. O'Connor, on Chevy Chase. She wondered irrelevantly what the V stood for. Vincent, Vic-tor? She wondered if he lived alone, or with a widowed mother, or a desiccated older sister. What on earth did it matter?

She dialed. And when his deep voice said in her ear, impersonally,

"O'Connor speaking," without thinking she said urgently, "Charles, this is me—Katharine. There's something—"

By morning at least they were nearly certain that no fatal accident had accounted for Gordon. As soon as the alarm went out, a crew of men started to comb the Rossmoyne area, paying particular attention to the street excavations up there. It was a difficult and exhausting search, especially in the dark; but before dawn the searchers were sure that wasn't the answer.

They also had a look in and around that half-built house.

The parents stayed home, in their lighted living room, waiting. All they could do. Varallo had asked a few questions.

"Did you ask the boy about what's been troubling him, Mr. Bicknell?"

"Sure," said Bicknell. He sat on the couch, grim-faced, chain-smoking. "But that was pretty obvious, he didn't have to tell me. He isn't getting along so hot at this new school, hasn't made friends, and the one he did make— Well, I guess it'd be a shock to a kid, even more than to us maybe, another kid getting killed like that. You can see how he's felt."

The woman just sat there crying silently, dabbing at her cheeks with a handkerchief.

"But that doesn't seem like a reason for his running away," said Varallo. Had the boy run away? "Nothing had been wrong here at home?"

"What the hell d'you mean, wrong? Of course not, we all get along O.K."

"Then maybe," said Varallo, "he's running away from something else. My God, I wonder if he *does* know something about that—"

"That's nuts," said Bicknell curtly. "Just nuts. He couldn't—or if he did, he'd have told us, see. Don't waste time on that."

"But if he has run away voluntarily, there's got to be a reason."

They sent out an alarm on him, county-wide. One ten-year-old boy, four feet nine inches, approximately ninety pounds, medium complexion, dark hair and eyes, wearing dark-blue slacks, light-blue shirt, brown shoes.

All through that night, nobody was sure that Gordon hadn't been taken away. By somebody, for some reason. That he wouldn't be found somewhere, like Paul Brandon.

Then, early on Tuesday morning, Mrs. Bicknell discovered that most of her housekeeping money was missing. She hadn't had occasion to look in her billfold all Monday, she said. So that settled it. Gordon had provided himself with running-away money.

On Tuesday, from early morning on, they had it in the news broadcasts. Anyone having any information, please contact Glendale Police Headquarters.

That turned up the bus driver, about noon, so then they knew where Gordon had got off the bus at least. And about two o'clock it brought in a vinegary old girl, Amanda Dawes. "And I don't thank Providence for interrupting my Tuesday bridge game, either! But as it is, well, I did see the boy, and at the time he looked at me so honestly—but I hope I know my duty as a citizen—"

So then they knew that Gordon was making for Los Angeles. Why? Just what had been in his mind?

And suddenly, right there, Varallo connected a couple of things. Miss Dawes: "He looked at me so honestly—" And the funny irrelevant way he himself had found a nebulous resemblance between that clear limpid look of the boy's and the hearty salesman Bradley's open grin. . . . It was the look, that of Gordon's, that he'd seen often enough on the juveniles he'd picked up. "Honest, I didn't do anything." It was the look of the liar putting over a convincing story.

They asked L.A. to have a closer look for him, but of course there was a lot of L.A.

And in the end, about four o'clock Tuesday afternoon, it wasn't any professional who caught up with Gordon. It was a ticket agent down at the Union Station, who called in to L.A. Headquarters to say this lone kid had been hanging around the station all day today and yesterday, he thought. At least he seemed to be alone; and it looked funny, two days in a row; and the kid had bolted off when the ticket agent asked him a couple of questions. And he'd just heard on the radio about this lost boy, and he thought he ought to tell somebody. It could be.

L.A. thanked him and sent a couple of men down to get a full description (by which it was probably the Glendale boy) and prowl the several large waiting rooms looking. They came across him in the restaurant, eating a sandwich. When they asked if he wasn't Gordon Bicknell, and told him who they were, the boy just gave them one terrified look and turned dumb.

They took him back to their own headquarters and called Glendale. Varallo, who'd just been leaving, said resignedly he'd be right down to pick him up, and had they got anything out of him?

"Not one damn word," said the L.A. man. "He's apparently been hanging around the station trying for a chance to slip onto a train somewhere—eating in the restaurant or a drugstore around there. Who knows why kids do things? He saw we had him, he didn't try to run, but he wouldn't answer any questions."

"Well. I'll be down."

Downtown, he found a rather dirty, rather tired-looking boy stolidly waiting, eyes on the floor. He tried, on the ride back, every way he knew to get at Gordon. He was friendly, sympathetic. "Nobody's going to do anything to you, Gordon. Your mother and father have been so worried, they'll just be happy to have you back safe. You must know that. Why did you want to run away, Gordon? What is it you're afraid of?"

Silence from the seat beside him. The boy stared stubbornly straight ahead and pressed his lips together.

He tried it tough. "Now look, boy, it's illegal to keep back any information you've got about a wanted man. If that's what you're doing, we could be pretty tough on you—"

Silence. What went on in a ten-year-old's head, anyway? Kids could get some funny ideas. Could it be that Gordon, for no reason, was afraid Paul's killer would come back and go for him? Kids this age got muddled ideas, projected fantasies of their own. Who could say? And the boy looked grimy and tired: probably hadn't got much sleep last night, dodging around the big, gloomy, echoing cavern of the station. And there'd been some kind of psychological upset to set him off like that. Poor little devil. And Charles's schoolteacher said that by all she knew there was no home trouble, his parents were fond of him and he of them. What was Gordon's trouble, a trouble so frightening, so imperative (to him at least) that he couldn't confide in them?

But he couldn't humanely press the boy any further now. He fell silent himself; parked at the curb in front of the Bicknell house on Rosemount, he just opened the door and took the boy's arm.

"Come on, Gordon," he said gently. "We're home." For a moment he felt the boy hang back, and then he came, stolidly, at Varallo's side.

The front door swung open. They'd been called, were expecting him.

"Gordon, baby!" Mrs. Bicknell ran out to put her arms around him. "Whatever got *into* you, honey—you come right in, I guess you must be hungry—we've been so worried—"

Bicknell just laid one hand on the boy's shoulder, hard. "Look, son," he said, "you gave us one hell of a scare. We're going to have a nice long talk about it, see, you and me, and get it all straightened out. Whatever it was set you off half-cocked. Aren't we?"

The boy raised his head slowly. "Yes, sir," he said in a whisper. "I'm— I'm sorry."

"O.K. You go in with your mother now." He looked at Varallo. "Thanks very much for bringing him home, sir."

"That's O.K., just glad we found him safe and sound. Haven't you any idea why he ran away?"

Bicknell shook his head. With his anxiety relieved, he looked less grim. "It's beyond me—unless it's just that all this has, you know, pressured him more than we realize, he just felt he had to get away. I guess we don't realize how a kid's mind works sometimes. But you can forget that jazz about his having any guilty info about your murderer—that's a real wild one. Thanks again."

"Maybe so," said Varallo.

It was a quarter to seven. He went home, and Laura said, "Finally. It's very frustrating, Vic. Policemen's wives never can plan anything for dinner that can't be warmed over or kept in the oven. Was Gordon all right? What did he say?"

"Nothing," said Varallo, frowning. "Just nothing. I wonder, you know, what *is* behind it? Because—oh, well."

CHAPTER 18

O'Connor collected Katharine at her apartment and took her to the Matador up on Foothill. He was a man who appreciated food himself, and he could work his way through a reasonably full meal enjoyably; but he watched, fascinated, as she put away an immense salad liberally mixed with Roquefort dressing, three rolls, an overly generous serving of rich beef tournedos with mushrooms, asparagus with Hollandaise sauce and French-fried onion rings, an enormous baked potato lavishly covered with sour cream and chives, another roll, two cups of coffee, and finally a large slice of cheese cake.

"I don't understand it," he said. "It's black magic or something. Most of the females I know are so terrified of the extra pound or two—counting calories and so on all the time. Waiters offer them cake or an extra slice of bread, they act as horrified as if it's poisoned. And you eat like a harvest hand and stay thin as a rail."

"Metabolism," said Katharine, finishing the cheese cake. "Maybe I was hungrier tonight because I've been worried about Gordon, and relieved to know he's all right."

O'Connor shook his head. "I couldn't see much difference. And I'm not female, but even I see it isn't fair. Being on a hell of a lot more sedentary job since I made lieutenant, I have to keep a little eye on it too," and he patted his stomach absently. "Awful example—uncle of mine, quite a beer drinker—he got up to three hundred pounds before he died. And I like an occasional beer in hot weather too, but I've sworn off it. I find, maybe, I've got up to one-eighty instead of one-seventy-five, and I have to swear off the bread and potatoes awhile as well. And sit and watch you gaily disposing of about three thousand calories at one meal and still stay so damn thin. It's adding insult to injury."

Katharine laughed, and the waiter came up and suggested a nice little glass of brandy to go with last cups of coffee. "That sounds rather nice," said Katharine.

"Another hundred and fifty calories," said O'Connor with a groan. "All right, I'll be reckless for once. But I never saw anything like it—it's so damned unfair."

They were just finishing the brandy when the waiter drifted up again. This was a very quiet, discreetly dim restaurant; O'Connor had said, one of his favorites, and the waiter had seemed to know him. Now he said hesitantly, "Excuse me, sir, but I remember you had a phone call here once before—do I remember right, it's Lieutenant O'Connor?"

"That's right."

"Well, you're wanted on the phone again now," said the waiter. "They said it was headquarters." He looked curious and interested.

"O.K., back in a minute, Katy," and he got up quickly.

It must be something urgent, thought Katharine, for them to check at his favorite restaurants to find him. Or maybe, like doctors, police officers left information as to where they'd be, so they could be reached if something broke in a current case. . . . Something about Paul's case?

He came back, threading his way among the tables with automatic physical efficiency; she thought irrelevantly he'd probably be a good dancer, he moved that way. He was looking astonished and excited at once; his eyes were very bright, his mouth a grim line, and urgency was in every inch of him. "Come on," he said. He slapped a ten and a five down on the table and without waiting for change he hustled her out to the main entrance, into the car. "My God, and no siren!" he said. He whipped them around the block fast and headed back down Foothill.

"What is it? What's happened? Is it something about Paul?" She was excited.

"The Goddamnedest thing," said O'Connor. "*The* very Goddamnedest thing— *Keep* over in your own lane, damn it— Who the hell could have imagined anything like— I don't believe it yet, I swear to God I don't, because how in the name of God, I ask you, can there *be* any link? It's just lunatic— What the hell is this joy rider doing in the fast lane? *Get* out of the way, you—" He blasted the joy rider ahead with a long warning on the horn; the joy rider speeded up to a cautious thirty, and O'Connor snarled, cast a glance behind to the right, switched on his directional signal and sailed around the car ahead. "Bastards that won't learn road rules," he muttered. "For God's *sake!* I just don't see how it can hook up, because, for the love of Christ, all those respectable ordinary people—that kind of neighborhood—it's not just impossible, it's ridiculous! *Look,* pal, you signal for a left turn, for God's sake make it, will you?" The Dodge ahead went on signaling and a block later swerved right into the middle lane. "For *God's* sake! The idiots they—"

"But what's it all about? What's happened? For goodness' sake, tell me—"

He was evidently still too full of his own astonishment and excitement to hear her, or make much sense. They were racing down Verdugo now, and by luck or good judgment making all the lights.

"It's worse than that, damn it, it's silly," he said. "It's like starting out to work a private assault and having it turn into a syndicate job. I *ask* you, for God's sake. What the hell is the connection? How the hell can there *be* a connection? Out of the way, damn it, out of the way— drive it or park it, sister! I don't *believe* it—"

"I'll scream if you don't tell me," said Katharine, bouncing in her seat.

He didn't answer. He whirled the Ford onto Wilson and gunned it down a block, to turn into Isabel and then again into the big lot at headquarters. He pushed her across the seat and out, taking her arm, slamming the door, and started at a trot for the nearest entrance.

Another car-door slam; somebody, a tall hurrying figure, caught up to them. "Charles? Jeff reached you, then."

"Damn right. You too? The very Goddamnedest thing I ever—"

"What the *hell,*" asked Varallo, "can the connection be?"

Detective Forbes, holding down the night desk, had been extremely bored up to forty minutes ago. It was usually a boring job; Glendale was a quiet town and didn't get much major crime. The other man on duty, Wayne, was still suffering with his neuritis and, being full of aspirin, half asleep and no company. Forbes sat reading a paperback crime novel, bored with that too and wondering where the hell these writers got their wild ideas about policemen.

Until, at about eight-fifteen, Sergeant Copeland on duty at the main desk downstairs toiled up to lay something on his desk. "Another flier from the Feds," he said. "Hell, you'd think it'd cool off some after dark, wouldn't you?" He mopped his face. "Damn climate. It's marked urgent."

Correctly taking this to refer to the flier and not the climate, Forbes glanced over it. A minute later he jerked upright in his chair and said aloud, "For the *love of God!*"

"What's up?" asked Wayne sleepily.

"All hell," said Forbes, and looked up numbers and started telephoning.

"Well, there it is in black and white," said the FBI man. His name was Burns, and he looked like a Hollywood version of a Fed but otherwise seemed to be a very nice fellow. "There's got to be a link, that's all."

"My good Christ," said O'Connor, "how can there be?"

"In that neighborhood?" contributed Varallo.

"A ten-year-old *kid*," said Forbes, still sounding astonished.

They all seemed to have forgotten Katharine. She looked around the big, bare, modern room with interest: a lot of desks around the walls and in the middle of the room, back to back: almost solid ranks of windows down one long wall: on this desk, probably O'Connor's, a gadget with a bank of lights, a light going on whenever a phone rang. Practical vinyl flooring, efficient strip lighting, and fluorescent lamps. But she still didn't know what they were all talking and arguing about. An FBI man (and, goodness, wasn't he handsome!)—

A flier, they said. Whatever that was. It seemed to be something to do with the single sheet of mimeographed paper there on the desk.

Katharine stretched out a quiet hand and picked it up. Nobody seemed to notice. She sat down in a chair a little way off and started to read it.

Further information, [it started out] has been obtained in re John Newhall, wanted as one of the Armagast kidnapers. [*That* terrible thing.] It is hoped that within 48 hours a photograph will be available. Newhall, who has also gone by the name of John Norman, is thirty-seven, average height, dark, and has a scar on upper left arm caused by removal of tattoo mark. He is a skilled drill-press operator. His hobbies are bowling and swimming. He was known in July to possess a new Colt Super .38 automatic and is a fair shot. He is a very moderate drinker, seldom drinks spirits but invariably orders Pabst beer. Said to be attractive to women. May have sadistic tendencies. He is known to have graduated from East Hampton High School in New Jersey in 1944, under the name of John Norman. Certain information suggests that his real name is John Neufeldt. He habitually carries a "lucky piece" which is described as a large silver antique coin with a figure bearing a lute or lyre on one side, a coat-of-arms on the other, and two Latin inscriptions round the edges. This coin is probably one from the old German province of Brunswick, as Newhall has been heard to say that it belonged to his grandfather who emigrated from Brunswick. It is suggested, pending the obtaining of the photograph, that all police authorities circulate . . .

But what on earth, thought Katharine—and then she remembered. Charles had told her—that coin, found under Paul's body in the hole. Almost certainly the murderer's, dropped as he arranged the body there.

One of the Armagast kidnapers— That awful thing, the little boy tied up and left to starve in the woods. And the kidnapers getting clear away.

She skimmed over the rest of it blankly, blindly. "Whereabouts of Kallman, second wanted man, not known— Kallman's Joliet record—the woman, Marion Stepp, whereabouts unknown but some indication— All police authorities urged to—"

One of the Armagast kidnapers. But—Paul? Paul Brandon? How could he have—

Up in that more-than-respectable Rossmoyne neighborhood. All those settled, quiet, respectable householders. What could any of those people have to do with a kidnaper from New Jersey? It just didn't make sense.

"It just doesn't make *sense*," said O'Connor passionately.

The FBI man said grimly, "It's got to. It's got to—sooner or later."

At least from now on they couldn't complain about lack of manpower. The Feds converged on them by the dozens, like bees around a botanical garden. Among other things, they annoyed O'Connor by taking over direction of the case. All very polite and deferential and asking cooperation, but that was what it amounted to.

But they couldn't get down to any real work on this new angle until morning. What they did Tuesday night was talk—and talk some more. O'Connor and Varallo had to give them every last little detail on the case, pass over every document—after O'Connor had remembered Katharine and, to her rage, taken her home. He got polite hell from Burns when he came back, Burns having discovered meanwhile that she'd been Paul's teacher. "But she doesn't know anything, and everything she thinks about it I can pass on—"

And after that they just went on kicking it around. More and more Feds kept coming in, from different offices around here, and had to be brought up to date. The Feds were feeling savage on this one; their pride had been hurt a little, to miss those three back in New Jersey, tail so far behind on them this long. By midnight the Detective Bureau was crowded with men and the air was blue.

"But how could anybody up there be connected with Newhall?" O'Connor demanded. "Everybody Paul knew and saw that day has lived there for years. Settled people. Most of the people up there— Vic, you can say better than I can—"

"Very settled people, sure. No newcomers in our immediate neighborhood that I know of. There may be a few farther away, and Paul could have known them. But I don't— The diary. Where's the decoded diary?" And they explained that. Burns seized it eagerly. "But I don't remember that there's anything in it about new acquaintances."

"Except the Bicknells," agreed O'Connor, "and we know where they moved from, other side of town."

"We'll look," said Burns. "Brother, will we look here. There are a couple of hypotheses. First, some honest-looking citizen may be sheltering Newhall, and the boy could have—"

"I don't see it, for God's sake. People like that! The Emmetts— successful honest lawyer. The moral Morehouses. The cat-loving Williamsons. That I just don't see, Burns. All the people we've remotely connected to this case so far are obviously ordinary honest people. How could there be a link to Newhall?"

"And another thing," put in Varallo, "practically all of them are living in the bosoms of families. Difficult enough to provide a hideout for a wanted man, keep his presence secret—how the hell could it be done when other people are living in the house? Because, grant that—*per l'amor di Dio!*—Keith or Bradley or Starke or somebody we can't name yet, up there, has some hook-up with Newhall, some reason to help him —how would he explain him away to the rest of the family?"

" 'Meet Mr. X, honey,' " said O'Connor sarcastically, " 'he'll be staying with us for a while. Only nobody must know that, see, because he's a big producer from New York planning to sabotage Paramount by signing up a dozen of their top stars in secret.' I ask you. I do ask you."

Burns said, "Hell, I know! It looks unlikely, it's a tough one, but this very hot lead—we'll go through that area with a fine sieve, and see what turns up. There must be a few people living alone the boy knew—"

"Ella Knox," said Varallo. "But if you're going to tell us that Mrs. Knox is aiding and abetting a kidnaper on the run—"

"Look," said Burns. "We run into these things, you know. Nice honest old aunts and uncles and grandmothers aiding and abetting the black sheep—lying to the police—because, they tell us tearfully, he was Nellie's boy and she said to look out for him, or, he was such a sweet baby and really deserves another chance. You've probably seen it too, occasionally. It happens."

"Sure," said O'Connor. "Sure, it happens. So maybe Mrs. Knox is Newhall's godmother, and she's hiding him in her spare room. She was fond of Paul too—she loved that kid, way his murder shook her up. D'you think, if she knew who'd done it—and if there is anyone hiding Newhall, he or she undoubtedly knew, probably witnessed the murder—she'd have gone on keeping quiet?"

"Intimidation then, maybe," said Burns shortly. "We don't know until we look closer." He had men out already on the legal angle, getting the search warrants. "We start out by going through every house the boy visited that afternoon. But here's another thing you may have thought of too. If it wasn't at any of those places he met up with Newhall, well, at the place he did nobody's going to be letting it out he was there."

"I don't know, we've accounted for his time pretty tight," said O'Connor. He picked up the sheet with the timetable typed out on it neatly: the record of Paul Brandon's last Saturday.

9:30 A.M.–Noon	at civic swimming pool. Bicycled home at
Noon–1:10 (app.)	had lunch, left home; to Mrs. Knox's home by
1:30–1:45	went home for bike, rode down to Verdugo to market by
1:55–2:20 P.M.	shopped for Mrs. Knox, started back.
2:45	left bike at home, went to Bradleys', mowed lawn.
3:25 (app.)	back to Mrs. Knox's for kitten.
3:50 (app.)	at Williamsons'. Left kitten.
4:10–4:15 (app.)	at Starkes' for very few minutes.
4:20–4:30	at Mrs. Knox's, took second kitten
4:50–5:15	at Rieglers'.
5:30 (?)	seen "walking up Rosemount" (no indication which direction) by boy, Johnny Keller.
5:15–5:45	received death blow.
7:30 (app.)	missing kitten found on Cordova Avenue by Mrs. Dyer.

"But he could have stopped somewhere else," said Burns.

"Oh, he could have," agreed Varallo. "But another thing—how did he learn anything dangerous? I take it we're assuming he found out something about Newhall, who he was, and that was the reason he had to be killed? Well, anybody sheltering a man like Newhall, you know, 'd be damn careful. Newhall out of sight most of the time, and so on. And, say Paul or anybody else walked in unexpectedly—Paul did, you know, habit of his to just walk in—and saw the strange man, how easy to say, Meet Mr. Smith. There's been publicity on the Armagast case, but as you admit, it's a tough one, you've spotted the guilty parties but you've only got pretty pictures on Kallman. Paul wouldn't know Newhall by his face. Are you supposing that just as he walked in somebody was saying in a loud voice, 'Isn't this exciting, hidding one of the Armagast kidnapers'?"

"I *see* all the objections," said Burns testily.

"There aren't many people living alone in that district," said Forbes diffidently. "It's single-residence zoned, no apartments. Family houses. A lot of fairly big houses, four bedrooms—like that. Upper-class family area. The angle I don't see is that one. How the hell could anybody introduce a guy like Newhall into a family group? I mean, even if he wanted to. Because, look—even say he could just get away with saying, This is my cousin Joe Smith, funny but I never happened to mention him to you before—even if that got swallowed, or some tale like that, how in God's name is he going to explain how come Joe Smith's got to stay in the house all the time, nobody knowing he's there? Because—"

"We don't know yet," Burns pointed out, "that some such situation doesn't exist. And you're forgetting the fact that Newhall wouldn't necessarily act like a fugitive. In fact, he'd be a fool to show like that. He could be the broke relative looking for a job, or just getting over a serious illness— Having that cover, he wouldn't be afraid of being introduced to the neighbors and so on. Actually, of the three, Newhall was in the least danger. No pedigree, and he hadn't been photographed very often, I gather. I might add, just to spur us on," added Burns grimly, "that the New Jersey boys figure he was the mastermind. Kallman's just a pro strong-arm guy, and they roped in the woman easiest to hand to ring the doorbell and keep the maid talking while they went in the back. She's just a nonentity, I gather that too. Well, we're going to take a long hard look at all these households"—and he tapped the timetable— "and after that, if nothing shows up, we'll take a long hard look at all the names mentioned in the diary—everybody the boy knew, in that area. I think we should hit pay dirt by that time, but if we don't, we're going to look inside every house within a ten-block radius, and if *that* doesn't turn up something—"

"Is there any possible loophole, though?" said Varallo. "Can we vi-sualize any possible way Paul could have stumbled across Newhall if Newhall *isn't* hiding out in that area? Because, on the face of it, that sounds so damn fantastic. Say just by chance Newhall's driving through the area—maybe he's parked as Paul walks by, asks him some question —maybe he almost hits him at a blind corner or something, and stops to—"

"How wild can you get?" demanded O'Connor. "How in hell would the boy find out anything dangerous to him in that case? I don't see how he could have in *any* case. As we've just said, there's been damn all in evidence on this Armagast thing. It isn't as if Paul had seen a picture in the papers, or even a good description. That's what *makes* this so damn fantastic, that the only possible deduction is that Newhall has gone to ground somewhere up there. That somehow Paul Brandon stumbled across the knowledge of who he was, and had to be got rid of. That—"

"And then," said Varallo, "there's another thing. They call it coinci-dence. I don't suppose that back there in sixteen-eighty-five those fel-lows working at the Brunswick mint, if they called it that then, struck just one nice big silver coin with all this decoration on it and called it a day. There could be a number of them still around. So maybe this is just a false alarm for you boys, Burns, and Newhall never was any-where around here. It could still be a private kill, with somebody else who had one of those coins playing X."

"Oh, hell," said Burns. "It *could* be, sure. But it's such a hot lead—"

"Well, you can look," said O'Connor. "And we're still on this, we'll be looking right alongside you. But I'm damned if I can swallow that somebody like Mrs. Riegler or James Keith or Bob Emmett has been hosting Newhall for—how long? a couple of months?—in, as Vic says, the bosom of the family. And of course that's another thing, the length of time cuts out all possibility that the hosting is involuntary."

"At gun point? Yes, obviously. One man couldn't keep that up longer than twenty-four hours or so. A whole family—even one person. But there must be at least a few people living alone besides this Mrs. Knox—widows, widowers who've stayed on in a big house of inertia. And there's another possibility too," said Burns thoughtfully.

O'Connor said, "You glamour boys are pretty good, but I've been a cop awhile. Sure. The hold over somebody, you mean. So maybe one of these people has a little black mark on their past record, something maybe he or she could go to jail for—and just by chance Newhall knows it, and said, You hide me out here or I'll tell the cops. That's not really—"

"If it is something like that," said Varallo wistfully, "how I'd love it to be Mr. Morehouse! Have it turn out that he's a bigamist, say. He'd certainly be in a better position than most men to introduce a stranger to the household. Quite the autocrat—no questions or curiosity allowed. Only, the way Steve's feeling right now, I think he'd have given it away."

"That," said O'Connor, ignoring him, "isn't really as plausible as it might look. The threat would be almost empty, because the threat would be all Newhall had as a lever—and how could he carry it out? Only by an anonymous letter or phone call. We get some of that—you boys get more. And we try to check it out if it looks serious, but without very definite details—unless it was something very damn definite, I don't see—"

"No," said Burns. "We'll look at everybody, but right now I'm inclined to say it's likelier somebody living alone. I want to look at Mrs. Knox hard. She's just the type to be aiding and abetting a misunderstood godson or nephew—and she didn't need to have known he killed the boy, you know. You say she's old and lame. He could have enticed the boy out to the garage, killed him there, told her Paul had gone home. . . . If we have to, damn it, we'll get a search warrant for every damn house in—"

"And draw blank," said Varallo. "It's ten days ago. Newhall may be anywhere by now."

"I *know,* damn it! But he might be still right where he was, too. So he knows you've fingered it for murder. He also knows you've got nowhere near finding out anything else, in this ten days—he could guess he's still safe. . . . I don't know how or where the boys actually working the Armagast case have been digging— They just hand out the relevant facts they get. But from the way this thing has broken, a great big blank for almost three months and then these little bits of information leaking out— I'd say a few of Newhall's friends, or the woman's, have put two and two together and begun to come apart. I say that because Kallman's pals would all likely be pro small-timers like him, and very unlikely to turn spady, especially on a federal count. Newhall and the woman, by what emerges, lived—on the fringes. Not exactly pro, not exactly not. They'd know people like themselves, people shy of cops, who wouldn't open up easy but might eventually come apart. You see the New Jersey boys are saying now they hope for a photograph. Reading between lines, I'd take a bet, some old flame of Newhall's they're being diplomatic with, trying to persuade. We like to try it that way at first."

"All right," said O'Connor. "Very interesting, but pending the photograph, that doesn't help us much here."

"By God," said Burns grimly, "we'll find out where he's been here, even if he's run on somewhere else—"

"At least," said Varallo, "he hasn't got his lucky talisman any more."

CHAPTER 19

On Wednesday morning a small army of men converged on the Ross-moyne area. Polite, well-dressed men primed to act diplomatic to out-raged honest householders who would protest the search warrants. They were starting out looking at the houses where Paul had been that after-noon; if they drew blank, they'd widen the search.

Varallo, somewhat to his annoyance, didn't join Wayne, Forbes, Poor and O'Connor in tagging along after the Feds. Headquarters still had other business than Paul Brandon; and at eight-ten that morning they got the first break on the school vandals. A Pasadena pawnbroker called in, saying he had some of the stolen items, had just discovered it.

Somebody had to follow that up, and the somebody was Varallo. He went over to Pasadena to see the pawnbroker and take charge of the loot, three of the stolen typewriters.

"I ought to have my head examined, not suspecting," said Campbell, the pawnbroker. "I didn't take them in, it was my part-time clerk. I didn't think to look at the serial numbers until I saw this latest flier—"

But the clerk, Wilanowski, careless though he'd been in accepting the typewriters, proved to have good eyes and an excellent memory. "I'd know both of 'em anywhere," he said. "Tall dark kid about twenty, ducktail haircut, and a loose kind of mouth—you know. And a younger boy, medium coloring, not so tall but chunky, one of those rabbity faces, teeth sticking out. He called the other one Don. I was a damn fool, Mr. Campbell doesn't have to tell me, but they told a plausible story, said they'd taken a chance at one of these storage-house auctions, you know where you bid blind on trunks and so on. Well, the lord knows you can pick up anything that way. My mother bought a trunk at a Bekins' actution once and it was full of brand-new women's shoes—all size three. Well, you see—"

Varallo said he saw, thanked them, signed a receipt for the typewriters, and went back to Glendale to look in Records for a Don.

Just as easy as that, Records turned up a Donald Grace. Twenty-one, Caucasian, male, six-two, a hundred and seventy, eyes gray, hair dark, complexion medium. Grace had been picked up as a juvenile for grand theft auto—probation: for shoplifting at Woolworth's—six months' suspended sentence, probation: and for siphoning gas out of parked cars—three months' suspended sentence, probation. These judges. All before he was eighteen. Then he'd been picked up, six months ago, for breaking and entering a market; he'd served two months for that, and that time he was of age so they could file a record on him and take his prints. He hadn't, apparently, been able to get along in regular high school; when he was first picked up he'd been attending the euphemistically named trade school where the difficult, backward, and incorrigible kids were transferred.

There was an address. Varallo went down to Prints and asked Burt to look at the prints they had for the vandals and at Grace's, see whether they checked.

While he waited, he wondered how the little army up in the Rossmoyne section was making out.

Theoretically, almost anything was possible; but it was very hard to conceive of, say, Mrs. Riegler or James Keith, having a black-sheep stepbrother or cousin, aiding and abetting him like that. It was difficult to swallow because of the kind of people who lived in that area, and the kind of criminal Newhall was. Very few people of any kind would knowingly, willingly, shelter a kidnaper—this kidnaper. . . . And it narrowed down to a fairly small area, too, when you looked at it straight: to the distance Paul might have gone, on foot, between five-fifteen and five-forty-five, starting from the Rieglers'. . . .

And he was still wondering (though his imagination couldn't come up with anything plausible) whether there wasn't a loophole. Whether Newhall hadn't been just passing through, and somehow Paul—

But wait a minute, he thought. No. It was definitely linked to that area, had to be. Because trouble had been taken over Paul's murder, to disguise it as an accident. To keep everything on an even keel. So Newhall could stay right where he was, nobody suspecting. It hadn't worked out that way; and possibly Newhall had got nervous enough, when it came out that they had spotted it for murder, to run on some-

where else. In which case, there'd be no traces now to say he'd ever occupied a spare bedroom anywhere in Glendale. . . .

The prints matched up. "Thanks so much," said Varallo, and had
lunch while the warrant was made out. He went down to Roderick Avenue and picked up Don Grace, who was lounging large as life on the
porch of his father's old house with a can of beer in his hand.

"Him one of the ones been doing *that?*" said Grace senior. "Can't say
I'm surprised. He allus hated school 'cause it showed up how dumb he
is. Listen, for God's sake, you put him in jail this time, will you? Don't
make no sense, pick him up and let him go next day."

"How right you are," said Varallo. And he might deplore this unnatural attitude, but at least it made more sense than the attitudes of the
parents who bleated, My Johnny'd never do such a thing. Don, of
course, was half sullen and half swaggering—and he wasn't going up before a judge alone; he came out with his pal's name right away.

"It was really Bill's idea, I just kind of went along— Bill Pitman, over
on Currier in Burbank—listen, I just—"

So presently Varallo went over to Burbank and collected Bill Pitman.
All the damn red tape . . . Nobody had called in excitedly, we've got
him, so presumably the minute search hadn't turned up anything interesting.

How could it? That quiet upper-middle-class neighborhood, my
God . . .

"September twelfth," he read, "the Balboa Elementary School. September twenty-second, Hoover High—September twenty-ninth, Wood-
row Wilson Elementary—October ninth, two in one night, Eleanor J.
Toll and Glenoaks Elementary—"

The two of them were listening sullenly to the formal charge, heads
down. A couple of louts. Useless louts. Who'd make a hell of a lot more
trouble for police before they died. While a boy like Paul Brandon—

"That's a damn lie," said Don Grace. "What you just said. That
school. Glenoaks? We never hit that. Sure, O.K., we was at Toll that
night— I guess it was that night. But not the other one. I wonder who
did. We didn't, Bill can back me up, can't you, Bill—"

The ferret-faced seventeen-year-old Bill said morosely, "Sure. That
wasn't us, bloodhound. Not that one. But no use try to sell it to you it
wasn't, I know that much. What the hell?"

Varallo looked at him a moment before going on. Some very small,
insignificant memory was trying to get past his subconscious— What?

The Glenoaks School—Fisher that morning—what a mess. . . . Nothing. Never mind; it would come to him.

Gordon was absent on Wednesday. Which wasn't too surprising, of course. With this kidnaper somehow linked up to Paul's murder—and what a farfetched thing that was—Katharine was thinking now that she must have been imagining things about Gordon. It was just Gordon's difficulties at school, intellectually and socially—and the murder would have shocked him perhaps even more than it had adults, and Paul the only friend he'd made here. With luck, and help, Gordon would catch up, get on an even keel. But, dutifully and politely, she called Mrs. Bicknell during her lunch hour.

"I was so glad to know he's all right. But as he's not at school today, I thought I'd—"

"Well, it's real nice of you, Miss Mason, be so interested. But, see, he picked up an awful bad cold, maybe even a virus the doctor said, and we figured better keep him in bed a day or so. You know."

"Oh, I see," said Katharine. Not very important, a couple of days lost from school; heaven knew he wasn't getting much out of it anyway. Only after a stiff several months' remedial-reading course (if he'd cooperate and try at all) could Gordon get much out of school. And how he'd managed to get by this long— "Well, I do hope he'll be better soon. I've got the addresses and schedules of the remedial courses being offered right now, for you—of course the sooner he's entered and starts work, the better. I thought I could drop by and give them to you and see Gordon this evening?" And she hadn't really much desire to give up even an hour to Gordon, but as an efficient teacher (whether she liked the boy or not) she knew that if he was convinced she was concerned about him, any teacher, it might be the one small thing that would encourage him to try, in the remedial course and his regular schoolwork.

"It's nice of you, take an interest. His dad thinks it's awful good of you too, Miss Mason. That'll be fine."

"Good, I'll see you about seven-thirty then," said Katharine.

As she went down the corridor to the teachers' room, to renew powder and lipstick before the afternoon session, she wondered avidly what they were finding out about the kidnaper.

Varallo sat at his desk and stared fixedly at the row of metal file cases against the wall. File cases, he thought. It was something to do with file cases. Just on the edge of his subconscious mind . . .

Six o'clock, and so far they'd drawn blank. They had covered, by now, all of the places where Paul had been that afternoon—meeting various responses, but most of the people up in that area were, as O'Connor had pointed out, honest citizens with respect for authority. They might feel a little indignant and more bewildered that the FBI wanted to search their houses, but they didn't argue too much in the face of the warrants.

"They ask why, of course," said a tired young man named Canaletti, limping in to report before taking time out for dinner, "and that gives us the opening." They were spreading the word—they were after Newhall; knew definitely he was or had been in that area. Without much doubt a lot of excited telephoning was going on. But so far, at least by what any of them could observe of reactions (and they were a pretty smart bunch, the Feds), they hadn't got any reactions except astonished excitement and, from the women, fear.

When they'd got through the list of addresses Paul had visited that day, they started out to go through the houses of everybody he had known up there.

It hadn't escaped Burns's attention that there was a space limit of sorts: the distance Paul might have walked from the Rieglers' within, call it at the outside limit, twenty minutes. He'd got the killing blow by 5:45; and it wouldn't have been delivered the moment he arrived wherever that was. Maybe quite soon after his arrival, but not at once. And 5:45 was the outside limit the doctor had given them. A good many of the streets up there were steep and curving; even an energetic ten-year-old wouldn't make as good time as on the level.

So they had looked at the map and at the actual terrain, and they had drawn a square provisionally enclosing the distance he could have covered, in whatever direction, the center of the square the Rieglers' house. The top line ran from the last half block of Harrington Road to its dead end; picked up on Hillcroft Road and ran down to Rossmoyne. The bottom line ran along Stocker Street from Cedar to Rossmoyne. Those two streets closed the square.

When they had covered all Paul's acquaintances, they'd start ringing doorbells inside that square.

They were not calling it a night until people would be going to bed. The men reported in, took a little time out for a meal, started in again covering the addresses on their lists. They were working in pairs, of course; the Feds never took chances on a thing like that. If by some heaven-sent chance they should come across John Newhall hiding in a closet—well, that last report had said, "is a fair shot."

"And would you have a guess," asked O'Connor, "how many houses there are in that mapped-out square? Ten square blocks, say? What a job—"

"We probably won't get to that," said Burns, "until tomorrow. But if we have to, we will. Something may break. That last teletype I had from New Jersey, the boys are getting warmer. We may get a wirephoto before midnight—they sounded optimistic. I take it you're planning to hang around awhile?"

"Damn right," said O'Connor. "I want to know the answer on this thing. It's so damn wild—"

"That's how the big ones look, sometimes," said Burns. "And then when you know, you want to kick yourself for being so damn stupid as to have missed seeing it." He looked at his watch. "I'm going out for something to eat and then take a run over to Burbank." The nearest FBI office was in the Burbank Hall of Justice. The Feds were using Glendale Police Headquarters as a base on this one, and all teletyped information would come directly here; but the wirephoto, probably, to Burbank, as in all the excitement Burns hadn't let New Jersey know that Glendale could receive one—not all police headquarters were equipped.

"O.K.," said O'Connor, "we'll hold down the fort." Burns went out, and he looked at Varallo. "What are you day-dreaming about? You haven't said a word in ten minutes."

"I'm trying to pin down an elusive idea I had—just for a flash. I can't remember it at all, except that it's something about the vandalism at that elementary school. Something to do with file cases. Damn it, all of a sudden I have the feeling it's important. Important about something else. And I'm damned if I can—"

"It'll come to you," said O'Connor.

"It hasn't yet. I must be getting old. Damn it. Oh, well—" He dialed home to tell Laura he wouldn't be in until late.

"I didn't really expect you," she said, "with all this going on. But it's incredible—*that* man! You and your G-men have certainly stirred up the neighborhood. Everybody calling everybody else to ask if *they've* had the house searched, and isn't it terrible, and what on earth gave them the idea such a monster could be living up here amongst *us*? But I gather you haven't got any more leads yet."

"It looks like a long job. And of course, he may not be here now."

"And also he may be," said Laura. "Vic. I don't usually say anything, because if you're married to a policeman, well, there you are— nothing you can do about it. You just gamble he won't run across the hopped-up hood with a gun. But this Newhall—listen, you be careful, will you? I don't want to be raising a fatherless child."

"Don't be silly," said Varallo. "Surrounded by all these tough Feds? If he *is* here, and anybody runs across him, just on the law of averages it'll be one of those boys, not me."

"That's all very well," said Laura. "But you listen, now. If you do go out on it, you take that fat Irish lieutenant with you, see? He may be a woman-chaser and an impossible autocrat, but he's also a sharpshooter, and I'd feel much happier to know that Charles and his favorite big-bore were right alongside you."

Varallo laughed. "Now that's a fine idea, me giving orders to the lieutenant! Don't fuss, *cara*. I'll be home when I can. Probably by eleven, at least." They'd shut down the work at ten or so; if anything really hot, or the photo, came in, the night-duty men could always drag them out of bed again.

Katharine cursed the weather, driving home; in any sensible climate, October would mean fall and cool weather, but it was the worst month for heat in Southern California. She dropped her bag and inevitable manila envelope on the couch and headed for a long tepid shower. After that she felt better, and got down to correcting papers with a show of briskness.

That task over, she looked at her mail—mostly ads, an invitation to join an alumni association, and a bill from the garage (heavens, that flat tire, hadn't she paid that when she should have last month?)—and set about getting herself some dinner. Chilled chicken salad ready in the refrigerator, lots of nice crunchy buttered toast to go with it, but that wasn't enough really—broil those two lamb chops? And maybe some instant mashed potatoes . . .

She wondered with violent curiosity what the FBI and police were finding out about Newhall. Such an unexpected, fantastic thing— She could have killed Charles, taking her home last night just as it was getting interesting. But of course she couldn't call up and just ask. Nothing but a private citizen—just because she happened to know a police officer—

It was maddening not to know what was happening. But sooner or later, if they did find anything more, it would all come out.

She tried to read over dinner, but her mind kept wandering from her book to Newhall, to that terrible Armagast murder, to Paul, to Gordon —to O'Connor. . . . She washed the dishes, and then it was ten to seven—she must hurry. It was a nuisance to have to go out again, but—

She stripped off her housecoat and put on a thin summer dress, slipped on sandals. Powdered her nose, renewed lipstick, combed her hair. Bag, keys—did she have that note of addresses and schedules? yes— She locked the door behind her and went down to the car.

It was 7:26 when she parked in front of the Bicknell house on Rosemount Avenue.

Mrs. Bicknell came to the open front door at the first ring, held open the screen. "Hello, Miss Mason. It's nice of you to take this trouble. Step in." Her voice was dull, and Katharine saw that she'd been crying, tried to mask red eyes with too much powder.

"How is Gordon?" she asked sympathetically.

"Oh, he's been pretty sick, I'm afraid. Doctor gave him a couple of shots, I guess penicillin or something, but he's been pretty sick. These viruses— He didn't sleep hardly at all last night, I was up with him a lot, and he's just now finally got off to sleep, so if you'll excuse it you'd better not see him—" She sounded oddly breathless.

"No, that's all right. I'm so sorry about all this, I know it's been an upset for you. But if—"

Bicknell came into the room then, and smiled at her: the smile that made him almost handsome. "Thought that'd be you, Miss Mason. We're sure grateful, you taking an interest in the kid like this. I guess my wife told you he's been pretty sick."

"Yes, I'm so sorry. No, I won't sit down, thank you— I really only came by to give you these addresses. I'm sure you'll find one of the schedules will be convenient for both you and Gordon, and I was just saying to your wife, if he'll try to cooperate, I think a remedial course would help Gordon a lot. I hope so, anyway. Here's the list."

"We appreciate it," said Bicknell. "Thanks. Can't you stay a minute? —offer you a cup of coffee—"

"Oh, no, please don't bother, thanks." She divided a smile between them, turning to the door.

And heard the little boy's voice say thinly, "Teacher—Miss Mason—"

She turned, and saw the boy on the threshold of the room: the boy clutching the doorjamb for support. She said, uncomprehending, "Why, Gordon—why, *Gordon*—"

CHAPTER 20

Varallo and O'Connor went out to dinner when Burns came back, empty-handed. Downstairs, a couple of Burns's men were hanging around monitoring the teletype. Nothing was coming in from New Jersey.

But the Feds were feeling happier—there and here. During the afternoon the New Jersey boys had had a hot lead on Kallman, and were following that up. Now if they could get a line on Newhall, the mastermind—

"But if he was here," said O'Connor, "is he now? We said at the time, they always underestimate us. He didn't think we'd spot it for murder, the way he staged it to look accidental. When we did, did it scare him into running again?"

"I don't know," said Varallo abstractedly, "but when you come to think of it, Charles, whatever his cover was here it must have been a pretty damn good one. Maybe, for the sake of retaining it, he's sat tight and taken the chance. He'd know we hadn't really much to go on, on Paul. He may have gambled on it, and stayed put. But I still don't see—that kind of neighborhood and people. Not to be snobbish about it, but—"

"I know, I know, haven't we all been saying it since last night! Added to which, of course, kidnapers are looked down on by even most pro crooks. Anybody who'd voluntarily help one like Newhall, I just can't see it being somebody like—" He shrugged and attacked his steak. "But this whole thing has been offbeat from the beginning."

They drove back to headquarters afterward in silence. But as O'Connor pulled on the parking brake in the lot, opened his door, Varallo said suddenly, *"Per l'amor di Dio— Certo!"*

"What's struck you?"

"Cattivo è quel vento che a nessuno è prospero—it's an ill wind, et cetera. File cases, file cases," said Varallo. "Those vandals. Sure, every school they hit, they did a lot of wanton damage. Mostly to the administrative offices, but also in classrooms. But while they overturned the file cases at the other schools, and so on, now I think about it—that's what I was trying to remember, what hit me about it—it was only at that one that they took such elaborate measures. Pulled out the files, tore them up, poured ink— And Grace and Pitman swore up and down that wasn't one of their jobs."

O'Connor caught up with him slowly. "Well, so what?"

"I don't know," said Varallo. "I don't know what it means. It just came to me—a funny little thing." He went on frowning to himself, thinking about it. They went into the building, climbed stairs to the Detective Bureau.

Men still hanging hopefully around the teletype. Upstairs, Burns was sitting somnolently at Forbes's desk, filing his nails. There wasn't anything to do but wait for the reports to come in. They'd said everything there was to say about this wild one.

Varallo sat down and stared into space. That one school, he thought, its records so savagely destroyed. Other damage, sure, but more time spent on destroying the files. The *records*. Just to annoy? That was a little subtle for vandals.

The Glenoaks Elementary School—

Burns said, "Be downstairs if you want me," and went out.

The Glenoaks School. All its records. What kind of records? of the kids, the teachers too, school affairs— He didn't know. And Grace and Pitman said—

A little offbeat. But what could it mean?

Hard steps pounded up the stairs: Burns, white and breathless. "Man from my office—just came in—here's the picture. Copy. I've got two men off to get reproductions as soon as—"

O'Connor snatched it; Varallo came up behind him. They looked at the wirephoto in silence for five seconds, and then Varallo said, hearing the naked astonishment in his voice, "But that's—"

And O'Connor said loudly, "Jesus H. Christ, *Katy*—" and exploded into action.

Varallo ran after him, flinging one name behind him at Burns. O'Connor plunged down the stairs, out, and into the lot: made for the nearest patrol car, keys always left, and flung himself in. He gunned the engine as Varallo slammed the right-hand door, and switched on the siren at the same time.

"Up Verdugo—quickest," snapped Varallo. "They haven't got that torn up yet."

O'Connor didn't answer. They were already screaming up Glendale Avenue. It was 7:27. But kill the siren when they were getting near—

"Why, *Gordon*—" said Katharine. Her voice was blank. And then everything—any comprehension, fear, astonishment—was swept out of her mind by the single emotion, for this somehow terribly hurt and frightened and helpless little boy. She started across the room toward him, impulsive, shocked, and compassionate. "Gordon, whatever—"

She heard, without comprehending that either, the screech of brakes, the sudden running footsteps on the porch, the violent crash as the front door swung back hard. She didn't turn; all her attention was on the boy.

Somebody was swearing obscenely in a low savage tone.

She heard O'Connor say, "All right, Newhall, we got there in the end—"

And she was seized bodily from behind, whirled around, and held in a rigid grip before the man. His left arm vise-like around her waist, and she was nearly as tall as he was, his body was well shielded behind hers. She felt something jabbed viciously into her right side. It all happened so fast she hadn't time even to gasp until then. "*What*—" she started to say in a high bewildered voice, "*what*—" That was a gun jammed against her. A *gun*. He was holding her so tightly she couldn't breathe. *Gordon's*— A gun.

She looked up wildly and saw O'Connor and Varallo in the doorway, ten, twelve feet away. O'Connor had his gun out, but it hung loose in his hand—an enormous gun, it looked two feet long, it—

"Hold it, bloodhound!" said the man behind her, sharp and cold. His grasp tightened; he was pulling her backward, toward the door into the hall, and he kept the gun jammed tight against her side. "One move to raise that canister, the girl gets it right in the guts—"

O'Connor was wearing a casual, rather thoughtful expression. She saw his hand move, and opened her mouth to scream. Then there was one incredibly loud explosion, and the man behind her screamed. He fell away from her onto the floor. She took three steps to lean on the wall, and looked down at him. There was something wrong with his right hand, it was mangled and bloody, and he'd dropped the gun—

Varallo swooped down on it. "A very pretty shot, Charles," he said, sounding shaken. And then there were sirens, brakes screeching outside, and men pouring into the house—

"You O.K., Katy? You'd better sit down," said O'Connor, and guided her to a chair. "Gave me a hell of a shock, damn you. I remembered you saying you were coming up here tonight, and when— My God, why do you have to be so damn conscientious about your kids?" He gestured angrily with the gun. "I damn near had a heart attack. I think I'll sit down myself." He did, and shoved the gun into his holster.

A crowd of men hauling the man up, grim-faced, half carrying him out. The man moaning obscenities—the man who must be—who must be—

The woman had fainted, ungracefully sprawled out. Men bending over her too. Katharine tried to pull herself together—it had all happened so *fast*—

"Please," she said, "Gordon—the boy—he's hurt, I—I think he's been beaten—terribly, he looked—"

"O.K., they're looking after him," said O'Connor. "I've contributed my bit for a while. Why the *hell* you had to—"

And full realization suddenly hit her of what *had* happened. She sat up a little straighter. She was suddenly and enliveningly furious at him. "I must say, you were certainly thinking more about getting your man than about my life! He had that gun actually jabbed *into* me! The second he saw you were going to shoot, he could've pulled—"

"Oh, no, he couldn't," said O'Connor. "We knew he had an automatic— I was expecting it. Damn fool sort of gun. And nobody but an idiot carries an automatic cocked. I saw him haul it out, I kept an eye on it. He hadn't cocked it yet. So he'd have to pull the trigger once to bring the load into position to fire—there was an easy two seconds' leeway, and I don't take that long to aim at a target."

"Two *seconds!*" exclaimed Katharine. "And his hand about three inches away from *me*—if you'd missed—"

"*Missed?*" said O'Connor. He sounded mortally offended. "Miss by three inches at ten-foot range? *Me?* Why, you damn little—"

"You've insulted him," said Varallo. "State champion after all, Miss Mason. Nevertheless, boy, it's a good thing you'd got in a few recent practice sessions."

"It was a very neat little idea, of course," said O'Connor in the growing dusk. The four of them were sitting here companionably in the Varallos' patio, long iced drinks at their elbows, the following evening.

Everything had turned out as satisfactorily as possible; they'd hardly got Newhall locked in before the teletype came in from Florida to say that Kallman had been dropped on too. . . . "Not Newhall's own invention. The Touhy brothers tried it once, back in Prohibition days. Go to ground by living like the do-good people. Get a regular job, a house, live a regular honest life. Lie low like that a year, longer, until the heat's cooled off. It was a dandy idea. Only on a couple of things he miscalculated."

"It still seems so— I *see* it," said Laura, "but what a fantastic—! And Gordon didn't belong to them at all?"

"Uh-uh. The woman—Marion Stepp—came apart and gave us the whole thing. That was the one artistic little touch that brought them to grief in the end. Newhall thought it was the one thing to raise them above any possible suspicion—who'd take a second look at a quiet couple with a kid? Marion Stepp is Gordon's Auntie May. His real mother is her sister, and the dad Gordon thinks so much of is one Artie Mayer, a pro elevator man now doing a three-to-five in Sing Sing. Gordon's been brought up the wrong side of the law, taught to hate and fear the cops, the bloodhounds. And in that kind of family, nobody cares much whether kids go to school regular— Gordon's got out of school as much as he can all the time he's been of school age. He probably hasn't attended one whole year, altogether. Naturally when he was expected to do fifth-grade work—"

"Which explains quite a lot," said Katharine, nodding. "Fantastic is the word. And this Marion Stepp—and I said she seemed like a nice woman!—just—just *borrowed* him from his mother, to—"

"To improve the cover, yes. We don't know much about the mother, but maybe with her husband away in the pen, she was just as happy to have the kid off her hands for a while. These people are like that. They came here," said O'Connor, "for a good reason. Newhall happened to know about this Bill Wegge. Probably from Kallman, who's done time. It emerges that about twenty years ago Wegge did a stretch for armed robbery. He's since settled down and turned into a respectable citizen, and his wife didn't know about his record, and he was scared to death of her finding out. That was Newhall's lever. All he wanted was a reference from Wegge, you see—in case anybody ever did come asking, Wegge was to say, sure, Bert Bicknell had been around Glendale a long while."

"It was odd about that address," said Varallo, rattling ice cubes in his glass.

"Not very," said O'Connor. "Wegge knows the town. On a street like Longa Way, people are coming and going all the time. Almost bound to be someone with a similar sort of name who'd lived along there awhile. People in a neighborhood like that don't remember very clearly what neighbors they had six months ago. He just took the chance, and it came off. And at that, if it hadn't—if I hadn't found a trace of anybody with a name like that there—I wouldn't have thought too much about it, you know—just figured maybe they hadn't lived there long, and the people who had known them had moved. Of course, if we'd ever had occasion to go looking really hard, it'd all have fallen through. No record of him at that agency garage, and so on. That's what he was gambling on, that no suspicion would ever be raised. What he wanted from Wegge mostly was the job reference. He knew he could get a job easy, he's a first-class mechanic. He came here, fixed things up with Wegge—whose wife, I'm happy to tell you, took his record in her stride, said, well, he'd always been good to her and the kids and she didn't care about anything else—and put a down payment on the house. Clever Mr. Newhall, lie low and work a regular job just like an honest man until the heat's off on the Armagast kidnaping. Put up the front, with the girl friend Marion, as a very ordinary couple. Only things started to go wrong—on account of Gordon."

"That poor little boy," said Katharine. "I can understand now— I suppose, coming from a family like that, he thought it was a great adventure at first, help out a real important big-shot crook—and his Auntie May. But what his mother was—"

"I will say," said O'Connor thoughtfully, "I doubt very much if his father hadn't been in the pen that Gordon could have been, um, borrowed so easy. Not even pro elevator-men have much sympathy with kidnapers. But women can sometimes be very damned cold-blooded."

"A woman like that, maybe. I never can understand— But of course once they were here, Gordon met some other kids—met Paul. And Paul —do you know how Paul happened to—?"

"As Charles says, she came apart." Varallo got up to renew their drinks. "Paul—" He looked sadly at the bottle in his hand— "Just bad luck for Paul, that he happened to walk in the kitchen door—as per habit—to offer the kitten to his new pal Gordon's mother, just as Newhall was saying something loud and boastful about having got clean away with the ransom money, the Armagasts'd never see a dime of that again, and how he'd have a ball with it when the heat was really off—"

"And Paul was a bright boy," said O'Connor. "He'd have read about the Armagast case. All the same, I wonder if he did really understand what he'd heard. It might have been passed off somehow, if Newhall had stopped to think— Paul wasn't expecting to run across a kidnaper, after all. But Newhall is the kind who hits first and thinks afterward. . . . The woman's just a nonentity, of course—infatuated with Newhall. She didn't like any of it—what happened to the Armagast boy, what Newhall was doing to Gordon—but she's the kind just stands around crying and saying, Oh, please don't. You know. . . . She says Paul just stood there, she didn't know if he understood what he'd heard, and then Newhall saw him and just made a lunge at him. Taking it for granted Paul had heard and knew who he was. He threw a punch and slammed him down to hit the edge of the kitchen table—" He stopped abruptly and drank. "We know what happened after that, no need to go over it."

"Gordon *there,* and knowing—" Katharine looked sick. "It's enough to— A ten-year-old boy."

"Two ten-year-old boys," said Laura quietly.

"Yes, of course. I've thought of something, too. That first time Gordon stayed away from school—I thought he was just being sullen when he didn't tell me or Mr. Harwell he really had an excuse, about the dentist. But that was a lie, of course—he just didn't know his supposed mother would back him up. . . . Yes, and—Newhall—must have beaten him for that, too, his face was all bruised next day— How—"

"Gordon worried Newhall like hell," said O'Connor. "Sure. He hadn't thought about it from the boy's viewpoint, he just saw what a beautiful cover it was for him. He hadn't figured that it might be kind of hard for a kid like Gordon to start behaving like an ordinary kid from a respectable upper-class home. A kid who'd gone to school regular, and so on. It worried him—and puzzled him—like hell when Gordon naturally attracted your attention," and he smiled sleepily at Katharine. "They *had* to keep looking ordinary." The smile vanished. "What with Auntie May just saying, Oh, please don't, I guess Gordon hasn't had just such a nice time with Mr. Newhall. And his sadistic tendencies."

"You needn't tell us," said Katharine, looking a little pale. "We can imagine. No wonder he ran away. But why didn't he *tell* somebody? Long before? A terrible thing like—and he *liked* Paul—"

"Katy," said O'Connor wryly, "you don't take into consideration that he's not an ordinary little boy, Gordon. He's a pro's little boy. He's been raised just naturally to look on the do-right people as marks, and the cops as his natural enemies. He's in on this thing, he's on a job with

Newhall and Auntie May—what, even think about turning spady and getting the boys in blue down on them? Even when he was so scared. He just tried to get out from under, and we saw what that got him. But he did break at the last, staggered out when he heard your voice, to ask for outside help at last."

"What's going to happen to Gordon?" asked Laura after a little silence.

Varallo laughed without much humor. "Why, he'll probably be sent back to his own mother, that's all. Newhall gave him quite a scientific beating up for calling so much attention on them—but he's going to be O.K. after a while in the hospital. And his mother hasn't any record. Legally speaking she's fit to stay his natural guardian. The fact that she was willing to lend him to her sister for a while—well, she can always claim, as she will, she didn't know a thing about Newhall, hadn't any notion her sister was mixed up in that case, just thought Auntie May meant to give Gordon a nice vacation in California—"

"It's not right!" said Katharine.

"No. But it's the law. Even if they do take him away from her, he'd end up in a state home somewhere. It's already a little late to do anything about Gordon—ten to one he'll grow up into a pro like his dad. Depressing as the thought is. They seem to be with us to stay, the pros."

"I suppose," said Laura after another silence, "that that other vandalism you were puzzled about—"

"Oh, yes, that was Newhall. You," Varallo smiled at Katharine, "let it out to him that in the ordinary way Gordon's former school would eventually pass on his records. In fact, you were wondering then why you hadn't already received them?"

Katharine nodded. "When there's a transferral like that, the old school sends over the records, usually, some time in the first month of term."

"Yes. That must have been a little shock to Newhall—that aspect of it hadn't occurred to him. Naturally the school had no records on a Gordon Bicknell. But Newhall was stuck with his story, and he did what he could. He'd have been reading about all the vandalism, of course, so he faked that attack on the Glenoaks School and destroyed all the records he could find. So, even if you asked specifically—when you didn't receive any records—there'd be no hope of finding any."

"But," said Katharine, frowning, "sooner or later I'd have found out, you know. With the records destroyed—if I'd asked who Gordon's teacher there had been, gone to see—"

"You could have, but would you? Have gone to that trouble? Just for one pupil?"

"I don't know," said Katharine slowly. "I might have, but on the other hand—we're kept pretty busy—"

"Well, it was all Newhall could think of to do. And then sit back and gamble that you wouldn't bother to check back in person. To go and see the fifth-grade teachers at that school and discover that none of them remembered Gordon. Newhall sat tight—but it worried him like hell that you took so much interest in Gordon—he hadn't foreseen that at all. Gordon was just a kid to him—good cover. He didn't realize that Gordon would attract attention at school because of his backwardness."

There was a longer silence. Gideon Algernon Cadwallader stopped batting at midges in the dusk and climbed up Varallo's trouser leg to peer into his glass. Varallo stroked him. Laura said, "*Oh!* Never mind, it's just got hiccups again. Some ways, I wish we'd never started this project. . . . Vic?"

"*Cara?*"

"Paul Brandon. Does it make any sense at all? Was it *for* something? Would you have got Newhall—in the end—anyway?"

"We haven't got him," said Varallo. "The Feds had first claim. Well, who can say? Do we say, something like destiny?" He shrugged. "And other lives changed too. Steve Morehouse's, for one. Wilma Starke's—I don't think Starke will put up with her much longer, and who can blame him? God knows the Brandons. I don't know, darling."

O'Connor said, his deep voice oddly gentle, "I think it was for something, yes. A very good chance that Newhall would have got away clean, except for Paul. Because, except for Paul, Gordon probably wouldn't have got so scared—with reason. Wouldn't have started acting funny enough to be noticed. And Newhall—Newhall is one bad man. The odds are he'd have gone on to kill somebody else. Maybe several somebodies. So Paul didn't get killed just for nothing, Laura. . . . You look at it square, I guess the right side even showed a little profit on this case," and he grinned at Katharine.

Gideon reached a paw into Varallo's glass before he could move it, touched an ice cube, yelled, and spat.

"Well—" Varallo sighed. "I don't know. The Brandons won't take comfort that maybe Paul inadvertently saved a few other lives. But there it is. . . ." He set down his glass suddenly, got up and handed Gideon to Laura, and inspected the climbing bush growing up the patio trellis. "Aphis, Goddamn it!" he said bitterly. "The first time Alida Lovett's had it this year!"

O'Connor edged his chair closer to Katharine's. (And what the *hell* had got into him? Not his type.) He said, "About Saturday night—"

DETECTIVE'S DUE

The qualities of a good detective are an abundance of physical and nervous energy; considerably more-than-ordinary persistence; imagination and ingenuity, with the initiative and force to apply them; and a broad background of experience with special reference to information sources. Psychological and physical tests may one day be developed to measure these qualities. . . .

ORLANDO W. WILSON,
Police Administration

Ah, take one consideration with another—
. . . A policeman's lot is not a happy one—

—W. S. GILBERT

I wish to note that one of the plots in this story was suggested by a story in *Official Detective Magazine* and I express my thanks to that magazine for the suggestion and for permitting me to borrow from it. Of course, any similarity between the characters in this work of fiction and any actual characters is purely coincidental and unintentional.

L.E.

CHAPTER 1

"All I can say is," said Varallo glumly, "I wish you'd get this *over* with. I'm getting damn tired of being a husband in name only, and besides—"

"You're getting tired of it?" said Laura. "Hah!" She looked at herself in the mirror over the bureau and grimaced. "How do you think I feel, going around looking like the circus fat lady? It must be quadruplets or at least triplets, Vic, the way—"

"God forbid," said Varallo hastily. "On a detective's salary? Don't even say such a thing, *cara!* And what about this doctor, anyway, is he any good at all? Saying it was due last week—"

"Well, you can't be sure to the exact day," said Laura. She sighed at the mirror. "I'd *better* hurry up and have it. At least you're out of uniform, but you do go out of the office on things, and every female who looks at you—" Resignedly, she looked at her handsome blond cop.

Varallo grinned down at her unself-consciously, running the comb through his tawny crest of hair. "Well, you've provoked a few whistles in your time."

"That," said Laura, cocking her brown head at him, "sounds like a left-handed compliment if I ever heard one. *Look* at me. I don't care whether it's triplets or—or sextuplets, I just want it *over* with! And we just have to *wait*. Why did I ever get involved in this project, anyway?"

"I have had the same thought," said Varallo, "myself. Just keep hopeful thoughts that it'll be soon. I don't mind so much when I'm on night tour, but this is my last night. I'm back on days Monday." He opened the top drawer, and took out the shoulder holster and .38 Police Special. "As you know."

"Well," said Laura, and sighed again. "Thirty-four *pounds*. I couldn't help it. Dr. Straw said not over twenty-five, but after all— I did try to stay on the diet, but I was *hungry*. And will I *ever* get back to a size fourteen afterward? Why on earth did I ever want a baby?"

"You sound very unmaternal." Varallo shrugged into his suit jacket.

"Right now that's just the way I feel," said Laura gloomily.

Varallo laughed and kissed her. "It's got to come eventually. Law of nature. And come to think, I'll be relieved to be off nights right now— you here alone. Now look, if anything does start happening you call Mrs. Anderson right away." The Andersons lived next door.

"I'll be all right. It probably won't come for *weeks*."

"*La finisca!*" said Varallo. "Don't sound so discouraged. Eventually—"

"Eventually," said Laura. "Take care, Vic."

"Just another boring night. Sit around the office and talk about Tracy. Nothing much exciting ever happens in Glendale. We've had our headline homicide for the fiscal year." Varallo walked back to the kitchen.

Laura giggled. "Poor Patrolman Tracy."

"It's not really funny," said Varallo, but he grinned too. "We'll have to do something about it. Don't forget to lock the door after me."

"I will, I will. Wait until I get Gideon." Laura made a dive for Gideon Algernon Cadwallader, who was hopefully under Varallo's feet with every intention of sliding out into the inviting darkness when the door opened. Gideon Algernon Cadwallader had a handsome black-on-gray striped coat, an immaculate white front and chartreuse eyes. Laura looked at him in her arms and said, "It's about time to have him done. He was three months in September when we got him, that makes him about seven months now. We'd better—"

"Well, I wanted to get that Granada and Lilac Dawn in tomorrow."

"You and your roses," said Laura. "So go and loaf around the office, cop."

Varallo waited until he heard the lock click into place, and walked across the patio to the garage. He detoured a few steps to sniff at Neige Parfum, which was doing well after its slow start, and then snapped on the spotlight on the garage and backed out his old Chevy. The street was very dark; this Rossmoyne area, one of the better (if older) areas of town, was usually quiet. He drove down Rossmoyne Avenue to Glenoaks Boulevard and down that to Glendale Avenue. It was Saturday, the fourth of January, and maybe everybody was still recuperating from the holidays, but there was little traffic and the town felt quieter even than usual. Glendale, the third largest incorporated city in Los Angeles County, was largely residential; it hadn't much serious crime, though since the population was going up—a hundred and thirty thousand now, or so—they were getting a little rise there too.

Patrolman Tracy, thought Varallo. Well, it wasn't really funny, but—

He went down Glendale to Wilson and turned right, and three blocks down turned left and immediately into the big parking lot behind the very handsome new Police Headquarters building on the corner of Howard and Wilson.

"My God!" he said, and involuntarily hit the brakes. The bare expanse of parking lot had suddenly ceased to be bare. Suddenly it was a grove of—what? Pots with tall stakes and vines growing up them—a jungle of vines. He blinked. Cautiously, he parked the car. Cautiously, he started toward the jungle.

Another car door slammed. "Vic?"

"Jeff." Forbes was the other plain-clothes man on night tour. "What the hell—"

Forbes's lanky tall figure ambled up in the glare of the overhead fluorescent lights. "Twenty of 'em," he said, deadpan. "Katz got such a kick out of it he called me at home. The truck driver wouldn't take 'em back, and the lieutenant didn't know what the hell else to do with them until we can send them back."

"You don't mean—"

" 'S right. Twenty ten-foot climbing roses, all ready for planting. C.O.D., of course," said Forbes solemnly. Then he began to laugh. So did Varallo. "I could almost hear the lieutenant from where I was."

"Oh my God!" said Varallo. "But we've got to do something about it, do you know, Jeff? Charles was going to write all the companies—"

"Well, Joe said between them they got three-four letters written and then Wayne came in with those hoods who heisted the liquor store last night, so they got sidetracked. Besides, Joe said the lieutenant had a date with that schoolteacher and took off early."

"Um," said Varallo. They walked up to the broad shallow steps and in the front door. Sergeant Copeland was on the desk.

"Hi. How d'you like Tracy's jungle out there?" he asked, and burst out laughing.

"It's not really funny—" Varallo burst out laughing.

"It's the most *interesting* thing that's happened since I've been on the force," said Forbes. "I like it."

Grinning, they climbed the stairs to the Detective Bureau. The Detective Bureau consisted of one large room well-lighted by continuous strip fixtures, with a lot of desks back to back and Lieutenant Charles O'Connor's desk off by itself. Nobody else was there. The day men were gone, of course. Glendale was a quiet town. It wasn't too often that the plain-clothes men on night tour got haled out of the office. Oh, once in a while a heist job, like that one last night: once in a while a break-in. Not often.

Varallo sat down at his desk and Forbes sat down at his. "No, but seriously, what do you think about it?" asked Varallo. "I mean, Tracy seems like a very nice guy. I admit, he hasn't got much sense of humor, but—"

"Would *you* have, about now?" asked Forbes. They both started to laugh again.

Patrolman Neil Tracy's strange ordeal had begun on December second, a little over a month ago. Although Patrolman Tracy had a perfectly good home on Doran Street, where he lived with his wife Margaret and his two-year-old daughter Diana, he suddenly began receiving mail at Headquarters. Mail, of a sort, you could call it, though some of it arrived by express too. The first parcel had contained twelve dozen tennis balls with his initials on them. Patrolman Tracy did not play tennis. The tennis balls had been sent C.O.D. and the postman had been persistent; finally O'Connor had had to pay for them. Called in and asked for an explanation, Tracy had none; he certainly had not ordered any initialed tennis balls. Nor had he ordered the twelve boxes of fine Havana cigars which arrived the next day, C.O.D., nor the hand-carved walnut humidor ($39.95 plus customs duty) from Israel, nor the case of fresh grapefruit from Florida. All of which arrived within the next week.

Patrolman Tracy was annoyed. He refused to accept the C.O.D. parcels. The post office and the railway-express messengers refused to take them back; the address was right, wasn't it?—he *was* Mr. N. Tracy, wasn't he?

Lieutenant Jensen of Traffic was annoyed. He was annoyed by the dozen specially aged prime steaks which arrived soon after the grapefruit, but he got good and annoyed about the dozen live tropical fish. "Listen, Tracy," he said, "this has got to stop. My God, fish yet! Live fish! Listen, Tracy—"

"*I* didn't order any damn tropical fish!" said Tracy. "Why, for God's sake, should *I* order—"

"Listen, write to these people," said Jensen. "Call the express and get the damn fish out of here!"

Patrolman Tracy wrote letters explaining that he hadn't ordered the merchandise and was therefore returning it. Before he finished writing letters there were delivered to him at Headquarters ten pounds of the best Florida shrimp packed in dry ice, a handsome set of tooled luggage from Mexico with a somewhat astronomical bill (including customs duty) attached, and the deed to a lot in Alaska. The messengers (from the post office and railway express) who were conferring all this largesse on him clamored for payment. Patrolman Tracy said he hadn't ordered— Yes, the address was correct, yes, he was N. Tracy, but—

Patrolman Tracy wrote more letters of explanation. By this time the answers to his first letters were coming in, and one and all the merchants were annoyed: why was he refusing perfectly good merchandise which he had ordered? Undoubtedly had ordered: they had the order blanks to prove it, please send to N. Tracy, C.O.D. Tracy started to write letters all over again, and while he spent his time off hunched over the secondhand portable he'd got to practice on (because he hoped someday to get out of uniform), there arrived at Headquarters, duly addressed to N. Tracy, an expensive three-speed record player, a crate of fresh river trout packed in dry ice and a cute little three-month-old silver poodle from a kennel in Oregon. All the delivery men clamored louder for money.

Detective John Poor, who was sentimental, said they couldn't send that poor little pup all the way back to Oregon. Might die on the way, he said. Besides, his wife had been talking about getting a poodle, and the C.O.D. was only fifty bucks, and he could manage that, he guessed. So that C.O.D. got paid, but the rest didn't, and everybody was writing Tracy sternly demanding payment, and Tracy got to feeling a little desperate.

By now he was spending *all* his off time writing letters. And while he toiled away at the typewriter, the lobby at Headquarters accumulated a tape recorder, seventy-five pounds of aged cheese from an outfit in Wisconsin, a notice sent from Paris, France, that his request had been received for a year's subscription to a certain Parisian girlie magazine, and he would start getting it as soon as they were paid, a case of Johnny Walker Black Label and a three-foot-high stuffed toy tiger. All, of course, C.O.D.

"Listen, Tracy," said Jensen. "Listen—"

"It's not *my* fault, Lieutenant!" said Tracy desperately. "What the hell am I gonna do about all this? All these different companies— I don't know what the hell's going on, they all say they *got* orders from me, but I never— And the damn post office won't—"

"All you have to do is write *Refused* on the stuff, the way you do with junk mail."

"Yeah, well, it's not so easy with C.O.D.'s, and the express people— What the hell *is* all this, anyway? Some joker—"

"Some practical joker," said Jensen, "and it's even unfunnier than most practical jokes."

"But what can I do—"

Patrolman Tracy continued to write letters, in the time he was not out riding a patrol car keeping the honest citizens of Glendale protected. Before he had caught up on the latest batch of firms which had trustingly sent him merchandise C.O.D., he became the unwilling recipient of an authentic kilt, size 42, from R. G. McIlheny, Ltd., in Edinburgh. The kilt was priced at $49.95, plus customs duty, and a note enclosed explained that the tartan was the Hunting MacDonald, the Tracys having been a sept to that clan.

The whole affair was providing a good deal of entertainment to all Tracy's colleagues, of course, and they got a lot of mileage out of that kilt. "Hey, Neil, you can wear it to mow the lawn, maybe, give the neighbors a treat?" they said. "Maybe the next time we hold a parade—"

Tracy snarled.

"Listen," said Jensen to O'Connor, "we've got to do something about all this, damn it! You're supposed to be a detective."

But as Forbes had just said, O'Connor had got sidetracked today; and so now there were all those climbing roses, ready for planting, sitting out in the parking lot. Patrolman Tracy, if he wasn't on night tour, was sitting at home writing letters.

"The damnedest thing," said Forbes. "The only thing I can figure, it's somebody who's got a grudge against him, wants to annoy him, you know?"

"But he says he can't think of anybody like that," said Varallo. "And he seems like a very easygoing fellow, Jeff—not the kind to put anybody's back up. He ought to know whether anybody's mad enough at him to—"

"Well, you might think so." Forbes rubbed his lantern jaw thoughtfully. "But there are some guys, Vic, can get riled up over some damnfool little thing nobody else'd think twice about. You know as well as me. Could be somebody like that. And Tracy never realized—you know —that the guy was riled."

"*È vero,*" said Varallo. "Have to do something about it, anyway. Charles said if we could get the firms to send us the original orders, maybe the handwriting might give us a lead. If it is somebody Tracy knows."

"Yeah," said Forbes, yawning. They fell silent; the office was very quiet. Night tour was usually a bore for the detectives on this force. Forbes said reluctantly he supposed he'd better get that report typed up, and ambled over to a typewriter. Varallo had brought along one of Laura's paperback mysteries, and started to read that. Funny, he thought, what peculiar ideas some people seem to have about cops. After a while he wandered down the hall and got himself a cup of coffee.

It would be a long time until eight A.M.

They were sitting around talking desultorily over more coffee at one A.M.

"I hate night tour," said Forbes. He yawned, and lit a new cigarette. "I wouldn't mind it one damn bit if I was on the L.A.P.D. or some place things *happen*. But about all we ever do here is sit round and yak to each other, if there aren't any reports to type. Take over in east L.A.," he added almost wistfully, "hardly a night goes by without a knifing or something."

Varallo grinned at him. "*Tanto peggio!* Bloodthirsty."

"Oh well," said Forbes philosophically, "I draw enough duty with you, I pick up some Italian anyway, and they always give educated guys an edge for promotion."

"Two birds with one—" said Varallo, and the inside phone rang. He picked it up. "Varallo."

"Vic, I got a call in from Barker and Harrison, they just got chased out to this address on Cumberland Road—" Sergeant Copeland added the number. "It's an ADW, what they say, not much on it yet but I gather it could turn into homicide. Boys asked for an ambulance pronto. You better get up there."

"On our way," said Varallo. A little action after all, assault with a deadly weapon. He relayed that to Forbes. They went down to the lot. Patrolman Tracy's climbing roses, ready for planting, stood stark under a gibbous moon.

"Crazy," said Forbes, shaking his head at them.

They took Varallo's car. They went the quickest way, straight down

Wilson to Pacific and straight up Pacific to Cumberland. Cumberland
ran through one of the more exclusive residential areas of Glendale: big
newish expensive homes. The one they wanted turned out to be a split-
level ranch with a lot of synthetic stone on its front; the porch light was
on, a spotlight somewhere in back was on, the black-and-white patrol
car stood at the curb, the front door was open and lights on in the
house. At the house to the right, the porch light was on and a couple of
curious neighbors were standing at the open door looking out. A big
white Caddy four-door hardtop was crazily parked in front of the
house, behind the squad car, with its front wheels canted up over the
curb.

It was fourteen minutes past one. A chilly January night, with a high
gusty wind getting up, another high restless wind, they'd been having a
lot of that sort lately, blowing down trees and power lines and breaking
windows—knock on wood, we can't afford any broken windows, thought
Varallo, what with the obstetrician's bill. God, would the baby *ever*
come? Come on, Laura, deliver!

He smiled at his own poor joke and went into the house with Forbes.

A house that said Money. A newish house, expensive furniture, rich
lush carpeting underfoot. A wide entry hall, and to the left a big living
room. Beige tone-on-tone carpet, a big walnut console TV with sliding
doors. A long quilted green couch. Synthetic stone hearth. The two patrolmen in uniform standing, one on either side of the man huddled on
the couch: they looked up with relief at Varallo and Forbes.

"Mr. Scott—"

The man looked up slowly. He was about forty-five, a good-looking
man, regular features, thick dark hair, a good firm mouth. He looked
wild right now. "Oh, God, if I'd been home," he said thickly. "If I'd
been *here*. Why did I have to be—"

"Mr. Scott?"

And there was the dwindling wail of an ambulance siren right outside, and the man sprang up to his feet. "What the hell took them so
long? We should have— Mother bleeding so—"

"We did what first aid we could, sir," said one of the patrolmen
gently. "Mr. Scott, I know you're concerned for your parents, but these
men are detectives from Headquarters, they'd like to ask you some
questions."

CHAPTER 2

"Just a second," said Varallo. "Let's get the picture here. Parents both attacked?"

The taller uniformed man straightened from Scott. "Yes, sir. I'm Barker. It's—" he looked a little sick suddenly—"in the first bedroom." Harrison went to hold the front screen for the ambulance boys and their stretchers. Varallo and Forbes went ahead of them into the hall again and down past the open door to a paneled study on the right, and came to an open door on the left.

"Christ!" said Forbes softly. Varallo felt himself grimace.

The room reeked of blood. There was plenty of blood to be seen, too. There were twin beds in the room, expensive Danish modern teak-wood, and a long double dresser to match, and a stepped night stand between the beds. There was more lush carpeting on the floor. There were heavy rose satin curtains on traverse rods pulled back from the two tall windows, and between the windows a small, rose upholstered chaise longue.

Both the beds had been turned down for the night. The one nearest the windows was still occupied, by a thin elderly gray-haired woman. The bedclothes had been pulled back—that would probably have been Scott or one of the patrolmen—and they could see what a fearful beating the frail-looking body had taken. She was wearing a sheer pink nylon nightgown. There was blood all over her, bruises and cuts, and she lay in her blood and moaned softly, sporadically, eyes closed.

Near the door to the hall, an elderly man lay on his back with his feet toward the windows, a tall, spare old man with white hair. He had on a navy-blue silk dressing gown over his pajamas. There was blood all over him and the carpet under him.

"We turned him over—he was on his face," said Harrison. Varallo nodded.

"Let us in, Mac," said one of the interns, and pushed past. "Jesus, what a mess." He knelt over the old man, reaching for one flaccid arm. In a minute he said, "This one's a D.O.A." He got up and went to the bed where the old woman lay. So it had turned into a homicide.

"Oh my God," said Harrison. "He had a pulse when I looked at him. I swear—"

"What've you got out of this Scott?"

"Not much yet. We called back as soon as we saw what it was. What a hell of a thing—he told us he'd just got home, about twelve forty, and when he turned in the drive he noticed his father's car out front—that Caddy—and he thought it was sort of funny because the old man always put the car away, but he didn't really think anything was wrong until he came in and saw the light was on in this room. Like a lot of old people —they're both in the late seventies—they always go to bed early, he said, about ten o'clock, and so he came to see if maybe one of them was sick, and found them. And called us."

"Yes," said Varallo. "The old man heard something maybe—somebody breaking in the back door—"

"I think that might have been it, sir. Only not breaking in. It's unlocked. I looked."

"So on the very off-chance that our boy hasn't heard of prints, we dust it," said Forbes. "And of course get nothing. But we have to go through the motions." He went to find a phone and call in for a lab kit. They hadn't, of course, known what they'd find, but maybe night tour was stunting to the brain or something—they should have brought one along.

"Where'd Scott been?"

"I don't know, he was so upset—"

"Yes," said Varallo. The interns had the old woman on the stretcher now, and were carrying her out. He followed them, and found Scott at the front door. Barker had evidently told him his father was dead; he looked gray, but was under better control.

"Please—how is she? Can I go—"

"Can't say right now, sir. You know the hospital—Glendale Memorial?"

"Yes—I'll come."

"Mr. Scott," said Varallo. "I know you're concerned for your mother, naturally. But she's in good hands now, and you can't do anything to help her. That's up to the doctors. But it's our job to find out who did this, and you can help us there, if you will. If you'll just wait a little while and answer some questions, then you can go to the hospital. The quicker we get on this—"

"Yes," said Scott. "Yes, I understand that." He took a deep breath. "Of course I want to help you all I can." He looked at Varallo with more attention. Standing, he was only an inch or so under Varallo's six one, a hefty-shouldered man looking younger than he probably was. "You understand, the shock of—of finding them like— My God, who would—"

"Yes. Would you mind giving me your full name, sir?" Forbes had come back and stood listening silently.

"Richard D. Scott. My father is—my father is—was—" he stumbled— "Robert Scott. He—"

"Suppose we go into the living room and sit down," suggested Varallo. Gently he steered Scott to the couch. Forbes ambled away into the dining room. "And your mother?"

"Frances—Frances Scott. D-Dad was retired. He was an attorney. He only retired last year—he'd always been so well, so active—"

"You live here with them? You're not married?"

"I—my wife—my wife," said Scott through stiff lips, "is dead. She's dead. She was killed in an accident—last year— Do you know, I'm not—not *used* to it yet? Wouldn't you think a man would get used to it after a year? But the house—every time I came—came home, I kept expecting her to be there. She always was—getting dinner, or dressing to go out—and then she wasn't. Of course. No—no Marcia. I couldn't—I thought it would be better—if I didn't have to come home to that house. You see?" Varallo nodded: he was letting him take his time. Forbes came back with a shot glass full of whiskey and handed it to Scott. Scott looked at it in vague surprise, said, "Oh, thanks," and swallowed half of it, and shuddered. After a moment a little more color crept into his face, and he said, "Thanks," again and sighed. "And Marty—Marty being just married, I didn't feel—I didn't want to break in on her and Jim. Young people don't—"

"Marty?"

"My d-daughter. She was named for her mother but we call—we call her Marty. She's twenty-two, she and Jim were married just before—before Marcia was—"

"Yes. So you came to live here. What do you do, Mr. Scott?"

Scott blinked up at him. "Oh, I'm an attorney too. With my father's old firm. Welker, Connally and Scott. Downtown L.A."

"I see. Well, you were out somewhere tonight?"

"Yes. God, if I hadn't— Yes, I had to see this woman, this Evelyn Clark, I had her will ready for her to sign and she works all day, she asked if I could bring it some evening. She's right here in town, so it wasn't too inconvenient—but God, why'd I have to pick *tonight*? Why—"

"Why did X have to pick tonight?" said Forbes. He shook his head. "No profit, Mr. Scott. Things happen."

Scott finished the whiskey and set the glass down unsteadily on the coffee table. "I know," he said thickly. "I know that. You're— I'd better know your names? You're being—"

"Detective Forbes. And I'm Varallo."

"Oh. Yes. There was something in the paper—few months ago. I remember your name. That—that little boy that got murd—"

"Yes. How did this Clark woman happen to go to you if your office is in downtown L.A. and she lives in Glendale?"

"Oh, she works there—she's an assistant treasurer at Horner and Bond. Brokerage house," said Scott absently. All this talk of irrelevant background had steadied him, as Varallo had known it would.

"So you went to see her tonight, and she signed the will. Where does she live?"

"Up on Verdugo Road—past the college. She lives with her sister, neither of them is married, but the sister is one of the legatees so she couldn't be a witness. Miss Clark asked in some neighbors—it's an apartment, these people live there too—a Mr. and Mrs. Bauer, quite— quite nice people. They witnessed the will. And I left and—"

"This was at what time?"

"Oh—let's see, I don't know, about nine to nine fifteen. I didn't—well, I was feeling low, you know. God, if I'd come right home! But I didn't. I didn't, and that's that. I went—I stopped at Pike's Verdugo Oaks for a drink. And I ran into a couple of friends—old friends, Marcia's and mine—Randy and Helen Sims. They'd just finished dinner. And we sat and watched the floor show and talked. It's their—their wedding anniversary, reason they were— So I didn't start home until about twelve twenty, around there."

"Yes," said Varallo. Forbes had wandered off, still listening, to tell the two uniformed men they could get back on tour.

"When I came up to the house, I saw Dad's car there. It's funny, it was in the garage when I left, he always—but it wasn't until I got in the house that—"

"Mmh. You didn't see anybody outside? Front or back? You came in the back door, yes. Anybody at all?"

"No, no, I didn't, if I had I'd have—" Scott looked up. "Why? Do you think—it was done just bef—?"

"Could have been." Break-ins like that usually didn't get pulled until late at night. The fact that the blood was still running said nothing, if the old man had been alive when Harrrison examined him; the surgeon would tell them more about that.

"Oh God," said Scott. "But after—after I called the police, I—there wasn't anything I could do for— I went out front, and you can see where somebody backed Dad's car out—right across the lawn into the street. Why? And why would a burglar—"

"Your father didn't have any enemies? Anybody with a personal grudge against him?" asked Varallo. Irrelevantly he thought of Patrolman Tracy.

"*Enemies?* Of course not. Of course not. How could— But it must have been a—a personal motive," said Scott. "I don't know how or why, but who else but someone who—who hated them would— But there isn't anybody like that! Everybody liked—"

Forbes was shaking his head sadly. "Wrong, Mr. Scott," he said. "With the random violence like this there needn't be any motive at all. Not what you or I'd call a motive."

Scott stared at him. "But such a vicious beating—to—"

"Um-hum," said Varallo. "Some young punk pulling a break-in, what he thinks is an empty house maybe, and being surprised by the householder, and we get things like this. Not often quite so bad, but— Young punk annoyed at being thwarted. Have you ever had a burglary here before?"

"Yes," said Scott. "Yes, about two years ago—before I was living here. Dad and M-Mother'd been away, when they came home they found the house ransacked. The police caught the man, he got a sentence. I don't remember his name, no." Records would turn him up.

"Did your parents keep much cash in the house?"

"Never. Of course not. Oh, Dad might have—ten, twenty dollars on him, ordinarily, and Mother about the same. That'd be all."

"Does your mother have any valuable jewelry?"

Scott put a hand to his head. "Not—not much, no. Her engagement ring—a few bits and pieces—there's a diamond pendant she wears a lot, and a pair of ruby earrings, but they're not large stones, I don't think very valuable—"

"Yes. Well, we'll be taking a thorough look around, Mr. Scott. You can get along to the hospital now. We'll be in touch."

"My God," said Scott. "It seems— To *beat* them like— Well, I'm not a criminal lawyer. You should know." He got up. "Th-thanks." He went out quickly, heading for the back door.

"Front, please, Mr. Scott. There just might be some prints back there." And maybe miracles could happen, thought Varallo.

"Oh. All right."

They heard a car pull up in front. "The lab kit. They took their time," said Forbes. "There's this and that—in the kitchen and the den." He went to let the man in. Varallo went back down the hall to the kitchen.

A big modern kitchen. Somebody in this family—maybe several somebodies—had made money. Or acquired it somehow. There was expensive marble-pattern vinyl flooring here, coved, a big electric range with two ovens and a rotisserie, an expanse of Dutch blue and white tile drainboard, tiled wall back of the stove, a pale blue refrigerator, a good many gadgets standing around—electric can opener, blender, ice crusher mounted on the wall. There was an alcove with a round glass-topped table and white metal chairs. A door to the right led to a large service porch where shutter doors discreetly hid a gleaming white washer and dryer side by side. Off the service porch was the back door, a louver door with screen inside. It stood a few inches open. Varallo looked at it sadly. There was a lock built into the knob of the door. To lock it, all you had to do was press in the little button. And because somebody had forgotten to do that one simple little thing— Because a louver door was a damn safe door, when it was locked. A burglar had to make a lot of noise and use a little time, breaking in a louver door, and without much doubt he'd have been heard and there would have been time for a patrol car to get up here before—

Forbes came back with the lab kit and said, "Once in a blue moon we do get a break. There could be prints. Somewhere." He opened the kit and started assembling materials.

There was blood in the kitchen. Blood, a little, had dried on the vinyl flooring; nothing, unfortunately, that resembled a footprint. There were, interestingly, a few smears of blood on the sugar canister—elegant stainless-steel canisters, sugar, coffee, flour, lined in a neat row on one side of the drainboard. "Went through the house after he'd put the Scotts out of commission," said Varallo. "Maybe his mother had the habit of hiding money in the sugar bin?" There were fainter smears of blood on the service-porch floor.

"Little dried blood on the door," said Forbes, squatting to manipulate his little camel's-hair brush. "Outside."

"Yes, he went out that way," said Varallo. "You said the den?" He went back there. This whole house was obviously kept immaculate and very tidy, so the disorder in the den was immediately apparent in grotesque contrast. A studio couch was pulled from the wall to stand crooked, its cushions on the floor. A large gilt-framed seascape had been torn down from the wall, and someone had put his foot through it. There was a kidney-shaped mahogany desk; all the drawers had been pulled out and dumped upside down, and a mound of miscellany scattered the carpet—old letters, a ledger, a stamp box, unused stationery, a check book, pens and pencils, a bottle of ink, a tube of glue—a duplicate income-tax return. Varallo bent and picked that up. It was the duplicate of Robert Scott's income-tax form for 1963; apparently he had been a businesslike old gent, sending in the last installment well before January fifteenth.

"*Per carità!*" said Varallo, looking at it. "We're in the wrong job, Jeff. You know how much they nicked him for? Nearly seven thousand bucks. And he'd have had quite a few deductions, wouldn't he? If he was over—what's the age, seventy or what?—a double exemption, and—It'd have to work out at the least to between twenty and thirty thousand net income."

"Is there that much money?" Forbes shook his head.

"Well." Varallo dropped the tax form. "Let's see the rest of the place."

There were three bedrooms, all spacious, well-furnished. Richard Scott's was the middle one, next to his parents' room. There, only the bureau had been ransacked, shirts, ties, underwear heaped on the floor. "Ask him to check if anything's missing," said Varallo.

Forbes said Yes absently. "Our boy didn't have a hunt through the parents' room at all. Leery of all the blood in there, after he'd shut them up? Could be. Could be he was nervous. I think maybe he figured rich people'd have cash lying around, that was what he was after."

"Looks that way. Print that Caddy out front, will you?" Varallo went into the main bathroom—there was a small pink lavatory off the entry hall, but that looked untouched. Here, the medicine cabinet was closed: no signs of entry here. So their boy hadn't been looking for dope, at least.

He went back to the front of the house. "Not a smell of a lead so far," he said, annoyed.

The Caddy, just as Richard Scott had said, had been backed out of the garage, down the wide straight driveway, and then swerved backward—violently, by the deep-cut tire marks—across the velvet Dichondra lawn, into the street.

"Why?" said Forbes. "When he didn't take it?"

"Afterthought," said Varallo. "He realized there'd be a call out on it. He has some rudimentary common sense. Which young and violent punks do not always—even very frequently—have."

"How true, how true," said Forbes. "These things kind of sour me on the idea that mankind's made all the great progress they claim, you know? Just senseless violence."

"You're just discovering this?" said Varallo dryly. "Well, you've only been a cop for what, nine years? I began to suspect that before I'd put in twelve months at this thankless damn job. And why the hell I didn't go into insurance or maybe flagpole sitting when I had the chance—" Varallo, with twelve years' service on a small-town upstate force, resigning as captain, had started a new career on the Glendale force.

They went through the motions. Forbes industriously printed all surfaces in the relevant rooms, and they sent a patrolman over to the Glendale Memorial to sit beside Mrs. Scott and take down anything she might say if she regained consciousness. They set up spotlights and searched the yard, back and front, and came up with the weapon—probably the weapon. A big wrench, with blood on it, probably tossed away as X ran—they found it just inside the low rear wall of the back yard. They questioned all the neighbors, who had seen and heard nothing. They had the Caddy towed into the police garage for examination, after Forbes had dusted it.

They got no leads at all, unless the wrench could be. Find out if it had come from the Scotts' garage, or elsewhere. There probably wouldn't be, when they came to sort them out, any useful prints.

Varallo went home at ten minutes past eight on Sunday morning.

He would be off all today, and then back on day shift tomorrow. He didn't feel really tired, and he intended to sleep until about noon and then get to work on his roses, get those new ones carefully planted.

These very new ones, just developed last year, and that Lilac Dawn was really something, if you could trust the pictures. He had the spot all picked for her, between Frau Karl Druschke and Golden Dawn—nice contrast. Granada was going in front, beside Golden Frills.

The damn aphis, he thought.

He let himself in the back door quietly and went softly down to the bedroom. It was just starting to get light. Very faint light from the open windows, and the tiny glow from the electric-blanket control, showed him Laura in the big double bed. Sighing, he started to get undressed. Five minutes later he got into bed beside her, and she stirred and said thickly, "Vic?"

"Who were you expecting?" said Varallo, knowing she didn't really hear him. He kissed the corner of her mouth lightly. There was his familiar, his darling Laura, until you got to midships, and there was the mound, the awful mound. God, it couldn't be twins. It could be quadruplets. And *when?*

Get a move on, Laura, he thought. Produce. Whatever it is.

So damn silly, he thought, getting involved with all those roses. Big tough cop Varallo.

Better get some more Aerosect—

He got up at twelve forty-five.

He got Lilac Dawn and Granada planted, carefully, with just the right amount of peat moss and rose food, in their appointed places. That Lilac Dawn—first and only really lavender ever developed—quite something. He hoped it would do well.

It was a nice sunny day, as January days quite often are in Southern California, and at four o'clock he was relaxing contentedly in the patio with a mild brandy-and-soda, admiring the new blooms on Alida Lovett climbing up the trellis nearby, when Laura called him to the phone.

"Charles," she said tersely.

"Oh hell," said Varallo, having premonitions. "What now?"

"Vic?" said O'Connor. His deep voice was hard and quick. "Sorry to break in on your day off, boy, but we've got a thing. Two little girls missing. Six and four. Up in that strip of La Crescenta that belongs to us. Everybody we've got we need. You know what it could be. Come to Papa."

"Oh God," said Varallo. "I'm on my way."

That kind of thing—indeed they all knew what it could turn out to be. It did.

CHAPTER 3

There was quite a lot going on up on Markridge Road when Varallo got there. It had only been discovered that the two little girls were missing about forty-five minutes ago. And that might have made them hopeful that the kids had just wandered off a little farther than usual, except for a few other circumstances.

The mother, Mrs. Jean Daly, said they were both very obedient children and had had it drilled into them that they were never to go farther alone than up and down this short block. Neighbors confirmed that, and then there was the woman who lived across the street, who said she'd seen a strange man talking to Judy and Lynn, at about two fifteen when she came home from the market. She couldn't say whether the man had a car, there were always cars parked along the block. But—

It was a big But. Judith Ann Daly, age six, dark brown hair, blue eyes, fair complexion, wearing red capri pants, a white cotton blouse, a red cardigan, white ankle socks and white sneakers. Lynn Carol Daly, age four, dark brown hair, blue eyes, fair complexion, wearing light blue capri pants, a red cotton blouse, a white cardigan, white ankle socks and white sneakers. Both girls average size for their respective ages.

The mother, of course, was still saying all over again what she'd said to the first officers to reach her. "Oh, God, if I hadn't—if I had only— I *thought* they were— I *do* keep an eye on them, anybody can tell you that, oh, God, if I hadn't—" She was a pretty woman about thirty, but disheveled and incoherent now.

Charles O'Connor, that wide-shouldered tough who had just squeaked in past the minimum-height standard at five nine, but made up for it in breadth, listened to her, asked a few questions and began to deploy his men. By the time Varallo got up there, there were five patrol cars along the block and nearly everybody on the block had been questioned. A few people weren't home. Jim Daly, who was the manager of the Thriftimart at the Glendale Plaza, had been called home and was demanding loudly that Something Be Done At Once. Varallo's first little job was to try to soothe him down.

In the first place, this was a rather funny stretch of residential area. It was ten miles above the rest of Glendale proper; it was a big piece of La Crescenta—which was not, of course, an incorporated city as yet—which for some reason had been taken into Glendale city limits on the map. Up here they were in the shadow of the great foothills of the Sierra Madre range, and all the north-south streets climbed steeply up past Foothill Boulevard. Markridge Road was the last cross street up the hill, and here it was a dead-end street. It was, like all the streets up here, a very quiet street of modest homes, mostly ranch styles; it was a street, like many streets up here, of neighbors known to each other and a lot of kids and dogs and cats.

The story was easy to piece out. Mrs. Daly had had a headache—a bad headache. She'd wanted to take a couple of aspirins and lie down, and so she'd called Mrs. Henry Slater who lived four houses down and had a little girl Judy's age, and asked if Judy and Lynn could play there for a couple of hours. Mrs. Slater had agreed, Judy and Lynn had been sent down there, and Mrs. Slater had thought the children were all playing in the back yard—a couple of other neighborhood kids were there too. It wasn't until a little past three, when she took out a plate of cookies, that she found the Daly girls gone, and her own small daughter said Judy had got mad because they wouldn't play the way she wanted, and she and Lynn had gone home—"a long while ago." Conscientious Mrs. Slater had called Mrs. Daly to check. So then—

By now, the whole block had been searched. By now, they had heard about the strange man Mrs. Polasky had seen talking to the children. She was vague on description, of course. It had been "about in front of Slaters'," and he was medium height, young, she thought, and neatly dressed in tan work clothes.

Everybody on the block was out—some of the women with Mrs. Daly, the men offering eagerly to help, the kids and dogs getting in everybody's way.

"So we look farther away," said O'Connor, hunching his shoulders. The bulge at his left shoulder stood out suddenly, where his favorite S.

and W. .357 Magnum reposed. "And damn it, Vic, if some bastard picked them up they could be miles away by now—"

"It'll be dark by a bit after six," said Fred Wayne, looking at the sky. It was just after five then.

"Let's cover the next blocks around here. They *could* have just wandered off—mother says not, I know, but that other woman says she only saw that fellow talking to them, it needn't have been— And let's get it on the air." O'Connor turned to the nearest patrol car and started using the radio.

They called up some more men and covered the six blocks down from Markridge. There wasn't anything but wild hill country above.

Varallo thought about that as he rang doorbells and asked questions. The people living up here were mostly neighborly, friendly; and most of them had kids of their own. They were concerned. A lot of the men volunteered to help look. As time went on, a number of the women got coffee going, and made sandwiches for the searchers, police and civilian.

And the local help was useful, because there were other, no less unpleasant possibilities besides a deviate.

"Like you read about kids getting caught inside old ice boxes and things," said one of the volunteers to Varallo. "I can't think of a place like that right around here, but some people don't keep up their yards too good, and you know how the junk accumulates in garages. Maybe an old trunk or something—we ought to look *good,* to be sure."

A lot of people did a lot of looking. As the sky began to darken, porch lights and yard lights and garage lights went on. Perhaps thirty cops and nearly a hundred civilians wandered through alleys and back yards, searching garages, and at frequent intervals called the little girls' names. As it got darker, all the different voices calling, "Ju-dy! Ly-nnnn!" got to sounding eerie, like lost souls calling lost souls.

God, what a thing to think, thought Varallo. He thought of Laura and the baby. Two little girls lost somewhere in the cold dark night, where, where? None of the possible answers was nice.

He walked streets and strange back yards, shouting too, and tension built in him, and he knew it was partly on account of Laura and the baby. Suppose— Parent or prospective parent, it got you, it reached you.

They hadn't found them at eight o'clock when Mr. and Mrs. Holland came home. The Hollands lived on the corner of Markridge and New York, six houses from the Dalys. They had been away since two thirty, having Sunday dinner with Mrs. Holland's parents. Finding the neighborhood in an uproar, they asked questions, and then they asked excitedly where the nearest cop was. As it happened, the nearest cops were O'Connor and Varallo, who were taking a break over Mrs. Slater's coffee.

"I *saw* Judy and Lynn, just as we were leaving this afternoon—it was a little before two thirty," Mrs. Holland gabbled. She was a pretty, pert little blonde; they hadn't been married long, Varallo judged. "They were standing at the corner—the corner of Markridge and New York, right across from our house. Just standing there. I w-waved to them—they're such nice little girls—oh, dear Lord, they've got to be all right! Oh, poor Mrs. Daly—nothing so awful could happen, could it? This is such a quiet neighborhood, nothing ever—"

"Did you see anybody else around? Try to think," said O'Connor urgently.

"I don't remember—" She looked a little uncertain whether this bluechinned tough was really one of Glendale's Finest. "I don't think so—oh, dear Lord, what an awful—"

"But *I* do," said Edward Holland. "I'll say I do. I don't remember especially noticing the kids, there are a lot of kids on this block, but I do remember that damn fool that almost nicked me." He nodded once, savagely, a thin dark young man with a crew cut and a long nose. "Look—" he pointed down the street to the house on the corner. "Well, I guess you can't see from here, but our drive comes out on New York. There isn't usually much traffic on New York, except sometimes on weekends—it's the steepest hill anywhere around, and the kids use it to test their damned hopped-up cars, like that. But naturally you look before you back out. I looked. There wasn't a thing coming either direction, so I started to back out. And this damn fool comes out of the blue —he must have just turned off Henrietta, that's just not half a regular block down, you know—traveling at a hell of a clip, and he never slowed at all. If I hadn't hit the brakes in a hurry when I saw him, he'd have caught me. Lot of damn fool drivers around."

"Well, if he was going as fast as that, he probably didn't see the kids—"

"Oh, he stopped," said Holland. "He ran by me, and across the intersection, and then he hit the brakes. God, you should've heard—some of these crazy kids—and stopped, right past Markridge on New York. I don't know why. I said something about that to Linda, and finished backing out, and started down New York, but in the rear-view mirror I saw the driver start to get out."

"That puts him just about opposite where Judy and Lynn were standing," said Varallo. He looked at O'Connor. "And at least a few minutes after Mrs. Polasky had seen the strange man with them. So maybe the strange man doesn't mean anything."

"Yeah," said O'Connor, "and maybe Mrs. Polasky isn't so damn sure it was two fifteen, maybe it was half an hour later so this damn-fool driver doesn't mean anything. Christ, women and time—! Do you know what kind of car it was, Holland?"

"Not to be positive, but it was solid white, a hardtop and if I had to make a guess I'd call it either a Ford or a Chevy about six or seven years old."

"What about the driver? You said, some of these crazy kids—was he a kid?"

Holland shrugged. "I don't know, it was the way he was handling the car that put a kid in my mind. I only had a fleeting glimpse of him. I don't really know."

So there was that, and what could they do with it?

"I'm also thinking about another thing," said O'Connor when the Hollands had started toward the Dalys' home. "Mrs. Daly says both kids had been repeatedly warned not to talk to strangers. Well, sure, my God, kids forget. But—it's happened before." He made a wry grimace. "Somebody they knew, right in the neighborhood?"

"You have nice ideas," said Varallo. "I'll tell you what I'm thinking about." He gestured. "All that wild country up there. Could they have for some reason wandered up there and got lost?" That was just a little bit more comforting to think about—two lost little girls out there in the hills, frightened and hungry, but—alive. Alive, waiting to be found.

"Mother says they never wandered. And there's a wire fence up there, at least one stretch I noticed—marks the city limits, you know, that's all county land back there. Christ, Christ, I hate things like this," said O'Connor softly. "The punks, the hoods, the pros, what the hell? The innocent bystanders—and I guess the damnedest innocentest bystanders are kids. Oh, Jesus, I hate this kind of thing. I'd better call in, see if anything's turned up from all the broadcasts."

It had been on the air and on TV since six forty. Two lost little girls. Descriptions, names. Anyone having any information—

There were nearly seven million people in L.A. County, and a surprising number of them were people of good will who wanted to help. A discouraging number of them had, by eight thirty, let their anxiety help stimulate their imaginations. A woman in Huntington Park was sure she had seen Judy and Lynn, both crying, in the company of a big Negro woman on Ascot Avenue. (Checked out, two kids with the family maid leaving a very sad movie.) A man in Long Beach had seen Judy and Lynn with a man and a woman at a restaurant on Telegraph Road. A woman in La Cañada had seen Judy and Lynn in a car in the parking lot of a supermarket. A woman in Hollywood had seen Judy and Lynn with a blonde woman who was "very cross with the children and slapped the little one," walking along Hollywood Boulevard. A woman in Pasadena had seen— Well, as was expectable, it went like that, and all those reports had to be checked out. The L.A.P.D. and a couple of other forces were very co-operative and helped there.

They weren't getting anywhere up here. It didn't help any that the street lighting wasn't too good, but most of the yards had lights and by nine o'clock they all felt, discouragingly, that all yards and garages for ten blocks around had been thoroughly searched. Such little girls couldn't have wandered much farther, could they?

It began to look pretty definite that they'd been taken away. By somebody. To somewhere.

They could be anywhere in the county. By this time, they could be in Santa Barbara.

That was when Gale Meredith showed up. She was a very pretty blonde, she was sixteen, she was a very bright girl and she owned a sorrel gelding named Melody, on whom she had won a number of ribbons for horsemanship and jumping.

"—And I just *thought*," she said breathlessly to Sergeant Fred Wayne, "I mean, if Dick or somebody had seen anything—up there— because if somebody *did*—you know—there's just *nothing* up there past the stables, it's all wild, and just maybe— So I called and asked, and of course they hadn't heard about it. But he *did!* Dick. *See* something. So I thought—"

What it came down to, there was a big private boarding stable up there, about a mile above the end of Dunsmore Avenue, up in the foothills. The stable owner and a couple of stablehands lived there; and Dick Pool, the owner, had seen something. Guided by Gale, very thrilled at a ride in a patrol car, O'Connor and Varallo went up to see Dick. A rough dirt road took them, eventually, to a cluster of buildings, a warm effluvium of horse, and Dick.

"Jesus, could it of been?" said Dick. "Two little girls—oh, Jesus, what a thing! I dunno, just tell you what I saw, hah? It was maybe about two forty-five, three o'clock. I was out exercising Thunder. Mrs. Thompson hadn't had him out a day or so, he was feeling his oats. So I took him out. I was over the first ridge—" he gestured—"there are horse trails around here, not much else—I was up toward the old reservoir. Not many trails up here good enough for cars, you know, but there's one off the end of Pennsylvania you *can* get a car up—old road up to that old winery, it's shut down now, years back, but the buildings are still there, of course. And I saw a car on the road. I was maybe thirty feet off, I guess. There was a man driving, and there was a kid in the back. I only saw one kid, sure, but if it *was*, there coulda been another in the front seat and I couldn't see. I'm sure the one I saw was a girl, I saw the long hair. In one o' these pony tails, see? Jesus, if it *was*— I was surprised, see the car, you hardly ever do on that road, but there's been talk lately they're gonna develop some land up there, subdivision you know, and I didn't think— Jesus, it *could* of been—"

So there was something to follow up, and what a thing. Up there beyond the very edges of town was just wild country—what Easterners would call mountains, what Californians knew as foothills—gentle peaks and valleys and box canyons all covered with the scrub growth of foothills, sage, low underbrush, a few scraggly California oak trees. There was, they saw on the map, Dunsmore Canyon, and Ward Canyon, and Cooks Canyon, and Shields Canyon, and Eagle Canyon—

That, of course, was outside Glendale city limits. That was all L.A. County. They called the nearest sheriff's station.

The sheriff's boys came out in force. That was a crack force, and it happened to be the largest law-enforcement body in existence. This wasn't really a very definite lead, but as any cop knew, you worked any lead you had, and when there were two lost little girls to be found, you worked it in strength, to hell and back. Maybe a hundred men had turned out by nine thirty, in addition to the Glendale boys and all the volunteers, and the sheriff's men brought bloodhounds with him, and by ten o'clock about forty of the sheriff's special posse turned up and begged horses from Dick Pool. Those were the only men who knew wild-country tracking: all the rest were city men.

"Look, I put on the ring lights," said Dick. "They show up a good long way." There was a training and show ring beyond the main stable, with big fluorescent lights all around it, thirty feet high. "Any o' you get turned around out there, you make for a high spot and look for the ring lights."

It was a beautiful, sparkling, clear night. The high winds had blown away all the smog, and up here you could see more stars than down in town. When the men got to the first ridge above Dick's stable, they could see the vast panorama in the distance, all the city lights below. It didn't seem possible, to many of them, that there could be this awful dark empty country within visibility of the city.

They made for the shut-down winery first. It was two miles back in the hills, a rough dirt track leading to it. There were a couple of old cobblestone buildings, dark—and empty.

Almost empty. In the smaller earth-floored building they found Judy's red cardigan.

So they fanned out; they brought up the bloodhounds and showed them the cardigan, and they spread out on foot and on horseback, and they called, "Ju-dy! Ly-nnn!" and every man among them was mortally afraid of what he might stumble over any next second. Two lost little girls, taken away by—

Sheriff's Deputy Ronald Weisenberg had two little girls of his own, and he knew how he'd be feeling if— Somehow, it was almost as if he was out hunting for his own lost little Rose and Marion, and he guessed every man among them who had kids was feeling the same way. He kept his flashlight moving as he ploughed through knee-deep underbrush, and every thirty seconds he raised his powerful deep voice—"Ju-dy! Ly-nnnn!" and all the while he knew they were dead, he knew some goddamned pervert had caught them and assaulted them and killed them, oh God, suppose it was— And it was a goddamned big lie to say cops got hardened to— Oh God, I hate things like this, he thought. And there was no end to this goddamned wide-open dark wilderness—

And he didn't believe it. He didn't believe it, but he heard a child crying.

"Judy!" he cried wildly. "Lynn?" He could see other flashlights pinpointing the darkness around him. He heard a bloodhound bay, back there a way. *"Judy!"* he cried, and the flashlight found them, ten feet ahead of him.

Two lost little girls, dirty and tear-stained, but two live little girls, stumbling tiredly down the mountainside. The little one crying.

"Oh *honey,*" said Sheriff's Deputy Weisenberg, and he went on his knees and gathered them into his arms, and they were Rose and Marion, safe. "It's all right now, we've found you now, darlings, don't cry."

"I want *Mommy!*" sobbed Lynn.

"Yes, honey, we'll take you to Mommy—"

"Bad man hurt Judy!"

"Judy, honey?" Oh God—

"I—was seeing the lights," said Judy falteringly. "A long time I was seeing the lights— I was trying to get Lynnie down to where the lights were, but it was so *far*. You're crying, man. I never knew growed-up men cried."

"Sometimes, honey," said Weisenberg. And he raised his voice and shouted, and the lights all started toward them, and the bloodhound bayed again.

Varallo got home at one forty.

"Did you find them?" Laura had heard the car and met him at the kitchen door.

"We found them," said Varallo tiredly. "Sheriff's boys, rather. Alive. Yes."

"Oh thank God. Vic—were they—"

"The older girl was raped. Judy. She's at the hospital. She'll be all right, but—"

"Oh God," said Laura. "What—was there any lead to—"

"We'll see," said Varallo. "Tomorrow. All we've got to do now is find the bastard."

CHAPTER 4

The first news that greeted Varallo when he walked into the office on Monday morning was that Mrs. Scott had died about three A.M. She had never regained consciousness.

"Hell," he said thoughtfully. "A double homicide. Nice. Did Records turn up who it was pulled the other break-in there?"

"One James Enright," said Sergeant Wayne. "Doesn't do us much good, though. I forget how many times he'd been picked up before, anyway that was his fourth conviction and the judge threw the book at him. He's still in San Quentin."

"Well, it was just an idea." Varallo sat down at his desk and sighed. "I see somebody took all Tracy's rose vines away."

Wayne grinned. "Isn't that a hell of a thing?"

O'Connor came in and said, "What the hell are you doing sitting around yakking on the city's time? God knows we've got enough on our hands." He picked up the inside phone. "Bill, you call the hospital? What? Oh. Sure. Maybe better that way. O.K." He put the phone down. "Judy. They've sent her home. She's got to be questioned. I don't think—" he rubbed his massive jaw thoughtfully—"a job for me. Like to take it on, Vic?" Joe Katz, Forbes and Poor came in together, yawning; they'd all been out on last night's hunt.

"No, but I will." It was better that the child be questioned by one man, not to confuse her; and maybe when she was in her familiar home surroundings it would be better too.

The inside phone rang on O'Connor's desk.

They hadn't got much out of either Judy or Lynn, last night. In all humanity, they couldn't try for much. Most of it had come from the four-year-old Lynn. The man said he'd take them up to see the horsies.

(They'd been taken up to Dick's several times, said Mrs. Daly, to watch riders in the ring.) But he hadn't, he'd taken them an awful place and he'd hurt Judy so she cried and then he'd gone and left them and they were lost and it got cold. . . . God, even the six-year-old, would she (in her shock and confusion, too) remember much more to tell them? But it had to be tried, and soon, very soon.

"Oh hell," said O'Connor on the phone. "All right, all right. For Christ's sake, maybe we're growing a new crime rate." He put the phone down. "Break-in at Webbs' overnight. They just discovered it, will we please send a detective over. Some of their real jewelry's gone."

"Webbs'?" said Katz. "The department store? They've never heard of burglar alarms? How could anybody—"

"Don't ask me, for God's sake, that's all I know. You and Vic chase over on it, will you?"

"Listen, this Scott thing," said Varallo. "I've got to see Scott again, find out if anything's missing, about that wrench—"

"I did that yesterday," said Forbes. "Before we got the alarm on the kids. Scott doesn't think X got away with anything, and he's pretty sure the wrench didn't belong to his father. Neither of 'em mechanical, they never tried to work on their own cars, and there weren't many tools in the garage. So maybe our boy brought the wrench with him. We ought to get an autopsy report on the old man some time today. Nothing from the prints."

"Helpful," said Varallo. "Why the *hell* did I deliberately join another police force? I need my head examined. O.K., you can go paw through Records for any punk who's pulled break-ins before and maybe showed signs of violence, and Joe and I will find out why Webbs' doesn't have burglar alarms in the store." He got up.

"You couldn't walk in on the Dalys at this hour anyway, damn it," said O'Connor. "We'll go looking in Records on that too, haul in all our deviates. But the sooner somebody sees Judy the better. And good luck on it, Vic."

"We'll need that."

"God," said Katz as they started for the stairs, "that thing. And they say with kids sometimes there'll be a kind of mental block—when she was so scared—would she be able to identify him if we get him? We don't get much of that sort of thing in Glendale as a rule. But the population going up—we seem to be getting all sorts these days."

"It's all these apartments," said Varallo. Up to recently, Glendale had been a settled residential town, with very few transients and a minority of renters. Now, there was a rash of apartment houses going up all over town, big ones, little ones, handsome ones, for the most part violently modernistic ones; every time you went out you found another lot cleared for another apartment to be built. "There can't be that many people coming in. I think myself a lot of big companies are putting them up to show losses on their books. I don't—"

"You been past that one on Glenoaks with the cement Aztec god out in front?"

"Please," said Varallo. "I come of the same race as Michelangelo and all those artistic fellows, Joe. I have a secret desire—some dark night I'm going to come down and paint a mustache and beard on that damned awful thing." Katz chuckled. They came into the big rectangular lobby and stopped, taking in the scene.

A man in brown uniform was wheeling a big dolly up to the desk. On the dolly sat a wooden crate about ten feet long and two deep. The man sat the dolly down flat, reached into his pocket for some papers and said, "You got an N. Tracy here, Sergeant?"

"You can't leave that here," said Sergeant Bill Dick excitedly. "It's all a mistake, he didn't order it."

"So how do you know? Looks all in order to me—and it's a C.O.D., Sergeant."

"That you needn't tell me," said Dick. "Take it out of here! Look, somebody's playing a practical joke on the guy, ordering stuff in his name, and it's a damned nuisance. Take it away, whatever it is, and tell whoever sold it he refused it."

"Look, Mac, on C.O.D.'s this isn't so easy," said the express messenger. "Where is this Tracy? I'd hafta talk to him personal about that."

"Oh, for God's sake, he's out on tour," said Dick. "How can I— The lieutenant'd hit the ceiling if I—"

"What largesse has poor Tracy been handed this time?" asked Varallo, coming up.

"Huh?" said the express messenger.

"What's in it?"

"So how would I know? There's customs duty due too. It came from Sweden."

"My God," said Varallo, bending to read the delivery form taped to the box. "It's a handmade Rya rug. Two hundred and sixty-eight— Oh, Tracy'll love that!"

They left Dick still arguing with the express messenger. "But we ought to do something about it, you know," said Katz, his round dark face serious. He looked up at Varallo; Katz had just got in over the minimum-height standard too. "It's malicious mischief or something, isn't it?"

"At least that. If we could get hold of some of the order blanks—"

"Yeah," said Katz.

They took Varallo's car and drove down to the next corner, turned left. Webbs' was on the corner of Brand and Wilson, but its parking lot was on Orange, which was a one-way northbound street, so they had to go round a block. They left the car; the store wasn't open yet and the lot was empty. They found the side door on Wilson locked, and rapped on the glass until a male clerk came and made grimaces at them to indicate that the store was closed. Patiently, they hauled out their badges. The clerk opened the door instantly.

"My goodness, about the burglar," he said. "Why didn't you say— Mr. Larkin was *most* upset— It's right over—"

There seemed to be quite a few people in the place, even an hour before opening time. Several men were mopping the old wooden floors, clerks were folding dust covers and arranging merchandise. Varallo and Katz were led past Notions, Gift Cards and Cameras, to a counter in the center of the store facing the stairs to the basement. The top of the counter was—or had been—glass, and two big panes of it had been smashed in. Shards of glass lay all over the rings, brooches, pendants, earrings, charms inside the case.

"The detectives, Mr. Larkin."

Larkin was a biggish, broad dark man wearing a good deal of jewelry himself; he was obviously upset but more indignant. "I never would have believed it," he said accusingly. He looked at Varallo and Katz as if they were personally responsible for whatever outrage he was contemplating. "Granted that the management here—um—is commendably trying to keep the overhead down—there's the matter of the safe too—still I never would have believed it! *Someone* was very careless, to say the least—it's not up to me to say who, but nevertheless— I'll bet," he added to Varallo, sounding friendlier, "you won't believe it either. But then too, Glendale's always been such a quiet town—not much serious crime. Come on, I'll show you." He came out from behind the counter and started for Stationery at the Wilson Street side of the store.

"We were going to ask if you haven't a burglar-alarm system, sir?"

"That's *just* the point," said Larkin testily. "Of course we've got a burglar-alarm system, we're not *complete* idiots! But somebody—well, I'll show you."

He took them behind a counter where a middle-aged woman was arranging boxes of stationery under a sign announcing a January sale, and past a curtained doorway into what was obviously the storeroom of this department. There were no windows at all, but up to the right, about three and a half feet up from the floor, was an open square hole in the wall. Larkin led them up there. "I can't *believe*—" he said. "But there it is. I hope I've done the right thing. I'd just left my car and was walking up Wilson, you know, toward the front door—when I noticed this display niche, that the glass was broken. If you'll bend down you can see—careful of that, that's what's ordinarily across the opening this side." "That" was a square of plywood painted black. "I came in and looked, and then I called you, and I didn't touch a thing because I know one shouldn't, and I warned everybody here to leave it alone too. You can see—"

They could see. Outside, built into the face of the building, was a little niche for the display of jewelry. It would be slightly below the eye level of a pedestrian, and it was about two feet square. And of course there had to be some access to it from inside, for the arranging of the displays. Right now, the niche contained a broken china figurine and several pieces of jewelry scattered around on its floor.

"You see, that's the way he got in. I saw at once—"

"Did you leave jewelry in there overnight?" asked Varallo. A couple of the pieces contained diamond settings. "Just behind a pane of glass? On the street?"

"Well, I daresay it seems—but we've never had such a thing happen before, it— And those niches haven't been in long. They were built in quite recently, as a matter of fact—smarten up the store, you know—and evidently when they were built, nobody thought to have them wired into the burglar-alarm system. Talk about *careless*. Well, in a way—it's heavy plate glass."

"Don't you have a safe?" asked Katz.

"Yes, certainly we have a safe. There wasn't any attempt made on that, I looked immediately. Of course the safe is—er—hidden away. Only a few people know its location. He just got in here and went straight to the counter and smashed—"

"You don't put every piece of jewelry away in the safe? Over the weekend?" Katz looked astonished; his father was a jeweler and he knew the business.

"The safe isn't big enough," said Larkin crossly. "We ought to have one twice the size, but there it is. We've got quite a lot of stuff here, you know. Anyway, I saw at once—"

"Yes," said Varallo. Katz sighed; he had brought along a lab kit, and now set it down and opened it. Dust for prints, anyway, empty a gesture as it probably would be.

"One thing," said Varallo, "whoever our boy is, he must be jockey-size. That thing can't be two feet square. Only a half-pint could get through it."

"Twenty-four inches," said Larkin, "by twenty-six wide."

"Well, let's have some definite facts. When does the store—yes, but yesterday was Sunday, it was closed. All right. Any cleaners in last night?"

"Not on Sunday. They generally come in, I don't know, around ten o'clock or so—the store closes at nine fifteen on the nights we're open, and six o'clock the other days—and the cleaning crew's gone by about two thirty A.M. But last night—"

"All the same," said Varallo, "he must have known something about this setup, Joe. That there was a backing he could push out. Isn't that thing ever locked in place somehow?"

"Well, no. No. The plywood just fits over and snaps into place, it—"

Varallo said, "You're all very trusting people around here. Never crossed anybody's mind that one of the clerks might be a little tempted?"

"Well—it's not often that anybody'd be alone here long enough— And all our clerks are— Good Lord," said Larkin, wiping his brow, "I know we must sound like fools to you—er—"

"Detective Varallo."

"—But we've never had a serious robbery here before."

"There isn't a night watchman?"

"Well, no, with the burglar-alarm system— And why nobody thought about connecting up these niches—"

"Yes. Do you have a rough idea of what's missing?"

Larkin nodded. "I'll want to go over everything and consult with Miss Porter, my assistant—but I started to make up a list at once. We'll have a complete list for you some time today, but right now I'd say there's about twenty thousand dollars' worth of stuff gone." He groaned. "Jewelry doesn't take up much space, you know, you can carry a fortune in both hands—and that's wholesale prices. Double it for retail. Chiefly rings and earrings, some watches, brooches."

"Yes. I suppose we'll find prints," said Varallo. "Several of you will have handled that plywood and the things in the window. We'll want your prints, sir, and anybody's who has handled—"

There were prints on the plywood, the niche, on the things in the niche. All of them turned out to belong to Larkin, Miss Porter and Mr. Lewis, who was also an assistant in that department—all but four nice clear unsmudged prints on the broken china figurine in the niche.

Katz lifted those very carefully, feeling a little incredulous, and he and Forbes started to go through records looking for a match. They sent a photograph down to L.A.P.D. headquarters, and also to the sheriff's office, because those boys had a hell of a lot more records than Glendale did. They also sent a copy to the F.B.I. in Washington.

When everybody had looked thoroughly, nobody came up with a match.

Evidently the burglar at Webbs' had no criminal record.

And Varallo, at one o'clock, looked at Judy Daly and thought, God, I'm no good at this sort of thing. Why did Charles have to pick me? I don't know much about kids.

Both the parents were there, of course. Lynn was taking a nap. The parents, looking about as you'd expect, he had been afraid would pose a problem. Jim Daly, a little belligerent, "Listen, I'm not going to have a cop asking her questions, just fix it in her mind is all, isn't it bad enough—"

But Jean Daly, quiet, "They have to, Jim. You must see that. They want to find him—whoever— And we ought to be—to be *thanking* them for the way they helped—all those men coming out to hunt—" Her face twisted.

"I don't want to ask her questions about—what was done to her," said Varallo. "All we want is whatever she can remember about what he looked like, his car, what he said."

"Yes, I see that. But you—you don't mind if we stay, do you? I mean —she's all right, you know, I—the doctor said she probably doesn't real-ize much about the—the connotations, if you—only six. But—"

"That's all right, Mrs. Daly." And now here was Judy, looking a lit-tle pale but otherwise just a nice little six-year-old, hair combed into a smooth pony tail, and he didn't know how to go about this, kids he didn't know much about, why the hell had Charles—

"You see, Judy, we want to find that bad man who hurt you, so we can put him in jail." She nodded seriously. "So, can you remember what he looked like?"

"Um-hmm," she said. "I wasn't—wasn't scared at first. I sort of remember. Are you a p'liceman?"

"Yes, I am, Judy." For my sins, he thought.

"Oh. What's your name?"

Varallo said helplessly, "Vic. You can call me Vic, Judy."

"Like for Victor? I know a boy named Victor."

"Well, no, my name's Lodovico, but—"

"Oooh, that's a funny name. I never heard that name before. But you've got pretty hair. I like goldy color hair, I wish mine was."

"Judy—" said her mother.

"His name was Bob," said Judy. She shuddered suddenly, her whole body shaking, and was still.

"The bad man—he said his name was Bob?"

"Um-hmm. He said—he said— Mommy always says not to talk to people you don't know but he said—he said he was our uncle. Our uncle we'd never met before. That's what he said. And I only know Uncle Les, but I sort of—sort of remembered Mommy saying about *another* uncle, only he's not here or something—and so—" She stopped suddenly and looked at the floor. She had pink-and-white skin and solemn blue eyes and he could see the clean comb marks in her brown hair and she looked as if she'd just been made new this very day, and he didn't know anything about kids, damn it. She sat on the couch and swung her feet back and forth, and she asked, "Have you got any—any children, Vic?"

"Well, no, Judy. Not yet. We're going to have a baby soon."

"Oh. Is it going to be a boy or girl?"

"Well, we don't know yet. Judy—"

"Would you like a boy or girl best?" she asked seriously. "Does your —your mommy want a boy or girl?"

"I guess it doesn't matter, Judy. Maybe—" he smiled at her—"I think it'd be nice to have a little girl." And then worry about things like this.

"I think so too," said Judy definitely. "A little girl with nice goldy color hair." And oddly, all of a sudden Varallo thought so too. "So when he said that," said Judy rapidly, "I just sort of remembered about Mommy saying about another uncle and I said was he our Uncle Bob and he said that's right he was and would we like a chocolate malted but I can't eat chocolate cause I've got a—a—a anergy."

"Allergy," whispered Jean Daly. "Oh my God—my brother Bob—he was killed in Korea— I never thought—"

Jim Daly was leaning forward in his chair, tense.

"Yes. Judy, did the bad man come up to you on the corne. you were standing there? You remember Mrs. Holland waving to Was it then?"

"I—don't—know. Yes. Sandy wouldn't let me have her old doll and . took Lynnie to go home but we went down to—to—to see Mrs. Holland's kittens, that's at the corner, only—then—"

"Judy, can you tell me exactly what the bad man looked like?"

"Um-hmm. He was growed-up and he had on a white shirt and his eyes looked funny. But that was after. He had hairs on his hands, all black and curly."

"What color was his hair?"

"Kind of—kind of— I don't know. Like mine maybe."

"Do you remember what color his eyes were?"

"They—looked—funny." She shuddered again.

Varallo thought, I don't know how. In his nearly fifteen years as a cop, he'd never run into this.

"Do you remember his car, Judy?"

"Um-hmm. After I said about the chocolate he said what'd we like to do and I said go see the horsies because Lynnie's just crazy about horsies and he said all right we'd do that and he'd take us because I knew Mommy had a bad headache and didn't want us playing around the house, so we got in his car. I got in the back and Lynnie was in the front. I wasn't scared then."

"What color was the car?"

"It was all white."

Like the car that had nearly nicked Holland: had screeched to a stop just opposite where Judy and Lynn were standing then. Because the driver had spotted two little girls alone?

"Did it have a top? Or was it—"

"Oh, it was kind of like Danny's car," said Judy. "Like the time our car wasn't any good and Danny took me and Mommy to market. It was almost azackly like Danny's car."

Varallo looked at the Dalys. "Danny Fields—he's a college boy up the block," said Daly. "But *Danny* wouldn't—it wasn't *Danny*, honey— the bad man?"

"Oh no, but the bad man's car was azackly like—"

"I think it's a Ford sedan," said Daly. "Fifty-five or fifty-six. You could—"

Judy slipped down from the couch. "I don't want to talk about that bad man any more," she said. "I don't want to." She was shaking again.

"All right, Judy," said Varallo helplessly.

CHAPTER 5

"And," said Varallo, "I found the Fields' house and asked what kind of car Danny has. It's a solid white two-door fifty-four Ford sedan. Which ties in with the car Holland saw stop."

"What the hell kind of goddamned lead is that?" said O'Connor. Varallo had long ago decided that O'Connor didn't really realize he was swearing; he just didn't listen to himself. It was as ingrained a habit as morning coffee or brushing his teeth. "Just how many damn cars like that you suppose there *are* in L.A. County? We don't know it's a fifty-four Ford. Not a hell of a lot of difference in line, fifty-four or fifty-five or fifty-six—not a hell of a lot of difference in line, Ford or Chevy or Plymouth."

"I know, I know. I tell you, Charles, I've got an idea that whatever we get from Judy we're going to get in bits and pieces. She was talking fine there for a while, and then—maybe talking about it brought it all back, and she suddenly dried up. I'm going to try to talk to her again—tonight or tomorrow—and have another session. But damn it, how does a six-year-old think? How do things look to them? She seems like a bright little girl, but *six*— Mostly everything's new to a kid that age, what kind of memory might she have?"

"God knows. You know, in all my fifteen years on this force I've never run into this kind of damn thing," said O'Connor. "I wonder if Katy would have any ideas." It didn't apparently occur to him that it was the middle of the last school period of the day and that Miss Katharine Mason would be hard at work with her fifth graders; he pulled the outside phone toward him, flipped open the phone book and found the number of the Verdugo Elementary School. And Varallo wondered if that would ever come to anything. Charles of all people:

O'Connor of the unlikely charm on the sex, O'Connor who had cheerfully played the field—preferring the cuddly little blondes—until he'd first laid eyes on Miss Mason last September. Katharine Mason was anything but a cuddly blonde, and it would be interesting to see whether—O'Connor was being passed around now, but he persisted; finally he said, "Katy? Me. Listen, just how good a memory would a six-year-old have, maybe? You'd know about kids, and—"

Varallo heard her deep voice say, "Did you call me out of class just to— Really, Charles!"

"No, now listen, maybe you can help." O'Connor went on and told her about it, and listened for long pauses, and at last said, "O.K., I've got that. That might help some. Thanks, Katy. I'll take you to dinner tomorrow night. Seven."

"Really—" said the telephone as O'Connor put it down. Treat 'em rough, thought Varallo; but O'Connor simply didn't know he did.

"She says it's mostly a matter of mental association," he said absently. "That it's all there in Judy's mind somewhere, maybe a lot of details, but it'll take patient questioning to get it. She says whoever talks to her ought to ask as few questions as possible, just get her talking. And that a lot might depend on who does the questioning, whether he understands kids and genuinely likes them."

"I'll buy that," said Varallo. "I don't know much about kids, Charles. Katz has got two boys, why not—or Poor—"

"I don't know, you're the one who's already talked to her. Somebody else might just confuse her. Jesus, *six*—" O'Connor shook his head.

"And she thinks I have pretty hair," said Varallo, smiling. "Where is everybody?"

"We turned up some possibles—both the Scott case and Webbs'. Out of Records. Same m.o.'s. Wayne and Katz and Poor went out on the break-ins—"

"But those prints— Oh well," said Varallo, "I know. They could belong to anybody who works in the store. We'd have to trace where that figurine came from—could be the prints belong to whoever packed it at the factory, something like that. Shall we run it down?"

"For Christ's sake, take the whole bunch of us six months!" said O'Connor irritably. "Larkin sent over a list. Pretty complete list. So I sent a copy down to L.A. headquarters and the sheriff's office, and it'll go on the pawnbrokers' list, and now we'll check the known and suspected fences. Eventually we'll get somewhere. I don't give a very big damn for Webbs' jewelry. My God, they're insured. Who I do want very goddamned bad is this bastard who raped Judy. We're really going to work that, Vic—to hell and back again. Because a thing like this, you don't get on him fast, nine times out of ten you don't get him at all. Jeff went out hunting up the local boys out of the sex file."

"And what invaluable aid have you been rendering us hard-working Holmeses?" asked Varallo, looking at the cup and plate on O'Connor's desk telling of well-creamed coffee and a club sandwich.

"I, for God's sake, have been writing letters to some of these goddamned outfits sending all the stuff to Tracy," said O'Connor disgustedly. "It's got to stop—we've got to find out what stupid moron with the sense of humor of a billy goat is— Those damn *vines*. And today a goddamned Swedish rug."

Varallo opened his mouth to say that if they could get some of the order blanks, the handwriting might help, and John Poor came in shoving a man ahead of him. The man was not a very prepossessing man: he needed a shave, and he needed a bath, and he was swearing in a low vicious tone. He was about thirty, a medium-sized man, very dark, with a thin face and heavy-lidded eyes and a pockmarked skin.

"Well, well, if it isn't Raimondo," said O'Connor. "I didn't know you were back among us. When'd you get out?"

"Son-a-bitch," said the man.

"He didn't want to talk nice and polite at home," said Poor, "so I brought him along. I found him in Records, and his file looked kind of promising so I thought we'd just see. He's new to me."

"He would be. Last time we had Raimondo in here," said O'Connor genially, "was about eight years back. If I remember right, you got a one-to-three for armed assault, and your parole officer told me later you'd gone to live on your uncle's farm up around Fresno. Rural life didn't agree with you, Raimondo? By Christ, if I'd known you were back in town—"

"*Che vuole?*" demanded the man sullenly. "Son-a-bitch—what I do? *Bastardos! Bravoccios!*"

"I haven't got three English words out of him yet," said Poor.

Varallo got up and went to stand directly in front of the man. "*Come vi chiamate?*"

"Don't bother," said O'Connor. "He speaks English all right. Too damn good he speaks English. Well enough to say 'Stick 'em up.' Excuse me—haven't introduced you. Raimondo Anoscurrio. Come on, Raimondo—talk up, damn you."

"Son-a-bitch," said Raimondo. Poor pushed him down into a chair.

"I done nothing. I come see my mama, my sister, I done nothing, this *bastardo* come, say p'lice. *Bruto!*" he spat at Poor. He had on a dirty white shirt with the sleeves rolled up, and Varallo looked at his thick brown arms with a mat of curly black hair, and thought of what Judy had said. But—wouldn't Judy have told about such a thick accent on the English? Would Raimondo have had the quick wit to tell that uncle story and would Judy have believed it, from him?

"Charles—" he jerked his head. They went over to the ranked continuous windows at the front of the office and Varallo communicated all that. "Hell," said O'Connor thoughtfully, rubbing his blue jaw. "I don't know. Say this—he puts on a lot of that accent. He had eight years of public school. He can talk O.K. when he wants to. Some accent, sure, but not that much. He just likes to make trouble however he can."

"Anything in his pedigree to suggest a thing like this?"

"Pay your money, take your damn choice. Picked up at fifteen for assaulting another kid on the school grounds with a knife. Picked up at eighteen for statutory rape." Which meant nothing; it was technically rape because the girl was underage, but the "statutory" said she'd probably been willing. "Picked up and charged at twenty-one with a heist job—that's when he got sent up. Record of violence, yes—he beat up the guy after he'd robbed him, and we had several cases of people held up and beaten afterward we never got anybody for, so we figured that was Raimondo too. Might be interesting to see what the Fresno boys have on him, if anything. We can ask."

"Let's try him, anyway," said Varallo.

"Sure."

They went back to Raimondo. "So we'll answer some questions all nice and easy," said O'Connor, and smiled. He looked about as friendly and amiable as a hungry shark. "Tell us about Sunday, boy. What'd you do all day Sunday?"

"I go mass, morning." Evidently Raimondo had decided to cooperate, if grudgingly.

"That was a good boy," said the irreligious O'Connor. "And then what?"

Raimondo looked at him uncertainly. *"Che vuole?* What happened Sunday? I done nothing Sunday."

Poor raised his brows at Varallo. He'd brought Raimondo in, because of his record of violence, with the idea of connecting him to the Scott homicide, and that had happened on Saturday night. Varallo nodded and said, "Judy," and looked at Raimondo, but got no flicker of recognition from him. "Where'd you go after mass, Raimondo? Come on—*avanti!*"

"Dirty cop. Always questions, questions. Some *uomo cattivo* done something, they say right away Raimondo. I been clean since I got out, cop. I didn't do nothing Sunday. I come home, I eat dinner, I look at TV, I go to bed." The accent had diminished surprisingly.

"Anybody with you?" asked Poor.

"My mama, my sister, I come visit. There's a law says I can't? Sure, they was in the house too. Mostly."

"When weren't they?" asked O'Connor.

Raimondo licked his lips. "One, two o'clock, go see women friends. I don't know. I looked at TV, that's all."

"And when did your mama and sister get back?" asked O'Connor gently.

"Oh, Jesus' sake, four, five, six, ask them! What the hell, just because you send me up once ever' time some punk pulls a job—"

"John," said O'Connor, "you pick up this bird at the same address in the file for nine years back? Some place over in the Atwater section, I seem to recall."

" 'S right. Larga Avenue."

"Yeah. House belongs to his mother. What kind of car you drive, Raimondo?"

"I got no car, cop."

"How'd you get down here from Fresno?"

"I walked," said Raimondo; and O'Connor moved in very close, studied him thoughtfully and said in a soft voice, "Don't you take that tone with me, you no-good son-of-a-bitch. How'd you get here?"

"My uncle's pick-up."

"All right, let's take it from the top again, and let's have some definite times. What did you do on Sunday?"

It was, like a lot of police work, deadly boring—the routine. Dealing with the punks. Pulling the words out of them by asking the same questions over and over again. But all of a sudden this looked like maybe being a hot one, so they worked it. Katz and Wayne came back with a candidate for the Webbs' job, and they left him sitting meekly downstairs under Sergeant Dick's eye while Wayne and Katz went over to Larga Avenue to talk to the women.

The women had been out, on Sunday afternoon, from one thirty until six o'clock. Raimondo's mother had a '55 white Chevy sitting in her garage.

Raimondo could have got up to Markridge Road by two o'clock easily, if he had left just as soon as the women had gone. This didn't really say one hell of a lot, because there was nothing in his record to indicate that he was a deviate of any sort—still, he could be the one. A white Chevy, a '54 Ford—but a six-year-old, my God—

So after a while they started to question him about Saturday night. Maybe he'd pulled the Scott homicide instead. He said he'd been to a party on Saturday night. Some old pals. Which old pals? There in the old neighborhood, on Larga Avenue. So they went out and found some of the pals; it had been quite a party, and everybody—including Raimondo—admitted freely that they couldn't say what had happened after about ten thirty. That kind of party. So, had Raimondo been there at all after, say, about ten o'clock? Had he really been drunk? Had he been getting fed up with rural life, and feeling mean, and thinking how to get himself a stake?

The mother had let him drive the Chevy, he admitted.

So where were they? Nothing to say this way or that way. He was sticking to his story stubbornly.

At five fifteen, they hadn't anywhere else to go.

"Do we keep him?" asked Wayne tiredly. "For the little girl to look at?"

Varallo lit a new cigarette. "I'm not liking him so much for Judy, Fred. Somehow I've got the feeling that whoever picked up Judy and Lynn had to be a lot smoother."

"A hell of a lot smoother," agreed O'Connor. They looked over at Raimondo, slumped sullenly in the straight chair beside Wayne's desk. "Hell and damnation, I don't know. He's never pulled a break-in either. Let him go and keep him in mind. Ask Fresno about him." They all nodded. You never knew how it'd turn out, but right now it looked as if they'd wasted most of the afternoon.

Varallo walked over to Raimondo. "All right, you can go," he said. "*Mi si levarsi dai piedi*—out."

"Go? So next time you need a fall guy you remember Raimondo some more—"

"We'll remember you all the time, little man," said Varallo. "We'll be thinking about you. Maybe it was you beat the Scotts to death. If so—"

"I never *kill* nobody! I never—"

"You came close a couple of times," said Varallo. He'd seen Raimondo's pedigree by then. "If you did, we'll find out."

"Son-of-a-bitch cops," said Raimondo, and walked out arrogantly. Varallo massaged the muscles at the back of his neck and reflected absently that he wasn't getting any younger. In fact, he had a birthday coming up, on the eleventh. A slightly depressing thought. Even if he had got out of uniform and made some rank again—they'd given him preference because of his experience—still occasionally it rang a little strange to his ears to be plain mister instead of captain. Thirty-five on the eleventh, he thought. Time marches on. A phone rang.

Raimondo. Yes, no? Well, that wrench. That anonymous wrench. Possible to trace it? Unlikely.

"Vic—phone. It's Laura."

"Oh. Thanks." Laura? She never— "What is it, *cara?*"

"Oh, Vic," said Laura, "I'm sorry to ask, but would you stop on the way home, please, and get some liver for Gideon and a half-gallon of milk and a pound of ground round—see they grind it fresh—and a pound of butter? Oh, and some of that Kitty Queen cat food—be sure it's that one, he doesn't like any of the other brands—the chopped heart."

Varallo held the phone away and stared at it. This was unprecedented. This was something new. All the time they'd been married, his efficient, well-organized Laura had never asked him to stop on his way home for something she'd forgotten. It simply was not a thing Laura did. "What?" he said. "I don't— Yes, I will. Wait a minute, let me write all that down—chopped heart, yes, but— *Amante,* how come? I mean, you don't—"

"Yes," said Laura. She sounded uneasy. "Well, the fact is, it sounds very silly, but I started to drive down to the market just now and—if you laugh I'll *leave* you, Vic—I can't get under the steering wheel. I shoved the seat back as far as it'll go, until I could just barely reach the pedals —and I still can't get under. The last time I had the car out was Saturday, and evidently I've added a couple of pounds since and that did it. I just can't. I'm— Are you laughing?"

"Yes," said Varallo. "My God, *cara,* could it be triplets or something? Well, I'm sorry, but—"

"*So* funny," said Laura crossly. "You sitting on the sidelines! You don't know how *I* feel, going around looking like a—like a walking pup tent or— It's easy enough for *you.* Yes, and when I think it's all your fault—"

"Sitting on the sidelines is damn right," said Varallo feelingly. "Can't you hurry this thing up? It's a damn nuisance."

"It's going to be even more of a damn nuisance," said Laura, sounding malicious, "afterward. Probably keep you awake all night."

"That'll be a change," said Varallo. "Ground round, milk, butter. O.K." He looked at his watch. "I'm just leaving. See you." He put the phone down and relayed the joke, which was duly appreciated.

Detectives Burt and Rhys came in; they were on night tour this month. O'Connor got up and said he'd take another look through Records. The rest of them started downstairs after him.

In the lobby they found a little crowd. The shifts were changing now at six o'clock, the Traffic men on night tour drifting in, in uniform, to check in and go down to the garage to be issued cars as the day men drifted in off duty. About fifteen men were in the lobby, and they were all acting highly amused over something, and in the center of the lobby stood Patrolman Neil Tracy, rather red in the face.

It was really unfortunate that it should have been Patrolman Tracy who was singled out for the unfunny practical jokes. Neil Tracy was that fairly rare thing, a dedicated cop. He had never wanted to be anything but a police officer, and he had devoted a lot of time even in high school to acquiring many skills which might come in handy to a dedicated cop. He knew shorthand; he had studied and religiously practiced judo; he had an excellent working knowledge of federal and California law; he was a qualified marksman drawing the eight extra bucks monthly for sharpshooting; and he took the physical-fitness program very seriously, being a nonsmoker and a teetotaler, exercising regularly and having a complete physical once a year. He was a good man, Tracy. He'd been on the force for three years, he was twenty-five years old, he'd had two years of college, and if maybe he took himself a little bit too seriously, that was a fault time usually cured.

He stood there now with a great big box at his feet, and there was a postman in drab blue uniform in front of him saying, "All I know is, it's C.O.D., ninety-eight seventy-five, and you gotta sign the—"

Tracy's colleagues were milling around grinning. "This is all you needed, boy—now you can move to Hollywood and compete with Elvis!" "Hey, maybe we get up a Policeman's Ball like they used to hold. Neil can provide the entertainment."

"Look, damn it," said Tracy, "I didn't order it. I—" Patrolman Neil Tracy was a fine figure of an officer, nearly six feet tall, broad and stocky; he had thick dark hair and a square bulldoggish face. He spotted O'Connor and said desperately, "Lieutenant— I— Look, we gotta do something about this! I can't—"

"Hootenanny Tracy they call him." "Better get yourself a good agent, Neil, that's half the battle." "How about a quick chorus of 'On Top of Old Smoky,' Neil?"

"All I know is, it's C.O.D. and I got to—"

"What the *hell?*" said O'Connor, coming up. "What is it this time?"

Mutely Tracy indicated the box. The manifesto was taped to it. One two-and-a-half-octave portable marimbaphone, with valuable book enclosed, *How to Play the Marimba in Ten Easy Lessons.*

"Pecos Bill Tracy they used to call me. Hey, Neil, how's about some lessons for my kid when you've—"

"For the love of *Christ!*" said O'Connor. "Listen, we've got to *do* something about this!"

CHAPTER 6

They had thought they knew what they were dealing with on the Scott thing. That was the toughest kind of case they got to deal with: the anonymous kill with no leads at all, no fingerprints, no footprints, nothing.

About all they had to go on there was that X had probably entered the Scott house looking for money, possibly thinking the house was empty, and when the old man heard him and got up and switched on a light, X had used quite unnecessary violence. If he had just run, ten to one the old man could never have identified him, because he hadn't had his glasses on and Richard Scott said his father had been very near-sighted. Of course, X didn't know that.

They had pretty well crossed out the idea that it had been a personal motive. There was just nothing in the background of any of the Scotts that suggested that. The neighbors, and friends, said they were nice quiet people, the elder Scotts entertained a good deal but in a quiet way, and young Mr. Scott seemed very much attached to his parents, who had been pleased he had come to live with them.

The only thing they could do on one like this was to look in Records for anybody whose pedigree indicated a predilection to violence on the job—especially the break-in artists—haul them in and question them. Get any alibis they had. Lean on them. That kind of pro hood was never very smart, and if you let them think you knew a little more than you did, surprisingly often they'd come out with the whole thing. But of course, when it was a homicide rap—

They did what they could on it. Sunday hadn't seen much work done on the Scott thing because of Judy and Lynn, but on Monday, in addition to the very-much-maybe Raimondo, they brought in and leaned on three smalltime pros, each of whom in the past had offered some needless violence to their victims. Hardly on such a scale as that offered the Scotts, but violence. Glendale didn't have any real slum sections, or much serious crime, no, but there were a few like that in Records.

Then, on Tuesday morning, the autopsy report on Robert Scott arrived and turned the whole case upside down. It was, as a matter of fact, waiting on O'Connor's desk when he came in. Everybody else was there, to check in before going off in various directions, except Varallo; Varallo had called to say he was going up to question Judy again.

O'Connor skimmed through the report and halfway through let out a wounded bellow. "What the *hell*—!" he said. And then he said, "Joe!" Katz was just going out. "For Christ's sake! All plans canceled. We'll all go up, and get some patrolmen too—my God! Listen to this, just listen! 'The anterior region of the cranium—' Oh, the hell with the double talk, what it boils down to is that that wrench wasn't the weapon, goddamn it! It didn't have one damn thing to do with either of the Scotts! The weapon, says Goulding, was something like a meat cleaver, for God's sake. Sharp striking edge—"

"But there was blood on the wrench," said Wayne.

"Bird blood!" said O'Connor disgustedly. "From a damn bird! Now how the hell— But anyway, my God, three days ago, but we're going to cover that terrain up there—any back alleys, all back yards—gutters—if there's a thousandth chance that he got rid of the weapon— And Goulding says he must have got some blood on his clothes too."

"Look," said Wayne reasonably, "we did look, you know. And I'd remind you that that's a very high-class neighborhood up there, Charles. Yards kept very neat, no alleys, even garages kept neat. You don't suppose, if he did drop the weapon on the run, somebody wouldn't have found it by now and reported it? A meat cleaver? With blood on it yet? Whether it was in somebody's back yard or right on the sidewalk or street?"

"Even so—"

"I'll remind us all of something else," said John Poor suddenly. "It's Tuesday."

"Well, for God's sake, I know it's Tuesday!" said O'Connor impatiently. "So what?"

"So you're not a householder," said Poor. "It's the day when all the refuse gets collected in that area. I was just thinking, you know. Like that one about the idiot boy and the lost horse. If you were a horse—"

"Have you got a point to make?"

"Simmer down, Charles," said Wayne.

"God," said O'Connor, "look at the report. He hit the old man on the head nine times with something like a meat cleaver—skull cracked open in five places. And probably went on hitting him after he was on the floor—right arm broken in two places, wounds on the body—"

"Not a nice lad, no. So what about the refuse, John?"

"Well," said Poor, scratching his sandy head reflectively, "so how do we have to figure? Did he panic when he saw the old man, or just get mad because he hadn't found any cash? I kind of think he panicked. We know it was before twelve thirty, maybe an hour before—autopsy give us anything there?"

O'Connor shook his head. "They were both still alive when Scott found them. Old man died about half an hour before the ambulance brought him in."

"Oh. Well, anyway, some people don't go to bed that early. We know he left the back way and went through a couple of back yards before getting onto the street—we found traces of him." They had. A few suggestive traces. Nothing very definite for court, but they could read it. It had been a dry year, and nobody watered lawns or flowers at night in January (as they would in summer), so there hadn't been any damp earth for him to step into. But down to the east from the Scott house, there was just a low little cement wall between the Scott yard and the next, and some rose bushes planted against it had been crushed, one limb broken off. In the next yard, there was a higher wooden fence leading into the second yard down, and there was a big scraped scar across the top of that, where somebody might have climbed it in a hurry —a fresh scar.

"Well?"

"Well, there he is with blood on him, maybe a lot of blood, and blood on this meat-cleaver thing, and he's cooled down a bit and wants to get rid of all that. Even if he lives alone, it's for ninety-nine percent sure it's a room or a cheap apartment, other people there, maybe to notice him. And you know, people get careless in a town like Glendale," said Poor. "Don't always bother locking garages. Which is where practically everybody keeps their refuse cans. And with them taking everything all together except garbage, and all the junk mail we get these days and all, most people have these big fifty-gallon cans. And who looks through all that stuff once you've dumped your wastebaskets and tossed in the tin cans and so on? You take out the cans on Monday night and the refuse trucks come by Tuesday and dump them and you carry 'em back to the garage. And anything that had been shoved down in the middle of a can, and stuff put back on top of it, it wouldn't be noticed."

"Jesus!" said O'Connor. "For God's sake, yes— Come on, all of you! And pray those goddamned city trucks haven't hit Cumberland yet!" He led the way downstairs at a run.

They were halfway lucky. The big yellow truck, with its complicated built-in grinding system that chewed up everything from tin cans to broken alarm clocks, was just turning onto Cumberland from Pacific when O'Connor's new Ford braked in front of the Scott house.

He got out and walked back toward the corner, flagged down the driver. "Sorry to spoil your schedule, boys." He hauled out his badge. "Come back here later—we've got to look all through this junk before we let you take it." And what a sweet hell of a job that would be. Well, Poor was a good boy and that had been a brain wave, but he happened to be wearing a new suit.

"Oh, for God's sake," said the driver. "Trust the fuzz to foul up things when they can." He surveyed O'Connor with sour amusement, and looked up the street to where the other men were deployed, each before one house where all the refuse cans sat waiting at the curb. "Not," he said, "that I've got anything against you boys, and are you gonna look just like that, pawing through all that stuff without gloves?" Both he and his partner were wearing thick canvas gloves. "I wouldn't advise it. You got no idea what people put out in their cans. Busted glasses, busted dishes, bottles, tin cans are damn sharp, you know, and knives with handles busted off, and I don't know what all. Well, have fun, bloodhound." He swung the huge truck from the curb and trundled it off down the block.

"Hell," said O'Connor. He wondered if Vic was getting any more out of Judy. He rejoined Wayne, told him to take the Ford and go get some gloves, and meanwhile they'd just try to be careful.

It turned out to be, of course, one hell of a job. At first people came out to ask what they were doing, and that made a delay; and when they got down to it, O'Connor (who just looked like a big tough cop and nothing more, but was something more) thought it was all very symbolic of police work *per se*. Pawing through people's dirt and muck. The inevitable refuse of humanity.

The big trucks collected everything but garbage, and that covered a lot of ground. They came across everything from tin cans which had held sauerkraut and chili to used sanitary napkins and old tooth-brushes. They thought they knew which way he had started running, but they didn't know how far he'd run through back yards, and so they looked, doggedly—with a dozen patrolmen to help—through every re-fuse can on that block, and it was a long block.

In the big blue plastic container at the corner of Highland Avenue, when they dumped it out on the tarpaulin they were using, they spotted a dirty white tee-shirt. When they examined it, it had what looked like bloodstains all over it. It could have been used as a rag, though it wasn't torn; it could have been used as an impromptu bandage, some-body cutting himself accidentally. They showed it to Mrs. Woods, who owned the refuse container, and she said she'd never seen it before.

So they had found a nice fat clue.

But they didn't find the meat cleaver or whatever the weapon had been.

About ten o'clock, when O'Connor and the rest of the boys were up there dumping out refuse cans and examining rubbish, a nice-looking el-derly couple came into headquarters and said they wanted to see some-body who was working on the case of that poor little Daly girl. Nobody was upstairs except Forbes, who'd been left to hold down the office, so Sergeant Dick sent them up and called him to warn him.

He put the phone down to face a man in brown uniform with a large crate balanced on a dolly. "C.O.D. for somebody named Tracy."

"Oh for God's sake," said Dick. "*Now* what?"

The man consulted his papers. "Case of fresh dates from Florida."

"Adding insult to injury!" said Dick. "Florida!"

Upstairs, the couple were introducing themselves as Fred and Martha Heffinger. "We'd have been in before," said Mr. Heffinger, "but the way it was, you see, we haven't been home. My wife's niece and her husband are here from Indiana, visiting, and while they haven't got much time, they did want to see Palm Springs. Haven't got a car with 'em, of course, so we said we'd drive them down, spend a night 'n' day there." He paused. He was a friendly looking smallish man with a round pink face and a fringe of gray hair round a bald head. "I'm re-tired."

"Yes, sir," said Forbes patiently.

"Well, we left Sunday afternoon, picked up Alice and Bob at their hotel in Hollywood and drove down there. Spent the night there, 'n' yes-terday, and Martha and I didn't get home till nearly eleven last night, so we never heard about this terrible, terrible thing till this morning. Little Judy and Lynn! Nice little girls."

"It just makes you sick to think about," said Mrs. Heffinger. "Just sick. These awful fiends—and it's such a quiet neighborhood as a rule, nice people—why these things have to—"

"Well, and right away I thought about that young fella," said Heffinger. "And I said to Martha, now it just *could* have been, and just in case we'd better go tell the police about it. Because I know you want to get that fella bad, whoever did such an awful thing."

"That we do, Mr. Heffinger," said Forbes. Was this going to be anything useful? "What do you know? You saw something?"

"I don't *know* anything," said Heffinger, "but—well, I'll just tell you how it was, Sergeant."

"Detective."

"Yes, I know you're a detective, Sergeant, that's why—"

Forbes opened his mouth and decided to let it go. Cops got used to the fact that civilians mostly knew damn all about the police. Come to think, the pros know more about us, he thought, than the do-right people, which is a funny thing. "Yes sir?" he said.

"Well, we were figuring on leaving about two thirty, see? And it was getting on for then, Martha was just putting on her hat, and I was going out to put the suitcase in the car. Oh, I should have said, Sergeant—we live on Markridge Road, right across from the Hollands—on the corner of New York."

"Oh," said Forbes. Mentally he sat up and took more notice. "I see."

"And I saw little Judy and Lynn on the corner there. Nice little girls —just makes you sick to think of— I smiled 'n' waved at them." Mr. Heffinger cleared his throat. "The garage is at the side—on New York— and I walked around there and put the suitcase in the trunk, and that's when I noticed this car. Across the street, parked, and there was a fella had the hood up, tinkering with the engine."

The car, thought Forbes, that had nearly nicked Holland, had screeched to a stop. A white car, could be a '55 or '56 Ford or Chevy— and Judy had said, a white car like Danny's, and Danny had a '54 Ford. "What kind of car, do you know?" he asked.

"It was a small car, not a sports thing but like a Ford or something like that—not new. It was all white. You know about this?" asked Heffinger.

"No. Just the car. What about the man?"

"Well, I thought the car'd died on him maybe. Stuck him up there. I try to be neighborly with people," said Heffinger, sounding aggrieved. "I strolled across to ask—thought maybe he'd want to use the phone to call a garage, you know. There isn't a public phone in blocks up there. So I said something like, She died on you, hah, you know, and this young fella just growled something back, real impolite—kids these days—"

"What'd he say?"

"Oh, something like he was just tuning her up, it was O.K. And he called me Dad. Disrespectful, you know. These kids! I was just trying to be friendly. Neighborly. But when we heard about Judy—" Heffinger looked distressed. "I never thought, at the time. That's—that's not the sort of thing you expect *or* think about. Is it? Such an awful thing! But when we heard, I did think—could it have been him? That kid? Because I went back across the street and Martha came out and locked the door and we drove off, and he was still there then. And—"

"And Judy and Lynn on the corner?" asked Forbes intently.

"Yes. Yes, they waved to us," said Mrs. Heffinger. "Oh, it just doesn't bear *thinking* about."

A little bit of corroboration, thought Forbes. "Mr. Heffinger, can you tell me what the kid looked like? How old and so on?"

"Well," said Heffinger complacently, "I can do better than that for you, Sergeant. I can give you his license number."

"The hell you can!" said Forbes, startled.

"I can. I just noticed it sort of casual as I come up, because it was a kind of funny one. JAD two three three."

"You *sure?*"

"Yes sir. Tell you why, right away it made me think of that old song, you know—'Ja-da, Ja-da.' And the two three three sort of put me in mind of 'Twenty-three-skidoo,' and it crossed my mind the whole thing had a kind of twenties flavor—" Heffinger chuckled. "You won't remember back that far, Sergeant, but that was why I remembered it. A fluke."

Forbes, who had been born in nineteen thirty, stared at him. A whole plate number. Was this going to break as easy as that?

A plate number, thought Varallo numbly. No—it couldn't be true. A six-year-old—

He had started out easy with Judy, trying to keep in mind what Katharine Mason had said, mental associations. "You know we want to catch the bad man, Judy. I don't like to ask you to think about him, but if we don't catch him, maybe he'll hurt other little girls. I want you to try to help me."

"I'll try," she said seriously. "I don't guess I'm very smart because I don't go to school yet, you know? I'm going pretty soon, though, in Feb-uary, and Mommy taught me all the letters and numbers. I know the alphy-bet."

"They say you shouldn't," murmured Jean Daly. "Silly. They wouldn't take her in the September semester because she wasn't six until December thirtieth. She's—" She looked at him with troubled eyes.

"That's fine, Judy," he said. He hesitated. Start with the car? Work up to the man? Association of ideas. "Where were you when the bad man came up to you? Were you at the corner?" Leading the witness . . . I don't know how to do this, he thought.

"Um-hmm. Mr. and Mrs. Heff-in-er came out and went away and waved to us. Have you got your little baby yet, Vic?"

"Well, no, not yet," said Varallo. Heffiner? That was new.

"Heffinger," said Jean Daly. "They live at the corner house there, opposite the Hollands. They're nice people."

"It was at the corner the bad man app—came up to you?"

"Um-hmm. He said Hello and I said we weren't s'posed to talk to people we dint know and then he said he was our uncle only we just dint know him before. And I said our Uncle Bob and he said—"

"Yes," said Varallo. "Now, when you got into his car, Judy, you sat in the back seat?"

"Um-hmm."

"Do you remember if there were doors in the back as well as in the front? Or did you climb over from the front seat?"

Judy thought. She sat on the couch swinging her feet back and forth, and her blue eyes were solemn. "I think it did," she said. "Do you want to know because bad men have cars like that? Daddy's car's got doors in back too."

"Well—"

"I'm not *azackly* sure," she said. "I wasn't scared then. And I found a sort of thing on the seat I was playing with then. A long sort of thing with numbers on it 'n' letters. I know the diff'rence. Mommy showed me. She said I was smart because I learned real quick. So's I wouldn't get *behind,* she said, on account of them not letting me go to school when Marlene started. I know the alphy-bet and I can count to a hundred."

"That's fine, Judy," said Varallo. And quite suddenly he felt as if he'd been struck by lightning. *A long sort of thing with numbers on it—*

Dear God, a license plate? What the hell would a license plate be doing in the back seat of a car? An old plate? But the D.M.V. would have records—

He swallowed.

He said very gently, "Judy, let's see how good you are at numbers and letters." He didn't dare look at Mrs. Daly; he willed her to be silent. "This long thing you were playing with—was it metal? Like—" he touched the brass pedestal of the lamp on the table beside him—"this?"

"Um-hmm. It was colored too. Orange and black."

A California license plate.

"Do you remember what any of the letters and numbers on it were?"

"Oh sure," said Judy brightly. "I remember them *all*."

"Oh, darling, you couldn't," said her mother. She looked at Varallo. "She does seem to have a good memory, and she learned the alphabet very quickly, but she *hasn't* been to school yet, only private kindergarten—"

"Judy," said Varallo. He brought out his notebook and a ball point pen. "Can you—can you—could you write down the numbers and letters you remember?"

"Um-hmm," said Judy. "I can write with a *pencil*. Mommy showed me how. Would that help you catch the bad man, Vic?"

"Yes, it would, Judy." Mrs. Daly got up and found a pencil in the desk drawer.

"It's absurd," she said almost crossly. "She couldn't possibly—"

"Judy, will you try? Please try."

"I don't hafta try, Vic," said Judy earnestly. "There's a kind of pitcher in my mind. I remember how it looked. Honest I do." She bent over the notebook, pink tongue protruding from one corner of her mouth, and painstakingly she drew the legend on the virgin page, large and shakily distinct—

CHAPTER 7

"Oh, I don't believe you," said O'Connor. "I don't believe either of you. My good Christ, a six-year-old remembering a six-digit figure she'd seen once—and after being raped? It just isn't possible. And you tell me—" he swung on Forbes—"this Heffinger remembered a plate number because it reminded him of a song! Hah!"

"Well, you know you *do* catch yourself noticing plate numbers more since we've had three letters instead of two," said Forbes. "Because a lot of them spell something pronounceable. There are a lot like that, HAH, and JIM, and JIP, and so on. In a way I think it's been useful to us—people tend to notice the letters if not the numbers, looking for words. I've done that myself. Anyway, I sent the number he gave me up to the D.M.V. in Sacramento. We should get an I.D. tonight or tomorrow."

"Well, miracles can happen, I suppose," said O'Connor. "But on Judy I simply damn well don't believe it, Vic."

"Oh, neither do I," said Varallo ruefully. He ran a hand through his tawny-blond crest of hair and looked at his notebook, where Judy's shaky big printing scrawled across the page. "SOS seven oh one," he said. "Damn it, *could* she, Charles? Some people have photographic memories. When I asked her to try to remember, she said she didn't have to, there was a picture in her mind. And she didn't hesitate over this."

"Oh, send it up to Sacramento," said O'Connor. "They've got nothing to do up there but hunt through Records. Send it. But don't, for God's sake, expect anything of it. Let's see that." He took the notebook. "SOS. They tried to weed out the combinations that sounded profane or made words that might—I don't know that I've ever seen an SOS plate.

Tell you what, Vic—not that I think you've got one goddamned thing here—you might ask the D.M.V. about SQS too. They slipped up there, the tail they put on the Q is so short you can't see it until you're on top of it, it looks like an O."

Varallo agreed with that. "But whatever this number is or isn't worth, Charles, she did see a license plate in the back seat of that car. *Perchè?* Or in other words, how come?"

"Funny," agreed O'Connor. "It wasn't, of course, an old plate off that car because they aren't handing out new ones every year. Just those little tags to put on the corner of— Wait a minute. We did get new ones last year, didn't we? And the sixty-five tags are getting handed out now. Damn, I haven't got round to registering the damn car yet. So all right, it could be this was the plate on the car from sixty-three. Or—there's another answer too, Vic. It could be X had junked a car, and stripped off the plates first. Why the hell he'd keep them I couldn't say."

"Yes. That could be. Funny all right. Well, I think this is too good to be true, but we'll get a make on it just for fun."

"I'm going to wash, I'm dirty as hell—what a morning *we've* had—and then let's go get some lunch."

"What've you been doing?"

"Tell you at lunch. Got something too."

They had sent the bloodstained tee-shirt to the lab at L.A.P.D. headquarters, where about every kind of test devised by science would be applied to it. They'd asked priority because it was evidence in a homicide; but that was a busy lab and they'd be lucky if they got something from it by Thursday or Friday.

There was enough to do without sitting on their hands waiting for the lab report. That might give them the killer's name right off the bat, but also it might give them nothing, if the shirt had been washed at home and was a national brand. So they spent the rest of Tuesday chasing down the known local deviates, hauling them in for questioning, and chasing down the burglars in Records who had a history of violence, and hauling them in for questioning. There didn't seem to be much of anything more to do about the burglar at Webbs' except to wait to see if he tried to pawn the stuff. And that might have seemed naïve—for of course in the one sprawling vast town that is L.A. County there are a number of fences in business who haven't been caught up to yet—except for those unknown prints. Fingerprints unknown to the Feds, unknown to anybody, said that the burglar at Webbs' probably didn't have a record, and that might say that he was an amateur, and that could have been his first job. And if that was so, it could equally be that he didn't know where to fence the stuff under the counter, and might try to pawn it. Two new pawnshops had just opened their doors in Glendale, and they as well as every pawnbroker in the county had the list and description of the jewelry stolen from Webbs'.

The police were more concerned with Judy, and the Scotts.

The six men they brought in for questioning that afternoon didn't take them any further. Two of them had what looked like pretty solid alibis; they let them go. The others— That was one of the maddening things about police work: you were working in the dark so much of the time, on the anonymous things like this. These four men— Any of the three deviates could have been the one who raped Judy: none of them had ever attempted rape before, two having got into Records for indecent exposure and one for stealing feminine underwear from clothes-lines, but that was how the dangerous deviates frequently started their careers. None of them had even a vague alibi—that kind were usually loners. They all had cars, none of them conforming to the description Judy had given them, but that car could have been stolen or borrowed. They could, and would, show Judy the mug shots, but if they couldn't get anything but an identification from her, any more solid evidence, that wasn't enough to take to court—judges had a habit of looking askance at the testimony of anybody as young as Judy, on such a charge. The fourth man they hauled in had a record of arrests for attempted break-ins, one burglary, and he had beaten up one of his victims. He could be the one who had killed the Scotts with something like a meat cleaver. He didn't have an alibi either, and if his wardrobe was missing a tee-shirt they didn't have any way to find out. They let him go. All four men denied any guilt, of course.

It seemed to Varallo, driving home tiredly at six fifteen, that police work could, a lot of the time, be described as trying to make bricks without straw. Something, some vague memory dredged up from a course at the university years ago, was nudging at his mind—"the shadows of the images." Was it Plato? God knew he'd never made much out of those supposedly deep thinkers, but—got it—". . . they see only their own shadows, or the shadows of one another . . ."

It was like that, he thought. All the police saw was the shadow cast by the criminal: the shadowy record of himself he left behind. Sometimes, when you were lucky, the shadow was tangible—fingerprints, footprints, a weapon, an article of clothing. More often, in the big city, the shadow was just a shadow. You know somebody was there casting it, but it was a shadow without shape. You just went groping for it as best you could, in the ways experience had showed might get you somewhere.

A meat cleaver, he thought. Funny about that wrench, ought to find out about that too, I suppose.

He put the Chevy away and went in the back door. Laura was standing at the stove stirring something in a saucepan; she looked hot and flushed. "Look," she said, "if this goes on much longer without producing results I won't be able to get the meals. I can hardly get near enough to the stove now."

Varallo turned her around and bent to kiss her. "You certainly are—"

"Say it. Enormous. Just enormous."

"It seems a damned long time since I've been able to get very near *you*."

"It is a damned long time," said Laura. "Dinner'll be a little late, I'm sorry. It's all in the oven. Let's sit down and have a drink beforehand, shall we?"

"Are you supposed to—"

"I *need* a drink," said Laura. "There's only your brandy, but any port in a storm. Sorry, I didn't see the pun coming." She took the saucepan off the stove. Varallo made two brandy-and-sodas. They sat down at the kitchen table. "Anything exciting today?"

"Exciting—" said Varallo, and told her about Judy and the plate number. "It's impossible, of course. I don't believe it. Too good to be true."

"Y-e-s, I suppose," said Laura. "Wonderful if it is, but—"

"Hell, I don't know much about kids," said Varallo uneasily. "I don't know what's possible or not, with kids. I do know that not one adult in a thousand would have total recall on a plate number under those conditions, and that seems to make it twice as impossible that a six-year-old would."

"Mhmm," said Laura. Her head was bent, the overhead light brightening her smooth brandy-colored hair. "Vic. *I* don't know much about kids either. I really don't. Only the two of us, and Paula's older, and she moved away when she and Tom were married, so I don't even know my own niece and nephew very well. Why did we ever get into this, anyway? When I think what's in store for us— It all comes back to conformity again."

"What's conformity got to do with it?"

Laura sipped brandy-and-soda. "Afraid to be different. People get married, they have children. They get married *to* have children, the dear winsome little creatures. Everybody adores children, you know. Anybody who doesn't is a monster of some kind. Whoosh, you made this strong."

"Well, you said you needed a drink. This is an interesting viewpoint, *cara*. You've decided maybe you don't want to go through with the project after all?"

"Very, very funny," said Laura darkly. "Either it's conformity or pure ignorance of what's in store—and with all the books out, no woman has any excuse for ignorance. When I think— Diapers. Millions of dirty diapers. And babies always get sick so easily, making messes to be cleaned up. And the yelling. At night, mostly. And all the horrible messy baby foods. And on a detective's salary, so I can't even hire somebody to do it all one day a week."

"Whoa, don't sound so discouraged."

"Oh, it's easy for you to talk! And neither of us knows anything about bringing up children! All the books sound perfectly ridiculous to me—double talk. We'll probably do all the wrong things and end up with a juvenile delinquent."

"*Non dubbio*," said Varallo, laughing. "People without any experience do manage to raise kids, and they mostly turn out all right. I expect we'll live through it somehow, but I wish to God you'd get on and *have* it."

"You aren't wishing any harder than I am. You don't have this damned baby kicking you in the stomach every five minutes. It's going to be either a heavyweight boxer or an acrobat. Um, that was nice. I'd better see about dinner." She hoisted herself up. "And listen, Vic—changing the subject—in a *kind* of way—we've got to get Gideon over to have him altered. I called Dr. Graehle today and he said seven months is the perfect time and to bring him in right away, because if we don't get it done before he starts spraying we'll never break him of it."

"You are not to go near that cat carrier," said Varallo firmly. "A good ten pounds with Gideon in it—" He crumpled up the empty cigarette package, and Gideon Algernon Cadwallader appeared from nowhere, crouched to spring, chartreuse eyes intent. Varallo laughed and threw the package; Gideon fielded it and started to bat it around the floor.

"Fine," said Laura. "Just where he can get between my feet and trip me."

"It can't," said Varallo suddenly, "be possible, can it? That she's right?"

"It couldn't be possible, damn it," said O'Connor. "I may be a cop, but that doesn't say I haven't got a few brains at least, for God's sake. A six-year-old—"

"Kids," said Katharine Mason, "are funny." She finished her martini and looked at him thoughtfully. He wondered suddenly whether she was thinking about Judy or just wondering why she let this crude Irish cop take her out. Me, thought O'Connor—with the absolutely finest collection of cuddly little blondes in L.A. County—falling for a schoolteacher. It was damn ridiculous. She wasn't his type. And so? And so there it was, for God's sake, and he'd never made a move at her —him!—because he was scared to death that'd end it right there, but would a girl like Katharine Mason even think once about marrying a cop? O'Connor was not at all used to feeling diffident with a female, and of course nobody—least of all Katharine Mason—would have suspected he did; but it made him mad. In fact, since he'd met Katharine he'd had a lot of feelings he'd never had before, and that made him mad too, because he'd thought he knew all about Charles O'Connor.

Six months ago, for instance, wanting to add that nice old Winchester six-shot to his collection, would he have taken a girl here to The Matador where he'd end up minus about twelve bucks? Hell, no. The handiest lunch counter and a movie. But here they were, and the Winchester would just have to wait until next payday. Absently O'Connor patted the bulge of the Smith and Wesson .357 Magnum at his shoulder. Ought to take tomorrow night off, do a little target practice if he wanted to hang on to the trophy as top marksman in the California Peace Officers' Association. He watched Katharine eat salad and sighed.

"How d'you mean, funny?" he asked.

"Funny," said Katharine. Damn it, she wasn't his type. A schoolteacher, for God's sake. She was only an inch shorter than he was, a tall, very slim, fine-boned girl with a mat-white complexion, and very black hair in a short smooth cut, and silver-gray eyes, and a too wide mouth. She taught fifth grade at Verdugo Elementary, and he'd gone there with Varallo last September to ask some questions, and something very damned funny had happened to him when he first laid eyes on her.

"Well, for Christ's sake, what *do* you mean?" he asked roughly.

"I don't suppose," said Katharine, "it'd be possible ever to civilize you, Charles. In a way, it'd be a pity. The perfect prototype just as you are—big tough cop." She surveyed him amusedly. The waiter came and took away the salad plates. Her smile faded. "Kids—" she said. "There's all the aptitude tests and intelligence tests and so on, and sometimes you feel it's all a lot of nonsense. Because, just like adults, they come all shapes and sizes and you really can't reduce them to a page of neat statistics. They come equipped with their own personalities. Capabilities aside. That poor child. I don't know much about that sort of thing, but isn't it apt to—to do some permanent harm? Emotionally? Oh Lord, I sound like one of the textbooks."

"I gather," said O'Connor absently, "that if there's a good stable home background, parents to talk sensibly and so on, it wouldn't. They seem to be intelligent people. And she's only six. They talk about the traumas and so on, I don't know, hell, would it mean anything to a six-year-old beyond the physical pain? I don't know, Katy."

The steaks came. "They always do them just right here," said Katharine, picking up her knife and fork hungrily. O'Connor gloomily watched her munch filet mignon. That was another damned annoying thing about Katharine; she could eat a seven-course meal and top it off with dessert and liqueur, and never gain a pound. O'Connor, especially since he'd ranked lieutenant and didn't get so much leg work, had to watch it a little.

"It *is* possible, you know," said Katharine.

"The plate number? I don't believe it. Not a kid. Even an adult, not one in a thousand would—"

"Memory is also a funny thing," said Katharine. "How do you remember things?"

"Like anybody else, damn it. I just remember."

"No, how does it come to you? In a sort of picture? A picture of somebody telling you something, or the page of a book where you read something?"

"Yes, I suppose so. Yeah, like that. As if you're seeing the original situation again."

She nodded. "Most people have visual memory like that. Some people have an auditory memory—they remember by hearing again, mentally. And some people have what's called a photographic memory, and that you could say is visual memory amounting to total recall. And that seems to be—what we know about it—a purely physical, mechanical thing. The mind just records what was seen, and the—the emotions don't enter in at all."

"Don't kid me. What I know about the head doctors' double talk, the emotions are always in the picture. Id or ego or whatever."

Katharine grinned at him. "Crude big cop, don't know from nothing. You're letting your I.Q. show."

"Never mind my I.Q. I can't believe that a six-year-old—"

"And there's another thing," said Katharine. "You said her mother's taught her the alphabet and numbers. Well—" she glanced around the restaurant—"I don't see any spies from the N.E.A., so I'll come right out and say in that case—from what the mother said about it—she's probably started Judy reading by the solid phonic method, and if so Judy's got about a thousand percent better basic grasp of the alphabet than the kids who started school last September. *Or* some of the kids in second and third grade, and if, Lieutenant, you quote me to the principal I shall categorically deny that this conversation ever took place. May I have some more butter, please?"

O'Connor beckoned the waiter. "God, you'd cost as much to feed as an army. I still don't believe it. A six-year-old."

"There are six-year-olds and six-year-olds," said Katharine, helping herself to her fourth roll. "Mind you, I'm not saying that all the testing and psychological statistics and so on are absolutely worthless. We've learned some interesting things, and found out some new techniques. For instance, we know now that some kids—the ones we used to think of as backward, or even uneducable—don't see quite like normal kids. We don't know why, but they may see printing upside down, or have a tendency to read from right to left. It's all very—"

"Shop talk," said O'Connor restlessly.

"Well, you asked for it," said Katharine. "Do you want that last roll? Well, then—"

O'Connor wondered what she'd say if he suddenly asked, Why do you let me take you out? Never made a move at her, for Christ's sake, *him,* and maybe she wondered— Because sure to God she hadn't got to be twenty-seven without—

He'd never felt like this with a woman. He didn't like it. It made him mad. He was O'Connor, he was proud of being a cop, he was a damn good cop, and he didn't like feeling that the man O'Connor, take him or leave him—that the job was any reason to think a girl would automatically turn him down. *Him.*

He said abruptly, "Well, we'll just have to wait and see."

There was a lot of that in police work. And maybe it applied to his other problem, too.

*

The telephone shrilled at him just as he came into his rather dreary apartment living room. He knew with certainty it couldn't be anything but headquarters, this hour. His right hand dropped from where it had been ready to strip off his tie.

"O'Connor."

"Rhys," said the phone. "The D.M.V. just came through with a make on that plate number Heffinger gave us. Looks like maybe he's got something after all. The JAD two three three. It belongs to a fifty-five two-door Ford, and the Ford belongs to one David Wagner, address on Mira Vista in Montrose. It's only eleven twenty. I wondered if you'd want to go and see if he's home. If he is important, you know—might surprise him a little, and sometimes when people are surprised—"

O'Connor grinned ferociously at the phone. "How right you are. Anybody else there?"

"Bill went out on a break-in."

"So, call Varallo. He isn't," said O'Connor, still grinning, "using his nights for anything but sleeping, anyhow."

CHAPTER 8

It was a middle-aged frame house on a narrow street of similar houses; Montrose was down the hill between La Crescenta and Glendale, an older little town than La Crescenta.

"You taking any bets," said Varallo as they got out of O'Connor's Ford and started up the dark front walk, "that Mr. Heffinger remembered the plate number wrong and David Wagner wasn't in miles of that corner on Sunday afternoon?"

"I'll take a bet. I had a hunch when Rhys called. Well, at least somebody's still up." The house was mostly dark, but a flicker of light showed in one front window and a steadier small glow from the other. "Watching TV," O'Connor added, and used a pocket flash to find the doorbell. They heard the chimes from where they stood on the front porch. They could also hear the TV.

There was a little pause, and then the TV volume went down and a surprisingly bright porch light went on over their heads. The door opened.

"Mr. David Wagner?" said O'Connor.

"No, I'm Frank Drecker. What—"

They both showed him their badges. Drecker's face changed. He was an ordinary-looking fellow in the fifties, a little overweight, with thinning gray hair and glasses. He had a stubborn jaw and very pale blue eyes. He said, "Is that no-good in trouble with the cops again? He's not here, but I suppose he will be some time. You better come in." He unlatched the screen door; they went in.

"What is it, Frank? Who—" A woman came in from another room, a bedroom probably; these old bungalows were often built without halls at all. She was about forty-five, a thin dark woman, who looked as if life had used her hard; she clutched an old terry-cloth bathrobe over her nightdress. "Who are—"

"Cops," said Drecker. "This is my wife Amy. It's her kid you want— my stepson. What's he done now?"

Varallo ceased to feel sleepy. "He's been in trouble before?" Offhand, he didn't recall the name from Records and evidently O'Connor didn't either.

"It wasn't so!" cried the woman. "He's just had—had bad luck, kind of. Davy never means anything bad, he's just a kid yet really, he don't stop to think. And after that first time, you all go *picking* on him." Her face crumpled. "What—why do you want to—"

"Sit down and let me do the talking, Amy," said Drecker, not unkindly. "You sit down too—uh—"

"Lieutenant O'Connor. This is Detective Varallo."

"Kinda like the United Nations," said Drecker, smiling. He went over and turned off the TV.

"You're always down on him too," she said drearily.

"Oh, damnation," said Drecker. He looked at her exasperatedly. You could see she'd been a pretty woman once, the madonna type, with thick dark hair and big brown eyes, but something had aged her too soon. Possibly Davy? "Look," said Drecker, pulling up a chair to face the couch where O'Connor and Varallo had sat down. "I can't get her to see it. I did my best, but the kid's just no good. He was fourteen when Amy married me. His own dad died in San Quentin. He was up for armed assault."

"But Davy isn't like—"

"I don't hold truck with the heredity bit, no," said Drecker. "But I guess it was just too late to help the kid get straightened out. I tried. But the neighborhoods they'd lived and all— For one thing, he's lazier than a pet coon. Yes, he's had cop trouble. First when he was sixteen."

"Where?" asked O'Connor.

"We was living over in Pasadena. They charged him with rape."

O'Connor said, "I see. How old was the girl?"

"He never did!" said the woman passionately. "I saw that girl in court 'n' so did you, Frank, and anybody'd take her for a good eighteen. Got her growth real early. And Davy swore to me—"

"She was twelve," said Drecker. "He got sent to that County Farm place a year and put on probation. That sort of finished him, I guess. He dropped outta school after that and took to running around. What you want him for now?"

"Just to question him about something. Has he ever been arrested again, Mr. Drecker?"

Drecker shook his head. "But they've picked him up and asked him questions four-five times—maybe more. When he was out late with other kids, you know. I don't figure he runs with such good kids. Catch him telling us anything. Gets free rent here—comes 'n' goes as he pleases, and that's all."

"Nobody gives him a chance," said Mrs. Drecker dully. "He does try to get jobs."

Drecker looked at them and spread his hands, shook his head. "I can't make her see the way she treats him maybe was half why he's turned out no good. Spoiled. Rotten. Expects everything handed to him. You're wondering why I put up with him, don't kick him out." He looked at his wife; she might not have been there, but his voice was kind. "She's had a hell of a rough deal outta life. I try to make it up to her. I put up with the kid—he's not around much anyway. I let her slip him the ten, fifteen bucks when he asks—and believe me he asks. I make a good living, got my own station and garage. But long ago I told 'em both, next time he gets in serious trouble, he's o-u-t out. And I mean it. Is he in serious trouble?"

"We don't know yet, Mr. Drecker. How old is he now?"

"Twenty-two."

"Doesn't have a job?" Drecker shook his head. "Do you know any of his pals—a girl?"

"Couldn't say if he even has a girl. He ever say anything to you, Amy?"

"I d-don't like to ask Davy things. He gets mad. You just don't know Davy, Frank. He's independent, 's all. He was the cutest baby—and a good baby too— He don't really mean—"

Drecker sighed loudly.

"Does he have a car?"

"Yeah. I don't even know where he got that. He said he made a deal. He did have a job then, at a bowling alley, but he wasn't making enough to buy the car on time. Sure, I asked him about it, but what's the good?"

"What's the car?"

"It's a fifty-five Ford two-door. White."

"License JAD two three three?"

"That's right. I get in the habit of noticing plates, see so many. So what've you got on him now?"

"Well, we've got some questions to ask him. You know where he is?"

"No, he never tells me anything."

"He said he'd be home early," said the woman. "I guess pretty soon. He don't usually get in till two, three. I listen for him."

Varallo asked, "May we take a look at his room, Mr. Drecker?"

"Sure." Drecker got up and led the way. But a glance was enough; the bare, dreary little bedroom was just a place David Wagner used to sleep in. A few clothes in the wardrobe, nothing fancy; no books, photographs, letters, diaries—it was as impersonal as a hotel room.

"Do you think he'll be home within the next hour?" O'Connor asked the woman.

She nodded. "He said something about there not being a game on tonight so he'd prob'ly just drop in a movie."

"What'd he mean by that?"

"I don't know."

"Well, I think we'll wait around a little for him," said O'Connor. "Thanks very much." He went back to the front door with Varallo.

"Are you going to take him in?" asked Drecker.

"Couldn't say until we've talked with him."

"You can't arrest him when he never done n——"

"Well, we don't know that yet, do we?" O'Connor opened the door and they stepped out onto the porch.

"You want me to leave the porch light on?"

"No, that's O.K."

"Well—" After a moment Drecker shut the door. After a moment the porch light went off. The street lights were bad along here; O'Connor got out his flash again as they walked down the dark path to the cracked sidewalk and the Ford. The Ford was dark green and was just a vague shape in the darkness. They got in and sat in darkness, in the front seat, and lit cigarettes.

"Something," said O'Connor. "Maybe Mr. Heffinger handed us something. Rape indeed. I'll be interested to hear what the Pasadena boys have to say about him."

"Twelve years old isn't six years old," said Varallo. "You heard what the mother said about the girl."

"Mothers like that," said O'Connor cynically, "can do better than the White Queen at believing impossibilities. As a cop, I am damn well prejudiced against females like that one. Responsible for raising more pro hoods than all the slums and orphanages and broken homes put together."

"We've all run into them," agreed Varallo. They sat there silent for a few minutes, smoking. All the houses on the street were dark now. There was a dim-burning street light, one of the old-fashioned short ones, about thirty feet up on this side of the street, and on the opposite side there was one about twenty feet down. Montrose was an unincorporated town and its taxes were low; it wasn't a wealthy town. Like La Crescenta, it had no force of its own and was policed by Glendale.

"Give him until one o'clock," said O'Connor. It was nearly a quarter past twelve.

There was another little silence, and then Varallo said suddenly, "This whole business of having kids— Oh, my God, Charles, I know it's silly, I tell myself not to be a damn fool, but I can't help—being so damn scared—for Laura. I don't let her see it, but—"

O'Connor said, "Oh. But these days, Vic—"

"I know, I know, tell me! These days, with all they know, women don't—don't *often*— And he's supposed to be the best obstetrician in town. But God, I don't know, he said it ought to have come last week, and if anything goes wrong, if—"

"Oh for God's sake, you've just got prenatal jitters," said O'Connor. "With all they've found out, and antibiotics and— Nothing's going wrong. Don't be a damn fool, Vic."

"That's what I keep telling myself. And, Christ, I know why but I still can't help it. Because they do—sometimes, Charles. They—do—die. Ginevra died."

He felt O'Connor turn to look at him. And he realized suddenly that it was the first time he'd spoken her name in years. Her right name. He heard himself laugh once, unsteadily. "That cr-crazy fight about her name," he said. "Dad called her Rita to the day she— He'd wanted to name her for his mother. But Ginevra was—her real—"

"Ginevra."

Beautiful fair Ginevra, golden Ginevra laughing in the sun. "My—my sister," he said. It was very quiet in the dark here. "She was three years younger. I—she—we were— I was closer to her than— Oh, goddamn it, Charles, I know that's why I'm scared, I know it doesn't happen often any more, but—it—happened—to Ginevra, she died and the baby died too, and I—"

"Listen," said O'Connor roughly, "you're a damn fool, deliberately borrowing trouble! For Christ's sake, stop jittering! Where was that, that little hick town upstate? Horse-and-buggy doctor, ten-bed hospital with practically no equipment. Use what damn brains you've got! She's got a specialist, she'll be in a good city hospital—"

"Glendale Community," said Varallo, as yet unaware that this was a lie.

"Well, there you are. Everything will be—" O'Connor gripped his arm. "Here's Davy boy."

The white car came down the street too fast for the darkness and narrowness. It screeched around violently to make the dirt driveway beside the house. The motor cut, the tail lights blinked off. In a second the headlights went off and the driver's door opened. By that time, O'Connor and Varallo were in position, Varallo at the right front of the car, O'Connor at the left rear.

"All right, Davy," said O'Connor unemphatically, "freeze right where you are. We'd like a little talk with you." He advanced slowly with the flash in his left hand.

"What the hell—" The flash showed Wagner to be middle-sized, wiry, with curly dark hair and a thin white face. It was a too narrow face, with a mouth too small, but he had his mother's big dark eyes. He said, "Fuzz. What the hell do *you* want? I'm clean."

"We'll just see," said O'Connor. "Up against the car, Davy."

"Who said you could call me Davy? Only my fr—"

"Up against the car, punk, and make it damn snappy!" said O'Connor.

"Oh for God's sake—" Davy had been through this bit before, obviously. He turned and spread eagled himself against the Ford, arms and legs apart. Varallo stepped in and went over him swiftly. No gun. A middling-fat billfold—it added to over fifty bucks—and a half-full pint bottle of vodka, besides the usual stuff.

"Is there a light in the garage?"

"Yeah."

"O.K. In. Turn it on. I want a little closer look at you while you answer some questions."

"Fuzz!" said Davy. "I tell you I'm clean. What the hell you think I done now?" But he walked into the garage and switched on the light. The light was over a littered workbench; already in the garage was a 1949 Packard De Luxe four-door sedan, glisteningly polished.

"The antique belongs to the old square Ma's married to. Don't think I—"

"Where've you been, Davy?"

"A movie—if it's any of your damn business, which it ain't."

"In Glendale?"

"Montrose. Why? I ain't—"

"Alone or with a girl?"

"Alone. If I reach for a cigarette, will you put a slug in me?" Davy brought out a pack of Camels.

"I'm holding no gun. Where do you get your money, Davy?"

Davy shrugged. "Ma. Odd jobs. I'm clean."

Varallo at his other side asked, "Where'd you get the money to buy your car?"

"I had a lucky day at Santa Anita along about then," said Davy, and blew smoke at him.

"Where were you last Sunday afternoon?" asked O'Connor.

"About two thirty?" asked Varallo.

"Sunday—what's with Sunday?" Davy's narrow face was tense with control. It is, thought Varallo, it's him and he never thought we'd get to him and he's— "I had the heap out, been tuning her up. I had her out for a run and then I went— I went to see a pal, that's all. What happened Sunday?"

"You know what happened Sunday, you bastard," said O'Connor hardly. "Two thirty, Davy. Sunday afternoon. You were at the corner of New York and Markridge Road up in La Crescenta. Why'd you stop there?"

Davy looked suddenly confused. He glanced from O'Connor to Varallo. He said cautiously, "I went up New York, yeah. To test how she was running. It's a pull up that hill, but, Jesus, she took it at seventy m.p.h., real sweet."

"That's nice," said O'Connor, "considering that the limit in town is forty-five and that only a few places."

"Yeah, well, there wasn't any fuzz around then."

"You stopped there. At New York and Markridge. Why?" asked Varallo.

"I stopped. Sure. I don't remember where exactly. Why the hell shouldn't I stop? I told you I was testing her. I wanted to adjust the carburetor a little bit. I didn't like—"

"You didn't stop, maybe, because you saw two little girls alone on the opposite corner?" snapped O'Connor.

"Two— Jesus, what do you—" Suddenly Davy took a step backward and dropped his cigarette. "Jesus God, you ain't talkin' about them two kids that was kidnaped and raped, bloodhound? You ain't tryina rope me in on *that?* Jesus, you think I'm a monster or something? For God's sake, I never laid eyes on— I wouldn't do nothing like—"

"You did a little time for rape," said Varallo.

"Oh for Christ's sake! That was just a bad joke," said Davy. "One hell of a bad joke. Take my word, cop, the little chick was eager an' willing, I never ast how old she was, but every guy in school knew that one could be had, and, brother, *had* she been had—if you get me. Then she gets p.g. and her folks raise a fuss, so she needs a fall guy and fingers me for rape. Believe me, it was— You don't really think—"

"Tell us about Sunday," said O'Connor.

"You stopped at that corner?" asked Varallo.

"I stopped to adjust the damn carburetor. Who knows it was that corner? I never saw two kids there. I wasn't lookin' for kids, why the hell would I? I was workin' on the car. I was there maybe ten minutes, I don't know." He was talking fast and free now. "Jesus, think I done a thing like— A guy'd have to be *nuts, want* to do a thing like— And then I took off again."

"Anybody come up and speak to you there?" asked Varallo.

"Oh yeah, this old guy comes up—from across the street, I guess—and asked what was wrong with the heap. There wasn't a damn thing wrong, I was just— And I took off, I never noticed exactly where I stopped, and I never saw no two kids, and that's God's truth, cops. Jesus, think I could do a thing like—"

Varallo looked at O'Connor in the harsh unshaded light. Davy was sweating. It had taken a little time to get Judy and Lynn up to that old winery, to rape Judy: and that might not have happened right away. By what they'd been able to sort out, the man had been with the two girls for at least an hour.

"So, go on," he said to Davy. "Then what'd you do?"

"I had a kind of date," said Davy. He said it reluctantly. "Just to meet a pal. He'll tell you. Sammy Pollack, he lives on Lamar Street in Burbank."

"What time did you get there?"

"Maybe three, a little bit before."

"How long were you there?"

Davy looked at O'Connor and then at Varallo again. He licked his lips nervously. "Uh—about two that morning," he said.

"Two on Monday morning? You don't say. Was there anyone else there except you and Sammy?" asked O'Connor.

"What the goddamn hell you mean? You sayin' now I'm a fag, for

God's sake? Goddamn cops— Yeah, there were other guys there. I give you their names, they'll say I was there alla time, except to go to the john. I wasn't never—"

"You sat around listening to records or maybe sharing out some reefers?" asked O'Connor.

"Goddamn cops. Take a fall, and every time some bastard pulls something, they— We got in a hot poker game, damn it! Is there a law against—"

"Yes, there is a law against," said O'Connor, "Burbank not being a town which has legal poker parlors, Davy. So give me the names of your pals."

Davy gave them, sullenly, and O'Connor wrote them down. When Davy gave him the name of one Gary Willetts, he looked up and said genially, "Charged with heisting a liquor store in nineteen fifty-eight. If I remember right, he got a one-to-three. Any of your other pals got pedigrees, Davy?"

"Go and ask, cop!"

O'Connor snapped his notebook shut. Both he and Varallo were conscious of the all-dark house a few feet from the garage: they could nearly feel the woman's eyes, through some dark window, watching the light here—the damn-fool, too maternal woman worrying about how the cops were treating her baby.

They looked at each other. Here was something else up in the air. Davy Wagner was placed on the scene—by Fred Heffinger and his own admission. He had once been charged with and convicted of rape, damn the other details to that. With the rape of a twelve-year-old girl. He had, in the classic phrase, no visible means of support: ran a good car: dressed fairly well: admitted joining in an illegal poker game. A gambler? Was that where his extra money came from? Poker game or crap game? The point being that if so, he ran with a bunch any of whose sworn words neither O'Connor nor Varallo would be inclined to accept as necessarily gospel truth.

"Overnight?" said O'Connor, raising his eyebrows at Varallo. "For Judy to look at tomorrow?"

"Jesus God, I wouldn't never do a thing like—"

"No harm," said Varallo. They could, under California law, hold him for twenty-four hours without making a charge. They had the gambling charge, if necessary—a silly law that was, most peace officers thought, but it *was* law.

"O.K.," said O'Connor. "We'll take you in, Davy. We'd like to hear what Judy Daly has to say about you."

"Oh, my Jesus Christ! *Me,* do a thing— Cop, you're crazy! I—oh my God, all right, all right, but Jesus I hope to God that little girl's got all her marbles and can say it *wasn't* me. Jesus, a guy'd have to be nuts—a *kid—*" Davy was white as a corpse. *"Me—"*

"We've got," said O'Connor amiably, "a nice comfortable new jail."

CHAPTER 9

The alarm went off and Varallo reached out for it blindly, with a groan. Laura was already up; he heard her in the kitchen. She, of course, had got to bed for good at ten thirty. He dragged himself out of bed and went down to the bathroom. He could, he decided, get by without a shave; there were advantages to being blond. He dressed and went out to the kitchen.

"You feeling all right? I wish—" It was the only time he'd confessed how he felt, last night to O'Connor; he didn't think Laura knew, but with wives you couldn't tell.

"I'm all right, don't fuss. I'm going to see Dr. Straw this morning, and I'm certainly going to try to pin him down. I don't see how I *can* go on much longer— Two eggs?"

"One," said Varallo. "Listen, you call and tell me what he says. Charles and I are taking Wagner up for Judy to look at this morning, but I'll probably be back in the office by eleven. You call. "

"Um," said Laura.

"How are you going to get downtown? You're not to take the bus— those rattly old heaps."

"No, Mrs. Anderson's going to drive me. You do fuss, Vic. It's got to be soon. *I* know," said Laura, "we'll make it on your birthday, shall we?"

"That's Saturday. You do that," said Varallo, forcing a grin. "Don't forget to call."

He got to headquarters at five past eight and met Burt and Rhys on their way out. O'Connor was already at his desk typing. He was a hunt-and-peck typist and swore whenever he made a mistake. He looked at Varallo with a harassed expression.

"The strange case of Patrolman Tracy," he said. "Jensen's yelling he's only supposed to deal with Traffic, we're the damn detectives, we ought to investigate. I'm trying to wangle some of those damned original order blanks from the outfits that've sent the stuff."

"And then we go and collect handwriting samples from everybody Tracy knows?"

"You have any better idea?"

"Well, nothing strikes me at the moment, no," admitted Varallo. "That is the damnedest thing. He says he can't think of anybody who'd have a reason to do such a thing, and he doesn't know any practical jokers." Wayne and Katz came in together.

"I don't know what's behind it, but I suppose we'll have to do some work on it. Hey, Fred, you want to carry on with this? Vic and I have to take that punk up for Judy to look at."

"Sure," said Wayne, strolling over. "Oh, that. Damn it, I don't type any better than you do. All right."

"That I know, I've read enough of your damn sloppy reports." O'Connor, who could put on a clean shirt with a neatly knotted tie and a sharp-pressed suit and five minutes later look as if he'd slept in his clothes, got up, kneed his chair in and yanked his loosened tie around more or less to where it should be. "Come on, Vic, let's do the great confrontation scene. Somebody call Mrs. Daly, tell her we're coming, or maybe she'll be out at the market."

"Has that D.M.V. report come in yet?" asked Varallo. It hadn't. It probably would some time today.

They went over to the jail on the other side of the building and collected Davy Wagner. Davy was subdued this morning; he said all over again that he hadn't never done such a thing, and he sure to God hoped the little girl would have sense enough to say so. He lapsed into tense silence before they got out of Glendale, and when O'Connor pulled up in front of the Daly house Varallo had to help Davy out of the car.

"Jesus, just a kid— Maybe she don't remember too good, it's three days back. I swear to God—"

"Just come along," said O'Connor. They climbed the steps to the porch. Mrs. Daly had been waiting for them; she opened the door before they rang the bell, and she didn't look at either O'Connor or Varallo. Her burning eyes fixed on Davy.

"They called from your office," she said stiffly. "Is—this—the one?"

"Lady, I swear to God I never— I done this 'n' that maybe, but thing like that—"

"We just want Judy to take a look at him. We don't have to come in. Where is she?" asked Varallo.

Mrs. Daly nodded tautly, still studying Davy. "She's—in the patio, playing. I'll get her." She turned from the door.

"Look—" said Davy. "If—if—"

"Relax," said O'Connor.

In a minute, Mrs. Daly came back holding Judy's hand. Judy was wearing blue capris and a white blouse today, and her pony tail was shining neat. She saw Varallo first and smiled at him.

"Hello, Vic."

"Hello, Judy. Would you mind coming out here a minute?" He held open the screen door. She came out and looked questioningly at the other two men, back to Varallo. "Have you ever seen either of these men before, Judy?"

She looked at O'Connor and something, some indefinable expression, came into her blue eyes; she stepped back a little toward Varallo, and he put one hand on her shoulder, and for a moment was shocked by the narrow frailness of her under his hand. How often had he touched a child? She looked at Davy, and then she looked at Varallo and said gravely, "No, I didn't. Did you think one of them was the bad man, Vic?"

"Well—"

"Him—" Judy nodded her head at O'Connor—"the bad man, he was all black like that man, but that isn't him. I mean—" she hesitated—"all like that on his face like that, all—all—all scratchy." She shuddered.

Davy let out a whistling little sigh. "Jesus, I don't want a scare like that in a while." He looked at O'Connor and grinned. "So you look more like him than me! That's a joke. You gonna let me go now, cop?"

"We'll even take you home," said O'Connor sourly. "O.K., thanks, Mrs. Daly." He smiled at Judy, but she didn't smile back.

"Have you got your baby yet, Vic?"

Varallo shook his head. "Pretty soon, Judy. I'll probably be back to see you again."

Mrs. Daly was still grave and intent, watching them out to the Ford. Davy gabbled on about the joke in a sweat of relief. They drove him down to Montrose, let him out in front of the house on Mira Vista.

"Thanks a lot, cop! And I hope I never see either of you again, ever."

"I have a hunch you will, punk," said O'Connor, and took his foot off the brake.

"So now we know he's one of the fellows who needs to shave twice a day," said Varallo, "and never looks really clean-shaven." O'Connor growled. "I hope that D.M.V. report's come in, I—"

"You don't really expect anything from it, do you? We don't get things handed to us on a silver platter like that, damn it, you know as well as me. I'll lay you a hundred to one there isn't even such a plate number in existence."

"I won't take you. You're too apt to be right," said Varallo. Laura's appointment was for ten o'clock; he wondered what the doctor— God, could there be anything wrong? He started worrying all over again. A first baby and she was nearly thirty-one—

They got back to the office at nine forty. Wayne was sitting at O'Connor's desk typing with two fingers, swearing under his breath. "Look," he said, "on that rug, do we write to the outfit that arranged for import or the one in Sweden? We don't know which one'd have the original order blank."

"Take the U.S. firms first," advised O'Connor. "Probably have enough trouble with them. Davy wasn't the bad man, by the way. Judy says he looked more like me."

"I always have thought," said Katz, looking up from a report, "you look more like the ones on the wrong side of the desk. But I never heard you needed to go in for rape."

"Jeff and Poor went out on the liquor-store heist," said Wayne. That was what had taken Burt out last night: a liquor store on North Pacific held up just before closing time. "Had both proprietors down looking at mug shots, they both saw the men—and got a tentative make on one. Oh, Vic, that D.M.V. report came in, I put it on your desk."

Varallo had just discovered it. "Hell," he said, reading it. "It's just as well we didn't lay that bet, Charles." There was no such plate number as SOS seven oh one. The plate number SQS seven oh one belonged to a 1960 Buick two-door, and the Buick belonged to one Mr. Hugh Merrill, who lived at nine twenty-four Buena Vista Avenue in Shafter, California.

"Where the hell is Shafter?" asked Varallo. He found an atlas on O'Connor's desk and looked it up: 8-F on the map of California; he found that and spotted Shafter. "Up a little beyond Bakersfield," he said thoughtfully. "So, all right, I'm stubborn. Let's check him out. It's about a hundred and sixty, hundred and seventy miles. What Californian thinks anything about driving that far? Maybe Mr. Merrill *was* here last Sunday. Maybe he's the type who likes to rape little girls. Let's see, that's Kern County."

"How stubborn can you get?" said O'Connor. "For God's sake—I tell you, she made up the number."

"Did she make up the license plate? It's a lead. It's one hell of a bad lead, but you can't drop it because you're sure it's hopeless. It *could* be Merrill."

"It could have been a Martian," said O'Connor. "So go, go send your teletype." Varallo went down the hall to send the teletype to the sheriff of Kern County, asking information about Mr. Hugh Merrill. A teletype was just coming in, for O'Connor: all the stuff on that Raimondo Anoscurrio. He'd been living with his uncle, Anastasia Anoscurrio—God, we Wops do have names sometimes, thought Varallo—on the uncle's truck farm outside of town. His former probation officer had sent them a routine report when he moved. He'd been picked up and questioned four times during the time he'd been there, when they'd had heist jobs of the kind he'd pulled down here, but they'd never gathered enough evidence to charge him. End of report. No suspicion of any rapes or molesting of kids. Well, Raimondo had looked like a better candidate for the Scott job anyway. Maybe he still was.

He sent off his own teletype and took O'Connor's back to the office. "Helpful," said O'Connor. "This is one of those damn times I wonder why in Christ's name I ever was such a goddamn idiot as to join the force. We just got the autopsy report on Mrs. Scott." He shoved it across the desk. "The same something like a meat clever. Sharp striking edge. Skull fractured in four places, left arm nearly severed above elbow, wounds in the body—" He dragged a big hand across his mouth. "Is this a nut, Vic? A schizo on the rampage? And not one single damn lead—"

The inside phone rang. Varallo picked up the autopsy report and grimaced, reading it. The senseless violence—and X hadn't got one damn thing out of it, not even the little cash that had been in the Scotts' bedroom, in his billfold, her handbag. A nut? Maybe.

"Oh," O'Connor was saying. "Well, why the sweet hell haven't they come in before? Civilians. The goddamn honest public we sweat to protect. Kids? Oh, well, send 'em up, send 'em up." He put the phone down. "Something new on the Scotts. We'll see. Joe's down hunting more deviates in Records. Jesus, not a smell on that either."

"Mr. Merrill," said Varallo.

O'Connor used a rude word. "We're going to lean on every boy like that in our files, and then we're going to have a look at L.A.'s records. And the sheriff's. What the hell good does it do us to have such a nice peaceful little place like Glendale, with a nice low crime rate, when we're bang in the middle of L.A. County, with one of the highest rates in the nation? How long does it take to drive from Boyle Heights to Glendale? And I'll tell you something else, too—the last few years, since they got back, thank God, to painting cars solid colors, for some damn reason you see about ten times as many solid white cars as any other color. And a *kid,* Vic. Six years old. How far can we trust—" He broke off as two people paused hesitantly at the door. He got up. "You'll be Edward Stillman? And Miss Sandra Brenner?"

"Yes sir," said the boy. He was about seventeen, and when he filled out a bit and acquired a little poise he'd be handsome. He was as tall as Varallo, and nearly as blond, and unexpectedly he had big dark eyes with lashes long as a girl's, and a good straight nose and a firm jaw. He was wearing gray slacks and a white shirt without a tie and a blue cardigan.

The girl with him was about the same age. She was blonde too, and she had a figure that was really something, and big blue eyes, and skin like cream, and she was nicely dressed in a navy-blue skirt and a light blue blouse and a white cardigan. Looking at the pair of them, both O'Connor and Varallo suddenly felt as old as God. The dewy aspect of innocence shone all over the boy and girl, and they looked around the big, light, clean Detective Bureau, a little awed, a little fearful, as if they expected to see a couple of big tough cops administering the third degree to some hapless suspect, but then there were a couple of TV series running which featured some pretty peculiar-type supposed cops.

"I—we talked it over, and we thought we ought to tell you, sir," said the Stillman boy. "I mean, yesterday I went back and looked, to be sure, and it was the same house, I know it was even if it was dark, and so I talked it over with Sandy at lunch period and we thought— And then I asked Dad about it last night and he said we ought to. So we went to the principal this morning and told him, and he let us both off class so we could come down and tell you."

"Tell us what, Mr. Stillman? Sit down, both of you, won't you? I'm Lieutenant O'Connor, this is Detective Varallo." O'Connor pulled up chairs.

"Well, thanks. This is— I've never been in a police station before," said the boy. He had blushed at the mister. "I don't know if it means anything, sir, but—it said in the paper—that awful thing, those old people getting murdered, the Scotts—it said that Mr. Scott's car had been taken out of the garage and left in front. And you see, I think—we both think—we saw whoever did it, do that."

O'Connor sat up with a jerk. "The hell you say! Sweet jumping—How and when?"

Sandra blushed. Varallo looked at her bare legs, primly together below the short skirt, and looked away hastily. Laura—before the baby, of course—had just as good a figure. God, the baby— He thought, two of the ninety-seven percent of all our teenagers who are O.K., don't get into trouble. Only the three percent get so much more publicity.

"Well, there was a rehearsal on Saturday night, sir. I drove Sandy—we've been sort of going steady anyway—we've just started rehearsal for the senior play, it'll be on the twenty-fourth and twenty-fifth, just before end of term, you know. I should've said, we both go to Hoover High."

"What—" began O'Connor, and the girl interrupted.

"You don't have to tell all that, Eddy. It's afterward is important. It was when we were coming home—"

"Well, they have to know how we came to be there. See, Sandy's a sort of second lead in the play, I'm only one of the walk-ons, but anyway we both had to be there. Oh, you'll want to know where we live, I guess. I live on Raymond Avenue and Sandy lives on Cumberland."

"Yes, Mr. Stillman," said O'Connor patiently.

The boy flushed again. "Well, the rehearsal broke up at nine thirty, see. Some of the kids were complaining because it cut into a Saturday night, but we didn't mind, there wasn't a good movie on in town or anything, anyway. But we didn't go right home, I had the car of course, and we went to Pike's for a hamburger."

"Pike's Verdugo Oaks?"

"Oh no—" Sandra looked a little shocked at that idea. That was about the nearest thing to a night club Glendale had, a fashionable—and expensive—place with, of course, a liquor license. "No, the Pike's at Brand and Glenoaks." A nice quiet little restaurant, family atmosphere, run by husband and wife. "I guess it was about ten thirty when we started home, Eddy?"

"Maybe a little later. Some other kids in the cast were there too—Roy Donahue and Mary Cass and Linda Stacy and that creep she goes around with, something Webster—"

"He's not a creep," said Sandra softly. "You always say that. Just because he can grow a mustache, the rest of you—"

"Yeah, yeah, and I heard Mr. Snavely say the principal was gonna make him shave it off, too." They both stopped and blushed.

"So?" said O'Connor. To his eternal credit, he said it gravely. But both he and Varallo felt older and older.

"Oh yeah, well—well, it was maybe about ten forty when we started home," said the boy. "I said I had the car. I went straight out Glenoaks, naturally, and up Pacific to Cumberland—to take Sandy home. I—did you say Lieutenant?—look, I know teenagers have sort of got a reputation of being damn-fool drivers, but gee, there's compulsory driver-education courses in high now, you know, and some of us have got *some* sense. I mean, I try to be careful, you get me? And anyway, it's Dad's car, I'll have to have a car of my own when I go to college, but I have to earn at least half of what it costs myself, which is O.K. I work summers. It's the principle, Dad says, even if he could afford—*which* is O.K. I mean, there's the insurance and upkeep and all."

"Eddy, you don't need to—"

"Oh hell," said the boy. "No, I know, it's only I was explaining. So I turned on Cumberland, see, this was maybe ten fifty, around there—and I'm going maybe twenty-five, maybe not quite that fast. Those streets up there are pretty dark. And all of a sudden this car comes backing out down this driveway like a bat out of— Well, it was going a lot too fast, anyway, and about halfway down the drive it swerved right across the front lawn of the house, still backing, you get me, and came out into the street over the curb. It must've been going thirty at least, and if I'd been going any faster, it'd sure have hit us. I just had time to swerve—"

"I think it was going faster than thirty," said Sandra. "Eddy's a good driver, but if he hadn't swerved that exact second, it'd have hit us. I was really scared afterward—you know how it is, it all happened so fast, but afterward—"

"It was a white car, all I can say. And its lights weren't on, I couldn't say at all about the driver, what he looked like. But when I saw that in the *News-Press* about that awful thing, the old people getting murdered, and the car backed out of the garage— Well, I drove back up Cumberland, and all I can say is I'm pretty sure it was that house where the Scotts lived. And I talked it over with Sandy and she thought so too—and so—"

"That's very interesting," said O'Connor. "This was about ten to eleven?"

"I think about then. I said something to Dad when I got home, lucky to have the Buick in one piece, one of these crazy kids who— He could say what time I—"

"A kid? I thought you said you didn't see the driver?"

Sandra was unobtrusively staring at Varallo, at Wayne hunting and pecking at his own desk.

"Well, I didn't, Lieutenant, not really—it was just because some kids *are* crazy drivers I said— But we thought we ought to tell you, just in case—"

It was a little something. At least it pinpointed the time for them.

CHAPTER 10

Laura called at eleven o'clock. "Well, he just says it might be any time and not to worry, there's nothing wrong, we just miscalculated a little is all."

"Oh," said Varallo. "Well—"

"We're going to have lunch at the new cafeteria and then I want to shop for—"

"Listen," said Varallo. "Wandering around town when it may decide to come any minute—you'd better go home, *cara*."

"I will," said Laura, "be sitting around home quite enough after it's here. Have you thought of any more possible names?" They hadn't settled on any yet.

Varallo said they'd been a little busy here and still were, and he hadn't given much thought to names. "You go home and—and rest," he said.

"And wait," said Laura, exasperated. "I might as well be window-shopping as twiddling my thumbs. I'll see you, darling. Early?"

"I don't know," said Varallo.

Between them, O'Connor and Wayne had written a dozen letters to the various firms which had bestowed the unexpected largesse on Patrolman Tracy. "And I think," said O'Connor, "I'd like to talk to him. Damn it, if he got some joker mad enough at him to go to all this trouble, sure to God he ought to know about it."

Varallo outlined Forbes's theory that the somebody had got riled over something very minor and hadn't showed it. O'Connor grunted disbelievingly and said he'd been up since six and was going out for an early lunch. Forbes met him in the doorway as the outside phone rang on Varallo's desk.

"Brought in another deviate. You want to sit in? He looks—"

"Not very damn much, but—"

"Glendale Detective Bureau, Detective Varallo."

"—Look very likely?"

"Well, he's had two charges of molestation, he's out on parole."

"—Is Sergeant Wright, Arcadia headquarters. Say, about this thing you boys've got, the elderly couple—double homicide?"

"Yes?" said Varallo.

"Oh hell, I suppose I'd better—" O'Connor's voice faded down the hall.

"Just occurred to me, when I saw it in the *Times*— I don't see your local sheet, of course, and I guess it got into the *Times* first time yesterday, which is when I saw it, last night. And it kind of rang a bell, so I had a look through the files this morning, when I had a free minute, and I thought maybe I'd better contact you. We had a thing a hell of a lot like that just four months back. Could be the same boy."

"You don't say," said Varallo. "I take it you didn't get a line on him?"

"Nope. Odds and ends. Elderly couple, Mr. and Mrs. Ronald Nesbitt —he was a retired banker, just retired and they'd just moved out here from Indiana. Married daughter lived here, see. They were living at the San Marino Motel until they decided on a house—plenty of money and then some. They had a rear unit, and there's an alley right back of the motel. Looked as if he came and went that way. Motel manager heard Mrs. Nesbitt scream—this was along about midnight—and went to investigate, and saw the kid running away."

"The kid? He got a good enough look to say—"

"Yeah. He thinks it was a kid, or a very young man, by the way he ran. That's all. But both the Nesbitts had been bludgeoned and hit with something sharp too. Old man D.O.A., wife died that night in the hospital. Old man's billfold missing, we found it on the next street—about forty bucks gone. But, while there isn't much there, the m.o. is enough alike that I just wondered—elderly people who wouldn't be likely to fight back, yet the unnecessary violence and the type of weapon."

"It makes me wonder too," said Varallo. "This was four months back?"

"September twelfth. Captain says you're welcome to our file on it if you want. I've given you the gist of it but there were a few more details."

"Thanks very much, maybe we'd better have a look," said Varallo.

And yet—Arcadia? And again, why not Arcadia? That was a very different kind of town from Glendale. A wealthy town, a town of expensive homes, a very classy town, with the Santa Anita race track in the middle of it and all that revenue pouring in. A lot of residents of Arcadia had pretty substantial incomes, and any potential thief might have picked that motel, probably a high-class one, as probably containing cash and valuables.

But it was still all up in the air. Not a real lead. Varallo sighed. And there was still Judy. That license plate—

The inside phone rang. "Varallo."

"Vic, I've got a pawnbroker for you. On that Webbs' thing."

"Oh. O.K., put him on." Varallo leaned back in his chair.

"No, no, he's here. I'll send him up."

The pawnbroker, when he came puffing and perspiring up the stairs, turned out to be Mr. Cornelius van Deering, and he filled the doorway. He must have weighed three hundred pounds. He was dressed in a sober black suit and a rather swashbuckling, wide-brimmed black hat, and he looked more like an undertaker than a pawnbroker. He stood and removed the hat, and mopped at a noble high forehead. "Stairs." He panted. "Stairs I don't like. You got this nice beautiful new building and no elevator?"

"Well, it's only two stories, sir—"

"Hah! I introduce myself." Van Deering presented him with a card. He hitched up his jacket and sat down in the straight chair in front of the desk, planting himself firmly. "To come to the point at once, there comes into my place about half an hour ago this—person—with a diamond watch to pawn. The watch is new. Hamilton watch. Good watch. Well, I have this list—all of us get these lists of stolen stuff, you know—and besides I see in the paper about this burglar at Webbs' the other day. Some Hamilton diamond watches taken. So I wonder. And—"

"You said 'person.' Man or woman?"

"Well, that's the funny thing. I think it was maybe a very young person. A kid. Right away he comes in I see he's not wanting I should recognize what he really looks like. He's got an old tattered man's hat, too big for him, pulled down, and an overcoat—in this weather, you know—too big for him also, and the little while he's there, he keeps up a handkerchief to the bottom part of his face, pretends he's got a cough. He just asks how much for the watch. And I think, this might be the burglar from Webbs' store, so I say I have to look at it close, and I'm trying to get a better look at him, do you see, when another customer

comes in and he says, Never mind, and snatches the watch back and out
he goes fast. And so I think—"

"Yes. How tall was he? Can you describe him at all?"

Van Deering shrugged. "How tall I can tell you. Measured by me, I
am six foot four. He was short. Maybe five foot five, six. Anything else
I couldn't say. He is all bundled up like I say, and I'm facing the light
from the door, behind the counter, and I couldn't even say what color
were his eyes. But I thought I had better tell the police."

"Yes sir, thanks very much for coming in."

And Varallo felt exasperated, watching van Deering lumber out. Just
what the hell use was it to know this, when the pawnbroker admitted he
couldn't recognize the man again? It didn't even say that van Deering's
would-be customer was the Webbs' burglar. It only said maybe, because
van Deering's pawnshop was here in Glendale. But wait a minute. If it
had been Webbs' burglar, that might back up the evidence—the negative
evidence—of those prints. They had said the prints, not being in anybody's records, might indicate an amateur, somebody who wasn't very
expert at burglary, and wouldn't know the fences. So—

And also, thought Varallo suddenly, yes—*per carità, cèrto!*—damn it,
that *was* the Webbs' burglar, because he'd seen at the time that only
someone fairly small could have squeezed through that opening at the
back of the niche. And here was van Deering talking about somebody
short trying to hock a new diamond watch.

O'Connor came in and said testily he wanted Judy to take a look at
this fellow. "He's done time for molesting kids. Twice. He's got no
alibi. He also—" O'Connor wrinkled his nose—"hasn't had a bath in
quite a while. God, I feel as if I need disinfecting."

"I wanted to see her again anyway," said Varallo. "But look,
Charles, this pawnbroker—" He brought O'Connor up to date on that.
"And the more I think about it, the more I think—as I said at the time—
that he had to know something about the store. He had to know that he
could push that plywood back out of the niche."

"The hell he did not," said O'Connor. "He could have knocked that
glass in just on impulse, to scoop up what was in the niche, and found
out accidentally the back of it would shove out."

"And that's right where I say you're wrong. You haven't seen the terrain, so to speak. That niche is about a foot deep, about two feet
square, *but* it's also about four and a half to five feet up the side of the
building from the sidewalk. Oh, hell, that isn't very deep and he *could*
have accidentally found out—but I don't see how. He'd be scooping up

what was in the window, as you said, and why should he even touch the back of the niche? No, I still say it's probable he knew that already. And look, Charles. They must have taken on quite a few extra clerks over the Christmas-shopping period, department stores always do. Temporaries. And they seem to be such nice trusting souls that they might not investigate those people very thoroughly. I think we ought to ask a few more questions at the store, anyway."

"Up to you," said O'Connor. "I am damn near starving to death. Did somebody mail those letters? Come on, let's go and have some lunch. Jeff's stashing our latest catch in jail, we'll pick him up later and let Judy take— And I already know what she'll say, damn it, but we have to go through the motions."

"*Perchè?*"

They started downstairs. "I had the very damned belated thought," said O'Connor, "that those two kids are from a pretty good home. That is, you know, parents talk grammatical English, the kids are taught manners and so on. So they're not going to take the word of some goddamned stranger who says he's their uncle, unless the stranger was fairly well-dressed and talked the way the parents and other people they know do. This bird, this Joe Uccello—" O'Connor gave a massive shrug. "He can barely read and write, and you can smell him a block away."

"Evidently he got some other kids to come up to him."

"In East L.A.," said O'Connor tersely.

"There's something else," said Varallo, and told him about Arcadia's double homicide last September. "They're sending over their files, but they don't seem to have got much on it."

"What, for the love of Christ, really bugs me is that damn wrench!" said O'Connor. "I know it's got nothing to do with anything, but how the hell did it come to be there, in the Scotts' yard? With bird blood on it, for God's sake?"

"If it's going to keep you awake," said Varallo, "we might just ask whoever lives on the other side of the rear wall in the Scotts' yard."

"Occasionally you do have an idea."

They stepped into the lobby.

"All I'm *saying* is," said the man in brown uniform, "it's a C.O.D. and I'm supposed to— Where is this N. Tracy?" There was a big wooden crate on the floor at his feet.

"Take it *away!*" said Sergeant Dick. "It's a mistake! It's a—"

"What is it now?" wondered Varallo.

The expressman asked, "You N. Tracy?"

"No, thank God," said Varallo. "What's in the crate?" It had a lot of papers pasted all over it, and rubber-stamp markings.

"It's a cuckoo clock," said the expressman. "A giant-sized cuckoo clock from the Black Forest. It cuckoos every fifteen minutes." Varallo and O'Connor started to laugh. "Personally, I think anybody'd have to be nuts. Imagine. Every fifteen minutes. If you weren't nuts to start with, you would be after a while. It's three feet high and the cuckoo's got real feathers. So the manifesto says. And it's also C.O.D., and—"

"I'll say one thing, Charles," said Varallo. "This joker has quite an imagination. In fact, he's showing great finesse in his choice. Of all the awkward useless things—"

"Yeah, that's how I think too," said the expressman. "But then I'm not this N. Tracy."

"For that," said O'Connor, "you can return thanks."

Neither of them especially wanted to sit next to the rich aroma of Joe Uccello in the back seat. They handcuffed him to the hand grip on the right side and Varallo got in front beside O'Connor. He said, "How come you have to finger two Italians? Stirring up my inferiority complex."

"All Wops are crooks," said O'Connor, "didn't you know? Of course, we do pick up a few micks now and then. I'm not writing the script."

Uccello, who looked as if he might possess an I.Q. of around 65, rode in sullen silence. Varallo very much doubted that he had been the one to play Uncle Bob, but of course you never did know and he had the right record for it.

They drove up to Markridge Road and repeated that morning's performance.

Mrs. Daly looked rather horrified at Joe Uccello, as well she might, and Judy didn't seem to like O'Connor any better than she had before. Varallo exchanged a look with him, and O'Connor bowed out and took Uccello back to the car to wait. "Mind if I come in a minute?" asked Varallo. He smiled at Judy and she smiled back. "You see, we're trying hard to find the bad man who hurt you, Judy. And you said you'd help too. But—"

"Yes. I would. So's you could put him in jail so's he couldn't hurt anybody else. Has your baby come yet, Vic?"

He shook his head. "Maybe it'll come on my birthday. I've got a birthday on Saturday."

"Oooh, that'd be nice." Charles's schoolteacher said, it depended a lot on the questioner. Whether he really liked kids. Because, as Varallo knew, kids sensed these things. Well, he really liked Judy. "How old'll you be, Vic?"

"Thirty-five, Judy."

Judy was silent, awe and puzzlement in her eyes. "Oh, that's pretty old, isn't it?" Varallo smiled and looked up to find Mrs. Daly smiling in sympathy.

"Yes, I guess it is. Judy, you said you remembered the letters and numbers on that pl——on that metal thing in the back of the man's car. But you didn't remember them right, you know."

"I did too! Honest I did, Vic!"

"No, we know you didn't, Judy. You see, that was a license plate from a car." She looked bewildered; he left that instantly, little use to try to explain. "We just know you remembered wrong, because—because we have a way to tell, Judy." Unless the very long shot paid off and it had been Mr. Hugh Merrill of Shafter, of course.

"I know I remembered right." She looked puzzled and hurt. "I *do*. Because—because—there was like a pitcher in my mind, like I was seeing it all over again, and I drawed it out just like it *was*. In your notebook."

"Yes. Well, I'd like you to do that again, Judy. Would you try that?"

"Sure, Vic. But I *know*—"

It was, he supposed, a waste of time. Impossible to believe that even a bright six-year-old would remember six digits, in the right order, after the considerable physical and emotional shock of rape, and that cold lost time up on the mountain. Judy was making it up, or imagining it, or—

But why should she invent a license plate?

"Judy," he said. He hesitated, running fingers through his hair.

"Can I get you a cup of coffee, Mr. Varallo?" asked Mrs. Daly suddenly. "I—I'd like to say we appreciate the trouble you're taking. I hope you don't mind, but I'm afraid you've—" she smiled—"rather intrigued Judy with your—your expected baby. I— Is it a first one?"

He smiled back. Damn the irrelevancy of females, interrupting. "Yes, it is, Mrs. Daly. Any day now. Coffee'd be fine, thank you." He didn't want coffee, but it would get her out of the way for a few minutes. He waited until she had gone out, and said, "Judy. This metal thing in the man's car, can you tell me about it? What color was it?"

"Orange and black," she said without hesitation. As she'd said before. A California license plate, orange figures on a black ground.

"Um. Did it have anything on it besides the letters and numbers?"

Judy squeezed her eyes tight shut, thinking. And he did not, reflected Varallo, approve of dressing little girls in pants the way so many mothers did. Reasonably, he could see it was easier in a *way*, practical play clothes, it wasn't that he felt it was exactly immoral, but little girls ought to be dressed—sometimes, at least—like little girls, and if the baby turned out to be a little girl, that he was going to insist on. He thought unexpectedly, *Sugar 'n' spice 'n' everything nice—*

"Yes, there was," said Judy, opening her eyes. "There was a little white square up at one corner, at the top, and it had black numbers in it, two black numbers only I can't see a pitcher of what they *were*— And right across the top in the middle, over the numbers you know, there was some *other* letters, real little letters, only I don't see a pitcher of them either. Just, they were there. All I see a real pitcher of is the real big letters and numbers."

So what did that say? By God, it said something. She had described a California license plate, all right. Orange on black. Across the top, above the plate number, CALIFORNIA spelled out full: in the left top corner the little plastic pasted-on tag, black on white, that would say 65, showing that the car had been registered for this new year.

Diavolo! What the hell? he thought. It had to be a '65 tag, because everybody in California who had a car had got new license plates in January '64. And this was only January eighth, and you had until February to register your car, pay the registration fee for 1965 and get handed the little '65 tag to put at the upper left-hand corner of the rear license plate. So how come? A plate in the back *seat* of a car, with a very new '65 tag on it—

And if she remembered that, and that little black and white tag made it look doubtful that she was just making it all up, then how come she was so wrong about the number? If she had that good a memory—

Hell, he thought. A kid. Six digits. She wasn't even in school yet. And unconsciously at least she'd have seen a lot of license plates, her father's car, cars parked up and down this block.

Charles's schoolteacher had said—

Mrs. Daly came back with two cups of coffee on a tray, cream and sugar, and set the tray down on the coffee table.

"Judy," said Varallo, "would you write the numbers and letters down for me again, the way you remember them?"

"Why, sure, Vic. I *know* I remember it. There's this pitcher in my mind. Mommy, can I have a pencil?"

Her mother gave her one from the desk, and sat down on the couch beside Varallo.

"Just cream, thanks." Varallo opened his notebook to a fresh page, not to let Judy see what she'd written down before, and handed it to her. She sprawled out in the middle of the living-room floor a few feet away and started laboriously to draw on the page.

"You said she was quick at learning the alphabet?" asked Varallo quietly.

"Yes, but she couldn't possibly remember— Oh, I don't *know*. I thought it was silly, their not letting her start in the September term, and I did start teaching her a little, so she wouldn't be too far behind. I don't care what they say, it's nonsense not teaching them the alphabet. Yes, she picked that up very quickly, but I haven't forced her or—or supervised her at all. She isn't reading yet, I just taught her the letters, the shape of them and so on. She knows them all. She seemed to pick up numbers herself, I think from listening to Jim. He does bring home a lot of the market accounts, and he *will* talk to himself." Mrs. Daly smiled. The smile faded. "They said she'd be all right—the doctor—she *seems*—" She fell silent.

"There!" said Judy. "I drawed it out just like the pitcher in my mind, Vic. I know I remembered it right. I *felt* them, you know. I felt the letters 'n' numbers with my fingers, like, besides *seeing* them." She handed him the notebook gravely.

He looked at the page. Thing called photographic memory, said Charles's schoolteacher. Maybe only partially: Judy didn't remember the "California" or the number on the '65 tag. But she wasn't reading yet, said her mother: just knew the shapes of the letters and numbers. And she had "felt" the letters and numbers too. As she would have: letters and numbers, orange on black, raised in relief a quarter inch or so on the face of the plate.

It was, in her shaky big drawing, the same six digits as she'd put down before, in the same exact order. You couldn't make them add up to anything else. The S's were a bit squarer this time, but there it was.

SOS seven oh one.

Hugh Merrill of Shafter? SQS seven oh one?

Diavolo, he thought.

He said, "That's fine, Judy, thank you."

CHAPTER 11

"An outsider?" said Larkin. "You're thinking now that somebody knew something about that—that using the niche to get in was deliberate? I don't see how, I'm sure."

"It could be like that, the way I see it," said Varallo. "That somebody knew, first, that the back of the niche could be pushed out, and/or, second, that the niche was not connected up with the burglar-alarm system."

"Well, *that's* out," said Larkin flatly. "I didn't even know *that* myself."

"I should think, when you—is it you?—changed the displays there, you'd have expected to have to disconnect that first. How is it you didn't know?"

"I never gave it a second thought," said Larkin, looking angry at himself. "In the few months since those niches have been in, I've been arranging the displays in the morning, before the store opens. That is, you understand, I've only changed the displays three or four times altogether, but it was always then. I'd come in a bit earlier even than usual, so the Stationery and Men's Wear people wouldn't be there yet—but naturally the store manager would be in first, and he'd disconnect the alarm system. I knew that, so it never occurred to me even to look for wires there. I'm—er—not very mechanical anyway."

"I see," said Varallo. "You were always alone when you arranged these displays?"

"Always." Larkin's deep voice went deeper with gloom.

"Never even one of your assistants with you?"

"No, sir. Both Miss Porter and Mr. Lewis are absolutely honest and reliable people in any case, but as it happened, as head of the department I arranged the displays myself, as I said. There's no chance that anyone could have seen me take down—"

"Wait a minute. Nobody with you in the store, but how about outside on the street? Somebody passing?"

"There'd be very few people on the street on any of those occasions, sir. It would be between seven and seven thirty or so. And leaning right into the niche, I'd have noticed anyone watching. No one ever passed while I was doing that."

"You're sure?"

"I'm sure. Wilson is the side street, you know. At that hour, people starting for work would mostly be in cars or waiting for a bus on Brand."

"Yes," said Varallo. "What about the clerks who use that stockroom? Do any of them know anything about the niche? Have you ever said anything to—"

"Sir," said Larkin impressively, "only myself, the store manager and my assistants know the exact whereabouts of our *safe*. I'm not a complete fool, and I'm aware that—um—human nature is sometimes frail. I have never been near that niche when any of the other clerks there was anywhere about, and neither has Miss Porter or Mr. Lewis. We all agreed on that. I should think, while most of them—the regular clerks—would realize that that plywood backing gives onto the niche, most of them would automatically assume it was locked in some way. And so it should have been," added Larkin with a groan.

"Yes. What about the temporary clerks taken on over the Christmas-shopping period?"

Larkin sighed, glancing down the jewelry counter to where a fat woman was examining a tray of pendants. "Rather a lot of those, especially over in Stationery. But we get a really nice type of girl as temporaries—college girls, high-school girls. This *is* the best store in town, you know. We've very seldom had any trouble with the temporaries, and if you're thinking of one of them perhaps discovering accidentally that that panel lifts out, well—" Larkin shut his eyes for a moment— "you just don't know what this place is like between Thanksgiving and December twenty-fourth. A madhouse, Mr. Varallo. That stockroom is used by Stationery, Men's Wear, Gifts and part of the Notions department, and I very much doubt whether any clerk would ever have been alone in it for more than ten seconds."

"Oh," said Varallo. "Well, nevertheless, I'd like to have another look at it, and I think I'd like to talk to somebody in those departments."

"Surely," said Larkin with a sigh. "Have to co-operate with the police." He glanced down the counter again.

The fat woman was saying doubtfully, "Well, I don't know. It seems like a lot of money, and just that one tiny little stone." Miss Porter, blonde and svelte, murmured reassurance that rubies were rather high, but after all—

"Ah-hum," said Larkin. "Perhaps you'd be interested in a garnet, madam? Those we just got in," he added aside to Miss Porter. "Coming into fashion again, garnets are, and of course far less expensive."

"Well, I don't know—"

Miss Porter whisked a black-velvet-covered tray to the counter and the fat woman bent over it. Larkin came out from behind the counter and led Varallo across to Stationery. A thin gray-haired woman at that counter looked at them but didn't speak, and there was curiosity and speculation in her eyes. The store didn't seem to be very busy; after-holiday, pre-inventory slump, Varallo surmised.

He looked at the plywood back of the niche again. "It is, by the way, connected with the alarm system now, so if you want to open it—"

"No, that's O.K. I wanted to check how it fits in." Varallo squatted down and studied it. The square of plywood was, he recalled, about three quarters of an inch thick, and fitted neatly over the opening with a lip of about half an inch all round; and at the top corners a pair of metal grips held it on, the top lip of the plywood being slid under the grips. Careless, he thought. If there'd been a different type of fastener top and bottom, ten to one it couldn't have been pushed out at all; but the bottom half of it would swing when pushed, of course, and give that away. And had that happened by accident, or had somebody known?

"When did you change the display last?"

"Oh well, I'm afraid not since around December twelfth. It was a Wednesday, I recall. I came in early as I said—we were doing a lot of business, and I had the open case to arrange too."

"Was anyone else here at the time?"

"Miss Porter had come in early too, but she was busy with the open case. There wasn't anyone over here at all. I do remember that Mrs. Coutts came in just as I was leaving. We just passed her out there—she's head of Stationery."

"So," said Varallo. "I think I'd like to talk to Mrs. Coutts."

Larkin sighed, led him out and introduced him.

"Oh—the burglary!" said Mrs. Coutts. "Have you got any of it back yet, Mr. Larkin? We've often had shoplifters, of course, but this is the first time since I've worked in the store we've ever had a *burglary*." She sounded more excited than upset, and was eying Varallo avidly.

"I'd like to ask you a few questions," said Varallo. "Are you free now, or—"

"*Me?* Questions? Why, I wouldn't know a thing. My goodness, how would I— But of course, anything you want to ask. I expect I could take my coffee break now. Mary!" A tall thin young woman drifted up: apparently the only other clerk there. "I usually go down to Newberry's—"

"Fine," said Varallo absently.

He told himself again that this was just a meaningless hunch; in all probability the amateur burglar had knocked in that glass on impulse and in reaching in had inadvertently hit that plywood backing and, seeing it hung loose, realized that this was a way into the store—for anybody his size. About five five, said Mr. van Deering. This funny hunch that the burglar had known all along about that way in didn't mean a damn thing. It didn't matter either that the store had been dark: practically everybody who lived in Glendale had been in Webbs' at one time or another, and would know where the real-jewelry counter was. And he may have had a flashlight.

Only—well, add up all the funny little things, maybe also meaningless, that had produced the hunch. Those niches, Larkin said, were lighted all night: just a little light, but a light. And while Wilson was the side street, still all the downtown streets were lighted better than most residential streets, and nobody could know when a patrol car would come cruising by. The amateur burglar had been a little reckless in his choice of a place to burglarize, hadn't he? Then, it had taken a hard blow (or a heavy tool of some kind) to break that double plate glass. A hand wrapped in a jacket wouldn't have done it. So he'd come here prepared. Or, of course, he'd discovered that he'd need a heavy tool and gone somewhere to get one, which said he was pretty damn determined to break into that niche. And the various items Larkin had tastefully arranged there had been all fairly inexpensive items, and only a few of them had been taken along with the rest of the stuff.

It just seemed possible to Varallo that the amateur burglar had had prior knowledge of the vulnerability of that niche, and if so, he must have acquired it somehow.

Mrs. Coutts, who had excused herself and bustled away, came back with fresh pink lipstick on and said, "I hope you don't *mind* Newberry's. Their coffee—"

"Well, suppose we find a place with booths, if you don't mind? There's that little place across the street, by the bank."

"Oh yes, that's nice. You know, I've never met a real detective before, Mr.—is it Varallo? That's Italian, isn't it? I didn't know there were any blond Italians. Oh, dear, that sounds rude, doesn't it? Do you think you'll catch the burglar?"

"Well, we hope so, Mrs. Coutts." I always get the ones with the tongue hung in the middle, he thought. He led her across the street and got her settled in a tiny booth at the rear of the little place. He offered her a cigarette; somewhat to his surprise she took one.

"But I just can't imagine how *I* could tell you anything to help."

"It's like this," said Varallo, and broke off as the waitress came up, to order coffee.

Varallo didn't know that he was about to hit a modest jackpot. Police work was like that: ninety percent of the time just damned dull slogging routine, with no surprises to it at all; and then sometimes along came a big surprise, or you started out questioning witnesses in the full expectation that you'd be at it for days before you got anything, and the first one told you what you wanted to know; or a little hunch proved out against all the odds. Or, of course, sometimes something showed up to cross out all the patient routine you'd been doing.

Mrs. Coutts listened to his theory about some outsider, and said at once that it was quite impossible. She said shrewdly that he was thinking about the temporary clerks over Christmas, but they'd all seemed like nice respectable girls, and the couple of young men taken on in Men's Wear were nice too. And anyway, nobody was ever alone in the stockroom. There was always someone else there because it served four departments. And while she herself knew in a vague sort of way that that plywood square was the access to the niche, as the other regular clerks would, she'd never given it any *thought* and didn't know any more about it. She'd always assumed it was locked. Nobody had ever asked her any questions about it, and if one of the temporaries—in *any* of those four departments—had asked about it, that would have been reported. She was quite definite that nobody would have had a chance to be alone in the stockroom during the hours the store was open. Not during the Christmas rush.

And of course it was possible, even if he was right, thought Varallo, that the inside knowledge had been acquired months ago and just casually remembered last Sunday night. But he was thinking now, a kid?— because of the unknown prints, because of the smallness, and the carelessness in leaving prints at all, and the evident lack of knowledge of the fences—and a kid, say a high-school kid, wouldn't wait around if he'd decided to pull a burglary, would he? Well, there were kids and kids.

"I shouldn't think any of the temporaries realized just what it was, you know. My goodness, Mr. Varallo, you just don't realize how *busy* we are over the Christmas season! You're busy every minute, customers lined up waiting, and I should think the temporaries would be even busier than the rest of us, because of not being as accustomed to making change and figuring up the tax and so on. Poor things, they do get run ragged, but we mostly get a very nice type of girl. Some of the customers are rude, and you've got to keep on your toes, familiar with *all* the stock, you know, and— My goodness, you just don't realize! None of us would have any *time* to be doing anything at all but wait on everybody! And Mary and I had to take all the orders for printed cards, of course—that was up to December tenth, they wouldn't take any printing orders after that—you couldn't leave that to inexperienced clerks—and what with keeping the counters filled with merchandise as it got sold off, and trying to keep your temper and be polite to everybody—" She paused, breathless.

"Yes. When did you begin to hire the temporaries?" he asked at random.

"Oh, before Thanksgiving. Most of them came on the Monday after Thanksgiving. But I don't see—" Suddenly her mouth fell open.

"You can *definitely* say that there never was anybody alone in that stockroom? What is it, Mrs. Coutts?"

She'd been drinking her coffee; the cup wobbled in her hand and she set it down unsteadily. *"Oh my goodness!"* she said. "But that'd be just crazy! A *burglar?* Why, Ted's an honor student! That simply couldn't be! Besides, I don't know that he even *looked* at—" She stared at Varallo, and under her modest make-up went a little pale, so that pink rouge stood out.

"Ted?" said Varallo.

"It just came *back* to me, that one night— But of course it's just crazy, to think he could have anything to do with— Why, he's an *honor* student! He's going to be an archaeologist. He's a very serious boy, Mr. Varallo, and he's been brought up right. My sister—"

"Who is Ted, Mrs. Coutts?"

"Well, my goodness, I see I'll have to tell you, but it's just ridiculous. It really is. Now, what day was it? It was either a Saturday or— No, it was Friday, I remember because I was supposed to be off at six but one of the temporaries didn't show up and I had to stay on. It was Friday the twentieth of December. A very busy night. And my car was in the garage, something had gone wrong with the transmission. Oh dear, it's just silly to think that *Ted*— Ted's my nephew, Mr. Varallo. Mr. Coutts and I never had a family, and since he died four years ago I've lived with my sister Cora and her husband. And Ted. He's a very serious boy, a nice boy. He's a senior at Hoover High. Well, and the store closes at nine fifteen, of course, but what with clearing the cash register—my drawer, I mean—and doing a little straightening up, I wouldn't be ready to leave until after nine thirty. And of course the buses have stopped running by then, and so I'd arranged that either Ted or Herb—his father —should come to pick me up. And—and Ted came in before the store closed, and waited round until I was—"

"And," said Varallo, "he was in the stockroom alone at one point?"

"It's *silly!*" said Mrs. Coutts crossly. "I'm not sure, but he could have been. I was the last one to leave—Ted and I. Most of the lights were out. I'd got in a muddle adding up the money, I had to do it over to make it come out straight. And while I was doing that, Ted was—just sort of wandering around. But you can't think *Ted*—"

Varallo didn't say what he was thinking. He asked, "What's Ted's last name, Mrs. Coutts?"

"Blair. But he—"

Well, it was something, thought Varallo. Did he have something here after all?

It was past three o'clock. But she'd said Ted was a very serious boy. Very serious boys—and honor students—have been known to join extra-curricular school clubs which met after school. On the off-chance, Varallo drove up to Hoover High and went in to ask questions at the main office.

The registrar's assistant wasn't much help to him, but a pimply-faced boy waiting to see the vice-principal was, offering the information that Ted Blair belonged to the Historians' Club and that met in Room 303 on Mondays, Wednesdays and Fridays at three fifteen.

Varallo climbed stairs and found Room 303. He went in and apologized to the portly middle-aged teacher presiding, and asked for Ted Blair. He was forced to produce his badge, which in turn produced quite a sensation, but he finally got Ted Blair out in the hallway and regarded him thoughtfully.

Blair looked older than seventeen or eighteen, and he looked intelligent. Varallo had checked, and there was no sign of him among the delinquents on record. He wasn't the type; he looked like a nice serious kid, not bad-looking, nudging six feet, with a dark-brown crew cut and brown eyes and a stubborn jaw.

At the moment he was looking at Varallo incredulously. "You're a *cop?* What on earth d'you want with me? I'm parked in the school lot."

Varallo said, "On December twentieth you called for your aunt at Webbs' to drive her home. Just before you left the store, while she was busy at the cash register, you went back to the stockroom there." He paused; Ted Blair was flushing slowly. "What happened then, Ted?" He had a small second hunch; he kept his tone conversational.

"Well, for God's— We must have a pretty sharp police force," said Ted. "But why on—" He stopped. "Oh," he said in a different voice. His eyes changed suddenly. "My *God,*" he said under his breath. "I just now connected it. My God, that burglary at the store. Aunt Milly talked about it but I never—" He looked at Varallo. "You don't think *I*— But, gee, I suppose that could have been how the burglar—"

"What happened then?"

Ted shrugged. "Silly little thing. I'd never been there before, I was just wandering around waiting for Aunt Milly. I spotted that square of plywood and sort of wondered what it was for, you know. I've been told—" he grinned briefly—"I've got an inquiring mind. Anyway, I went over and looked at it, and just touched it—the top edge—I saw the clamps—and, my God, the whole damn thing fell down and I saw what it was, all that jewelry in that alcove thing. I put it back in a hurry, and I expected I'd set off the burglar alarm and there'd be cops down on us in droves, but nothing happened. That was all. I didn't say anything to Aunt Milly, of course. But—"

"No, but I think you told somebody about it?" said Varallo. Talk about jackpots! So whoever Ted Blair had told knew about that plywood, and knew the niche wasn't connected up to the burglar alarm. Not for sure, that last, because for all Blair knew, the store just closed, the alarm system might not have been switched on yet. But—

Blair said thoughtfully, "Gee, it *could* have been the way. I guess it was careless, all right, but who thinks anybody you know is gonna pull a burglary? Well, some kids I know are fairly wild, but not *that* wild, you get me." He looked at Varallo. "It could be that somebody who heard me *did*— But how would *I* know anybody there would— And I don't suppose, if it was like that, it'll help you much, Sergeant or whatever."

"Detective. Why not?"

"It was in the gym locker room, the Monday afterward. I was telling Jim Frenier what a hell of a scare I'd got. That's the only time I remember ever mentioning it. Well, it was just a silly little thing, you know. I suppose," said Ted Blair, "there were maybe three-four other guys around, getting dressed, who could have heard. I remember Bob Carter was around somewhere, matter of fact we'd just finished a set of singles together—and I think Mike Kroeger was around too. If they did hear me, well, I don't know. I wouldn't say either of 'em's exactly the burglary-type, but they could have mentioned it to somebody else. I wouldn't know why, but you do get talking, you know—"

So there was his jackpot. So? Varallo said, "I'd like your fingerprints, if you don't mind."

Ted Blair looked interested. "Sure, that's O.K. You want me to come down to headquarters now? O.K. Be very interesting, see how you guys go to work."

Varallo very much doubted that it had crossed Ted Blair's mind to use his inadvertently discovered knowledge to pull a burglary. And those other kids, hearing about it casually, could have as casually relayed the information to anybody. Not thinking much about it.

Why the hell, he thought, didn't I go into insurance or something?

"What do you think yourself?" asked O'Connor.

"I don't know what the hell to think, Lieutenant," said Patrolman Neil Tracy. "I'd call myself an easygoing guy, I don't know of anybody with any reason to want to—to annoy me like this. Annoy me— Boy!"

"Nuisance value, all right. Haven't had an argument with anybody lately? Over anything?"

Tracy thought. He wasn't a good-looking young man, Tracy, but was honest and open-looking, with his bulldog jaw and serious eyes. The tan uniform looked good on him, as if it were tailored. This was the first time O'Connor had really met him, talked to him, and he thought Tracy was the kind they wanted, a really good man. He said suddenly, "You got permission to wear the gun that way?" Tracy was carrying the holster on his left hip, back to front, with the grip to hand for a cross-body draw.

Tracy flushed. "Yes, sir. I think it's a better position for a quick draw."

"Agreed," said O'Connor. "If you're fast at all. What d'you shoot?"

"Average about ninety-four, sir."

"The hell you say. I'll have to get in some practice— You'll take that damn trophy away from me." O'Connor grinned. Tracy relaxed a little. "Arguments?"

"Well, my God, sir, what's arguments? My brother-in-law doesn't agree with me on politics, what the hell's that, I ask you? This guy down the street, he lets his dog run, I've told him about the leash law, but the damn dog comes and digs up my nasturtiums, and I tell the guy— But what kind of idiotic reason for all this is that kind of thing? I don't see it, sir."

"Who knows?" said O'Connor. "Funny damn business. You're a gardener? Funny damn hobby. Vic and his roses. Well, hell, I don't know—"

"My wife," said Tracy, and stopped. "I told her it was ridiculous. But you know women."

"That I damn well do. She's got an idea? About the joker?"

"Well, it's crazy. I mean, nobody would—just for *that*. But she says, nobody except somebody with a petty mind would conceive such a —a campaign, sort of. Just, like you say, for the nuisance value. She thinks—" Tracy shook his head.

"Spill it, for God's sake! *Any* idea—"

"She thinks," said Tracy, and shrugged, "it's some guy I wrote a ticket for once. A traffic ticket."

CHAPTER 12

What Varallo should have done, of course, then at twenty minutes to four when Ted Blair gave him the names of the boys who had possibly overheard what he'd said, was to go and look up all those boys and ask them. Sizing them up while he listened to their answers.

But that was another thing about police work. Police officers and housewives had in common that their work was never done: there was always more of it to do. Housewives, however, could maintain some control, because the individual housewife could make the big decision, wax the kitchen floor on Wednesday, wash the windows on Friday. Cops, no. Especially if you happened to be a cop on a fairly small force. There you were, maybe just getting a lead on a homicide, when some punk pulled a heist and you found yourself asking new questions of new witnesses.

They had the heist job from Monday night, the liquor store on Pacific, and Poor was out on that; the proprietors had identified one man from Records, and they were still looking for him. There had been a hit-run yesterday, out on Colorado, and Jensen had turned that over to the Detective Bureau this morning; Wayne and O'Connor had been doing some work on that.

So at twenty minutes to four on Wednesday afternoon, Varallo brought Ted Blair back to headquarters with him, and took his prints for comparison with the four nice prints they had from the broken figurine in the niche at Webbs', and took down the names of all those boys, and drove Ted Blair back to Hoover; and then he went back to headquarters, because he'd asked Forbes, who'd just come in, to have a look in the records and see if any of those names showed up in their delinquents file. He intended, after finding that out, to go and locate them and ask the questions.

But just as he came into the building, he met Forbes, O'Connor and Wayne running down the stairs, and O'Connor grabbed his arm and snapped, "Come on—there's a heist going on at Fidelity Federal!" Outside, a patrol car with a uniformed driver had just screeched out of the lot, and they all piled in, and the siren started as the driver made a U-turn and started down to Broadway at seventy m.p.h. Along Broadway, a block down, all traffic was stopped—there was another siren coming from the other direction. Three blocks up the squad car screeched to a stop behind another one with its door hanging open, in front of the modernistic brick-and-glass and blue-painted building at the corner of Louise and Broadway.

There was a little crowd, with a uniformed man trying to break it up. "You want to get *shot?*" he kept shouting.

There were a couple of shots from inside the building. Another patrol car came up and its siren died, and out of it got Patrolman Neil Tracy, his gun already out.

"What's the story?" asked O'Connor. "The dispatcher just got the automatic alarm." He had the .357 Magnum out too, and it looked enormous compared with the .38's the other men carried.

"I don't know, sir," said Tracy. "They just sent me over—"

The other uniformed man said, "I just came up, but the boy from that car must be in there. I've counted four shots, I was starting in but all these damn people came crowding up and I thought—"

"All right," said O'Connor. "Side door?"

"No," said Tracy. "This is my beat. Back door on the parking lot."

"You go and take that. Jeff, you go with him. If possible, try not to get yourselves shot—we're shorthanded as it is, damn it." O'Connor started toward the front door. A woman screamed inside the building and there was another shot and a man came running out, clasping one arm.

"Thank God, cops," he gasped. "Shot—they came in the back door, they've got Mr. Hill, using him—as shield—made all the girls open their— I stepped on an alarm and one of them saw—three of them— My God, I'm *shot!*"

"Let's go," said O'Connor. "Goddamn it, crime *is* going up here—all these damn apartments." It was a plate-glass door and it gave on an empty vestibule with another plate-glass door ahead giving onto the main office of the savings-and-loan company. They could see, in the instant of time they rushed the second door, that to the left and rear of the enormous room an oval marble counter ran, with tellers' windows at intervals, and to the immediate right soared a spiral staircase in front of an alcove leading, presumably, to the basement stairs.

Then they were in. "Hold it right there!" shouted O'Connor, diving for the partial shelter of the staircase. Varallo went with him; Wayne dived to the left and crouched behind a desk. Bullets came at them and the inner glass door exploded into fragments.

The three men, all wearing Halloween masks, were at the rear and side of the room. One of the two at the rear was holding a man in front of him, a very frightened-looking smallish man in a neat gray suit. The second was holding a big paper shopping bag, and a girl had frozen stiff in the act of dropping money into it. She was a pretty brunette, but right now she looked like something in a waxworks museum, mouth distorted and open, absolutely motionless, her fingers still clutching a big roll of bills. The third man wearing a mask was a little way down the left wall, behind the counter, holding the rest of the tellers in a bunch before him —awkwardly, all the tellers between him and Wayne.

Sprawled in the center of the floor on his face was a big man in tan uniform, his gun near an outflung hand. There was a good deal of blood spreading out from his right hip.

"Sweet Christ, what a *hell* of a position," said O'Connor disgustedly.

The third man took his gun off the tellers for a moment and fired at the stairs. Varallo heard the slug go by and smack against the wall behind them. He'd never claimed to be a marksman, and that one was maybe fifty feet away, and it would be an angled shot. If O'Connor could get a good clear view—

The stairs were modernistic, without backs to the treads. Not, in fact, very good cover. The other two men were perhaps sixty or seventy feet away, at the very rear of the building. The one holding the hostage fired at the stairs and Varallo heard that slug go by very damn close and wondered academically whether Laura would be raising a fatherless child, and snapped off a shot at the second man up there and missed him.

"Out of the way, damn it, out of the way," said O'Connor, and rushed the few feet from the stairs to where the right-angle wall jutted into the alcove. He was in full view of the third man holding the tellers, who lifted his gun, but the third man didn't know that O'Connor didn't waste time fooling around when he had a clear target. The .357 Magnum went off with a full-throated roar, and as the slug hit the third man he was knocked off his feet and slammed back against the marble wall. He slid down it slowly and disappeared. Wayne stood up and the man up there holding the hostage fired at him, and then a door behind him opened in a hurry and Tracy and Forbes came in. "Freeze right there!" barked Tracy, and both men whirled and fired. Four guns went off almost simultaneously, Forbes yelped, both the heist men went down, and in the sudden silence the little gray-suited man said, "Oh dear me," and fainted all over his recent captor.

"The son of a bitch got me," said Forbes, clapping a hand to his right upper arm. "Damn it to hell, this is my best suit!"

O'Connor thrust the .357 Magnum back into its holster and ran up the room. The man who had taken the slug from that was very, very dead, and somebody would have a nice job cleaning the marble floor where he lay. The other two were alive, but bleeding, one having a bullet in his leg and the other a bullet in his shoulder. The one who was conscious was swearing obscenely.

They laid the little gray-suited man out and called an ambulance. Everybody in the place was talking at the top of his or her voice. They would have to get statements from everybody: the law was very fussy about that sort of thing. Meanwhile, after they'd rendered some first aid to the uniformed man, they pulled off the Halloween masks to see what they'd captured, and O'Connor said, "Well, I will be goddamned if it isn't Henry Albert Mortensen. Off the Ten Most Wanted. I was looking at your ugly mug on a flier just the other day. And a damn shame I didn't get you instead of your pal, but you're wanted on a homicide back in Jersey, aren't you, so I guess it's six of one, half dozen of another." The conscious man swore at him viciously.

The ambulance came. The interns looked at the dead man and one of them said, "Jesus, what hit him, a cannon?"

"I don't know why you carry that thing, Charles," said Varallo. "The little shooting we have to do is generally at fairly close range, and that big a bore—"

O'Connor patted the bulge at his shoulder and said absently he liked to know he had the range and weight, was all. He used the radio to call up some more patrolmen, a couple to accompany the two live ones to the hospital and a couple to clear away the crowd. The male teller wasn't seriously hurt. The slug that had hit Forbes had just creased his upper arm, but of course it hadn't done his suit any good.

"There are invisible weavers," said Wayne. "I think you're right,

Charles, the rate is going up. When's the last bank robbery we had? I'd just made Detective, I seem to—"

The patrolman who'd been shot would be O.K.; he just had a broken leg.

They were busy there until nearly six o'clock, taking all the statements; some of the girls were so upset it took time and patience to get them to make sense. After they were finished there, Varallo called Laura and then they went and snatched a quick meal. O'Connor and Wayne were carefree bachelors, and so, of course, was Forbes, who rejoined them about five o'clock with his arm bandaged.

Then they went to the hospital and printed the second man, and looked for him in their own records, but he wasn't there; so they sent copies of the prints down to L.A., and to the sheriff's office, and to Washington. Both Mortensen and the other man refused to talk.

Over dinner, Varallo told O'Connor about Judy. How he'd got the same exact six digits out of her, and that made it look as if she had a damn good memory, so how come it was the wrong number? Unless, of course, the rapist *had* been Hugh Merrill of Shafter. And as long as he was doing overtime anyway, he was going to try to locate a couple of these boys Ted Blair had mentioned.

O'Connor said that was a hell of a queer thing, the inside knowledge, and if Varallo was going to turn into one of those goddamned superstitious detectives who worked by hunches, he could just knock it off. About once in a thousand cases, a hunch might turn up aces. The rest of the time—

"All right, all right, I know," said Varallo. "I've been at this just as long as you have, boy."

"What you ought to do is some target practice. You missed that bastard by three feet. Just because you're out of uniform— If there's one damn thing I hate, it's sloppy shooting."

Varallo exchanged a look of resignation with Forbes and said they couldn't all be marksmen.

"That Tracy," said O'Connor, "is a damn good man. God, I'll find out what idiot is doing that to him if it's humanly possible."

Varallo found Jim Frenier at home: the others, he'd have to get their addresses from the school, but Ted Blair knew Jim's address because they were close pals. It was up on Virginia Avenue above Olmstead, a pleasant big house older than its neighbors.

Jim Frenier was home, working on algebra homework in his room.

The parents were alarmed to find a cop on the doorstep, but Varallo soothed them down: just routine questions. Jim Frenier wasn't especially alarmed, just interested. He was Blair's type, a little more mature than most kids that age. He was a big solid kid, built like O'Connor, with massive shoulders, and he'd probably—like O'Connor—had to start shaving at fifteen or so.

He had to think to remember Ted telling him about that thing at Webbs'. Then he said, "Oh yeah, I remember that. It was just a little thing he mentioned. Little thing that happened. For God's sake, you think that had something to do with that burglary? I don't see—" He didn't remember all the other kids Ted had mentioned as maybe being in earshot, but he remembered one Ted hadn't—a Roger Byrd. "I'm pretty sure about that, because just as I was finishing dressing this Byrd character comes up with some of his—uh—feelthy peectures, know what I mean. He's always got a pocketful. He's a queer anyway. He could have heard Ted, I guess."

"Oh really?" said Varallo. "Real pornography?"

"Well, I guess I'd call it that," said Jim. He looked apprehensively at the closed door of his room; Varallo had persuaded the parents to let him talk to Jim alone. "God, Mother'd have a fit," he said, and grinned. "But not being a queer myself, I don't go for that stuff."

"You said a queer. You mean a real fag?" asked Varallo, unthinkingly using the pro slang. "That is, I mean—"

"Oh Lord, I don't know if he really is," said Jim, and Varallo was surprised again at how the pro slang drifted into use so quickly by the non-pro population. "I don't know. He just smells that way."

"Um," said Varallo. And Glendale was a nice quiet town, up to recently a very respectable town, jokingly known as Los Angeles' Bedroom because so many people lived here and worked in L.A.; but with the increase in population, and in transient population, they were getting all sorts. Hoover High—in a good residential district; but they'd had a pusher there last year, trying to make customers for his stuff. These days—

"Well, thanks very much," he said. "Mind having your prints taken? Just for the record. Sometime tomorrow." He doubted very much that Jim Frenier, who was also an honor student, had utilized the knowledge gleaned from Ted to pull a burglary—but there was that deadly thing, Routine. You had to cover all the possibilities.

*

He went home and asked Laura how she felt. "Like a dirigible," said Laura crossly. She was sitting in a straight chair embroidering a bib. "My back is *killing* me, and this infant is bouncing around like a—like a ballet dancer."

"You don't suppose—" said Varallo worriedly.

"No, I don't suppose. Nothing resembling labor pains." Gideon Algernon Cadwallader was sitting on the arm of the chair making occasional passes at the embroidery silk. Laura squinted down at him. "When's your next day off? We really ought to take him to be altered."

"Monday," said Varallo. "All right." He'd meant to do some spraying of the roses tonight, but he was too tired. He yawned. "You hear about our bank robbers on the radio?"

"*No!*" said Laura. She dropped the bib. "*Bank* robbers? For heaven's sake, Vic—"

"Well, there was some shooting, but Charles was along. . . . I *cannot* make out about Judy. When she could remember so many other details, why should she—"

"The bank robbers!" said Laura. "Was anyone shot? What happened?"

Belatedly Varallo worried about telling her. "Oh, now, look, I wasn't in any danger, I said Charles was there. It's really quite rare for a cop to get shot, *amante*—don't—"

"Don't," said Laura, "talk the baby talk, darling. I knew when I married a cop the possibility of sudden widowhood was slightly higher than if I'd married a shoe clerk. Yes, I worry. Fact of life—nothing to be done about it. I just want to hear about the bank robbers, please."

Varallo smiled and told her. "Feather in our caps, getting Mortensen. The Feds have got priority on him, of course. But you should have seen— Well, never mind. Not to dwell on horrors. But I'm damned if I know why Charles carries that cannon. I think he sleeps with it."

"That O'Connor," said Laura. "By all the books, the truth is that he's got a terrific inferiority complex and has to bolster up his ego by acting tough."

"Charles?"

"Mmh, yes, knowing Charles," said Laura, "I'd say he's just doing what comes naturally. *Oh!* Nothing, it just kicked me again. My back is *killing* me. Won't it *ever*—"

The phone rang. Gideon, who hated loud noises, shot off the chair and down the hall to the kitchen. Varallo got up, yawning.

"Varallo here."

"Hi, Vic," said Rhys. "Kind of slow down here. I just thought you'd be interested to know that Washington made the other live guy. He's one Antonio Ragalucci, and New York wants him for homicide."

"Another Italian," said Varallo. "This is unconstitutional prejudice against a minority. I'm going to write my congressman."

"You can always change your name to Smith," said Rhys.

"There's just one thing against that," said Varallo. "Smith is my congressman's name."

O'Connor walked into Katharine Mason's apartment, tossed his hat on the couch and sat beside it. "I could," he said, "use a drink, Katy. What were you doing before I arrived to enliven your evening?"

"You needn't really ask," said Katharine. A little pile of uncorrected papers sat on the desk, where she'd shoved her chair back to answer the bell. "And you're corrupting my morals. The most any N.E.A. spy might have found in my cupboard six months ago was a chaste bottle of sherry. And I've still got twenty papers to do, and you can stay exactly half an hour." She went out to the kitchen and came back three minutes later with a highball glass.

"Now, Katy, you know I don't like to drink alone."

"Oh all right." She got herself a glass of wine and sat down in the armchair opposite. "I heard on the radio you had a little excitement this afternoon."

"A little." O'Connor gulped rye and water and looked at her, but damned if he could tell whether that had upset her any, O'Connor under fire. He thought gloomily that of course she wouldn't have cared much. A girl like Katharine Mason—oh, a nice ten-dollar wreath for the funeral. Let him take her out now and then, what the hell, a *cop*— He took another swallow and said, "Not altogether a social call, Katy. Wanted to pick your brains. This little Judy Daly—"

"That." She looked serious. "Haven't you got a lead yet?"

"Hell, how does a thing like that go?" O'Connor was angry. "How do we start looking? Routine, sure. Whatever description that kid can give. Which isn't much usually, as it isn't here. We made a damn thorough search of that building—part of the old shutdown winery—where we found her sweater, where we think the attack happened. The lab went over Judy's clothes. All that told us was, she'd been raped." Katharine made a sick sound. "We rounded up all the deviates in our records—still have a few to look at. But unless we come up with something fast, right away, on a thing like that—a damn positive make from the kid, or—it can be a hell of a tough one. A six-year-old kid—you ask for a description and she tells you his eyes looked funny. Christ, I hate these things." He swallowed rye. "I guess Vic's doing all right questioning her, but— It *is* a hell of a funny thing. Katy, I don't know much about kids." He looked at her.

"Anything I can tell you," she said. "That poor child—"

"Look, she gives Vic a good description of this license plate. By all he's got, she's an observant kid, she's got a damn good memory—maybe almost photographic, the way you said—and she says there's 'a picture' in her mind of the letters and numbers. She draws out the same exact damn plate number she gave him Monday, the day after. SOS seven oh one. Or just maybe it *is* SQS seven oh one and Mr. Hugh Merrill of Shafter, which I do *not* believe," said O'Connor. "Do we need a deviate driving all the way from Shafter when we've got plenty right here in L.A. County, for God's sake? But if she's got such a damn good memory, how come she's wrong on the plate number? Her mother says, incidentally, that Judy isn't reading yet, just knows the alphabet and the—you know—look of the numbers and letters. You got any suggestions?"

"Well—"

"Because a bastard like that we want to get," said O'Connor.

"For once I'm with you. The only thing that occurs to me," said Katharine, "is that she might—if she's just learned the alphabet and numbers—have confused this for that. What might she— Let me get some paper. What looks like what? She might have mistaken a nine for a seven—or even an O for C or G—"

At eight fifteen Thursday morning, as Varallo was just leaving headquarters for Hoover High to get those other boys' addresses, Sergeant Dick downstairs called the Detective Bureau. O'Connor took the call.

"Listen, I just had a call," said Dick. "From the sexton or caretaker or whatever they call him at the Grandview Cemetery. You know, up at Grandview and Glenwood. I guess you'll be interested. He says he's just been out to prepare a new grave for a funeral tomorrow, and he found an ax with a lot of blood on it, lying up against the wall. Well, the damnedest thing, but I told him—"

"For Christ's sake! An *ax?* An— All right," said O'Connor abruptly. "I'm on the way. Vic! An *ax,* for the love of—"

CHAPTER 13

The Grandview Cemetery was a big walled plot of ground four blocks down from Cumberland Road. As they got out of O'Connor's car at the mausoleum, Varallo voiced the fact of their proximity; O'Connor said, "An *ax*? God, the Scotts were cut up—you saw the reports—but if somebody had used an ax on them it'd have been a damn sight worse."

The caretaker or sexton or whatever he was showed them the ax. "I didn't touch it. Not when I saw all that dried blood on it. I just called you right away. I thought about them folks got murdered last Saturday, not too far from here either, and—"

They squatted down and looked at the ax. It was a wicked-looking thing about two and a half feet long; it was an old ax, its handle scarred, and all over the blade was a long-dried mess of what could only be blood. The ax lay just inside the ten-foot wall on the Grandview Avenue side, at the far end of the cemetery from the administrative buildings; it had been a five-minute walk here from there, and there were only a few graves nearby.

"Well," said O'Connor thoughtfully, "if the damn thing *has* been here since last Saturday night, how about prints? If there were any, ten to one they're gone now. We've been having some heavy dews in early morning. Looks as if it might have been thrown over the wall from the sidewalk—it could have slid on the grass, too."

The caretaker said helpfully that it could have been there since Saturday night. Neither he nor any of his assistants had been down here since before that.

So they handled the ax very carefully, touching it as little as possible, and encased it in a plastic bag, and took it back to headquarters. O'Connor was convinced then that it had been the weapon in the Scott homicide, because when they'd turned it over they saw that the handle, on the other side, bore a large, crudely burned-on N.

"Nesbitt!" said O'Connor. "For God's sake, could it be the same boy? Could he have stolen this damn thing from those Nesbitts he also chopped up?"

"They were living at a motel," objected Varallo. "It doesn't seem likely they'd have had—" The Arcadia boys had sent over all they'd got on that; it wasn't much and it hadn't helped.

They dusted the ax, or rather Katz did, and found there were no prints on it at all. So then they took it over to Dr. Goulding's office on the ground floor of the jail and asked him about it.

Dr. Goulding cocked his bald head at it and said, "Well, it could be. The lab can tell you the blood type, and that should tell you for sure right away, because the Scotts had different types. He was O and she was AB, which is fairly rare. If you find both types here, bingo." He prodded the ax with a spatulate forefinger.

"But according to the wounds, doctor—"

"Hum. Well, I will say if the ax was the weapon I'd rather have expected to find more and deeper wounds. In the first place, anybody who picks an ax as weapon is usually, um, a rather violent type. And an ax being a fairly heavy weapon, with striking edge— Well, I know they were badly cut about, but the only very deep wound was on the woman's left arm, and that could have been a fluke—and then too, she was attacked from above, she was still in bed, and gravity would help there. What they both actually died of was loss of blood." Dr. Goulding took off his plastic-framed glasses and pinched the bridge of his nose absently. "If you want something definite," he said, "I'll say that if this turns out to be the weapon used on the Scotts, then I think whoever used it wasn't a very strong person, or very big or hefty."

"Oh. That sounds damn funny," said O'Connor. An ax murderer you naturally thought of as being a Neanderthal. However, there it was. They handed the ax over to their little lab, and Varallo said he was going out to see those boys.

O'Connor called Arcadia and asked whether the Nesbitts had owned an ax that had turned up missing after the murder. The sergeant he talked to had no idea, but would find out. "And—wait a minute," said O'Connor. "Stick around, Vic, I've got something for you. Sergeant? I read through those files you sent—just comes back to me, the people who owned that motel, damn it, their name was Naylor? Be damned. Look, will you find out if *they* missed an ax after the homicide? An old ax with an N burned in the handle. Fine, thanks." He put down the phone.

"I really ought to—"

"Sure, but just think about this. Katy's idea, that just maybe Judy isn't quite as familiar with letters and numbers as she claims, and mistook this one for that one. We came up with a few possibilities." He passed a scrawled half sheet to Varallo.

"That could be, sure as she seemed— I want to talk to her again, I've got a little idea of my own there too." Varallo looked at the combinations on the page. SCS. SGS. Nine oh one. SDS. He said, "I kind of like SDS. Because as you know the style of those letters is square and modern—whatever you call it—and the D doesn't have points beyond the vertical line. That could be the likeliest. I can't think of another number she'd mistake for seven except nine."

"Neither could we. You might get a make on all those, anyway."

"Just in case, yes." Varallo wrote down all the possible combinations on a fresh sheet. SCS 701. SCS 901. SGS 701. SGS 901. SDS 701. SDS 901. He took it down the hall to Communications. There was a teletype coming in, addressed to him. He read it off and said mildly, "Damn."

The teletype was from the sheriff of Kern County, and what it said was that Mr. Hugh Merrill was a well-known lawyer in the town of Shafter, and from six o'clock on last Sunday night he had been the speaker at a testimonial dinner for the mayor, a function which the sheriff had also attended.

So Judy was wrong. They'd said from the first it was too good to be true. So, try these possible combinations. He sent off the request to the D.M.V.

Then he went out to see these boys and find out if one of them had been the burglar at Webbs', or had casually repeated Ted Blair's story to somebody who might be the burglar.

At least they had some patrolmen back. The F.B.I. had sent some men over to take Mortensen and Ragalucci off their hands, and arrange for guards until they could be moved. They hadn't identified the dead man yet. He was no loss.

O'Connor, with a little time to himself to think, used it and then he drove over to the new county courthouse at the corner of Glendale Boulevard and Broadway. He got passed around but finally reached the highest custodian of their records, who regarded him curiously. "Traffic tickets?" he said.

"That's what I said." It would be a hell of a hunt, but— When a patrolman wrote a ticket, he handed it to the driver or, in the absence of the driver, he stuck it under the windshield wipers. The driver had to take it to Traffic Court if it had been a moving-violation ticket, but if it wasn't, he could mail in the fine or come here and pay it personally, with the ticket. Part of the ticket was torn off for a receipt, and the rest went into the files. For how long, O'Connor wasn't sure; they must weed them out at intervals or they'd gradually swamp the building. The carbons were turned in by the patrolman at headquarters and an individual count kept monthly, and then they were destroyed. The headquarters building was just so big too. Records, thought O'Connor, were the curse of the twentieth century. But sometimes helpful.

"Well, you'd have to get a court order if you want to take any away."

"No, that's O.K. I just want to look at them now."

There were, of course, a hell of a lot of them. And unfortunately they were filed under the drivers' surnames—naturally. But a quick glance at the signature, along the bottom line, of Issuing Officer, was sufficient; and by the time he'd seen a dozen of Tracy's tickets, he felt he was getting somewhere. Maybe.

A very petty little thing for the lieutenant to be working when they had a double homicide and a child rape on their hands, but all the lieutenant was supposed to do was organize the work anyway. Like hell, thought O'Connor, on a force the size of this one. He drove back to headquarters and stopped at the desk to ask Sergeant Copeland—it was Dick's day off—where Tracy was, on tour or what.

Copeland looked at the duty chart and said it was his day off, he was probably writing letters. "Nothing's come for him today, but it's still early. The damnedest thing, isn't it?"

"The damnedest." O'Connor went upstairs, looked up the number and called Tracy.

"What? Oh, Lieutenant. What's come *now?*" asked Tracy resignedly. "Did you hear about that damn cuckoo clock? Listen, I've had another batch of letters from some of these companies and they're all being tough about it. I—"

"You write many personal letters?" asked O'Connor.

"Why, no, not so many. My family's right here in town, and—"

"I mean formal letters. Like—oh hell, to the bank about something, or ordering things sent—really, I mean—or maybe a letter of recommendation for somebody. You know."

"Why—now and then, sure, we all do. Why, Lieutenant?"

"How'd you sign a letter like that?"

"Well, how *would* I sign it? Neil Tracy, or Neil G. Tracy, I guess."

"But when you write out a traffic ticket," said O'Connor, "you always sign it N. Tracy. I've been looking at some."

"Yes, that's right. It's quicker and easier, and all they want is some—"

"I've got," said O'Connor, "every damn respect for female intuition, Neil boy. Females can be damned annoying sometimes—in various ways —and they're at their most damned annoying when they tell you something like they know perfectly well it was Mrs. Smith who robbed the women's club treasury because of the way she had her hat tilted—and you tell them females are illogical, and then they turn out to be absolutely right. The dear scatterbrained little wenches."

"What?" said Tracy.

"I thought about that idea your wife had," said O'Connor. "It may sound damned silly at first thought, but you know drivers. So do I— I did my stint at riding squad cars too, and many's the ticket I have written. And this is just the kind of damn-fool stunt somebody might start because you gave him a ticket and he got mad. Nine thousand, nine hundred and ninety-nine drivers will cuss about it, or get mad at first and then calm down and admit they were wrong—but this could be, and evidently is, the ten thousandth. And why didn't you spot it yourself? You always sign your tickets N. Tracy, and that's just how all this C.O.D. stuff has been addressed, damn it."

"Well, I'll be— For God's sake! It never crossed my— Hell, you write it so automatically. That's sure as hell right, Lieutenant, and I feel like a damn fool for not spotting it before. But—some guy I just gave a ticket? Would anybody go to those lengths? I mean—"

"If I can just get hold of an original order blank from one of these damn firms. The idea there before was to prove it's not you. Now, if he maybe paid the fine by a check— And then too, it probably wouldn't have been long before this started. We'll see what turns up on that angle."

"One thing I've learned," said Tracy. "I had absolutely no idea, Lieutenant, you could order so *many* things by mail. So many *different* things."

O'Connor laughed and hung up. Immediately the inside phone rang. "O'Connor."

"Copeland. I've got a call for you—and you'll never guess what's just come for Tracy. You'll never in God's world. I swear I don't understand the *mentality* of anybody who'd—"

"What is it?"

"A genuine antique cigar-store Indian. The express bill alone is forty-nine bucks."

"For Christ's sake," said O'Connor, awed. He agreed with Varallo: the practical joker at least had one hell of an imagination. "Who wants me?"

"Richard Scott."

"O.K., put him on." When Scott said his name, he said, "Yes, Mr. Scott? We're still working on it, and we may be getting some place soon." An *ax*—

"I know you won't give up on it." Scott sounded tired; there'd been a double funeral yesterday. "But what I called about—it's something damned queer, Lieutenant. I told you there wasn't anything missing. Well, I didn't notice it was gone at the time, because naturally I was looking for missing valuables, Mother's jewelry and so on. But it isn't anywhere around. Once I noticed it was gone I went hunting, but it's nowhere in the house. And I distinctly remember it being there in the living room when I—when I left Saturday night."

"And what is it?" asked O'Connor.

"It's crazy, that's all," said Scott, sounding bewildered. "Dad paid something like seven ninety-five for it postpaid. Mother'd admired it in a catalogue that came—junk mail—objects of art from all over the world. It's a brass crane from India—painted a lot of different colors, mostly on the wings. . . . I said a crane. The bird, you know. With long legs and a long neck and a long bill. It's about a foot high. Mother used it a good deal in flower arrangements."

"I will be goddamned," said O'Connor. "Could you identify it?"

"Well, I suppose other people in town might have one like it. I don't know. And it's crazy, the thing's not worth anything."

"No, but it might have just struck his fancy," said O'Connor thoughtfully. "They do the damnedest things sometimes, Mr. Scott. Thanks very much, you never know what'll give us a lead."

"I just thought you ought to know," said Scott.

"Yes, thanks," said O'Connor, and put down the phone. Jeff Forbes came in.

"L.A. called just as I came in downstairs," he said. "So I took it there. They think they've found that elevator man we want—one of the proprietors of the Pacific Avenue liquor store picked out. He's in their records too. Who's here besides you? You want to come along and help put the arm on him?"

"Fred is somewhere around—no, he went out to pick up another deviate." O'Connor scowled, thinking about Judy. "Where've you been, anyway?"

"Out solving another mystery," said Forbes, and felt his bandaged arm, wincing. "It kind of bugged me too, you know—that wrench. All covered with blood, in the Scotts' yard the night they got murdered, but not the weapon—and bird blood. And Vic made sense when he said— Because, from the signs, we know our boy went to the *side* fence, over into that yard, not over the back fence which is where the wrench was. So I went to the house back of the Scotts'—it's on the next street up, Meadows Drive—to ask some questions. The guy told me all about it."

"All about what, for God's sake?"

Forbes draped his lank seventy-four inches against O'Connor's desk. "The pigeon," he said. "I kind of know how he felt. Fellow named Stoner. Retired grocer. He's got a poodle, spoiled as hell, cute little thing. He says—Stoner, that is—that on Saturday night when he came home—he'd been out playing golf, it was about six o'clock he drove in— he hit a pigeon in his driveway. You know how they're all around town, and pretty tame, but it isn't often one gets killed in traffic, they get wise. But it happens. Anyway, he said the poor damn bird wasn't quite dead even though he'd run over it. You slow down, you know, but you expect the birds to get out of the way—and he knew he had to put it out of its misery, it was all crushed and flapping around—and he just ran to the garage and picked up the first tool that came to hand. He said he couldn't bring himself to touch it, wring its neck. He has a thing about blood. He hit it on the head and killed it, and then—having this thing about blood—he just fired the wrench away. As we know, it went over the wall to the Scotts' back yard, but he didn't realize that. And he buried the bird, and that was that."

"Well, I will be damned," said O'Connor. "Coincidence. Just to mislead us a little."

"You want to come and help make this collar?"

"O.K.," said O'Connor. He got up and patted the bulge at his left shoulder. The inside phone rang. "O'Connor."

"Copeland. We've got a suicide. Probably. Over on Jackson. Apartment manager just called. I sent a car. Woman, a Mrs. Bennett. Usual thing, mail accumulating, not seen the last week, so the manager used his passkey. Says she cut her throat."

"Oh Jesus," said O'Connor, making a face. He was a cop, and a good cop, and you had to get used to some things, *as* a cop, but he didn't really like blood any better than Mr. Stoner. "O.K." Wayne came in and underhandedly O'Connor dispatched him to Jackson Street and the cut throat.

He just hoped it was a suicide, not another murder.

The crime rate was definitely up.

At the main library, little brochures left out invitingly among the other brochures: Civil Service Opportunities. The city of Glendale is urgently in need of new recrutis for the police force: good salary, automatic increase in six months, opportunity for advancement, see requirements below.

"Come on," he said to Forbes.

Varallo was still up at Hoover High, where he'd found the boys. Bob Carter and Mark Kroeger and Roger Byrd. The first two were just ordinary kids, average students probably, average-looking and average-talking. They were both a little nervous, called out of class to talk to a cop.

Neither of them remembered much about that gym locker room talk. Ted Blair talking casually to Jim Frenier about a funny little thing that happened to him when he went to pick up his aunt at Webbs' department store. They didn't—or said they didn't—remember any of the details.

Neither of them was in the J.D. records. Which didn't really say much, Varallo knew. There had to be a first time.

Now, in the vacant vice-principal's office, he was talking to Roger Byrd and not liking his smell.

Roger Byrd was the hail-fellow-well-met. A medium-sized kid about seventeen, with untidy blond hair and a big mouth in two senses. Varallo had gone over him and found the feelthy peectures, which Frenier had mentioned. The usual crude, immature thing; he wrinkled a lip at them.

"Not exactly the sort of thing we like to find a kid your age buying," he said. "Where'd you get them?"

"Find out," said Byrd. "What's the beef, cop? You don't like sex? I think sex is just dandy."

"Sure," said Varallo. "The right kind, Byrd. I'm taking you in on this." And he knew what would happen: a first count, and not a crime against property, so this loudmouth punk remanded in custody of his parents. What were the parents like? "But what I want to ask you about otherwise—"

Byrd was a loudmouth in a couple of senses too. He snarled at Varallo over the threatened charge—"It's a crime to *have* them? I wasn't *peddling* the damn things." But he just naturally had his tongue hung in the middle, wagging at both ends; incipient con-man, thought Varallo. He couldn't help talking.

That bit about goody-goody Blair scared he'd set off the burglar alarm at Webbs'— Sure, he'd heard that, that time. It was a laugh, that one. Passed it on? Well, hell, it had been a thing—sure he'd talked about it. Boy Scout Blair, the good boy, so scared of the fuzz— Maybe he'd said something to Harry, or Mike. Yeah, and come to think that little creep Jerry had been around when he was yakking with Mike. Why the hell?

"Full names, punk," said Varallo tiredly. It was getting on for half past eleven. He wanted to call Laura some time.

"Cops," said Byrd. "Harry Foster. Mike Hand. That creep Jerry Hunter. I don't know nothing about— It was just the joke, see? Those go-to-church-Sunday good boys like Blair, they give me a pain."

He also wanted to see Judy some time today. He had a little idea there, to test Judy.

He wondered if those new plate numbers would turn up anything interesting.

He said, "O.K., Byrd, let's go down to headquarters and call your parents."

"Which is one on you, cop. I got none. I dunno who they were. I'm in a foster home on the county, they only take me for the forty bucks a month. The old lady's prob'ly out at the corner bar anyway, she won't come down."

Which maybe, thought Varallo, explained much. Well, the county tried. In a fumbling kind of way.

Laura and the baby—

Judy.

At three twenty the lab called. Fred Wayne was alone in the office, typing up a report in triplicate on the Jackson Street suicide. Which had turned out to be a bona fide suicide.

The long-dried blood on the ax, said the lab, was of two types—type O and type AB.

The ax had been the weapon which had killed the Scotts.

In the hands of a not very big, not very strong individual.

It was funny. Funny-peculiar.

An individual who had stolen an Indian-made brass crane a foot high, worth eight bucks. Even funnier.

CHAPTER 14

"It does make you wonder," said Poor, lighting a cigarette. "They do come all sorts."

Varallo sat down at his desk and pulled his tie loose. They could still hear the woman delivering a tirade at the top of her hoarse voice as she and the boy went down the hall toward the stairs. "And how'll he end up? On the wrong side of the line because nobody ever took any real interest in him, had any real affection for him? Sometimes I go halfway with the psychiatrists, John."

They had haled Roger Byrd's foster-mother down to headquarters. Mrs. Phelps. She wasn't tight, but you could tell she'd had a few drinks. She said she washed her hands of the boy, just a bad boy to start, always trouble, always being impudent, and now *cops* after him, bringing her to a police station!—she was going to ask the county to take him away, she'd had enough.

All the while, the boy stood smiling contemptuously at all of them.

And there wasn't, of course, a charge: no evidence that he'd attempted to sell the pornography. They took it away from him and sent him home. Home, thought Varallo. God. What could you expect from a kid raised like that?

He said, "I want to call Laura. I also think it'd be a very nice idea to call the County Welfare Board and drop a few gentle hints about Mrs. Phelps. I'd hate to think of them sending her a replacement for Roger. Don't they screen these people?"

"They can never find enough, I understand," said Poor. "Sure, but the ones like Mrs. Phelps take care to put up a good front when the social worker calls. And they haven't got enough of those either, to keep a regular check. I'll do that." He sat down at his desk and started looking in the phone book.

Varallo called Laura. "You all right, *cara?*"

Laura said she was just the same. "I'm beginning to think it's a false pregnancy. I understand that does happen."

"Don't say things like that!"

"Well— And about Gideon, Mrs. Anderson's going to drive us over on Saturday morning, so you can have your whole day off for your roses."

"You're sure you're O.K.?"

"I feel like a captive *balloon,*" said Laura. "Don't keep reminding me. Will you be home on time?"

"Probably, unless something drastic happens. You take care, now. If anything starts happening—"

"You don't know how much I wish it *would*. Don't fuss, Vic."

But he really couldn't help it. And he sat with his hand on the phone, knowing objectively it was because of Ginevra, his lovely Ginevra, and unable to stop his inner jittering. God, he'd be glad when this was over.

If it ever *was*.

"Well, come on," said Poor, putting down his phone. "Best I could get out of 'em, they'll reinvestigate, thank you very much. So, back to the salt mines, find these other kids. Funny setup in a way, Vic. Chasing down all these kids— What Blair said needn't have a damn thing to do with the break-in. It could be—"

"It could be, but it adds up a little too neatly," said Varallo. "I want to chase it down a bit further."

It was twelve forty. They stopped at Pike's at the top of Brand on their way and took twenty minutes for sandwiches and coffee. Then they went on up to Hoover High, and asked to see the boys' vice-principal. What did he know about any of these boys, Mike Hand, Harry Foster and Jerry Hunter?

Mr. Reilly, an amiable-looking, tubby little man, was disturbed. Glendale, and Hoover High, had such a good record in general—very little delinquency, and nothing really— He hoped there wasn't going to be any trouble. He couldn't say offhand about the first two, he'd look at their files, but— He shook his head. "Hunter," he said. "A difficult boy. We're constantly sending out truancy notices to the guardians. An aunt and uncle, I understand. I think myself the boy needs psychiatric help. And perhaps medical. He has problems of his own, and adolescents— For one thing, he has a very bad case of acne, and you know how sensitive boys that age are. Not a good-looking boy even aside from that, and he shies away from people. He's a loner—possibly for just that reason. I don't think the aunt and uncle handle him very sensibly." Mr. Reilly shrugged. "We try. But with the number of boys and girls we have— Well, we can't do as much as we'd like."

Varallo and Poor exchanged a glance. "Well, we'd like to see all three of them, if you don't mind."

Reilly shrugged again and went out to give orders to the secretary.

Jerry Hunter—"the creep"—was absent from school. He was younger than the other two, only sixteen. Mike Hand and Harry Foster were average-to-dull types who looked a little nervous when Byrd's name was mentioned but also did a little furtive snickering. Byrd talking about Ted Blair? Naw, they didn't remember that. What he'd said or anything. About Webbs'? They had to be reminded there was a department store of that name. Byrd was kind of a nut, they said, they weren't really pals, and what was this all about anyways, cops and all, had Byrd done something?

Varallo surmised that that was more or less gospel. They didn't think much of Byrd, but they'd been interested in his dirty pictures. He asked them about that (*had* Byrd ever tried to peddle them?) and they both said in a hurry they didn't know what he was talking about.

"But I think," said Varallo, when they'd gone—also in a hurry—"we'd like to have a chat with Jerry Hunter."

"I think so too," said Poor.

They got his address from the school files; it was over on Garwood, an older section of town over toward Burbank. They found it, an old frame bungalow on a block of old frame bungalows, the kind of houses that had been put up cheaply forty years ago; a succession of owners had done the minimum in the way of necessary repairs. Along blocks like this, if you went through and counted, you'd find a fine collection of leaky toilets, dripping faucets, loose screens, termite-ridden floorboards. More visible to the casual eye were the trodden brown lawns where little grass grew, the litter of children's toys in front yards, the thin slinking cat dodging under a parked car, a broken front window.

The aunt and uncle's name was Dunne.

The house badly needed painting. The steps to the porch shook under their weight, and there was an old-fashioned doorbell instead of chimes.

The doorbell brought them, presently, a thin woman in a bedraggled-looking blue housedress. Her legs were bare and her bare feet were thrust into dirty white rubber thong sandals. Her brown hair was streaked with gray and hung lank about her unmade-up face, but her eyes were still beautiful—big violet-blue eyes with long lashes.

"Mrs. Dunne?" They showed her their badges.

"*Oh!* Is it my husband? Something's *happened*—" A dirty hand flew to her heart. "Oh, what—"

"Nothing like that, please don't get upset, Mrs. Dunne. We just want to talk to Jerry. Jerry Hunter."

"Oh, dear, is he in some *trouble?* With the *police?* I just don't know what to do. Mr. Dunne and I have tried our best, I'm sure," she said helplessly. "He's my own sister's boy. I will say his father didn't amount to much, but we've tried to raise him right. He's never been in any real *trouble,* only this staying away from school."

"Is he here now, Mrs. Dunne?" asked Poor.

She stared at him. "Why, no, he went off to school this morning."

"He's not there."

"Well, then I couldn't say where he'd be, I'm sure. Not at school again?" She shook her head. "Mr. Dunne'll just have to give him a good talking-to again, but I don't know what good it'll do. That boy. He never gave us any trouble till a year or two ago, you know. Seems like he changed overnight. What—what d'you want to see him about? Do you think he's—*done* something?" Fear in her eyes now. "We've always been respectable people."

"We just want to ask him something about another boy," said Varallo mendaciously. "Would you—"

"Oh. Oh well, that's all right then." She looked relieved; she smoothed her untidy hair back. "You'll have to excuse how I look, I was just washing the kitchen floor. We've always been respectable, like I say, if we haven't much money—it'd be awful to think, Jerry *doing* something. We've always seen he goes to Sunday school regular, ever since we had him and that's nearly six years. Since May got killed in an accident on the freeway. Her husband'd run off, left her, when Jerry was just a baby. And it's best a boy should have a man around. I'm sure Mr. Dunne and I have tried our best. Never had any of our own. I've kind of left it up to Mr. Dunne on account of Jerry being a boy, see— just try to fix nice meals and like that, you know. And he was a good boy up to a year or so back. I'm sure I don't know what's got into him." She poked at her hair again.

Varallo had met the Mrs. Dunnes before. They were born, he thought, already defeated by life, and they stood on the sidelines wringing their hands and exclaiming that they couldn't think what had gone wrong. The high whining voice betrayed her. Mrs. Dunne's life would be a succession of little failures, the roast she somehow didn't get in the oven on time, the dress that didn't turn out like the picture on the pattern, the— While Mrs. Dunne stood wringing her hands helplessly.

"Didn't a counselor from the school—"

She looked vague. "Oh, yes, along about Thanksgiving it was. Asking me to come to school. It was the day I picked up our turkey. It's a pity Bill don't like turkey any better, it being so cheap—that's my husband, Mr. Dunne—but he says once a year is plenty. Mr. Courtney, the man's name was. He seemed real nice, but honestly, those people earning eight, ten, maybe fifteen thousand a year, they—"

"Well, teachers really don't earn that m——"

"—just don't understand. And a waste o' money even if we had it to spare. My husband works at a gas station. I mean, he doesn't own it even, just works there, and he don't earn much. Steady, but not much. That man at the school saying as how we ought to take Jerry to some kind of specialist about his pimples. Most kids in their teens got 'em, they grow out of 'em. But I guess—seeing Jerry's not here—you don't want to listen to me ramble on." She stepped back and started to close the door.

"Does he usually come home on time for dinner?"

"Oh, yes, he'll be here then. He knows he's s'posed to be here by five. We keep an eye on him all right, he's not allowed to go rovin' around after dark like *some* kids."

"Well, will you call us when he does come home? And meanwhile, don't tell him we were here. Call when he can't hear you."

"But I thought you said it was just— *Has* he done something? Oh dear—"

"Just do that, please, will you?" Varallo frowned at her.

"Oh, I s'pose," she said defeatedly. "Mr. Dunne won't like it. We've never had anything to do with the *police.*"

"Could we come in now and see Jerry's room? He does have his own room?"

She stepped back farther. "Oh, I don't think Mr. Dunne'd like it if I let you do that. I really don't. You better just—just come back when Jerry's home."

"All right, Mrs. Dunne." They heard the front door shut loudly as they came down the steps.

"Taking any bets?" asked Varallo.

"Uh-uh. He sounds like a good prospect. Might have had some nutty kidlike notion about getting enough money to pay the skin specialist himself."

"That occurred to me too," said Varallo. "Well, I suppose we'd better check back at the office. Have to prime the desk about her call anyway."

They started back up Garwood in silence, and caught the light at Glendale Boulevard. "Damn it, those plate numbers," said Varallo. "If these new combinations turn out dead ends, I think we'll have had it, John. Except for combing through all L.A.'s deviates. God, what a thought!"

"Those boys are usually co-operative," said Poor. "We may have to, all right." Varallo parked in the lot and they went in and briefed Sergeant Copeland on the expected call from Mrs. Dunne. "Pass it to the night men too."

"Will do," said Copeland. They climbed stairs. They went into the Detective Bureau. O'Connor, Katz and Wayne were standing around an unshaven, sullen-looking tough in a straight chair.

"—know it was you, Rudy, why waste time on these goddamned silly lies? Listen—" O'Connor broke off and grinned at Varallo and Poor. "My wandering boys." He came over to them. "Got a job for you."

"I want to go up and see Judy," said Varallo.

"You can do that later. Right now you're both going over to the county courthouse and hunt back through the files—take it from October first—and make up a list of everybody who got handed a traffic ticket by Neil Tracy, through November."

"For God's sake, why? Traffic tickets—" said Poor.

"The joker is somebody he gave a ticket to," said O'Connor, and explained. "Think it over and you'll begin to see it isn't as crazy as it sounds. Drivers—"

"I'll be damned," said Varallo. "But do you have any idea, Charles, just how many tickets got handed out in those two months? We do patrol Montrose, La Crescenta and La Cañada as well as Glendale, you know. And all filed under the drivers' names. Thousands—considering drivers, as you just said."

"Sure," said O'Connor. "So go and start the treasure hunt, boys. He's there somewhere, damn him, we're bound to run across him eventually. Doing the routine. Questioning everybody Tracy gave a ticket to. And I don't think he brooded on that ticket long before starting his little campaign—early November is most likely. Why else did you join the force if you aren't crazy about routine work?"

"We had to walk in just now," said Poor resignedly. "What a hell of a job."

Varallo sighed. He'd meant to get home in time to do some spraying. The lawn would have to wait until Monday, but damn it, he hadn't even fed the new ones since planting them—that Lilac Dawn, really something—hardly had a chance to look at them, see how they were doing. Damn. Well, of course, all this was a little more important than roses. But— He sighed. He asked, "Who's your friend?"

"Oh, him. One of the guys pulled the heist job on the liquor store up on Pacific. We're hoping he'll sing a pretty song about who *his* pal was. On your way, on your way. Have fun."

"Routine being too lowly for a lieutenant," said Poor. "Or you've got a date with your schoolteacher and'll take off early."

O'Connor scowled. "Week night. She's got papers to correct. Damn it, go!"

They went. At the county courthouse, finally, left alone with the files, they started the boring routine job.

Poor said, "A *traffic* ticket. I ask you. . . . Did you hear about the cigar-store Indian?"

The elevator man went on refusing to talk. They got tired of him eventually, and Wayne still had some paper work to do on the suicide, and there was more of that to clear up on the bank robbers, so they took him over to the jail and booked him in.

O'Connor had just got back to his desk when the inside phone rang and Copeland said there was a fellow here wanting to see a detective about the little Daly girls. Name of Stanley Tronowsky.

"Send him up," said O'Connor interestedly, and handed the paper work over to Katz.

Stanley Tronowsky, when he came hesitantly into the big room, was a big burly fellow, dark and balding, about thirty-five. He had on neat working clothes, tan cord shirt and pants. He looked at O'Connor and swallowed nervously.

"You the one I—I can talk to?"

"That's right. Sit down, hmm? I'm Lieutenant O'Connor. You think you know something about how the Daly kids were—"

"Jesus, no," said Tronowsky. He collapsed suddenly into the straight chair beside the desk. "Mister, I been having the blue devils ever *since.*

I tell you. My God. I got visions of you guys hauling me in and beating me up, and I wouldn't *blame* you, a guy do a thing like *that*. Those two cute little kids!" He swallowed. "You don't know me from a hole in the ground, I mean. How would you— Well, anyway, Annie—Annie's my wife, mister, we got two kids of our *own*, you think I'd— Annie says I'm crazy, see? Says the cops don't do stuff like that, you're regular guys and smart and all, you'd listen. And I should come and tell you. Well, she convinces me, see, so here I am and I hope to hell she's right."

"Well, we like to think we're fairly damn smart these days. Here to say what, Mr. Tronowksy?" O'Connor offered him a cigarette and he took it with a shaking hand.

"I had the jitters so bad— I hope to God Annie— Well, I'm—I'm the guy that dame said she saw talkin' to the kids. The Daly kids." He looked at O'Connor piteously. "Jesus, as if I'd do a thing like— The one it said in the papers, strange man seen speaking to children. It was me."

O'Connor sat up. "You don't tell me. So fill me in. When and where? Why were you up there?"

"Oh Jesus," said Tronowsky. "I'm a plumber, mister. I go out on Sunday calls— I'm about the only one around here does. I got my own shop, see, and three guys working for me. I do O.K. Annie said I oughta come in, so you could stop wasting time trying to find that guy the dame told about. Because it was me, and I got two kids of my own, you think I'd hurt a *kid?* I was on a call. I can show you the bill. I got it right here, Annie said I should bring it along to show." He produced it and laid it gingerly on the desk. "People named Johnson, forty-one twenty-six Markridge. They had a stopped-up toilet, it wouldn't flush. Called me about one fifteen and I come right out. We get double time on Sunday. It came to seventeen sixty."

"So?" said O'Connor.

"So, hell, I fix the toilet. Johnson writes me a check and I come out, start down to where I hadda leave the truck. House or two down the street. And there's these two cute little girls, mister. I *like* kids, I got two kids my own, I stop and say Hi, give 'em a smile, is all. So what's wrong with this? The little one smiles back but the other one says they're not s'posed talk to strangers, so I think they got good parents, good and careful because that's what Annie's always telling our two, like you got to in the city these days—Jesus, you don't know what kind of nuts are around—and I go and get in the truck and drive home, we're at 12566 Evergreen in Burbank, and I musta got home about three and

Annie was there and she could say and the kids too only they're only four and seven, but I saw George Grover next door about three thirty when I was cutting the lawn and Jesus am I glad to have all that off my conscience—" He stopped and looked at O'Connor dumbly.

O'Connor said softly, "Hell and damnation. Another very little damn lead gone. After those very dubious plate numbers, you were our last bet. Hell."

Varallo didn't get up to Markridge Road until six o'clock. He and Poor had worked over those files of tickets, locating the ones Tracy had written, copying the drivers' names and addresses, until nearly five thirty. Such funny ideas the public had about cops: even the ones on the cops' side: glamorous job. Glorified file clerks, thought Varallo.

He called Laura and said he'd be late. "All right," said Laura. "Like all police wives, I rely on casseroles that can be reheated indefinitely. Yes, I'm all right. Just the same."

Well. Would it ever—

Mrs. Daly was busy in the kitchen, and not overpleased to see him. "We do appreciate the effort you're— But it's rather an inconvenient—" A singing tea kettle began to scream in the kitchen and she said, "Oh dear," and fled.

Varallo looked at Judy. Judy was sprawled out on the couch looking at a picture book. "Hi," he said.

"Hello, Vic." She scrambled upright. "Has your little baby—"

"No, not yet, Judy."

"Oh. I'll bet your—your mommy is hoping it'll come soon."

"We both are," said Varallo. "Judy, would you play a little game with me?"

"What kind of game, Vic?"

"Well, I'd like to see if you really do—remember things. Letters and numbers. Have you got a pencil?"

"I know where one is." Judy went to the desk in the corner of the living room. "Do you want a piece of paper too, Vic?"

"We'll use my notebook, O.K.?"

Mrs. Daly came to the door between living room and kitchen. She said softly, "You must know she couldn't possibly—she's not reading yet. She doesn't really—"

Varallo ignored her. The plate number—the possible plate number—was their last resort. This was, in a way, another little hunch—he couldn't say what kind—just, he liked Judy and somehow had faith in her. This was just something he wanted to try.

"O.K. Now, I'm going to write down some letters and numbers," he said. "And then I want you to look at them, how they look to you, and then I'm going to take away the paper and I want you to write them down just the way you remember them. Without looking at them again. O.K.?"

"Well, O.K.," said Judy. She looked a little puzzled. "Sure, Vic."

Did she really have that good a memory? And would this be at all a valid test? Then, her memory might well have been numbed by the physical and emotional shock; now, she was safe at home, in familiar surroundings. A child's memory— Would this prove anything?

He didn't know.

He opened his notebook. At random, he printed large across the page a fictitious plate number. TJM three four three. He tore the page out and gave it to her.

"Just look at it a minute," he said.

"But she couldn't possibly—" said Mrs. Daly.

"Well, O.K., Vic," said Judy. She gave him the page. "I looked at it."

"You think you remember all those letters and numbers?" Not in school yet, not really reading yet, my God—

"Yes, I remember. It makes a kind of pitcher in my—"

"So, can you put them all down for me?" He gave her his notebook, open on an empty page.

"Sure," she said. She sounded a little impatient with the vagaries of grown-ups. She bent over the notebook, pink tongue protruding.

"Six figures," said Mrs. Daly. "I don't think—she can rattle off the alphabet, yes, but—"

"We've just got to try everything, Mrs. Daly," said Varallo. She nodded.

"There!" said Judy. "I drawed it all down just like the pitcher in my mind, Vic." She handed him the notebook. He looked at it. He felt suddenly as if he'd been struck by lightning. He shut his eyes for a second and stared at it again. In her big shaky printing—

The fictional plate number he'd given her. *Reversed.*

CHAPTER 15

"Charles? You hear what I said? It's fantastic, I don't—"

"I was thinking. Why the hell, Vic? In reverse? And why are you so damn excited about it, for God's sake?"

"It's the answer—it's got to be, don't you see? I seem to remember reading about it somewhere, how some kids, for some reason, see things in reverse like that. Anyway, what it's got to mean is that she gave us the original number in reverse too, and—" Varallo looked at the page on the desk before him; he was smiling excitedly. It was seven fifteen; he'd done a few minutes' work on this and then started calling around to locate O'Connor, and had found him at one of his favorite restaurants.

"That I do not see," said O'Connor. "If she'd done that, we'd have spotted the numbers being first, ahead of the letters."

"That's just the beauty of it," said Varallo. "Get out your notebook and write it down, and see. If it had been almost any other combination, my God, of course we'd have spotted it! But as it is, there's only one possible right plate number it can be. Look for yourself. What else looks like an S except a five? We just thought her S's looked a little squared-off, but a kid who's just learned the alphabet— And what the hell else could we have mistaken for a seven except a T—a T with one short cross arm? And O and I, damn it, can be either letters or numbers, so—"

"Be damned," said O'Connor. "Wait a minute. I *will* be damned! If it hadn't been—yes, I see, it's got—"

"It's got to be IOT five oh five. Yes. I've just sent it up to Sacramento, marked Urgent. We can only wait and see what they give us on it. Personally, I'll be convinced if it turns out to be a car registered in L.A. County."

"If Judy remembered the plate number in the right order, damn it. I suppose it could be TOI or something like—"

"Oh, don't be such a wet blanket, Charles! I tell you, we've got him. All along I've had a hunch that Judy was that smart. If it hadn't been for the funny business about seeing right to left— What? I don't give a damn what the plate was doing in the back seat, that we'll find out when we pick up the bastard. We should get the word some time tomorrow."

"Yeah. So let's all do a little finger-crossing that Judy's as smart as you think. If so, well, it is a hell of a funny thing, all right. Coincidence, would you call it? A bad one for the boy we're after."

"The damnedest thing, yes. Look, right now I'm meeting John to snatch a sandwich or something, and then we're going up to see the Hunter kid. I called Laura—" He'd told her about Judy, and she'd been nearly as excited. It had looked so hopeless, and then this fantastic break.

"O.K. You think he looks good for that break-in at Webbs'?"

"He looks hotter than anybody else we've run across. Which isn't saying much," admitted Varallo, "I know. But I want to see him. I'll call you at home later if we get anything."

"Try Katy's," said O'Connor abruptly. "I want to ask her about this right to left bit. Never heard of such a thing, of all the goddamned offbeat cases I ever— Well, keep our fingers crossed. See you, Vic."

"The trouble with you is you simply don't listen," said Katharine. "I was talking about it just the other night, when you first asked me about Judy. But how *terribly* queer—just the one little girl who had that inversion— Why, you'd have had him the next day if—"

"If," said O'Connor gloomily, "that plate belonged to him. And why the hell was it in the back seat of the car in the first place? And did Judy remember the right plate number even if she did write it down backward? I never heard of—"

"I *told* you about it, practically. We're finding out a lot of things like that, about some of the children they used to think were uneducable. That inverted reading is commoner than you might think, and now it's curable—special classes, you know, you have to teach the child deliberately to train himself to read from left to right, but it can be done. We had a case of it just last year, in Miss Salisbury's first-grade class. Fortunately she's very quick at spotting things like that, but in a school where the classes are large and teachers can't give individual attention, a thing like that can keep a child classified as retarded or even uneducable for years, until it's spotted. Judy's lucky hers got spotted now, if in a very funny sort of way."

"Funny is hardly the word I'd pick," said O'Connor. "I will be goddamned. I will be—"

"But if it *is* the right one, now— And *how* odd," said Katharine, "that it should have been a license number where you could misread figures for letters like that."

"Very damned odd all round," said O'Connor, "and I'm not waving any flags until we've heard from the D.M.V. and taken a look at who belongs to IOT five oh five."

"When will you know?"

"Probably some time tomorrow, unless they're swamped with other requests up there."

"Oh. Charles, will you call and let me know? Please? It seems," said Katharine thoughtfully, "like the classic retribution, doesn't it? The innocent victim holding the one vital clue."

"If," said O'Connor. "Wait and see."

Varallo and Poor parked in front of the Dunne house on Garwood Drive at twenty to eight. As they got out of the Chevy, Poor said, "It would also explain why none of the stuff's showed up. This kid's got no record, he wouldn't know any fences."

Varallo agreed. Mrs. Dunne had phoned the desk at five fifteen and said Jerry was home. But what with seeing Judy, and all that excitement, and contacting the D.M.V., and stopping for a meal of sorts— They hoped Jerry was still home, but Mrs. Dunne had said he wasn't allowed to go roaming around at night, so—

"How about their keeping him in the way she said?" asked Poor as they climbed the steps.

Varallo made a derisive sound. "A kid of sixteen? Lay you any amount he's got a window to get out of, *and* uses it. I don't think Mrs. Dunne would be too quick to suspect anything. We'll see what Bill's like." He pushed the doorbell.

Its angry old-fashioned buzz, this time, brought a man to the door. He threw open the inner door and at the same time snapped on the porch light. He stared at them. He was a big man running to fat, he'd lost most of his hair and he had a square face (reminiscent of Tracy's), with an underslung jaw. He was wearing a soiled tan shirt without a tie and wrinkled tan pants.

"Are you the cops?" he asked aggressively.

"That's right," said Varallo. They showed their badges. "We'd like to talk to Jerry Hunter."

"Nobody's talkin' to Jerry until I know what the hell this is all about! Cops, coming asking about Jerry. Listen, we're strict with the kid, he's never been in no trouble, what the hell put you on Jerry's back? Oh, for God's sake, come in!" He stepped back from the screen door. They went straight into the front room; it was a typical bungalow, without an entry hall; there was a long combination living-dining room across the front. As expectable from outside, the furniture was old and shabby, but everything looked very clean and neat. It was, also expectably, an unimaginative room, the inevitable mirror over the old hearth, a cheap framed lithograph of a garish seascape over the sagging couch.

Mrs. Dunne sat on the couch. She had changed her dress and combed her hair, but otherwise didn't look much different. She said dully, "I told you he wouldn't like it."

"Damn right I don't like it! We done our best by the boy. When Ruth told me about your comin', I like to fell over. Jerry! He's been raised right, anybody tell you. Sunday school ever' Sunday regular, and he's never been a wild kid, like some these days. Too quiet, ask me, just the opposite. Never runs around in no gang. I guess he's even a little backward for his age, I don't mean in his brain, but—you know—" Dunne hesitated.

"Emotionally?" said Poor.

"Yeah, yeah, like that. Why the hell— What's your names?"

"I'm Detective Varallo and this is Detective Poor. We—"

"Hell of a name," said Dunne. "Jinx sort of name, Poor. So why are you after Jerry?"

"Where is he, Mr. Dunne?"

Dunne jerked his head. "In his room. Studyin' or something."

"But you've had a little trouble about his staying out of school, haven't you?"

"Oh hell, all kids play hooky now 'n' then. Besides, I'm no great believer in all this damned schooling for some kids. Kids like Jerry. Sure, the ones got a lot of brains, want to be scientists and teachers and like that, O.K. But a lot of people ain't realistic about it—not *every* damn kid is like that, some of 'em just naturally not very smart *that* way, the book stuff. I guess I'm smart enough, take me, I always got a job, but I'm better with my hands than like sittin' at a desk adding numbers or something, see. I only had to eighth grade myself, and I get along."

"Eighty bucks a week," said Mrs. Dunne with no particular expression in her voice.

"Well, we eat, don't we? Listen, you guys. Jerry's not my kid or any relation o' mine, but we took him and we've done our best by him. Not like I didn't treat him right just because he's *not* my kid, see? I did. I've spent time with him, played ball with him, talked to him about how a guy should act and all. We even been kind of strict with him, not like the way some people—"

"But a year or so ago, he started staying away from school, maybe acting a little queer?" asked Varallo.

Dunne fell silent suddenly and rubbed his massive jaw. Suddenly he looked a little uneasy. He said absently, "I tried to talk to the kid. That teacher or whatever Ruth saw up at the school—well, that sounded fairly crazy to me, sayin' about a specialist and all. *I* don't know. Kids all go through times o' acting queer, maybe, when they're growin' up. I tried talk to him, say, go out and play, go out see a movie maybe, have fun, instead o' stayin' cooped up in his room all the time. Look, I got him a bike, I think maybe that'll kind of get his interest, you know? I paid thirty bucks for it secondhand, it's a good bike. Well, *I* don't know. You ain't said why you want to see him."

"Just a few questions," said Varallo.

"Like about what?"

"Several things."

"Well, I think I'm gonna be right there to hear you ask them, see."

"That's your privilege," said Varallo. "So, will you take us to Jerry's room?"

The woman blurted out, "You know yourself, Bill, it's not *natural*—a boy of sixteen stayin' in his room with the door shut all the time he's home, which is mostly. You said yourself—it *is* queer. And been getting worse."

Dunne didn't look at her. He said heavily, "I'll take you." He turned and went out of the living room, through the front bedroom into a short hall. There were just the two bedrooms in the house. The first contained an old-fashioned cheap bedroom set, walnut veneer, and a straight chair. There were four doors giving on the hall: three were open, to the front bedroom, kitchen, and bathroom. Dunne hesitantly opened the fourth and said, "Jerry?"

"Let's all go in," said Varallo, and reluctantly Dunne led the way. They looked at Jerry Hunter, "the creep."

He was sitting on the bed. There was a book beside him, but he wasn't reading it; he was just sitting. He looked up very slowly.

He wasn't a very big boy. He was, in fact, just about the size Varallo was looking for. Hadn't started to get his growth yet, maybe never would be very big: he was about five five, and a thin boy. An unhealthy-looking boy, with, as they'd heard, a serious and very ugly case of acne. The festering, raw, open and partly healed sores spread all over his face from forehead to chin, inflamed and angry looking. You saw that—that jumped out at you—before you noticed anything else about him. His brown crew-cut hair, his pale blue eyes, his narrow mouth looking rather weak, his pointed chin. He was dressed in jeans and a blue shirt.

"What—who're these guys?" he asked. He didn't sound very interested.

"Look, Jerry, I'm right here now, you don't need to be scared." But Dunne was the one who sounded nervous.

The boy looked at them, mildly inquiring.

"Detective Varallo, Detective Poor," said Varallo, and they showed their badges to Jerry. He blinked. "We want to ask you a few questions."

"So go ahead." The boy wasn't impudent: just apathetic.

"Do you know Roger Byrd?"

After a moment Jerry said, "Oh yeah. From school. I don't know him so good. He's always carrying around these pictures—" He stopped.

"Yes, we know about those. Do you remember hearing Byrd say something about Ted Blair?"

"No," said Jerry. He returned his gaze to the floor between his feet.

"About how Ted Blair went to pick up his aunt, around Christmas, at Webbs' department store, and while he was waiting for her after the store was closed, he accidentally opened the back of one of those outside niches where jewelry is displayed, and how he was afraid he'd set off the burglar alarm, but nothing happened?"

Jerry shook his head. "I never heard about that."

"I think you did," said Varallo.

"Who are these guys?" asked Dunne, bewildered. "What—"

"Jerry. Did you read in the paper about Webbs' having a burglary last Sunday night?"

"I don't bother read the papers."

"Did you know about it?"

"No."

"Then you don't know that the burglar was small enough to get through that niche after he'd smashed in the glass. And evidently the burglar knew that he'd be able to shove in that plywood backing without setting off an alarm. And anybody who'd heard Ted Blair talking about what had happened to him would know that—or anybody who'd heard Byrd talking about what happened to Ted."

"I don't know Blair. He's a senior. Real big shot."

"And you don't know that the burglar got away with about twenty thousand dollars' worth of jewelry."

The boy looked up again. His eyes had looked glazed; but the pupils were normal—no sign of dope showed. Now there was expression in the eyes, but Varallo couldn't define it before the lids came down and Jerry said expressionlessly, "Yeah? That's a lot of loot."

"It is. And you don't know that the burglar left four nice clear fingerprints for us to find? Where he touched a broken figurine in the niche."

"Oh," said Jerry. "Well, then I guess—I guess you'll catch him easy."

"I think we have," said Varallo.

Dunne seemed to wake up suddenly. "A *burglary?*" he said. "A— *Jerry?* You think he—that thing at Webbs'— For God's sake, that's crazy! I never heard such a— Listen, Jerry's never out the time o' night that musta been pulled."

The boy looked at him fleetingly. It wasn't half a second, but Varallo caught the expression, and was suddenly very sure. Beside him, Poor shifted his weight and sighed. He had caught it too. The look that said, half contemptuous, *That's all you know.*

"Jerry," said Varallo, "we'd like you to come down to headquarters so we can take your prints." The boy was silent; he stared at the floor.

"Hey, you can't *do* that!" said Dunne. *"Jerry?* This is just crazy. But I *do* happen to know that, you can't take the prints of nobody under eighteen, and Jerry's only sixteen."

Which was quite true, and goddamn all the tenderhearted lawmakers concerned with the reputations of the kiddies. Varallo ignored him.

Poor said, "I think we'd also like to search this room, you know, Vic? And maybe also the garage. Though I think it'd probably be in here somewhere." He looked around the room speculatively.

A plain enough room, sparsely furnished: about twelve feet square, with a walk-in closet. A single bed with a neat white cotton bedspread, a painted chest of drawers, rag rug on the floor, painted straight chair with a cushion before a cheap painted student's desk, which bore a lamp and a blotter: a framed picture above the bed, a cheap reproduction of a Winslow Homer. It wasn't much, but it was, thought Varallo, a hell of a lot nicer room than he'd had at sixteen; he'd never had a room to himself at all until— And then too, of course, he'd never had a case of acne, let alone one like Jerry's. But what the hell? You got born this way or that way. Circumstance, environment, could change some things, but not the basic things.

"Hey, hey, what *is* this? You can't do that either—you got to have a search warrant. Just *crazy*—"

Varallo turned to Dunne. "Look, Mr. Dunne. I know we can't take Jerry's prints unless you consent, as his legal guardian. I know we need a search warrant. But if you'll give us permission, it would clear this whole thing up right away, we'd know yes or no right now, and I think you'll agree with me that that would be the best way to handle it."

"For God's *sake!*" said Dunne wildly. "That burglary—*twenty* thousand— I don't— For God's sake! Yeah, yeah, I see what you mean. Just *crazy*, say Jerry— Yeah, I get you. You better. You go right ahead, look all you want, you'll find you're way off, fellas, I dunno where you got such a crazy idea, but—"

"It's in the closet," said the boy, staring at the floor. "I didn't know what to do with it. I hadn't thought about that before I got it. I tried to sell one of the watches at a pawnshop, but—"

Dunne froze, mouth open, looking at him.

Varallo opened the closet door. A meager assortment of clothes, one good Sunday suit, shoes on a rack. "Where?"

"Oh, in the pockets of my suit." Jerry's voice held no expression at all. "I didn't know it was—worth that much."

Varallo brought out the suit, dumped it unceremoniously on the bed; he and Poor emptied the pockets. It was all there, the loot from Webbs'. Diamond watches, rings, bracelets, earrings, jeweled charms. It made quite a display.

"You'd heard Byrd telling what happened to Blair?"

"Yeah."

"So you figured, that niche not being hooked up to the alarm system, you could get in that way?"

"I didn't think about the alarm," said Jerry dully. "I thought at first, just the stuff in the little window. Then I remembered—what Rog said, you know—so I figured—"

"Oh, my God!" said Dunne. "Jerry—no—you couldn't've."

The boy raised his head and stared at Dunne with faint curiosity.

"You get out one of your bedroom windows?" asked Poor. There were two.

"Yeah."

"Have you been doing that long? Often?"

"Sometimes. After I'm s'posed be in bed."

"How'd you get downtown?"

"On my bike."

"Oh Christ, oh my God," said Dunne, "this isn't *so!* Ruth—I don't believe— After all I said, all we done for you, tried to—"

"Have you ever done anything like this before?" asked Varallo.

The boy moved slightly. "No."

"Why did you pull this one?"

"I—I—I don't know."

"Come on. You must have had some reason. Did you have some idea," asked Varallo gently, "of being able to pay a dermat——a skin specialist yourself, to cure the acne?"

Jerry's eyes moved nervously. "Yeah," he said, still without expression. "Yeah, that was it."

They had to book him, of course. Glendale didn't have a separate juvenile facility, but it was a nice new jail, he'd have a cell to himself. And be out on bond in twenty-four hours after he was arraigned.

As they had to do, Varallo explained all Jerry's rights to the Dunnes. "As a minor, he'll come under the Juvenile Court. If you can't afford a lawyer, the court will appoint a public defender. And of course it is a first charge, that'll be taken into account. He'll probably be arraigned next Monday. Maybe Tuesday. There'll be bail, as I say. You can—"

"Why?" asked Dunne. He was looking dazed. "I can't— I can't take it in— Listen, we raised him right. We did our best by him. *Why?* Christ, I never believed in all this heredity crap, his own dad was an ex-con but he never *knew* him! We did our best by him, Sunday school and all. Will you tell me *why?*"

Varallo couldn't tell him why.

He called O'Connor at home and told him the Webbs' thing was wrapped up, at least. He hoped to hell he'd built a fire under the D.M.V. on IOT five oh five. That hell of a peculiar thing.

He went home to Laura.

CHAPTER 16

The baby hadn't yet decided to come by Friday morning. "If anything *does* start," said Varallo, "you get Mrs.—"

"How I wish it would!" said Laura. "I'll keep my fingers crossed for you, darling—about that plate number. It's just got to be. Take care."

"And you, *cara*." He'd got up early and managed to do a little work on the roses. The two new ones seemed to be doing fine. On Monday, better start pruning them all back, that was the January job: and feed them too. Better stop on the way home for some rose food.

He got to the office at eight ten. O'Connor was there alone. "No, it's not in yet," he said before Varallo could ask about the D.M.V. report. "They sent all the others you'd asked about, when we were still thinking it could be SCS or SGS. That's no good unless we find out Judy was wrong all along the line, which is also possible, so we'll just, damn it, have to wait to see who belongs to IOT five oh five. What—"

"Damn. Where is everybody?"

"Seems we missed a little excitement last night," said O'Connor. "That big Thriftimart out on Glenoaks—break-in. It'd closed at ten, but the manager was still there, inventorying stock or some damn thing. Anyway, he was a surprise to the breakers-inners, who banged him over the head with a flashlight or something, and got away with about three thousand bucks. Manager's in the hospital—not bad—they said he could answer questions this morning, so Fred and John are over there. Forbes —oh, here he is now. Oversleep, Jeff?"

"Go to hell," said Forbes amiably. "The battery's down on my car, I thought I'd never get it started. What's new and what are the plans for the day? Has that D.M.V. report—" They'd all heard about that offbeat one by now.

"No. This joker," said O'Connor. "Let's spend some time on it—that one I want to catch up to." He rummaged among papers on his desk. "John left me his list."

"Yes," said Varallo, and sat down and lit a cigarette. "Do you know how many tickets Tracy wrote in October and November? One hundred and twenty-four."

"Zealous young officer," said Forbes.

"And we don't even know that the joker is among those. He might have brooded awhile before embarking on the campaign, damn it to hell," said O'Connor. "I don't think so, but he might have. Yes, I see, very damn awkward." He stared at Poor's list of the drivers Tracy had tagged. Suddenly he said, "Oh hell. I slipped up there. Should have had you take down what these tickets were for. Because it isn't very damn likely that anybody got mad enough at a patrolman for all this business over a parking ticket or some damn fool thing like that. A two-buck or five-buck fine."

"For God's sake, if you're going to chase me back to the county courthouse again—those damn files—" said Varallo.

"Tell you something else," offered Forbes. "I can see one hell of a lot of time spent, however we do it. So we go see all these people—we can't eliminate the women, I suppose, in fact it might even likelier *be* a woman. We have to get handwriting samples. Suppose they say no? We can't force that. And at least some of the men are going to be working in L.A., Hollywood, Pasadena—hell of a job."

"Now wait a minute," said O'Connor. "Let's not, for God's sake, lose our heads here. Let's use some common sense. I see all that. So all right, Vic did his stint at the files, you can go over there and get all the information on the tickets, Jeff."

"Oh, for—"

"Because that could be important. Look, it'll be easier because now we've got all these names. Vic, copy the list for him, hah? Surnames only, unless it's Smith. Then I think you and I can do some phoning, find out which of these people work in Glendale, start the easiest way."

"All right, all right." Varallo took Poor's list from him and got out his own, swiveled around to face his desk and pulled the typewriter toward him. Like most of the men in the bureau he was a hunt-and-peck typist, but practice had made him fairly fast. He got the string of names on Poor's list down, in three columns, in about twenty minutes, shutting his ears to the desultory talk of the other two men, and started on his own list. The tickets were filed by the month, and he'd taken October and Poor November.

He typed rapidly, only looking at the carriage occasionally, swearing when he hit the wrong key; and then suddenly he stopped.

"*Che diavolo,*" he said. "Here's a duplication. Norris L. Fenway. He got a ticket from Tracy in October and another one in November. So, have we hit something?"

"I'll be damned. That sounds very damn likely," said O'Connor, sitting up. "And, damn, that name rings a bell. I can't place it, think I saw it in the *News Press* maybe—prominent citizen? Damnation, you know this could be the break. Especially if they were both moving-violation tickets. Look, it won't do any harm to chase him up first—this might be a short cut. Where the hell's the phone book?"

Norris L. Fenway lived up on Olmsted. "One of our more substantial citizens, by that," said O'Connor, slamming the book shut. "You stay here in case anything comes in, Jeff. We'll just check Mr. Fenway out."

"Pleasure," said Forbes, and took the new *Reader's Digest* out of his pocket.

"Talk about half-assed cops lazing around on the city's time," said O'Connor. They went downstairs. In the lobby stood a brown-uniformed expressman with a large crate at his feet.

"But that's the address, plain as day," he was saying. "N. Tracy, at—"

"Take it *away!*" said Sergeant Dick.

O'Connor went over. "What, for the love of God, have we now?"

The expressman turned. "It's a portable kiln for this N. Tracy, and it's C.O.D., and this character says— I'd hafta see this Tracy personal, if—"

"Listen, Lieutenant," said Dick, "will you guys up there pretend to be detectives for once and catch this bird? It's a pain in the—"

"Think of poor Tracy," said Varallo. "We may be on target right now, Bill. Preserve calm and keep your fingers crossed."

They took O'Connor's car. "How's Laura?"

"Tired of waiting. So am I. And *is* that damn doctor any good? Oh Christ, I'll be happy when this is over. I can't help—"

"The things you worry about don't happen. Wise sayings from folklore."

"I know, I know. Easy enough for you to talk."

Olmsted was only a couple of blocks down from Cumberland; the address they wanted wasn't too far from the Scott house. It was one of the dignified older houses up there, the kind of house where no one could afford to live unless there was a substantial income, so the initial reaction they got was all the more surprising. A pretty woman in her mid-thirties opened the door to them, smiling; she was smartly dressed, groomed and coifed to the nth degree, and very conscious of her own charm. And when O'Connor had got out, "Mrs. Fenway? I'm Lieutenant O'Connor of the police depart——" her smile vanished and her eyes turned cold and for a minute they thought she was going to slam the door on them. Which was odd, because most honest substantial citizens respected the police.

"What do you want?" she asked coldly.

"To see your husband, if—"

"What trick are you planning to play on him *now?*" she asked. "It's rank persecution, I swear. He was *not* drunk, he'd had exactly four cocktails, and of all the *inconvenient—*"

O'Connor looked at her thoughtfully. "Mrs. Fenway, where is your husband now?"

"Where would he be? In his office, of course."

"In Glendale?"

"Certainly not, he's the junior partner in Orde, Blake and Fenway in L.A."

"Address? Brokers?"

"Find out for yourself!" she snapped, and did slam the door.

"Well, well, well," said O'Connor. "I think we've got one jackpot coming up, Vic. What's your first reaction?"

"The nearest Central phone book."

"On the nose," said O'Connor.

Orde, Blake and Fenway turned out to be architects, and they had offices on Beverly Boulevard. O'Connor took the freeway; they left the car in a public lot, rose through synthetic marble walls to the ninth floor in a plush-carpeted elevator and stepped out into more marble halls and chaste Philippine-mahogany slab doors.

"Money," said Varallo.

"Damn right. Loosely translated, maybe, a mere cop hasn't any right to order a big man like me around?"

"Could be, could be."

"Which way is nine eleven? Down here—" Suddenly O'Connor began to laugh. He stopped and leaned on the wall and howled.

"What the hell—"

"I—just happened—to think," gasped O'Connor. "You know what, boy? We haven't got one damn thing to charge him with! Have we? You know the only damn thing he can be got on—we'll have to bring the U.S. Post Office in to make a charge of using the mails to defraud. Call it six months' probation and a thousand-buck fine. Oh, my God—"

Varallo said he'd be damned, that was about it, and began to laugh too.

"Mr. Fenway?" said the dazzling blonde receptionist. "I'm sorry, you'll have to make an appointment, sir."

"We don't have time for that," said O'Connor, and walked past her to the slab door bearing the legend in gold, NORRIS L. FENWAY. He opened it and they walked in.

The receptionist chased after them agitatedly. "Oh, Mr. Fenway, they walked right past. I don't know who— Oh, should I call the *police?*" She stared fearfully at O'Connor.

O'Connor and Varallo brought out their badges simultaneously.

Norris L. Fenway was a rather jolly-looking smallish man with receding blond hair, a pair of amiable, friendly blue eyes and a long mobile turned-up mouth which looked as if it had been made expressly for smiling and no other activity.

He looked at the badges, and his smile quavered, and he said, "It's O.K., Gloria, these *are* the cops." And then he leaned back in his desk chair and laughed and laughed. His laughter was infectious; both Varallo and O'Connor felt themselves starting to smile.

"Oh dear, oh dear," gasped Fenway, and took off his glasses to wipe his eyes. "How did you find me?"

"The traffic tickets, Mr. Fenway," said O'Connor gently. "Occasionally even cops have a bright idea."

"Oh dear me, yes. I didn't know what the N. stood for, of course. There are three Tracys in the phone book with that initial. Well, I suppose I'd better apologize to the poor man. But it *was* a good joke, wasn't it?"

"If you happen to like practical jokes," said O'Connor. "You've caused one hell of a lot of trouble, Mr. Fenway. And just why in Christ's sweet name did you start such a—"

"Well, it was damned annoying, you know," said Fenway. "Damned inconvenient. It still is. This Tracy—he acted a little puritanical about it too, writing up that drunk-driving one. I was *not* drunk. Sure, I'd had four martinis, but I wasn't, my God, incompetent to drive! And just by a fluke, I suppose, he was the one handed me a speeding ticket—forty in a thirty-mile zone. I'd take a bet you've done that yourself—er—"

"Lieutenant O'Connor. No bets."

"And on the second one, the judge revoked my license for a year. Marlene's still grousing about it, and it *is* damned inconvenient. You know the damned buses in this place! Have to get up at some ungodly hour to catch— Well, I was mad. I said *was,* Lieutenant." He started to laugh again. "I wanted to get back at this—this puritanical cop. I thought about that—it was a really diabolical thing, wasn't it?—and I tell you, I admit it, I got carried away. It was like an obsession, to find the most outlandish things to order."

Varallo bit his lip. "Well, I hope you realize your little game has come to an end."

"Oh yes. I hope *you* realize that you haven't got a charge. Only the Post Office. My father was a lawyer. Oh dear, I *am* sorry—do apologize to Mr. Tracy, won't you? But you've no idea what fun it was! That cuckoo clock—" Fenway mopped his eyes. "Yes, I know, it'll probably be a stiff fine. It was worth it. Every penny of it. I assure you." He blew his nose, and his long mouth twitched, and he asked, "Has the live baby burro come yet?"

"Oh Jesus," said O'Connor and then they all started laughing.

About noon, the L.A.P.D. lab sent up a report on that bloodstained tee-shirt. They hadn't got much out of it except a definite link to the Scott homicide. There were two types of blood on it, O and AB. No laundry marks. No other stains of any interest.

The D.M.V. in Sacramento remained silent.

Forbes was still reading the *Digest*. The routine on Judy was held up until they'd checked out IOT five oh five. If that was a dead end, they'd start sorting through L.A.'s deviate records, and the sheriff's. Routine cleared up a lot of cases, but it was always nice to be offered a short cut.

O'Connor held down the office while Varallo and Forbes went out for lunch. Varallo called home; Laura said she was just the same, but in the middle of wrapping up his birthday presents just in *case,* and that Gideon was being a great help with that job.

O'Connor went out when they came back, and ten minutes later Fred Wayne and Poor came in and said they were just looking in to report. "Occasionally," said Wayne, "the miracle happens. We lifted some prints off that safe at the Thriftimart, and lo, they show up in L.A.'s records. One William Lee Manfred, out on parole from a seven-to-ten for burglary—his second count. L.A. gave us his mother's address, also his ex-wife's, so we're going out hunting."

"He do the job alone?" asked Forbes idly.

"No, manager says there were two of them—gave us a vague description. People," said Wayne. "I sat through enough sermons as a kid to have had my fill, but sometimes Holy Writ has the word for it. *They have eyes and see not.* At least we've made Manfred, maybe when we pick him up he'll open his mouth."

"Have a nice time," said Varallo. For the tenth time he went down the hall to Communications to see if anything was coming in from the D.M.V.

Such a damn peculiar thing. He was hoping hard that Judy had—incredibly—remembered right, not only because it made a short cut for them but because it would be, in a way, poetic justice. The victim providing the one needful clue . . .

"Katy said that," said O'Connor. "Said this—what the hell did she call it—inverted reading isn't as rare as you might think. Damn funny, ask me. I never heard of such a thing before."

"Well, as a bachelor you're not—"

"I suppose." O'Connor looked suddenly irritated.

And Forbes, who had wandered down the hall a few minutes before, came back in a hurry, looking excited. He had the long yellow strip of a teletype in one hand. "Here it is."

They all bent over it excitedly. *"Per Bacco!"* said Varallo. "I buy it, I buy it! By God, Judy came through all right! For one hundred percent—"

IOT five oh five belonged to a 1959 Dodge, and the Dodge was registered to one David Fernald at an address on Fairmount in La Crescenta. About two miles from where the Daly kids had been picked up and abducted by the man who'd said he was their Uncle Bob.

"Christ, I wouldn't have believed it," said O'Connor softly. "I wouldn't have *believed* it. A six-year-old kid— So let's go take him, boys." He patted the bulge at his shoulder absently.

They all went. Nice quiet town like Glendale, it wouldn't matter if the Detective Bureau was empty for a couple of hours.

They went in O'Connor's car, up Glendale Boulevard past the college where it turned into La Cañada Boulevard and then left to La Crescenta Avenue, and up to Fairmount.

It was a new house, a modern ranch style. Pink stucco and redwood. The lawn immaculate and green. A flagstone path to a tiny front porch.

As they went up that, Forbes said, "Damn the political party, the governor agitating for outlawing capital punishment. Talk about soft hearts—soft heads is more like it."

"Few civilians," said O'Connor, "see it from our viewpoint. *Or* see the hoods up close. The nuts. The perverts. A waste of time keeping them shut up—waste of time and money."

"On the other hand," said Varallo, "if they did just send them all to the gas chamber, Charles, we'd all be out of a job."

"Be damned, we would at that. The city fathers so damn chary of granting us any more money, let's hope they don't think of that for themselves," said O'Connor, and pushed the doorbell.

After a few seconds he pushed it again.

David Fernald, who presumably lived in this house, had just had his future discussed by three cops. A number of states had laws whereby rape—of any variety—was punishable with the death sentence. California was not one of them. But California had its "Little Lindbergh law," whereby anyone who committed an abduction with intent of bodily harm was subject to the death penalty, and David Fernald—very probably—had been the one who had taken away Judy and Lynn in his car, promising to take them up to see the horsies.

"Yes?" A stout elderly woman swung the door wide and looked at them.

"Does David Fernald live here?" asked O'Connor.

"Why, yes—he's my son— What do you—"

In silence they showed her their badges. She looked at them, looked up to broad stocky O'Connor between the other two tall men. "Police," she said. "He's done something else again, here. He always promises but it never means anything. My husband left me nearly two hundred thousand dollars, do you know that? And about three quarters of it going for lawyers, for— But I don't understand why you never *keep* him." Her voice was dull, with no particular expression. "When we all know he'll just go and do something again." She looked down at her clasped hands. "And I don't know why, about him. I—I was nearly forty when David was born, but that's no reason, is it? He seemed like a normal baby, it wasn't until he was fourteen he— You'd better come in. What—what has he done now?"

These were the ones to feel sorry for, thought Varallo. These were the ones to try to help. The innocent bystanders.

"We think he's the man who abducted those little girls and raped one of them," said O'Connor. He said it gently.

"Oh my God," she said heavily. Her florid face paled. "I get to wondering—if I'd never married Henry—? I was thirty-five. It's like living on top of a load of dynamite. He's my *son*. I don't know what he is. Psychopath, that one doctor said. But why can't you people just *keep* him? What am I supposed to do? He won't work—his father left him money too, an annuity. Isn't it better I should live with him, try to keep some sort of eye—? He does these things—ever since he was fourteen—stealing things, and he's raped children before too, and attacking people, mugging they call it. They put him in jail and then they let him out. And he always promises— I haven't been soft with him, but after Henry died it wasn't easy. Moving all around—every time he—so people wouldn't know, maybe he could make a fresh start. Something always happened again. He seemed—pretty quiet and good this time. Since he got out last —that was back in Indiana—and we came here. I let him have his car— he seemed— But I knew it would come. I guess this is the last, I'm too tired to go on like this with him."

This was the last. Because they'd come to California, with its Little Lindbergh law.

"Where is he?" asked O'Connor.

"Out in the—the patio." She pointed wordlessly.

They went in that direction, across an uncared-for-looking living room, to a side door. It was a pleasant patio, flagstoned and sheltered by a big alder tree.

David Fernald was about twenty-five. He wasn't a bad-looking young man; you wouldn't look twice at him; he looked anything but dangerous. He was about five nine, and very stocky; he was black-haired, with a very heavy beard staining his jaw, though he was nominally cleanshaven; his shirt sleeves were rolled up, and his arms were covered with thick curling black hair. He had blue eyes and heavy brows and a thin narrow mouth and he looked like anybody you might pass on the street any day.

They looked at him and held out the badges, and he looked at them and said tiredly, "Fuzz." He was sitting in a rattan armchair smoking; he didn't move. "So?"

"So," said O'Connor, "you son of a bitch, get up on your feet! You had your car out last Sunday. You picked up the two little Daly girls at Markridge and New York. You drove up into the hills and you raped Judy. Didn't you? *Didn't* you? Talk up, you bastard!"

David Fernald stayed where he was. He looked at his cigarette. He didn't say anything.

"Talk! Didn't you? You didn't know that Judy has a photographic memory, did you? Didn't know that she remembered the plate number she saw on the license plate in the back seat? But she did, and that's how we got to you."

The woman had followed them out there. Fernald remained silent; his head was bent. Varallo was reminded, oddly, of Jerry Hunter last night, silent, staring at the floor.

"I expect you'll have to know," whispered the woman. "You'll want to know—about all the other times. In Pearl River, that's New York—and Brunswick, New Jersey. And Syracuse. And Rochester. I didn't know what else to do. He's my son. It was my—my responsibility to *try.* But when all the police must have known he'd just do something else, why they can't keep him—"

"What the hell," asked O'Connor savagely, "was the license plate doing in the back seat, for God's sake?"

And David Fernald raised his head slowly and said in a mild tone, "It came off when I was putting the sixty-five tag on. Nuisance. I tossed it in the back seat. I put it on again that next day, Monday. Yes, I'm the one you want. I'm sorry. I don't know why I did it."

Jackpot. Judy had come through for them.

"He's my *son,*" said the woman. "What was I supposed to do? Are you—can you keep him for good—this time?"

O'Connor shoved his hat back, regarding Fernald pleasurably. "Lady," he said, "this kind we don't keep in this state. We send 'em straight to hell, and that's where he's bound for. Come on, punk!"

CHAPTER 17

They took him downtown and booked him and printed him. Mrs. Fernald went along. In the charge room, O'Connor asked her if she wanted to call a lawyer for David.

She shook her head numbly. "It's no use, is it?"

"He'll have to have one," said O'Connor.

"I keep thinking," she said, "suppose I'd never married Henry. You know? I suppose it's no good my staying. You'll let me know when—?"

"Yes, Mrs. Fernald." They took him up to the Detective Bureau then, to get some sort of statement out of him. He didn't give them any trouble; he came out with it without any prodding.

"I just happened to see the kids on the corner there. I wasn't heading any place special, just riding around. So I stopped and talked to them and I guess you know about the uncle bit because I saw it in the papers, so—"

"Get it in the statement," said Forbes tautly. He was taking it down in shorthand.

Fernald sighed and told about that formally. "They got in the car, and I already was thinking about finding a place where nobody could hear if she yelled, the bigger one you know, so I drove up in the hills, I couldn't find a road at first and then I did. I was hoping she would yell when I did it because I kind of get a kick out of that too." No special emotion in his tone. "And after a while the bigger one saw we weren't on the way to where I'd said, and—"

They listened to it all, impassively, because cops have to get used to things like that; and Forbes went away and typed it up and Fernald signed it, neatly and carefully, and initialed each page. They took him back to the jail again, and delivered him to the jailer.

And as they turned for the door, they heard Fernald ask, "Could I have a couple of Hershey bars? I want the kind with almonds in them, please. You got any of those?"

They went back up to the office in silence. "Well," said O'Connor, "so that's that. We seem to be making a little progress here. Now let's concentrate on that damn peculiar homicide. . . . A brass crane, I ask you, and two people killed." He sighed. "We've got time to have another hunt around for the ones we picked out of Records and haven't located yet." It was three forty.

That was where you started, the routine: matching up m.o.'s out of records, hauling the indicated people in for questioning. There were three or four ex-cons who looked good for the Scott homicide on those grounds—men with pedigrees for burglary, who had in the past used unnecessary violence. They hadn't found all of them yet. Men like that tended to move around.

"I want to call Mrs. Daly," said Varallo. "Yes, there's that Stafford—he looks pretty hot to me. The one who attacked the old couple when they surprised him by coming home early. Give me ten minutes on the phone."

"*And* the market job," said Forbes. "We haven't checked Records on the second man." He drifted out, and Varallo sat down at his desk and pulled the phone toward him. . . .

"Mrs. Daly? Detective Varallo. I just wanted you to know that we've got him—just now. And we probably never would have if it hadn't been for Judy. She did remember that plate number absolutely right. But a very funny thing—"

Mrs. Daly listened, exclaimed and was incredulous. "But it hardly seems possible—a child her age— Oh, I'll most certainly tell the school about that, I've heard of it but I never dreamed— M-Mr. Varallo? Will she have to—to testify? At the trial?"

"No. Not very likely. He's made a full statement admitting it. May I talk to Judy a minute, please?"

"Yes—" she said hesitantly. There was a longish pause before Judy came on the line.

"Hello, Judy."

"Hello, Vic. Is your baby come yet?"

"No, not yet. Judy, I wanted to tell you that we've caught the bad man who hurt you. So he won't be hurting any other little girls again. And it was all because you were so smart and remembered those letters and numbers right."

"Oh well, that's good," said Judy matter-of-factly. "Why'd you keep saying I didn't? I *told* you I did."

"I know, Judy. I guess we weren't quite as smart as you were."

She giggled. "But I don't even go to school yet!"

"Well, anyway, you're a very smart little girl, Judy. You just forget about the man now, will you?"

"Mhm-hmm," she said. "Well, I've got to go and drink some milk now, Mommy says. And I'm not really smarter than you, am I?" She giggled again and hung up.

Smiling, Varallo got up and stretched. Thomas Stafford, he thought. Next on the agenda. Last known address over on the east side of town. He pulled his tie into a neater knot and turned to the door, as Wayne and Poor came in.

They looked tired and disgusted. "We stayed about one jump behind him all day," said Wayne. "God, I could use a drink! Then we lost him. So we went to see the ex-Mrs. Manfred, and played in a little luck again —he's due to show up at her apartment about eight o'clock. She was on the point of taking up with him again, but when she heard he'll be going back to jail she changed her mind, I guess. Anyway, she'll let us in to wait for him. Good-looking wench, too," he added absently, yanking his tie loose.

"So we thought we'd take a little time off," said Poor. "Seeing as how we'll be putting in some overtime."

"Wouldn't it be nice," said Wayne dreamily, "if we got actual overtime pay like all the union boys? Has anything exciting been happening here, by the way?"

"What you missed," said Varallo. He sat down again to tell them. None of them quite believed the Judy thing, but there it was—one of those things they'd go on talking about for years, the really offbeat one. As for Fenway—

"My God," said Wayne suddenly, and started to laugh. "There was an express truck just turning into the lot when we drove in. I wonder—"

Without a word they went out of the office, downstairs and around to the lot. A brown-uniformed man was just climbing out of the truck, consulting some papers. There was a great big wooden crate in the back of the truck.

"Say, any of you know an N. Tracy here?" asked the expressman.

They all opened their mouths to explain, and were nearly deafened before they got anything out.

"HEEE-AWWWW!" said the wooden crate hoarsely.

Patrolman Tracy's last—presumably—strange gift had arrived.

"Good God!" said Wayne, shaken. "That's a *baby* burro?"

Varallo collected Forbes from Records and they went over to Delaware Street to see if they could locate Stafford. It was an old house that had been cut up into four apartments, and Stafford had lived in one of them, with a woman he claimed as his wife, up to last October, but neither of them was there now and nobody knew where they'd gone. Nobody remembered where or if Stafford had held a job. His parole had ended, significantly, on October thirtieth.

"Well, there are a couple more like that," said Forbes philosophically. One of them, Peter Gold, was still on parole and so he'd probably be keeping very clean—on the surface—until that was over. He was currently living over in Eagle Rock, so they drove over there and found the address. He wasn't home; he worked at a bowling alley but had Friday afternoons off and his landlady didn't know where he was.

"So I vote," said Forbes, yawning, "we knock it off now and meet at the bowling alley at eight o'clock."

"O.K. I had the *chance* to try another job, that's the idiotic thing," said Varallo. "So what do I do? Martyr-complex Varallo they call me. Straight as a homing pigeon I walk into the nearest police station and say please can I be a cop again." He shook his head.

"You're just dedicated," said Forbes. They got into the Chevy and headed back for Glendale. Varallo dropped Forbes at headquarters and drove home to Hillcroft Road and Laura.

Who said rather crossly that it couldn't possibly *be* a false pregnancy, could it? Her next appointment with Dr. Straw was on Monday, and she'd certainly ask him. "It's kicking me every five minutes. Hard. No, *not* like labor pains. Don't be silly, Vic, anybody'd know the difference! And my back is *killing* me, and I've had indigestion ever since I was idiot enough to eat those radishes at lunch."

"Well, it was your idea," said Varallo reasonably.

"And I certainly do hope it is twins or triplets, so I won't have to endure all this again."

"*Per l'amor di Dio!* You're not intending to—"

"Well, we said two, and besides it's not good to have an only child. But I'm borrowing trouble. I'm just so *tired* of this infant—where it is, I mean."

"Not any more than me," said Varallo. "Oh, but I didn't tell you, *cara—*" He began to tell her about Fernald, which took her mind off the baby. . . .

He met Forbes at the Eagle Rock bowling alley at eight o'clock; they went in and talked to the manager. Peter Gold was the night cashier, the manager relieved him at the desk and they questioned him in the manager's office.

Thinking of what Dr. Goulding had said, that considering the weight and size of the ax that had killed the Scotts, he'd think that X hadn't been very big or strong, Varallo eyed Gold thoughtfully. Gold was about five four and a scrawny little man. But he'd been sent up for a heist job on a small hotel and pistol-whipping the night manager who'd resisted him.

Gold said aggrievedly he was clean, real clean, and why they had to suspect him of every two-bit job that got pulled—

"This one wasn't two-bit," said Varallo. "Those Scotts who were beaten up last Saturday night—"

"Oh my God, you're not pinnin' *that* on me!" said Gold in a hurry. "A murder, for God's sake—*me?* Oh no, you don't, bloodhound! I was with my girl last Saturday, all night, she'll say I was."

"Naughty, naughty," said Forbes. "You're not supposed to be up to anything like that while you're still on parole. Don't you work on Saturday nights?"

"Well—uh—we hadda few beers, just sitting around, you know, and I —uh—just decided to skip it, I hadn't been feelin' too hot, I was maybe comin' down with the flu, and—"

"Which is what you told the manager," said Varallo. "All right. What's the girl's name?"

"She'll say—it's—"

"She'll say. Probably," said Forbes as they went out. "Does it mean a damn?"

"Depends on the girl. I don't suppose Gold would pick up a very high type."

They went and saw the girl, who was forty if she was a day, but then Gold was no chicken either. The girl coyly admitted that Petie had been with her. And it could be that that didn't mean a damned thing. Varallo drove Forbes back to where he'd left his car and they said good night.

Varallo went home.

He heard the phone ring as he came in the back door, and nearly sprawled flat as Gideon raced between his legs, complaining loudly about Sudden Noises. He came into the living room to find Laura saying, "Well, actually I'm feeling *awful,* but it can't go on much longer. Oh, here he is now. Charles," she added to Varallo, handing over the phone.

"Don't tell me something new has come up?" asked Varallo. Damn it, he hadn't been able to do any work on the roses all week, and in January of all important times of the year for roses—

"Well, just a little something," said O'Connor's heavy voice. "Little damn nuisance, but that we get a lot of. Fred and John picked up that Manfred at his wife's apartment, and he sang a very pretty little song. We've just been listening to it. The guy who pulled the market job with him is one Fred Lees—no pedigree—and Manfred doesn't know where he's living. They split up after they halved the damn take, and all Manfred could tell us was the place where Lees used to live, and about one of Lees' girl friends. So don't bother checking in first thing tomorrow, hah?—you meet me over in Burbank, Keystone Avenue—" he added the number. "Girl friend's place."

"Um. O.K.," said Varallo.

"You get anything out of Gold?"

"An alibi. Of sorts. Worth what?"

"One of those goddamned things. Well, see you."

"See you," said Varallo, and hung up.

"You're not going out *again?*" said Laura.

"I am not. I am," said Varallo, "going to bed."

"To sleep," said Laura bitterly. "No sleeping pills, the doctor tells me, and so I lie awake with this damned infant rampaging around like a—like a TV wrestler. Honestly, I *can't* go on much longer, can I? It's two hundred and seventy-six days now, we figured it out the last— *Oh,* there it goes again! I don't know, Vic, maybe an only child after all."

Varallo met O'Connor at the address on Keystone in Burbank at eight fifteen. O'Connor was armed with the girl's name and Fred Lees' description. It was a newish one-story court of only six units, and Miss Coral Mills lived in the one farthest down the flagstoned walk.

Miss Mills was apparently not an early riser. She took five minutes to get to the door, and eyed them blearily, clutching a pink nylon peignoir over her nightgown.

"*This* ungodly hour," she said. "What the hell you want?"

"Have you seen Fred Lees lately?" asked O'Connor producing the badge.

She stared at it. "Oh. Fuzz. At *this* hour. You boys certainly get up with the chickens." She squinted up at Varallo. "You're in the wrong business, Handsome. Ought to be on TV. I'll mention you to my agent, you like me to. Fred Lees? Oh, him. No, I haven't seen Fred in a month of Sundays."

"Are you sure?" asked O'Connor.

"I'm sure. I went around with him a little bit, but he got a little too handy and I'm particular who I let get like that. In fact, you want to know, I smacked his kisser for him, but good, and I haven't seen him since. Which is no loss to me." She blinked. "Gee, I haven't been up *this* early in—" She was, even unkempt, a very pretty girl, with a lot of wild black hair and melting brown eyes. "Did he *do* something?"

"He did," said Varallo. "Do you know where he's living now?"

"You sure are a real doll," said Miss Mills frankly. "You married, Handsome?"

"I am. Do you know—"

"That's always the way," said Miss Mills gloomily. "I meet one with everything I could go for—it isn't so often you see a guy really blond— Gee, I'll bet if you got sisters they all got the mousy straight hair, it's always that way."

(Ginevra, his lovely, flaxen-haired Ginevra—dead so long ago—and Laura—)

"—And he turns out to be married, and I got a rule, I don't play with married guys. I mean, we girls have got to stick together, you know. Men got enough of an edge as it is." She stared at Varallo solemnly. "But the offer still goes about my agent, you get tired of being a cop."

Varallo smiled and thanked her. "You know where Lees is living?"

She thought. "It was some place in Glendale. I don't know the address. I haven't seen him for maybe three weeks, a month."

"Well, thanks very much," said O'Connor. "So that's that."

"Get me up at the crack of *dawn*," said Miss Mills. "You think it over, Handsome. The TV." She shut the door on them, yawning.

"Goddamn," said O'Connor. "Well, check back at the office, see what Fred and John came up with." He started down to where he'd left the Ford. Varallo had parked behind him. "You thinking of taking up that offer, Handsome?"

Varallo grinned. "Sure, what else? At least I could set those producers straight on some details. I think the pay's better too."

"But think of the damn income tax."

"*Deh,* I'd forgotten that. I guess I'll skip it after all."

*

They landed back at headquarters at nine o'clock to find that Wayne and Poor had just come back triumphant with Lees in tow. He had skipped out of his cheap apartment on Myrtle Street a month ago, owing two months' back rent, and the landlady had astutely laid hold of his clothes and a tenor sax he'd left, in lieu of the cash. Wayne and Poor had shown up there this morning just before Lees rang the bell, now armed with the cash—from the market job—to redeem his belongings. They'd collared him pleasedly, and he sat now in a chair beside O'Connor's desk with the tenor sax across his lap.

"Goddamn," he was saying mournfully, "I didn't care so much about the clothes, it was the sax. I'm pretty good on this sax, yeah, man. I really am. Only I can't get jobs often—one-night stands, like that—on account it's against my principles to join the union, see?"

"You don't believe in unions?" said Wayne.

"It ain't that. Sure I believe in unions—done a hell of a lot for working men's rights, fine," said Lees. "But I don't believe in no organization tellin' me I *got* to join it or I don't get a job. This is all wrong, see? It's un-American. Against my principles." He looked up at O'Connor and Varallo, who'd just joined the rest over him. "My God, it takes five of you big bloodhounds to ask me stuff?" Forbes was hanging around too. "My God, look at you. Big bastards, aren't you? Well, so I walked into it. Just wanting the sax back. So that's the breaks." He shrugged. "I mighta known better than to go into anything with Willie Manfred. Strictly smalltime, and open his mouth the minute a cop looks at him."

"Have you been in cop trouble before, Lees?" O'Connor tossed his hat on the desk.

"No, no," said Lees in a hurry. "I never, honest to God! It was just, I was strictly from Brokesville, see. I'd had a couple jobs blowing with a combo, one-nighters, like that, but the damn union— It's a monopoly, I thought we had laws about that! Damn bunch of dictators. So I meet up with Willie, and he says this is a cool deal, no hitch, these markets are big time, they take in thousands, he happens to know this manager'll still be there after it's closed, he heard him say somethin' to one of the clerks, see, so the take won't be in the safe yet."

"Oh, you knew that?" said O'Connor interestedly. "I see. Were you planning to knock him off just to get at—"

"Jesus, no, nothing like that, my God! What you think we *are*? We went in about a quarter of ten— Listen, don't crowd me, I'm *telling* you, ain't I?—and we found a place to hide so's they wouldn't see us, while they closed up the store."

The inside phone rang on O'Connor's desk. Wayne picked it up.

"—And when we was pretty sure everybody was gone except—"

"Vic! Outside call."

"Thanks." Varallo took the phone. "Varallo."

"Oh, Mr. Varallo," said a man's pleasant deep voice. "This is Doctor Keith at the Los Feliz Small Animal Hospital. Your wife came in some time ago with your cat—er—"

"*Yes?* What—"

"We had a little crowd in as usual— Well, she's in labor, all right, I've got her on the table just in *case,* but of course I've called an ambulance, and I think—"

"For God's sake!" cried Varallo wildly. "But you can't—she can't—"

"Now relax, Mr. Varallo. Please. We have to take a pre-med course, you know. I'm—er—quite competent to deliver the baby if the ambulance doesn't— I think. In any case, I'm quite sure the ambulance will be on time. She'll be taken to the Glendale Memorial Hosp——"

"But she's got a reservation at the Glendale Community—"

"Sorry, the Memorial is the emergency hospital."

"Doctor!" said an agitated female voice in the background. "Oh, Doctor—"

"—Memorial Hospital," said Dr. Keith, and the line went dead quite suddenly.

"Oh my God!" said Varallo. "My God—Laura's having the baby at the *animal* hospital. I've got to—" He bolted out.

"The—" said Wayne.

"Well, be damned," said Fred Lees amiably. "I always knew detectives weren't quite human, but I never stopped to think about their wives."

CHAPTER 18

And in spite of all that hurry and bustle, it was nearly ten o'clock before he found anybody who would *tell* him anything. By the time he got to the small-animal hospital the ambulance had come and gone, and all they told him there was that there'd been an older woman with Mrs. Varallo who'd gone with her in the ambulance.

He rushed up to the Memorial Hospital and by asking questions along the way, in that rabbit warren of old and new wings, he finally found Obstetrics and was thrust by a busy, no-nonsense nurse into a waiting room. Mrs. Anderson was already there, and greeted him with relief.

"I'm so glad they got in touch with you—they said they would, or of course I'd have—"

"Where is she? Has it come yet? What—"

"Oh, it may be a good long time yet," said Mrs. Anderson comfortably. "The vet took her into the examining room because it came on so suddenly, you see—but they were about ten minutes apart then, so it may be a while. My goodness, Vic, don't look so scared—she'll be all right. You sit down and relax."

"Did anybody call Dr. Straw? Damn it, he's the one's supposed to be looking after her, not God knows what butchers in this place."

"Now," said Mrs. Anderson in a motherly tone. "They know what they're doing."

"Well, if it isn't going to come right away—" as if anybody could know!—"they ought to take her where she's *supposed* to be, over at the Community." The nice new modern hospital.

"I expect they think she'd better just stay here until the baby's born, they wouldn't want it to come in the ambulance, and maybe—"

Varallo went out to the hall and tried to find someone with any information. Nobody seemed to know a thing, and the no-nonsense nurse came by again and thrust him back into the waiting room. "I take it," she said, "this is the first experience for you. You just settle down and relax, Mr.—"

"Varallo, my wife is—doesn't anybody know anything about her being here?" God, maybe she'd just been left somewhere, everybody thinking somebody else was—

"Yes, yes, the ambulance case. It may be quite a while, Mr. Varallo. With a first baby. Though starting so suddenly— Well, you just sit down and relax." She bustled away.

Varallo sat down on the edge of a chair and Mrs. Anderson got up and patted his shoulder encouragingly. "I'm as sorry as I can be, but I've got to be getting home, Jean and the family's coming for dinner. Now you call the minute you *know*, won't you? And don't you worry, Laura'll be fine."

"Your car—if you came in the ambulance—"

"Don't fuss over that, I'll just call a cab to take me back there. Don't you forget to call."

"No, no—thank you for—"

And then he sat there alone, and the damned room must have been soundproof, because it was silent as the grave. *As the grave,* don't think things like that. Nobody came near him. He ran out of cigarettes in the first hour, and found a vending machine and a young intern who didn't know anything about Mrs. Varallo, down the hall.

He went back to the waiting room. Presently another man came briskly in, sat down and pulled out a paperback book. The title of the book was *How to Play Successful Golf.* The man seemed absorbed in it.

"Look—" Varallo cleared his throat; the man looked up inquiringly. He was a nice-looking fellow about forty, well-dressed. "How long does this usually take? Nobody seems to know anything about— I don't even know where she *is*—and—"

"Oh. Your first time," said the other man. "How long've you been here?"

"Since—God, I don't know, years. Ten o'clock." He looked at his watch and was surprised to see it was only ten past twelve.

"Oh, my," said the other man. "You may be still sitting here twenty-four hours from now, buddy. With a first one."

"Oh Christ, I hope not. I—which is this for you?"

"Which—oh. The fourth. *And* the last," said the other man unemphatically. "Relax, buddy. Just relax."

Varallo stared at the floor and entirely against his will began living over that day when Ginevra had died.

At three o'clock a nurse looked in and told him brightly his wife was getting on nicely and Doctor was quite pleased, but it'd be a while yet.

He tried to ask her if that was Dr. Straw, but she popped out as fast as she'd come in.

He lit another cigarette.

At four minutes to five, another nurse looked in and said, "Mr. Burrows? You have another nice little girl and your wife's just fine."

"Well, that's just swell!" The other man's face lit up. "We were sort of hoping it'd be a girl, make it come out even, two of each. Can I see her?"

"In about twenty minutes, sir."

Varallo lit another cigarette. Burrows rambled on happily about his family, announced that he was going to buy himself a drink when he'd seen Alice. Sure a relief to have it all over—

Varallo wished desperately that he could have a drink. God, could he use a drink. Calm down, he told himself. They must know what they're doing. A hospital. Yes, but the wrong hospital. Hell, it was a *hospital*, wasn't it? The thing was to think about something else.

Think about the Scott homicide. Try to come up with something.

A brass crane—

Burrows went out and a wild-looking, distraught young man came in. "Nobody'll *tell* me anything!" he said. "They just took her away on a damn table and they won't say when—or— These damn hospitals! I never did like doctors! She's got to be all right, don't you think?" he asked Varallo anxiously.

"I don't know," said Varallo. His voice sounded rusty with disuse. "I—"

"—Just tell me to relax and wait, and take her off somewhere— Doctors!" said the young man.

Varallo felt great sympathy for this discerning fellow. He felt the same way about doctors and hospitals. He wished he had a drink to offer the young man. He said instead, hollowly, "I've been here since before ten o'clock."

"Oh my God," said the young man. "I'm sorry we ever got *into* this thing! What's all the fun in a family, for God's sake? My God, I wish I had a drink. They ought to install bars in these damn places."

Varallo agreed with him violently. He was by now feeling rather peculiar physically, as if he were absolutely hollow inside and paralyzed outside. He lit another cigarette. Well, he wasn't paralyzed; his hands were shaking as if he had palsy.

Another nurse looked in the door. "Mr. Varallo?"

"*Yes?*" He leaped up, dropped the cigarette and knocked over the table beside the chair.

"Oh dear me, that's burning the carpet," said the nurse, and hurried over to restore order.

"*Ciò che*— What—my wife—"

"She's quite all right, Mr. Varallo, and you have a fine little—"

The roaring in his ears drowned out the rest of that. He leaned on the chair, feeling weak. "*È vero?* Are you sure? Are you— She's all right, and—"

"Yes, of course, sir." She looked at him concernedly, a little amusedly. "Shall I bring you a glass of water? You can see her in about twenty minutes. I'll come and tell you."

"Thank you very much," said Varallo, and suddenly felt like a damned fool. Of course it was all right. Everything was quite all right. He sat down again.

"Oh my God," said the young man despairingly. "I wish I was you, that's all. I just wish—"

"It'll be all right," said Varallo largely. He felt slightly drunk.

"How do I *know?* Doctors! Hospitals! Hell, I'm out of cigarettes."

"There's a machine down the hall," said Varallo kindly.

And when they finally let him in to see her, she looked fine, just fine, even with all her make-up washed off and her hair still wet with perspiration, and he leaned over and kissed her very gingerly, and Laura smiled and said, "Happy birthday, darling. I finally made it. I hope you approve of the result."

He hadn't noticed the result, tucked in at her other side. She moved, and he stared down into a face he knew. A small pink face, the eyes set just so, and the mouth and the chin—and a glistening flaxen soft down—

"*Ginevra!*" he whispered.

"You're not sorry it's a girl? Vic—what do you mean? Oh," said Laura. "Is she—is she like her? So much? You look—"

He nodded, quite unable to speak for a moment. "Do you mind, *cara?* If we—if we—call her—Ginevra Margarita?"

Laura considered. They hadn't decided on any names really. "I like it. Yes, Vic, we will." She yawned and shut her eyes. "I've had rather a strenuous day, darling. You go away and get yourself some dinner. We'll still be here tomorrow, unless they transfer us to the other hospital."

Varallo realized suddenly that the hollow feeling was just plain hunger; he hadn't had anything since breakfast. He said, "Yes, *cara.*" But his eyes kept going back to his new Ginevra, so incredibly tiny but so like—so like, in the uncanniest way—

The nurse came back and said he'd have to go, they had a patient coming into the second bed in the room. Laura was already half asleep.

Coming out of the hospital, he felt fine. In fact, he'd never felt finer in his life. He wanted to tell people about it—all about his new darling Ginevra. His stomach was growling fiercely.

He'd forgotten to tag the car as the property of a police officer, and there was an overtime parking ticket tucked under one of the windshield wipers. That was very funny indeed, and he laughed aloud over it, folding the ticket away in his billfold. He got into the car and made for the nearest restaurant, which was actually a glorified coffee shop. But a modicum of common sense was left to him and he knew if he went in and sat down he'd start babbling like a damn fool to the waitress or anybody else handy, so he bought two hamburgers to take out and wolfed them down in the car. Then he drove up to the Western Union office and sent a wire to Laura's older sister, and found a public phone and called Mrs. Anderson. And then there wasn't anybody else to talk to, so he naturally headed back for the office where there was.

Burt and Rhys were playing gin on Burt's desk. O'Connor and Forbes were still there, for some reason—probably just inertia, neither of them having anything but an empty apartment to go home to.

"—Thought you'd have a date with your schoolteacher, Saturday night," Forbes was saying as Varallo came in.

"She had some goddamn teachers' meeting to— Vic! Everything O.K.? Is Laura—"

"Oh yes," said Varallo, smiling idiotically. "Oh, Laura's fine—but wait until you see Ginevra. Charles, she's exactly like—the damnedest uncanniest thing." He went on talking, and after a while O'Connor began to grin, and exchanged looks with the others.

"I can see we're going to be hearing about nothing from now on but Ginevra, every damn spare minute. Take a breather and sit down, will you? So O.K., we're all very happy about it. Calls for a drink, hah?"

"If you're not hanging around for any reason, I'll buy," said Varallo. "Really, Charles, it's the most incredible—she's really the sweetest—"

"Yes, yes," said O'Connor. "Let's go and get that drink." He'd taken off his jacket; he picked it up, and the inside phone rang on Burt's desk.

"Burt . . . Oh. Yeah? O.K." Burt looked at O'Connor. "Richard Scott on his way up."

"Oh?" O'Connor tossed the jacket onto his desk. Varallo went on staring dreamily at the blank windows.

Scott came in quickly. He looked tense and excited. He had a big paper bag in one hand. "I thought I'd better bring it in right away," he said. "The damnedest thing. Because there might be fingerprints. I thought of that right away when I spotted it, so I only handled it by the legs."

"What—" said O'Connor.

"That—that brass crane I told you was missing." Scott set the bag down on O'Connor's desk, very carefully. "I haven't—I suppose—been exactly operating on all cylinders this week, since—and anyway, I always put my car in the left slot, away from the workbench. Well, about half an hour ago I needed a pair of pliers, I couldn't get the top off—oh hell, never mind, the point is I went out to the garage and spotted the crane. It was right at the very back of the workbench, where you wouldn't see it unless— And I *know* the damned thing was in the living room when I left—that night. It was sitting in the middle of a flat bowl of camellias on the coffee table. So that looks as if he— Why? It's crazy! Started to take it, and then left it in the garage instead. Crazy, but then this whole thing—" He brushed a hand across his eyes. "And I just stared at it, and then I thought about fingerprints, so—"

"Be damned," said O'Connor. They all looked at the paper bag as if it were full of dynamite. "You can finish that hand later, Bill, hah?"

"Damn right," said Burt. "Don't tell me, a break in that case? The ax handle was too rough to take prints, but—" Very gently he picked up the paper bag and went out with it.

"Do you think there could be?" asked Scott. "When will he be able to say?"

"Few minutes. Take a bit longer to check through Records, see if we have 'em listed—if there are any damn prints at all. Now why in hell's name would he have done such a damn silly thing? Realized belatedly the thing wasn't very valuable?"

"Why did he back the car out?" asked Scott wearily. "I think it must have been a psycho, that's all. The kind who doesn't need a reason really." He lit a cigarette. He wouldn't sit down; he wandered around the office uneasily, smoking.

Varallo smiled at him. "I've got a new little girl, do you know that? Her name's Ginevra. She's about an hour old."

"Oh," said Scott. "Well, congratulations, that's nice."

"For God's sake, don't encourage him," said O'Connor. "Talk about maudlin!" He sat down heavily at his desk and lit a cigarette.

"But honestly, you know, Jeff," said Varallo to Forbes, "it was *uncanny*. The first second I looked at her—my God, I hadn't even heard the nurse when she said what it *was*— And it just *was* Ginevra! It was—"

"Quite a coincidence," said Forbes kindly.

"I suppose he could have thought at first it was valuable, and then—" said Scott.

"I don't— *Well?*" demanded O'Connor as Burt came back. Prints *per se* would be a hell of a step forward; they'd have places to ask if they weren't in their own records.

Burt stood in the doorway with a rather peculiar expression on his face. He said, "Some nice prints. On the body of the thing."

"Ah!" said O'Connor contentedly. "So you've got a night's work cut out for you, studying all the pretty loops and whorls out of our modest little collection. Mr. Scott, thanks very much for—"

"No, I haven't," said Burt. "I made them already."

O'Connor stared at him. "Boy, I know you're good but you're not *that* good. Five minutes' looking?"

"Well, I'd been looking at the other ones so recently," said Burt, licking his lips, "and there are a couple of distinctive— You won't have to go hunting either. We've already got him. Locked up nice and cozy over there, waiting to be arraigned on Monday and let loose on bail."

They were all staring at him now. "And maybe you won't want to believe it, boys," said Burt, "but fingerprints don't tell lies. They're Jerry Hunter's prints."

"Jesus H. Christ," said O'Connor very softly.

"Oh," said Jerry Hunter. "You found out about that."

He stared at the brass crane O'Connor had laid on the neat cell cot. It was a graceful, handsome ornament, the brass gleaming, the iridescent colors on wing and head brilliant. "I guess I sort of forgot about that," said the boy. "I had it, and then when I saw the car— Anyway, I guess Aunt Ruth'd have asked where I got it."

"Suppose you tell us all about it, Jerry," said O'Connor.

They hadn't, of course, let Scott come with them as he'd wanted to. They'd left Burt and Rhys to hold down the office and come straight over to the other side of the building to see Jerry. They didn't quite believe this thing yet. Jerry Hunter, the kid they had all felt a little abstractly sorry for.

Jerry Hunter, sixteen, a scrawny little kid not looking even sixteen. Just a kid, with the angry inflamed ugly acne sores spreading all over his face. He sat there lax on the cot, dull and resigned as he had been when they picked him up for the Webbs' break-in.

Varallo thought absently about the Dunnes. They wouldn't believe it either. . . .

"I don't mind," said the boy dully. "I thought maybe you'd come about that, the other night. It was the other thing, though. But I been sort of wanting to talk to somebody about it, because it was funny the way it happened. I don't know why it happened really." He looked up furtively at O'Connor and immediately dropped his eyes to the floor again.

"Where did you get the ax?" asked O'Connor quietly.

Jerry drew a deep breath. "I had that about—about a month, I guess. It was in Arnie's garage—Arnie Nalley, I know him at school. I walked home with him once, not that we're really pals or anything, we just did, we were fooling around his yard and I saw it. The ax. In his folks' garage. I saw it and—and—and that night I went back, the door was open, and I took it. I don't know why I wanted it really, only—only—I'd been thinking—if I could get some money—and there wouldn't be any way to do that except stealing stuff, and so I thought— That's sort of dangerous, and you'd want to have something to—to protect yourself, like."

"To protect yourself," said Forbes without emphasis. "So?"

"So, well, I got it." Jerry blinked. "I hid it at the back of my closet. I was thinking about all those rich houses, I got to ride past some on my way to school—like up on Olmsted and Cumberland, around there. I thought rich people like that'd keep money around. You know. And maybe be out somewhere nights. I went out a lot o' nights. I was—you know—getting up my nerve, like. I don't know why it happened like it did, though."

"You wanted the money for a skin specialist?" asked O'Connor.

"Well, yeah." Jerry blinked nervously; he hadn't once looked up since that one glance at O'Connor. "I mean," he said, and suddenly the words came out in a torrent, as if they were shoved out by some terrible inner pressure, "I saw this house was all dark and so there wasn't nobody home so I left my bike up the street and I went up the drive and the back door wasn't locked, I tried it, so I went in and I had the—the ax with me because I thought too if there was a safe like rich people have sometimes like it says in books, and I went down the hall— I had the flashlight too, see, Uncle Bill's flashlight—and I was looking for a den or something where maybe a safe would— And all of a sudden there's a light goes on and there's this old guy in a bathrobe standing there yellin' at me and I don't *know* why but next thing I swung at him with the ax and he fell down and I went on hitting him and I see the old lady in bed and she seen me too and could tell but that wasn't the reason really, I guess, but I went over and hit her too. And I found the den and looked behind the picture where safes always are but there wasn't none. So I looked some more and then I seen there wasn't any money anywhere. I was sort of scared, go back in that room where— So then I went out to the kitchen—and I—and I was by the back door and I touched a switch or something and all of a sudden the garage door went up, out there. Like magic, kind of, it was. One of them electric-eye things. And I—I took—that—thing—" he nodded at the brass crane— "only then I got thinking about the car. I'd sure like to have a car. Some guys at school got cars, you know? The girls like those guys the best. Only even if I *had* a car—" His hands came up to cover his face, but he wasn't crying. "I—I—went out and the keys were in it. In the ignition. I'd never drove a car, gee, it was a Caddy, you know? But I got the engine on and I found where it said Reverse and I backed it out. Only I was kind of nervous and turned the wheel and went over the lawn. Only then I thought, gee, what'd I do with the car? A Caddy. There wasn't no way I could keep it and not have people ask—"

He looked up then and slowly took his hands away from his face. "So I—just left it. And there hadn't been no money or anything and it was all just for nothing. So I went through some back yards there because there was a car going up the street and I thought they'd see, and I got my bike, only then I saw all the blood on my shirt—gee, I didn't think I hit them that hard, to bleed—only I don't remember so good just how that was, about hitting them—and it was all over the ax too. I was sort of scared then and there hadn't been nobody in the yards I went through, so I took off my shirt and went back and stuck it under a lot o' trash in the can in that last garage, and then on my way home I threw the ax over—over—the wall of that—you know—that cemetery place. I never thought I *killed* them. Those people. I didn't mean— I don't know why," said Jerry Hunter.

"Never done a thing like that before?" asked O'Connor conversationally. "Maybe at a motel, out in Arcadia? Last September?".

"I never— What? I never been in Arcadia." The boy seemed disinterested now he'd got it out. "No. I don't know where that is."

"Over the other side of Pasadena."

"Oh. I guess I couldn't ride that far on my bike."

True. O'Connor sighed. The Arcadia boys still had an unsolved homicide on their hands. He touched the brass crane. "Why'd you pick this up, Jerry? Think it was valuable?"

"No," said Jerry. He looked at it. He reached out a hesitant hand. "It had," he said, "such a nice—sharp—beak. Like a knife. Like a knife."

They stood at the entrance to the jail. It was a nice clear night, with a little cool wind.

"Psycho?" O'Connor lit a cigarette.

"Who knows what the head doctors will say?" sighed Forbes. "Double talk. Repressions, frustrations, what the hell. What a thing. Sixteen. Could be he's a schizo."

"The Dunnes are going to be—" O'Connor sighed too. "The poor goddamned innocent bystanders. What a hell of a thing. Yeah, sixteen." He looked up at the stars. "There's that. They'll stash him away somewhere, as a minor—unless he's definitely nuts—until he's twenty-one, and then try him. And by that time everybody'll have sort of forgotten about the Scott couple, and ten to one they'll give him a one-to-three or maybe just let him go altogether—these goddamned judges—and whatever he is or isn't, he's got the violence in him. He's one of the dangerous ones. I wonder how many more he might do before—"

"You do have such optimistic ideas," said Forbes.

I must, thought Varallo suddenly, call Judy and tell her about the baby. Dear little Judy, who'd been interested in the baby. Tell her it is a little blonde girl, my own darling Ginevra. I'll call Judy in the morning, after I've been to see—

"Join the force and see human nature in the raw," said Forbes. He dropped his cigarette and stepped on it.

"It gets," said O'Connor, "pretty damn raw sometimes. Well, leave the formal statement-taking until tomorrow. Vic—"

"Um?" said Varallo. "I was just thinking I'd call Judy and tell her, you know. She was interested. I tell you, it was the *uncanniest* thing—the second I—"

"Oh my God," said O'Connor, "I see you're going to be very little damned use around here until you've recovered a little bit from the shock of becoming a parent." He grinned and clapped both of them on the shoulder, and linked arms. "Let's go out and celebrate, boys—Saturday night, all the current mysteries solved, *and* the baby! I'll even pay for the drinks."

They turned and in step headed for the parking lot.

THE NAMELESS ONES

. . . They lay wait for their own blood; they lurk privily for their own lives. So are the ways of every one that is greedy of gain; which taketh away the life of the owners thereof.

—PROVERBS 1:18–19

CHAPTER 1

When Varallo came into the headquarters building at five to eight, Sergeant Albert Duff was still there, leaning on the main desk talking to Copeland, who'd just come in. Sergeant Duff was on nights this month.

They both said, "Morning, Vic."

"Nice quiet night?" asked Varallo.

"Well, a couple of things," said Duff. "I was just telling Bill. We got a call to a child-beating out on Chevy Chase—"

Varallo grimaced and said, *"Deh.* I will never understand—"

"—But," said Duff, grinning, "when Harrison got there it turned out it was a false alarm. Just a nervous new papa, and mama had left him with baby while she went to see her sister, and he was just trying to change the baby, which same he'd never done before. Stuck a pin in wrong or something, baby yelled, and one of the neighbors got excited."

Varallo laughed, starting for the stairs. "Nice quiet night. Any more heist jobs?" They had somebody around pulling a few; not much of a lead on him yet.

"Uh-uh. Well, I'm off," said Duff, yawning. The Traffic shift had already changed; the headquarters building felt quiet and a little sleepy. Katz came in with Poor just behind him, and as Varallo started up the stairs Copeland was telling them about the false alarm. Varallo grinned again, feeling superior: not that Laura let him in for the diaper bit very often, at that. And besides, his darling Ginevra was such a good baby and hardly ever did yell. Much. Of course, most babies—but Ginevra wasn't like most babies. Equally of course. Their darling Ginevra—

"I can't get over it," said Katz behind him. "Just look at him."

Varallo turned in the doorway of the big Detective Bureau which spread all across the front of the second floor of the new police building. "*Look* at him," said Katz, shaking his head. "Our big handsome blond Eyetie. No bloodshot eyes, no yawns, no snarls. With a two-month-old baby at home. It's not natural. You don't mean to tell me she slept right through again?"

"She always does," said Varallo, feeling more superior. "I told you. Since the week after she came home from the hospital. Eight to six thirty, no trouble at all. She—"

"It's not *fair*," said Poor.

"That's what I say," said Katz gloomily. "My God, it aged me ten years. Both times. With Joe Junior and Johnny. Ten years. Going off like time bombs at two-thirty every single damn morning, and keeping it up for hours. I swear, there were times I like to fell asleep questioning witnesses. She hasn't even *once*, Vic?"

"No, I told you. Of course not. She's—"

"Please," said Katz hastily, "no raptures. All right, all right, she's the most beautiful baby ever, if she still does need her diapers changed. Sleeping right through. God, when I think—"

"Not fair," said Poor again. "I tell you, Joe—you'll remember—I had to take sick leave, get caught up on my sleep. There was nearly three months there—just like you said, a time bomb. Every morning, two, three o'clock, the baby yelling." They both looked at Varallo enviously, crossing to their desks.

"Well, Ginevra just—"

"Spare us the raptures," said O'Connor from the door. "I'm a tender plant this morning." He slapped his hat on the rack and sat down heavily at his desk. "Anything new in?"

"Don't tell me you've got a hangover, Lieutenant," said Poor.

O'Connor just looked at him. O'Connor the tough, who couldn't open his mouth without swearing, was curiously puritanical in some directions and was rarely known to take more than one drink. "I don't feel so hot," he said querulously. "I just don't feel so damn hot. I feel as if I might be coming down with a cold, damn it. For God's sake, I haven't had a cold in five years!" He sounded aggrieved. He felt his throat tenderly.

"Lots of cold around," said Poor. "Flu too. I tell you what it is, the change in temperature. March, after all. That little hot spell at the first of the month like we usually get, and then going down to the fifties again, and all the wind. Is your throat sore?"

"It feels a little bit sore, damn it. I think," said O'Connor.

"You ought not to come in. Spread it all around."

O'Connor growled. "Goddamn it, I'm all right! Just a damn *cold*. If it is. Maybe I've just been smoking too much." He swallowed experimentally.

"Now listen, Charles," said Varallo. "If it is a cold, I don't want to be carrying it home to the baby. You ought not to—"

"Oh, for God's sake!" said O'Connor. "I'm all *right*. With this kite flier wandering around, and the heist man, and that Goddamned homicide—"

Forbes ambled in and over to his desk. "I think we can give up on that, Lieutenant. Not one smell of a lead. Ask me, and Wayne thinks so too, that was the random, impulsive thing, and it might have been anybody, from some moronic j.d. from over in east L.A. to some ditto transient just passing through."

O'Connor growled again. "Where's Fred?"

"Gone back there to question the neighbors again. With Rhys."

Varallo sat down at his desk, with a slight effort removed his mind from that best and most remarkable of all babies ever, certainly, vouchsafed to any set of parents, and frowned at the top sheet on the blotter. That homicide . . . Forbes was probably right. It looked like that sort of thing.

Glendale, California, that nice quiet town, third largest in L.A. County but possessing nothing that could be called a slum, didn't as a rule have a very high crime rate. As the population climbed so did crime, but not really very high—compared with lots of other places. In the last eight months they'd had six homicides and three of those had been suicides. The petty break-ins, the vandalism, the purse snatching, once in a long while a mugging on some dark street—that was how it went in Glendale.

Right now they had this homicide. Elderly woman who lived alone, a Mrs. Martha Collins, owned a modest house on Geneva Street. An inquisitive neighbor had wondered why she hadn't been seen in her yard for several days and eventually called the police. Mrs. Collins dead on her dining-room floor, dead about four days, beaten to death, and the house ransacked. Back door broken in. And no lead at all, as Forbes said. Might have been anybody. Anybody, among the too many types around—a few right here, a lot more over in L.A. and Hollywood and environs—who, maybe hopped up on H. or not, wouldn't think twice about doing a thing like that. Or even at all.

You got them. And it was cops had to cope with them. Only—

Varallo shook his head. One like that, crawl back into the jungle, and just how did a poor damned cop put the finger on him?

Then they had the kite flier. Or rather in the plural, because the smooth fellow wandering around town passing checks not worth the ink on them seemed to have a girl friend who'd helped pass a few. That precious pair had strayed over into Burbank too, and that set of cops was looking for them as well. Checks for pretty sure printed by the passers, nice-looking, impressive-looking pay checks—and other kinds—fancily printed up with the names of nonexistent corporations.

La é cosí, reflected Varallo sardonically. All the paper: the sea of paper the entire economy rested on and perpetuated: my God, even places like dime stores taking checks these days (and inviting charge accounts, for God's sake). All busily accepting the checks, the credit cards: the paper maybe even more commonplace than the coinage. In a way, only themselves to thank for the bouncy checks. Lodovico Giovanni Varallo, maybe from a poor and rural upbringing and maybe just by nature, distrusted the paper; and having the ability to figure percentages of interest, never bought anything on time if he could possibly avoid it.

However. Then there was the heist man. He had—successfully, from his viewpoint—robbed a drugstore, a dry cleaner's, a small movie theater downtown, a second drugstore and a hole-in-the-wall malt shop. He hadn't got much of a haul except at the theater. They had a description of a sort: the citizenry sometimes seemed to be all blind, but this and that they gave them. A young man, middle-sized, dark, with a gun. So they were looking for that one too.

It was about par for the course, in Glendale. A quiet town as a rule. Maybe today they'd get called on an overnight break-in, or a car theft, or a piece of vandalism. Maybe the night men would get called out to a fight in a bar. Maybe—

"It can't be a cold, damn it," said O'Connor. "I don't get colds, for God's sake. I'm never sick, you all know that, for God's—"

"Look, anybody can catch a cold," said Poor.

"*I* don't," said O'Connor. "I just damn well don't. I've just been smoking too much." He swallowed again and felt his nose.

"I suppose," said Katz, "somebody ought to go see that Melvin again. The guy who took the latest check, at the Pep Boys'. He was so mad when I talked to him yesterday he couldn't give me any description, but maybe when he's thought it over—"

"Go, go," said O'Connor gloomily, hunching his wide beefy shoulders. "Did somebody call all the local papers to pass on all the god-damned phony corporation names—and this joker's aliases?"

"I did," said Varallo. "The *News-Press* was very upstage. They might find space or not. The *Independent* was very cooperative. But even so, Charles, will everybody take the trouble—*or* remember a third of them?"

"People!" said O'Connor. "I know, I know." Katz had gone out, looking unhopeful, and Forbes was starting to type up a report on the heist man. The phone rang on O'Connor's desk and he picked it up. "O'Connor . . . What? Where? . . . For Christ's sweet sake. All we need. O.K., thanks, Bill, we're on it. You call Goulding? For *God's* sake." He put the phone down. "I tell you, boys, it's all these new apartments—different class of people coming in. Damn town's changing. Now it seems we've got another homicide. A murder yet."

Varallo jerked upright. "Where and who?"

"Barker called in just now. Jeweler's up on North Central—" O'Connor passed over the scrawled address. "You and John go look, hah?" He swallowed, felt his throat and squashed out his cigarette.

"If it is a cold," said Poor as they went down the stairs, "he's got no business to come in—spraying germs all over."

"You expect he'd ever admit any little thing like a cold could get him down?" Varallo grinned. "My wife says he's obviously got a king-sized inferiority complex and is just compensating for it. You know, the big tough cop."

"*O'Connor?*" said Poor.

"No, I know, even Laura doesn't believe it," said Varallo.

"And I wonder what more we've got now," said Poor. "Could be he's right, all these apartments. Another homicide. Want to take my car? What's the address?"

Up here on North Central Avenue, in the midst of a large and mixed residential area, was a little pocket of business. Old business, which had been there for years. There was a good-sized market on one corner, with a large parking lot; across the street was a gas station, a plumbing company and a dry cleaner's. Across the intersection there was a small dress shop, an ice-cream store and a photography shop, and across from there, on the same side of the street as the market, was a drugstore on the corner, a small coffee shop, a large furniture store and rather un-expectedly a small jewelry shop.

The jewelry shop had a faded sign over the door, KESSLER'S FINE

JEWELRY. The same legend in dingy gold paint was on the one display window, and under it, *Engraving to Order*. Kessler's was their destination, by the squad car and the little crowd outside.

"Funny place for a jeweler," said Poor as they got out of his car. Varallo agreed. Kessler's was the end shop in the small block of stores; down from it the block was entirely residential, single houses, old and fairly well-groomed houses, mostly frame. The one nearest the block of store fronts, he saw, was empty, with a FOR SALE sign on the front lawn.

A dozen people stood outside the jewelry shop, and the tan-uniformed Barker stood close outside the narrow front door. He hailed Varallo and Poor with relief. "You call the doctor? The guy's dead in there. Could be our heist man, looks sort of like that. This is Mr. Vincent Moore, you'll want to talk to him."

Mr. Vincent Moore looked at the two tall detectives a little nervously. "*I* don't know anything about it," he said, licking his lips. Mr. Moore was perhaps twenty-five, weedy and pale, with narrow shoulders and what he obviously hoped might turn into a real mustache someday. "I just, it being Saturday, you know, I don't work Saturdays, I'm a clerk at Hornblower and Weeks, that is I'm studying accounting, but anyway it was for Marjorie's birthday which is on Sunday. Tomorrow. Four fifty a week I'd been paying on it, and I came to make the last payment so as to give it to her, my wife I mean, Marjorie's my wife."

"Yes, Mr. Moore," said Varallo patiently.

"I came, and the door was open, and I went in and saw him. The proprietor." Mr. Moore gulped. "On the floor. And I hope I know how to keep my head, I went right to the drugstore, the pay phone, and I called—"

"Yes. If you'll just wait a few minutes," said Varallo, "we'll want a statement. Did you touch anything in there?"

"I did *not*," said Moore.

Barker moved him away from the door. Varallo and Poor went in, glancing at the door which had been obviously forced with a jemmy or something like that.

It was a very small shop, no more than twenty by fifteen feet. It was an old building, and though some effort had been made to keep this little shop clean and neat, the hardwood flooring was scuffed, the walls needed painting. There was a single display case, its glass top and sides shining clean, which served as a counter; against the wall behind it hung a variety of wall clocks, and under those a metal table bore an old cash register. At the far end of the shop, down from an inner door, was a long table bearing more clocks.

He was sprawled on his face, legs twisted, halfway behind the display case, as if he'd tried to run toward that inner door and hadn't made it. They couldn't see his face, but Varallo could almost imagine it from the rest of him: a little man, about five-five, a scrawny little man wearing a pair of shabby dark slacks and a white shirt; the slacks were pulled up and his socks were handmade Argyle-pattern socks and the heels of his old black moccasins run over badly. He was nearly bald. His arms were flung out over his head and he was wearing a plain gold wedding ring on his left hand and a Masonic-order ring on his right. Bending over him, Varallo saw that his soft-looking white hands were well-manicured.

He had been shot. In the back—probably more than once there—and high in the left shoulder, and in the back of the head, low toward the spinal column. He had bled a little, not too much, and from that Varallo could deduce one fact at once.

"First shot probably killed him," he said, straightening. "The one in the head."

"Um," said Poor. "So maybe, Vic, is this our elevator boy taking his first shot at somebody?" The heist man who had held up the drugstore, *et al.,* had not yet taken a shot at anybody; but there was always a first time.

"Could be," said Varallo. He looked around too.

Barker had followed them in. "I heard this and that while I was waiting for you," he said. "The guy's name is Horace Kessler. He's had this place maybe twenty, twenty-five years. Quiet little business, looks like. Doesn't seem like he'd get an awful lot of business—just enough to get by. His wife's dead—most people around here knew him. The pharmacist at the drugstore says he lived in an apartment upstairs, over the store."

"Oh," said Varallo. "Any other apartments upstairs besides his?"

"I couldn't say."

"Funny," said Poor, "nobody heard the shots, Vic. At night, maybe? Last night?"

"Maybe. If there aren't any other apartments. Or if they're empty," said Varallo. He looked at little Mr. Kessler, pathetically sprawled out behind his counter, thoughtfully. Most of the shops along here—possibly not the small coffee shop next door—would be open until nine or so in the evening, on Friday nights. If they all conformed to Glendale custom. Which, of course, they might not. This was some way from downtown proper, where Friday night was shopping night. The market at least would be open, probably the drugstore. But even if Kessler hadn't been open, living on the premises he might well answer the bell downstairs; or equally he'd have come down if he heard somebody trying to break in. He was dressed. So, after the market and drugstore were closed, but some time before midnight, say? And the nearest house empty: no one close to hear the shots.

Dr. Goulding would narrow the time a little. Maybe be able to give an educated guess about the caliber, if no slugs were available from the body. Just *as* a guess, Varallo thought it had been a fairly big caliber, and the slugs might be smashed in consequence.

And it was a very long chance, of course, that X would have left some pretty prints on the glass case.

"It looks," said Poor, nodding around, "kind of open and shut. Which doesn't take us far finding him."

"Yes," said Varallo. Either the heist man—one man they knew was wandering around town with a gun—or somebody else breaking in (maybe not knowing Kessler lived upstairs?) and being surprised. Open and shut you could say.

The drawer of the cash register was open and at first glance the register looked very empty. One side pocket of Kessler's slacks had been pulled inside out. One section of glass on top of the case had been smashed in, and shards of glass lay over the remaining expectable items in the case. A few birthstone rings in boxes; a few watches; a few fancy little bedside alarm clocks and a couple of pen-and-pencil sets. There were empty spaces in the case where other items had obviously been snatched. Apparently none of the clocks had been touched. Which figured. Varallo looked at the wall clocks; only one was running, a large clock with a polished walnut case and Roman numerals, which informed him that it was twenty minutes to nine.

Of a nice sunny coolish March morning in California, and looking at Mr. Kessler, Varallo wondered all over again why on earth he'd deliberately chosen to be a cop.

"Yes," he said. "Very open and shut." He went out to the sidewalk and found Mr. Vincent Moore obediently hanging around. "You didn't notice the door had been forced, lock broken?"

"No, it was open just as it would be with the store open for business, and I was just a little surprised, tell you the truth, because you see it was early, we ran out of cigarettes over breakfast and I just came up to the market for cigarettes. I hadn't figured on stopping in here for Marjorie's ring until later, we live just over on Melrose, it's handy, but long as I was here, and I found a place to park on the street, just down there, so I passed Kessler's on my way to the market and I just thought —I don't know what time he usually opened, no, sir."

A white-smocked young man in the little crowd spoke up eagerly. "Nine o'clock, Officer, I know. Set your clock by him, like they say. Anybody around here could tell you. Old Kessler, he'd been here longer than anybody else. Opened at nine A.M. and closed at six on the dot. Poor old boy. He's *dead?* He have a heart attack or what? Must've been seventy-five if he was a day."

The heist man, no, thought Varallo. Or not very likely. Late at night, after everything around here was closed, and ten to one, when they came to find out, nobody but Kessler living upstairs. Nobody to hear shots. Ten to one, somebody breaking in—using a tool on the door—and Kessler hearing it and coming down.

"He's *dead* in there? Horace?" It was a stout woman in a voluminous white apron over a pink-printed cotton dress, and normally her fat face would be florid, but it was pasty-white now and she stepped out of the crowd to confront Varallo, her crookedly-lipsticked small mouth working. "Horace! As wouldn't hurt a fly—why, I run my Cheery Nook Tea Room right next door fifteen years—anybody knew Horace *I* do—a nicer, kinder man there never was, mister—helpin' me out time my sister was in the hospital—and no chick or child of his own, and all the trouble 'n' sorrow he had with his poor wife dyin'—cancer it was an' the doctors' bill just awful, but he just said to me, Myra, it's the Lord's will. *Horace?*" She began to sob noisily. "It's not right, him dyin' all alone like that. *Was* it a heart attack?—'n' no chick or child—an' all the little bit he had left to the Red Cross."

Well, thought Varallo. Somebody to mourn Mr. Kessler, anyway. And this looked like just more of the same they already had with Mrs. Collins. The very anonymous kill. He sighed.

"Here's the doctor and Rhys with the lab kit," said Poor. He sighed too.

CHAPTER 2

"Say eight to ten hours," said Dr. Goulding tersely. Which went right along with what Varallo and Poor were thinking. Eleven to one A.M. last night. The break-in, and Kessler coming to investigate. The punk with the gun.

On a force like Glendale's, there weren't any specialists; they were all competent to do the printing and so on, but in practice the printing usually fell to Burt or Rhys. When the body had been taken away Rhys started dusting the shop while Varallo and Poor asked questions; after a while Varallo went upstairs to the apartment.

The block of shops was owned by the man who owned the furniture store; and except for the little apartment over the end shop, the second floor was used for storage for his stock.

Kessler's apartment told the same story as his shop. The door at the top of the stairs was open: he'd come out in a hurry. There was a neat and shabby small living room, a smaller bedroom, a tiny kitchen, a miniature bathroom. The bed was turned down, a lamp burning on a bedside table. A lamp burning on the scratched kidney-shaped desk in the living room, the desk chair shoved back. Kessler sitting there writing when, presumably, he heard the intruder. Both lamps of low wattage, and only the one in the living room could be noticed from the street. And the punk hadn't known about the apartment upstairs so he hadn't looked.

Nothing looked out of place here. Kessler had been, Varallo discovered, writing in his diary: a lonely, self-contained man, maybe the type to keep one. Varallo looked around the place desultorily: obviously the punk hadn't been here: and ended up back at the desk, looking down at the open pages of the dime-store exercise book a little vaguely and reflecting that unless X had left some prints downstairs this would turn out another one like the Collins thing: where to find a lead?

> . . . do trust I have not taken cold. Throat a trifle sore, I took precaution of having whiskey in a little honey. Mary's old standby. Sold remaining cuckoo clock. Glad to have it off my hands; shall not reorder. . . . Very queer about that Worthington engraving job, but as saying goes, customer always right. Was sure he meant 1939, as for anniversary or some such. Did not charge for correction of course but it made a little trouble for me. Hand not so steady as it was, I fear. *Anno domini.* Next Sunday would have been our golden anniversary if Mary had lived. It is hard to realize. . . . Must remember to buy new ledger soon, current one nearly used. Do not feel that—

That was when he'd heard the punk, thought Varallo. He'd been using an old-fashioned side-filling fountain pen, and cast it down on the blotter uncapped.

Varallo went downstairs and reported his findings. "Yeah," said Poor. "Open and shut, only how do we go looking for who?" It was a rhetorical question; they both knew the answer to that one. They'd look in records for men who had pulled break-ins, and/or similar violence before, find them and haul them in and question them. They might get a hunch who, and question that one hard, in relays, hoping he'd break; or they might never get a smell.

"We got a slug out of the wall," said Poor. "Went right through him, probably. Big one, thirty-eight or forty-five. I tell you, Vic, we're getting too much of this kind of thing. A hell of a lot too much. The random violence, you know. In Glendale, my God. I was just thinking, the first five years I was on this force, we had exactly two murders."

"A while back," commented Rhys sardonically.

"Oh, it was."

"Mess of prints here, probably customers and his own. Are we going to check 'em all out?"

"You know the routine, Bob," said Varallo wryly.

And there'd be a little job for somebody—he hoped not him—routing out Kessler's latest inventory, comparing it with what was here and the books, to make up a list of what had been taken, get some idea of how much cash was missing. Routine! They were indeed getting entirely too much these days of the random violence. . . . He lit a cigarette, watching Rhys dust the shards of glass from inside the case. At least, he reflected, this wasn't a school night. . . . Passed the lieutenant's exam once, but that was a while back too, and a man with any ambition had to keep up with new facets of his profession; so that dedicated cop Varallo was going up to Glendale College two nights a week taking one of the advanced Police Science courses. This semester it was state and federal law; and thinking of that, and the random violence, brought a frown to his regular lean features. Connections, he thought, all right: the damned lenient judges, and the damn-fool new laws so solicitous of criminal's rights, so careless for the rights of all the damn fools idiotic enough to be career cops protecting the honest citizenry.

That was a profitless reflection. They had done about all they could here. See what a ballistics man could tell them about that slug; and any others Goulding might get. Have a look at records.

Kessler, by what the tea-room woman told them, hadn't had any relatives. She had known the name of the lawyer who'd made a will for him: let the lawyer deal with the arrangements. While they looked in records, the strictly routine job.

And meanwhile typed up reports on it. Sometimes a cop got to feeling like a glorified clerk.

They left Rhys still dusting the shop, and went back to headquarters to find O'Connor, alone in the detective bureau, under siege by an outsized and enraged female citizen.

"—An' I'd like to know what I pay taxes for, that's all! What's the good of you dumb cops sittin' around here prob'ly playin' poker all day, with bums like that goin' round stealin' honest people's money? Thirty-four ninety-seven it come to an' I'm here to tell you I'm a workin' woman as can't afford to—"

"Mrs. Shaw," said O'Connor. "Please, Mrs. Shaw—" He threw a goaded look at Varallo.

"—An' just how was *I* to know? I'm expected to have X-ray eyes maybe, he's a nice gentlemanly sort o' lookin' fellow, says it's for his wife, and for heaven's *sake* I know the May Company, big store like that, am I gonna suspect right off a check from the *May* Company? I ask you."

"Please, Mrs. Shaw," said O'Connor. "You're not the first and only one's taken one of those g—those checks, Mrs. Shaw. We know they're being passed, we're looking for—"

"A perfeckly good *refund* check—merchandise returned, he says, and it looked absolutely on the level, an' then the bank tells me—"

"Yes, we know, Mrs. Shaw. If you'd—" Suddenly O'Connor began to cough. He put down his cigarette; his face got red and he glared imploringly at Varallo, who grinned at him behind Mrs. Shaw's broad back and stepped into the breach.

She was fiftyish, much too fat, raddled of complexion, and she didn't like O'Connor at all, but she thawed under Varallo's benign eye, and turned dismayingly coy. Mrs. Myrtle Shaw, it seemed, owned a dress shop, and this perfectly all-right-looking fellow had come in—things for his wife, he said. Oh, he'd passed out other bad checks too?—and she couldn't *afford*— What say? Describe him? Well, she'd know him again if she saw him, but she wasn't much hand at describing—

O'Connor recovered his voice and sat up. "If you're free tomorrow morning, Mrs. Shaw, I'm taking about a dozen people down to head-quarters in L.A. to look at mug photographs." L.A., of course, had many, many more such to look at than Glendale had. "It could be among you we'll spot him, because we think he's a pro. If you'd—"

Mrs. Shaw shied back a step. "I don't know as I care about goin' such a place. All you cops just sittin' here while an honest woman—"

"But if you could identify him," began Varallo persuasively, and she sniffed.

O'Connor started to cough again.

"I don't s'pose I'll get my money back anyways." She looked at O'Connor sourly, glanced back at Varallo. "So thanks for nothin'." She went out stiff-legged.

"Lady a little leery of the L.A. cops?" commented Poor, rolling a form in triplicate into his typewriter.

"Could be," said Varallo. "That's a nasty cough, Charles."

"I've been smoking too damn much," said O'Connor defiantly, "that's all. What about the homicide?"

Varallo told him about the homicide. "Hell," said O'Connor. "Hell and damnation. Another thing like Collins. Couldn't be the same boy, you think?"

"I do not. Break-in sure, but this one used a gun, not just his fists. Only the shop ransacked—he was after the stock, whatever cash there was. It's just a little funny that anybody should have picked that shop— small place, not much stock, not an obviously prosperous place, you know. But on the other hand—" Varallo drove fingers through his crest of blond hair— "it could be even more the random impulsive thing than Collins." He groped for a cigarette. "With Collins, somebody could have picked her because she lived alone, was old and wouldn't put up a fight. Who knows? But Kessler—" He shrugged. "It could be any punk out joy-riding, maybe high on liquor or H. or maybe not—maybe just a punk with empty pockets—all of a sudden spotting a jewelry store and getting the impulse."

"Yes," said O'Connor, "and if he hadn't had the damn gun, would that have made any difference to Kessler? That kind—"

"Probably not," agreed Varallo. "The violent ones. No. Whoever killed Collins didn't need one. Wayne get anything new on that?"

"Oh, for God's sake, it's dead," said O'Connor disgustedly. He flung himself back in his desk chair, which squeaked protestingly; his jacket fell apart to show that cannon he was reputed to sleep with, the favorite S. and W. .357 magnum with the custom rosewood grips, snug in its outsize holster. "He could be in Timbuktu by now—more likely just lying low in the jungle someplace, and we'll never drop on him. Now. It's nearly two weeks ago."

"Wayne didn't get anything new."

"What the hell d'you expect? It was just a last gasp. That kind of damn thing. And so now we go through all the routine on *this* damn thing. I swear to God, Vic, something's damn well gone wrong with people. All these punks—" He started coughing again and Poor told him he ought to go home. "I'm perfectly all right, goddam it! Yeah, and the goddamned purblind citizenry—haul that bunch down to Central tomorrow and they take ten hours looking through all the mug shots of known kite fliers and say, Well, I can't be positive." O'Connor snorted.

But that was how a cop's job went; and all of them tried to be run-of-the-mill good cops at least. So Poor typed up the first report on Kessler while O'Connor, who was still experimentally swallowing to test the not-quite-sore throat, typed up a new report on the kite flier, and Varallo went and pawed through their records looking for anybody and everybody who had ever committed a crime of violence, particularly with a gun. He found seven possibles right away, but he had a vague recollection that one of them was still in Quentin; he'd check. Three of them had local addresses, one in Burbank, one in Van Nuys, one in Hollywood.

That took them up to lunchtime, but Varallo hadn't had lunch yet when Dr. Goulding called. "I'm sending over three slugs. Not too much damaged, you can probably get a make on them."

"Thanks very much," said Varallo. Their little lab already had the one they'd dug out of the wall.

"For what it's worth, I think the first shot killed him. He hadn't bled much. Very healthy old fellow for his age, he looks."

"Yes," said Varallo meaninglessly. "Thanks, Doctor." For no reason he remembered Horace Kessler's diary, left open there on the shabby desk. The lonely old man, no chick or child— Hell, he didn't know

Kessler; the old fellow might have been a bastard, for all he knew, despite the tea-room woman's tears. But whatever he'd been, he hadn't deserved to die for trying to protect his own property.

And Varallo wanted lunch, but he called the lab and asked if they'd made the gun yet.

"I was just about to call you," said Thomsen. "You psychic? Yes, I spotted it for you—slug wasn't much damaged. She's a Combat Masterpiece. S. and W. thirty-eight. Chambered for that thirty-eight Special ammo. And this particular baby's seen a lot of shooting, Vic—she's an old one."

"That so?"

"She's either been knocking around awhile—S. and W. haven't made that one quite some time—or, if she's newer, she's had a hell of a lot of use. And hasn't been taken care of the way a good gun ought to be."

"Oh," said Varallo. "Well, thanks very much."

"Welcome," said Thomsen.

And while it was nice to know that, of course it didn't take them very far as of the moment. Say this Thomas John Holly—with a record of armed assault, latest known residence (1963) on Clark Street in Burbank, should turn out to be in the possession of an old, or mistreated, S. and W. Combat Masterpiece, well, very nice indeed. Once in a while it was just as easy as that.

More often it wasn't.

After lunch, Varallo went out to look for Thomas John Holly, but he had moved. He was now off parole, so nobody knew where he might have gone. His nearest relative was his mother, Mrs. May Holly, and that address proved n.g. too.

Poor was out looking for Jay ("King") Ettman, also from records, also once up for armed assault. Varallo trailed in at three o'clock to find that, surprisingly, Ettman had been right where records said he would be, and Poor and O'Connor were questioning him. Ettman started out snarling and ended up smiling. Last night, bloodhound? I'm but real clean, you got nothing on me. Last night—

Last night Jay Ettman had been in the drunk tank downtown at L.A. Central. As a call to Central established. From eleven ten to eight this morning.

Which was depressing, but a lot of police routine was. They were all used to that kind of thing. They let Ettman go. They lit philosophical cigarettes and looked at other names from records. James Quait, armed assault. Richard Newcomb, assault, rape, armed robbery. Two bets, and no guarantee: you never did know: Kessler could have been a first job for somebody. But you had to work it the tried and true way.

Varallo got home, to the house on Hillcroft Road, at twenty past six, and detoured from the garage to examine Neige Parfum, which was doing splendidly, not a sign of aphis and four new blooms to show him. He sniffed in satisfaction. Still a pretty ridiculous thing, big tough cop Varallo turning into the rose fancier.

"Daddy," said Laura, smiling, opening her arms. His lovely Laura, again his nice slender brown-haired Laura, but— He kissed her.

"Don't you dare," he said severely. "Ever. Of all the pernicious habits, *cara!* I disapprove. Implying I'm *only— La finisca!*"

Laura laughed. "I was only—"

He shook her a little. "Only! Get into a habit like that— I disapprove."

"Well, I do see what you mean. I suppose I do too," said Laura meekly. "I won't, Vic, all right."

Varallo kissed her again and wandered down the hall, to the second bedroom which had become the nursery. Most certainly the best and most beautiful baby ever any set of parents had produced, and even after two months it was still quite uncanny to him how she did resemble her namesake—his lovely golden Ginevra, his lost Ginevra, the younger sister dead so long ago.

She was awake, and he picked her up. The vague blue eyes tried to focus on him. *"Buona sera, carita. Che dice?"*

Laura said from the door, "Quite the expert papa."

"You forget I'm the oldest of seven."

"I'm so terribly glad she's got *hair,* darling. So many babies seem to stay bald until they're practically grown. And I really think it's going to be curly."

"Sure it is. I told you. Just like—"

"Heavens, the potatoes!" exclaimed Laura, and fled. . . . And dutifully asked, over dinner, "Tough day, darling?"

And Varallo shrugged. "Another homicide. Crime rate still going up. Another senseless random thing. With a very small chance of getting X, unless the routine pays off—as it often does, sure. Just keep on looking." Finishing his coffee, he took the last cigarette out of the pack and crumpled the cellophane, and Gideon Algernon Cadwallader appeared out of nowhere, chartreuse eyes intent; Varallo laughed and tossed the crumpled pack to him, and Gideon pounced delightedly, all claws extended.

"He chased the Forsythes' beagle halfway down the block this morning," said Laura. "You'd never know he was neutered."

"Che gatto!" said Varallo.

And it was good to be home, with his lovely Laura and his new darling, but as long as he'd been a cop, sometimes—like any cop—he couldn't just shelve the job at the office, and at the back of his mind there, still, was Horace Kessler sprawled out on the floor of his little shop. Dead, for trying to protect his property. Dead at the hand of one of the nameless ones, the violent ones, after the quick easy loot, and no remote understanding of any basic moral law in them.

The ones the cops had to cope with. Somehow.

And while Varallo finished Thursday night's police-science lesson, and later made love to Laura—and while O'Connor went on telling himself it couldn't be a cold—and while Forbes watched an old movie on TV and John Poor checked his wife's budget and found it as usual exactly on the nose—and Rhys, who lived with his mother, helped her deliver her champion Cairn terrier bitch of six puppies—and the men on night duty sat around the office down there feeling bored—overnight, another woman died. . . .

She always washed her hair on Saturday night. A long time ago, she'd used to go to a beauty parlor to have it done, but Harry did fuss so. Two twenty-five then, and you had to leave a little tip. Probably a lot more now; she wouldn't know. Not as if she'd ever spent much on herself, but Harry—

Oh, well. Maybe it'd have been different if they'd ever had any children, she thought wistfully. The way it was, the business was just everything to Harry, and that was all right too, if he'd just be a little—well, a bit more—well, she didn't know how to put it exactly (even to herself), but she'd read something somewhere once that, in a kind of way, explained it, and made her smile. Had it been in the *Reader's Digest?* Some magazine. People don't change as they grow older—something like that—they just get more like themselves.

It had made her smile. And it was *true.* That was just exactly what people did do, just get *more so.* Like themselves.

So in all likelihood Harry just couldn't help it. It was just Harry. And she hadn't exactly been a silly young girl when she married him—she'd been twenty-seven and Harry twenty-eight. And anyway, Agnes Mac-Donald Gardiner had had a proper bringing up and knew that marriage vows had to be honored . . . *for better or worse,* it said, *in sickness and in health.* . . . Nearly forty years ago— And heaven was her witness she *had* honored them. Harry no more difficult, this way and that way, than most men. A good man, in the main.

And he had built up the business. Trust Harry! They'd never have to worry about old age or illness or such. Thank God, both of them still with their health, even if she was pushing sixty-seven. Strong and well as she'd ever been, she felt.

All that was just at the back of her mind as she busied herself about the house. Their own place, all paid for long ago; and prices up now, they could get a lot more for it if they wanted. But they never would. A nice snug little place, home; nothing fancy because neither of them believed in spending on a lot of show, but a nice house and she kept it just so; she'd always liked things kept neat and clean.

Harry wouldn't be home until around nine thirty. Like always, he'd close the store at nine sharp and then straighten things up some, maybe bring the books up to date, before coming home. The business was to Harry all the family they'd never had—everything. Which was all right.

She glanced at the clock as she unbuttoned her housedress. Six thirty. They always ate early, roundabout five, and Harry'd hurried a bit over it tonight, wanting to get back to the store; he didn't really trust that part-time pharmacist he hired to spell him, but then Harry never really felt anybody could do things the way he did. She smiled, hanging the dress away.

She undressed just to her slip, reflecting that maybe that new diet would help her shed a few pounds. She laid out the towel ready, on the little bench in the bathroom, and got out the bar of old-fashioned pine-tar soap. Say what they did about these new cream shampoos, the old-fashioned—

She heard the little noise at the back door. It always stuck a bit. She was surprised, not frightened. She'd never been a nervous woman, and besides it was early—dark, this time of year, but not quite seven o'clock.

She listened, and came out of the bathroom into the hall.

"Harry?" she called. He couldn't be home at this hour.

She heard the back door open with a little crash. But it was locked, and Harry'd be at the store—

She started down the hall. He must have come home, just a minute, to get something—

She came into the kitchen, and saw the vague shadowy outline of a man in the doorway of the service porch.

"Harry!" she screamed as the first blow descended.

But there was no help from Harry.

CHAPTER 3

So that was waiting for them on Sunday morning. Sunday is just another day for a cop. Once in a long while, by the coincidence of duty, a cop gets Sunday off. Technically, O'Connor had Sundays off this month; but he lived alone in an apartment, and he hadn't much personal to do today until he took his schoolteacher out to dinner tonight, and anyway O'Connor, who was half Scot, not only looked a little like a bulldog but was. Once he got his teeth into a thing— And the kite flier annoyed him. O'Connor, still surreptitiously testing the sore throat, shepherded that bunch of citizens who had innocently accepted the bouncy checks down to Central L.A. headquarters to look at the mug shots.

But Burt and Harrison, on night duty, hung around a few minutes before going off duty to brief the day men about their new homicide.

"Husband came home and found her," said Burt, yawning. "We got called about ten thirty, after the patrol car got there. It looks just exactly like Collins."

"Oh, hell," said Varallo and Katz together. Poor just looked glum.

"Yeah. I printed the whole place," said Burt. "It was a mess. I don't have to tell you. Ransacked. We've got photographs too—all that bit's done, and I suppose you'll get something out of Goulding today or tomorrow about the body. Naturally we couldn't press the husband too hard, time like that."

"Neighbors hear anything—if any?"

"That is a little funny," said Harrison. "But I guess not really, if he knocked her unconscious first thing. Neighbors close on both sides, but nobody heard anything. Back door was forced."

"Um," said Varallo. "Much taken?"

"I ask you, how could we press the poor guy?" asked Burt through another yawn. "He comes home from work and finds his wife beaten to death. A mess—like it always is. Drawers dumped out all over the floor, blood all over—can we ask him to start taking inventory? Couple in the late sixties, married nearly forty years I gather. He's a pharmacist, has his own store out on Glenoaks. So you take it from there, boys."

"Thanks so much."

"Prosperous?" asked Poor laconically.

Burt shook his head. "What maybe makes it worse. Like Mrs. Collins. Little people. Getting along, but not millionaires. This Gardiner, maybe pretty substantial, modest sort of way—the kind doesn't throw it around—but nothing big. Well, the address is Fifth Street. Ordinary middle-class district. It could for my money very well be the same joker who took off Collins. Same exact m.o., if you can say there is much m.o. about breaking in a house and beating somebody to death and robbing the place."

Katz said reflectively, "There were four-five repeaters we had in to question on Collins who are still up in the air. Haul them in again?"

"Yes," said Varallo. "Just for kicks." That was one of the depressing things about police work, in a free country. The citizen was presumed innocent until proven guilty. So, on Collins, there had been that Theodore Reinfeld, for instance, with a record of burglary and armed assault, just the type of boy who might be X; so they found him and questioned him, and he said on the night of February 18 (when Mrs. Collins had probably been killed, but Goulding couldn't pin it down within twelve hours) he'd been alone in his apartment, and all next morning too. With no exact time of death, what did they have? A great big nothing. There were others like that. There were, of course, still the pawnbrokers' lists: if some identifiable loot from the Collins house—and now Harry Gardiner's house—should turn up, and the pawnbroker could identify Reinfeld—or another man—as connected with it, fine and dandy. But X might know a fence, say over in L.A., and the loot never show. And a lot of the loot wouldn't be identifiable: cash, old diamonds taken out of their mountings.

"One thing," said Harrison. "The intern said she'd been dead between three and four hours. Well, you know interns—cocksure sometimes. See what you get from Goulding. But if so, that puts it between six and seven, about, which is kind of early for that sort of thing. In a neighborhood where the houses are that close."

"Oh, really?" said Varallo. "Yes, indeed. Dark, but there'd have been lights on."

"I guess. Well, have fun," said Burt. He and Harrison went off. At least nothing new had been heard from the heist man. O'Connor was doing what could be done about the kite flier; and there wasn't anything else to do about Horace Kessler except the tiresome routine: making up a tentative list of what was missing from his stock, and also collecting the prints of everybody who'd been in his place recently—if possible— thus hoping to isolate any strange ones Rhys had picked up. Naturally Joe Katz came in for the first job; his father being a jeweler, he was familiar with the business; and Rhys went with him to start asking around all the other places as to who might have been in Kessler's shop lately.

Varallo and Poor took Varallo's old Chevy and headed for their new homicide on Fifth Street.

"I can't get over it," said Poor. "She doesn't wake up at all?"

"Eight to six thirty, right through," said Varallo. "That first week she did wake up for a meal at two A.M., but no fuss. And even if there was, it wouldn't concern me—Laura's nursing her."

"Brother, it would concern you if she was a normal ordinary baby," said Poor feelingly. "Stevie you could hear for blocks. I'm telling you. You just don't know how lucky you are, that's all. Jean keeps saying— well, it'd be kind of nice to maybe have a sister for him, if it turned out that way of course, but the idea of going through all that again—brother. I never heard of a baby that didn't yell at night."

"Well, you have now," said Varallo complacently. It was nice to hear confirmation of the fact that his darling was so exceptional.

"You want to turn at Grandview."

"I know."

Fifth Street was a rather odd little street running off at an angle. The funny thing about Glendale, Varallo thought, was that you could stand up there on Mount Hollywood looking over the valley and the city of Glendale looked like a chessboard: ruler-straight, criss-cross streets, up, down and across. But actually driving the streets, you found all sorts of jogs and dead ends and streets shooting off diagonally. Glenwood Road, along here, stopped dead at Grandview and turned into Fifth Street, which shot off at an angle. It was a street of solid middle-class houses, frame and stucco, middle-aged houses, most of them well kept up with green lawns.

The one they wanted was a frame house painted white with green trim. The driveway was the old-fashioned kind, twin cement strips with a stretch of grass between. The separate single garage was closed. There was a cement walk up to the narrow front porch across the width of the house. They left the Chevy at the curb and went up the walk.

The house on the right was a stucco box with pink curtains showing at the front windows. Varallo saw one of them twitch and felt eyes on them. Naturally.

Poor pushed the bell, and they heard chimes inside. They waited. Presently Poor pushed the bell again. In about thirty seconds the door opened.

"Mr. Gardiner?" said Varallo politely. "We're from headquarters, we'd like to talk to you if you don't mind. We're sorry to disturb you at a time like this—"

"I suppose it can't be helped," said Gardiner thinly. He stood looking at them for a moment. "You're not the same ones who were here last night."

"No, sir. Those were the detectives on night duty. I'm Detective Varallo, and this is Detective Poor."

"Oh, of course," said Gardiner. "I see. I suppose you would have—shifts, like that. Not like being in business for yourself. Well, come in. I've hardly got things straight yet—you can see how it is."

He was a tall old man, a little stooped, thin and going bald, with just a fringe of gray hair around his head. He was neatly dressed, if shabbily, in a pair of ancient olive green slacks and a frayed white shirt, tieless, and his brown shoes were polished if cracked. He blinked at them from behind horn-rimmed glasses, shepherding them into the living room, and he said, "Agnes would have a fit. Just a fit. I will say she is—was—an orderly housekeeper. I hardly know where to start. That doctor gave me a sedative, you see, and I only woke up about an hour ago. The kitchen floor—"

Varallo looked around the living room and felt depressed. He had an orderly mind himself. He'd seen such sights often enough before to have reached the conclusion that, even excluding murder, the ordinary burglar added insult to injury by leaving the mess behind.

It was, or had been, an ordinary middle-class living room of the kind such a couple could be predicted to own. There was the old overstuffed sofa and matching armchair, dark green, two smaller armchairs, green and beige, and a large stuffed ottoman. There was a mantel with a clock on it and a rectangular frameless mirror hung over it. There was a large lithographed landscape over the couch. There were lamps with ruffled shades, there was an American Oriental carpet underfoot. And there were handmade antimacassars on all the chairs and the sofa.

But chaos had struck the prim old-fashioned order. All the chair cushions had been dumped on the floor, the chairs overturned; the seat cushions from the sofa ditto. The clock lay on its face. All the drawers of a little maple chest serving as a lamp table had been yanked out and upended on the floor. There was a blank space in one corner where, probably, a TV or radio had stood. And the bedrooms would look the same.

Varallo remembered that he hadn't asked Burt whether the bathroom medicine chest had been ransacked. The one in Mrs. Collins' house had been, and that said that their boy could be on dope, looking for same.

"I guess you'd better sit down," said Gardiner. He picked up a cushion and fitted it back into a chair, began replacing the cushions in the sofa. "I really don't know where—" He shook his head. "Agnes would have a fit. I suppose I haven't really taken it in yet." He sat down in one of the smaller chairs and touched his glasses nervously.

Varallo and Poor sat down on the couch. "You understand, we don't like to bother you, Mr. Gardiner, but if we're going to drop on whoever did this we have to ask questions. Could you—"

"I understand that, sir. Of course. The men who came—last night— were very nice about it. I know. Do you—do you think it could have been whoever—did that—to that other poor woman, the other side of town?" He touched his glasses again. "It—just occurred to me. From what I read in the paper, you know. It seems—well, it's hard to imagine anyone doing such a thing."

"Yes, it is," said Varallo sympathetically. "That could be, Mr. Gardiner. Now, could you give us any idea of what's missing here, what's been taken? Would there have been much cash in the house?"

Harry Gardiner blinked and touched his glasses. "No, very little. I—we were always careful about that. As a professional man, and I think I may say a good businessman too—I have built up my own little place quite well, you know—I never like too much cash around." He touched his glasses. "Yes, I can tell you that—what you asked. I don't suppose Agnes would have had over five dollars in her purse. Saturday, you know. She always does—did the weekly marketing on Saturday." Involuntarily he glanced across the room: on one corner of the mantel stood a leatherette-framed photograph, obviously an enlargement of a snapshot. It showed Gardiner, unsmiling, beside a neat, rather dowdy little woman. She was a trifle too plump, but her smile was cheerful; she had graying brown hair in an old-fashioned style, parted and hanging loosely to her shoulders, and she wore a plain printed cotton dress. "I'd give her a check for fifteen dollars, usually, and of course she'd spend most of that at the market." Gardiner frowned, looking down at his interlaced hands. "Oh, during the week she'd shop again for a few things, but the main marketing—call it eight or ten dollars in cash. And—" He blinked around the room. "Whoever it was took the TV set. And—"

"Can you give me a description of that, please?" Varallo got out his notebook.

"Well, it's an RCA—just a small one—portable, they call it, I think. A beige color," said Gardiner. "I didn't care for it myself, a waste of good money I call it, the silly shows they put on—but Agnes kept at me. I paid a hundred and thirty-nine fifty for it a year ago."

"I suppose you don't know the serial number, sir?"

"No, I don't."

"Was there a guarantee with it, Mr. Gardiner?" asked Poor. "The serial number would be on that, or if so the store would have a record."

"Oh. Yes, I suppose so. I kept the guarantee until it was up—that was just last month. No, I don't know. I got it at a discount house." He named it. "And there's Agnes' jewelry, that's gone too. Some of the costume jewelry too. She hadn't much, but some. Her engagement ring, that's a very good stone, a diamond of course, twenty-five points. I paid three hundred and fifty dollars for it, of course that was a long while ago but diamonds—"

"Can you describe the mounting, Mr. Gardiner? Was it yellow or white gold?"

"Yellow." Gardiner touched his glasses. "A plain sort of mounting, I suppose you'd call it. Not a Tiffany setting. I don't know much about jewelry, but I know that. And there was a garnet pin—it was her grandmother's—several large garnets—and a garnet and pearl ring she used to wear a lot—and a pair of amethyst earrings—all family things, you know. I suppose you'd say old-fashioned things—and one of those wide engraved gold bracelets, and her watch—"

"What sort of watch?"

"Oh, a Hamilton. She'd had it for years. It's yellow gold, on a gold band. No diamonds, no, of course not. And then there was a little cheap jewelry. Not much. What they call costume. Pearls—not real ones, I mean." Gardiner looked around the room. "That's all gone."

"Mr. Gardiner, if there was any liquor in the house, was it touched?" asked Poor. "Or—"

Gardiner looked faintly outraged. "I am a teetotaler," he said stiffly. "No, of course not. Why—"

"Just wondering," said Poor.

"Can you give us a more detailed description of this jewelry?" asked Varallo.

"Oh, I suppose so. The garnet pin, it's one of those old-fashioned sunburst pins. The ring—" He pondered. "There are four or five garnets in the middle, and pearls all around. I don't know what they'd be worth."

Varallo absently reached for his cigarettes and then thrust the pack back into his pocket. No ashtrays here.

"I suppose I haven't taken it *in*," said Gardiner. "It's really very odd to think, you know. I couldn't help thinking about it." His tone was absent. "I suppose some people might have thought—leaving Agnes alone so much—but if you have a business, a profession, well, you work at it. And I have built it up. She wasn't a nervous woman, she never minded being alone, the evenings the store's open—and I was always home by ten at least, you know. Not very late. But that young intern—I remember, last night, he said she'd been killed three or four hours ago then. That would be between six and seven o'clock, wouldn't it?—and there I was in the store, as it might have been making up a prescription or something, right then, and not knowing at all." He shook his head.

Poor muttered sympathetically.

"And she always kept both doors locked after dark. No sense inviting burglars," said Gardiner, "is there? She was probably just getting ready to wash her hair—she always did that on Saturday nights. I'd have been home earlier, I usually am, but I stayed to bring the books up to date. I like to keep them up." He smiled thinly. "To know where I stand. I closed the store at nine, of course—or a few minutes later, old Mr. Coulter had been in quite late, for his reserpine—but I stayed to work on the books. It was nearly ten when I got home—and found her. It seems queer to think—while she was—was being killed, there I was just maybe quietly making up a prescription."

"Yes, sir. Do you mind if we look around a little?"

"Oh, no, whatever you like. I just hardly knew where to start—you'll have to forgive how things look."

"That's all right, Mr. Gardiner," said Varallo. "This is all you can think of that's missing from the house?"

"Yes, I think so. I—Agnes and I've never been much for spending on luxuries."

Varallo put his notebook away; he and Poor got up. Gardiner trailed after them listlessly as they went into the front bedroom, where chaos had also struck: bureau drawers dumped out on the floor, a sparse collection of female cotton underwear, sweaters, stockings tumbled out: male underwear, old and mended, socks. Clothes pulled out of the closet, in a heap. In the second bedroom, the bureau drawers had evidently been empty. Guest room. The front bedroom furniture old-fashioned, but walnut: in the other bedroom, cheap painted pine, and no rug on the floor.

Varallo opened the middle door in the hall. A small square bathroom: blue and white plastic tile, a chipped but spotless pullman washstand, medicine cabinet above. He opened that: everything had been printed last night. Two plastic tumblers each containing a toothbrush, a lone bottle of aspirin, a Schick razor in its plastic case.

"Would there have been anything else here, Mr. Gardiner? Any prescriptive medicines, codeine or—"

Gardiner said, sounding surprised, "Oh, no. No. I'm afraid—" he touched his glasses—"I'm the wrong side of the counter for, you know, dosing myself with this and that. And Agnes was very healthy."

They went on down the hall to the kitchen. And on the threshold Varallo stopped and—as long as he'd been a cop, and all the things he'd seen, the blood and dirt and ugliness and sin—he felt a little unaccustomed sting in his eyes.

Gardiner, that orderly man, had started to wash the kitchen floor. There was a plastic pail of soapy water and the rag he'd been using left on the floor.

Varallo tried to imagine how it would be, and he couldn't. The woman (Laura, his lovely Laura) you'd fallen in love with and married, and lived with (*in sickness and in health*—well, of course they'd driven over to Vegas to get married by a judge, but—) for nearly forty years, and you came home one night and found her beaten to death on the kitchen floor. By one of the violent ones, the amoral animalistic hoods. You called the cops, and they were nice and kind, the police doctor gave you a sedative, you were in shock, and then inevitably you woke up. Next morning.

With life, your ordinary quiet workaday life, lying in ruins.

What did you do?

Well, a man like Gardiner, you started to wash the kitchen floor.

You thought numbly, Agnes would have a fit. All the mess. The chaos in what had been your quiet orderly home. (The personal laundry done on Monday; beds changed on Saturdays; weekly marketing for staple items; the planned routine.) You thought, Agnes couldn't leave the place that way, and so you started to clean it up. To wash away Agnes' blood.

The linoleum was ancient, but it had been polished. It was light blue and white, and the tile on the drainboard was plain white. From here he could see into the service porch: an old semi-automatic washer, and there were splinters of wood on the floor where the outside door had been forced—crudely, hastily, even as Horace Kessler's front door had been forced—and Mrs. Collins' back door.

The violent ones.

"She was in the kitchen," said Gardiner, "you know. She must have heard him—whoever—breaking in the door. And came to see. She—she wasn't a nervous woman. I think she was just about to start washing her hair, she was—partly undressed."

And it could very well be the same joker who had broken in and killed Mrs. Collins two weeks ago.

Varallo thanked him. "If you think of anything else that might have been taken, Mr. Gardiner—when you're straightening things up—will you let us know? You know we'll be on it—we'll be after him."

"Well, I hope so. Yes. Yes, I'll do that, but I think I've told you about all there is." Gardiner blinked at them.

In the Chevy, Poor said, "It's a bastard. For my money, the Collins boy."

"That I'll buy," said Varallo. "It looks like. So, a local?"

"So," said Poor, "we talk to the neighbors first, and then haul in Reinfeld and all the other possibles again, find out if they've got alibis."

"So," said Varallo, "we do just that, and see. Join the cops and see life."

"Yeah," said Poor. "In the raw."

CHAPTER 4

"Oh, my, that poor woman. That *poor* woman. I can hardly believe it."
Mrs. Pearl Glover looked at the two detectives avidly. "And us right
here all evening and never heard a *thing*. *Beaten* to death? You mean
like that other woman, couple of weeks ago, I saw in the paper? I can't
get over it—Mrs. Gardiner!"

Mrs. Glover lived next to the Gardiners on the right side, in the
stucco house with pink curtains. She was a big-boned woman, only a
couple of inches under Poor's five eleven, she might be forty-five, she
had a lot of rather wild hair of the color called pepper-and-salt and she
was the kind of woman who was very simply and genially interested in
everybody. But she wasn't being much help to them.

"I told the officers last night when they came—different ones they
were—we didn't hear a *thing*. I can't get *over* it. Mrs. *Gardiner*. Such a
nice respectable soul—a nice woman. Never heard her say an unkind
thing about anybody, and I must say it doesn't seem fair—a thing like
that—after what she had to put up with! That husband of hers. Now
mind you, Jim and me, we aren't extravagant for all he brings home
good pay, I don't mean to say I hold with wasting money on things like
liquor and big cars and, you know, fur coats and all like that. But there's
a *limit*. I mean, my Lord, there he's got his own drugstore, a good substantial living, and she didn't even have a regular washing machine! *Everybody's* got a washing machine, even some of those hillbillies down
South! Never saw her with anything on but a cotton dress, she did her
own hair you could tell, and she invited me in sometimes for coffee,
mornings—a nice woman, I think she was awful lonely with him gone so
much—and I've seen the house, not even a rug in the bedroom! Grudges
every penny, that man. And she never complained. Never said a word
against him. Just how *careful* Harry was about money, she'd say." Mrs.

Glover sniffed. "Miserly, I call it. I got a new washer-dryer last year—the all-in-one kind, you know—and she did admire it, and don't tell me they couldn't afford one—him with his own store and all."

"Well, Mrs. Glover," said Varallo, "some people just like to save money. You didn't hear any unusual noises—say between six thirty and seven thirty?"

"I did not, and I can't get *over* it. Right next door while *that* was going on! Well, Micky barked, but he barks at anything. He barks a lot. I don't take any notice. When I told the other officers that they went out in our back yard and looked, but there wasn't any footprints or anything, I guess, or they'd have said. . . . No, sir, Micky's a real friendly dog, he wouldn't go after anybody, stranger or anybody. Just bark—he barks a lot, for no reason. Mr. Gardiner complained about it a couple of times. No, Jim got home usual time, about six thirty, and I had dinner most ready, we ate about seven and I had all the dishes done by eight or so. And never suspected a *thing*. Well, it was dark, of course, I saw Mrs. Gardiner's kitchen light and the light in the front room. He came home like always about a quarter of five, it was light then and anyway I hear the car even if I'm not in the kitchen, like you see their drive's on the side toward our house—and off back to his store he goes a bit after five thirty, and the kitchen light on while she did her dishes I suppose, and then off. And Jim and I watched TV and never a noise or anything until I hear Mr. Gardiner drive in about ten o'clock, and pretty soon—we was just going to bed—the cops' cars and all. I can't believe it yet—in *our* neighborhood! Always been a nice quiet neighborhood—and a nice woman like Mrs. Gardiner."

They got away from her eventually. The people on the other side were named Willetts, and Varallo and Poor caught them just leaving for church, but there was nothing to be got there anyway because, it transpired, the Willetts always went out to dinner on Saturday nights, had left at six and didn't get home until eight-thirty.

"I think," said Varallo, getting into the Chevy, "we want to have a little conference with Wayne."

"Good idea," said Poor. Both of them had been on night tour up to the last week, and didn't know much about the Collins thing; Wayne had been on that from the start. This did look very much like the same thing. The average break-in did not include murder. And the likelihood, in a town this size, of two jokers wandering around who were the type to beat to death the surprised householder, couldn't be very high. That sounded like the psychopath. The random killer-on-impulse. The real violent one.

They went back to headquarters to see if Wayne was in. He was. He was sitting at his desk reading a report on the heist man, and put it down without reluctance to listen to Varallo.

"You can see it looks like the same boy. From what I've heard on Collins. You were on that, what do you think?" Varallo propped himself on the desk opposite, lighting a cigarette.

"It does indeed," said Wayne thoughtfully, straightening up in his chair. Varallo wondered academically how Sergeant Fred Wayne had succeeded in staying a bachelor: he wasn't more than average good-looking but he was built like Tarzan, and could have earned a living posing for life classes. As he stretched now, the big muscles rippled under his shirt. "I could use a cup of coffee," he said.

"I'll go get some." Poor went down the hall.

"Yes, indeed," said Wayne. "What loot did he get?" Varallo passed over his notebook and Wayne studied the entries interestedly. "Hum. Not a hell of a lot compared to what X got from Collins. And it's a little funny he wasn't heard there either, that house is pretty close to neighbors too. Fifty-foot lots—old part of town. Pretty much the same kind of neighborhood. Substantial middle class. It was just our damn bad luck she wasn't found for so long. As it was, we couldn't pin down the time of death. Anywhere from Tuesday night to Wednesday night. She was a widow, sixty-nine, lived alone. Her husband had been a bank teller. They'd saved, and she had real estate. The kind that can be a gold mine—low rental property." Poor came back with paper cups of coffee and he took one with a grunt of thanks. "I could also have a guess that old Mrs. Collins had learned a lesson from the Depression—or somewhere. About the tangible assets. Because she didn't spend much on herself, or the house—by what we got—but her daughter could tell us plenty. Mrs. Collins a very canny old lady, and the daughter had a duplicate inventory of everything valuable in the house. What Mrs. Collins spent money on—" Wayne drank and swore, setting the paper cup down— "My God, that's hot! Why didn't you warn me?—spent money on was diamonds. And she kept 'em at home. I've got a list—show it to you. Upward of ten grand worth."

"*Per carità!*" said Varallo. "You don't tell me."

"I do. Daughter—who lives over in Hollywood, married—was kind of resentful about it. I don't blame her. There were odds and ends of other things—another portable TV, an old fur coat, wrist watch, little hoard of coins she'd been saving, a couple of clocks, lot of little stuff like that, but the diamonds were the main haul. Windfall for him. Daughter says nobody but her knew about them—old lady didn't wear them. Daughter also says mother was very careful, always kept the house locked up—but they want in, they're going to get in. That kind."

"Yes. How did he get in?" Varallo sipped coffee.

"Forced the back door. It took some strength, Vic, because she had one of those patent bolts on it—you know the kind, not a regular long bolt that slides across but the little one that fastens on the jamb and folds back across the door. Door was also locked. And that kind of bolt is really the best kind, because while it isn't as long as a regular bolt horizontally, it's a good two inches long vertically and exerts that much more resistance. X tore it clean out—inch-and-a-half screws holding it. With a jemmy of some sort, tire iron or what have you."

"You don't say. A Samson."

"Well, with a good strong tool and the right leverage, the average man could do it. But it would make a little noise. And this is another reason why I go along with your thinking on Gardiner." Wayne cautiously sampled the coffee again. "We couldn't pinpoint the time, but on Gardiner you can—between six and seven, give or take some. Now I thought about the Collins thing, and I don't think our boy broke in that house very late at night. *Because* she wasn't found for four days, if you take me. It's a quiet neighborhood, and houses close. Middle-aged people, old people—not much noise, even cars passing, say after ten o'clock. I think if he'd broken in at say midnight, it'd have been heard. The back door is just across the driveway from the nearest neighbors' bedrooms."

"Oh," said Varallo. "Oh, I see. Yes."

"Yes, indeed. Mrs. Collins would have heard and got up, maybe had time to call us. The neighbors would have been waked up. When that bolt gave, Vic, it made a little racket. Not to mention the jemmy being forced in to start with. It'd be a loud sharp crack—like a cap pistol. Now I got from the daughter that Mrs. Collins liked her main meal in the middle of the day. She'd have a cup of tea, a sandwich, some cookies, something like that, about five o'clock, and then another snack before she went to bed about ten. So any time between, call it, six and nine thirty, she wouldn't have been in her kitchen, near that back door. *And* the neighbors, between five thirty and six thirty or seven, wouldn't have been in their bedrooms near Mrs. Collins' back door. *And* by then it'd be dark, this time of year. *I* think," said Wayne, "that he came some time between six and nine. Even six and eight."

"I get you," said Varallo. "Where was she found and what did the autopsy say about stomach contents?"

"Whoosh, we do have at least one bright cop around," said Wayne, grinning at him.

"*È come!* You forget I resigned as captain upstate—it's just more experience."

"You'll make sergeant yet. She was found in the dining room, which is in the middle of the house between the bedroom wing and the kitchen wing."

"Yes. Heard him, some strange noise at least, and was coming to investigate. Or—where's the phone?"

"Oh, please, not *so* brilliant, Vic. I can't take it, you'll give me an inferiority complex. The phone's in the kitchen."

"Very neat," said Varallo. "So she could have been coming—posthaste as they say—to call the cops. And?"

"And there were tea and pound cake and what was probably a lettuce sandwich in the stomach."

"Which sort of clinches it, doesn't it?" said Poor. "Between five and ten anyway, that says."

"Well, it says so to me," said Wayne, "whether it was Tuesday or Wednesday night. And I don't know what more that says to our genius here, but it says to me—" he hunched his wide shoulders— "a real wild one. A psycho of some kind, moron or whatever. You know the kind—cops on big-city forces see more of 'em—the kind who just lash out and kill, no rhyme or reason. Or go berserk when they see the blood. In both of these cases, there wasn't any need to kill the woman, my God. Both elderly women, couldn't put up much of a fight if they tried. Easy enough to knock 'em out, maybe tie 'em up and go through the house at leisure. But instead—murder." Wayne grimaced. "The Collins woman, God, she had taken a beating—there were bones broken. Goulding said he doubted there was any weapon used, just fists, but he thought she'd been picked up and slammed against the floor, against the furniture."

"My good God," said Poor mildly.

"A Samson," repeated Varallo.

"Well, she wasn't very big, Vic. Only weighed ninety-eight pounds."

"Nevertheless, that's what it says to me, Fred. Somebody big and strong. Considering that bolt. He didn't have as much trouble at the Gardiners'. No bolt on the door, just a lock—and an old one. A Samson could break it in with a few jolts from the shoulder. But it does very much sound like the one we want for Collins, doesn't it?"

"Yes indeed," said Wayne. "I wouldn't want to think there were two like that running around loose on our beat. And another little thought I had, Vic—"

"Yes, I know," said Varallo absently. "Could be it's not our beat. Could be it's some psycho from the big city over the hill. They have got more of them over there—let's see, the county population's up to around seven and a half million, isn't it?—and almost everybody's got access to a car. And so, it might be a halfway smart idea for somebody to take a little trip down to L.A. Central H.Q. and say, please, may we peek at your records? Because about a thousand to one, a joker like this has *got* some kind of record of violence."

"Oh, I may as well shoot myself," said Wayne. "A genius yet. Yes indeedy, you may go to the head of the class, Detective Varallo. That was just exactly the thought I had."

"Did you get anything suggestive?"

Wayne shrugged. "About twenty-five more punks to look at. If we'd been able to narrow down the time, something significant might have showed. As it was—all up in the air."

"I understand there were a couple of likelies in our own records."

"That too." Wayne sighed. "I don't know, boys, seems to me the jungle just gets junglier all the time. That kind. What's the answer?"

"We don't have to make the answer," said Varallo. "We're just here to catch them. I don't think there is any answer, except human nature."

"Then it's getting more damn human all the time," said Wayne; and Jeff Forbes came in, looking mad. His dark hair was ruffled madly as if he'd been running fingers through it. He flung his lank six two into his desk chair abruptly.

"This arrogant bastard," he said. "Do you know he just pulled a heist in broad daylight—on a Sunday morning—at a church!"

"A *church?*" said Varallo, Poor and Wayne together.

"I'm telling you. A church. A Catholic church. The Church of the Immaculate Heart up on Brand. He timed it after Mass, when everybody was gone and the priest had time to get back into his house which is next door—this bastard rings the bell cool as be damned and holds up the priest and his housekeeper. He got the whole damned collection," said Forbes.

"Well, I will be damned," said Wayne. "Do we get any description? Sound like the same boy that took off the other places?"

"Oh, for God's sake," said Forbes. "What else? Yes, it sounds like the same boy. Young man, medium-size, medium-to-dark coloring, take your choice about eyes, dark slacks, blue shirt this time. And a gun."

"Helpful," said Wayne.

"You say it twice! Rhys is bringing them both in for a session with an artist and the Identikit, but you want to bet we'll get anything useful?"

"No bets."

"I never heard of anything like—holding up a church! He got about fifty bucks. I ask you." Forbes slammed the triplicate blank reports into his typewriter.

"And no leads on him at all?" asked Poor.

"Oh, we've got *leads*. Out of records. I suppose we'll drop on him eventually." Forbes started to type, referring to his notebook.

"Well," said Varallo, standing, "I suppose we'd better follow up what leads we've got on Samson. Did you mention somebody named Reinfeld, John?"

"For a start. And also we'd better look at all the thugs Fred turned up from Central's records. "

They found Theodore Reinfeld, a big slob of a punk with a long record, from little to big—Grand Theft Auto as a juvenile, to armed robbery—and they asked him questions. He was living with his mother, who was a lush, over in the Atwater section, and he had a part-time job at a car-wash place. He was currently on parole, and he protested that he was real clean, he hadn't done nothing.

Last night, he said, uh, well, last night he'd been right here, hadn't gone no place. Watching TV.

His mother said so too. Which of course said nothing. But while Reinfeld was a big one, and had the record, Varallo didn't feel that essential violence in him. The kind of violence that went berserk. Reinfeld, he thought, the run-of-the-mill pro, which meant essentially the lazy slob. The drifter. Irresponsible and allergic to an honest day's work, given the wrong kind of associates and environment, they just naturally turned into the pro hoods. They were usually—like Reinfeld—pretty stupid. Once in a while they graduated to murder, but it was usually by accident. That kind wasn't the kind who, breaking violently into a house to steal, battered the householder dead with that kind of fury.

There were others to find and question. They went looking. One name took them clear out to Van Nuys, and when they found their quarry he was in the hospital and had been for four days. They didn't get anywhere, but they put in a full day.

Varallo had just got back to his desk at five thirty when Dr. Goulding called.

"The Gardiner woman. I got right on it—occurred to me it could be the same boy accounted for Mrs. Collins."

"It occurred to us too," said Varallo dryly. "What've you got on it?"

"Well, she was banged up," said Goulding inelegantly. "I think this time he used a weapon. Maybe whatever he used to break in the door. Something fairly sharp, anyway—a wrench, a jemmy, take your choice. What actually killed her was a blow on the temple—simple language—but she took some punishment otherwise. She'd bled a good deal. It'd be my guess—not that I'm trying to do your job for you, but I gather she didn't scream, didn't have a chance—that she was knocked unconscious almost at once, and didn't move much from where she was first struck down. Judging by the blood."

"Yes. Can you pin down the time?"

"Within fairly narrow limits, yes. We got her quick enough. Let's see, she was found about ten o'clock, on Saturday night—yes, well, she didn't die earlier than six or later than seven thirty. We know she had a meal about five o'clock," said Goulding cheerfully, "by what the husband says. Ground beef, green salad, mashed potatoes, corn and coffee. That's O.K., all present and digested roughly about two hours."

"Yes," said Varallo. "Thanks very much." He had been feeling hungry.

"Hope you catch him," said Goulding. "Not one to have running around loose."

"No, Doctor," said Varallo. Rhys came in with Katz and announced sourly that they'd got damn all on Kessler.

"Just a lot of prints that mean nothing. The tea-room woman had been in Kessler's place, but she's the only one we've marked. Advertise in the paper for everybody who set foot in the place the last few days? Argh!" said Rhys. "One thing. The cash register was wiped clean."

"So you don't waste time advertising and comparing prints," said Varallo. "That tells you right off he took no chances, he wiped everything."

"I can add two and two," said Rhys.

Wiry little Katz slumped into his desk chair and contemplated ink-stained fingers. "I couldn't get his books to balance. There's an item of six seventy-five I couldn't account for," he said wearily. "But there's a line blanked out in the ledger for February twelfth. I can't figure it—maybe a mistake, or maybe some customer decided at the last minute not to buy something Kessler'd already written the bill on. What I do come up with, there's about a grand missing. In value. It was a piddling little business, Vic. Peanuts. He didn't get an engraving job once in a blue moon. The synthetic birthstone rings, the alarm clocks, the cheap wedding sets—fifteen-point diamond engagement rings—the twenty-nine ninety-five wrist watches for graduation presents. Like that. What's gone is worth about a grand. Wholesale. I made up a list. Some synthetic rings, watches, a few diamonds. A fence might hand him two fifty for it, maybe not that much."

"Well," said Varallo thoughtfully, "which in a way makes it look all the more like the punk joy-riding around and all of a sudden spotting a jewelry store."

"And he died for it," said Katz. "For that. What makes sense, Vic? Just because the punk happened to have a gun on him. . . . Sometimes I get tired."

"Don't we all," said Forbes over the clatter of his typewriter. O'Connor marched in, stopped at his desk, and started to cough. He pulled out a handkerchief.

"How's the throat?" asked Poor.

O'Connor coughed, swallowed, with a supreme effort regained control and straightened to beam at them. O'Connor's beam was like the smile of a hungry shark. O'Connor, the prototype tough cop, who had just squeaked by requirements at five nine but made up for it in breadth —O'Connor still the holder of the top trophy for marksmanship of the California Peace Officers—O'Connor was pleased and happy. Despite his incipient cold.

"I am," he said hoarsely, frowning at Poor, "perfectly all right, goddamn it. We do cuss the citizenry, but sometimes they come through. They made him—by God, they made him. Looking at all the damn mug shots. They did damn well make him, bless their little hearts." He pulled out a typewritten page. "By Christ, we've got an official description and a mug shot and his prints. And guess who—just guess. Off the Ten Most Wanted, FBI. George Leland Hollison—got a record to hell and back—he dabbled in counterfeit awhile back—and he lands in Glendale of all places. We even, for God's sake, made his girl friend. She's got a record too."

"Congratulations," said Varallo. "Now all you have to do is catch them."

O'Connor scowled at him. "Goddamned comic, aren't you? Now we know who they are—"

"Go and pick up your schoolteacher," said Varallo, grinning at him. "You need a shave and a clean shirt, but she's probably used to you by now."

CHAPTER 5

Varallo took off a little early and drove across town to the only hardware store he knew of which was open on Sundays to nine P.M., and bought a pair of those little patent bolts.

"And look," he said to Laura, getting out the screwdriver from the little chest in the service porch where they kept the tools and extra light bulbs, "you use them, *cara*. See? I want these shot by the time it's dark every night."

"For heaven's sake, Vic!" said Laura. "It's dark before you're home now."

"So you can come and let me in when you know it's me. Look," said Varallo, "we've got this wild one loose. He's killed two women right here in town. One on Geneva Street, which is only about a mile away from here. God alone knows where he might go wandering, and in both cases we know about it's been early when he broke in."

"Oh," said Laura. "Well, I do see what you mean."

"Yes. You just don't know with one like that. He could turn up anywhere." Varallo got the first screw in tight and started on the second. "Never does any harm to take precautions, you know."

"I suppose not, but it'll be a nuisance."

"So you cuss it, you're still alive. You and our hostage to fortune."

"How does it work?"

He illustrated. "You just lift it and fold it across the door. And see you remember to do it."

"Oh, all right," said Laura, and went back to the stove. "Dinner in about ten minutes, darling."

Varallo went to the front of the house with the second bolt to put it on the front door, but passing the nursery on the way discovered his new darling awake, chuckling to herself and playing with her toes, so he

spent the ten minutes playing too. Really uncanny, how she looked—
even at two months—like his lost Ginevra; and anybody would take to
calling her Ginny at their own peril. Such a good baby: such a strong
healthy baby, said the doctor. . . . *Piacesse a Dio,* his Ginevra come
back to stay with him. . . .

He put the bolt on the front door after dinner.

John Poor drove across town to the only hardware store in Glendale
open Sundays, and brought home three of those patent bolts: they had
a side door as well as a back and a front.

He put them all on after dinner. "And see you use them," he said to
his wife. "With one like this running around—after what I heard from
Wayne—"

"Oh, all right, but what a nuisance," said his wife.

Joe Katz was a little late leaving the office; he'd wanted to get out
that list of what was missing from Kessler's, and he phoned his wife that
he'd be a little late. When he did leave, he was thinking about what he'd
heard from Varallo (good man, their Eyetie) and Wayne about Collins
and Gardiner; and he went a bit out of his way to drop into the only
hardware store he knew of that was open on Sundays, to pick up a couple of those patent bolts. Well, Glendale a nice quiet town, and not
much crime; you got out of the habit of— Why, some of the bad summer nights last year they'd left the front door open, just kept the screen
door hooked. But with one like this joker running around loose—

He wasn't very handy with tools but he got the bolts screwed on after
dinner. "And you remember to use 'em, too," he told Anne.

Rhys had been thinking about what he'd heard from Varallo too, and
he thought a little harder because his mother's house was on Balboa
Avenue only about four blocks from where Mrs. Collins had lived.
When he left the office he drove across town to the only hardware store
that was open on Sundays, and carried home a couple of those patent
bolts. Better safe than sorry, he thought, wielding the screwdriver.

"But Bob, what a nuisance," said his mother.

"With a wild man like this running around—you see they're both shot
by dark, hm?" said Rhys. "How're the pups doing?"

Dr. Goulding, who had seen the corpses, felt a little worried too: he
had an old place up on Mountain, a big house somewhat isolated from
its neighbors, and his wife had a little arthritis and wasn't too quick at
getting around. And they'd just lost their old German shepherd. Dr.
Goulding stopped at the main desk to confer with Sergeant Duff, who'd

just come on duty, and Sergeant Wayne was just going off and stopped to say good night. And the upshot of that was that Dr. Goulding drove across town to the only hardware store that was open on Sundays and brought home four of those useful little patent bolts; they had a side door and a door into the patio as well as a front and back door.

He screwed them firmly into place with his clever surgeon's hands before they sat down to dinner, and told his wife to remember to use them. "And I know we've said it was too soon, hon, but let's think about another pup."

"—I know he hasn't hit an apartment," said O'Connor hoarsely, "but two dead women is two too many, damn it. I was going to get you one of those patent bolts—damn it, I went all the way across town to the only damn hardware store open on Sundays—reason I was late—and would you believe it, they'd sold out of the damn things just in the last hour. I'll get you one tomorrow. Because—"

"You," said Katharine Mason, "have got no business being out, Charles. Spreading cold germs all over."

"I'm all *right,* damn it. It's just a cold," said O'Connor, having resigned himself in the last six hours to the fact that it *was* a cold. His first cold in at least five years, he was never sick.

"Now admit it," said Katharine. "You feel lousy."

"So I feel lousy. It's just a damn cold—it'll go away."

"You're terribly hoarse. Are you taking anything for it?"

"I don't go in for dosing myself, Katy." O'Connor swallowed Scotch and water and opened the menu.

"More fool you," said Katharine. "Really, Charles, everybody knows you're a big tough he-man cop, you don't need to play it to the hilt every minute." And the funny thing about that was, of course—as even Katharine knew by now—that O'Connor didn't know he was. It was just Charles Vincent O'Connor *au naturel.* "You sound as if you're about on the second day. By your voice. Now look, if you've got any sense at all you'll have a nice bland omelette or something." She sipped her Martini. "And you will then take me home and go home yourself and go to bed. And—what? Oh, I'll have the tournedos of beef. Blue cheese dressing, please. Coffee later."

O'Connor relayed the order, adding a steak for himself which he didn't particularly want, but he always had a steak at the Matador. "I'm all right, for God's sake. Just a little cold, and we've got this and that on our hands, I can't—"

"So you pass it on to everybody else in the detective bureau," said Katharine with asperity. "If you'd use some sense, Charles—"

"And isn't it easy to see you're a schoolteacher! I ought to be over the infectious stage tomorrow, damn it."

"Yes, and come to think I only hope *I* don't catch it and pass it on to the whole class before I realize it," said Katharine.

"Now, Katy. You know better than to pick up things that don't belong to you."

"And when you get home—have you got any whiskey or is that a foolish question?"

"Yes, I have got some damn whiskey. Why, you going to advise me to get drunk and forget it?"

"You have a very heavy-handed brand of humor, cop. No. Have you got any honey?"

"Any what, darling?"

"Oh, God," said Katharine, closing her eyes. "I was out of my *mind* ever to go out with you. These sprightly little jokes. Well, have you? All I'm trying to do is help you, Lord knows why. Look. You take some whiskey and you put it in some water and get it boiling hot and put in about a tablespoon of honey and a tablespoon of lemon juice, and drink it. Slowly. Very good for a cold. For the sore throat."

"Teach your grandmother. My mother gave me that whenever I had a cold." O'Connor coughed.

"Well, then, why don't you take *care* of yourself? It's silly—a couple of days in bed would—"

"We've got all this on our hands, damn it. This wild man running around—" O'Connor finished his drink and from habit got out a cigarette, but didn't light it. He'd got to the stage where cigarettes tasted like hell. "And listen, Katy—" he coughed, managed to stop coughing after thirty seconds—"listen, you be careful, damn it. Take care of myself *I* damn well can—but with one like this around—and you're coming home after dark sometimes, too—"

"Oh, the apartment drive's lighted, I'm always careful."

O'Connor coughed some more. He thought, bent over his handkerchief, he'd like to come right out and say, Let me take care of you, Katy; but not only, he guessed, was it not a very propitious moment to propose to a girl, but he'd be scared to death. In spades. Him, for God's sake. O'Connor. Well, something very damned funny had happened to him last year when he first laid eyes on her, that was all. His schoolteacher. Oh, they kidded him, but— Something very damned funny. Not the type he'd ever gone for, he'd always liked the little dumb blondes.

Damn it, she was only an inch shorter than he was, and too thin. He cast a surreptitious look at his schoolteacher across the table from him there, Miss Mason, tall and slim and rather elegant-looking in gray chiffon, her short dark hair smooth and her silver-gray eyes large under arched heavy brows, her too-wide mouth looking serious. He wondered why she did go out with him. Never made a move at her: he knew, with Katy, that'd end it unless— Him, O'Connor, and just how the hell did you let a girl know you were *serious?*

He controlled the cough and put the handkerchief away. "Yeah, well, you just be careful, that's all. I'll come and put that bolt on for you to-morrow night."

"You're not fit to—"

"Oh, for God's sake," said O'Connor roughly. "Just a *cold.*" And he thought irrelevantly about Varallo (damn good man and they were lucky to get him, twelve years on a force upstate and resigning as captain) and the new baby—O'Connor didn't know much about babies, but she was a sort of cute one, all that blond hair, and he'd kicked in a couple of bucks with the rest of the boys to get a present—and he wondered if he'd be exactly suitable, ever, for all the domesticities. Maybe a little wistfully he wondered it. Said his mother used to give him that cold remedy, sure, she had, but it was one of the few things he remembered about her. She'd died when he was seven and he didn't remember his father at all: old man had walked out on her long before. Not many people knew that Charles O'Connor had been a ward of the county, in and out of a lot of foster homes mostly pretty indifferent, before he turned eighteen and worked his way through a couple of years at L.A.C.C. and then joined the cops. It wasn't a thing he bragged about. And sure, there had been that couple of years of college, but, well, Katy a teacher, and besides any woman might think twice about marrying a cop. These days.

"You really have no sense at all, Charles," said Katharine warmly. "You aren't tasting that four-fifty steak at all, are you? No. Well, you can take me home and I'll *give* you some honey and you go home and—"

"Yes, I am tasting the steak. Think I was a damn four-year-old!" growled O'Connor.

Varallo got to the office at three minutes to eight and got together with Poor and Wayne. Katz and Rhys seemed to have fallen heir to the Kessler thing, and while that was a boy they'd like to get—a punk with a gun and not averse to using it—the Collins-Gardiner boy seemed a lot more important.

Varallo handed over to Katz what they had on those two out of records they still hadn't found, on Kessler—James Quait and Richard Newcomb—and kicked around this and that on the other two homicides with Poor and Wayne.

"I had a thought overnight," he said. "Don't know what you'll think of it, but try it for size. Can either of you think of an instance where we've had a break-in that early at night?"

"I thought about that too," said Wayne. "It's unusual. The pro burglar usually looks for a house where people are away, or at the very least waits until they're likely to be asleep in bed. But—"

"È vero. I—"

"But what does it say, Vic, except that he is a wild one?"

"It might say two things, Fred. One from out in left field. A juvenile. If you ever read the true-police magazines, you'd know how frighteningly many of that kind show up. The quiet mannerly kids who never gave anybody a minute's worry, all of a sudden running amok and killing. The unsuspected schizos, and we all know that the schizos go off the rails finally during the teens oftener than at any other age. Well, like that one we picked up in January—murdered the elderly couple. I just thought—one like that, a Jekyll and Hyde thing, some teenager from a good home maybe, where he's checked up on and can't be out late."

"Left field let us say. Sure, they exist. Let's hear your other idea."

"I can guess what it is," said Poor, looking at his cigarette. "Because I had it too. Somebody who knew them. Knew that Mrs. Collins lived alone, and maybe even knew her eating habits—knew, anyway, that the next-door house has its bedrooms on the side toward her back door. Which would be easy enough to figure for anybody who had a legit occasion to walk up the drive or even past the house. I had the idea last night so I drove by the place this morning. Anybody can see which are the kitchen windows in the next-door house. Kitchen's on the front. And somebody who knew that Mrs. Gardiner would be home alone on Saturday nights. Knew—and this is important maybe—that the Gardiners ate early, about five, and Gardiner went right back to the store. Because that too is fairly unusual."

"Yes," said Varallo. "And just conceivably it could be both. Both the juvenile and someboy who knew them—that much about them."

Wayne wrinkled his brow. "You are really reaching, genius. Both of you. That's far out. Well, a little far out. Sure, I see that about the time. That does still throw me—unusual. But in the first place, I do not see—even if you're both right—that it gives us any new handle to reach for, any way to find him—and in the second place we have got, for God's

sake, enough possible louts out of records to look at. From ours and
L.A.'s."

"If you think it through, Fred," said Varallo gently, "if John and I
are right, it could say something very damn depressing. It could say that
maybe he's not in anybody's records, because he's never gone off the
rails before."

"Oh, God give me strength," said Wayne. Absently he flexed all
those muscles. "I pray to the good Lord you're wrong, Vic. I know, I
know. I do occasionally read the official detective stuff."

Varallo leaned back in his chair and stared at the ceiling. "There was
that high-school girl raped and murdered back in Rochester, New York.
When they dropped on him, a nice quiet high-school kid from a substantial home, never given his family an instant's worry. Nobody could
believe it until he confessed. There was that mother and daughter, elderly and middle-aged, both widows, back in Indiana somewhere. Abducted and murdered—beaten to death. When they picked that one up, a
nineteen-year-old farmhand—sure, not very bright, but he'd never so
much as had a fight with anybody before. Didn't know why he'd killed
them—he just had. There was— But you know what I'm talking about."

"It happens, it happens, there they are, I know," said Wayne. "Let's
not make it harder, Vic. You know as well as me—" He paused, rubbing
his jaw.

"That it's likelier to be somebody out of records," said Varallo
softly, "somebody we've got a name for? I don't know that at all, Fred.
I don't often pull rank on you boys—" He grinned: Wayne knew as well
as he did that, all told, Vic Varallo had longer experience as a cop than
most of them. "But if I've learned one thing, it's that a cop can't indulge
in wishful thinking. We've got a thing here. A wild one, as you say. The
one that runs berserk. And at least one unusual circumstance—the time
of both murders. Which we can't close our eyes to. It's easy to say the
routine thing, Look in records for the possibles. But let's not shut our
eyes to the possibility that these could be first jobs for somebody. *Or* to
the fact that they were both elderly women."

"Um, yes," said Poor. "Just now and then the psychiatric jargon does
make a little sense. I thought about that too. I just wondered, Vic—
don't know how you feel about it—if it might be any use to us to have
a look at the sex files? The latest naughty boys who've been stealing
feminine panties off the clotheslines and purveying the feelthy peectures?"

"Oh, my God, you two," said Wayne. "You scientific modern cops!
I've got at least one thing to come back at you with. I *worked* the

Collins bit. Damn it, where is it?" He scrabbled through the cardboard-backed Collins file on his desk. "All right. Here. Howard Nelson Burke. Out of L.A.'s records. Latest known address, Dover Place in the At-water section." Which was, of course, between Glendale and Holly-wood. "He's a psycho—I won't bother you with details—diagnosed as a schizo at sixteen. Record of attempted assault on other kids on the playgrounds, and so on. Two years in Atascadero, but of course he's a minor, they remand him in custody of his mother. These damn soft-headed judges. Charges of attempted assault on two elderly women, neighbors. Not pressed. He is now twenty-one, and still loose. He had no alibi for Collins—but of course nothing else hooked him up to it. He has got a doting mother and he's got access to a car. This is just one out of records, boys. You think we shouldn't check him on Gardiner? Are you saying—"

"Check him, check him," said Varallo mildly, putting out his ciga-rette. "All I'm saying, Fred, is that we've got to keep all possibilities in mind. Our boy isn't for a hundred percent sure in anybody's records. He could be one just like the one John and I have been speculating on."

"All *right!*" said Wayne. "We run out of possibles from records—which is practically impossible, because you know as well as me most of 'em won't have solid alibis—you have any ideas about how to start hunt-ing for your hypothetical schizo who's only just gone off the rails?" He sat back disgustedly. "God," he said, "and the citizenry calling us names! I just wish some of 'em could have the job to cope with awhile."

"Well, if it was somebody who knew both of them," said Poor medi-tatively, "some common denominator ought to show up, if we—"

"For God's sake! Milkman, bakery-truck driver, mailman, no, the addresses too far apart. I ask you! So all right, it could be, but I don't see—"

"Common denominators," said Varallo thoughtfully. "Yes. All I say is we ought not to overlook any lines of inquiry. Newsboys? I don't know how large an area the *Independent* carriers cover—for instance. And there was that case back in Muncie, Indiana, where a fourteen-year-old boy assaulted and murdered the beauty-shop operator—"

"Oh, for the love of God!" said Wayne. "Talk about the wild blue yonder. Look, this Burke hasn't been checked. On Gardiner. Let's get *on* it, boys. On the routine. It does usually pay off."

"In the end," agreed Poor, getting up. But he exchanged a glance with Varallo.

They'd still be thinking about the newsboys—and so on—too.

CHAPTER 6

"I don't know what call you got to come suspecting Howie of any- ·
thing," said the woman fearfully, angrily. "Howie—people always saying
things about him. Telling lies—I never did believe he did do what that
Mrs. Oliver said—just because he's different. Just different. That one
doctor, he did say that's how I ought to think about it. Different. Howie
never means to do anything wrong. What do you want with him now?"

She was a small dumpy woman in her fifties, and she'd been very
pretty once; her blond hair had faded to dirty brown mixed with gray,
and she had on a little too much make-up, and at nine thirty in the
morning she wasn't dressed, had on an ankle-length cotton housecoat
that had seen better days, and a pair of rather dirty pink terrycloth bedroom slippers. She looked at Varallo and Wayne with secretly terrified
eyes, and she said, "He's just different. And he hasn't—done anything—
lately. He hasn't. What you want with my Howie?"

"Just to ask some questions, Mrs. Burke. Your son has been diagnosed as a schizophrenic," said Wayne gently, "and has spent some
time at Atascadero. After charges of assault."

"People tell things. Half the time lies. He's all right with me. What do
you want to know, anyway? *Police* coming."

"Is he at home? We'd like to see him."

"He don't like strangers. I can ask," she said dully, and trailed out of
the room. Varallo and Wayne exchanged a glance.

A modest and shabby house in the Atwater section. Old furniture: a
twelve-year-old Ford sitting in front. A defeated shabby woman. Home
of Howard Nelson Burke, schizo. A vagary of nature, and lives ruined.
Varallo wondered about Howard's father. They waited.

He was with her when she came back. A big young man, but thin and pasty-faced. And a wildness came into the room with him, a nearly tangible feel of the something wrong which accompanies that kind like an aura. He stopped just inside the door, across the room from the two detectives, and his eyes showed white.

"You be good now, Howie. They said just some questions."

"Why?" he asked sharply, in an unnaturally high-pitched voice. His eyes moved too much, and too fast. You might not turn to look at him in the street, but if you did, a second glance showed all the little wrongnesses: the moving eyes, the hands clasping and interlacing into different positions, the small mouth working. And there was that wrong smell. "I don't like you," he said suddenly. "Tell them to go away, Ma."

"Howard," said Wayne. "Do you remember where you were last Saturday night?"

He just stared at them.

"Howie—please."

"Who are they? I don't like them," he said.

"Do you know where he was on Saturday night, Mrs. Burke?" asked Varallo.

"Saturday—why, sure I do. Howie, you know! You were right here playing rummy with me and Mrs. Keats."

"Between what times, Mrs. Burke?"

"Oh, I guess about six thirty or so we started. After dinner. Howie— We were all right here all evening, so Howie couldn't have—"

"Tell them to go away!"

"And was this Mrs. Keats here all the time? To when?"

"I guess about ten o'clock. Howie couldn't have— What did you think he did? Howie—"

He suddenly turned and bolted from the room. Somewhere at the rear of the house a door slammed. "You got him all upset," she said. "You see? He didn't—"

"Where can we find Mrs. Keats?"

"Why, right out back, she rents the rear house. She can say, Howie was right here all that evening. I don't know why you should think he— If everybody'd just leave him alone—just different, like—"

"Mrs. Burke, the doctors must have told you he's potentially dangerous?" said Wayne.

She looked at him, and there was fear in her eyes she didn't know was there. "People tell lies. Just because he's different. He doesn't *mean—*"

Varallo thought there was almost touchable tension in the very air in-side this house. As if an invisible bomb was ticking quietly away. And essentially, of course, there was.

Nobody could get through to the Mrs. Burkes. Had she ever looked up "schizophrenia" in the dictionary? Instinct filled her with fear; but she had lived with it for a long time and maybe she didn't know it was there any more. And maybe pushing it down below consciousness was the only way anyone could live with it.

They didn't try to talk to her. They went out and around the house to the little ramshackle house in the rear, and found Mrs. Keats. Who was a fat, placid old lady with a fat, placid old yellow cat, and couldn't be talked to either.

"For the land's sake," she said when she finally understood who they were and what they wanted. "As if poor Mrs. Burke hadn't enough trouble, now the police. What with her boy and all. Just a little touched, like—pity he can't hold some kind o' job, help her out some. But just God's will, some come like that. Funny too, he's quick enough at playin' cards, and like that—real bright at arithmetic he was in school, she said. What say? Saturday night? Why, yes, I was there. Playin' cards. I don't hold with gambling, but just a friendly game of cards. What say? Yes, he was. Yes, I did see him, every minute up to about ten o'clock when I come home. I must say I don't see why—"

"Mrs. Keats, do you know Howard is a schizophrenic? That he's been violent before?"

"Well, Mrs. Burke said something—allus people to tell things about one afflicted like that. Just a little off." She rocked comfortably, the cat asleep on her lap.

"Mrs. Keats—" said Varallo, and then shrugged at Wayne. They'd got what they wanted to know. Howard Burke was not the boy they wanted for Mrs. Gardiner. Alibi.

In Wayne's car, Varallo lit a cigarette. "You wonder," he said. "You do wonder. Like to make any predictions?"

Wayne thrust the key into the ignition, shoved in the dashboard lighter and sat back. "I could say this and that about mother love. Of course she's not a very intelligent woman to start. Or the other one. But somewhere along the line, somebody must have tried to tell her some basic facts. That it's a purely congenital, physical condition that can't be cured. That they practically always end up violent. That quite often the violence is inflicted on their nearest and dearest. I could damn well make a prediction. They'll leave him loose until he kills somebody.

Then they'll shut him up for good, it is to be hoped. Mama may not know it—or accept it—but she's gambling with her life."

"But he's not our boy on this one."

"At least we know that much."

Varallo felt depressed. They had others to go and see: too many others. The possibles. A couple of them were counterparts of Burke, mental patients. One of those retarded, with a record of attempted violence; another manic-depressive with a like record. The rest were just the ones with violence in their pasts, who couldn't take refuge behind the insanity plea. The ones just naturally violent.

And not all of them would have alibis for Saturday night, and so there'd be more routine. They'd get search warrants and look for anything to hook those men up to Mrs. Gardiner. They'd hope that some of the loot would show up at a pawnbroker's or somewhere, to give them some lead.

"Look," he said to Wayne, "let's save some time and split up. This is going to be a long job as it is." Cops, he thought, saw so many more of the Burkes—and the just plain no-goods, of every type—it was a wonder they didn't all live in a permanent state of depression over the human race.

But they could cross one off their list, anyway.

The various addresses were as far apart as San Fernando and South Pasadena; up to twelve thirty Varallo had chased down just two of the possibles. By a fluke, both of them had alibis; one had been at a wedding reception and the other in a crowded bar with a party of friends. Cross off two more. Progress.

But the other thing was at the back of his mind—not just one of the violent ones, but something nearer home. Somebody who had known both women? Somebody running amok for the first time?

Because, take this next name on the list at random—Stanley Keller. He was in the Glendale police records because he had once broken into a house in Glendale, with a pal who lived in Glendale; but he'd never lived there. He lived in Sunland fifteen miles away, and he was currently on parole—he'd served two short terms for burglary—and that said he had a job of sorts. His only record of violence was the official "resisting arrest," and that might mean anything from a little scuffle when he was picked up to a real berserk effort. But why should Stanley Keller all of a sudden drive down to Glendale and commit murder during a burglary? It wasn't really likely. Keller was a small-time pro. Whoever had battered those two women to death was, for Varallo's money, somebody like Burke: off the beam upstairs, he put it to himself rudely. A wild one.

Only, of course, they had to check out all the ones like Keller, just to be sure.

And Varallo had been a cop for a long time, he was a good cop, and he knew reasonably that about ninety-nine percent of all police work always consists of the routine. The plodding, patient routine that so often, in the end, turned up the answer. That was why records were kept. But only long discipline and experience had taught him that, for by all temperament and instinct Vic Varallo was what he thought of as a Jumper. There were people with another type of mind who proceeded painstakingly from A to B to C and so on, cause and effect, all very logical; and then there were people who jumped, maybe from A to F, on pure inspiration. It was, he supposed, essentially the feminine type of mind in a way; which reflection only made him smile: everybody with both male and female bits in their personalities. Maybe, to make it sound more dignified, you could say that some people (for whatever reasons) got the nuances from anybody they met: and it was experience of human nature that set them jumping to inspired conclusions.

All he knew was that almost every time he'd come up with the answer to a real puzzle—and there'd been a few like that, even up in Contera, that one-horse burg, his years on the force there—it hadn't been by the routine, but by some sudden funny hunch, or a reasonless certainty that took root in his mind. Something that said to him, Look there; or, Ask about that.

Cops couldn't go all out on hunches; but you pinned any experienced cop down, surprisingly often, he'd tell you, the little hunches paid off.

And something was saying to Varallo now, that the X they wanted on Collins and Gardiner had been closer to home than this impersonal list of possibles out of records. That X had known something about the setup at both those places. Even if only that the women were alone. And if that little hunch was so, it meant that there had to be a common denominator somewhere. Because Fifth Street and Geneva Street were way across town from each other, a good two miles apart.

He dropped into Pike's at Brand and Glenoaks for a sandwich, and he thought. Milkman. Bakery-truck driver. Fuller Brush man. Any door-to-door salesman. Somebody who for some logical reason would be calling at both addresses—somebody whom both those women might get a little chatty with. No, I'm a widow, I live alone. Oh, my husband has his own drugstore (and every drugstore in town open Saturday nights). Like that. All right. Who else?

Ask Laura, he thought, nodding to the waitress who offered a refill of coffee. Ask who came to the door these days. He suddenly remembered that Laura bought eggs at the door, on a regular basis, from a man who had a chicken ranch in the valley. Such a nice man, she said, friendly and pleasant. Which didn't sound like X—but there could be other such.

He finished his coffee thoughtfully, and temporarily forgetting the list of possibles in his pocket, he looked up the address and drove up Glenoaks to Harry Gardiner's drugstore. Possibly Gardiner wouldn't be there: only two days after his wife had been murdered, after all. But it was in the same general neighborhood as the Gardiner house.

It was, in fact, a convenient eight blocks away from Fifth Street. It was open. It was the corner store of a short block of shops. Glenoaks Boulevard was zoned in a rather odd—but convenient—way: each block alternated, residential and business. So the preceding block was all nice-looking, middle-aged apartment buildings with green lawns and flowering shrubs in front, smallish apartment buildings; and so was the block up from here; but this block was all business. A Shell gas station on the corner, a realtor's, a beauty shop, a hardware and paint store, a bakery, a liquor store, a small variety store and on the other corner Gardiner's drugstore.

A fairly prosperous-looking little place, it was. The block of buildings had been painted not too long ago, a pleasing warm tan. Along here, away from downtown, there would nearly always be parking spaces available. Varallo parked in front of the drugstore and went in.

The usual drugstore. Two aisles toward the counter at the rear, a large magazine stand up front. A fat woman was looking at the magazines. Cosmetics, hair products, cologne; stationery, wrapping paper, twine; a small stock of wine and liquor; candy; shelves full of all the nonprescriptive drugs and medicines; a rack of greeting cards. Varallo went back to the counter where the cash register stood. There was a partition behind the counter, a little room back there, and he could just see another half-open door beyond. Somebody must be here to wait on customers.

In a moment Gardiner came through that half-open door, a small bottle in his hand. He recognized Varallo and nodded.

"A few more questions, if you don't mind, Mr. Gardiner."

"Anything I can tell you," said Gardiner gravely. "If you'll excuse me a moment, sir. Mrs. Lambert, your prescription is ready."

The fat woman came up the aisle with several magazines, and rummaged in her handbag. Either she didn't read the papers or didn't know Gardiner's name; she didn't mention the murder. It had, of course, got headlines in the *News-Press*. Her gaze passed over Varallo incuriously; she paid Gardiner, received her change and went out.

"I don't know what you'll think of my—er—being here," said Gardiner, touching his glasses. "Perhaps you'll think, callous. But life does go on. And I think it's best to keep busy. Agnes wasn't a person to brood. Either." He looked at the counter and absently rearranged rows of chewing gum in better order. "After I'd got the house cleaned up—" He sighed. "And the one man I employ to spell me as a pharmacist—well, I'm afraid he could be more reliable. One does have the regular customers, and I feel a certain responsibility." That was without emphasis; he blinked at Varallo. "Have you—have you found out anything?"

"We're working on it, Mr. Gardiner. What I wanted to ask you was whether your wife had milk delivered?"

Gardiner blinked faster. "The milk? Why on earth— Well, no. Of course not. It costs more that way. It would amount to quite a bit more over a month's time, and we never did. Do you think—"

"Well, we have to check out everything," said Varallo vaguely. "Did she usually buy from one of those bakery trucks that comes around? Like Helms'?"

Gardiner took off his glasses and began cleaning them with his handkerchief. "Well, really I don't see the point, but again I have to say no. For the same reason. It stands *to* reason—what with the overhead of the trucks and the drivers' wages and all, that they have to charge more. Quite a bit more. No, she never did. . . . Fuller *Brush?* Oh, indeed, no, sir, she never bought at the door. Anything you buy at the door is more expensive. Until I built my place up, you know, we had a little struggle, to keep up payments on the mortgage and the rent here and all, we got in the way of looking after the pence, as the saying goes." He slid his glasses back on. "You do have to think of these things. I always cautioned Agnes about buying at the door."

Varallo thought of the next-door neighbor talking about poor Mrs. Gardiner and her miserly husband. Well, people. Careful, thrifty people: maybe the nonconformists these days, but the kind of salt-of-the-earth people who had built this country, he thought. And it seemed to be one of the rules about human nature that there wasn't much happy medium in that sort of thing: you were either too much one way or the other. He regarded Gardiner indulgently.

"Did you have a gardener?—your wife ever belong to any clubs?—do you take a newspaper? Which one?"

He drew a real blank. . . . "Any way I can help you," said Gardiner humbly. "But the more I think—not that I'm presuming to tell you your job—you know more about these things than I do, after all—the more I think, the more convinced I am that it must have been the same terrible criminal who killed that other woman, and we'd scarcely have *known*—"

Varallo sat behind the wheel of the Chevy and looked at his note-book. The Gardiners took the *Independent,* the less expensive of the two local sheets. Mrs. Gardiner had never belonged to any club, never bought anything at the door, never ate a meal out at a restaurant alone or with her husband, had no close women friends, and no correspon-dents—neither of them had any living relatives—and no hobbies.

His immediate reaction was, that poor damned woman. What a joy-less sort of life *that* must have been. Saving and scraping, at first, to build up the nice little independent business: and getting so in the habit of it, both of them, that when things were easier and they could have enjoyed life a little, they just didn't. Typical, maybe. Poor damned woman, a life of that and then the senseless random death.

Random? Well, if X had known she'd be alone, available, he hadn't known that in that house there'd be very little of value by which he could acquire the easy loot. No.

But that he had known a little something, Varallo would bet. So there had to be a common denominator somewhere. Somehow.

And he thought dismally, then, the link could be that next-door neighbor. Mrs. Glover. The jovial extrovert interested in people. Mrs. Glover probably had a lot of close female friends. And talked about ev-erybody she knew—kindly, genial, interested. Conceivably X could have known a little about Mrs. Collins because he lived in roughly the same neighborhood—and heard a little about Mrs. Gardiner because his mother or sister or aunt or fourth cousin twice removed knew Mrs. Glover.

Diavolo, he thought, let's not make it harder.

There must be more possible common denominators.

It was getting on for two o'clock. And he had a lot more of the rou-tine to get through. Checking out the possibles from records.

Often, it did pay off.

Varallo sighed and started the engine.

*

He ended up back at headquarters at six o'clock with nothing significant. None of the other possibles he'd found to question had anything like an alibi. So they were still up in the air. He wondered what Wayne and Poor had got; and he had a little project in mind, in pursuit of which he wanted a private glance at the file on Mrs. Collins.

He plodded up the stairs to the detective bureau and found O'Connor at his desk, Wayne at his typing a report and nobody else there.

"I've got damn all," he said to Wayne.

"That's nice," said Wayne. "So have Joe and Bob on that Kessler."

"How's the cold, Charles?" Varallo glanced at Wayne's desk; the Collins file sat off-center, carelessly, on the edge of it. "You catch the kite flier for J. Edgar yet?"

"You can go straight to hell," whispered O'Connor hoarsely. "He passed another one at Webbs' this morning. Sharp-eyed teller spotted it an hour ago and called in."

Varallo stared at him. "It's a secret?"

"Straight *to* hell!" whispered O'Connor. "The cold's fine, Vic boy. Me, that's something damned different."

"By tomorrow," said Wayne, "he won't be able to talk at all. Which will make a lot of difference around this place. I only hope to God he hasn't passed it on to every last man in the building. Talk about devotion to duty."

"You'd better go home to bed, Charles," said Varallo with a grin, and casually picked up the Collins file and flicked over pages.

"Hell and damnation," whispered O'Connor. "Got to go put the damn bolt on Katy's door—said I would. Got it 's afternoon. This damn joker running around—you go to hell."

"Certainly make a change around here," said Wayne without stopping typing. "Silence is golden."

Varallo laughed. "Better stay home tomorrow, Charles." He had what he wanted; he put the file back on Wayne's desk.

Mrs. William Ferris, Silverlake Terrace in Hollywood. Mrs. Collins' daughter.

CHAPTER 7

"Laura." Varallo was stretched full length on the living room floor tickling Miss Ginevra's ribs while she rolled on a blanket and chortled. "Who comes door to door these days? I'm trying to think of some link between those two women."

"Five more minutes and into bed she goes," said Laura. "Dinner's almost ready. Yes, I know, I've been thinking too, since you mentioned it." She wrinkled her small straight nose. "Honestly, Vic—I'll have to press those slacks all over again if you— Well, just very occasionally there's some man with fresh fruit or vegetables. Not nearly as often as there used to be. Obviously they wouldn't shop at the same market, Mrs. Collins and the other one I mean. You said the Gardiner woman didn't drive, didn't have a car, so she'd shop at the nearest one. . . . I did have a thought on that. If the Collins woman did, and if she was one of those—those eagle-eyed bargain hunters who follow all the supermarket sales—you know, using ten cents' worth of gas to save two cents a pound on coffee—they could have met at the market Mrs. Gardiner—"

"No," said Varallo. "Mrs. Collins didn't drive either." He rolled Miss Ginevra over and patted her bottom and she squealed. Gideon Algernon Cadwallader stalked by and she made a vague grab for his tail which he didn't deign to notice.

"Oh. Well, I can't think of anything else—there are obnoxious people coming round trying to sell encyclopedia sets. And, Vic—common denominator as you call it—they could have gone to the same doctor or dentist. Or chiropractor or something like that."

"*Per Bacco!*" Varallo rolled over on his back and peered up at her thoughtfully. "Now that is an idea. Thanks very much. Though what could it mean? Another patient—true, people do get to chatting in waiting rooms. But—well, that is a thought. I'll look into it."

"And you can put her back in bed while I make the coffee. How's Charles's cold?"

Varallo got up and swept Miss Ginevra up with him, blanket and all. "Doing fine. I don't think he'll be in tomorrow." He deposited Miss Ginevra in bed and tucked her in, and she chuckled at him happily. The best baby there ever had been. Out of the dim past he did remember—most of them did yell at night. . . . Doctors? Dentists? Well, what could that say? Another patient? It was possible. . . .

He told Laura the other boys who'd been through the fatherhood bit were green with envy at a baby who slept all night. "Of course she *is* exceptional. The next one might—"

"Whoa, you just wait a minute there, buster," said Laura, pouring his coffee. "Don't say it so glib."

"Well, I wasn't suggesting we embark on the project right now. But you always say an only child—"

"I know what I always said. I can change my mind, can't I?" Laura offered him a dish of asparagus. "At least give me time to enjoy wearing a size fourteen again. . . . And you know better than to beg at the table," she added severely to Gideon, who was watching every mouthful they took.

"I'm not rushing you," said Varallo mildly. "I want to see Mrs. Collins' daughter tonight. And mind you shoot those bolts after me. . . ."

He drove over to Hollywood, after phoning to be sure Mrs. Ferris would be home, and talked to her, but he didn't know that it was much use to him. Mrs. Ferris was an angular blonde with a permanent expression of discontent, and she had a grievance. "I never did approve of her going on living there alone in that big house. She could have come here with us, or had a nice little apartment, but no, you couldn't shift her. Said she'd lived there for forty years and no place else would seem like home. Well, a woman alone—an elderly woman—she's always in danger of burglars. They get to know. And besides, she shouldn't have had all that housework to do at her age. But you couldn't tell her. Not that I expected such an awful thing as *did* happen—" She touched a handkerchief to her eyes.

She answered questions without interest. Her mother had been a Christian Scientist and didn't go to any doctors. She had gone to a dentist, a long while back, to have her teeth out and dentures. A Dr. Rheingold, Mrs. Ferris thought. She shopped at the supermarket a few blocks up on Glendale Avenue. Once in a while she went downtown in the afternoon to see a movie, not often. She took the Los Angeles *Herald,* an evening paper. She'd never driven a car. Usually some friend picked her up and took her to church on Sunday: a Mrs. Bridges. She had belonged to a small bridge club years ago, but not within the last ten years since her arthritis had been worse. Well, she didn't spend much on herself, but when she did buy new shoes or a new dress, it wouldn't have been at any special place. She didn't buy from strangers at the door, but she had liked the Fuller Brush products and bought some of their things; and because it was more convenient, she had dairy things delivered by Knudsen, and bought some things from the Helms' bakery truck sometimes. No, no one had ever tried to break into the house before.

"And I usually called her nearly every day, but as it happened we'd been away—my husband had a business trip to— And when the *police* called and told— Well, it was such a shock, my own mother, I couldn't believe it! But there, if she hadn't insisted on going on living there alone —*as* I'd told her time and again—"

Varallo thanked her and started home. Just a handful of nothing, he thought. No common denominators, unless Agnes Gardiner had gone to Dr. Rheingold too. And on that very long chance, probably Dr. Rheingold would take a very dim view at being asked for a list of his other patients because—about ten thousand to one—there just might be a berserk killer among them.

How ridiculous could you get?

He slid the car into the garage beside Laura's, and walked up the flagstones past the covered patio, pausing to examine Alida Lovett climbing up the trellis, in the moonlight. Doing fine, after he'd finally got round to cutting them all back in January. His very favorite, the Duquesa de Peñeranda, was doing well too, after a slow start. But he'd noticed yesterday that Charlotte Armstrong had a few little holes in her leaves. Those goddamned aphis. Well, Thursday was his day off. Do some spraying then.

He had his key out, and struggled with the door a little while before he remembered the bolt and pushed the bell—just like, he thought, any door-to-door salesman.

Katz and Rhys collared him when he got to the office on Tuesday morning. "Listen," said Katz, "you and John took the original call on this Kessler thing, and then just blithely hand it over. Let's do a little work for a change, hah?" Poor came in and he beckoned him over. "It looks like one of those things we go on working until it just dies a natural death."

"What've you got?" asked Varallo. It had looked like that at the time, of course.

"Hardly anything but the make on the gun that shot him," said Katz. "But one thing does strike me as funny, Vic. None of the loot has showed."

"Well, he was only shot last Friday night, after all."

"Words of one syllable," said Katz, hoisting one lean hip on Forbes's empty desk and lighting a cigarette. His thin, shrewd, dark face wore a faintly mournful expression. "Now what does Kessler look like? The punk—the little thing, not even a pro, maybe just a j.d. on impulse hitting the jewelry store. The closed jewelry store. Punk not knowing the owner lived upstairs. Nobody, but nobody, Vic, would have picked out Kessler's place to knock over *but* a punk. No burglar, even small-time, would go for it—not worth the while. I tell you, a piddling little place—if you cleaned it out, you wouldn't get a grand out of it from a fence."

"You should know."

"Yeah. I do. So all right. We got the list of what's missing to the pawnbrokers all over the county on Sunday. And none of them had seen any of it up to last night. Why?"

"Well, only two full days—some of it might— Oh," said Varallo. "Oh."

"Bright cop finally arrives at the point. So, sure, this is not surprising if it was a real pro burglary. A pro burglar has got contacts—he's got a reliable fence—or fences—to offer the loot and see who gives him the best price. And he's lucky if he gets a third of what the loot is worth. Naturally the loot vanishes, the fence also having contacts. Any really good pieces are broken up, in the jewelry line, which is what we're talking about here, and the stones sold separately. Mostly a long way off. But this isn't like a slick break-in, say at the Glendale Jewelers, some big outfit like that. This—" Katz waved away Mr. Horace Kessler's humble business venture with a disdainful hand— "this isn't even small-time business, Vic, it's a hole in the wall. Do you know how many carats of diamonds he had in stock? Three! Three, I do ask you. A twenty-point engagement ring, a quarter-carat gent's ring, a three-point pendant, a— I *ask* you. The biggest stone was twenty-five points. Call it a hundred and twenty-five bucks retail, *including* the troy weight of the gold. Big deal, this is."

"What you're saying," said Varallo, "is that even a small-timer, if he wanted to knock off a jewelry store, wouldn't likely have picked Kessler's. Well, we said right off that it was probably a punk—quite likely a j.d.—getting the impulse. And just bad luck for Kessler that the punk had a gun."

"That's so," contributed Rhys. "But if you think that one over slowly, Vic, it does make it sort of funny that none of the loot has showed."

"You tell me," said Katz cynically, "you just tell me how the punks do, Vic. We know 'em. He's out joy-riding, he comes past the little jewelry store—night, and the place closed—hey, man, loot for the taking! The punks, who haven't graduated to pros yet, they don't give a damn what loot they take. Big or little. It's strictly on impulse and they don't —or can't—think five minutes ahead. They pick up the ten or twenty bucks to pay for the night's liquor and a dame, they're happy. Right?"

"Right," said Varallo ruefully. "And too many of that kind around."

"All right. Tell me what the punk does, after breaking in and getting surprised by Kessler and shooting him—*which* the average type like that wouldn't worry about much. I'll tell you. He grabs up what loot he can in one load—just in case somebody has heard the shots and comes running—and he drives it to the handiest pawnshop, to unload for what the man will give him. If he's got just a little more brains, he goes to six or seven pawnshops to get shut of all of it, because the average pawnbroker would spot such a collection as loot the minute he laid eyes on it."

"All right," said Varallo. "What you're saying is that in spite of all the county's efforts, there's a crooked pawnbroker somewhere in the county. Unless it *was* a more than usually stupid small-time pro, and there I think I agree with you because very few of that kind carry guns around."

"No," said Rhys. "The gun does sound more—considering everything else—like the wild punk kid."

"And the county regulations are pretty stiff, Vic, and the sheriff's boys pretty good about keeping tabs. Sure, in a place the size of L.A. county, one bad one could slip through— God knows they have before. But also think about this," said Katz. "It says nothing if the punk was from Boyle Heights or Vernon or some place. And they are all pretty mobile these days. But if it was a punk from right here in town—and the

punks are always eager to get their hot little hands on the dough and
start to live it up—I think he'd have tried to pass at least some of the
loot off to local pawnbrokers, and he hasn't. I know the two in Glendale, the couple in Burbank, all perfectly on-the-level guys. It hasn't
showed."

"So he's not local."

"I don't know," said Katz. "I've got a funny feeling about this
Kessler thing, Vic. You ever have a funny feeling about a case?"

Varallo didn't smile, or Rhys or Poor. All of them had been cops
awhile. Sometimes you did get a funny feeling about a case. Often there
wasn't one damn thing you could do about it.

"What kind, Joe?"

"I don't know, damn it. Just a funny feeling. That it's something
offbeat," said Katz. "Something different."

There was a little silence. Jeff Forbes came in and glanced at O'Connor's empty desk. "Boss staying home today?"

"Well, he hasn't showed," said Poor. "Best thing for him. . . . So,
have you got any suggestions on what else to do about Kessler?"

"I have not," said Katz. "I just pass on conclusions to you. We might
call the sheriff and ask if they've had any little suspicions about any
pawnbroker lately."

"If they had they'd crack down," said Varallo. "No leads out of records, Joe?"

"Negative, all we've tried. Of course it could be one of the ten-twelve
j.d.'s we've checked, if he got rid of the gun meanwhile. But again, that
gun—" Katz shook his head. "Maybe that's what gives me the funny
feeling. Of course any punk can pick up any kind of gun— And I do get
so damn sick and tired of all the agitation about new gun laws. I ask
you. Any hood who wants a gun can always find one. They just make it
tougher for the honest citizens to protect themselves— But your run-of-
the-mill punk who gets hold of a gun, it's practically always a cheap
one. A little one. Not a cannon like that Combat Masterpiece. Even
secondhand, or under the counter, you'd pay a little something for it—
and for the ammo."

"And it's not a gun you'd pick up for the fun target practice," said
Poor. "I see what you mean, Joe. But funny feelings be damned, there's
not much more we can do on it but continue to check records."

"Oh, I know, I know," said Katz. "I just thought I'd share some
gloom."

O'Connor didn't show up. They got to work on all the routine again, and depressingly, as the day wore on, it was evident that they weren't going to escape another March heat wave. It seldom lasted long, but as a foretaste of things to come later it was depressing.

Varallo went to find two possibles from records over in Burbank, didn't find either, drove out to Van Nuys to see a third and found he had a nice alibi for Saturday evening. After checking out the alibi, he came back to Glendale, had lunch at Pike's and dropped into the office to see if O'Connor had come in. He hadn't. Nor had he called in.

"I suppose," said Forbes, who was the only one in the office, "somebody ought to call, or stop by his place, to see if he's dead. I mean, it isn't his day off and you know how he is. He always does call in—even on his day off sometimes—and he's pretty hot after this kite flier."

"*È vero*," said Varallo. The job constituted a very large part of Charles O'Connor's life, and Varallo liked O'Connor quite a lot; quite a boy, Charles O'Connor; thinking of what he had, his Laura and his new darling, Varallo felt suddenly immensely sorry for O'Connor—which he would never say.

The phone rang on O'Connor's desk, and the little light marked the main desk downstairs. Varallo picked it up. "Yes, Bill?"

"Another heist job—fellow just called in. Drugstore up on North Pacific," said Copeland succinctly. "I sent a car. Better take an Identikit along with you just in case. Sounded like an old guy, but he had all his wits about him. A Mr. Butterworth—Carl Butterworth."

Mr. Carl Butterworth was sitting on a stool in the little back room of the North Pacific Pharmacy, and a concerned squad-car man was bending over him. "Now you take it easy, sir, you've had a little shock—" The uniformed man turned as Varallo and Forbes came up and squeezed behind the counter to the narrow aisle. "Connors, sir. Say, you won't believe this, but he chased him off. He didn't get a damn thing this time. My God, I don't know that *I'd* have taken such a chance. I know he hasn't actually taken a shot at anybody, but— Mr. Butterworth? You all right? You like a glass of water or something?"

Mr. Carl Butterworth said, "Oh, dear. Yes, I believe I would—it's very kind of you. You'll find a tap in the lavatory—just off the stock room there—and there are paper cups. Thank you." He looked at Varallo and Forbes.

"We're from headquarters, sir. If you could just tell us what happened here."

"Yes, of course." Mr. Butterworth might be seventy, or older than that. He wasn't a very big man, about five seven, and thin, and he had a few wisps of lank gray hair still left, and a neat small-featured face, and old-fashioned rimless glasses. He was very neatly dressed in a gray suit with a discreet tie. "Dear me," he said. "I must call Mr. and Mrs. Weddemer and tell them. Such an upset. I'd read in the paper about this hold-up man in town, but after all one doesn't *expect*—and really I suppose it was very foolish of me. Oh, thank you." Connors came back with a paper cup of water, and Mr. Butterworth took it and sipped.

"I mean, it's a hell of a good way to get shot, sir," said Connors earnestly. He looked at Mr. Butterworth incredulously, and at Varallo. "Just ordered him out. Imagine."

"Very foolish, I suppose," said Mr. Butterworth meekly. "Yes. But really, one doesn't expect— I really don't know what got into me, because if anyone had asked me what I'd do, if this hold-up man came into the store, I'd certainly have said I wouldn't— But you see, it isn't my store." He blinked myopically up at Varallo. "If you understand me, sir. It belongs to Mr. and Mrs. Weddemer—such nice people. I'm only here part time, as the extra pharmacist. To relieve them. And I really don't know what got into me. At least, I do know, but really something outside myself seemed to take hold of me— The crime rate going up dreadfully, I've read—"

"You just take it easy, sir," said Connors.

"He came in—quite a young man, he was—and he asked for some cleaning fluid. There wasn't anyone else in the place. I went into the back room to fetch it, and when I came back he had this gun in his hand, and he said something about this being a hold-up and to open the register. Well, really, gentlemen, it was as if something just took hold of me. The idea of this—this lout, this criminal, simply walking away with Mr. and Mrs. Weddemer's money—because he had a gun. There's far too much of that kind of thing these days, these violent *louts* wanting something for nothing—no morals, no moral training at all—and the Weddemers have worked hard to build up the business. Really something beyond myself rose up in me," said Mr. Butterworth, and sipped water. "And I have never been a man to curse, either, but—really I wasn't conscious of planning to do it—I merely looked at this—this fellow, and I said to him, You can go straight to hell, sir, I said—and—"

"Jesus," said Connors. "I don't know I'd have had the *nerve*."

"Good for you, Mr. Butterworth," said Varallo with a grin. "Though I don't know that I'd have had either. And?"

"I wasn't myself, sir," said Mr. Butterworth earnestly. "Or perhaps—

yes—I *was*. A good moral bringing-up I had, sir. *Thou shalt not covet.* Yes. Altogether too much of it these days. All these poor young people with no moral training. Something for nothing—take whatever you want, any way you can get it. These violent people." He sipped water. "Mr. and Mrs. Weddemer worked hard for this place. As I worked for mine— I sold out when I retired, to a chain, but I had my own place. They've worked hard. Raised a fine son and daughter. Good people. And this lout, this criminal, comes and steals their money with his gun." Mr. Butterworth shook his head.

"And you told him to go to hell," said Varallo. He looked at old Mr. Butterworth affectionately. The average citizen who, when all the chips were down on the board, did stand up in all his moral indignation for all the old-fashioned basic values.

"Well, really," said Mr. Butterworth, handing the paper cup to Connors, "I hadn't time to be frightened. I expect it was foolish, but I simply was *not* going to hand over Mr. and Mrs. Weddemer's money to such a—such a— Well, he seemed rather surprised, you know. When I said that." Varallo and Forbes grinned; as well he might have been. "I don't think he knew what to do next—I just got that impression—and really, gentlemen, *I* scarcely knew what to do next, except that I was *not* going to hand over Mr. and Mrs. Weddemer's money to him. And just then the deliveryman came in with a box of new stock—from the California Wholesale Drug Supply—and the young man just turned and went out. And I expect it was the reaction, really I don't know what got into me, but do you know, I had to ask the deliveryman to dial the police, my hands were shaking— Just the little shock," said Mr. Butterworth apologetically. "Afterward. Such a thing to happen."

Mr. Butterworth was quite an old boy, thought Varallo. He liked Mr. Butterworth, the solid citizen with moral values ingrained.

"Hell of a good way to get shot," said Connors.

"Can you give us a description of the young man, Mr. Butterworth?" asked Varallo.

The old man straightened. "Oh, yes, I can do that, sir. Nothing wrong with my eyes, with my glasses on. I can give you a *good* description."

CHAPTER 8

As Varallo climbed the steps to the front door of the apartment build-ing on Chevy Chase, a woman came briskly up behind him; he held the door for her and she thanked him. At second glance he tentatively identified Charles's schoolteacher and said, "Miss Mason?"

She glanced at him: a tall girl, and definitely not O'Connor's type—up to now, apparently. "Oh, you work with Charles, don't you?"

"Detective Varallo."

"That *man*," said Katharine as they came in. "Do you know the apartment number? Oh, good. He looked perfectly awful on Sunday night and if I know him he's been doing nothing for it at all, which is silly. If there is one thing that annoys me, it's these big would-be he-men trying to pretend they're not sick when they are." She had a large paper bag in one arm.

"It's upstairs." They climbed the short flight and Varallo knocked on the door. Silence from inside. He knocked again and called O'Connor's name. In a moment the door opened and O'Connor stood looking at them silently.

Any alert cop would have arrested him on suspicion after one look. He looked villainous. He hadn't shaved, and with his heavy beard even one day's growth stuck out in all directions, wild and black. In the mid-dle of the beard his nose, not small to start with, was swollen and red. His eyes were bloodshot and red-rimmed. He was wearing wrinkled blue pajamas with a silk dressing gown over them.

"Well, I'm glad to see you're not dead," said Varallo cheerfully. "I was deputized to drop by and notify the coroner if you were. I ran into Miss Mason on your doorstep."

O'Connor sneezed and groped in the dressing gown pocket for a handkerchief.

"Honestly, men," said Katharine. "I thought you'd be feeling like this about now, and either eating all the wrong things or not at all. I've brought you some nice hot chicken broth. That being the proper way I was brought up—to invalids you bring homemade chicken broth."

O'Connor sneezed again. "Manners, Charles," said Varallo. "Aren't you going to ask us in and thank the lady?"

O'Connor glowered at him over the handkerchief. He stepped back, they came into his little living room and O'Connor shuffled across to the desk, found a memo pad and pencil, scribbled and showed it to Varallo.

"Ah," said Varallo, enlightened. *"Lost my voice.* Damn it," he added for O'Connor. "Well, Fred did predict it. That will make a little change."

"It certainly does," agreed Katharine amusedly. "It must be very frustrating for him not even to be able to swear every time he sneezes." O'Connor sneezed again and nodded violently. "What have you had to eat today?" O'Connor shook his head, spread his hands and sneezed. "Nothing at *all?* Really, Charles! You'd better have this right now while it's hot. Where's the kitchen? I'll find a bowl—"

O'Connor sneezed, blew his nose and scribbled on the memo pad, *Thanks very much.* Katharine went out to the kitchen. O'Connor looked at Varallo and raised his eyebrows, made an abortive effort to croak something and tugged on an imaginary string.

"What? Oh, no, they haven't picked him up yet. The status quo still very status," said Varallo. "Aren't you taking anything for this?" O'Connor pulled a bottle of aspirin out of his pocket. "Oh. Well, they do say it lasts about the same time whatever you do for it. I suppose you're past the infectious stage now, but you really do look like hell. I suppose you feel that way too." O'Connor nodded dolefully. Katharine came back with a bowl and spoon on a tray. "Well, now I know you're still with us, I'm off to school. I leave you to the tender ministrations of Miss Mason."

"Heavens, I'm not staying," said Katharine. "If I hadn't run into you I'd never have come farther than the door, Mr. Varallo. Whatever would the superintendent of schools say! One of his teachers— Now for goodness' sake, Charles, sit down and drink this while it's hot. It's all there—I emptied the thermos—and if you don't feel like all of it now you can warm it up again. I don't suppose you want any crackers with it." O'Connor shook his head and felt his throat. "No, I don't suppose so. It certainly does make a change, doesn't it?" she asked Varallo. O'Connor shook a fist at them, sneezed, put down the spoon and reached for his handkerchief. "Yes, indeed," said Katharine thoughtfully.

"I expect he'll live," said Varallo.

"Oh, I should think so. Though it is rather like sea-sickness—or, I understand, hay fever. You know you're not going to die of it but you wish you would. Now listen, Charles. You finish as much of that as you can and take three aspirin and go straight to bed. Oh, with some hot whiskey and lemon if you feel like that. In a couple of days," said Katharine briskly, "you'll be fine."

O'Connor nodded meekly and held up his thank-you note again.

"We got on just fine today without you," said Varallo. "You'd better stay home tomorrow too." O'Connor glared at him over a spoonful of chicken broth.

On the steps outside, Katharine laughed. "Quite heartless, but he *is* a spectacle. Poor Charles."

"He's just getting past the worst of it. I'll reserve sympathy for who-ever else he's passed it on to—and I hope devoutly I'm not one of them," said Varallo.

He drove on up to Glendale College and sat through two fairly bor-ing hours of a lecture on the various legal clauses regarding entrapment. Every other man in the class was a cop on some force: six patrolmen on the Glendale force, a couple from Pasadena and one plain-clothes man and four patrolmen from Burbank. At the midway break they talked a little desultory shop and Varallo detailed some of their current troubles to the detective from Burbank. The two towns were indistin-guishable from each other except on a map and the bad boys from one frequently pulled jobs in the other. The Burbank detective, whose name was Billings, said he'd have a look in their records for any possibles, both on the Kessler thing and the berserk killer. He added that they all had their eyes peeled, since Glendale had sent out the fliers, for George Leland Hollison, that kite flier off the Ten Most Wanted. "I was look-ing at the current *Official Detective* yesterday. They've got the usual offer of a hundred bucks' reward on him. Pity cops can't take rewards, I could use that." He yawned and rubbed his eyes. "God, I could sleep on my feet—apologies. New baby. At least three months. Going off like a time bomb at two A.M. every single damn night. You married? Any kids? Well, then you know how *that* is."

"Afraid not," said Varallo, smiling gently. "*My* daughter's a very exceptional baby. She sleeps through every night. Has since she was 2 weeks old."

"My God!" said Billings, staring at him. "I didn't know any of them ever did. My God, you just don't know how lucky you are."

Varallo got home at ten twenty and rang the bell to be let in.

When he caught up with Poor and Wayne just entering the building at eight o'clock, again they found the night men hanging around waiting for them.

"Don't tell me something new," said Wayne.

"Relax," said Burt, yawning. "Maybe a break. Patrol car brought in this j.d. about one thirty. Spotted him acting a little funny right smack on Brand Boulevard, did a little recon—it was Norman, on his regular beat—and surprised him trying to break into a dress shop. That fancy one next to the California Hotel. Point is, the kid had a gun on him."

"Oh," said Varallo. "What was the gun?"

"Little Hi-Standard twenty-two. But the kid has also a little pedigree, which includes some violence, and the bright thought hit both Ray and me that anybody who has one gun might have two, and also—forgetting the gun and remembering Collins and Gardiner—anybody who's pulled a little violence might pull a lot."

"How right you are," said Wayne. "He's sitting over on the other side of the building in a cell, I trust?"

"Oh, yes," said Harrison, sighing. "Technically, thank God, he's not a j.d. any more—over eighteen. But we had a little hassle even so. We had to get mama out of bed—there's no papa—and she had the whole office awash with tears, and all very careful we told her three times over he could have a lawyer while we questioned him, and she even routed one of those out to come down. He finally convinced her, her darling boy wasn't going to get beaten up overnight. We let the girl go home."

"Girl?"

"He had a girl with him." Katz had come up to hear most of that, and stood listening silently. "He was also very, very high—no dope, just rye, judging by the smell—so we just dumped him in a cell and left him for you boys. I dug out his record, it's on my desk," said Harrison. "Have fun with him. Anybody find out how the boss is?"

"He'll live," said Varallo, "but I don't expect we'll see him today." Burt and Harrison went off and the rest of them climbed the stairs to the detective bureau and crowded round while Wayne read off the punk's record.

Edward Everett Horstman. Turned eighteen last December. Drop-out from Hoover High. First contact with police at the age of fifteen, evidence that he attacked another boy with a knife on a junior-high-school playground. Probation. After dropping out of school, picked up at age sixteen with four other juveniles in a stolen car: all of them had been drinking whiskey stolen from the parents of one boy. Probation. The same year, picked up for Grand Theft Auto. Three months on the sheriff's farm and probation. (There, Wayne broke off to swear at the damn judges.) At age seventeen, again charged with assault—on another kid, a fight over a girl; but knives were pulled. Three months later, picked up for loitering in a suspicious manner, with three other kids, outside a house whose owners were on vacation: a neighbor had called in, spotting them. Currently, he was on probation ("My good Christ!" said Wayne disgustedly) on another Grand Theft Auto charge. Description, as of the time of the last charge, six one, one-eighty, Caucasian male, sandy hair, blue eyes, tattoo of snake on upper right biceps, no birthmarks.

"Could possibly be a Samson," said Varallo.

"Yes, and here's something else," said Wayne. "He is, by what Norman reported when he delivered him, one of those that turns nasty with a little liquor in him."

"Oh, really," said Varallo. "Well, if we're right on the time on Mrs. Collins, that seems a bit early for anybody to have had a skinful, but on the other hand this one seems to have acquired a taste for it young, so he could have. And that could have been the reason somebody did go berserk, Horstman or not."

"I'd also like to know," said Katz, "if he's got another gun—"

"Or maybe traded an old Combat Masterpiece for the one he had last night," said Poor.

"You pays your money and you takes your choice," said Wayne. "He looks fairly hot, anyway. Shall we try some questioning in depth?"

They had him brought up from the jail, they sat him down on a straight chair and before they started to ask him any questions they told him he was entitled to have his lawyer there. They asked him twice whether he wouldn't like to call his lawyer.

"Oh, what the hell?" said Horstman. "The answers won't be any different. Look, I was high. I didn't know what I was doing. I'm real sorry I tried to break in that place, it was just the kind of fool idea you get when you're high. I was gonna get Sally a new dress, see?"

"Sally's your girl?"

"Yeah, yeah, Sally Harris. We was on a date, and I was high, was all. It was just a fool idea." He shrugged. "I didn't really steal nothing, you can't hold me on that."

"No, Eddy," said Wayne, "but we'd like to ask you some questions about a couple of other things."

He just stared up at the big sergeant, and faint sullenness showed in his eyes. Varallo felt a little tired, looking at him. The pattern was set, for this one. Nothing was going to change him—except for the worse. Where had he gone off the rails? Why? Doting mother, said Harrison, but while that kind of indulgence wasn't good, plenty of men had survived it without turning into punks or pro criminals or alcoholics. No papa, said Harrison, but plenty of men had survived that and turned into responsible citizens too. Well, was there an answer? Or any combination of answers? Varallo didn't know. He just knew Horstman made him feel tired. Very tired of human nature, which could get so very damned human.

"Do you remember where you were last Friday night, Eddy?" asked Katz.

The sullen blue stare shifted to him. "Friday? What's with Friday? Yeah, it's anything to you I was with Sally then too. . . . Well, I guess from about six. To maybe two A.M."

"Have your gun with you then, Eddy?" asked Poor genially.

After a minute Horstman said, "I keep it in the glove compartment. Now you bastards took it, I suppose I don't get it back. All I wanted it for was protect myself."

"You want to carry a gun around in this state, you're supposed to have a license for it, Eddy. I don't see you getting one." Wayne. "Where'd you get it?"

"I bought it off a guy."

"Who?"

"I don't remember who. Some guy."

"When?"

"Oh, for God's sake, six months ago or about then. I never even fired it, for God's sake! . . . I don't *remember* who. I didn't know him, another guy I knew knew him. . . . No, I never had another gun. . . . No, I—"

"What about Saturday night, Eddy?" asked Varallo. "Where were you then?"

"Oh, for God's sake," said Horstman. "You guys. A guy does a couple little things and every time something happens you pick on him. I haven't done anything. It's a crime to get high? None of you ever been high, hah, I'll bet!"

"Saturday night," said Varallo, feeling tired.

"Oh, hell, it was Sally's birthday. No. No, that was on Sunday. On Saturday night—on Saturday night I went to get her a present. That's all. Downtown. At—I forget the store."

"What'd you get her, Eddy?"

"I got her a ring."

There was a little silence. "Is that so?" said Katz softly. "What kind of ring?"

"Just a ring, for God's sake. With a blue stone in it. She likes blue."

"Where'd you get it?"

"I forget. Some little store on Brand."

"How much did you pay for it?"

"About—about thirty bucks. Around there."

"How'd you happen to have that much money?" He didn't have a job at the moment; he lived with his mother, who was a salesclerk at a chain dime store downtown. "Well? Where'd you get the thirty bucks?"

Horstman said, "For God's sake. Bully a guy till he can't think. I—a guy owed it to me, he paid up."

"Who?"

"What d'you mean?" Stalling.

"Who paid you the thirty bucks?" asked Wayne patiently.

"I—oh, a guy named Don. I don't know his other name."

"Now look, Eddy," said Katz gently, "we've been on the merry-go-round rides before. We know all about you and all the little punks like you, so don't think you can con us even the first time round. There's no guy named Don. Where'd a punk like you get thirty bucks to lend a guy you didn't know? Don't be any stupider than you can help, Eddy."

"I tell you—"

"Tell us straight, Eddy." Absently Wayne flexed all those muscles. "Where'd you get the thirty bucks?"

"This guy paid me back, I said."

"Oh, God give me strength," said Wayne. "We do earn the pension, listening to the punks. You don't remember the name of the store? Did you keep the receipt for Sally's pretty ring?"

"I think," said Katz meditatively, "I'd like to see that ring."

Horstman looked at him from under heavy eyebrows; and back to Wayne. "What? Re— Oh, no. No, I don't guess I did. Why should I? I was giving the ring to Sally next day."

"What time on Saturday night did you buy it?" asked Katz.

"I guess—about—it was after dinner I went—about seven. I—"

"Well, that's a lie anyway," said Katz. "Nothing's open Saturday night in Glendale except Sears, and the drugstores, and Webbs'. Take your choice, Eddy. You buy the ring any of those places?"

Horstman looked at him and shut his mouth to a hard line. "I'm not saying anything more."

And after a futile little while prodding at him to reconsider that, they had to send him back to his cell. Probably some time today fond mama would get him out on bail; it could be—he hadn't actually succeeded in breaking into the dress shop—in the end, charges would be dismissed. But—

"But," said Katz, "I would like a look at that ring."

So he and Varallo went to call on Sally Harris. Who was, in a sort of way, a counterpart to Eddy Horstman; and Varallo, the new father of a daughter, looked at her sadly and wondered and deplored, and renewed a silent vow about proper discipline and what old Mr. Butterworth called moral training.

You didn't like to think, typical. She was seventeen and she looked twenty-five. She had a towering beehive hairdo of bleached platinum, and an accumulation of several days' make-up, and chipped blood-red nail polish, and her neck was dirty. She'd be a little too fat in another five years if she didn't watch it, and she was wearing soiled blue stretch capris and a ruffled pink cotton overblouse and thong sandals, and she batted false eyelashes at Varallo's tall blond handsomeness, and he felt tired all over again.

He thought, Babies. Most babies cute, and cuddly, and always, a new beginning. A new Somebody.

His darling Ginevra.

Once this one had been all new, too. Was there an answer?

Before her mother went to call Sally from her room, she had looked at them a little fearfully and said, "I didn't like her goin' around with him—one like that. Been in police trouble. Like that. But you just can't talk to Sally. Not no ways." She was a small, defeated and unhappy woman. "She just don't listen to me," she said. "I sort of give up trying. I go get her."

Sally batted the eyelashes at Varallo. "Sure, Eddy give me a ring for my birthday. Not that we're engaged. I go round with Eddy some but I guess I can do better than Eddy Horstman, it comes to getting married. . . . Why you wanna see it?" Sudden suspicion and greed flared in the shallow blue eyes. "You gonna tell me that jerk went and stole it someplace—you're gonna take it back?"

"We don't know, Miss Harris. We'd just like to look at it. We can get a warrant."

"Oh, for—"

"Sally, if they just wanta *look* at it," said her mother timidly.

"Yeah, yeah, cops I know!" And then she relaxed, put on the languid sophistication. "Oh, *well*. Cheap little thing like it is, I guess, what's it *matter?* O.K., I'll get it." She moved to the door, swaying her hips.

It was Katz who looked at it, thoroughly, with a jeweler's loupe. Then they thanked Sally, handed it back and left.

"Verdict?" said Varallo, thrusting the key into the ignition.

"Well, it could be, Vic. The hell of it is, of course, we haven't got exact descriptions of all the Kessler stuff. The cheap mass-produced stuff like that is fairly anonymous. Even with Kessler's manifests from the wholesaler. That ring is a very anonymous bit—the synthetic aquamarine set in a perfectly plain fourteen-karat mounting. It'd retail for about thirty bucks, sure. Among the Kessler list is such a ring, sure. But I'm not turning any handsprings, because almost any jeweler in town would also have such a thing in stock, there's no identifying mark on it, *and* we haven't got one single other thing to hook up Eddy with Kessler."

"No. Go look up all his pals? See if we can hook him up with a Combat Masterpiece? He is just the type we decided on, Joe."

"I know, I know. I continue to have the funny feeling about the Kessler thing," said Katz. "We'll do that, sure. Make the effort. But even so, Vic—even if he gave one piece to Sally—just the typical punk— where's the rest of it?"

"I don't know, Joe. I guess I've got a kind of funny feeling about Kessler too. As well as the Collins-Gardiner thing."

"Which is *a* thing," said Katz.

They went back to the office. Just as they came in, Wayne put down the phone. "Out you go again, genius," he said. "We just got a call from this pawnbroker. Benjamin Lefkowitz over in South Pasadena. He's got a portable RCA television which just might belong to Harry Gardiner. Go talk to him."

CHAPTER 9

"How about it, Mr. Gardiner?" asked Varallo.

Harry Gardiner looked at the portable RCA television. He was in a surly state; Varallo had decided to take him along in the hope of a possible identification, and Gardiner had been very unwilling to close his drugstore. Yes, of course he wanted whoever had murdered his poor wife found, but on a business day—and his usual part-time employee not available. Varallo ought to understand that in business one had a certain responsibility— Losing a little patience with him, Varallo had been curt, and Gardiner had reluctantly agreed to come with him.

Now, Varallo could admit he'd been in the wrong. The television was the counterpart of God knew how many others of the same make and model. Barring the presence of any distinctive scars, nobody could identify it absolutely as having come from anywhere.

Unfortunately, more precise means of identification were not available. Gardiner had thrown away the written guarantee when it expired, and the discount house where he had bought it had since gone out of business. There was no record obtainable of the serial number of Gardiner's TV.

Gardiner looked at this one. It sat on a shelf in the back room of Mr. Lefkowitz pawnshop; Mr. Lefkowitz, a brisk good-looking young fellow with alert eyes and a friendly manner, watched eagerly. Varallo thought Mr. Lefkowitz, thank God there were some left, was one of the many citizens who still thought of the cops as the Good Guys and enjoyed helping them out.

"You understand, I can't say," said Gardiner. "I really couldn't. It could be the one—it's like it. But I don't know." He sounded petulant. "I was never interested in it—a silly extravagant waste of money. I never watched it. It was Agnes kept at me and at me, everybody had one, she'd watched the Glovers' and liked some of the silly shows. And so it was, Why couldn't we have just a little one, and so on and so on. A hundred and thirty-nine fifty, for a thing like that. I never paid any attention to it. And Agnes knew how I felt—the electric bill, too—she didn't put it on while I was home." He fell silent, staring at the TV.

Mr. Lefkowitz cocked his smooth dark head and gave Varallo a hint of a wink that said, Miserly old fellow, no? "It's a fairly new model," he contributed.

"It looks like the one I bought," said Gardiner. "A hundred and thirty-nine fifty. Outrageous. I said so at the time. For *that*. But that's all I can say." He went on staring at the TV, as if it reminded him of the original outrage.

"Well—" said Varallo. It was really all he could expect. If they only had the serial number, damn it. "So who brought it in?" he asked Lefkowitz.

"First customer this morning," said Lefkowitz promptly, ready for the questions, confident. "I'll confess to you, I didn't spot it then—I've been away, only got back last night, and I hadn't read over the latest hot list. When I did, at lunch, I spotted it. It was two young fellows. Early twenties. The one who pawned it gave his name as James Currier. About six feet, slim build, sandy, blue eyes. Crew cut. He's got a tattoo on his left forearm—Navy—anchor and U.S.N. The other one was shorter, maybe five nine, darker, could be a year or so older, I won't swear to his eyes, ordinary-looking duck."

"You ever think of joining the force, Mr. Lefkowitz? That's pretty good."

"I'll tell you the truth," said Lefkowitz sadly, "I tried to get on the L.A.P.D., and your force, and Pasadena. They won't have me. My eyes. You know about the requirements. I've got to admit, blind as a bat without glasses. So what else, I give in to my old man and manage one of his businesses for him."

"Oh. Well, that's too bad—we can always use a camera eye. Did Currier give you any address?"

"Yep. One reason I called in. On Maple Street, only I looked in the phone book and he's not listed. Anywhere." Lefkowitz mentioned the address.

Varallo eyed the TV. Some heartbreaking work had been done, on the Collins murder, by both Burt and Rhys; the whole place dusted and everybody she knew who'd been in the house recently checked out. No strange prints had showed. Ditto the Gardiner house, with the same result. So it'd do no good to dust this very-much-maybe TV, because they hadn't any prints to compare.

"And they cost to repair," said Gardiner suddenly, still looking at the TV. "That guarantee wasn't a guarantee at all—that was outrageous too! When something went wrong with it—I don't know what—Agnes called the company and a man came, but he charged me eleven dollars and thirty-four cents for parts. And all the satisfaction I got when I complained was to be told the guarantee didn't cover the cost of new parts."

"Some guarantees written up like that," said Lefkowitz easily. "Tough luck . . . As I say, when I did look over the new hot list and spotted that TV, I thought this might be it, so I called."

"We appreciate it." What else was there do on the TV? Check out Currier, of course. And while Currier's description vaguely matched Eddy Horstman's, Horstman had different tattoos. Of course, Horstman might be hooked up to Kessler instead; in fact, Varallo was feeling that he was a very likely bet for Kessler. Considering that ring.

"*Prices,*" said Gardiner. "It's terrible, do you know? Just terrible. Why, just the prices for the very food we put in our mouths—and Agnes wasn't always as careful as she could have been. I tried to tell her. But with the business, I couldn't always go shopping with her. Milk alone. Even skim milk. And bread. I was *always* telling her. And then such a foolish extravagance as—as *that.*" He nodded at the TV. "It was a long while before I gave in—and then I insisted that she save at least part of the cost from what I gave her for the house. I believe she hadn't bought any new clothes for several years, saving for that. And as I told the fellow; it's morally dishonest to give out a guarantee which isn't a guarantee at all. Agnes had paid it—I daresay she had to, the man right there —and she was almost afraid to tell me. Disgraceful. But I got no satisfaction from the company at all." His voice, which had been shaking a little, trailed off into silence, and while Varallo and Lefkowitz watched him, he suddenly began to tremble, and put both hands to his face, and said in a muffled voice, "*Agnes!*"

"You sit down a minute, Mr. Gardiner," said Varallo gently, and shoved a chair forward. . . . People made the way they were made, he thought. . . . It got to be a way of life for the ones like Harry Gardiner, scrimp and save and put away and keep an eye on the pence, everything to life seen from the one viewpoint— How much will it cost? How much will we save on it?—put away, get the interest, save for the comfortable secure old age and easy retirement and maybe the necessary doctor bills, save, save, save. It got to be a religion, and maybe Agnes Gardiner converted too—forty years—and almost as bad. (Only she'd backslid over the TV.) And then all of a sudden the blind violence struck—one of the greedy ones, unlike you wanting something for nothing—and left your life in chaos. And maybe, looking at the little TV which was like the one Agnes had enjoyed, you realized all of a sudden how little use it had all been, what a waste of life it had been. You thought, maybe, of the pretty clothes Agnes hadn't had when she was younger, the movies you hadn't seen, the vacation trips you hadn't taken, the too-expensive sirloins you hadn't enjoyed— And now Agnes dead, never even to enjoy the quiet benefits of security earned. And you broke down, thinking about it.

They eased the old man onto the chair and he kept his hands over his face and rocked a little.

"Poor old fellow," said Lefkowitz compassionately. "Hell of a thing. These punks. You think this is any lead?"

"It's up in the air. If we had the serial number of the TV— Oh, well, we'll see how this Currier checks out." Varallo looked at Gardiner. "I suppose I'd better take him home first. Waste of time to drag him over here, but you try anything."

"Thankless job," said Lefkowitz sympathetically. "I'll wish you luck on getting one like that. Beating people to death, my God."

"You feeling better, Mr. Gardiner?"

At the touch on his shoulder Gardiner sat up. "I'm all right," he said stiffly. "I beg your pardon."

"I'm sorry I had to ask you to come, sir. I'll take you home now," said Varallo.

But in the car, Gardiner insisted on being taken back to the drugstore. "Life does go on. And one has a certain responsibility to regular customers."

And that whole bit proved to be a waste of time—as so much of police routine always is. Varallo went back to Pasadena and sought out James Currier on Maple Street. James Currier was quite surprised to see him and his badge, but let him in and answered questions readily. Currier had just been discharged from the navy after his first tour, and was temporarily living with his married sister Ruth, and Ruth's husband Frank had just lost his job and there were the three kids and all, it was tough, and Ruth was looking for a job but so far no luck, and she'd asked him to take the TV in and pawn it because of course he could carry it easier than she could, and Frank was down at the employment agency. It'd been a friend of his with him, old school friend, Ernie Bauer. Did Varallo want Ernie's address? He'd got twenty bucks for the TV, buy a few groceries at least. And he'd been thinking of signing up for another tour of duty—he liked the navy fine—but seeing how things were, he figured he'd better get a job and try to help out here until Frank got something steady again.

Varallo wasted the next three hours tracing the TV back to the place Frank Lamont had bought it. The business had changed locations twice, and it was a big discount house where every known variety of household item was sold, and while the personnel were willing and eager to help, none of it was very efficient, and it was some while before the serial number was run to earth.

When he finally got it he went back to Mr. Lefkowitz' pawnshop and checked. The TV was the one Frank Lamont had bought.

"I don't know why you want to be a cop, Mr. Lefkowitz," he said. "I don't know why anybody does, frankly. I've wasted nearly the whole day on this and it doesn't mean one single damn. We're right where we were before."

"Not quite," said Lefkowitz. "You know somebody else who didn't do it. And all my fault—apologies."

"You needn't apologize. Next time you spot something on the hot list, you call in again. In the end, we always do depend on the cooperation of the citizens. Even if you're not always right."

He went back to the office and discovered—it was getting on for three thirty—that the rest of the boys had had an abortive day too. With the help of a cooperative lawyer they'd got Mrs. Horstman to postpone yanking her darling boy out of his cell; under the law they could hold him twenty-four hours without a charge; and as Horstman refused to open his mouth, they'd set about the tedious task of locating his closest pals to question.

Mrs. Horstman—whether truthful or not—disclaimed any knowledge of her son's friends. But they had some names from records, kids he'd been picked up with, and they'd started to check those out. Poor and Rhys were still out looking for a couple of those. The hopeful point being that quite often a punk like Eddy would boast to pals about a job: and quite likely, if Horstman had been the X on the Kessler thing, one of his pals would know something about the gun.

Just before Varallo came in, Katz and Wayne had come back with something that looked more helpful than anything else they'd found. The various pals of Eddy's they'd had in had all disclaimed any recent association with him, and that was only what had been expected; but now they were hearing it again and it sounded very much like the truth, seeing who it was coming from.

"I tell you," Steve Miller was saying honestly, "I don't want anything to do with any of those guys. Not since last year. You're not going to be having any reason, haul me in here again. But—" He was a nice-looking boy, medium-sized and dark, with a fresh complexion.

"I should hope not," said his father beside him, and smiled. Fred Miller was a big jolly-looking man, neat and clean in good sports clothes; but his jaw was solid and his expression a trifle grim right now. He was the manager of a men's clothing store downtown, and had a nice house up on Olmsted. "I'm a practical man, gentlemen. I don't know what any of you might advocate in such a situation, but me, I think I used logic." He turned a benevolent gaze on his son. "I'd figured we'd brought him up O.K., but I realize adolescence can be—and all the pressures on kids these days— But it did really rock me when I found *my* kid getting hauled in by you fellows on a stolen car charge, even if he was just with the other kids. Well, it rocked me. I just tried to use my head."

"I guess you did all right," said Steve. "I guess you got me using *my* head, Dad." He grinned at his father.

"Sure." Miller grinned back at him. "My kid, running around with no-goodniks like that, *and* high on whiskey. What do I do? I'll tell you, gentlemen. I take him downtown to Georgia Street emergency, I let him have a good look at all the people bleeding and dying, they've got run into by some fool drunk, or got drunk themselves. At all the idiots on dope. I take him to police court, give him a good look at all the bums and the hoods, how they live, how they always get caught up to in the end. I take him down to Central Jail—I got a friend in the D.A.'s office— I let him look, I say, This is where you want to end up? So, imagine, he starts to think twice and he decides he'll go to college and be an engineer instead. But then he's a fairly smart boy, being my boy."

Steve laughed. "Well, I did," he said. "I mean, all that does make you think."

"Mr. Miller's a fairly smart man," said Varallo dryly, drifting in to hear that. The heat wave was still with them; he took off his jacket and hung it over the back of his desk chair.

"So I couldn't tell you anything about Eddy Horstman lately—that I know, you know, firsthand," said Steve. "But if it means anything—I'd told Dad this before, see—I still see this Bob Oestreicher in school. We're both first year at Glendale College. And Bob's brother Ken, he used to be one of Eddy's pals when—when I was still sort of in that crowd, see, only Bob doesn't want anything to do with them either, he tries to get Ken out of that bunch but— But anyway, from Bob I know this, that Eddy hasn't been teaming up with any of them in quite a while. He's got a bunch of new pals, some of 'em over in Hollywood, from what Ken says. Ken told Bob the last time he saw Eddy—which would I guess be a couple of months back—Eddy was talking about some really big deal, way he said it, a real—you know—crime job. Like a hold-up or something. Well, the way I say, I don't want any part—or does Bob—he tries to straighten out Kenny, just the little things that bunch does like stripping cars and—"

"None of it's little, Steve," said Wayne.

"No, sir, I guess not. But you see what I mean."

They saw what he meant. In a way it was discouraging. It meant that Eddy, graduating or about to graduate to the bigger-time jobs than hopping cars and so on, had teamed up with a variety of new, unknown pals—but "some of 'em over in Hollywood." That was a fairly large piece of territory, but on the other hand, if Eddy's new pals were on the verge of being real pros, it just could be that some of them would be in Hollywood's records.

They thanked the Millers, and the Millers departed. Varallo related his saga about the TV set, which was received in gloomy silence. Seeing that no citizens were present to notice their public image, Joe Katz took off his tie and unbuttoned his shirt.

"It is a little funny about all Mrs. Collins' diamonds," he said. "About ten grand worth, you said? Sometime I'd like to see a description. Because we said, on the Collins-Gardiner thing, not very likely a pro. Very likely a nut. Considering the autopsy reports. House cleaned, and Collins was fourteen days ago—fifteen—but none of the loot has showed. Only a pro would know a fence—as I pointed out on Kessler. But—"

"Oh, hell," said Wayne, loosening his tie, "we could be wrong six ways from the ace, Joe, on both cases. First glance, kind of ordinary cases—according to what we know is ordinary—but you look at them closer, a little offbeat. We're going to have to make up our minds about Eddy pretty quick. Charge or no charge."

"That's no problem, Fred." Varallo sat down, leaned back and lit a cigarette. "We've got not one single damn thing to make a charge. The D.A. would just laugh at us. He could have been the one, on Kessler. But—"

"There's nothing, just that ring," said Katz. "I'd take a bet on the manufacturer. Either Crown or Regent. The two biggest outfits, and I could march you into any jeweler's here or in Hollywood or L.A. and show you the same damn ring in stock. So Eddy tells us a fairy story about the ring. What does it say? It says it could be Eddy bought it from a pal who shoplifted it—or at a pawnshop where somebody who'd stolen it hocked it. Or Eddy shoplifted it himself. It doesn't put Eddy at Kessler's."

"You'll have to let him go," said Varallo, blowing smoke at the ceiling. "He's on probation—could be they'll stick him back at the sheriff's farm, but I rather doubt it."

"Hell!" said Wayne. "I know, I know that. Search warrant for the Horstman house coming through, but I take no bets on finding that old Combat Masterpiece under Eddy's mattress."

Nobody took any bets on that. They'd spent most of today on what had turned out to be wasted effort, and they were annoyed, but as experienced cops philosophical about it. A lot of days turned out that way. At least they had a few things going for them: old Mr. Butterworth had given them such a very good description of the heist man that they had had a provisional sketch made up from the Identikit; and a lot of citizens who read the papers had their eyes peeled for George Leland Hollison, the check artist.

"I just wish—" began Katz, and a man came into the big office from the corridor. He was a big man, with just the beginnings of a paunch, a man maybe forty-five, in a rather tired gray suit and a shirt that had been clean this morning, and a blue-and-crimson tie that had seen better days, and he stopped to mop his forehead just inside the door.

"Must be ten degrees hotter over here," he said in a pleasant voice.

And they all knew without any telling that he was another cop, one of them, one of the Good Guys doing the dirty thankless job of protecting the citizenry. It was a funny thing how they all knew. Not just by the little unnoticeable bulge of the gun at the left shoulder; not just by his taking-for-granted air of the big untidy desk-filled detective bureau. Something intangible. Like the secret grip of lodge brothers. They just knew.

"Sergeant Wayne?"

"I'm Wayne." He stood up.

"Hanrihan. I'm from Wilcox Street." He proffered his I.D.

"Sergeant," said Wayne. "Sit down. What can we suburbanite cops do for you?"

Hanrihan hoisted a hip on Poor's desk. "Well, I'm afraid I've come to take a little punk away from you, unless you've got a heavier charge on him. One Edward Everett Horstman. A pal of his—Dick Garnette— came sort of unstuck an hour ago and parted with this and that, so I chase over to Glendale to pick up Horstman, and surprise, surprise, his doting mama tells me you've got him. So—"

"Oh-oh," said Wayne dismally. "Talk about coming unstuck—I have a premonition. What've you got on him?"

"I know what they've got on him," said Katz gloomily. "A burglary. Burglary of a jewelry store. And among the loot is a synthetic aquamarine ring in a plain fourteen-karat mounting. Which means—"

"Psychics you've got on the Glendale force," said Hanrihan. "How'd you know?"

"I've got a crystal ball," said Katz. "Oh, hell. You've got evidence, Sergeant?"

"Some dandy evidence. Well, the usual circumstantial—but it could be he's still got some of the loot. Little place over on Hollywood Boulevard knocked over last Friday night. The usual bastard to work—the anonymous thing, you know—but we got, believe it or not, a couple of prints. Turned out to belong to this Garnette, who has a pedigree. We just picked him up this afternoon, and he's been singing. Loud and clear. Brings in Horstman and another guy, a Rex Heliker. Ring a bell? No? Anyway—"

"Maybe you'll want to talk to a Sally Harris here," said Wayne. "Horstman claims he was on a date with her Friday night. I'll give you her address. . . . Hell *and* damnation. So the ring hadn't anything to do with Kessler, and we're right back where we started."

"Not quite, Fred," said Varallo. "Hollywood's cleaned up a break-in and got Eddy on a big-time charge."

"I've got a warrant for him," said Hanrihan. "Have I upset something, boys? Apologies."

"Never mind, never mind," said Wayne mournfully. "I only wish the boss was here—his vocabulary's better than mine. We'd just decided we hadn't any legit charge on Eddy, anyway. Take him. Take him, you're welcome, Sergeant."

"Oh, well!" said Hanrihan, grinning. "That's the way the ball bounces. We'll hope to get some nice evidence on Eddy, if you haven't."

And, Varallo reflected, tomorrow was his day off; he could for a while forget the thankless job.

CHAPTER 10

He got up later than usual and took the baby out to play in her play pen, carefully in the shade, while he did some weeding and spraying of his roses. It was hot again, but not quite as bad as yesterday, he thought; probably the heat wave was broken. Thank God. It was really adding insult to injury at this time of year.

Brandywine needed spraying as well as Charlotte Armstrong—that damned aphis knew no seasons—and Frau Karl Druschke was drooping a little. Lilac Dawn hadn't bloomed yet, and he gave it a feeding, hopefully; that was a new one and should be really something to see, a true lavender. Otherwise it looked healthy enough. . . . Damn silly thing, big tough cop Varallo turning into a rose fancier, but you got interested.

Laura came out with her bag in one hand and keys in the other. "I'm just going down to the market. Any errands?"

"I'm almost out of cigarettes." He refused to smoke filters, as she did. "You might pick up a carton."

"Will do. Is Gideon around?" They looked. Gideon, so catlike otherwise in matters of self-preservation, had no caution about cars. Varallo finally spotted him hopefully stalking a butterfly behind Ulrich Brunner at the rear of the yard, and held on to him while Laura backed out.

The mail came while she was gone, and when she came back with an armful of groceries he was stretched out beside the play pen looking through a gardening catalogue.

"*Look* at this," she said, pausing beside him. "Not even a full bag, Vic. A bag I can carry in one arm, supposedly the weaker sex. *Nine* dollars and forty-three cents. It's outrageous."

"I know, *cara*," said Varallo, with a fleeting thought of old Harry

Gardiner. "There's a new spray out, I think I'll get some to try. They swear—of course you can't depend on a guarantee, but on the other hand the Tropico Nursery's a good one, always reliable and it stands behind its—"

"Oh, damn," said Laura suddenly.

"Don't—"

"Swear. Not ladylike. Must set a good example to the child. I *am* sorry, Vic, I forgot your cigarettes. I ran into Mrs. Stewart and we— I *am* sorry."

"Don't try to kid me," said Varallo, getting up. "You're just getting miserly with the grocery allowance. Let me pay for my own coffin nails. It's all right, *cara,* I want to go and get some of this new stuff to try. Just for fun." He followed her into the house and went down to the bedroom for a tie, from force of habit, and then realized on his day off he needn't bother. He picked up his billfold and car keys.

"Gideon's in. Having lunch. Fix you anything special for when you get back? No, come to think," said Laura, "you'll hang around at the nursery and get talking to somebody and forget all about lunch."

Varallo laughed. "I won't be long." He cast a fond glance at the very exceptionally good baby, who was happily chewing on a plush toy kitten, and backed out the Chevy.

He stopped at the market and got the cigarettes. Drove on down Glendale Boulevard to Wilson, again force of habit, and glanced at the new headquarters building as he passed. He turned on Pacific and went down to the Tropico Nursery on San Fernando.

Sometimes it was quite crowded, less often not: a big nursery, and they operated a landscaping and gardening service too. The elderly Japanese named Sam came up to serve Varallo, and they discussed the new spray. "It's good, all right, Mr. Varallo. I think even better than Aerosect. Look, you try one can, and if you don't think it's better, I give you your money back, O.K.?"

"Fair enough," said Varallo. "Oh, you'd better give me some more of that rose food too."

"You be careful with that, Mr. Varallo, especially in this heat. O.K." Sam went off to the back, and Varallo lit a cigarette and stood waiting.

A thin woman was being waited on by Sam's very pretty and very much on the ball daughter. A fat man was looking at the counter of stone garden ornaments, fingering a statue of St. Francis. Another woman was arguing with Sam's nephew over snail repellent. And another man was just standing around a little way from the counter with the cash register on it. Varallo's gaze passed over him and then snapped back. . . .

Old Mr. Butterworth had sharp eyes. For all his shock and upset, he'd given them such a good description of the heist man that they'd got a provisional sketch. And Varallo had, of course, seen it: had, of course, been one of the detectives using the Identikit with Mr. Butterworth to come up with the closest approximation to set of eyes, ears, line of jaw, shape of face, and so on and so on. Now, something about this fellow rang a faint but clear bell in his mind. Something? There was the general description—medium-sized, dark, sports clothes and so on; but also, that sketch— The same long-lobed ears, and the lantern jaw, and long thin nose. The man was standing in profile to him; Varallo waited, watching, until the man turned restlessly; and then he was nearly sure. By God, he thought, is it? Have I—a cop, casually on my day off—run across our boy? In a town of over a hundred and thirty thousand population? Well, it could be, it could be. Coincidence took a hand in things sometimes.

In any case, he thought, this fellow didn't look or act like a regular customer of the nursery—any nursery. He didn't seem interested in anything here, as the average gardener who came in would be—he wasn't, while waiting for a clerk, looking at the various ornamental planting tubs and pots, the large variety of garden ornaments, or the counter of weed killers and sprays and snail killers and rose food and camellia food and azalea food and prepared mulch and the different kinds of nozzles for hoses and the ant repellents: nor the various potted plants sitting around. He didn't—as practically every gardener did who came into this place—wander down past the porch at the rear to inspect the hundred and one growing plants for sale under the big net canopy over the yard. He just stood near the counter, waiting.

And by any logic, of course, he could be a non-gardener whose mother or aunt had said to him, "Oh, please stop by the nursery and pick up some rose food"—or spray, or ant repellent, or anything else. On the other hand, there was the sketch. The fellow really did resemble that sketch. Yes, the same shaped face—an odd shape, if Mr. Butterworth was right (and Varallo would lay odds Mr. Butterworth was): a face very wide at the temples, sloping abruptly with hollow cheeks to a long pointed jaw. And the eyes wide apart, and dark eyes, as Mr. Butterworth had said. And he had on dark slacks, not very clean or well-pressed, and a blue shirt, and—at about eighty degrees—an imitation leather jacket half buttoned up.

Varallo wondered very hard. He was nearly, nearly sure. It wouldn't do any harm to find out a little more about him, if possible. Because the heist man had been hitting a variety of places, not choosing all drugstores or all theaters, and conceivably he could be planning to hit a nursery.

While Varallo debated, trying to visualize the sketch from memory, the man made up his mind for him. He turned again, looking over the one big inside room of the nursery with one comprehensive glance, scanned the people there and then glanced back to the counter with the register, and sent one quick glance out the back door. And to any experienced cop, he might just as well have spoken his thoughts aloud.

This was their boy. He'd cased the nursery; he probably knew that the back was all fenced on three sides, no quick way out there. It could be when he'd cased it, there hadn't been any customers in and—as was often the case at slow times—only old Sam sitting on his high stool behind the counter. So the nursery had been marked as a place to hit, and here he was all ready to pull the job.

Only, a hitch. Four customers in here, and some more—Varallo could hear them talking—out in back, wandering among the rows of plants; and probably at least one of Sam's nephews out there, and in here Sam's daughter Mary and Sam's nephew Joe. And Sam himself. Too many people. Right now the heist man was wondering whether to hang around hoping that eventually there'd come a moment when he was alone with Sam, or whether to skip it and get out.

And, Varallo thought, for about a hundred percent sure there was a gun under that imitation leather jacket. And he wished to hell it wasn't his day off and that his own gun, the nice solid hefty thirty-eight Police Positive, wasn't innocently resting at home on top of the pile of clean handkerchiefs in the bureau drawer. . . . But then he remembered old Mr. Butterworth, who had indignantly, in the face of the heist man's gun, told him to go straight to hell—and thought the heist man had been a little taken aback. . . . First jobs? thought Varallo. Well, a gun was a gun—and as the patrolman Connors had said, a hell of a good way to get shot. Who could say whether Mr. Butterworth would have ended up shot or not, if that deliveryman hadn't happened to come in just then?

Sam came back, short, stocky and stooped of shoulder, with a can of spray in one hand and a bag of rose food in the other. The thin woman went out. The fat man was nodding at Sam's nephew over the statue of

St. Francis. The heist man took a couple of steps farther away from the counter and fingered a box of ant poison.

"Three sixty-six, Mr. Varallo," said Sam.

Varallo gave him a five. "Sam, do you know that fellow over there in the black jacket?" he asked in a low voice.

"Never laid eyes on him before," said Sam, and rang up the sale. Two women came in, and a middle-aged couple came back from the yard with Sam's nephew Jerry behind them.

Varallo saw the man make up his mind. This crowd was too much. He turned and started out rapidly. Varallo started after him.

"Hey, Mr. Varallo, your change—and you forgot your—"

Varallo gestured back at him hushingly; Sam's voice died, uncertain.

The man turned right at the door, and Varallo debated for one agonizing moment. Toward a car? This was practically certain in Southern California. Varallo's car was parked up to the left. Run back there, yes, and do what? Start the engine and wait. X's car might be on a side street, facing the other way, and never a glimpse to be caught. There was a long chance that there wasn't any car, and you couldn't tail a man on foot in a car. Varallo almost turned, to be in the Chevy ready, hoping that he'd have a clear view of X getting into a car parked along San Fernando here. He never knew why he didn't. Possibly, he thought afterward, at sporadic moments some guardian angel watched over the affairs of good cops who kept up to standard on the range and never lost patience with the irrational citizenry. Possibly the protective spirits of cops in the great beyond, still cooperating as good cops should.

Anyway, he didn't go back for the car. He followed X on foot, down San Fernando. And after a block, he was sure X wasn't heading for a car. A lot of empty parking spaces along here, and if X had a car he'd certainly have left it as near as possible, anticipating a getaway from a heist job.

And now Varallo was sure of him. Mr. Butterworth had said, "When he walked out, from the back he had a funny sort of walk—as if he was rocking a bit back and forth." The man ahead of Varallo on the sidewalk rocked from one foot to the other, just slightly, an odd lurching gait; but he was walking fast. There were no other pedestrians on the street. There seldom would be, along this block. On up from here, behind them, San Fernando Boulevard was mostly industry: small manufacturing. Here, they were heading toward Los Feliz, and more neighborhood shops and small businesses.

And Varallo started wondering about something else. Was X, having missed pulling one job, thinking about another right away? Had he passed his own car parked outside the nursery there, and headed at random toward those small shops two blocks down? On the spur of the moment? Anxiously Varallo wondered. On the next corner was a small tavern; next to it a dry cleaner's (and the heist man had hit one of those before), then a laundromat and then—unlikely—a wholesale lighting fixture store. The tavern? Better to approach X now, show the badge pinned inside his billfold, ask for I.D.? Call up a car, take him in on suspicion? He might come meek as a lamb; on the other hand he might not.

And also on the other hand—eyewitness evidence. Sometimes it was worth just damn all. Varallo would trust Mr. Butterworth, he thought; but direct evidence was always nice. If X now walked into the tavern—it was a good time to hit a tavern, especially a small one off the beaten path like this, the lunch crowd not yet in—and attempted a job, very nice to catch him in the act.

Varallo felt naked without the gun. He kept twenty feet behind the man, who lurched ahead surprisingly fast, crossed Acacia Street which dead-ended at San Fernando and stopped on the opposite curb. Varallo slowed.

The man stood irresolutely for thirty seconds and then went into the tavern. Varallo crossed Acacia and followed him in.

It was a small dim room, redolent of beer, with a long curved bar at the end and a few booths against two walls. And at a quarter of twelve this hot Thursday morning there wasn't a soul in the place but the bartender, a little fat fellow in a clean white apron. He was at one end of the bar, lethargically packaging sandwiches in cellophane bags for the lunch trade. He looked up and smiled at the sight of customers.

The man in the imitation leather jacket moved up to the bar. Varallo didn't think he knew anyone was behind him. He prayed the bartender wouldn't do or say anything to call attention to him.

It went as if it had been rehearsed, after that. For the next forty-five seconds, that was.

"Beer," said the man in the jacket.

Varallo was ten feet behind him, standing still.

"Coming right up," said the bartender genially. He took a clean glass from the shelf behind the bar. "Tap, sir?"

"O.K."

The bartender went to the far end to decant the tap beer. He trotted back and set the foaming glass before the man, and then the glass skidded before his fingers let go of it and his eyes got wider and he said with a little gasp, "What—"

"—is a holdup. You just act nice and quiet, you don't get hurt. You go open up the—"

"Hold it right there!" said Varallo, and lunged for him. He got him by one shoulder, pulled him around—*what hand was the gun in?*—and there was a loud crack and something buzzed angrily past his left ear leaving a little sting. Gun in right hand; he grabbed for it, intent on the gun—naked without a gun (for the first time he appreciated how O'Connor felt about that favorite .357 magnum), he got his left hand tight round the barrel of the gun, a very damned good way to get his hand shot off—

"Hey!" yelled the bartender. "Hey! What's—"

"Call the police!" Varallo yelled back at him. He shoved violently at the man; he shifted his left hand to the man's wrist and twisted with all his strength, heard something heavy drop to the floor. The gun. Good. He kicked at it blindly, couldn't find it. Man to man, and Vic Varallo was six one and weighed in at a solid one eighty and wasn't any stranger to hand-to-hand fighting— Only he'd never run up against anything like X before.

The next five minutes were confused in his mind. The fellow wasn't as big as he was, but he turned into a wildcat. They were on the floor, they were banging up against the bar, and rolling—teeth in his right hand, he swung and connected hard with something, and then there was a fighting, screaming weight on top of him, and blows—on his face, neck, ribs. With a violent effort he clutched, and rolled; and then a squirming body under him, a knee trying for his groin, nails clawing at his face—he jerked back involuntarily, and the knee found its mark, and he gasped in agony, again on his back, trying to breathe, and then quite suddenly nothing. No noise, no nails or teeth. He was on his back looking up at a dim dirty ceiling above him, his knees drawn up, trying to get some breath into his lungs. He was conscious of a strong smell of whiskey and nameless dirt and dust on the floor under him.

He managed to draw one long breath. Cautiously, he relaxed his knees.

"Mister, you all right?" The anxious face of the little bartender swam into focus, peering at him. "Jesus, I thought you was dead! Jesus, who is that guy, anyways? Try to hold me up, and you—"

Varallo accepted his hand and sat up slowly.

X was stretched full length on the floor, drenched with whiskey and breathing stertorously. The bartender was clutching the broken top third of a fifth of Johnnie Walker. The whole place smelled like a bootleg still.

"Jesus, I couldn't get a clear crack at him—fighting like a she-bobcat, I swear— You all right? Jesus, mister, you got an artery cut or something? All the blood—"

"You call the police?" asked Varallo.

The bartender looked at him reproachfully. "Jesus, have I got *time*, you 'n' him rolling all over my floor and me tryin' a get a clear crack at—" He looked at the neck of the bottle in his hand. "Oh, Jesus H. Christ!" he said. "Why in hell did I have to grab a bottle of the expensive stuff?"

"Where's the phone?" croaked Varallo.

It was Wayne and Poor who came over in a hurry. Wayne took one look at Varallo, who was hunched over a table in one of the booths, and immediately began to check him over, hurried and efficient, for the cut artery. Varallo fended him off.

"I'm O.K., Fred. Bullet nicked my ear. You know ears."

"Oh," said Wayne. "Oh. My God, Vic. You look as if you'd been wallowing in a slaughterhouse. My God."

"I don't doubt," said Varallo. He could see his shirt: ears would bleed, and there was the bite, and assorted scratches, and he was fairly gory. "But there he is. Our heist boy. Caught in the act. Just by a fluke."

"He came in here," the bartender was gabbling excitedly, "I never seen him before—nobody else in the place—the other big blond guy comes in just after—and orders a beer, the first guy I mean, and I get it, and he's got this gun, and he says— And then the blond guy piles onto him and Jesus I never *saw* such a— Like a she-bobcat—and I grab the nearest bottle and why the *hell* it had to be the expensive stuff, and I try to get a crack at—"

"Sort it out later," said Varallo, getting up slowly. "My God, I'll bet I'll have a nice shiner, he connected once."

"You're certainly a candidate for first aid," said Poor. "Sure you're O.K.? How'd you happen to spot him?" He stared down at X. "He's a dead ringer for that sketch all right."

"A fluke," said Varallo, looking at his right hand where the teeth marks showed. "Just a fluke."

They called an ambulance, whose interns said X didn't need hospitalization, just a crack on the head, but if he acted thus-and-so when he came to, it could be concussion. They delivered X to the jail with instructions to watch him and call Dr. Goulding when he did come to. Varallo was delivered to first aid where he was washed and disinfected and painted with various unguents and bandaged, and then he climbed the stairs to the office to see what, if anything, they'd found out about X.

They had, of course, emptied his pockets. They had hit a minor jackpot, and they were—Wayne, Poor and Katz, the only men in the office—excitedly speculating.

"What do you bet?" Poor was saying. "On Kessler, no, I still think that was the punk—but on Collins and Gardiner— Look at this, Vic—my God, he did mark you, you look like a gangster—and that *is* going to be a nice shiner. But just look at this! Francis John Conway—some out-of-date I.D.'s, driver's license and so on—a discharge pass from Camarillo dated December last year. My good God, the head doctors saying so-and-so has made a good adjustment and is suitable for—my *God*. So he's our heist man, our elevator boy. That old pharmacist gave us a good sketch, all right. But what else is he too? The nut—"

"I don't know, John," said Wayne. "I suppose it could be. But once they pick some lay, they don't often vary—"

"A nut! Who knows what a nut—— Look at the way he lit into Vic! Talk about berserk—"

"That sort of convinces me, in a way," said Katz. "You feeling O.K., Vic? You look like hell."

They kicked it around some, until the phone rang on O'Connor's empty desk and Wayne, answering it, said, "Oh, he's here. He's O.K., Mrs. Varallo—at least—"

"Vic? What on *earth*—on your day off. Well, I didn't really think too much about it—you *do* get talking—until Sam phoned. Sam Nagao, you know. From the nursery. And he said you'd acted very odd, and gone out without— What on earth happened? And I thought I'd better— What are you doing at the office? Are you all right? After all, it's getting on for three thirty, and—"

Varallo looked at his watch and discovered that it had stopped and the crystal was broken. "Is it? A little excitement, *cara*. I'm O.K. At least— And damn it, the car's still sitting in front of the nursery, and I'll have to— I'll be home, *cara*."

"You'd better warn her what you look like," said Poor.

CHAPTER 11

Laura took one look at him and asked in a faint voice for explanations. Varallo explained.

"All I can say is," said Laura, "that I think you are mentally deficient. You had a *chance* to do something else than be a cop. After you resigned up in Contera. And you walk into the nearest police station—"

"I know, I know," said Varallo. "And say, Please can I be a cop again. All cops are stupid or they wouldn't be cops, didn't you know?"

"And," said Laura, "you'd better not go near the baby, you'll frighten her into a fit. . . . Hadn't you better put something on that eye?"

They got this and that from the papers Conway had had on him, and they sent off teletypes to Oakland, which was his home town, apparently. Intermittently on Friday they got teletypes back. And of course—considering the way he had gone after Varallo—he could be a candidate for the X on the Collins-Gardiner murders too. He had been around town, they knew; the first heist job had been pulled on February thirteenth.

The first teletype they got from Oakland outlined his background. He had quite a little pedigree for a fellow not yet thirty. The usual Grand Theft Auto as a j.d.—more heist jobs—two burglaries, and assorted muggings. He'd only served one term—for burglary—as an adult; and the latest time he'd been dropped on, for a mugging, a smart lawyer had convinced the judge that Conway was sick-sick-sick, and he'd been shunted up to Camarillo. Where he hadn't stayed long. They sent, and received, teletypes from Camarillo too. Conway, said that report—once they translated the jargon—was not mentally ill in any sense: he was mildly neurotic, but had no compulsion to perform criminal acts, and it was felt that his case would be better dealt with by ordinary penological methods.

"Best stash him in the pen," Poor translated that, "so they blithely turn him loose because he isn't a nut. Head doctors I will never understand."

Oddly enough—they got that from his Oakland record—he had only one count of violence on him; and that had been an occasion when he'd been accosted unexpectedly from behind by a patrolman. He'd gone wild then too, and put the patrolman in the hospital.

"Probably," said Wayne to Varallo, "if you'd just walked up beside him and said, 'I'll trouble you for that gun, sir,' he'd have handed it over meek as could be. Tough cop Varallo had to jump him."

"With a gun in his hand, I remember my manners?" Varallo had taken a certain amount of kidding, at his evening class the night before, and grinned reluctantly.

"And I still say—even if it was only twice he hair-triggered off like that," said Poor, "he could be the one, on those two women."

"Well, I don't know, John," said Wayne. "There's no sex count on him at all, and the times he pulled break-ins, it was on empty houses, with people away." He looked back at the Camarillo report and grunted. "Wonder they don't tag him as a psychopath. Not that there aren't such things, God knows, but so often they will hang the pompous title on the just plain pros, too stupid or too lazy to work a regular job. I don't know, John. We can tackle him on it, of course."

But the bartender had struck pretty hard, and it turned out Conway had a concussion; he'd been transferred to the hospital and they couldn't talk to him yet.

O'Connor came back on Friday, an O'Connor still hoarse and still sneezing, but announcing robustly that he was over the worst of it and perfectly all right to come in, and what the hell, everybody sitting around maybe playing Deuces Wild with the boss not there? "What *about* this Hollison? We know he's around town—why, for God's sake, hasn't anybody spotted him? Yeah, just fine and dandy we've got Conway, and my sympathy, Vic—you do look like hell. But Hollison—"

"Don't kid me, Charles," said Varallo. "You're just out for more glory, that's all. After you got that bank robber J. Edgar was agitating about, back in January, you're just itching to catch somebody else off the Ten Most Wanted. Picture J. Edgar sitting there back in Washington saying, 'Hm, this Lieutenant O'Connor must be a pretty smart boy.'"

"You go to hell," said O'Connor, and sneezed and groped for a handkerchief.

About three o'clock that afternoon, just as Varallo got back from interviewing a couple of Eddy Horstman's former pals—the bright thought had struck him that, while Eddy had teamed up with some new pals over in Hollywood, the bad boys he'd run with were still right here—Sergeant Hanrihan wandered in.

"Thought you'd be interested in a follow-up on Horstman," he said. "And thanks very much for letting us use your search warrant. Found some of the rest of the loot from our break-in in his room, so we've tied him in nice and tight. First big job for all these boys, they were pawning the stuff a little at a time. We couldn't tie in that girl. God, what kids are coming to these days—that girl. Oh, well, that kind always with us, I suppose. She says Eddy told her to say she was out with him Friday night if anybody asked, but she wasn't getting mixed up with cops on Eddy's account. Which could be so."

"I think it is," said Varallo, remembering what Sally Harris had said. "She's gone off the rails other ways—and she'll go farther off the rails, possibly into our territory. But she isn't there yet."

"Yeah," said Hanrihan thoughtfully. "That could be. Well, anyway, Eddy'll be tucked away for a little while—and be just a little smarter when he's let loose." He drifted out.

"Any luck?" asked Poor. "On those former pals?"

"You tell me," said Varallo. "Two of them say they were at the late movie at the Alex last Friday night. The other one was home alone. He says. He lives with his mother—divorced mother—and she works nights as a nurse."

"Oh, how nice," said Poor. "No reason at all to ask for a search warrant, and have a look for the Combat Masterpiece. This is a dead one, Vic. It could be, it probably is, one of the how many young punks we've talked to, who broke into Kessler's and shot him. But we'll never know who—we'll never be able to prove it."

"I continue," said Katz from his desk, "to have a funny feeling about Kessler. Maybe you're right—I'd agree it's dead, we'll never get him. To prove it. But I don't know that I think— Oh, hell, I don't *know* what I think about Kessler. I just feel funny about it."

The phone rang on O'Connor's desk; O'Connor was down the hall after coffee, and Wayne picked up the phone. "Yes, Bill . . . Oh. Address? O.K., I've got that." He looked at Varallo. "I guess you and

John can go out on this one—at least you won't scare a corpse with your
ugly mug, Vic. Suicide. Little hotel down on South Brand."

Varallo swore; he and Poor got up resignedly. A suicide is sometimes
messy and always a nuisance. There is very little for the cops to do
about it except type up a lot of reports, whereas in the live case—from
Grand Theft Auto to murder—there is at least a little interest and sometimes excitement in the puzzle, in the chase. A suicide just meant a lot
of tedious paper work.

They took Varallo's car and drove down to the little hotel. A very
cheap little walk-up hotel, on the second and third floors of a block of
office buildings: a hotel with a narrow entrance door on the street giving
on a flight of steep narrow stairs up to a minute lobby with an old desk
serving as a counter, and a cold-eyed, middle-aged woman behind the
desk. From $1.50 per night. That kind of hotel.

"She came on Wednesday," she told them, all business. "We charge
by the night, she paid for Wednesday and Thursday. Registered as
Marion Thompson. . . . Yes, she paid in cash. Three singles. And our
time for checking out is two o'clock, so when she hadn't come to pay by
then, and I was pretty sure she was still in, I took my passkey and—"

Varallo had left his watch at Webbs' for repair, but he looked at the
dirty face of the old wall clock above the desk significantly. It was three
thirty-seven. She followed his glance with an eye quick as a snake's.
"Well, it was after two but I couldn't say how much. I mean, we're not
as quick as all that, right on the dot if a guest don't— It could've been
nearer three."

Poor sketched a shrug to Varallo. And it was another thing they'd
never prove, but both of them knew what Mrs. Marcia Coldfield had
been doing in that while before she called the cops to take a corpse off
her hands. Discovering the corpse, she'd had a good long look through
the dead woman's luggage for anything of value.

Conceivably it would be necessary to challenge Mrs. Coldfield on
that, and make her sweat enough to break down and admit it, and dis-
gorge whatever she'd taken. Neither of them would relish that job. Neither of them was going to start it unless it did prove necessary.

They went down the dusty, uncarpeted corridor of the old building to
the room where Marion Thompson, if that was her name, had died. The
ambulance was already there, the interns were in possession. It was a
dreary, bare, shabby room, about ten feet square; there was an old single iron bedstead with a thin mattress on it, and an unpainted pine
three-drawer chest, and a straight chair that had got separated from a

dining-room set made around the turn of the century: its upholstered seat was gaping its stuffing. There was one double-hung window, very dirty, with the bottom half open: no curtains, only an old torn window shade across the top half. There was an ancient rag rug about three by five in the middle of the floor.

Varallo thought, What a hell of a place to die. What a hell of a place to come to the end— And maybe, as with many suicides, there had been one moment for Marion Thompson (or several such moments) when a push one way or the other would have been enough. One cheerful word of friendliness might have sent the scale up on the right side—and if that was so, maybe a long look around this room had been the last thing to set the scale plummeting. If this is all—

He looked at her there on the bed, over the bent backs of the interns, and felt pity. The one thing a cop learns early—but only if he is a very good cop—is compassion. She couldn't be over thirty, maybe younger: and not bad looking even in death. Her face was clean of make-up (odd for a suicided female: they usually wanted to look their best), and she was wearing only an old faded peach-colored slip with one strap fastened with a safety pin (and that a little odd too).

"What's it look like?" he asked.

"Just at a guess, barbiturate of some kind." The sandy intern jerked his head at a dirty glass on the pine chest. There was sediment of some sort at its bottom.

Varallo sighed and got out his notebook. Just some poor damned female who decided to take her own way out—and all the reports to be written up in triplicate, and filed away. . . .

O'Connor, in between bringing himself up to date reading all the reports of the last couple of days, was swearing about Hollison. It was a little funny Hollison hadn't been spotted, what with his official mug shot plastered all over the second page of the *News-Press* and the first page of the *Independent;* but then, a lot of the citizenry seemed to be, as O'Connor said, purblind.

"I see you've been working this damn Kessler thing into the ground. Goddamn punk kids running loose, and— But that is a very damn funny sort of gun for one like that to get hold of, for God's sake. I—"

"We all said that too," said Katz. "A cannon like that. If it was— which it does look like—a not-quite-pro, probably a j.d. But it says nothing. Anybody can get hold of any kind of gun if he wants to, and

God only knows how many different ones are floating around under the counter. I said to Vic—"

"You're supposed to be a goddamn detective!" said O'Connor. "Use some imagination, damn—" He sneezed, reached for his handkerchief, coughed until his eyes watered, made a supreme effort and controlled himself, and sat up, putting the handkerchief away. "You know what that damn well could say, Joe? If you'd used an ounce and a half of brains on it, for God's sake. Combination of probable j.d. with a cannon like that? Have you *got* any imagination, Joe?"

Katz sat up slowly. "Oh," he said. "You mean—"

"Just now he gets there, the great detective. That's just exactly what I do mean. Some j.d. whose dad, or uncle, or big brother or whatever, has got that cannon all legit, for protection, or because he's a night watchman or carrying a payroll for somebody, or a doctor who's out nights or— And for *God's* sake, he might have a license for it. All legit. If he's carrying it around at all. And Junior swiped the damn gun one night so he'd feel big and brave pulling his first break-in. I do mean, Joe, we like to explore every damn avenue and—"

"Turn over every damn stone," said Katz. "Yes. I've only passed the sergeants' exam once, I hadn't quite got that far yet. I see what you mean."

"So, go," said O'Connor. "Just on the off chance, Joe, go look at the licenses. If there just happens to be one license for the damn cannon we're after—"

"Yes, Lieutenant. I'm on my way, Lieutenant," said Katz.

O'Connor sneezed, reached for his handkerchief and grinned at him. "We can't all be as smart as a good Irish cop."

"And *shalom* to you," said Katz. "Me you accuse of no imagination. A fairly smart Jew."

"Oh, you'd have got there in the end," said O'Connor; and the phone rang. "Yes, Bill?"

"I got a call from the house dick at the California Hotel," said Copeland on the desk downstairs. "A real brawl going on in one of their suites. Husband and wife—a Mr. and Mrs. Alfred Clark. Wilson— the dick—says it's their most expensive suite and I guess aside from that he's smart enough to hold off interfering in a domestic spat—but he says you can hear them all over the fifth floor and will we please—"

"So chase a patrol car over, damn it! I'm the lieutenant, Bill."

"Well, Wilson did say something else, reason I called you. He'd only caught a glimpse of this Mrs. Clark just this afternoon, even though they've been there nearly two weeks—they're out a lot, apparently. He says he almost called in then, because she looked a lot to him like that Sonya Horvath who—couldn't say for sure, but—"

O'Connor leaped up like a startled fawn. "I'm on my way!" he barked. He beckoned Katz violently, charging toward the door, feeling the .357 magnum at his shoulder. "Come on!"

"Something up?" Katz followed him.

"Something, hell!" Downstairs he shoved Katz into the new Ford sedan and sent it as fast as traffic allowed down Wilson. He made the light at Brand by cheating a little on the amber, roared across the inter-section down to Orange, turned up to the right, circled two blocks and braked the Ford in the loading zone in front of the California Hotel at the corner of Brand and Lexington.

Wilson, the house dick, was waiting for them in the lobby. "Look, Lieutenant," he said, "if you'll be *discreet*—this *is* the best hotel in town, and after all that suite is thirty dollars a day—the desk clerks tell me this Clark couple, nothing but the best, he's a big businessman from back East, by his card—and two weeks they've been here, no trouble at all, but— *I* think he's a little high, that's all—and you know the kind of guests we get, all quiet respectable people."

"You thought this female looked like the Horvath dame? You told—"

Wilson shied back. "Oh, well, I shouldn't really have said. I only thought, the newspaper picture—just a little similarity, but people like that wouldn't come *here,* Lieutenant— The hotel wouldn't—"

"What's the room number?"

"Five-twenty," said Wilson, capitulating. "It's quite a row, Lieu-tenant."

It was. They stood outside the suite door, and it was quite a row. Male and female voices, slams and bangs and crashes. Listening to it, O'Connor began to grin pleasedly.

"Please, Sonya—now, darling, please don't do that— You know I was only being polite to the w— *Ow!*—now, Sonya, you know I'd never— *ouch!*—be unfaithful to— Please, Sonya."

"Married couples," said Wilson. "You know. If we can just quiet them down—"

All up and down the corridor of this very quiet, very respectable hotel, faces were peering out of doorways in various stages of indigna-tion and interest.

O'Connor motioned, and Wilson bent to use the passkey. The door opened and O'Connor shouldered in with Katz and the house detective behind him.

"Well, well, well!" said O'Connor, with his hungry-shark grin. "What have we here? As I live and breathe, Mr. George Leland Hollison! Nice to make your acquaintance, George."

The row stopped as if God had suddenly struck them both dumb.

Sonya Horvath, also no stranger to the FBI, was the girl friend of George Leland Hollison.

She stared at them, a leggy blonde simply clad in black lace bra and panties, and she said flatly, "Oh, hell."

"I *told* you, Sonya," said Hollison. "Make *such* a row over nothing at all. You shouldn't lose your temper like that. Now look what you've done. Called the fuzz down on us." He looked at O'Connor mournfully. She'd connected a couple of times—by the look of the room she'd been throwing everything she could lay hands on at him—and he had the start of a nice black eye and a lot of scratches. He was a good-looking man about forty, the distinguished touch of gray at the temples, the nice firm jaw, a reliable-looking man, a gentleman—when he was dressed for the part. At the moment he was wearing a pair of blue nylon jockey shorts and nothing else, and his chest was hollow and his shoulders stooped and she'd knocked his glasses off and he peered nearsightedly at O'Connor and said, "Of all the lousy luck. Just as we were figuring to move on, too. Of all the goddamned lousy luck! Just because you had to lose your temper. Women! *I* never lose my temper. It doesn't pay. I told you—"

"Listen, you two-timing gigolo bastard, if you hadn't started making eyes at that— Try to con me! I guess I know—"

"Break it up, break it up," said O'Connor genially. (And maybe—only he knew—he did have a little vision at that, of J. Edgar thinking, Hm, this lieutenant out in Glendale, California, must be pretty much on the ball, two off the Ten Most Wanted in three months.) "We going to need the cuffs for you, or will you and the lady come quietly?"

"Oh, for *God's* sake!" said Hollison despondently. "Of all the luck. In two hours we'd have been on the way to Honolulu. All right, all right." He turned to the bed and picked up a clean shirt laid out ready. "So that's the way the ball bounces." Typical con man: a rabbit, it came to the physical fight: a gentle man, one sense of that. And the funny thing about the con men, the best of them could retire on their loot, but they never could resist the fascination of the game of wits. It wasn't essentially the loot they were interested in, but the game.

The FBI figured that Hollison had taken from the marks, over twenty years, close to a million.

They went over the room, and he had just six dollars and forty cents in cash. The blonde had under twelve bucks.

They let them get dressed, and took them downstairs, Hollison resigned and Sonya icily aloof. As they came past the desk, the desk clerk eyed the little party and cleared his throat delicately. Etiquette in such matters is a no man's land; the California Hotel such a very respectable place: the California Hotel simply did not have its guests removed by the police; but the desk clerk was as well drilled as a bank teller, and neither did the California Hotel have its guests renege on their bills. The clerk rose deferentially. O'Connor, Katz and Wilson might have been invisible.

"Er—Mr. Clark? If you are—er—leaving us, I'd—er—remind you—"

Hollison turned from O'Connor's light grasp on his arm, and old habit and custom took over automatically—the essential con man. "Oh, my bill," he said, and gave the clerk a beautifully reliable warm smile. "Of course. Just a moment, I'll make you out a check."

("Don't you *ever*—" so the manager of the California Hotel was to ask all his desk clerks later, "don't you EVER look at the papers? That man's official police photograph plastered all over—")

And O'Connor was still laughing—which set him coughing all the more—over Hollison and the desk clerk, when on Saturday morning they got a further-information teletype from Oakland on Conway.

On February 18 and 19—the dates on one of which somebody had broken into Mrs. Collins' house on Geneva Street and beaten her to death prior to ransacking the house—Francis John Conway had been in Oakland. Sure, he could have been—undoubtedly had been—in Glendale and environs before, pulling a few holdups. But on those dates he'd been in Oakland, maybe visiting a pal in the home town, since he hadn't any known relatives. The Oakland police knew. They'd had him in both days, for questioning—abortively—on a break-in that had happened on the seventeenth. Had him in, of course, on account of his record.

So Conway—a kind of improbable possible—was out, on the Collins-Gardiner thing.

They'd have to go on looking elsewhere, for the maybe j.d., maybe unsuspected schizo, the maybe first-time-out X, on the Collins-Gardiner thing.

The X who had—maybe, by a far-out hunch thinly shared by Varallo and Poor—known a little something about both those women?

CHAPTER 12

"Twenty-four years is just how long we've lived here," said Mrs. Ray Bessemer. "It's a nice quiet neighborhood, hasn't changed much. We raised our four kids right here. Kind of rattle around in the house now they're all gone off, but it's been home a long time, you know?"

Varallo said he knew. "I've got a few questions for you, Mrs. Bessemer, and no matter how peculiar they sound I wish you'd do your best to answer—"

"Anything to oblige. You still looking for that awful fiend that broke in and killed Mrs. Collins?" She eyed him avidly.

Varallo admitted it. It was Monday, getting on for lunchtime, and he was taking today on a last (probably) intensive look at this thing from the viewpoint of the hunch he shared with Poor. If they were right, some kind of common denominator there had to be. So he took the west side of the street and Poor the east, and they were covering all the neighbors again, this entire block on Geneva Street where Mrs. Collins had lived. He noticed that Mrs. Collins' house now had a FOR SALE sign on the front lawn.

This was his ninth visit, and several of them had duplicated. They had started with a couple of premises. Regardless of common denominators, this and that about the Collins murder made the premise pretty plain: the probable hour of the attack, and the fury of the attack, said first that X could be a juvenile, could be a juvenile from the neighborhood (if there had been some knowledge of Mrs. Collins personally) and could be, probably was, unstable in some way, to go berserk like that. So what they were trying to get today—after they'd about exhausted the list of possibles from records—was any information about young people in this neighborhood, or people who had moved recently, in or out of the neighborhood, or anybody from outside who came into the neighborhood regularly for some reason. Like that. Anything, in fact, the neighbors had to relay about each other, gossip and all.

He had so far heard some duplication, gossip and otherwise. He had no doubt Poor had too. He'd met only one uncooperative housewife who'd regarded him suspiciously; in a neighborhood like this, the people were mostly all respectable upright middle-class, and friendly to police. They'd all been shocked at Mrs. Collins' murder, but one and all —of course—they said, as Mrs. Bessemer was saying now, "But you can't be thinking it was anybody lives around here did that! Why, that'd be just impossible—must've been some fiend, or dope maybe, from over in the L.A. slums—"

But most of them, once he'd got them talking, talked willingly. And right now he was hearing some of what he'd heard from Mrs. Taylor, and Mrs. Cox, and Mrs. Stanley, and Mrs. Webster. It was a neighborhood, these quiet middle-class blocks along here, of largely middle-aged and elderly people. At one time there had been children, and teenagers, here, but few were left. Glendale was, of course, the kind of town where people tended to stay put. The Taylors' and the Bessemers' and the Coxes' and Stanleys' children had all grown up here, were now married and living elsewhere. The Carterets in the middle of the block had a boy—the youngest of four, still at home—going to Glendale College. Don Carteret, a nice boy, said Mrs. Bessemer. (Mrs. Taylor had complained about his noisy sports car.) There were a couple of teenagers in the house just back of the Bessemers, that'd be over on Howard, but Mrs. Bessemer didn't know the name, just heard them out in the yard on summer nights. Not really too noisy—just kids having a good time. Some people named Holt who had lived across the street toward the end of the block had a high-school boy, but they'd moved away a couple of months ago. Mrs. Bessemer didn't know where: hadn't known them too well. Then there was a youngish couple had just moved in—the house the Holts had owned.

"Houses don't change hands often, a neighborhood like this. As I say, we've been here twenty-four years, and my sister and her husband— Mr. and Mrs. Lawrence—they lived here nearly twenty-nine all told. Reason Jim and I bought this house in the first place, Dora and Kent living here—the corner house, other side of the street, was theirs. They just moved last year when Kent retired. Insurance, he was in. I told Dora they'd likely get sick to death of it, after living in a decent-sized town with all the markets near and so on, but Kent always had a yen to live in a little town, and they've moved up to a little place called Clovis, near Fresno—retired there."

"Any children, Mrs. Bessemer?"

"Oh, yes—Dora and Kent, you mean? Yes, they've got their daughter Marla, she's married to an air force man and lives somewhere back in Florida—and the boy still with them, young Bill. Some people named Randolph bought their house, but I don't know much about them. They seem to have quite a lot of company. Haven't any kids. Say, what are you asking about kids for, anyway? No kid did that to Mrs. Collins! I tell you, since that happened we're all pretty careful about locking up, and I know Mrs. Taylor and Mrs. Cox, they stay with each other evenings their husbands are out, like at lodge meetings and so on. You can hardly believe a thing like that—old Mrs. Collins. Some fiend it must've been. A nice old lady—oh, set in her ways like they get, and I suppose someday they'll be saying the same thing about me." Mrs. Bessemer smiled: a fat, pleasant woman. "It was me called you, you know. Because every day it was nice, whenever I passed on my way to market or somewhere—I believe in walking, good exercise—she'd be out in her front yard puttering around. She liked to garden. I'd always see her. And when I didn't for a couple of days, and happening to know her daughter and son-in-law were away—she'd mentioned it just that week—well, I asked Mrs. Taylor, who's right next door, and they hadn't seen her either and we thought she might've been taken sick, or— So we called. Just a horrible thing! You can't— Pardon? No, they asked everybody that before, if we'd noticed any strangers, and nobody had. . . . Well, of course, like I say she was set in her ways, and she could be a bit sharp sometimes. I heard her once complaining to Mr. Taylor about their dog, getting in her flowers in front. And she'd scold my nephew, young Bill— of course that was years back, he's grown up now—about playing ball on the sidewalk and sometimes running into her yard. Old people—you know. . . . No, nobody saw any strangers hanging around that week at all. But of course he'd come after dark. And most of us along here being older and all, and most of the men still working, you know, we all get to bed fairly early. Even on weekends there isn't much partying and so on. I don't know what any of *us* can tell you. It couldn't be anybody living around here, naturally. . . ."

The only thing there he hadn't heard before was about the teenagers in the house behind the Bessemers. And of course, when you said "neighborhood," logically it would cover more than one block. If there was a link somewhere here, it might be two, three blocks away. Needle in a haystack . . . The Holts and their son who had moved away he would follow up. He might take a look at the Randolphs, who had moved in last year. But otherwise, what did he have? A lot of odds and ends that meant, probably, nothing.

A neighborhood where people were friendly but didn't run in and out of each other's houses. A neighborhood of ordinary people—office men, shop foremen, a bank teller, a personnel director—who lived quiet ordinary lives. *But,* Varallo thought, also a neighborhood which, in one way, confirmed his conviction that there had been some knowledge of it on X's part. In the three hours or so he'd been walking from door to door here, exactly four vehicles had passed down the block: a visitor to the Coxes' in a beat-up blue VW; a Good Humor truck; a TV repair truck which had stopped at the Randolphs' and a parcel-post truck which had stopped at the Bessemers'. This stretch of little Geneva Street wasn't a street you'd find yourself on, on the way to somewhere else.

He thanked Mrs. Bessemer, came out to the sidewalk and paused, looking over his notebook. He felt his eye; it was a lot better but still showed even under Laura's pancake makeup. And he couldn't have his watch back until tomorrow, damn it. Oh well, at least the heat wave had gone away; it was back to ordinary March weather, cool and sunny.

Poor came across the street, jaywalking diagonally toward him. "You get anything suggestive?" asked Varallo.

"I got something I think is very suggestive," said Poor thickly. "Oh, damn. I've *got* it all right, I—ah—ah—" He sneezed explosively. "I told you my throat was sore on Saturday, and Anne made me gargle with aspirin and all that, but I've *got* it all right." He brought out a handkerchief.

"Well, don't give it to me. What did you pick up?"

"That woman over there—Mrs. McCowan. Awful gossip," said Poor. "Every neighborhood's got one. Kind who keeps track of what kind of new stove the Smiths get and how often the TV repairman calls at the Joneses'." He sneezed again and swore. "I feel like hell. I'm starting to ache all over. Just like flu."

"So?" said Varallo.

"So," said Poor, "she's the only one on the block I've talked to who knew where the Holts had moved to. . . . I didn't think this was such a hot idea, Vic—I didn't think there was anything more to be got. Fred worked it, after all—though not from exactly the same angle, somebody local. After all—well, I know what we said about the nice mild kids that all of a sudden blow their tops, but as a rule any potential nut has acted funny enough in some way that it'd be noticed—"

"Not always by any means, but so?"

"Well, it just could be, Vic my boy, that we've dropped on our common denominator," said Poor. "That woman—should be named town crier. She had everybody in the block down pat, I swear to God she could tell you what brand of lipstick every female along here uses. And what does she come out with when we get to the Holts? Moved in January— January twelfth—over to the other side of town toward Burbank. I—" Poor sneezed and snatched for his handkerchief.

"*Per caritá!*" said Varallo. Over toward Burbank—other side of town, which was where Fifth Street and the Gardiners' house was. "You don't tell me."

"There's a teen-age boy, I suppose you also heard."

"I did. Bob Holt. Well, well."

"It's nothing on the surface."

"No. But just for fun, let's see where the Holts have moved to, shall we? Did she know the address?"

"Even Mrs. McCowan didn't know that, no. I should think they all know what she's like and don't go out of the way to annoy her. She said the Holts were very standoffish and unfriendly, by which I deduce that they didn't like her and kept their distance."

"Yes. You can't really depend on a woman like that except for facts. Those, they always know. How they interpret them is something else again. What time is it?" asked Varallo.

"Twelve thirty. You want some lunch? I'm not hungry. I feel like hell. My throat's raw." Poor felt it. "You want to bet, O'Connor's passed this damn cold on to every man in the office, one by one we'll all come down with it."

"They say will power helps. Let's hit the post office first. Oh, hell," said Varallo. "I haven't seen that Mrs. Carteret yet. I suppose, to round the thing off, I ought to."

"She'll tell you nothing new."

"I don't know that." Varallo hesitated, but years of experience had ingrained the orderly routine in him. You started a thing, you finished it. "You do look like hell. Go home and let your wife cosset you."

"Not on your life. Tomorrow, maybe. I've got interested in this thing now, and I'm O.K. for the rest of the day. Because I do go along, whoever it was had to know a little something—and it'd be one in the eye for Fred if we do turn up the common denominator. Him and his routine."

"Mostly it is the routine thing, so routine hands us the answer. Just now and then it isn't," said Varallo.

"Um. Tell you what, I'll take the post office. Meet you back at headquarters in an hour."

"O.K." And Varallo expected nothing new from Mrs. Carteret; he was just being thorough in his canvass of the neighborhood. And what he got he hadn't expected at all.

She was a small dark untidy woman, rather scatterbrained, and she seemed a little bewildered as to what he wanted of her. She didn't, she said, mix much with any of the neighbors; friendly and all, but the Carterets had their own friends and—

He had interrupted lunch. And what he got came from young Don Carteret, who strolled in with a glass of milk and a king-sized sandwich, to listen. He eyed Varallo with admiring interest, and when his mother paused, asked, "Gee, you don't mean you think it was somebody right around here killed the old lady? That sounds just cr— well, I mean, I guess you know better than me, but I can't see anybody around here—"

At least Varallo was interested to get a look at Don Carteret; and he doubted very much that it was young Don who had gone off the rails. Though you never did know. A big healthy, good-looking nineteen-year-old, with an open friendly grin.

"Well, we have to look everywhere," he said mildly.

"But around here—an awful murder like that! Well, gee, nobody that lived— I guess the only really odd sort of guy ever lived around here's moved away, and he wasn't as odd as *that*. I mean, he wouldn't—" Don crammed the rest of the sandwich into his mouth.

"Darling, such big bites," said his mother. He grinned at her amiably, chewing, swallowed and poured the rest of the milk down his throat.

"Who was that?"

"Who— Oh, Bill Lawrence. When I say odd, I don't mean like *that*. Just dumb, maybe. I wouldn't know. It's funny, but Bill Lawrence kind of straightened me out a couple of years ago." He had all the frank egotism of youth, assuming that the strange police officer would be just as interested as he was in the affairs of Don Carteret. "You get to thinking it's a drag, you know, school and all—when you could easy get a job at a market or somewhere, union wages, and make enough to run the car and—you know. But seeing Bill Lawrence around, well, it kind of made me think twice. I'm in first year at Glendale College now."

"What had Lawrence to do with—" Bill Lawrence. Son of Mr. and

Mrs. Kent Lawrence, who had moved away to a little town named Clovis, up near Fresno. Nephew of Mrs. Bessemer.

"Oh, well, sort of as an *example*," said Don. "You see what I mean. He dropped out of high—of course he's older than I am, he'd be about twenty-two, twenty-three now, I guess—and I never really knew him. Just saw him around. But the way it's turned out for him—seemed like he wasn't getting any place, all right. I don't know if he's just stupid or what, but he'd have a job and then he wouldn't, just be hanging around all day, and a couple of times I knew he went off from home awhile and then he'd be back, out of a job again. And I got to thinking, this is also a drag, no? You get qualified for something, you're always pretty sure—the education bit and all, you know. And I just—"

"I understood Lawrence was living at home and moved away with his parents?"

"Oh, sure, I guess so. But I know he came back once, to stay with his aunt and uncle awhile—the Bessemers. Then I guess he went back with his folks again, I don't know. No, I don't remember seeing him around just lately. But you can see why—"

So there was another one Varallo would check out. Just to be thorough. When you got a thing that wasn't—or might not be—quite the ordinary thing, it was good policy to explore every avenue and turn over every stone.

When he got back to the office Poor informed him that Mr. and Mrs. Robert Holt and their teen-aged son were now living on Winchester Avenue. Varallo sat down at his desk and opened the County Guide.

"By the address, about twelve blocks away from the Gardiner house," he said. It was unsatisfactory. As a common denominator it was nothing very solid at all. Even if they found out that the Holt boy perhaps had to pass the Gardiner house on his way to school, or—that would say nothing. No direct contact. Unless he delivered the *Independent* to the Gardiners, what chance of direct contact could there be?—and the Holt boy was in his senior year of high school, and the *Independent* carriers were all younger—kids of eleven and twelve.

"Well, it's something," said Poor.

"It's not anything I like very much. Oh, we'll check him—go see him, see what he looks like. But—"

Katz came in. He was wearing his slight one-sided smile. "Another of the boss's brain waves didn't pan out. All the legit gun licenses. Not a Combat Masterpiece in the lot."

"I never claimed to be infallible, for God's sake," said O'Connor, looking up from a report.

"That thing," said Poor through a cough. "Kessler. It's dead. We can make guesses, we'll never get any evidence."

O'Connor growled. "You might as well see this, Vic. Autopsy report on that suicide. Damn all. There wasn't any note, you said?"

"Nothing but the dead woman on the bed. Two suitcases, a few cheap clothes, no jewelry. Anything unusual in the autopsy report?"

"Not one damn thing," said O'Connor. Rhys came in and opened his mouth to say something and then shut it as O'Connor went on. "Healthy young woman, this Thompson—no organic disease, no pregnancy. Had never borne a child. Not a virgin but how many are at that age— Goulding tags her at about thirty—death due to, et cetera, et cetera. What it boils down to, sleeping pills. He's got the damn brand earmarked. Prescriptive, sure, but how hard is it to get them? Walk into a doctor's office and say, Doctor, I'm *so* nervous, I can't sleep, and bingo, he writes the damn prescription. We've sent her prints to Washington— she didn't show in anybody's records here—so with any luck we should find out if she really was Marion Thompson. . . . *I* never can figure them," said O'Connor, sounding incredulous, disgusted, belligerent. "They're all mean to me, Life's no fun, I can't stand it, goodbye. Goddamned bleating cowards. No guts."

"I can imagine a couple of situations, Charles," said Varallo, "where it'd take a lot of guts to commit suicide."

"I can't figure it," said O'Connor. "Anyway, there it is. She checked into that cheap hotel, she spent a couple of days brooding, apparently, and then on Thursday night she dissolved a lot of sleeping pills in a kind of hefty Scotch-and-water and drank it. End of story."

"Just say that again," said Rhys, coming up to his desk. "Is that in the autopsy report? Scotch-and-water?"

"Why? Yes. 'Stomach empty except for heavy traces of Scotch whiskey, water, barbiturates detailed above undoubtedly dissolved in drink.' He goes on to say that the alcohol in the blood was about point six percent, reason I say a hefty drink. She wouldn't be drunk, but damn well on the way. A lot of them do that."

"So they do," said Rhys, "but maybe this one didn't. I will be damned eternally."

Poor began sneezing again. "What the hell are you talking about?" asked O'Connor.

"I photographed that room. You know the routine," said Rhys.

"Record of everything. No Scotch. No liquor of any kind. No bottles."

"For God's sake!" said O'Connor. "For—you sure?"

"Sure. So where'd she get it? That's a pretty casual sort of place, I'd guess. People wandering in and out. Though that Mrs. Coldfield that manages it has a gimlet eye, all right. The Thompson woman have a visitor, maybe? Who happened to have a bottle on him and kindly donated—you said point six percent blood alcohol?—about eight fingers of Scotch for Marion to suicide with?"

"I will be *damned!*" said O'Connor. "That's the queerest damn— Vic! You were out on that first. Was the room door locked?"

"No," said Varallo, thinking back. "No. I took it for granted Mrs. Coldfield had opened it with a passkey."

"I asked her," said Poor. "It wasn't locked. She expected to find it locked."

"It just could be we've got another little murder here," said Rhys thoughtfully. "Have we got the lab report on the glass yet?"

"No. And that I damn well want to see," said O'Connor forcefully. "Of all the funny damned—look. Look, she could have emptied the bottle and thrown it out the window."

Rhys sniffed. "Me, I'm not only a well-trained detective, but I've got a naturally orderly mind. I looked that room over. I took a lot of pictures. Awful little hole of a place. And I doubt that window'd been washed these five years, and the screen's rusted on tight. It'd take Samson to move it. We can look, but I'd take an oath it hasn't been opened in years. Nobody threw anything out of that window. Take my word."

"Well, that's about the damnedest offbeat thing we've had in a while, isn't it?" said Varallo thoughtfully. "Either an accomplice to a suicide— which I refuse to believe, at least until we know more about it—or an absent-minded murderer who sets up a nice plausible suicide and then forgets to leave a piece of vital evidence."

"This I'm on," said O'Connor. "This I want to know more about!" He snatched up the phone. "Get me the lab. . . . Listen, you damned lazy bums down there sitting around telling blue jokes instead of working. What about that glass you've got—out of the suicide's room Friday? —what have you—"

And having turned up his possible common denominator on Collins-Gardiner, Varallo didn't like it much; and his foreboding proved true.

He drove out to Winchester Avenue—after they'd all kicked around that very damned odd Thompson thing awhile; the lab had promised to get busy on the glass—to check out Bob Holt, Junior. Who had lived in Mrs. Collins' block and then moved across town with his parents.

Holt Senior was a partner in a tax-accounting firm. Solid upstanding citizen. Mrs. Holt a rather reserved and pretty woman, quite obviously wrapped up in husband and son. The boy was an honor student at Hoover, majoring in mathematics; he was home, and he impressed Varallo. A boy very mature for his age; a boy who had, obviously, had a sensible bringing-up and a good solid home background; and a boy who had, depressingly, an alibi on both Collins and Gardiner. On February 18—the Holts were orderly people living orderly lives and keeping records—Bob Holt had been at home, hosting a party of young people: birthday party for his closest friend. And the following night he had been at a Christian Endeavor class at the Holts's church. And a week ago Saturday night he and his parents had gone to see a performance of *The Mikado* at the West Ebell theatre in Hollywood.

And, damn all common denominators. All *right,* thought Varallo. It was, likely, as dead as the Kessler thing. It had been the random wild thing—no, by God, the hour and everything else, X must have known something—but barring a miracle, they'd never know who. Or why. Likely not much why about it. One of the greedy, violent ones wanting something for nothing . . .

O'Connor called his schoolteacher at six o'clock and said, "I'll take you out to dinner if you haven't had any yet. I've got the goddamnedest offbeat homicide, and a woman and all, I could bear to get maybe the female viewpoint on—"

A sneeze interrupted him. "I," said Katharine in a thick voice, "am going nowhere. I've got your cold, damn you. A good three days off, and I—" She sneezed again. "Why I ever took up with a cop!" she said crossly, and banged the phone down.

CHAPTER 13

"I tell you what it is," he said to Laura on Tuesday night, drying the dinner dishes for her. "Maybe we're not thinking simple enough. God knows the average thing like Kessler or Collins or Gardiner is damned simple, but maybe we're just being too sophisticated—about Collins and Gardiner. All I can figure." He stacked the plates in the cupboard and came back for the cups and saucers.

"How d'you mean?" Laura took off her apron.

"Well, we said the times and so on made it look as if he had some knowledge of the woman. Could be we're being one step shrewder than the random killer, *cara*. Could be it was just his blind luck that when he got the impulse, picked the house, he found the women alone. It gets just that simple sometimes."

"I know," said Laura. "I suppose it could be. I'm *terribly* curious about that funny suicide, Vic."

"Oh, so is Charles. So are the rest of us." Varallo hung up the dish towel. "Scotch and water in the glass found there, all right. No bottle of Scotch in the room. Charles is going after that Coldfield woman hip and thigh—he'd like to think she just ransacked the room after finding the woman dead, and thriftily appropriated everything of value down to the half bottle of Scotch. And that could be just that simple, too. Anyway, I don't see—"

From the nursery came wails of distress. And Miss Ginevra did so seldom wail (that best of all babies) that they both rushed down the hall to investigate.

"She couldn't have fallen out of—"

"Don't be silly, Vic, the rails—"

In the nursery, Gideon Algernon Cadwallader was sitting on the white-painted chest of drawers next to the crib, remotely contemplating himself in the mirror hung over it. He was a handsome sight, his gray tiger stripes smooth and his white shirt front immaculate, his chartreuse eyes half-slitted in admiration. As far as the front half of Gideon was concerned, he knew absolutely nothing about that fascinating striped, white-tipped tail which was hanging enticingly down into the crib, and neatly twitching away in the nick of time each time a small starfish hand grabbed at it. Miss Ginevra was feeling frustrated.

Varallo laughed and went to comfort her. "*Su, su, hon importa, carita.* That cat!"

"Gideon," said Laura severely, "that's not being nice to the baby. Bad cat!" Gideon glanced round in vague surprise, as if noticing them for the first time, and coiled the offending tail tightly around his solid bottom. Miss Ginevra, distracted by being picked up, forgot the tail and made a grab for Varallo's open collar.

"You'll be late," said Laura, taking her. "You don't see what, you were going to say?"

"What? Oh, I don't see anything much more to do on it. Either of them. Damn, I *will* be late if I don't— I'm off." He bent to kiss her, stopped on his way down the hall to snatch a tie from their room, and left by the back door.

Ambitious cop. School night. Thank God the heat wave had gone; it was a nice cool night. He hoped to God he wouldn't get that damned cold; Poor was laid low with it at home.

The class was from eight to ten. He supposed he could have skipped it tonight; it wasn't a regular class, there was a guest speaker. And he found several had skipped it; Billings wasn't there, or another man from Burbank, or two of the Glendale patrolmen. After the first twenty minutes, Varallo began to wish he'd skipped it. The guest speaker was an attorney from Hollywood, one Montague Armstrong, a tubby little man impeccably dressed, with a bald head and a very active tongue. He was supposed to be talking about some oddities of law still on the books as they affected law enforcement; but he was evidently an extemporaneous speaker and he kept wandering off onto certain queer and unusual cases he'd had or heard about.

"—And speaking of what we sometimes call blue laws, gentlemen, I well recall—it was in nineteen forty-seven, or was it nineteen forty-eight —I ran across a rather queer specimen of . . . It was called to my attention by a Mr.——. . ."

Varallo's seat mate slumped lower and fidgeted with a pencil. Varallo tried to shut his mind to the chatty voice, debating about going home after the first hour, and his mind wandered.

That suicide. If it was. Funny, and no handle. Washington didn't know Marion Thompson's prints. O'Connor could, of course, be right—he often was; that Coldfield woman a fairly rapacious female. A search warrant for her room, and nothing suspicious there; but she'd had time to stash the loot away elsewhere.

Kessler was dead. In both senses, thought Varallo grimly. And as for the Collins-Gardiner thing, as he'd said to Laura, he was now coming round to think that he and Poor had been just a little too smart. A little too logical. Giving too much credit to X, who had been just, and only just, one of the violent people out for something for nothing, who might have just at random picked on Mrs. Collins' house and found a woman alone; and ditto on Gardiner. Maybe third time round would be unlucky for him; maybe the next time he had the impulse, he'd pick a house where there was a big strong man waiting for him. So maybe then they'd have him to question, and finally break him down into admitting it.

Because nothing, absolutely nothing, connected those two women. Aside from their ages. If X had known something about Collins, Varallo couldn't see any way he could also have known something about Gardiner—beyond overhearing something on a bus or at a lunch counter, and that kind of thing was just impossible to figure, or find out about.

He had—having the name—gone so far as to teletype an inquiry up to Clovis, on young Bill Lawrence. Not that that was a lead, even a poor small lead. But for the sake of thoroughness. No big deal, he teletyped to that sheriff, he's not hooked up to anything, don't alarm the parents, but is he there, and if so, has he been down here recently? Job? Reputation?

And that would be a dead end too. It was fairly cold-blooded to think, but—considering that one like that, who could go so very berserk, didn't often manage to control himself long—their best bet might be to sit back and wait for the next time.

God, what a thing to think.

"—In the matter of torts, of course, it is a very ancient precedent in law—"

Boring little man.

And, of course, that particular wild one might have come visiting from Hollywood or L.A. or— Ask some other precincts over there about anything similar going on, on their beats. The L.A. boys always right on the ball, and cooperative. That Hanrihan, a good man.

He wondered if Charles would break down that Coldfield woman. He felt a little sleepy. An awful woman. Harpy. Just the type to do that.

"—inheritance. Of course it is something of a no man's land, and all too often the individual judge will be arbitrary one way or the other. One rather queer little case which is on the calendar at the moment, I happen to have personal knowledge of, as I am acting for the litigant . . . very wealthy man who died intestate, and as is always the case several claimants have come forward. My client, Mr. George—"

Varallo suppressed a yawn.

"—Worthington Woodruff . . . Possession of old family articles, as well as his mother's marriage license and a few other documents, but his case immeasurably strengthened by his ownership of . . . great-grand-father's hunting-case watch with the name and date engraved, June eighteen thirty-nine—and an old family Bible with inscriptions on the flyleaf. . . . analysis of the ink from the flyleaf proved to be . . . Estate of Franklin George Worthington—"

Varallo sat up as if something had stung him. *Worthington.* That rang a loud clear bell in his mind. What the hell? *Worthington.* "The Worthington engraving job—" The—

Kessler. Kessler, writing in his diary, hearing a noise below, getting up—the break-in— "Was sure 1939 the correct date . . . made a little work for me." *Worthington.*

Without realizing it he was on his feet. "Mr. Armstrong! Excuse me, but let me hear that over—a claimant to an estate—and some of the things he's backing the claim with, an old watch engraved with the name of Worthington and the date eighteen thirty-nine?" But what the hell was this? That had been the obvious random break-in—

Armstrong, halted in mid-stride, stared at him. "What? Yes, that's correct—most interesting case, rather circumstantial as most unfortunately the courthouse back in East Newburg, Connecticut burned down with all its records in nineteen eleven—but together with the marriage certificate, and his birth certificate, *and* these family possessions— Of course, any one item any person might inadvertently acquire at an antique shop or somewhere, but the cumulative value of a number of such —the watch and the Bible and the old bracelet which is also engraved, with the name of his great-grandfather's wife—and— I really think a substantial part of the estate should be awarded—"

"To whom?"

"Really—why, my client, of course. Mr. George Worthington Woodruff. I'm afraid I don't—"

"You've seen this watch. When did you first see it, Mr. Armstrong? Prior to—" God, when—"about the middle of February?"

"What? What? Well—it would be about three weeks ago. The case is just in a state of preparation, you understand." Armstrong stared at him, bewildered. "I don't understand—"

"By God, I don't know that I do either," said Varallo, "but it could just be that you've broken a case for us, Mr. Armstrong." And this was one hell of a long jump his mind was making—from A to Z, maybe—but— "Excuse me," he said, and sidled out of the aisle, went out to the corridor and made a run for the pay phone at the end of the hall.

He got Katz at home. "Listen, Joe. Kessler. He'd been writing in his diary just before he was shot. Don't ask me why, just tell me—what happened to all his effects? You mentioned a lawyer. Do you know if he kept the diary?" It was only ten days or so ago.

"How the hell would I— Yes, it was a lawyer. He didn't think there were any relatives. How would I know what happened to the diary? Why? What's up, Vic?"

"Something very damned funny, Joe, and I may be seeing ghosts, but such a damn funny coincidence I can't— Yes, by God, and there was that item. Six seventy-five, you said had been crossed out on the day book—engraving job?— Of all the offbeat things— It could be, my friend, if I'm not seeing ghosts, that Kessler was a private personal kill. What's the lawyer's name?"

"A—oh, now, look, you go home and sober up," said Katz.

"I know, I know. Crazy. I may be. I just want to find out more about it," said Varallo. "What's the lawyer's name?"

"I don't— Daly," said Katz. "Daniel J. Daly. In town. Vic—"

"And if you're really a dedicated cop," said Varallo, "meet me at the office in say an hour. I'm calling Charles too. Thanks." He put down the phone and began hunting for Daly in the book. This was crazy, it was reaching so far—but the coincidence of dates, and that passage in the diary—and God, if there *was* anything to it, was there any evidence left lying around to be got?

"Mr. Daly? Are you the attorney who took over the affairs of Horace Kessler after he— You are. You don't know me, sir, my name's Varallo, I'm a detective on the Glendale force. I'd like to ask you, please, if you remember—"

*

It was crazy, it was offbeat, but the more they heard about it the more interested they got. Varallo explained enough to little Mr. Armstrong that he summarily closed the class session and followed Varallo down to headquarters, where they forgathered with O'Connor and Katz.

"Just on a damn date, you jump to the conclusion—" Both O'Connor and Katz were looking incredulous.

"Not just on a date. You saw that diary, Joe? It was just a couple of sentences, but the implication was plain. And once you put it with Mr. Armstrong's client— Kessler had done an engraving job and made a mistake in the date. He thought the customer meant nineteen thirty-nine. He doesn't say what the customer wanted instead, but if that engraving job was on Mr. Armstrong's client's old watch—which turns up with a date in eighteen thirty-nine on it— Well! *È vero,*" said Varallo. "Sure, I jumped. But Kessler also put down the name of Worthington. If that's the name engraved on that watch, probably that's the name the customer gave. And Mr. Armstrong's client is claiming an estate left by a man named Worthington. I only—"

Armstrong kept up a series of startled little exclamations. "God bless my—but it is quite a good claim, you know—his mother's—and he seems quite a— I don't understand, but if you think Mr. Woodruff—"

"Look, for God's sake," said O'Connor, "you don't tell me I can claim to be the great-grandson of some millionaire and get handed the estate because I can show a damn gold watch engraved with his mother's maiden name or—"

"Not at all, Charles. But it's like the evidence we depend on all the time—circumstantial," said Varallo dryly. "And every little bit helps."

"I most certainly regard it as a valid claim, sir," said Armstrong agitatedly. "Until it's proved otherwise, I still— No, of course not. Of course not. But there is a cumulative value in such possessions, you can see that. He has documents too—his mother's marriage license—there was an estrangement in the family, his grandfather was disinherited by the old man—but research has shown us that there can be only one male heir in this generation—we know for certain that the grandfather's sisters both died childless—and naturally the possession of such family relics *is* a good piece of cumulative evidence—the Bible, and the watch, and the bracelet, and the wedding ring, which is also engraved inside with initials and a date—and— God bless my soul, I'm not sure what you're suggesting, but—"

"Of value," said Varallo, "especially to a possibly sentimental judge."

As you said awhile ago, that sort of thing is all up to the judge, and they are not infallible. Oh, really? All that. I just wonder if your client, Mr. Armstrong, has been quietly and busily canvassing the old-gold dealers and buying up odds and ends of Victorian jewelry—and patronizing the little out-of-the-way jewelers for the little engraving jobs. Just to bolster up his claim to—how much?"

"What? What? Well, it's an estate of over four million. I never expected to get all of it for him, of course, but Mr. Woodruff is the only serious claimant who has evidence. I hope to get him awarded at least a quarter of it, with what—"

"I leave it to you, Charles," said Varallo. "By the grace of God Mr. Daly thinks he still has Kessler's diary—meant to destroy it, stuck it in a drawer. You tell me whether we haven't got a little reason to go and talk to Mr. George Worthington Woodruff. Because a million dollars is still a good-sized piece of money. For which some people would go to some lengths. And I can see Mr. Woodruff, in the process of acquiring all the plausible family heirlooms, to bolster his case, inadvertently picking Mr. Kessler to do one of his engraving jobs—going far afield to another town—"

"He'd have been smarter," said Katz, his dark eyes absorbed and interested, "to go to one of the big department stores downtown. So many jobs they get, and who's to remember one from the other? To Mother with love. Bob and Sue, June nineteen sixty-two. Graduation, anniversary, wedding, birthday, just names and dates, who remembers? But if that's so, Vic, I can see a fellow like that—trying to be smart—going to the little hole-in-the-wall ones like Kessler. Who, God knows, might not have remembered it either."

"And he might not have, but he made a mistake," said Varallo. "He assumed the date the customer wanted engraved on the old watch was nineteen thirty-nine instead of eighteen thirty-nine. Possibly the customer wrote it down for him and he thought the customer had made a little mistake. And when he had to do the job over, possibly he'd have done a little wondering anyway—any jeweler might—that old a watch. He—"

"We have verified the maker," said Armstrong mournfully. "It was a model made before eighteen thirty-nine."

"Sure. It'd pay Mr. Woodruff to bone up a little on all that. Hunt around the old-gold shops," said Varallo. "You see all sorts of antique stuff in those places. What is Mr. Woodruff's background, Mr. Armstrong? Do you know?"

"Oh, for the love of Christ," said O'Connor. "Reaching out into thin air— I've told you before, Vic, the detective that goes by hunches is a damn bad detective, and I—"

"But they help sometimes, Charles. And listen to the evidence to back up this one."

"—Perfectly honest fellow," said Armstrong faintly. "He is a printer by trade—he has his own small business in Hollywood. But, gentlemen, the utmost care has been—the writing on the flyleaf of the Bible, the ink has been analyzed, it has the correct ingredients, ink made before that date—and the Worthington name inscribed—"

"And who would be more apt to have such information—or know where to look it up—than a printer?" asked Varallo. "I don't suppose it'd be much trouble to mix up a batch of old-fashioned ink."

Katz scratched his jaw. "It also occurs to me," he said, "just using a little imagination—" he glanced sardonically at O'Connor—"that a case involving a sum like that might get a little mention in the papers, and it'd be a kind of human interest bit that it was partly decided on these old family relics—and Kessler might just notice it. Kessler and not the other jewelers who'd done the little engraving jobs for him. Because of that little mistake about the year, which would have fixed it in Kessler's mind."

"You've got something there, I think. Or Kessler may have asked some innocent questions about it, showing Mr. Woodruff that he would remember it," agreed Varallo. "In any case—"

"Dear me, gentlemen, I can't help thinking you are all— Leaping to such unwarranted—"

"—The little coincidence, which I don't think it is, of the date and the name, make me think we'd better pay a visit to Mr. Woodruff," said Varallo. "What do you think, Charles?"

"Oh, for God's sake!" said O'Connor. "I do, I do. Even if it's only a hunch. Just every now and then, I admit it, a hunch—"

They took George Worthington Woodruff, printer, completely by surprise. And his attorney unwittingly just made matters worse for him. "—Quite unwarranted conclusion, Mr. Woodruff, but I feel—as your representative—it will clear this foolish question up much more quickly if you will answer their questions freely, and although they have not got a search warrant, I do advise you to allow them to—"

Woodruff stared at his attorney. "What? No! I won't—"

"Oh, really I do think you would be wise to— They could *get* a search warrant, I daresay. Really much wiser to— If you'd just let me speak with you confidentially while they—er—"

Woodruff, a big sandy man in his forties, interrupted in the middle of breakfast, peacefully contemplating a successful claim to at least a million bucks, and now all of a sudden invaded by cops, stared and spluttered. "I—listen, what is this? I—"

"Thanks so much," said O'Connor. "Just once over lightly, boys."

And in the top drawer in the bureau in Mr. Woodruff's bedroom they found an old Smith and Wesson Combat Masterpiece in poor condition, and about twenty rounds of ammo for it.

And ballistics told them it was the Combat Masterpiece that had killed Horace Kessler.

And O'Connor growled at Varallo, "Jumping to conclusions! I will be damned. The private, personal kill. To protect his little con game. When it looked exactly like—"

"What he set it up to look like, Charles. A halfway smart fellow. Just halfway. Though at that," said Varallo, "he'd have got away with it, if I hadn't just happened to—"

"Would he?" asked Katz. "I don't know. The trade I do know. If he'd taken his engraving jobs to the big impersonal places, well, no bets. And Kessler must have let him see he was curious, would remember the job—so Kessler had to go. Obviously the victim of the random break-in. But I'd take no bets that, if it had all gone off the way he planned—seeing that he picked the little hole-in-the-wall jewelers—that one of them wouldn't have noticed the human-interest story in the *Times,* and remembered the unusual little job—and eventually have talked."

"That could be, Joe."

Eventually they were to find the old-gold dealers who had sold Woodruff the watch, and the bracelet, and the wedding ring. Eventually they were to track down the jewelers who had done the other engraving jobs. They were never to trace the old Bible.

But it was the Combat Masterpiece that pinned Woodruff down. That was solid evidence, and that he saw.

And eventually he talked.

"For God's sake, talk about unfair! I *am* that old guy's great-grandson, I know—things my mother said—and her maiden name and how she gave me Worthington for a middle name and— Her marriage certificate, and—but it wasn't enough really—and I'd seen a case in the paper, this Judge Ford, how he awarded a claim like that, and it'd been things like that, family things, to prove who he really was—some papers too, but mostly—and I thought—and after I'd got all that— I looked it up, about the ink and so on, and I can imitate that Spencerian script, they call it, pretty fair. I knew all the family names, of course. Of all the lousy luck! I had it made! I asked Armstrong, and he said the chances were the case'd come up before that same judge. That damn snoopy little jeweler! Thinking I meant nineteen thirty-nine, and then asking questions— such a well-preserved old timepiece, wasn't it, and was it a relative, the name I wanted— Remember it! I could just see him, spotting a couple of lines about it in some paper and— When I'd got that close! I *am* the old guy's great-grandson. I had a legit claim, only—only—" He pounded one fist impotently on his knee. "That damn little old-maid jeweler! What *was* he? Old man alone—he talked—I knew that. Lived over the shop. What the hell *was* he? He was old—he'd had his life! And me—I'd had nothing. Ever. And I could have—I could have—" He stopped and wiped his lips.

"There's a commandment, Mr. Woodruff," said O'Connor hardly.

"Yeah—yeah—there's a million bucks maybe, too! Rightly *mine*. Who was he?"

"Another man," said Katz, and he sounded sad.

"Yeah—yeah. A million bucks. If he didn't talk. And he would have remembered, and talked," said Woodruff. "I set it up. I took the gamble. You shouldn't ever have *suspected*. I don't know how you ever came to."

"Maybe," said Katz gently, "it was just God's will, Mr. Woodruff."

CHAPTER 14

Friday morning, and Wayne came into the lobby just after Varallo. "If it isn't our great little jumper to conclusions, on time for once. Morning, Vic. Bill."

"Morning," said Copeland mournfully. "I think I've got that damn cold. My throat's sore."

"Oh, don't mention it," said Wayne. "I'm pretending mine isn't, too. Go through the whole damn building eventually." He and Varallo climbed stairs to the detective bureau and said good morning to Katz.

"I have an awful suspicion," said Katz, "that I've got that damn cold."

"I told you," said Wayne. "Through the whole force, I swear." Poor had been laid low for three days, had come back yesterday and had gone home at noon, still feeling shaky and running a little fever. He couldn't, he said, seem to shake it off.

Katz looked at Varallo and shook his head. "The picture of health. Our famous jumper to conclusions—and what a hell of a funny business that was. It isn't fair."

"I'm using will power," said Varallo. "I haven't had a cold in nearly six years."

"I didn't mean that. You'll get this one too eventually, want to bet? I just can't get over that baby," said Katz. "Every single baby I have ever known or heard about—and I've got three sisters and assorted cousins, all married—has waked up to yell at night. It's just another fact of life, babies waking up to yell at night."

"Always the exception to prove the rule. She's just," said Varallo smugly, "got an exceptionally good disposition."

"Well, all I can say is," said Katz feelingly, "that I hope the second one is a hellion. Teach you to be smug. Brother, you just don't know how lucky you are."

O'Connor came in, frowning, absently patting the bulge of the .357 magnum. "John still off? Damn, I wanted—"

"And whose fault is it?" demanded Wayne. "You've passed this thing around so damn generous, Charles. Joe's got it and I think I'm coming down with it. Have we got the paper work cleaned up on Kessler? And what an offbeat one—"

That had kept them busy, principally, since Tuesday night; it was about all cleaned up now, unless whoever had sold Woodruff the Bible should turn up to make a statement; it wasn't important.

"This goddamned Coldfield woman," said O'Connor, scowling. "I'll break her down, damn it, if it's the last thing I do. It's got to be the answer, on Thompson. Oh, Vic, there's a teletype in for you. From some place in Madera County. What would that be about?"

"Nothing much, I don't think. Little inquiry that came up on the last look around on Collins." Varallo went down the hall to look at the teletype.

He had really only made the inquiry to be thorough. That Bill Lawrence had showed up unexpectedly; they'd heard of the Lawrence family who had moved from Geneva Street last year, but until Varallo had talked to young Don Carteret they hadn't known that Bill Lawrence had come back, visiting his aunt and uncle. Bill Lawrence, twenty-two, twenty-three, a school dropout—that said nothing in itself except that he was either backward or lazy, and that kind always more apt to get into trouble. But they didn't always. There wasn't one thing to say that Bill Lawrence had ever been in any trouble, and the only reason Varallo had made any inquiry about him was simply that he had showed. A shadow—a very-much-maybe possible. Just as Varallo had, being thorough, gone to see the Carterets.

So he didn't expect much from the teletype from the sheriff of Madera County, where the little town of Clovis was located; and he read it with surprise and growing interest.

The sheriff of Madera County seemed to be a chatty type. Or much interested in Bill Lawrence . . . The Lawrences had moved to Clovis a little over a year ago. The son came with them. Bought a little house on the outskirts of town; elder Lawrences quiet people, well enough liked mostly. The son held a job in town for a couple of months, working at a gas station, and then got fired for arguing with customers and making wrong change. Son had then vanished from Clovis; said to be staying with aunt and uncle back in Glendale. He came back to Clovis in June, didn't get a job, didn't look for one, hung around the bars and was involved in a few brawls, evidently the type that turned belligerent with a little drink inside. One count of D. and D. in Clovis.

Varallo's eyebrows rose. *"Per caritá!"* he muttered. "Can I have struck pay dirt here?" He went on reading.

Young Lawrence didn't have much of a reputation in Clovis except for making trouble—for his parents and other people. Some people in town unfriendly to all the Lawrences in consequence. The sheriff thought charitably, elder Lawrences all right, just saddled with a wrong one for a boy. Did young Lawrence have any record down in L.A. County? Last July, up in Clovis, he'd beaten up another young fellow pretty bad, the other fellow swore Lawrence had rolled him after knocking him out, but that couldn't be proved, and Lawrence had got only ten days in jail. While he'd still been around town, last September, there'd been a break-in at a local drugstore, overnight, and about eighty bucks stolen. They'd had Lawrence in to question along with some others—just on the natural suspicion of any such young drifter without a job—but no evidence had showed. Lawrence away from Clovis October to December, said to be in Fresno working. In January, he'd been home briefly, tried to get a job around town, but nobody would hire him. Absent from Clovis since about the middle of January, said to be with aunt and uncle. Sheriff sympathetic to the parents, who acted in such a way that the sheriff—evidently a shrewd character as those rural sheriffs mostly were—suspected it was nothing new to them to be questioned by peace officers about young Bill. Which was the reason he wondered, did Bill have a record down there?

"Diavolo!" said Varallo. Pay dirt? He certainly never had expected— from such a background as Geneva Street, and Mrs. Bessemer had seemed like a pleasant, ordinary woman. Upright middle-class. But the Bill Lawrences came from anywhere these days. And this could just be a big break.

Because it was largely unprofitable to try to put yourself into the criminal's shoes—think, what would I have done if I were—because it was impossible for an intelligent and honest man to imagine just how stupid and unreasoning the small-time hood can be. But all the same, Varallo thought it was asking a bit too much of the blind luck that the X on Collins and Gardiner had by utter chance found two women alone at that early hour, unprotected. One, he would swallow. Gardiner, if by a long and lucky chance it had been Bill Lawrence, who, knowing a little something about old Mrs. Collins, had been the one who broke into that house.

This could indeed be a little something.

He went back to the office to talk it over with somebody and Katz told him O'Connor had gone out to tackle Mrs. Coldfield again. "And I wish him joy of her. Awful female. Kind who makes you understand monks."

"Yes," said Varallo. "Joe, we checked all the juvenile records on Collins, didn't we? The first time and when we reworked it after Gardiner came along?"

"All but the sex files. I always said we should have—it's not too late now. Two elderly women, and—"

"Yes. I suppose so. But there isn't anything says he— I'll tell you something else," said Varallo suddenly, looking at the teletype in his hand. "How foolish can I get? Bill Lawrence hasn't *been* a juvenile in a while, and we didn't go pawing around in the past."

"What? Who? You starting to work it all over again from scratch?" asked Katz. He swallowed experimentally and felt his throat. "Damn, I've got it all right. Give it another forty-eight hours to develop—"

"Try will power. I might just do that, Joe," said Varallo absently. He went down to records. There wouldn't be any harm—

They had only so much space. Every so often they weeded out the records; these days, now, they were trying to get all the back stuff on microfilm, to save room; that hadn't all been done yet, something of a job. And there were the cross files with prints, too. The juveniles under eighteen brought in for anything couldn't, legally, be fingerprinted. *Deh*, no, he thought, give the poor little darlings a police record so young, just because they'd been mugging elderly strollers or committing some other high-spirited high jinks? Unthinkable. But records otherwise were kept on them, of course. And Bill Lawrence hadn't been under eighteen for five years or so.

And if Bill Lawrence, who sounded like the usual lout, was on the point of graduating to the serious break-ins, Varallo would take a bet that he had, so to speak, given the warning rattle as a juvenile. They mostly did.

And he had. In the under-eighteen records of seven years back, finally, he found Bill Lawrence. Age sixteen, Grand Theft Auto; probation to parents. Three months later, attempted assault on another kid; probation. The year following (a notation tagged him as a dropout then) D. and D., and another attempted assault. Three-months sentence, suspended, probation. God, these judges. And that was it. As it didn't look, by what the sheriff up in Madera County said, as if Bill had straightened out much—a drifter, holding a job seldom, of sufficient reputation that they hauled him in to question on that burglary. Varallo wondered if Bill had just been lucky, in between then and when he moved away. The chances were he had done this and that in between. Could be he was in somebody else's records around here.

He pulled the file, went back and showed it and the teletype to Katz. "Now isn't this interesting," said Katz, sitting up. "Where'd this come from? How'd you happen to drop on this Lawrence? I never heard of him."

Varallo told him. "Evidently the parents—and the Bessemers, who must have known about this—managed to keep it quiet. Even from the inveterate gossip of the neighborhood. We didn't get a smell of this that day we canvassed the block. But it is an interesting little something, isn't it?"

"I take it you're thinking among other things, you'll swallow one coincidence," said Katz acutely. "I think I go along. If. He knew Collins, but picked the Gardiner house at random."

"You're psychic, Joe. Damn, it's all up in the air. It could be our Billy boy, all right. He's the type, and if he was tight at the time, well, evidently he gets fighting-mean with a little inside. But it's nothing like evidence."

"No. But I guess we could both bear to know Billy boy's whereabouts at the moment."

"I'm just about," said Varallo, "to look into it. And even as an experienced peace officer, Joe, I do sometimes find myself wondering about people. Nice quiet middle-class town, Glendale, and we like to think most of the residents think of cops as the Good Guys—happy to cooperate. Just the little I talked to Mrs. Bessemer—and I suppose Fred or whoever talked to her before'd say the same—I'd have taken my oath she was cooperative. Anxious to oblige. But she must have known about this—her own nephew—a little record of violence at least—and she didn't speak up."

Katz grunted. "She might not have known, Vic. Parents might have kept it a dark secret to themselves."

"Living on the same block! For God's sake, I don't see how—"

"And then too, even knowing that, would she think it was possible? Billy she'd known as a baby? Doing a murder? That murder? A lot of people don't reason, Vic—they just feel."

"I know that, for God's sake, but—"

"And it seems to be a respectable family. Probably all of 'em—you know—at a loss to know what to do about Billy. How to straighten him out. I sometimes think it's a tossup," said Katz wryly. "You try to bring 'em up right, but some of 'em just go off the rails regardless. . . . And then again, does it occur to you that she might have thought Billy was with his parents up in Clovis when the Collins job happened? We see he wasn't, but he needn't have been here either. There are a lot of places to be besides Clovis and Glendale."

"That," said Varallo, "is what I'll try to find out."

As he turned to the door, O'Connor came in looking grim, and trailing behind him a sullen, trap-mouthed Mrs. Coldfield. He planted a chair close beside his desk and pointed to it silently. She sat. O'Connor sat down in his desk chair, unfastened his jacket and leaned forward, whether by accident or design affording her a nice view of the outsized holster, and gave her his amiable-crocodile smile. "Now, Mrs. Coldfield, you're going to give me some nice straight answers, damn it, and stop tying to con me. . . ."

Varallo went out to the corridor and nearly collided with Bryson from records, just coming in.

"Oh, Varallo. Just coming to see you. Two birds with one stone, I wanted some coffee anyway." The machine was down the hall. "After you left just now, all of a sudden it came to me that we had a request to copy that file on Lawrence just awhile ago, for the L.A.P.D. Back in January it was. I looked it up. The Wilshire precinct."

"Oh? Thanks." Varallo went back into the office, sat at his desk, looked up the number and dialed.

"—*told* you the truth! Damn suspicious bloodhound—"

"Well, well, the pro slang. Have you got a little pedigree somewhere, Mrs. Coldfield? All I want are some straight answers. Why did you delay in calling the police when you found the Thompson woman dead?"

The Wilshire precinct desk sergeant answered; Varallo explained, and got shunted upstairs to a Sergeant Kallenburg. . . . "Lawrence? Just a minute, I'll ask around, doesn't ring a bell with me. . . . Here's Sergeant Stone, he's the one can tell you about it."

"—And you can't say I *did,* because I did no such thing. I don't *know* anything about any Scotch and you can't—"

"—Got his name from one of the birds we picked up for it," Stone was saying. "Overnight break-in of a liquor store on Pico Boulevard.

January twentieth. The owner was there, making up the books, and got banged on the head and concussed. We got an ident from him on one Walter Craig, whose pedigree we had, and Walter told us finally that a couple of pals had been with him—this Bill Lawrence and another guy named Sidney. Which of couse is not evidence but we wanted to talk to both of them. We've got a little record on Lawrence over here too, from four years back or so, but we took a look at yours—just for fun. We never picked him up. You any idea where he is?"

"Unfortunately, no. You've got a record on him too? What kind?"

"Not us personally—Wilcox Street. Oh, little j.d. stuff—brawls, one count of D. and D., suspicion of attempted break-ins—no charges. Why? Are you looking for him now?"

"I am. I want to talk to him about a murder."

"Jesus," said Stone, "is that so? He got into the big time pretty quick, didn't he? Well, I wish you luck."

Varallo put the phone down. All of a sudden, Bill Lawrence looked very hot. He thought angrily, impotently, The family must all have known this: what he was, what he might do. I'll bet he had temper tantrums as a kid, he thought. And either, as respectable upright reputable people, carefully keeping the dark secret, or of course as Katz said, thinking blindly, Billy was such a cute baby, naturally he couldn't have—

People. Just by being people, hampering the cops . . .

"All *right*, all *right!*" she screamed suddenly. Varallo and Katz jumped. "All *right*, damn you, there was a man in her room that night, I'm gonna come out with it so you maybe take me in as a madam or— *I* don't care what the hell transients do, I keep a young ladies' school?— why should *I*— All *right*, make whatever you damn like of it but that's every last thing I know. No, I don't know when he came or went, I just happened hear a man's voice I passed her door. Damn cop bullies—"

Varallo glanced over at O'Connor, who was glowering up at the Coldfield woman, suppressing surprise and annoyance. The Thompson thing. Well, well, Varallo thought, so that was what she'd been covering up. Charles had got more than he bargained for: a real little puzzle.

A man in Thompson's room. Accomplice to a suicide? Or a murder? An absent-minded murderer who forgot to leave a vital piece of evidence?

That, for the moment, was Charles's business. His was Bill Lawrence. Suddenly looking so hot for Collins and Gardiner. Well, another possible, at least—true, that much violence wasn't in his record, but there was always a first time.

"Dragging all that up!" she said angrily, fearfully. "I don't see why you all have to go picking on him. It's not right. Any boy can be led into a little mischief by bad company. . . . Of course I didn't say anything about Bill to you, why on earth should I?"

"Mrs. Bessemer," said Varallo. "I don't understand this. Let's be quite clear. Your nephew Bill has several charges on his record as a juvenile here."

"Years ago it was."

"But not so very long ago he got in trouble over in Hollywood too. He's been tied into a burglary there quite recently."

"I don't know anything about that. You could just be saying such a thing, I never heard— Bill wouldn't—"

"And among the counts on him, both as a juvenile and afterward, are several involving violence. He lived on this street all during the time he was growing up. Are you telling me that, knowing all this as you admit, it didn't even cross your mind to mention your nephew when Mrs. Collins—"

"No, it didn't, and it doesn't now! Couple of harmless boyish pr—and the police always picking— *Not a thing like that!*" She looked at him wildly, and put both hands to her mouth. "Dora and Kent just *sick* about it, they tried— And *drinking!* Why, he never saw that at home— good Christian upbringing, they— And Marla such a nice girl, a good girl and married with two fine children—and up there—a small town, that's what Kent said, quiet settled atmosphere, he'd settle down and be all right, he'd—it'd be better for—but he couldn't—he couldn't— *Not a thing like Mrs. Collins!*" Quite suddenly Mrs. Bessemer began to cry. Not noisily, or hysterically; she just rocked back and forth, there in the overstuffed chair in her neat old-fashioned living room, the tears streaming down her cheeks, and sobbed.

And compassion rose in him. Not the stubborn denial, the purblind denial, the blurring of present fact with the remembered fat cooing baby —but stark fear kept rigidly inside, and the family pride, and, just a little, that incorrigible and all too human tendency of human nature—if I don't look at it it'll go away.

"Mrs. Bessemer." He touched her arm gently. "I understand how you feel—but please, you know I have to ask questions."

She nodded, groping for a handkerchief, blowing her nose.

"Your nephew visited you last fall? Yes, and went up to Clovis again. But he hasn't been there since the middle of January. Have you seen him since then?"

After a minute she said in a thick whisper, "About the end of January, he—Bill—came and asked for a loan. He was looking for a job—he said."

"Where, do you know?"

"Over in—Hollywood somewhere. We gave him twenty-five dollars. My own nephew and—" She looked at Varallo piteously— "*Not*—he couldn't be the one—a thing like that! Stealing, maybe but—"

"Do you know where he was living then?" She shook her head. "Have you seen him since?" She shook her head again. "Well, if he turns up here at any time, will you please call us?"

She nodded obediently, wiping her eyes. "I see we'd better . . ." She looked up slowly. "We all tried, with him. I don't know why. I don't know *why* he's— But it was all little things—nothing very bad. Not *really*. He *couldn't* be the one—a thing like that. . . . Could he?"

And Varallo went home and told Laura he wasn't sure they should have embarked on this project at all. Children. "I don't know but what Joe's right—you can try your damnedest, instill the morals into them and all, but they do come equipped with their own personalities, and in the end it's a tossup how they turn out." He stripped off his tie.

"Don't be silly, Vic," said Laura, who was looking especially attractive with her bright brandy-colored hair freshly washed and waved, and her cheeks flushed from bending over the oven. "Of course it matters how they're brought up. Bending the twig and so on. Essential personalities, certainly, but even in nine and a half weeks I can tell you exactly how this daughter of ours is going to turn out." She laughed. "The essential Pollyanna. One of those obnoxious people who can always see the bright side, and loves doing Good Works, always happy and laughing. Quite obnoxious. I got some soap in her eyes when I gave her her bath, and she yelled once and then looked at me forgivingly, I swear, and I could have smacked her. She's too good to be true. . . . Dinner in fifteen minutes."

Varallo laughed and went in to see his darling, who cooed at him softly. Surely the very best baby any set of parents— She was going to have long eyelashes. And, he thought, a dimple, in the same place as his other, lost Ginevra. Really uncanny . . . And of course it *did* make a difference how you brought them up, and he would definitely put his foot down about dressing her in pants. At least sometimes, little girls should be dressed like little girls. . . .

And O'Connor swore about the new puzzle Mrs. Coldfield had handed him; and he wasn't at all sure she wasn't lying about *that;* the simple answer could still be the true one, and Mrs. Coldfield just covering up with more lies.

And Katz came down with the cold, a day after Copeland did, and Wayne succumbed the day after. Which made the rest of them a little more work, because there was a holdup at a liquor store out on Glendale Avenue on Sunday night, and a burglary of a private house on Monday night while the owners were at a party, and a hit-and-run on Sunday afternoon which got handed over to the detective bureau by Monday, and there was no doubt that the crime rate was going up, even in Glendale.

The paper work got finished on the very offbeat Kessler case. Poor finally came back to work, cured. Rhys came down with the cold on Tuesday.

They had a wanted flier out on Bill Lawrence to every force in the county. And in Clovis, Madera County, just in case he showed up there.

On Wednesday Katz, who had been laid low with the cold, came back in. "You and your will power," he said to Varallo. "You'll get it yet. I managed, of course, to give it to Anne. They do say husband and wife should share things. Any trace of that Lawrence punk yet?"

"Not yet." Bill Lawrence Varallo would very much like to lay hands on. Just to question. Eventually—

On Friday, at about ten minutes to six, there was a phone call for Detective Varallo at the detective bureau. "Stone, Wilshire precinct. Say, we've had your flier on this Lawrence. We just picked him up—by a fluke—in a hot car with a couple of other punks, both with pedigrees. You said something about a murder. You still want him?—he's all yours to talk to. Of course we want to ask him this and that about that break-in, but a murder—well, that's the heaviest charge there is. Shall we expect you?"

"I'm on my way!" said Varallo. "Charles, call Laura and tell her I'll be late."

CHAPTER 15

The Wilshire Boulevard precinct station was a rabbit warren of a place, and Varallo had never been there before; asking his way, he found himself at the entrance of a big shabby room looking oddly familiar. Nothing really could have been less like the new, fluorescent, strip-lighted, smartly vinyl-floored detective bureau at Glendale Headquarters, with its steel desks and scientific-posture typing chairs and its modern wall of windows looking out over the town toward the line of foothills. This was an old building, and the floor was scuffed bare boards, and the tall narrow windows were old-fashioned, double-hung windows, and the lights were ordinary desk lamps and overhead fixtures, and the desks were old wooden ones. It looked familiar because, in some mysterious way, all places where the law enforcement boys work at the thankless job got to look and feel and smell alike.

There were four men there around a desk and a couple of chairs, up at the end of the room. A fifth man sat in one of the chairs and stared up at them.

One of the men detached himself from the group and came over to the door. "Varallo? I'm Stone." The other three deserted their catch temporarily to join them. "Briggs. Stanton. Galluzo."

"Well, *paisano*," said Varallo. They shook hands all round.

"My God," said Stanton, "glamor cops they got over in Glendale. You'd make more on TV, Varallo."

"I've been told. Just a glutton for punishment, me. That him?"

"Lawrence. Yeah. We haven't got much out of him yet. Did you say you're after him for murder?"

"I don't know, it could be." He gave them a breakdown on the Collins-Gardiner thing. Stanton looked dubious.

Galluzo rubbed his jaw. "What we've got on him, it's little stuff. But I will say there's violence in his pedigree. What a thing. Look, you want to take him home with you? It's a heavier charge than we've got, if he comes apart."

"I haven't got any charge on him," Varallo pointed out. "I just want to question him."

"See that. O.K., suppose you sit in and stick in your oar where it might do the most good," said Stone with a grin. They all went up to the end of the room where Bill Lawrence sat and stared at the floor.

"O.K., Lawrence, back to the old grind," said Stone. "Walter Craig tells us you and Sidney helped him break in that liquor store on January twentieth. You remember back that far, Lawrence?"

"I remember. He's a liar. I didn't have anything to do with it, and you can't prove I did."

"You know Craig?" Stanton, conversational.

"Yeah, I know Craig. That doesn't say I pulled any jobs with him."

"Do you remember where you were on January twentieth?"

"I was here in town. I don't remember where I was that night, do you? I'd take a bet you don't remember, bloodhound."

"How'd you know it was night?" asked Galluzo.

"You said a break-in. These get pulled in broad daylight? You think I'm a nut?"

Varallo looked at Bill Lawrence. Sometimes it did make you wonder. He'd grown up in a good solid family background, with people who'd tried to bring him up well. Say he was weak, say he got into bad company, say he was just born that way, still it did make you wonder. Not a bad-looking young man: about six feet, wide-shouldered, slim-hipped, dark hair and good features, if at the moment he was affecting the exaggerated sideburns. He was foppishly dressed, dark-plaid slacks, a fancy sports shirt with French cuffs and gold cuff links. And he was playing it cool: cops he had some experience of, and he knew they hadn't any real evidence on him.

Another one of the greedy ones, thought Varallo. The ones who wanted it the easy way. "Lawrence," he said.

"New boy," said Lawrence easily, looking back at him. "So what's your question, Handsome?"

"You get over to Glendale much?" asked Varallo.

Lawrence's mouth tightened involuntarily. "No, why? I grew up in that hick town, why I want to go back?"

"But you did, didn't you, about the middle of last month? You broke
in old Mrs. Collins' back door and you—"

"I never did," said Lawrence automatically. His eyes moved, once,
and suddenly, viciously, Varallo was sure. It had been Lawrence. And
he was only trying to play it cool, talking up like the characters in
movies he'd seen, cheap paperback books he'd read, the way his greedy
and boastful little small-timer hood pals told him how they'd talked up
to the cops. He had graduated to the big time before he was ready for it.

"Who the hell is Collins?"

"You remember Mrs. Collins, Billy," said Varallo coldly. "Right on
the block where you lived up to last year."

"Oh, that old dame. Sure. Somebody break in and rob her? That's
sure too bad," said Lawrence. He smirked up at Varallo. "Snotty old
dame, always yelling at people to get off her flowers."

"So you thought you'd get back at her, maybe. Was she mean to you
when you were a kid, Billy? And what'd you do with all the diamonds?
Don't tell me a punk little kid like you knows a real live fence? What
about it?"

"I don't know anything about it," said Lawrence.

"You didn't remember where you were on January twentieth. Where
were you on February eighteenth and nineteenth?"

"I was here, I was here, damn it, who remembers what he was doing
that far back? I don't know anything about—"

"Ten grand worth of diamonds, Billy. That was quite a windfall,
wasn't it? Bought you your fancy clothes and the pretty gold cuff links.
Real gold, Billy? Where'd you raise the price? Don't tell me you've got
a job?"

"I— Oh, for God's sake, I got lucky at poker down in Gardena.
What's it to— What's with a job? You—"

"No, you don't stick to jobs very long, do you? They expect you to
do a little work at a regular job, and that you're allergic to, your kind.
Real gold links—you got a lot lucky at poker? Let's see, with what else
was missing from Mrs. Collins' house, I figure a fence might have given
you about thirty-five hundred. How much of it have you got left, Billy?"

"I—"

"Answer the nice man, Lawrence," said Stone.

"I don't know what the hell he's talking about." But again his eyes
moved whitely.

It went on like that for a while, in relays: the Hollywood men hammering at him about their break-in and then Varallo taking over; they

gave him cigarettes, and the glass of water he asked for, and nobody
went near him to lift a hand, but they bothered him. He hadn't, even
with his record, much experience of questioning in depth; and he began
to get tired, and just a little rattled. At around eight thirty he settled
down to mumbling, "I don't know, I don't know," to every succeeding
question; and they let him alone for a while and drifted out to the corridor, lighting cigarettes.

"I kind of think you've hit pay dirt, *paisano*," said Galluzo. "He re-
acts to the name."

"I thought so," said Varallo. "And he'll know the charge."

Stone looked at his cigarette. "It's my opinion we'll never pin him
down on this burglary charge. All we've got is Craig's story. If
Lawrence goes on saying, don't know nothing about it, we can't charge
him. But the insolent little small-timers like that—I do try to be a nice
polite gentlemanly cop, but I admit, they make my fists ache. I'd like to
see somebody pin him down on something."

"Not too small-time, Jim," said Galluzo, "if he's done two murders.
Yeah, the way he reacted—to the Collins name at least—I think you may
have something there, Varallo."

"So put it on the line," said Stone. "We can hold him legally until
about four P.M. tomorrow. I don't think we want that much of him.
He's just going to go on saying I don't know. Oh, we'll go at him some
more, but that I'll predict. Would you like to join another session and
take him home with you around midnight? Or we can turn him over to
you in the morning."

Varallo laughed. "Six of one, half dozen of another. I agree with you,
on your charge. He knows he can duck that one. But on ours, he is running a little scared, for some reason, I think." He yawned; he was tired
and hungry, but he felt very pleased, for he was certain now: just little
things, a movement, an expression, a silence, but he was sure now—it
had been Bill Lawrence on Collins-Gardiner. The incipient violence
showing up before: and it could even go back to what Poor and Katz
had suggested, the suppressed sexual motive. Elderly women. A symbolic striking-back at adult authority? Hell, you could read that into almost anything. But that Lawrence was X he no longer doubted.

Funny, he thought: in one way it pointed up the moral of how the
patient, plodding routine nearly always paid off; and in another, the occasional value of the hunches. He had felt all along that whoever broke
into Mrs. Collins' house had known something about her. . . . Evi-

dently on Gardiner it had been just blind luck, and he hadn't got much loot there.

He said suddenly, "Tell you something else just occurred to me. It could be those diamonds were fenced—or just pawned—elsewhere. He's moved around. He might know a fence up in Fresno. Though of course there'll be more of them in the big city, and one of his pals might—"

They agreed. "Well, boys, I'm hungry and I think I'll go home. Have fun with him. We'll be over to get him in the morning. Where?"

"New facility down on Alameda," said Stone. "And we all wish you luck in pinning him down."

"Me," said Varallo, shaking his head, "I should never have been a cop. I don't scare people very easy—they take me for a gent. But we've got a very, very tough lieutenant over in the sticks, by the name of O'Connor. One look at him, nervous women faint and the toughest hoods come apart. I want to turn him loose on Billy. He's feeling a little annoyed over another homicide at the moment, and he should be just in the mood to swallow Billy at one bite."

Stone grinned. "Would that by any chance be the O'Connor that won the association's marksmanship trophy second time running last year?" asked Stanton interestedly.

"That's our Charles. I really do believe he sleeps with that favorite cannon of his."

"He does look quite a boy. I watched him shoot that day. Let's hope he scares hell out of Billy."

On that note Varallo came away and went home. He had to wait for Laura to come and turn the little bolt. "And I think it's a needless precaution now," he said, kissing her. "I think we've got him. The one on Collins-Gardiner."

"Oh Vic! Who?"

"Tell you over something to eat. You did save me something?"

"What, and me such a good dutiful housewife? Don't be silly. Beef stew and wild rice. Fifteen minutes," said Laura. Varallo started to mix himself a brandy and soda. "And she's sound asleep, so you needn't go disturbing—"

What with retailing that to O'Connor and Katz and Forbes the next morning—Wayne was still out with the cold along with Rhys—it was eight forty before Varallo and Katz took off for the new jail facility on Alameda downtown to pick up Lawrence.

They didn't do any talking on the way back; and he rode in sullen silence. It was after nine forty-five when they led him upstairs to the detective bureau; and at the door they met a big dark man of middle age who was fidgeting on the threshold. He looked at them anxiously.

"This the detectives? The guy told me downstairs—"

"Yes, sir, who was it you wanted to see?"

"I dunno. Somebody about—about Marion. Marion Thompson."

"Oh," said Varallo. He exchanged a silent glance with Katz. That one was really bugging Charles; if they could clear it up, maybe he'd tackle Lawrence all the tougher.

"Come on, Bill," said Katz gently, "we'll wait downstairs awhile. Give you some more time to get nervous." He led him back the way they'd come, and Varallo took the newcomer in to O'Connor.

"So what do you know about the Thompson woman?" O'Connor pounced on him when he heard that. "Name, sir? What—"

"Oh, that don't sound right, the Thompson woman. Marion was an awful nice girl. My name's Solquist, John. J. Solquist. I work at Penney's, the men's department." He sat down gingerly. "Gee, I just didn't believe it, I see it in the papers. Last night. Marion! Well, she hadda lot of trouble. I guess she was pretty low when I left her that night."

"When? What do you know about her, for God's sake?" snapped O'Connor.

"Now take it easy, I tell you, give me time. I been away—when I said the papers last night, I mean it was about her funeral I saw. I couldn't hardly—but she *was* pretty low. And it said you was looking for a man she'd been with that evening, well, it was me, see? Nothing *wrong* about it, I don't mean, that way, I just felt sorry for her, see? She used to work at Penney's too, how we knew each other. And she'd had trouble. Lost her job there—she was only part time anyways—and she had trouble finding another, it wasn't like she could type or anything, she'd been taking domestic jobs and anything else she could get, and that ex-husband of hers, he'd skipped and quit paying alimony, and she was out of work and feeling low. We ran into each other at the hamburger joint just down from where she had a room in that hotel. Not that I knew she did then, see? See, I'm a bachelor, I live alone, apartment over on Elk, that same neighborhood, and I drop in that hamburger joint sometimes. She told me she hadda give up an apartment, couldn't afford it. Well, I tried to cheer her up, see? Felt sorry for her. She says to me, Sol, she says—that being what they call me—Sol, she says, sometimes a person just doesn't feel like going on, and I tried to kid her, I said you don't mean that, I said, Look, I'd just picked up a fifth—I'm not a drinking

man but now and then I like a little one, I keep it on hand—I said, For
you, Marion, I open the bottle and take the risk of getting picked up by
a cop on my way home. We went up to her room in the hotel—nothing
wrong about it, don't get the wrong idea—and I open the bottle, she's
got just the one glass, but I don't especially want one right then anyways, so she had a nice stiff drink alone, see, and she thanks me and
says she feels better, and so I wish her luck and I go home. And I been
up in San Francisco, my younger sister she just got married up there,
but when I land back here last night and see in the papers— Gee, I
never thought she meant it! But when I saw that about the man—me, I
mean—well, I thought I'd better— Gee, that poor woman, she—"

"Oh, for God's sake!" said O'Connor. So that was the answer to the
little puzzle, and a very natural answer too. She'd had the hefty drink,
first, and used the same glass, unrinsed, for her final drink.

They listened to him repeat it all, anxiously; they thanked him for
coming in. No, no need for a formal statement. This cleaned that one
up; it was dead. "And I am damn glad to have it off my mind," said
O'Connor, when Solquist had taken himself out. "A little queer thing
like that can bother the hell out of you. I was wondering if maybe we
had a real mystery. So that's that. Where's your double murderer?"

"Waiting downstairs with Joe. Charles, I swear he's it. You say little
things—you know how the little things tell you. The expression, and the
hands, and how he answers yes or no. You know. He's the boy we
want. Let's go all out to pin him down."

O'Connor sat back and absently patted the bulge at his left shoulder.
"Yeah, I know. I know what you mean. Is he tough?"

"On the surface only. He got big-time all of a sudden—you've seen
his record. He's run with the little ones, the bad boys just graduating
from being j.d.'s. He's been picked up and questioned, but the real interrogation in depth he hasn't had. He didn't enjoy it last night."
Varallo put out his cigarette, stabbing it out a little viciously. "He stood
up to the L.A. boys about that burglary because he knew all they had
was Craig's word. But the way he reacted to me, and Mrs. Collins'
name, for some reason he's running scared about— Or," said Varallo,
"it could be there was—there is—some emotional tie-in there, with Collins. He said something—she was a touchy old lady, evidently. He grew
up on that block. Maybe she used to—yell at him to get off her flowers,
he said. Yes. Something like that. Anyway, he is the boy we're after,
Charles, so let's get on it and try to get him to sing. *Al lavoro!*"

"Go fetch him," said O'Connor, sounding pleased and ominous; he reached up and loosened his tie.

"The eighteenth and nineteenth of February, Bill," said Varallo harshly. "Here. Right here in town you were. The old home town. What bars had you hit? How high were you?"

"How much did you have on you?" O'Connor, fast and grim. "Broke, weren't you? And you thought you'd pull a quick, easy job. For the fast loot. You thought of the old lady—Mrs. Collins. Had you heard some gossip about there being big loot in her house? You didn't like her, did you? Come on, come on, speak up!"

Lawrence muttered, "No. I don't know what you mean. Don't—"

"You went up there—it was dark. What'd you use to break in that bolt on the back door? Were you driving? A borrowed heap—a hot car? It doesn't matter how much we don't know, Bill—we know you pulled that job. You're giving yourself away every time you look at us, and we're going to keep at you until you spill all of it! We know, hear me? You punks think you're so goddamned smart! We know—"

"You thought about old Mrs. Collins, Bill," Katz took over, "and you knew she was alone, you probably knew she had her dinner at noon and wouldn't be in her kitchen—at that side of the house. It was after six o'clock and before eight o'clock, wasn't it? And you had a—"

"No," said Lawrence. "No. Please." Suddenly he laid his arms out on Poor's empty desk alongside him and put his head down on them. The detectives looked at each other in silence.

It was a quarter to two and they had been at Lawrence ever since ten thirty. They were tired, but not as tired and confused as Lawrence, the small-timer with a little pedigree who'd suddenly graduated to the big-time. His shirt was soaked with sweat and his eyes looked unfocussed and he was shaking.

"Please," he said. And then, "Duke. It was when I was a kid and I had Duke. My dog. He just ran up on her grass to smell the tree and she hit him with a broom. He just wanted to smell the tree."

"Sure, Bill," said Varallo gently. "She didn't hurt him, did she?"

"No, but she might have. She might have. All her damn flowers. No, I didn't like her," said Lawrence. "All right. All right, I'll tell you. I was broke, sure, that job Micky talked about didn't come off and I'd got in a crap game on Monday and cleaned out, I was staying with Sid then —that liquor-store deal was all sour, Walt skipped with most of the loot, and we didn't know where—and first off I thought I'd hit Aunt Margaret for some dough, but when I got over here—in Sid's car—that was why I came over here, see—I didn't like to—on account of she'd cry and carry on and all about the regular job and all that, what a drag, and I was sort of putting it off and then I thought about old lady Collins. Like a kind of inspiration. My mother always said she was sort of a miser and I thought— And I found a couple of tools in the trunk, it was dark then, and I went up there and it was a hell of a job to break in that door, but I was there then and *on* it, and I kept trying and finally it broke and I—and I—"

"Went in, and found her there all ready to scream," said O'Connor, "so you just started to beat her. Just to shut her up, Bill? Or were you just a little tight and feeling mean? Beat her until she died there on the floor, her bones broken, and you—"

Lawrence leaped to his feet and his eyes rolled wildly at them and his mouth opened wide, horridly, and he staggered forward and brought up half-leaning on O'Connor, who stood there like a wall, and he uttered a strangled half-scream. *"Dead!* She's not *dead!* I didn't— I didn't go to make her *dead!* She can't be *dead!* Oh Jesus, oh Jesus, I never knew she was *dead*—you aren't sayin' you call it *murder*— I didn't I didn't I didn't—"

O'Connor pushed him down to the chair again. "It was in all the papers, Bill. Listen—"

"I don't—read so good. She can't be *dead*. Oh Jesus, oh Lord, no— I never—"

"Lawrence!"

But that was the end of that session. Lawrence slid off the chair in a dead faint.

But of course there was Mrs. Gardiner too. They started all the paper work; they charged him formally with the Collins murder, and they'd get him to sign a formal statement—if they could—all that he'd already come out with. Unless an attorney by then advised him not to. But just in case they could get him to confess to the Gardiner one too, he had to be questioned on that.

When Varallo and O'Connor got round to doing that tiresome job, at the jail on Monday, they found Lawrence anxious to talk—about Mrs. Collins.

"Look, look, you got to believe me, I never knew she was dead. I never meant to *kill* her—anybody! Look, I tell you everything—those di-amonds, the fence—Sidney knew a fence—I didn't, I gave Sidney a third of it for telling me about the fence, I never knew she had all those diamonds, but a *murder*—I never did any *murder!* It wasn't a *murder*, for God's sake! I never meant— I never knew—"

"Take it easy," said O'Connor unceremoniously. "Sit down. We don't want to talk about Mrs. Collins today, Bill. We're going to talk about Mrs. Agnes Gardiner."

Lawrence collapsed on the straight chair in the interrogation room. "Who—who's Mrs. Gardiner? I tell you—"

"The other one, Bill," said Varallo. "The second woman you murdered by beating to death. Over on Fifth Street, on March eighth. A Saturday night. After finding all that nice loot in the Collins house, you decided that was a pretty good lay, you thought you'd try another one. Picked a house at random, did you?—which turned out to be the Gardiner house—"

Lawrence began shaking his head violently. "No— No—that not so. I never meant to kill old lady Collins, I didn't know—you've gotta believe me—I don't know anything about this other thing. Oh my God, you damn cops—every unsolved case on the books you shove off on me. I don't know—"

"Now look, Bill," said O'Connor. "We're not fools, damn it. The same exact damn m.o., and sure, you knew a little bit about Collins and the Gardiner house you maybe picked at random, your good luck and hers bad that she was alone, but don't try to—"

"It's a lie, a goddamn— I don't know anything ab— *What* day did you say? Oh my God, what *day* did you say?" Lawrence grabbed O'Connor's arm. "*What*—" O'Connor shook him off.

"March eighth," said Varallo. "A Saturday. Why, Bill?"

"Oh God," said Lawrence. "Oh my God." He sank back in the chair, and raised an arm to wipe his forehead. "Oh my God." He was dead white and shaking. "Then I can prove it. I can prove it. I never—oh my God. March eighth. I was—in Fresno that day. Sid and I, we'd driven up— I got a couple pals there, I thought maybe—but we got tagged. Oh my God, thank God, we got tagged—in a beer joint. There was a little brawl, the cops— They took us all in, we didn't get let go till next day— thank God—"

And Varallo and O'Connor looked at each other.

CHAPTER 16

"So let us use some goddamn order and method here," said O'Connor. "We've got to check it, for God's—"

It was Varallo who put in the call to Fresno. And it checked out on the surface, with one Sergeant Klaus. "But are you sure it *was* William E. Lawrence you had, Sergeant? We've got to be sure, because it's an alibi for a homicide rap. If."

"Oh, you don't say," said Klaus. "I'll check with the arresting officer and ask around—do our best for you. I'll call you back."

"I don't believe it," said Wayne. He was still coughing, but back to work; which was more than Rhys was. Rhys had called in yesterday afternoon just for somebody to talk to; he said he felt like a leper, his mother was so afraid he'd pass the cold on to her nursing Cairn mother and the pups—valuable pups—he was being treated like an outcast.

"I think we'd better start to believe it, Fred," said Varallo. "I have an awful premonition—"

It came true half an hour later when Sergeant Klaus called back. "Afraid you'll have to go on hunting your killer down there. Whoever it was, it wasn't Bill Lawrence, if it happened any time after about four P.M. on March eighth. Coleman—the arresting officer—knew him. He'd picked him up before. D. and D., and brawls. Same like this. They picked up three others with him and they were all in the cells overnight here."

Varallo thanked him, and relayed that news. They looked at each other. "Oh for God's sake," said O'Connor. "What are we all thinking? For *God's* sake. No."

Wayne got out a cigarette and looked at it. "There are a few basic rules about detective work, Charles."

"Yes, and also exceptions to the rules. And if *so,* damn it, how do we prove it?" O'Connor looked incredulous, annoyed and disgusted all at once.

"You take that thing," said Varallo, leaning back and blowing smoke at the ceiling, "and if it had happened out of the blue, all by itself, wouldn't we have wondered? At least wondered. And done the elementary checking? Just on account of the basic rules. But it just naturally tied in to Collins, so we didn't. In fact, it never crossed our minds."

"All right, all right," said O'Connor, exasperated. "Was it supposed to, for God's sake? Why should it? Talking about alibis—"

"Listen," said Wayne. "Awhile ago, Vic, you said to me, maybe you'd been thinking a little too logical—not simple enough. The birds who pull this kind of thing are usually, God knows, simple—not to say primitive. Let's not outsmart ourselves here. It could be one of those we've hauled in to question, who spelled out the newspaper stories on Collins and thought, That's kind of a good idea, and went and did likewise."

"It could be, Fred," said Varallo, "but I've got a little hunch it—"

O'Connor groaned.

"—wasn't."

"Hunches!" said O'Connor.

"Because even with what it looked like—if Collins hadn't come before—wouldn't we at least have considered it? It so often is, you know," said Varallo.

"Why?" asked O'Connor. "I don't mean why *that,* anybody can see there are reasons, but why, on this one? Not that we have to show motive, of course."

"If it was," said Varallo, "I could have a funny guess, Charles. But I'm doing no more guessing unless and until we collect a little evidence."

"And has our jumper to conclusions any bright ideas about how to do that?" asked Wayne mildly. "Before we start pawing through records again and bringing in everybody with a suitable pedigree to question?"

"I think," said Varallo, "we'll do it direct and open, Fred. The easy way. We may get some interesting reaction right off."

O'Connor gestured savagely. "Offbeat! Damn it, I hate these goddamned unexpected offbeat things! So go and look. Jumping to conclusions. You'll waste time proving another solid alibi."

"Want to bet?" said Varallo. "I thought you were more of a cynic, Charles!"

*

And he didn't make any objection, or ask any questions or raise any little fuss at all. Touching his glasses in habitual nervous gesture, a little shaky, just looking a little surprised. "Well, of course I know you have to ask about everything—just to be sure. I believe I can remember. Some of them will be in my records. I'll try to help you."

Names he gave Varallo and Wayne. They went to find the names, splitting the list.

Mr. Henry Coulter—"I'm afraid I was rather late. To tell you the truth I hadn't noticed that I was nearly out of my high-blood-pressure tablets until my wife called my attention—it would have been nearly nine o'clock when I—" N.g.

Mrs. Helen Constantine— "Oh goodness, I suppose it was around a quarter to six, I just popped in for a minute to pick up some shampoo, on the way from work—oh, I was home by six or a few minutes after, getting dinner." N.g.

Mr. George Wilhem— "My wife's . . . prescription it was, I don't take stock in dope of any kind, but she gets these migraine headaches— she'd run out, asked me to go get it filled—oh, roundabout seven thirty it'd 'a' been, after dinner anyway." N.g.

The Misses Jean and Linda Harvey, round-eyed teenagers with apprehensive parents in the background— "Well, we weren't there but a few minutes, why d'you want to *know?* What's it *about?* Well, Mother wanted some sherbet and Lindy's just learning to drive and Dad said it'd be good practice at night driving for her, he went along too because she's just got a learner's license, and he sat outside and waited for us—it was about a quarter of eight we left the house." N.g.

Miss Genevieve Burton, schoolteacher— "Yes, I can tell you the time, Officer. Though why you should want to know I cannot imagine. That poor man. One finds it difficult to understand the absolutely primitive mind capable of such things—and in our advanced culture, too. There were a few little things I wanted to pick up—small necessities, you know, hairpins and so on—and I was going out that night to attend a lecture—a most interesting lecture at the Church of Religious Science —it was at eight o'clock and I stopped to do my little shopping on the way. It would have been about seven twenty when I went in. I always like to allow myself *plenty* of time, one never knows when some little delay will occur, and I— Not at all, Officer. I am only too happy to be of any service." N.g.

It was Varallo who, late on Tuesday afternoon, came across Mrs.

Beryl Gillis. Mrs. Gillis lived in an apartment just down from Graynold on Glenoaks Boulevard, and she was a pretty little woman of plump and cheerful middle age who hospitably asked him in, introduced her two small black poodles and her Siamese cat and her husband, in that order, and asked what she could do for him. "Quite thrilling, to help the *police,*" she said. Varallo explained, and she exclaimed, and said she was no good at all at remembering dates.

"I am," said her husband, regarding Varallo interestedly. "It was the eighth all right. You had two prescriptions from the doctor that day."

"Oh, was it? If you say so, dear. But I couldn't say at all about the time. I never can. I just browsed around the magazine rack and looked at the greeting cards—such fun, those tall humorous ones, aren't they? He said it'd take a little time, and I seem to remember it *did*—but I—"

Her husband smiled. "We were going out to dinner that night. Eight o'clock, at least twenty minutes' drive off. I was noticing the time, knowing how you can fritter it away. You left the apartment at five minutes to six and you got back at about five minutes to seven. The drugstore is about five minutes' walk."

Varallo got out his notebook. "Would you swear to that, Mr. Gillis?"

"Yes, I would. I'm sure. Why?" Gillis looked interested.

"Oh dear, was it as long as that? I really wouldn't have said so, but you are so good at times and dates, darling."

"Have to be," said Gillis, winking at Varallo.

"I know he said one of them would take a little while—I didn't really notice. I looked at several magazines and then I looked at all the cosmetics and remembered I needed nail polish and there was a new Coty's color chart on the counter, and I do remember I hesitated between two shades but I finally—"

"No time sense," said Gillis. "She won't wear a watch. Spend hours doing that—two shades of nail polish." He looked at her indulgently. "Oddly enough, quite an efficient housekeeper," he added. "Female."

Varallo smiled back, but he was feeling a little excited. If that was the word for it. Female, he thought. It could only have been a female. Of this special type. Because he was concentrating right now on the how and forgetting the why.

"Mrs. Gillis, do you go to the drugstore often?"

"Well, it's so convenient. Just a block away and I don't have to take the car, you see. Yes, I do, quite a lot. For all the prescriptions, and there's your hay-fever stuff, dear, and my sleeping tablets, not that I have to take them often, and these new ones for tension Doctor Walker gave me, and I usually buy cosmetics there and all the odds and ends one *does*. But I must say I don't understand why. Is it something about that terrible murder? Have you caught him yet?"

"Well, Mrs. Gillis—"

"Mustn't ask," said her husband. But his interested glance was shrewd. "What? Yes, I'll swear to the times. Rather fancy it *is* about that, eh? Well, I will be damned. I will be damned." He looked at his wife. "What a godsend for him," he said, and laughed shortly.

"Jumping to conclusions, sir," said Varallo. "I'll ask you both to come down to headquarters and sign a statement, if you will."

"Oh dear, how exciting— If you'll wait while I powder my nose." She fluttered off.

"Happy to oblige," said Gillis. "Jumping to conclusions be damned. I can add two and two."

And Varallo thought but did not say, so can we; and I only hope the real answer isn't five. But he didn't think it was. He really didn't.

They brought him down to headquarters that evening. Varallo skipped the police-science class; he was a good deal more interested in this. Burt and Harrison were silent and rather incredulous witnesses.

"Mr. Gardiner," said Varallo, "just when did you first get the idea of killing your wife? I think it must have been a little while—maybe a long while—before Mrs. Collins was murdered. But we'd like to know for sure."

Harry Gardiner blinked up at him from behind the heavy lenses of his glasses. "What—what did you say?" He touched the glasses nervously.

"We can guess what you did, Mr. Gardiner. Some of it. But we'd like you to tell us. You know, we let you drive here in your car with Sergeant Wayne, and we've got a warrant to look at that as well as your house. You know what Sergeant Wayne's finding down there in the lot?" And that was more jumping to conclusion; O'Connor frowned at him from the other side of Gardiner's chair.

"Oh," said Gardiner. He stared up at Varallo. "Oh. I—" He looked blank and bewildered. Little strokes? wondered Varallo. Brain damage? The man was an old man. Let the doctors sort it out. He knew. And it was, of course, another offbeat one.

"We won't talk about the why right now, Mr. Gardiner—just what you did. You read about Mrs. Collins' murder in the paper, and you thought if you could make it look as if the same man had killed your wife, no one would ever suspect it was really you. Didn't you? You thought about how you could do it, and maybe several plans occurred to you, but only one was really workable, wasn't it, and you saw that. You had somehow to make it seem your wife had been killed while you were in your drugstore, at work. And eventually you thought of Mrs. Gillis. A good customer, a regular customer. And you knew, the kind of woman who'd have no vague idea how long you took—to make up a prescription, Mr. Gardiner! There in your little back room, out of sight —with the rear door of the store at hand. You knew she'd stay out in front there, looking through the magazines, no idea of time passing—and when you came out and said, 'Mrs. Gillis, your prescriptions are ready,' she'd have been quite ready to swear you'd been there all the time, making up the prescriptions. It was a chance to take, that another customer might come in, want something in a hurry—even if Mrs. Gillis said, He's in the back making up a prescription, such a customer might call out for service. But—while you didn't choose the time—it was an ideal time to take the chance, wasn't it? As it worked out? Between six and seven, not many people likely to drop into a drugstore in that quiet little block of business."

Gardiner touched his glasses. "That's quite true," he said. "I certainly never thought you'd suspect." His voice was expressionless. O'Connor suppressed an oath, and Burt looked at Varallo incredulously.

"No, you didn't. You hadn't any choice about the time—you just had to wait for Mrs. Gillis to come in. But she generally did drop in at least once a week. And after you'd planned it, the first time she came in, you —used her. It was a lucky time for you—in more ways than one. A medical examination would show that your wife had died several hours before you came home—officially. And you delayed deliberately getting home that night, to underline that. . . . You told Mrs. Gillis her prescriptions would take a little while to make up—and we'll check that, and I think we'll find that both were just a matter of counting pills into bottles. And you went into the back room, and out the rear door. Or perhaps you made up the prescriptions first, to be all ready when you got back. Did you, Mr. Gardiner? You got into your car and drove most of the way home. I think you parked the car on the street behind Fifth, and went through back yards, quietly, to your own back door. Unlocked it and went in, and met your wife coming to investigate, and— And afterward you broke the lock deliberately, to make it look as if it had been forced. . . . The only real coincidence was the time. You didn't know, because it wasn't in the papers, the approximate time Mrs. Collins had been killed. You had to use the time when Mrs. Gillis came into the store, and it just happened to be roughly the same time. That did throw us off a little. Mr. Gardiner—"

"But why *couldn't* it have been the same one?" asked Gardiner in a reasonable tone, plaintively. "Last night's papers said you'd arrested somebody for it. I don't see why—"

"He has an alibi for the time of your wife's murder," said Varallo gently. "Quite a good alibi. Mr. Gardiner, won't you tell us about it?"

Gardiner said, "Oh." He took his glasses off and began to clean them meticulously with his handkerchief. "Oh, I see. I really did think it was a good plan." He sighed. "And I *did not like* to do it. I—I *did not like* the idea at all. Quite an efficient housekeeper, Agnes was, and I was—I was—I was *used* to her. But first it was one thing and then another. That foolish television, and then something going wrong with it and the repair bill. And she was *not* careful about the marketing. I thought I had her trained, but she was *not*. Frozen vegetables instead of fresh—so much more dear—and trying to tell me it was an economy because they'd been picked over first! And she would buy that one brand of coffee—three cents more a pound—said it went further! Things like that. I had been worrying about it—I had spoken to her—and then just after Christmas she began talking about an automatic washing machine! Like the one that woman next door had. Such outrageous extravagance! You must understand," said Gardiner fussily, "I'm a very patient man, but that was too much. One has to save to build up security, it is a—a basic moral principle. 'Agnes,' I said, 'that is too much.' And in an idle way at first I began reckoning up how much—how much I could save *without her*. If she wasn't— Why, it came to quite a nice round sum," said Gardiner, his eyes lighting up. "Less than half the grocery bill, it would be, because *I* should be much more careful, you see—and the soap, and wear on the sheets and so on. *Quite* a sum." He touched his glasses.

Wayne came in and said baldly, "It's all there. Locked up in the trunk of his car. The TV, and all the jewelry he described."

"It'd be worth something," said Gardiner. "Of course, I was going to sell it."

"You—" Varallo swallowed. He'd felt sorry for the old man. Washing the blood off the kitchen floor. That morning at Lefkowitz's pawn shop. *Sorry* for him. "You didn't dare be gone too long. I think you pulled out all the drawers, stashed the supposed loot in the car, after you came home openly at ten o'clock, didn't you? It was dark, and you could carry it all out in one load, in three minutes, from the rear door to the garage."

"There was a wrench too," said Wayne. "Looks like—what he used."

"Oh, yes. Did you, Mr. Gardiner?"

"I certainly never thought you would suspect. No. Yes, that's right. I *did not like* to do it," said Gardiner earnestly. "I must insist on that. It was a *most distasteful* thing to have to do. But there it was in black and white, the really nice round sum I should be able to save if Agnes wasn't *there,* and the more I thought about it— Well, she was a very healthy woman, you know, and there was really only one way to—to accomplish her not being *there,* you can see that. And when I read in the paper about that Collins woman getting killed like that, really it seemed most providential. And then of course, Mrs. Gillis—"

"Mr. Gardiner," said Varallo, "you'd been married to her for forty years. She was your wife."

"Quite true," said Gardiner. "She had learned about the saving—but only up to a *point.* I was very, very sorry to have to do it. And it made quite a little mess to be cleaned up, too. One has to take care of property—another form of investment, of course. I was *sorry*—but the figures were quite definite. If she wasn't *there*— You do understand?"

Even O'Connor had nothing to say. They all just looked at each other. And the head doctors would probably say, Brain damage, strokes. The single obsession.

"We understand, Mr. Gardiner," said Wayne heavily.

"I'm glad of that. And really, now I *consider* it," said Gardiner—and his eyes lit up and he smiled— "think what I shall be saving in food bills, in prison! They do feed and clothe you quite free, don't they?"

"They do, Mr. Gardiner," said Varallo.

"But, Vic, what an awful thing! He must have started to go senile or something."

"I would guess. He'd almost have to, wouldn't he?" said Varallo. "I know we come all sorts, but how could any man who'd lived with a woman forty years— *Deh!*—I mean, *cara,* even if it hadn't ever been the great romance, and I don't suppose it ever was with Harry and Agnes Gardiner—"

"You don't know," said Laura. "It's always so hard to imagine old people as they must have been, Vic." She laughed, leaning on him. "Us.

Aging. And—how we were. That awful time up in Contera when we'd had the fight. And you *wouldn't*—"

"I got some sense in the end, *amante*." He hugged her hard.

"And there's the baby *ten* weeks old already and before we know it she'll be in school, and then going out on dates, and married, and all of a sudden we'll be grandparents," said Laura, starting to untie his tie, "and I'll have false teeth and you'll be bald and the grandchildren will never, never be able to believe—emotionally, you know—that Vic and Laura were ever young and in love with each other—or ever made love."

"Whoa, now!" said Varallo. "They wouldn't *be* there if we hadn't. *Which*—"

"I said emotionally," said Laura. She looked up at him soberly. "Vic. I—I hope she didn't know. Mrs. Gardiner. That she just went out to her kitchen to investigate a noise and saw—an intruder. A strange man. Do you think it was like that for her?"

"I think maybe, *cara*. Probably. There wasn't a light on."

"Well." Laura sighed. "I hope so. I hope she didn't know. Because that would be the—the last most awful thing."

Varallo kissed her. "To change the subject—I have an awful suspicion I've got that damn cold. My throat's been a little sore all day." He swallowed experimentally.

"So you come home lovingly spreading the germs," said Laura. She looked up at him and laughed. "So at last I'm going to find out."

"Find out what?"

"Well, all the six years I've known you," said Laura, "including the two and a half we've been married, I've been thinking occasionally that —just like this daughter of yours—you're too good to be true. Now I'll find out whether you're just as provoking and sorry for yourself as most men when they're sick. I'll bet you will be." She turned him around and gave him a brisk pat. "So go take some aspirin, cop. I'll mix you up some lemon and honey."

"It reminds me," said Katharine thoughtfully, "of a story my mother used to tell. About the couple who were married for sixty years and had about ten kids, and the wife died, and on the way back from the funeral the husband said to the funeral director, 'You know, I never did like that woman.' "

O'Connor laughed. "I've heard it said marriage does bring out your worst qualities. Martini, and Scotch-and-water," he said to the waiter.

"Mmh. But what an awful thing. Charles?"

"Well?"

"I hope she didn't know. That it was *him*," said Katharine. "How could he? *Forty* years. I mean, even if he'd stopped—loving her, that way—the way when they were young—mere habit, you'd think—being used to having someone around."

"It makes you wonder," said O'Connor. He wondered if she'd just got used to having him around. The convenient date: the platonic thing. Hell! Him, O'Connor. But he didn't know either that he'd be very suitable material for the domesticities. He thought fleetingly of Varallo, and his pretty brown-haired wife, and the new baby; and he said absently, "If you think about it, it scares you, Katy. People. How they change. Strokes, whatever—senility—like Gardiner. I suppose, damn it, he did—love her, once. Married her. Maybe not exactly the great romance, but—" He shrugged angrily. The drinks arrived and he took a swallow. "I mean, damn it—"

"Yes," said Katharine. "I don't know, Charles, but I think it's a thing like hypnotism—you know. You'd never do anything that wasn't *in* you to do anyway. Incipient."

"Maybe," said O'Connor. "Maybe." He looked at her across the table, and anyway how the hell would he do as a husband, him, O'Connor, not very domesticated the good God knew—all the indifferent foster homes and so on—coming home and maybe that belonged in quotes to the cold little apartment (but by God he had *got* somewhere, he was O'Connor, O'Connor the good cop, the top marksman) and anyway (after all the succession of cuddly little brainless blondes), anyway just how did you let a girl know you were serious? The thing for keeps? And how the hell did she feel about him, his Katy he'd never made a move at, but—

"Katy," he said. "Katy, I—"

She made a little face at him over her drink. "Why you have to call me—nobody *does*. What?"

"Would you like to order, sir?" Obsequious waiter. And he guessed it wasn't, anyway, a very propitious time. People all around. He guessed not. Right now.

"Nothing," he said. "Damn it. What'd you like to eat?"